SO
FAR
FROM
PARADISE

A novel

1

Caged Potential, PO Box 12746, Kansas City, Kansas 66112

So Far From Paradise / LANE

First Edition

Library of Congress Control Number 2010908331
ISBN 1453712801
EAN – 13 9781453712801

CONTENTS

Acknowledgements		5
Prologue		6
PART ONE: FILTHY ROUTE		8
1.	A Gangsta's Nightmare	10
2.	Patience	26
3.	The Initiation	44
4.	Granting Wishes	66
5.	Personal Friend	86
6.	Putting In Work	102
7.	Running Out The Crack House	128
8.	Disclosure	164
9.	Fugitive	182
10.	My Brother's Keeper	200
11.	Hardheaded Decisions	216
PART TWO: FOOTPRINTS IN THE SAND		232
12.	Certification	234
13.	No Way Out	260
14.	Face To Face With The Devil	274
15.	From Elementary To The Penitentiary	290
16.	Rock-A-Bye Baby	310
17.	Out Of Sight And Mind	336
18.	Justice Or Just<u>us</u>?	358
19.	Ad-Seg	382
PART THREE: THE PATH		398
20.	Siddiq	400
21.	Elevation	430
22.	For The Sake Of Allah	442
23.	9/11	460
24.	The Board	478
PART FOUR: THROUGH THE FIRE		496
25.	No Ways Tired	498
26.	Compensation	530
27.	A Special Person	550
28.	A Taste Of Paradise	570
29.	EPILOGUE	580

ACKNOWLEDGEMENTS

Alhamdulillah! Thanks Bobbie, for believing in me and making seeing this book into fruition one of your New Year's Resolutions. I also extend my deep gratitude to the reliable crew you assembled: Jacqui, Carla, and Amy for all of the painstaking typing, editing and support as a whole. I really appreciate it ladies! My family, especially my father, my two brothers Rico and Muhammad, Tazz, Yah Ya, Lil-John the Mafia Don, D.O.A..None of this was possible without your support. Everyone who read bits and pieces of the manuscript, encouraging me with your commentary along the way. Lastly, much love and respect to CAGED POTENTIAL.

PROLOGUE

My name is Atif. I am a young man of African descent, born and raised in (and by) the streets of Kansas City, Missouri.

I have a story to tell.

It is not your average everyday tale filled with sex, drugs and violence narrated by an individual who never even lived such a lifestyle, thus being totally out of touch with realistic inner-city life. Nor is this a talk about a successful "African American" and his experiences within the middle-class workplace and dating fields.

This is the story of my life. My pain, my joy. My innocence, my guilt. My confusion, my understanding. My love, my hate. My stagnation, my growth. My struggle, my resilience. My accomplishments, my failures. My losses, my gains. My grudges, my forgiveness. My rebellion, my submission.

I want to welcome you into the mentality of that young man you saw on the news last night who was arrested for taking another person's life over drugs, money, a color, or what have you, something that seems so petty. You know, the one from the hip-hop generation that you see on the street corner with the baggy clothes, smoking weed and selling dope instead of in someone's classroom? Well, this story is about him. Your son, your brother, your cousin, your client. If you have ever seen or had an encounter with this individual and wondered how someone could possibly have such a disregard for their future and the law, a willingness to sacrifice so much for so little, especially with the end results being so clear and inevitable, then this story (my story) is something you should read.

My story is not full of accusations directed towards blaming the "White Man" and his unjust system for my actions and circumstances. I am not a college graduate with a Ph.D. or a doctorate in psychology. I am writing this from my heart and experiences. My story is not derived from text books and statistical studies. It is simply written , clear for all to understand and is not filled with ten to fifteen letter words that would keep even some of the most

6

intelligent people flipping through a dictionary. I use the native slang of the streets when necessary in order to capture the essence, attitude and emotion of certain incidents as I attempt to transfer my memories onto these pages, painting a clear picture for you to see and understand in its rawest form without being diluted. In other words, the language and certain incidents get a little ruff at times, but I am sure that you will not read anything you have not heard, seen, or experienced before.

May Allah forgive me for my stubbornness.

So, do you think you know me? Do you think you understand why I made the decisions I made and did the things I have done? Do you think you can relate and identify with where I come from?

Humph, you have no idea. Lets get started then, shall we?

PART 1:

<u>FILTHY ROUTE</u>

"Ridin' down the filthy route,
what will be the future for me?
Will I see the penitentiary
or stay free?"
-Soody Mak

"I know this ain't the way
my mama raised me,
but I've drifted off to the other side;
so Mama please forgive your baby!"
-Tazz Mania Devil

A GANGSTA'S NIGHTMARE

"I gotta few hommies,
that didn't get a chance to live their life.
I'm lookin up outta my curtain like Malcolm X;
Somethin' just ain't feelin' right."
-*Tazz Mania Devil*

1

June 6, 1992. You know, it's a trip how much this still hurts after all these years. Even with all of the knowledge and understanding I have acquired pertaining to death, the tragic and pivotal events that transpired during the wee morning hours of this day will forever be engraved in my memory bank and psyche. I remember everything in full detail. It was Friday, the last day of my eighth grade school year. After this day I would be making my transition from Jr. high school to the next level.

The previous two years were pretty cool. I enjoyed the small freedoms that Jr. high school had to offer compared to elementary. No more eating lunch in the classroom with the teacher, there was a cafeteria for that. No more P.E. class only on Tuesdays and Thursdays, it was an everyday thing. Music class, etc. were electives, I was given the choice between them, shop class, home economics, R.O.T.C., art and typing. This was a good thing to me because I always felt like music class, along with all of its singing and carrying on, was for the females. My inability to carry a note more than likely had a lot to do with my misconception.

That transition had its drawbacks as well. There were no more field trips, field days, or recesses. P.E. everyday compensated for the recesses in a sense, but it was not the same.

The thing that I had missed most about Jr. high school, now that I reflect, was the park directly across the street known to all of us as "*The Battle Ground*". This park was the scene of all the drama. If someone had a problem with anyone, boy or girl, it got dealt with on *The Battle Ground* after, and even sometimes during, school hours. Sometimes kids would skip class and come back to school the next hour with bloody noses and busted lips. Word of a potential throwdown would spread quickly throughout the school like a wildfire, amazingly without alerting the teaching staff. By the time the combatants made it to *The Battle Ground* it would already be packed with anxious spectators, especially if it was after school hours. Some

11

kids would miss their bus, having to walk all the way home after the fight.   So if one had any doubts about their abilities or the outcome of the match, he or she would have probably tried to schedule the match during school hours. This way not as many people would actually see them get "smashed". Everyone would hear about it but it was not as difficult to deal with the funny looks and whispers of those who were not in attendance as it was when they came from those who were. You weren't really labeled a punk if you lost a fight, depending on just how bad you lost it. Many reputations were made and shattered on *The Battle Ground*. Respect was won, lost and sometimes simply maintained. It was an unwritten law that once two combatants stepped foot on *The Battle Ground* premises there was no turning back. They had to fight. All reasoning was exhausted so you can imagine why there was not a whole lot of talking and arguing once *The Battle Ground*'s thresholds were breached.

Me?   I had my share of "funk" on *The Battle Ground*. I must say in the humblest manner I can muster that I was somewhat of a legend and highly favored inductee into *The Battle Ground* Hall of Fame. I had an undefeated record of 7-0-1, the draw being with a light skinned mixed kid name Kev.

Kev lived over on 24th street and Brooklyn. My affiliation with the 27th street Piru Blood Gang and his with the 24th street Crips laid the foundation for a wall between us that we both refused to let down. Throughout the years we had numerous altercations but had only recently actually fought one-on-one. We went at it. That was the longest and hardest fight I had ever fought up to that point. Over the years our rivalry escalated and is still talked about to this day.

"Man, I wish this dude would hurry up so I can go to sleep." I remember saying aloud to myself. It was sometime after one in the morning and I was standing at our bedroom window looking out into the quiet night. The full moon in the sky cast an eerie glow over the front lawn and reflected off of my mama's 1983 Chevrolet hatch-back in the driveway, giving the rusty tan spot plagued factory paint job a fresh recently painted by "A Touch of Class" kind of look.

Across the street, two houses down, I noticed a dark colored two door 1987 Cutlass parked in front of Old Lady Jenkins' house. This was peculiar to me when I thought about it because Miss Jenkins didn't play that. Naw, not at all. I can remember times when we would be playing an innocent game of football and miss a pass resulting in the ball landing in her yard, and that would be the end of the N.F.L. on N.B.C for the day. All we could do was hope that she was in a decent mood, looking out of her front window like she did everyday all day with her nosy self, and felt like coming outside when she seen it topple into her yard. She would pick the ball up and launch it with amazing strength, seemingly trying to take one of our heads off in the process, making Joe Montana look like a second string quarterback for the New Orleans Saints. Then she would holler out, "Keep yo baseball outta my front yard and off my grass you little bastards!" knowing that her front yard consisted mainly of dirt like everyone else's in the neighborhood. If it was a football, she called it a baseball. If it was a basketball, she would call it a football. If it was a baseball, she called it a basketball. Go figure. And if you went in her yard to get the ball yourself you were liable to catch a couple of buckshots from her 12 gauge, of which every man, woman and child that resided on 28th and Monroe was able to describe the grooves on the inside of both barrels because of various confrontations with Old Lady Jenkins. That woman was old, lonely and did not discriminate between children or adults; she was a trip.

I thought to myself that the Cutlass had to have just arrived there between 11:30pm and 12:00am, in between the time span in which Old Lady Jenkins goes to bed and I myself began looking out of the window waiting for my brother Malik. If it had arrived anytime before that, Old Lady Jenkins would have called the police and had the car towed off from in front of her house. She didn't have any family and rarely had any visitors, none at this hour. I would not have put any money on it at the time, but I could have sworn that there were two people sitting in the driver and passenger seats. I kept thinking that maybe I was sleepy and my eyes were playing tricks on me. Why would somebody be sitting in front of her house? People were always sitting in cars around the neighborhood, smoking weed and freaking with females or whatever. But not in front of her house. Everybody in the hood knew better than that.

My thoughts switched to how tight I felt I was going to look that day with Malik's *1 and a ½* inch thick, 14 karat gold herringbone around my neck. This was my sole purpose for waiting up for him to come home. It took me at least two whole weeks in order to convince Malik to let me wear it on the last day of school.......

"Why? So one of them little crab ass niggas can take it from you?" Malik had asked me with that sarcastic smirk on his face that made him look like an image of Lucifer often rendered in old European paintings, painted black with braids and minus the horns.

"Naw! Come on man," I pleaded, resenting the verbal insult on my boxing skills but dismissing it for the moment, "you know you ain't gone go to school on the last day anyway."

"How you know what I'mma do?" Malik asked with that smirk still on his face.

"When was the last time you went to school on the last day?" I asked. Malik thought to himself silently. "Matter of fact, when was the last time you went to school period?" I offered, mocking my brother's smirk and returning a sly dig of my own in retaliation.

"Probably around the same time you got your funky ass in the tub." He answered. We both laughed at this.

"What's up man, you gone let me bust the necklace?" I asked seriously.

Malik looked into my eyes and saw how much I really wanted to wear his necklace. It meant a lot to me. I wanted to go out in style I guess you could say. He knew what I was up to and understood how I felt at the same time. He had been in the eighth grade once too only a few years before me. If he had an older brother who had a

14

herringbone like his and let him wear it on his last day of Jr. high school, every female in attendance would have been on him.

For a brief second I saw a flicker of reminiscence in his own eyes. As if he was yearning for the innocence of his Jr. high school years. So much had changed so quickly for him since then. Maybe he was thinking that if he could go back in time he could find a way to avoid this dead-end road that he felt so trapped on and destined to crash upon. He could see the dead end approaching fast in the distance, and deep inside I know that he knew it represented death or life imprisonment. He felt he was too deep in the game to turn around now. Once you started banging you rode until you reached that end result. No ifs, ands or buts about it. At least that is how we perceived it to be at the time, but in reality we had a choice. Not much of one, but it was still a choice no matter how one twisted it up and turned it around. It was just an extremely difficult one for an adolescent to make when all of the peer pressures and temptations were considered, which had to be before a just judgment could be made. At times I also sensed that he felt bad about my following in his footsteps. I never really knew my father, and from what Malik did tell me about him he was not much of a role model himself. I never did use that as an excuse, it was simply the truth.

"I'mma let you bust it on the last day dawg," Malik started to my delight. "But if it come up missin' you gone come up missin' right along with it." He finished, putting that devilish smirk back on his face. He then let out a "sss-sss" sound, the sound a professional boxer makes when he exhales while throwing a punch, and gave me a quick, stiff left-right combination in the chest, forcing me to stumble backwards.

"Aahh, fag!" I yelped in pain, massaging my chest area with my right hand....

I would have just waited until later that morning to get the necklace from Malik, but trying to wake him up after an all-nighter filled with females, alcohol, dope slanging and weed smoking was like trying to wake a dead man. I would

15

rather catch my brother while he was good and high. That was the best time to get anything from Malik.

Sometime later I noticed a car turning onto Monroe with its left headlight out. It was K-Red's Pontiac Grand Prix, Malik's best friend.

Malik once told me about when him and K-Red were riding and smoking one day and they bumped into some 43rd street Crips they were at war with. He said that they were standing outside on the corner of 43rd and Cleveland, in front of the liquor store in a group of about ten, and began throwing up gang signs when they noticed K-Red's Grand Prix. K-Red said, "Watch this" and swerved up onto the sidewalk all of a sudden, pushing the gas pedal to the floor at the same time, causing everybody on the corner to stop set tripping and dive for cover like some U.S. soldiers in Vietnam under Vietnamese gunfire. K-Red ran over a stop sign and a fire hydrant, busting the left headlight, then sped off like a bat out of hell. Malik said that they were too busy laughing at the looks on those Crips' faces to wonder about the damage they may have inflicted on the vehicle.

"Bout time." I said as I turned away from our bedroom window. I was on my second step away from the window when I heard a car start its engine. I turned back around and walked up to the window, looking out at the Cutlass sitting in front of Old Lady Jenkins' house. K-Red's Grand Prix was coming down the street and the right headlight shined on the Cutlass. I knew I wasn't trippin' now, all of this time there *were* people sitting in that car!

I took my attention off of the Cutlass in an absent state of mind as I observed K-Red's Grand Prix pulling to a stop in front of the house. K-Red turned off his headlights, then the passenger door opened causing the interior light to come on.

Malik was in the passenger seat with one foot out of the car. He wore a white tank top, revealing the big 27th street brand on his left biceps that had been foolishly burned into his flesh with a hot hanger the night he was initiated. Around his neck was the gold herringbone I had been up all night waiting for. Malik also wore a red

16

bandanna on his head tied Aunt Jemina style with long, black braids dangling from the rear.

My attention was drawn back to the Cutlass parked in front of Old Lady Jenkins' house. All of a sudden it hit me. My stomach filled with butterflies and I could taste bile in my mouth.

"Aw shit, Malik!" I screamed as I started banging on the window with my clenched right fist. The glass was thick, but even if it wasn't I was not concerned with it breaking.

"Atif? Boy! What the hell are you in there doing?" My mother yelled angrily from her bedroom across the hall, startled out of her sleep.

"Malik!" I screamed again, steadily beating on the window while ignoring my mother's question and ignorance of what I knew was about to go down.

"Malik......!"

******

"Man that bitch looked like a big bag of groceries with her fat ass." Malik said, causing K-Red to burst out laughing and choking on the marijuana smoke that he was in the process of inhaling. "Why you do me like that blood?" Malik asked with a smirk on his face.

"I told you dawg," K-Red replied in a wiry thin voice, still trying to recover from the coughing fit that brought tears to his eyes. "I didn't know what she looked like. I ain't never seen her before tonight. Here you go." He passed the joint to Malik. Malik took the joint in between his forefinger and thumb. He took a long puff, followed by a short puff, then inhaled with a deep breath and held it.

"I ain't fuckin with you and Chantel like that no more dawg, no more blind dates." Malik exhaled slowly. "I should've knew though. She told me on the phone that she was short and thick, 5'4 and 200 pounds." This made K-Red burst out laughing again.

17

"Nigga, what are you, like six-foot and what? 180? Nigga please, you should've put two and two together. Or should I say 5'4 and 200 together!" K-Red laughed at his own joke. "Let me hit that blood."

Malik took another hit, inhaled and passed the joint to K-Red. "I know, call it wishful thinkin'."

"Call it what?" K-Red asked in a thin voice, trying to hold the smoke in his lungs while talking at the same time.

"Don't trip." Malik replied. "I forgot, you kind of dense." He then said with a smirk.

"Fuck you nigga." K-Red replied. "I don't know what dense is, but it don't sound like a compliment." K-Red never did have an extensive vocabulary. "So fuck you." This time it was Mailk who burst out laughing.

Tupac Shakur rapped about the hypocrisy of those who were so quick to label individuals like us as being violent in a song entitled "Violent" from his 2Pacalypes Now album, which emitted from the speakers in the back and the tweets in the dash of K-Red's car.   It had been an interesting night. Malik was not attracted to big girls but he had a somewhat sensitive side to him when it came to women in general, at least while in their presence.   Of course he would deny the existence of it, but it was this side of him that allowed him to show Chantel's friend Kim a nice time despite her obesity. She was actually a good person though. I in turn came to meet her on an occasion or two myself later on in my life.

K-Red passed the joint back to Malik and as he was about to take a hit, he noticed the Cutlass parked in front of Old Lady Jenkins' house.

"A, Red." Malik said.

"Wha'sup?" asked K-Red, bobbing his head to the music.

"Do you see that car in front of Old Lady Jenkins' house?" asked Malik.

"Yeah, what about it?" K-Red asked in return.

"Isn't somebody sittin' in it?" Malik asked. K-Red peered into the darkness at the car.

"Naw nigga, them the front seats." K-Red answered in dismissal.

"No they ain't." Malik said. "I know you can't see, I don't know why I asked your blind ass anyway. Won't you roll me up a lil' somethin' to wake up to." He finished, squinting at the Cutlass.

Unlike me, my brother did not think that his eyes were playing tricks on him. Somebody *was* sitting in that car. The question was, why? Maybe they were doing the same thing him and K-Red were doing, Malik thought. If so, who was it? He could not really tell what kind of car it was, it looked to him like a Regal or a Cutlass. What he did know was that he had not seen it sitting there anytime before then. And in front of Old Lady Jenkins' house? Malik began to feel uneasy. He did not like the way this looked. Something told him to tell K-Red to start the car and roll out; to go to his house for the night or at least roll past it and see what was up. Malik was usually one who believed in following his first mind. *Naw*, Malik thought silently to himself with a slight shaking of his head, *that nigga's mama be trippin' and I ain't in the mood for no late night sermon.*

K-Red's mother was a devout Christian woman. I myself had a few encounters with her. She was the type that made one feel guilty for every little thing he or she may have done that went against the grain. She kept a Bible in her possession, and like Red Fox's nemesis on the old hit television series "Sanford and Son" (I forget her name), she was quick to hurl some passages from it at you. Her and her son were on two totally different pages in life.

What my brother did feel like doing was getting a little closer to one of his firearms he had left underneath his mattress to go out with the ladies. His reasoning had a lot to do with Chantel's wanting to go outside the city limits to Blue Springs on their night out. That and the fact that they would be riding around a middle class area with only one headlight, which is just about all the probable cause a police officer needed in order to pull over a car full of young blacks, convinced him to uncharacteristically leave his weapons behind.

"Let me see your pistol dawg." Malik requested. K-Red could have cared less how far away from the city they were going, he would carry one or a few of his many guns with him. He had so many enemies that he was beginning to lose count.

"Ain't nobody in that damn car blood; what you so scared fo' nigga?" K-Red said, retrieving a charcoal grey Colt .45 semi-automatic from his waistline. "You need to quit smokin' this bud.   You get high and get to gettin' all paranoid, seein' shit. Boa, I tell you." K-Red said, shaking his head as he handed it to Malik. He then began sprinkling marijuana into a folded EZ wider rolling paper. "Where your shit at anyway?"

"In the crib." Malik replied.

"What good is it gone do you in the crib?   Didn't Eazy-E tell you to never leave the pad without packin' a gun? You should've brought it with you, maybe then you could've shot a couple pounds off Kim." K-Red said, lightening the mood. They both laughed at this.

Malik began to calm down, he felt better with K-Red's pistol in his right hand. The whole time he kept his eyes on the car parked in front of Old Lady Jenkins' house. Malik took the weapon off of safety and checked to make sure that there was a bullet in the chamber.

*****

"Atif!" my mother yelled again as she burst into my bedroom.   "What is your damn problem?"   I continued beating on the window. "Why are you hollarin' and beatin' on my window like you crazy?"

I then, ignoring my mother's string of questions, observed the Cutlass in question as it slowly began creeping up the street. I could clearly see movement from the two individuals seated in the front seats then. It was no longer a question of whether or not someone was actually in the vehicle, but who they were and why were they about to attempt the assassination of my brother? If it was K-Red that they were looking for then they would have been sitting on K-Red's block instead of ours. It was at this moment that I leaped from the windowsill and bolted from our bedroom into the hallway, almost knocking my mother to the ground in the process.

20

"Atif, stop!" I remember my mother screaming frantically behind me as I raced down the dark hallway. I had to warn my brother of the impending danger of which I assumed laid only a few seconds into the future. Malik didn't even have any of his firearms with him. I knew this because me and my hommie D-Mack had been crossing Malik's boundaries just a few hours earlier that day and we saw that all of Malik's weapons were left behind. This was strange to me because the Malik I knew would carry a concealed weapon along to church with him; if he went. These thoughts made me run even faster through the house. I could hear my mother calling out and running right behind me. I didn't care. All I cared about was trying to get Malik's attention before what I thought was almost the inevitable occurred. As I reached the front door, I unlocked the doorknob and tried to open it but it didn't budge.

"Damn!" I cursed aloud. I then turned around, colliding with my mother whom I had forgotten was running directly behind me just that quick. "Mama, where the key to the dead-bolt at?" I asked with a terrified look in my eyes. A look that she had never seen there before.

"What is it Atif? What's wrong?" she asked worriedly in response, noticing the fear in my eyes as she dug into her robe's right pocket for the key. Whatever anger she had been feeling for being awakened in such a fashion and at such an hour in the middle of the night was erased instantaneously by the premonition of some kind of danger. "What's wrong with Malik?" she asked, moving me out of the way and inserting the key into the dead-bolt. She then turned the key and opened the front door.

I didn't want to waste any time trying to explain the situation to my mother so I ran out of the front door waving my hands and screaming my brother's name. The Cutlass was almost right up on K-Red's car now with someone hanging out of the passenger side window while gripping what looked to me to be an AK-47 assault rifle. I then looked backed towards K-Red's car and I didn't see Malik in the passenger seat.

"Where the hell did he go to that fast?"   I remember thinking to myself as I tripped over the last step leading away from our front porch, falling to the ground.

*****

"Oh shit, watch out nigga!" K-Red exclaimed, swatting at Malik's left pant leg.

"What the ...?   Ssss, ah man!" Malik grimaced in pain, feeling a burning sensation on his left upper thigh. "Watch what the fuck you doin' man, you tryin' to set me on fire or somethin'?" Malik asked, brushing the lit joint out of his lap and onto the floor.

"My bad blood, I was tryin' to hand it to you.   Grab it man before it burn a hole in my floor mat." K-Red said. Malik bent over in his seat and began searching for the joint.   He then heard K-Red chuckling.

"What you laughin' at ?" Malik asked, still bent over in his seat.

"Your brotha' man, he just tripped and fell flat on his face.   What the fuck is he doin' out here any-"

K-Red was interrupted by the crackling sound of rapid gunfire.   It was deafening, mixed with a scream and the sound of shattering glass, it created a sense and scene of absolute panic.   We all were used to the sound of gunfire, but to experience it up close and personal was a different story indeed.   Instinctively K-Red opened his car door and dove out onto the sidewalk, using his car for cover.   Malik, however, wasn't so lucky.   By the time he went to follow suit, the dark blue Cutlass seemed to be right up on him.   Malik turned his head back and was staring down the long dark barrel of the assailant's assault rifle.   As he looked up into the beholder's face he could make out not much more than a skin tone and what seemed to be a grin behind a blue ski mask.   It was upon seeing this grin that transformed my brother's panic into blind rage.   Malik raised K-Red's .45 and attempted to fire a shot, but he saw a flash of fire that seemed to jump out towards him.   He felt an excruciating stab of enormous pain in his right shoulder blade simultaneously that felt like Bo Jackson had hit him

22

with a baseball bat, causing him to drop the pistol. Malik cried out in pain. It was a type of pain that is almost impossible to describe. One would have to experience it for themselves in order to even begin to comprehend just how much it hurt. It was a sense of pain that he had never even imagined feeling before. All Malik wanted in life at that particular moment was to get away from that pain or at least the source of it. He didn't even think of trying to recover the gun he had dropped, all he knew was that he didn't want another dose of the medicine his assailant was dishing out. He rolled over onto his stomach and tried to crawl out of the driver's side like K-Red had done.

"Hold up cuzz, I ain't dismiss you! Where the fuck you think you goin'?" Malik heard someone say followed by two more shots. The first one missed and the powerful AK-47 slug ripped straight through the driver's side car door which was left partially ajar. The second one struck my brother in the lower-back. Malik's whole body tensed up and his legs seemed to go numb, giving out on him. "Here nigga, I ain't through. Take this with you!" Malik heard the same voice say as three more shots were let loose. By this time my brother, with the assistance of K-Red, had almost made it completely out of the vehicle and out of the line of fire. Unfortunately his legs were the only part of his body that remained in the car and it was his right leg that caught one of the most recently released bullets. K-Red pulled Malik out of the car and onto the ground. Malik's heart was racing and he was beginning to lose consciousness. He felt cold and his body was shaking uncontrollably. The sound of tires burning rubber on the pavement and laughter echoed eerily as the dark blue Cutlass sped off into the dreadful night. Malik heard the sound of footsteps running towards him as he slipped into a sea of darkness.

"Go call the ambulance!" K-Red exclaimed towards me as I ran up to his side. I just stood there frozen in horror with my eyes wide and my mouth open at the sight of my brother laid out across K-Red's lap leaking blood from everywhere it seemed. He looked dead. I felt sick to my stomach. "Come on Malik, wake up dawg! You gotta stay woke blood!" K-Red pleaded, smacking Malik across the cheek.

"Is he dead?" I managed, shakily.

"What are you still standin' there fo' man? I said call the damn ambulance!" K-Red retorted.

"Why don't we just take him, they gone take too lo-"

"Go!" K-Red cut me off. I snapped to attention, turning around and running towards the front door. I don't remember what I was thinking on my way. I was in a state of shock and total disbelief. Malik was laying on the ground dying. *My brother!* When I got halfway up the front steps I noticed that the glass from the screen door was shattered and most of it laid askew on the front porch. I raced up the rest of the stairs and snatched open the screen door, running inside. Upon my entrance into the dark foyer, I tripped and fell again.

"Damn, what was.." I tried, turning to see what it was I had tripped over. What I saw crushed me. I mean it felt like someone or something just drained all of the adrenaline my body had been pumping through my veins during the course of events that had taken place as my knees got almost too weak to stand. My mind went blank and I simply stood there staring down at my mother as she laid there sprawled out in a puddle of blood with a facial expression that once held a scream eternalized on her face.

*****

PATIENCE

"You make me want it when I see you flaunt it,
Gotta get up on it.
If you don't wanna get bit by a dawg,
You shouldn't taunt it.
Girl when you smiled
Off in my direction,
I felt some type of affection
Deep in my mid-section.
Can you feel this connection
That I have been stressin?
Yo' thick hips and complexion
is givin' me an erection."

-Soody Mak

2

"Atif!"

"Hmm?" I mumbled groggily, still partially asleep.

"Ati-"

"Okay, okay. I 'm up, I'm up." I sat up in my bed, trying to recall whatever it was that I had been dreaming about. Frustrated with myself for not being able to do so, I stood up and stretched the rest of the sleep from my body and then headed to the bathroom down the hall.

It was the morning of the much anticipated first day of high school for me. I was officially a freshman. Now that the day had finally arrived, it didn't seem too much different from any other. The last three weeks were spent hastily running in and out of all the local malls; the Landing Mall, Banister Mall, Independence Center, Ward Parkway Mall, the Blue Ridge Mall and the Oak Park Mall with my grandmother in tow trying to find the right clothes to start high school in. I wished that my mother was there to take me school shopping, but at the same time I knew that she would not have spoiled me like Big Mama.

I missed my mother dearly. I would have given absolutely anything to bring her back if I could but I understood the finality of death and I knew that bringing someone back from the grave was beyond my capabilities. After three months I still could not fathom why our Creator would allow my mother to be murdered like she was. She was so innocent and had nothing to do with the reasons why her life was taken. Things had not been the same either.

Malik pulled on through to the surprise of his surgeons whom had stated how unlikely it was for him to recover from surgery. So even though I was somewhat upset with our Creator for my mother's death, I was at the same time thankful to Him for allowing Malik's survival to be incorporated into His Will. The doctors also said that if by chance Malik did survive, it was doubtful that he would ever walk again. But my

27

brother, with strong determination and an almost primitive instinct to survive, pulled through nevertheless. After only a month of physical therapy he was on his feet, walking with a slight limp against all odds.

"When do you plan on makin' yo-self presentable down there man?" I said aloud to my penis while urinating. I was fourteen years old and my pubic hair seemed to be taking its sweet time with filling out. "You know, it is about that time for us to break our virginity and I ain't tryin' to do this lookin' like no amateur."

Yes, I was still technically a virgin. More so out of fear. I had my chances and opportunities but my humility and fear restricted me from taking advantage of them. I was not afraid of the act of having sex itself, I yearned for it honestly, it was my inexperience that frightened me. It was the chance of not doing something right or not being "big" enough that got to me. And if news of something like that made it back to Malik or D-Mack or whoever, then I would have been better off crawling into a hole somewhere and dying because I would never hear the end of it. That is what I was afraid of.

I shook myself clean and flushed the toilet. Then I went over to the sink and began washing my hands. While doing this I heard a knock on the bathroom door.

"I'm usin' it." I said, spreading toothpaste on my toothbrush.

"Open the door, punk. I gotta piss." Malik said from the other side of the door. I went and unlocked it.

"Get out, sissy." Malik said, stepping into the bathroom.

"Ugh man," I replied, repulsively pinching my nose with my thumb and index finger, "Your breath smell like hot garbage." I finished, knowing that just seconds ago my breath was probably just as bad. But with my toothbrush in my right hand and a mouth full of toothpaste, I felt like I had room to talk.

"A'ight," Malik warned with a smirk on his face, "don't think that I won't send you to school with a black eye on your first day."

"Aw yeah?" I asked, stalling for time so that I could place myself out of my brother's reach, knowing from experience what kind of assault my next comment would bring on.

"Yeah." Malik responded as he began urinating into the toilet.

"Well, I would rather start the first day of school with a black eye than have to go to school knowing that I am in the same grade I was in last year!" I said. This was supposed to be Malik's senior year but according to his credits he was still considered a junior.

"You little...!" Malik started. He forgot what he was in the process of doing when he lunged at me, sprinkling urine down the front of his boxer shorts and on his fingers. "Damn." He muttered to himself after I slammed the bathroom door in his face, laughing and running down the hall.

*****

My new bus stop was on the corner of 26th and Prospect, directly in front of Kevin's Cleaners and across the street from a club that my mother used to frequent called The Green Duck Lounge. It was nice out, your typical early fall weather. I stood there wearing a black Karl Kani Jeans outfit with red trim. Under my Karl Kani Jeans jacket I wore a solid red T-Shirt tucked into my jeans. On my feet were a pair of black Rockport casual boots. My new outfit, my skin fade with the crisp lining, oh I was ready to make my entrance. I had hoped to do so with my brother but he never went to his first hour classes, if he went at all. He got up and went to school when he felt like it.

There were four other people standing and waiting for the bus to come. After ten minutes of speculating on how high school would be amongst the group, a big yellow school bus pulled up to the curb in front of us

29

with the number sixteen on the side. The bus driver was a black woman in her mid-thirties with long extensions in her hair. She wore a pair of dark gray slacks with a uniform shirt, which was a lighter shade of gray, buttoned all the way up to the second to last button with a white patch over the front right pocket that read RYDER. She smiled, showing off a gold cap on her left front tooth with a cursive letter "L" on it, welcoming us all aboard. Afterwards, she closed the doors and stood up, waiting for us to find a seat before she spoke.

"A'ight, after I pull off from here there will be no more stops until we get to Central." She said. Everyone stopped talking and focused on her. "My name is La'nay and as you can see I am your bus driver for this year. I noticed some new faces and thought that I'd introduce myself and explain how I do things on my bus. I don't mind y'all talkin' to each other as long as y'all keep it down and don't be hollerin' outta my windows. Y'all can chew gum and eat y'all's little candy or whatever, I don't care. Just don't leave no trash on my bus, take it with you. Once you get on this bus, find a seat and stay in it until we get where we goin'. No fightin', no cussin' and no gettin' off at other people's stops. Any questions?"

"I got a question." D-Mack said, standing.

"What is it?" she asked.

"They call me D-Mack, and I was wonderin' if you might need a fresh dressed young playa' like myself in your life?" D-Mack asked. Everyone on the bus erupted in laughter.

"Well D-Train, or whatever you call yo-self, you are a little too young for me. Look me up in another fifteen years or so." She replied.

"Are you sure?" D-Mack asked. "I'm young and full of endurance *now*." More laugher from the kids on the bus.

"Yeah, I'm sure." she said, joining in with the rest of the kids in their fit of laughter. "Now sit your crazy self down boy. Your name should be De-lirious." She finished as she turned around, taking a seat herself and pulling off.

I was seated next to my hommie D-Mack, his birth name was Darion Nichols. He was dressed in some black Levi jeans with a Blackhawks hockey jersey. Around his neck he wore a gold rope necklace with a gold Old English letter D as the emblem.

"You aint' got nothin' comin dawg, she ain't messin' with you." I told him.

"Aw man she just frontin' cause all y'all was watchin'. You know me, I 'm a pimp by nature." D-Mack said, grabbing a hold of the three hairs on his chin. "If I really wanted her I could have her. Don't be surprised when you see her pulling up on the block in this big raggedy ass bus handin' me a fistful of money. Malik and them a be like, 'Look at lil' pimp!'" D-Mack finished. Sometimes it seemed as if Darion thought that his whole purpose in life was to earn Malik and K-Red's approval.

"Yeah, right." I said. We rode in silence for a couple of blocks with the both of us staring out of the window at nothing in particular. After a few more moments, D-Mack turned to me.

"A man, I know we ain't never really talked about it, but that was messed up what happened to Rose." D-Mack said.

It had been three months since that fatal night. I don't know why he chose to wait until then to offer his condolences. Our relationship was strange after my mother's death. I mean we spent a lot of time together like always, we just did so in silence. Over the summer I had been in a state of withdrawal. Darion was the only person outside of my brother and grandmother whose company I didn't mind. He was just always...there, and his presence alone was comforting to me. There were times where I would begin to cry softly out of the blue and I never felt the need to hide it. We had seen each other cry on countless occasions. We grew up getting whoopings together. I don't know how I would have made it through all of that without

31

him always being around. Malik and I, we distanced ourselves from everyone on the block. Especially Malik, he seemed to be suspicious of everyone. As if the whole neighborhood played a part in our mother's death. When the situation was looked at from our point of view and given some thought, our isolation and peculiar way of carrying ourselves throughout that summer was easily understood. K-Red did for him what D-Mack had done for me. This all brought us closer together.

"Yeah, I know." I said, wondering how many times I would hear that throughout the day.

"Do y'all know who did it yet?"

"Naw." I answered. "I mean, Malik might know but he won't say nothin' about it." Silence. "I thought that you was gone wear that Nike suit today." I said, changing the subject.

"I was, I changed my mind this mornin' though." D-Mack said. "A, I heard that Kev got out of Juvenile a couple of days ago." It was rumored that Kev had been apprehended for carrying a concealed weapon and was detained at the Juvenile Justice Center on 26th street.

"Nigga you always hearin' somethin." I said. He was, too. Whenever something went down he always seemed to have the latest on it. "What you tellin' me for anyway?"

"I was just sayin', shit, if he did get out then he will probably be up at the school today. If he is, what you gone do?" D-Mack asked.

"What do you mean what I'm a do? I ain't trippin' on him."

"You know everybody gone be anticipatin' a rematch. I was gone jump in when y'all was fightin' last year bu-"

"But what?" I cut in.

"It didn't look like you needed no help or nothin' to me. It ain't like you lost."

"It ain't like I *won* either."

We rode the rest of the way in silence. Darion never was off into a lot of fighting. He could and would, he just was the type who avoided confrontations. I always sensed that Kev put a little fear into his chest though for some reason or another.

As we got closer to the school, I wondered to myself if Kev would be holding a grudge. Then again, who was I kidding? Our whole relationship was a grudge. I didn't fear him, in fact I believed that I would win if we were to fight again. Kev was no match for me when it came to boxing, but I in return was no match for him when it came to wrestling. He was bigger and stronger than I was. It was my speed alone that kept him at bay during our last match. I just had enough on my mind already without having Kev to worry about.

Moments later the bus turned into a spacious parking lot filled with the teachers' cars and eleven other buses lined up in front of the school. The school itself was a brand new two story brick and glass building. It had Central High School engraved in stone across the top of the front doors. An American flag flapped in the wind atop a tall silver flag pole. There were bushes along the sidewalks and flower beds up under the classroom windows.

I stepped off of the bus with D-Mack in tow, together we fought our way through the crowded entrances. Once inside we noticed an eagle painted on the floor in the main hallway. CENTRAL EAGLES was stenciled around the eagle.

"We got a big bird for a mascot?" D-Mack asked mostly to himself. "I hope they don't plan on puttin' that thing on our football jerseys."

There were six hallways on the first level, three on the left and three on the right. The walls were lined with lockers and classroom doorways with the teachers standing outside giving directions and conversing amongst themselves.

"Do you have any idea where our lockers is?" D-Mack asked me.

"My locker number is three-fifty-six, I'm a go see if that means it is in the third hall."

"If that's how it go, then my locker should be here in the first hall somewhere. I'm a holler at you in the cafeteria durin' lunch. Save me a spot if you get there before I do." D-Mack said.

"A'ight then." I said, offering my right fist for some dap. We bumped our fist together lightly and split up. D-Mack headed on up first hall and I made my way to third hall.

I found my locker in between two other lockers whose occupants already had them open.   Without paying attention to whoever was on either side of me, I began turning the dial on my locker, entering the combination that was typed on my class schedule. Failing to get it open with the first try, I started to put the combination in again when I heard the locker on the right side of me slam closed. I looked up and there stood Kev glaring at me.

Kev wore a pair of black Dickie work pants sagging way below the waistline and a blue Kansas City Royals sweater. On his feet were a pair of blue and white Nike tennis shoes. He had a nose ring in his nose and his natural curly hair was cut short with the sides faded and parts on the right side.

"Sup cuzz?" Kev asked.   He was trying to start something.

" I ain't no kin to you, nigga." I answered. This was almost exactly how the last fight started.   I really wanted to enjoy my first day at Central in peace, but at the same time I was not about to back down if he wanted to go there with me right then and there. Kev smirked at me as he turned and walked away. I noticed a blue bandanna hanging neatly out of his back pocket. I shook my head and went back to the task of trying to get my locker open.

After failing for the second time, I heard the locker on my left hand side slam shut. I was so busy re-entering the combination with my tongue protruding out of the corner of my mouth, like I always did and still do to this day while concentrating, that I didn't bother to see who the locker belonged to. I heard a female giggling and when I looked up I saw who just had to be the prettiest girl in the whole school.

She was holding an American History book with a pink notepad across her chest with her left arm and she was covering her mouth with her right hand to muffle the laughter. She was beautiful. Light skinned with long, silky, black hair down to the middle of her back. Her eyes were light brown, hiding behind long luscious eyelashes deep set into a very pretty face. Her eyebrows were arched and evenly separated on both sides of a perfect nose. She wore some tight fitting white Guess Jeans that looked as if they were painted on with a paint brush. She had on a white T-Shirt that read: IDAHO? NO, UDAHO! Across the front in big bold black letters. The shirt was tied in a knot at the bottom in the front, showing off a pair of thighs and hips that was sure to cause more than a few cases of whiplash throughout the day.

"Are you laughin' at me?" I asked, turning my head from left to right to make sure that I was the only one standing there.

"Yes." she answered in between giggles. That voice! She even talked sexy. Her voice had just the faintest little trace of bass in it, it wasn't all high-pitched and childlike. Hearing her speak made me think of T-Boz from the group TLC.

"For what?" I asked.

"Why do you have your tongue sticking out of your mouth like that? Are you thirsty?" she asked in proper English, laughing softly at her own question.

"No, it's just a habit I got. I do it whenever I'm concentratin' on somethin'." I answered. If she was not so fine I would have had something real slick to say about her laughing at me like that. I was a little too infatuated to get offended.

"Why are you concentrating so much on opening your locker? It really is not that hard, you know."

"Well, it might not have been that hard for you to open yours, but there is somethin' wrong with mine."

"Can I try?" she asked, holding out her right hand. I handed her my class schedule and stepped to the side. "Hold this." She said, handing me her things. She then looked at the combination on the schedule and began turning the dial. I was standing behind her admiring the view when I heard a sharp click.

"It looks just fine to me." she said, opening my locker.

"Looks just fine to me too." I mumbled under breath.

"Did you say something?" she asked me, turning to face me. Damn she had some pretty eyes. "He-llo." She said, waving her hand in front of my face. I had lost myself in them. "Are you with me?"

"Aw, yeah...uh...I said thank you." I lied, thinking to myself that with her was exactly where I wanted to be.

"We have the same home room." She said, handing me my schedule and reaching for her stuff.

"Aw yeah?" I asked, maybe with a little too much enthusiasm, grabbing my schedule from her and taking a look for myself. That meant that she was more than likely a freshman just like me.

"Yes. Can I have my history book now?"

"Aw, yeah, here. My bad." I apologized, handing her things to her. She took them, smiled and then turned to leave. I could not let her just walk away like that. "A, won't you let me walk you to your class? Well, our class?" I offered. That had to be the oldest line in the book.

" Do you know where it is?"

"No. We can find it together though."

"I can get lost on my own." She said, walking away. I stood there at my locker watching her walk seemingly right out of my life. When she reached the end of the hallway she looked back at me and smiled as she turned the corner. To this day I believe that was the prettiest smile I have ever seen in person. In hindsight, I think that I was supposed to catch up to her. Maybe she was playing one of the many games females play. I was way too naïve then to catch on to something like that.

*****

My first hour teacher was a middle aged black man by the name of Mr. Williams. On first impression I believed that he was pretty cool despite the fact that he had the nerve to assign homework on the first day of school.

Patience. That was her name. I made sure to find a seat near Patience in our homeroom class. As Mr. Williams took roll call, I anxiously waited to see exactly which name Patience would answer to, and when my name was called in return I could have sworn that I saw Patience out of my peripheral vision seeming to be waiting for the same thing. Ever since I had first seen her at my locker earlier that morning my whole train of thought revolved around her. I had never been so affected by a girl like that in my life. Who was she? Where did she come from? These were some of the questions that I asked myself throughout the day.

The day seemed to be passing by slowly as the excitement of being in high school began to recede like George Jefferson's hairline. I knew a lot of people up at Central. I was approached countless times even by individuals whom I did not know inquiring about my brother. There were a lot of different cliques from different sets at Central. There were more Bloods than Crips but the latter stuck together whereas the former seemed to only associate with people from their own neighborhoods. I enjoyed the attention, especially from the females who were in my brother's grade. They all would tell me how much I looked like Malik, which didn't bother me since this was clearly attractive in their eyes. One girl even wrapped her arm around my shoulders and insisted on showing me to my third hour class. She was an aggressive senior by the name of Niki. She patted me on my butt when she dropped me off.

I found myself weaving through traffic again on my way to the cafeteria for lunch. I was amazed at how big the lunchroom was when I got there. Adding to my surprise were the numerous vending machines filled with snacks and soft drinks lined up against the wall to the far left. The cafeteria was loud in volume as bits and pieces from the many different conversations blended into one like a symphony. I stood in line and got my lunch which consisted of a chili-cheese dog and curly fries. I then went and found a table that was partially empty and took a seat. Half-way into my chili dog I heard a voice from behind me and recognized it instantly.

"Hello Atif."

Patience. I turned toward her as my heart sped up and butterflies began to fill my stomach. When I faced her, she reached for my face and for a hot second I thought that I was about to be kissed! I instinctively closed my eyes. Patience then took her thumb and wiped my bottom lip with it.

"You had some cheese hanging off of your lip." She said, smiling down at me. There was that perfect smile again. I was *too* embarrassed. "Do you mind if I sit here?"

"Naw, go ahead." I replied, pulling the chair off from under the table for her. She then sat down and placed a bag of Cheetos and a Sprite on the table before her.

"That all you gone eat?" I asked, gesturing towards her chips.

"Yes, I don't like hot dogs. Plus, I am not very hungry anyway." She answered, opening her bag of Cheetos.

"You don't know too many people here, do you?" I asked after a few moments of silence between us.

"No, why do you ask?"

"Because every time that I saw you today you was by yo-self and I can tell by the way you talk that you ain't from down this way."

"How do I talk?"

"Proper."

"And what exactly is wrong with using proper English?" she asked me with her arched eyebrows raised.

"I didn't say nothin' was wrong with proper English, I just said that that is the way you talk." I answered. "I like the way you talk, it makes you sound....."

"Intelligent?"

"Naw. Smart."

"Is there really a big difference between smart and intelligent?"

"No, not much. Intelligent just ain't the word I was lookin' for."

"Whatever. You are just mad because my word was bigger than yours." Patience said. I laughed at this.

"Where your boyfriend at?"

"I don't have a boyfriend Atif."

"Ooh girl, say that one more time."

"What? I don't have a boyfriend?"

"Naw. My name."

"Atif?" she said, giving me a look that said, "What is wrong with you?" I gripped the edge of the table with both of my hands and closed my eyes. Then I made my body quiver as if the very mentioning of my name from her lips brought me to the highest point of sexual climax. "Stop, boy!" Patience exclaimed, laughing as she playfully slapped me across my right biceps. She looked around the cafeteria to see if anyone else had seen me. "You are a freak, you know that?" she stated more than asked.

Moments later, to my disappointment, a bell sounded throughout the cafeteria signaling the end of first shift lunch break. Patience began to gather her trash from the table.

"Don't worry about that, I will take it up Patience."

"Ooh boy, say that again." Patience said. The two of us laughed at this. "I have to go Atif, I will see you later." She said, turning to leave. I remember wondering if she had a little freak in her herself as I

39

watched her hips sway from side to side in an undercover seductive way that was almost rhythmic.

Later on that day I bumped into Darion in the main hall after seventh period.

"Sup blood? I ain't seen you all day, where you been hidin' at? "D-Mack asked me.

" I ain't been hidin' nowhere. Where was you at durin' lunch?"

" I got algebra for fifth hour and my class is in the third hall, so we eat last. I got hungry like a big dog waitin' until it was time for us to go to lunch." Darion answered. "You get any phone numbers?"

"Nope. You?"

"Naw."

"You a poor excuse for a pimp, you know that?" I asked. Honestly I was surprised by that. I would have guessed that Darion would've had at least five numbers from five different females by then.

"I was just peepin' the scene today, you know, seein' who's supposed to be goin' with who. It is some *ho's* up at this mutha' fucka' man, damn! They everywhere. I got this one light skinned chick in third hour nigga. She tuff, I'm tellin' you. Light brown eyes, long black hair, thick-"

"You talkin' about her right there?" I cut in with my head tilted to the left, indicating Patience. We were not too far from my locker.

"Yeah, that's her. I wonder where she came from with her fine self." Darion commented as we turned into third hall, heading in her direction. "Is that Kev she talkin' too?"

"Yep." I answered shortly, feeling a slight pang of jealousy.

Darion noticed that we were heading straight towards Patience and Kev, he then asked, "What you finna do dawg?" first looking at Kev and then back at me.

"The same thing I was finna do in the first place nigga, go to my locker." I replied smartly. "Lay on back with your scary ass." I finished with a smirk on my face.

Kev was turning to leave as we approached my locker, "mean mugging" us both as he passed. We both refused to falter under his scornful gaze by looking away. In a way we were being challenged, and if we had lowered our gaze Kev would have been the victor. Patience witnessed the exchange and looked curiously between the three of us.

"Hi Atif." Patience greeted as the three of us watched Kev retreat up the hall. D-Mack arched his eyebrows in surprise with the mentioning of my name from Patience. "What was that all about?"

"Nothin'." I answered shortly. I then turned towards my locker and began to turn the combination dial.

"Wha'sup?" D-Mack asked Patience.

"Hi."

"How you doin'?"

"Fine."

"What's your name?" Darion was using his so called mack-daddy voice. It was pitiful, but it did seem to work the majority of the time I must admit.

"Patience."

"That's *sexy* girl, who named you that?"

"My mother." Patience answered shortly, not acknowledging the compliment.

"Damn!" I cursed at my locker as I began to re-enter the combination for the third time. D-Mack told me later on that I interrupted his mack. Please, it was not intentional. What do you think? Did it read to you like she was picking up what he was dropping down?

"Here Atif, let me help you." Patience offered, welcoming the chance to discontinue the conversation between her and Darion before he got around to asking for her phone number. I stepped back and stood beside D-Mack, allowing her to get at the combination lock.

"Ain't you gone ask me for the combination?" I asked as she began to work the dial.

"I don't need to. I have it memorized."

"You only saw it once." I pointed out.

41

"I know."

"So if somethin' come up missin' I should holler at you then, right?" I asked her with a smirk on my face.

"Boy you do not have anything that I want." Patience said while opening the locker. "At least not in your locker, that is." She finished, looking me up and down. Darion chuckled excitedly in the background. "Here," she said, working the dial again. "I am going to set this so that all you will have to do when you get to school tomorrow is turn the dial to the last number of the combination and open it up. I don't want you to bite the tip of your tongue off in concentration."

"Aw yeah? That 's cool, I appreciate that. It don't like me for some reason." I said, referring to my locker.

"Well, I will see you tomorrow Atif, I don't want to miss my bus." Patience said after an awkward moment of silence.

"A'ight, I'll see you then." I said, putting my Modern Science book in my locker and retrieving my American History book as she turned and left.

"Why you didn't get her number Atif?" Darion asked as we watched Patience retreat down the hallway.

"What?"

"Her *number* nigga! You was supposed to ask her for her number. That's what she was *waitin'* on!"

"Think so?" I asked, feeling kind of square.

"Man, come *on* man! She stood there and *told* you she wanted you." Darion said, grabbing himself and jumping up and down.

"No she didn't. " I said doubtfully.

"*Boy you do not have anything that I want, at least not in your locker.*" D-Mack stated, mimicking Patience's proper English and looking me up and down like she had done. "Ain't that what you heard?"

"Yeah, I guess that *is* what she said." I replied. I did hear her say that but it wasn't until Darion pointed it out that I *really* heard it.

"You damn right that's what she said. I see I gotta give you a few more lessons in pimpology."

"Nigga please. *Simpology* is more like it." I replied, shutting my locker. We both laughed and headed back down the hall.

What a nice day that was. I will always remember it for two reasons: it was my first encounter with Patience, and it was the beginning of me losing my innocence. My freshman year was significant because it was during this time in my life that I decided to take a detour. I begun to lose my sense of patience and my life seemed to all of a sudden take off at one hundred miles per hour, spiraling down a road full of sharp, twisting curves and speed bumps.

*****

THE INITIATION

"It ain't hard to believe
that she was manipulated,
her temple robbed of its sanctity
when she was penetrated.
She once was a beautiful black baby beamin'
With aspirations and hope,
Abased to a thugged-out Ghetto Queen
Only motivated by sex, gettin' high, and sellin' dope."
-Soody Mak

3

The weeks seemed to fly by as all of us freshmen at Central High got comfortable and made ourselves at home. Darion and I tried out for the jr. varsity football team and made the cut. Darion was the second string quarterback but he felt cheated because he was a far better quarterback than the sophomore that made the starting position. I, being the fastest runner on the team, won a starting wide receiver slot. Kev made the team also, and was the starting halfback. With the assistance of me and Kev, Coach Turner believed that we could go undefeated that year and he said so to anyone that would listen. The team had been in a slump ever since Malik and K-Red moved on up to varsity, quitting soon afterwards. Even they never went undefeated.

On the morning of the day that the first home game was to be played, Darion and I were approached by Patience and a girl whose name was Tamika, but we called her Teebaby. Teebaby stood about 5'3, her skin was the color of honey and we called her Teebaby because of her smooth, baby like face and her real soft, baby like voice. When people heard her speak, they would often make the mistake of assuming she was shy not knowing that she was the exact opposite, outspoken with an acid tongue when she felt like it was necessary.

"Hi Atif!" Patience greeted with a warm smile as her and Teebaby approached.

"A, wha'sup Patience? Wha'sup Teebaby?" I returned the greeting to the both of them.

"Nothin', wha'sup with you?" Teebaby greeted in return.

"Nothin,' I'm chillin'." I answered.

"Damn, y'all act like y'all don't recognize a pimp in y'all's presence. Can I get a hello, a fuck you or somethin? What?" D-Mack asked sarcastically.

"Hi Darion." Patience and Teebaby said in unison while rolling their eyes at the same time.

"Y'all ridin with us today?" I asked the young ladies. They both were on the cheerleading squad.

"Yes, we will be cheering for you and Darion." Patience answered.

"Darion?" Teebaby asked, mocking surprise.

"Yeah, D-Mack. I'm the quarterback, you ain't hip?"

"If you the quarterback, why you always on the bench?" Teebaby asked Darion. "Who did you bribe to get on the team anyway?"

"Girl you sleep on me. I can throw that ball almost as good as you throw that ass when you walk." D-Mack answered. I burst out in a fit of laughter. Teebaby did have a behind like a grown woman. That was my hommie there though, he kept a slick comeback. It was all comedy watching those two go at it.

"Shut up boy." Teebaby said to D-Mack, giving his shoulder a push with her fingertips. A bell sounded throughout the halls signaling that the students had five minutes to get to their first hour classes.

"Why you don't ever walk me to my class like Atif be doin' for Patience?" Teebaby asked Darion.

"Three reasons. For one, I ain't no trick ass nigga like Atif. For two, I ain't your man. And last but not least, *I'm* the shit! You should be walkin *me* to *my* class!" D-Mack answered. Teebaby rolled her eyes and turned to walk off. "Come on girl, you know I'm a walk my baby mama to her class."

"I ain't yo' baby mama boy. Lets go, you gone make me get a tardy. We will see y'all later girl." Teebaby said to us. She then grabbed D-Mack by the arm while turning to leave. "Here, carry my books." She said, thrusting her books into D-Mack's unsuspecting arms.

"What you trying' to do to my rep? I can't be seen carryin' your books for you. That go against everything I stand for." D-Mack said. Teebaby elbowed him in the ribs. "A'ight, a'ight. I'll holler." Darion said to us as they left.

"Those two are going to make a good couple. I think that Teebaby is the only girl in this school who can stand to put up with that boy." Patience said to me as I closed my locker. I then took Patience's books from her arms, adding them to my own, and we ceremoniously walked to Mr. Williams' class together.

*****

"It is now twenty minutes till, I am going to let everyone call it quits a little early today.   Everybody understand the homework assignment?" Mr. Williams asked the class, taking a seat on the edge of his desk. He wore a pair of creased black slacks with a white T-shirt that read Central Eagles Spirit across the front. He also wore a pair of gold rimmed prescription eyeglasses on his face. His hair was cut short to the scalp displaying a pattern of waves that disappeared into a skin fade on the sides. "I will take that as a yes." Mr. Williams commented, referring to the chorus of groans that accompanied his question.

"Since we have a little time left before class is dismissed, I thought that I would share some American (he indicated quotation marks with his fingers) history with you that you will not find in your history books. You see, I don't follow a predetermined curriculum because I believe that the curriculum offered for us to follow, as far as history teachers are concerned, does not relate to the majority of the students who attend Central High School. If you study the history books that were issued to you on the first day of school from cover to cover, you will find that it is full of Caucasian American history. And that would be fine if this were a class full of Caucasian students, but that is not the case here in room number 128. As a matter of fact, I don't see one Caucasian face in this classroom at the present time." Mr. Williams said. Patience raised her hand above her head in response to this statement. "Yes Patience?"

"My mother is Caucasian, so technically you do have at lease ½ of a Caucasian face in your class." Patience commented, smiling.

"Well...not necessarily, more like ¼." A student by the name of Rakim said.

"Excuse me?" Patience asked perplexed.

"Your father is a black man, right?" Rakim asked Patience.

Here *he* go. I thought to myself. Rakim would try to convince you that the Caucasian race was grafted from a

47

group of Africans isolated on an island by a big headed black scientist some six thousand years ago if you let him.

"Yes," Patience answered.

"The black gene is dominant, white is recessive. So you are still considered to be black." Rakim finished.

"Oh please, you think you know everything don't you?" Patience asked Rakim with a sour look.

"Wait a minute now Patience, Rakim does have a point." Mr. Williams cut in with a smile on his face. Patience rolled her eyes. She did not like to be wrong about anything. "Now, I don't know about the black gene/white gene concept. I am not a science buff so I am not going to comment on that. But, you are still considered to be black despite having a Caucasian mother. In fact, if you were born back during slavery you would still be looked upon as a black slave in most cases. However, we are straying from the subject. This is not a black or white issue. What I am saying is just because Patience has Caucasian blood flowing through her veins does not mean that Caucasian history is all that Patience needs to learn.

"In this class, we are going to dig off into some of Patience's *father's* history also. The only thing that these history books have to say about our ancestors is that they were either slaves or running around butt naked in the jungles of Africa with bones in their noses practicing cannibalism." This brought laughter from the class. "Has anyone ever heard of Black Wall Street?" The students looked amongst themselves with a shake of their heads.

"Does it have anything to do with some kind of riot that happened a long time ago?" Rakim asked.

"Yes Rakim, as a matter of fact it does. But it was much more than just a simple riot. It was a *massacre*. Sometime after the Civil War there was a small section of the state of Oklahoma set aside supposedly for the Natives and ex-slaves. This small area was located in part of what is now the city of Tulsa. During this time period beginning with the turn of the century, a lot of blacks migrated to Tulsa and built a strong and prosperous black community. Money is said to have circulated at least one hundred times before making its way out of the community; nowadays the black dollar does not last a mere fifteen minutes. By the year 1921 this community thrived with over 600 successful black owned businesses; 21 churches, 21 restaurants, 30 grocery stores, 2 movie theaters, a hospital, a bank, a post office, libraries, schools, law offices, a ½ dozen private airplanes, even a bus system.

"Well on June 1, 1921 a young black man was falsely accused of touching a white woman and all hell broke loose when a band of Caucasian vigilantes attempted to hang this brotha' without a proper trial. You see, a lot of whites had just made it back from the war years before and they came home to poverty while this community of ex-slaves was over here living it up. They didn't like to see this and it brought on feelings of jealousy and envy. When the local blacks objected to the hanging, this gave these envious whites the excuse they were waiting for the take down what is now known as Black Wall Street. The community was burned to the ground and over 300 blacks were killed in the melee."

It is difficult to express how I felt at that particular moment. I will say this though, hearing about Black Wall Street for the first time in Mr. Williams' class that morning ignited a passion within me to learn more about such incidents that would not fully surface until later on in my life. School was not like it was in Mr. Williams' class. If it was, I believe that the drop out rate for young blacks would reduce tremendously. None of my teachers had ever piqued my interest in such a way before.

Mr. Williams looked at the many sorrowful facial expressions throughout the class. "How does this revelation make you guys feel. Angry? Sympathetic? Inquisitive? It should. Actual facts like these are deliberately hidden or covered up. History that is forgotten will only repeat itself."

"Coach Turner speaks very highly of you Atif. How do you think the game will turn out tonight?" Mr. Williams then asked me, changing the subject after a moment of thoughtful silence from the class.

"We will beat'em." I answered, full of confidence.

"Grandview High School, isn't that your old neck of the woods Patience?" Mr. Williams asked Patience.

49

"Yes."

"From what I've seen over the years, they are a pretty good team, don't you think?"

"Yes, the um...what do you call it does not allow the other team to score a lot of points."

"The defense?" Mr. Williams asked.

"Yes, the defense. There is this real big guy. His name is Mike and he always tries to hurt the person he tackles."

"Yeah, I know who you are referring to and I have seen him play. He hits pretty hard. I hear that you are pretty fast though Atif," Mr. Williams said to me. "But you might want to look out for this guy."

"I doubt if they got anybody on they squad that could hold my nuts in a briefcase." I said and the class began to laugh. I got that one from Darion.

"Watch your language in my class son." Mr. Williams told me with a smile on his face. Patience reached over and gave my forearm a slight pinch. At that moment the bell rang and the class was dismissed.

*****

The Principal, Mr. Bowie, canceled seventh hour and hosted a pep rally in the auditorium for the football team. The cheerleaders danced a few routines and the teammates were announced by threes from behind a curtain on stage. When me, D-Mack and Kev were introduced, we came running from behind the curtain amongst loud whistles and roof, roof, roofs from the audience.

The game itself drew a nice sized crowd. Kev and I started while D-Mack rode the bench for the first two quarters. During half time Patience and Teebaby approached me and Darion as we sat on the bench. The score was tied at 7.

"You were looking good out there Atif, I didn't know that you could run so fast." Patience said to me, rubbing the back of my head.

"Not as good as you was lookin' over there cheerleadin,' I seen you." I replied.

"Y'all can miss me with all that mushy talk. What y'all need to do is quit playin' with all of our emotions and gone and hook up." Darion directed towards us.

"Why don't you mind your own business?" Patience asked D-Mack.

"Yeah, wasn't nobody even talkin' to you." Teebaby cut in.

"Wasn't nobody talkin' to you either!" D-Mack pointed out.

"I thought you was supposed to be quarterbackin' anyway. Why you been keepin' the bench warm all game? Over here lookin' like the *waterboy*!" Teebaby said. The ladies laughed at this. I joined in, I couldn't help it. That was a good one.

"A lil' nigga!" The four of us turned towards the sound of the voice.

"And here come your brotha' with his fine ass." Teebaby said as Malik walked across the track in our direction. He wore a pair of black Dickie work pants and a red hooded sweatshirt. On his feet were a pair of the latest red and white Nike shoes endorsed by Deon Sanders. He walked with a slight limp and had that devilish smirk on his face.

"Wha' sup?" I greeted Malik as he approached us.

"Wha' sup y'all?" Malik greeted, looking around the group.

"Wha' sup blood?" D-Mack said.

"Hi." Patience greeted cheerfully.

"Heeeyyyy." Teebaby said, tilting her head while lustfully looking Malik up and down. My brother smirked at her.

"What you doin' up here?" I asked.

"Big Mama wanted to see you play so I drove her up here."

"Where she at?" I asked.

"Over there." Malik answered while pointing towards the bleachers. Big Mama waved back at me with a big smile on her face. "Why come you ain't playin' lil' dawg?" Malik asked Darion.

"I'mma play in the second half."

51

"Where K-Red at?" I asked Malik. One was rarely seen out in public without the other.

"He at the tilt." Malik answered. The "tilt" was what we called the crack house that my brother and K-Red operated a block or two up the street from Big Mama's house. "Is this that female you be talkin' about?" he then purposely asked to my embarrassment, looking at Patience. I silently vowed to get him back for that one.

"When y'all gone let me and Atif sit in the tilt and get some of that money?" D-Mack asked him, coming to my rescue.

Malik and K-Red did a lot of talking while my brother was recovering from surgery. Malik felt that it was time to step up and gain complete control of the neighborhood. No one had currently held complete control, that wasn't where the problem laid. The problem was that there were too many outsiders operating freely in the neighborhood and not only did these individuals bring a lot of unnecessary heat from the law, but it also made it difficult to decipher who did what when something tragic occurred. There was a lot of money to be made in the neighborhood and it did not make sense to allow people from any other neighborhood to come in and accumulate a large sum of this currency. Especially when some of these outsiders were Crips. After these talks, K-Red went to work on the proposed task. With the assistance of Smack Man, the neighborhood was fumigated of all individuals whose left arm did not bear the 27th street brand. Most went peacefully, but some had to be forced out with violent intimidation tactics. As time passed by, Smack Man liked the way K-Red and Malik had gained control of the neighborhood, like he had been insinuating the need for them to do so for awhile, and he showed his appreciation by giving the two the tools needed to monopolize the area. Within a month's time Malik and K-Red were dealing with tens of thousands of dollars on a weekly basis.

"You niggas ain't ready to get no money for real. If-" Malik was interrupted by the ringing of his cellular phone with a black rubber antenna. "Wha'sup?" he answered. "Yeah.....I'm up here watchin' Atif and them play.....He right here....." There was a long pause as the person on the other end was apparently explaining something. We all kept quiet, not so much out of respect as being plain nosy. "A'ight, tell her to chill for a while, I will be there after the game." Malik then pushed the power button on the phone and placed it back in his pocket with a smirk still on his face. "A Darion, I want you to ride with us when y'all finish playin'. I got some business at the tilt I want y'all to handle," he told D-Mack.

"A'ight." Darion replied, looking at me. He was going to ride with us *anyway* after the game. I shrugged my shoulders beneath my shoulder pads with a curious expression of my own on my face. We had never actually been invited to the tilt, we always just popped up on our own accord. Both of us were leery and wondering what Malik had up his sleeve.

"Y'all better not let these sissies beat y'all. I didn't bring Big Mama up here to watch y'all lose. They couldn't fuck with us when we was playin'." Malik said as he turned to leave.

"Lets go, huddle up guys." Coach Turner said to the players on the bench.

"Good luck." Patience wished us both. Her and Teebaby then joined the rest of the cheerleaders.

Coach Turner followed up on his promise to let Darion quarterback the team through the second half. The third quarter passed by with Kev doing most of the damage by pounding the opposition with running the ball up the middle. Late in the fourth quarter we were trailing by a field goal. With 58 seconds remaining in the game, Darion called the team in the backfield for a huddle.

"A'ight y'all, it's third down and we only need four yards for the first down." D-Mack said, kneeling down on one knee. He then went "old school" on us and began to draw in the grass with his index finger like we used to do back in the day on the block. "They gone be expectin' for me to give the ball to Kev, and this is what the coach just signaled for me to do, but fuck that. We runnin' outta time. So what I'mma do is fake it to Kev and Atif I want you to run straight up the sideline like you do when Big Mama be after your ass with a switch in her hand." The team laughed at this. "I'mma throw it to you. Don't miss it man, if you do Coach gone kick me dead in my ass." D-Mack finished.

Me? Miss the ball? Yeah right. I didn't do that very often at all.

"Man fuck all that cuz, give me the ball." Kev said.

"We ain't goin' for the touchdown, I'm just tryin' to get us close to the end zone while they slippin'. We all know that Marcus can't kick no field goal from back here." Darion said. We all shook our heads in confirmation. Marcus, our field goal kicker, could not kick the ball as far as I could spit. "When we get up there you can run it in, and if you can't do that, we will just go for the tie." D-Mack finished.

"I'mma get it in." Kev assured.

"A'ight, lets ride on three." D-Mack said. All of the players rushed up on the line of scrimmage. "Down! Set! Hut hut..hut!" The center snapped the ball and Darion took three giant steps back. Mike, number 66 for the defense, came crashing through the offensive line anticipating the run. Darion faked the hand off to Kev and then turned in the opposite direction, concealing the ball with his body. Kev continued running bent over with his arms clutching his chest as if he really had the ball. He saw number 66 coming and met him in a head on collision, ending up on his back with number 66 on the top of him. Meanwhile, I was sprinting up the sideline at top speed, leaving my defender five feet behind in my wake. Coach recognized the play fake and began to jump up and down on the sideline, protesting the deliberate change of play. Patience and the cheerleading squad went wild and the crowd stood up on the bleachers to get a good look. Darion pump faked the ball, causing a linebacker coming his way to forget about the sack and jump in the air going for the interception or deflection instead. Darion side stepped to the right and launched a perfect spiral thirty yards up the field. The ball looked like it was overthrown to the spectators and just as they began to give up hope on the play, I sped up and leaped for the ball, catching it in mid-air with the very tips of my fingers. I hit the ground landing on my stomach and rolled out of bounds to stop the clock. The referees blew their whistles and stopped the clock with 29 seconds remaining.

D-Mack started jogging up the field in order to congratulate me on the catch. After jogging about five yards, he noticed that I was not getting up from the ground. He then picked up his pace and then ran full speed until he reached me.

"What's wrong man?" D-Mack asked me, kneeling down beside me. I was rolling from left to right, clutching my stomach with my eyes closed. I had spit my mouthpiece out of my mouth. Coach Turner then appeared on the scene with Patience in tow.

"..can't...breathe!" I tried, gasping for air.

"Lie still Atif. You hit the ground pretty hard and knocked the wind out of yourself." Coach Turner coaxed. Malik then appeared on the scene.

"Is he alright?" Patience asked, gasping for breath herself.

"Yeah, he cool. Get up nigga, you ain't hurt." Malik said. He then reached and grabbed me underneath my armpits, bringing me to a sitting position. I began to breathe again and stood up with the assistance of my brother. When I reached my feet, the crowd began to cheer as we all walked over to the sideline.

"Hey baby, you alright?" Big Mama asked me, placing her arm around my shoulder pads.

"Yeah, I'm cool. I just couldn't breathe for a second."

"That was a good catch, I'm proud of you!" Big Mama complimented, hugging me.

"Thanks Big Mama." I said, squirming as she kissed my cheek.

Coach Turner took advantage of the time out called by the officials and motioned for the team to huddle up quickly on the sideline.

"Darion! Hustle up!" Coach shouted. Darion seemed to be taking his time making his way across the playing field. He was in no hurry to receive the tongue lashing he had coming for the deliberate change of play. "That," Coach began when D-Mack made it to the huddle, pointing out onto the football field. "is why you are second string instead of in the starting position. And you will remain there until you learn how to follow my directions." He said, staring Darion down. Darion lowered his gaze. "This time you do what I say. Run a full back swing. Ready? Break!"

The players trotted back onto the field. Darion ran the play prescribed by the coach and Kev scored on the first down. It was his first touchdown of the day, I scored the other one. We won our first home game 14-10.

*****

After the game the three of us were in the process of dropping Big Mama off at the house. "Where do y'all think y'all goin?" she asked us.

"I'mma take'em out to do a lil' celebratin'." Malik answered. Darion and I looked at each other and shook our heads, knowing this was a lie. Big Mama glared at Malik for a moment.

"Don't you get them boys high, ya'hear?" she warned.

"Me?" Malik asked. "Why I neve-"

"Gone boy, get on away from here. You make sure you get these boys back home before too late. They have to get up for school, unlike some people I know." Big Mama said, turning to leave on that note. We laughed in the back seat.

"What you faggots laughin' at?" Malik asked us through the rearview mirror with a smirk on his face.

"We ain't no fags." I replied.

"Yea, we will see. Get in the front blood, lets go."

Malik popped in the new Click tape as he pulled off. He then reached into the glove compartment and grabbed a sandwich bag full of marijuana and a pack of ez wider rolling papers.

"Roll me up a joint." Malik said, handing me the weed papers. "Put me somethin' in there too man, don't be rollin' my shit all tight and skimpy." he finished.

I didn't get high very often up to that point in my life, but I long ago mastered the art of rolling joints while listening to Malik and his hommies in the basement telling war stories. Everyone liked the way I rolled and would always ask me to roll up the weed.

The tilt was a one story house mostly built from bricks. It sat up on a hill and had stairs made of concrete that led up to the front porch. The front door hid behind a thick screen door made of steel. It had a large dead bolt lock; Malik and K-Red had this addition made in high hopes that it would slow the Drug Task Force down whenever they decided to do a kick in, giving them time to flush the dope.

Malik knocked on the steel screen door and then fired up the joint I rolled for him.

"You don't have a key to your own tilt?" D-Mack asked Malik.

"Yeah man. It's a 2 by 4 across the door on the inside so he gone have to let me in anyway. You been up here a million times, you knew that." Malik replied in a strained voice while inhaling marijuana smoke through his nostrils.

"Who is it?" a voice asked from inside the house.

"It's me blood, open the door." Malik replied after exhaling.

We heard the board being removed from the door and locks being unlocked before the door swung open. K-Red stood there at about 6'0. He was brown skinned and he wore a red and gold San Francisco 49ers sweat suit with a pair of red Reeboks. On his head he wore a red bandanna. In his right hand he held a chrome and black 9 millimeter down at this side.

"Wha' sup blood?" K-Red greeted Malik, giving him the standard 27th street handshake as we stepped in. "Let me smoke with you." He said to Malik, reaching for the joint Malik had in his mouth. "Wha' sup with you lil' niggas?"

"Nothin'." We replied in unison.

"Make sure you put the board back on the door behind you Darion. Y'all follow me." K-Red said to us.

We followed K-Red and Malik into the living room which consisted of nothing but a couch and a radio. NWA's EFIL4ZAGGIN blasted from the speakers. There were three people down on one knee in the middle of the floor shooting craps.

"Who got me faded?" Money Mike asked, shaking the dice in his right hand. Money Mike was twenty-four years old and was called by that name because his Cadillac and everything else he owned was green, the color of money. He was dark skinned and wore a full green Dickie suit. On his left ring finger was a big gold nugget ring and around his neck he wore two gold donkey ropes with dollar signs as emblems. Money Mike usually gave me money whenever he saw me and I planned on hitting him up before he left.

We made our way to the kitchen. In here there was a wooden table with four mismatching chairs surrounding it. At one of the chairs sat a girl by the name of Kesha that we all knew from the neighborhood.

Kesha was seventeen years old but looked as if she was already in her twenties. She had a somewhat mocha like complexion and she stood about 5'5 with dark brown eyes. Her body was well proportioned; she had a pair of nice round breasts and a butt that you could see from the front. I used to grab it and take off running when I would see her on the block when I was younger. She would chase me down, pin my shoulders to the ground with her knees, and tickle my armpits until tears would come out of my eyes.

"Sit down y'all." K-Red said, pulling a chair off from under the table for himself and sitting down. We then took a seat and Malik leaned up against the stove.

"Roll up some more weed, Atif." Malik said, tossing me his bag of weed and papers.

"Let me hit that," D-Mack said to K-Red, indicating the joint he held in between his index finger and thumb. "You gone let it go out." K-Red turned and looked at Malik through half shut red eyes.

"Don't look at me, shit, I ain't his daddy." Malik replied to that look. K-Red then handed D-Mack the joint.

"You better be careful nigga, that ain't that homegrown shit you used to." K-Red cautioned. Darion, intent on proving that he could smoke with the best of them, took a big puff and inhaled. He then broke out into a fit of choking and gagging. This brought an orchestra of laughter from the rest of us.

"K say you wanna be put on the set." Malik said to Kesha.

"Yep."

"Why you wanna do this?" Malik asked her.

"I been hangin' wit y'all since I was little, y'all might as well gone and put me down."

"That ain't the thing girl. This shit ain't no game. You see us gettin' bread, smokin' good, shoppin' and shit all the time but it's more to it than that. You gotta be down to ride for this shit here." Malik said, throwing up 2-7 across his chest.

I can't believe how long it took for me to see how silly this mentality was. Down to die for what? A block that we didn't own a single blade of grass on? A color? Dope? None of it made any sense. Especially when there was (is) so much injustice in this country that was (is) worth "riding" for. Our anger was mis-directed and this stemmed from ignorance and a lack of proper guidance.

"When we see crabs, we bomb on site." Malik continued. "We at war right now with them Duece-Fo niggas because them bitch ass niggas popped me up and killed my mama in the process." I looked up at this, it was the first time that I had heard Malik say anything about who killed our mother in a long time. "You think you ready to go to war?"

"Yeah nigga. You know I ain't scared to pop that thing." She wasn't, either. Kesha would tear the club up when provoked. She was well respected by the other females in the neighborhood.

"Yeah, we know that. Just don't be thinkin' that you won't have to put no work in just because you a female." K-Red cut in.

59

"I-" Kesha started, but was cut off by some shouting in the other room. K-Red grabbed his pistol off of the table and stood up.

"Nigga, my point is five! We bet ten on the five or nine and twenty on the straight make! I just rolled a nine, so that twenty dollars over there is all me, if you wanna bet it back then drop ten more dollars!" Money Mike roared from the front room.

"Man roll the damn dice! You's a cheatin mutha' fucka'." Trigga yelled back.

"Boa, them niggas is best friends but turn into bitter enemies when they get to shootin' them dice." K-Red commented, sitting down and placing his pistol back on the table.

"Duece-Fo', that's what Kev be reppin'." D-Mack said, passing the joint to Malik. I nodded my head, licking the gum on the ez wider paper as I finished rolling up another perfect joint.

"Who is Kev?" K-Red asked me.

"He is the runnin' back on our team."

"Is that the lil' crip nigga you was fightin' with last year?" Malik asked me.

"Yeah."

"I know you whooped his ass, didn't you?" K-Red asked me.

"Nope." I answered shortly, handing Malik another freshly rolled joint.

"Here, let me fire that up." Kesha interjected, grabbing the joint from me.

"It was a tie." Darion said to K-Red.

"What was a tie?" K-Red asked D-Mack, forgetting the subject of the conversation that quick. It was some good weed.

"The fight, nigga." Darion answered and began to chuckle.

"Aw, yeah. Anyway, what do you think blood?" K-Red asked Malik.

"What do I think about what?"

"Man you niggas is dense." I commented, shaking my head in pity. That right there was why I didn't smoke a lot of weed.

"Man what the fuck do dense mean? I'm tired of you niggas callin' me that shit." K-Red said. His question went unanswered.

"I'm hip. This is your brain on drugs." Darion said. Me, D-Mack and Kesha laughed at this.

"About me. What do you think about me?" Kesha asked Malik while still giggling to herself.

"Aw, yeah. There are two ways you can get initiated." Malik said, holding up two fingers. Darion and I looked nervously at each other, wondering what we had to do with it. Gang-banging as a whole was on the decline back in 92. Initiating someone into the set was really played out by then. Game was being run on Kesha. Her desire to be a part of something and her greed was being taken advantage of in a sick way.

Malik then began counting off with his fingertips. "You can get your ass whooped by the hommies or you can get fucked." He finished with a smirk on his face. Darion and I glanced at each other again and smiled as understanding dawned on the both of us.

"Fucked?" Kesha asked with her eyebrows raised.

"Fucked." K-Red said.

"Fucked by who? I ain't finna let all you niggas fuck me. Y'all crazy than a mutha' fucka'." Kesha let us know off the top, looking between Malik and K-Red. Malik then looked at me and Darion. Kesha followed his gaze. "Aw naw, hell naw!" Kesha said, shaking her head in refusal. Honestly, she told me later, she didn't mind the thought of having sex with me. But Darion? He would tell everybody in the neighborhood about it and she would never hear the end of it. She didn't want to take that route.

"Quit frontin' girl, you know you wanna play hide the salami with me." Darion said to Kesha, grinning mischievously from ear to ear.

"Boy please, you ain't had no pussy since pussy had you." Kesha retorted. We all laughed at this. "I would rather get my ass whooped." She said to our disappointment. "Y'all ain't gone do me bad is y'all? I can't be goin' home with no black eyes and shit."

"You want a sample?" K-Red asked her.

"A sample?" She asked in return, looking questioningly between K-Red and Malik.

"Yeah, a sample." K-Red replied. "Stand up."

"Why? What you think you finna do?" Kesha asked K-Red. Malik still wore a smirk on his face.

"I'm a hit you in the arm, give you a lil' sample." He answered, moving his chair out of the way as the both of them stood up.

"Don't hit me hard K." Kesha said.

"I'm just gone give you a sample." He said, smiling. I thought that I would go crazy if he said the word "sample" one more time. "Are you ready?"

"Yeah." She answered, gritting her teeth and closing her eyes.

K-Red threw a right hook with lightning speed, connecting with Kesha's upper right arm before she had a chance to change her mind. Kesha cried out in pain as she fell backward, the kitchen sink was the only thing that saved her from falling to the ground. D-Mack burst out laughing, smacking the table and clutching his stomach.

"Ssss, ah punk!" Kesha hissed, slapping K-Red across his chest with an open hand.

"Man you didn't have to hit her like that." I said to K-Red, picking up the joint Kesha left burning in the ashtray and taking a puff, feeling a slight buzz almost instantly. She wasn't going to want anymore of that so I thought that maybe the weed would give me some confidence. Kesha was massaging her arm, giving K-Red a sour look.

"Why you lookin' at me like that?" K-Red said, laughing.

"Cause you didn't have to hit me that hard, *that's* why!" She answered, swaying her head from side to side with an attitude.

"I was just keepin' it real with you. We don't wanna do you like that for real. Gone and give the lil' hommies some pussy and get it over with. It ain't gone take nothin' but two seconds for them to bust a nut anyway, you know they still some virgins." K-Red said.

"I ain't no virgin." D-Mack commented. I remained silent.

"What you gone do?" K-Red asked Kesha.

At that moment there was a knock on the front door. "Give me some dope Malik, let me bust this serve." Darion asked hopefully. Malik pulled out a medicine bottle full of crack rocks. He removed the lid and poured five stones into Darion's open palm, which seemed to be shaking with anticipation.

"You bring me back seventy-five dollars off of this and keep the rest. If you let one of them geek monsters gank you, I'm a fuck you up and it's gone come out of your check. That ain't gone last long, so when you run out come and get some more. A'ight?" Malik asked.

"Yeah, a'ight," Darion said gratefully, staring down at the crack in his hand with a smile. He had forgotten all about Kesha for the moment. Fantasizing about all the money he planned to make, he turned to leave.

"Wait nigga, take this with you." Malik said, handing Darion a black .380 caliber pistol. "Don't ever answer that door without a strap in your hand, and if it is somebody you ain't seen around the hood before, then tell them to get the fuck away from here and don't serve them shit. I don't care how much money they got or who they say sent them." Malik finished. Darion then grabbed the pistol and left to answer the door.

All eyes were on Kesha again as Darion left the room. She had her shirt sleeve pulled up and was examining the spot where K-Red hit her. I had now smoked a good portion of the joint and was in a bliss. My mouth felt dry and my lips were white and ashy. As I looked at Kesha, I began to get excited. In my mind she was standing there naked.

"Girl, you too black to bruise." K-Red said to Kesha. She gave him the finger in return. "Speakin' of fuck yous, what you gone do?"

63

Kesha looked up and rolled her eyes at Malik and K-Red. She then turned and retreated to the back bedroom. Malik and K-Red laughed and then turned to look at me.

"Didn't I tell you I was gone get you some pussy nigga?" K-Red asked me. He had said so a few weeks ago when he found out that I was still a virgin. "What you waitin' on, scary ass nigga?"

"I ain't scared." I lied. In reality I was scared to death. It was so sudden and unexpected. I also knew that if I went about it as if I didn't know what I was doing, which I didn't, then I would become the joke of the neighborhood. The only experience I had was what I had seen watching porno flicks. "I'mma finish smokin' this joint." I offered in procrastination.

As soon as the situation began to look like it was really about to go down, whatever confidence I had mustered up by getting high fled with Kesha's departure from the kitchen. In the back of my mind I was kind of hoping that she would have chosen door number one or at least let Darion go first.

"Take it with you nigga, gone back there. She might suck your lil dick for you while she at it." Malik commented, smirking. I could not hide my fear from him. He knew me like he knew the back of his own hand. I looked at my brother, then to K-Red, and stood up. My knees felt weak and butterflies filled my stomach. I then smiled at the two and walked out of the kitchen.

*****

<u>GRANTING WISHES</u>

"Do you wanna be in love
Wit' a thug like me?
One who love to smoke bud
And sell drugs like me?
Do you wanna be in love
Wit' a thug like me?
One who love to mean mug
And bust slugs like me?"
-*Soody Mak*

4

"Hello?" I answered the ringing telephone. It was Saturday morning and I had just finished mowing the lawn for Big Mama.

I really miss those good old Saturday mornings. I would wake up to the sweet aroma of bacon frying and the even sweeter sound of Big Mama humming some old Christian song. After breakfast I would help her clean the house and we would talk about any and everything while we worked.

"Wha' sup nigga?" Darion greeted through the receiver.

"Nothin'. Where you at?"

"I'm at the crib. Di-"

"You wanna go see Menace to Society?" Teebaby cut in.

"Damn you rude! Ain't got no manners." Darion scolded.

"Shut up Darion." Teebaby retorted back.

"D slash Mack, D-Mack. Y'all gone quit callin' me Darion and tellin' me to shut up." D-Mack predicted.

"Shut up Darion." Teebady repeated.

"Teebaby?" I asked, recognizing her voice.

"Yeah, that's her raunchy ass." D-Mack answered.

"I'mma hurt you boy, watch." Teebaby threatened. "Are you goin' Atif?"

"Tonight?"

"Yeah."

"A'ight, I will go."

"Click over and call Patience." Teebaby said. I clicked over and called the number on the three-way.

"Why did you ask me if I wanted to go first?" I asked her as the line began to ring. I could see that Teebaby was trying to arrange a double date of sorts.

"Because Patience ain't gone wanna go unless I tell her that you gone be there."

"Let me ask for her y'all, be quiet." D-Mack said.

"Hello?" a female voice answered.

"May I speak to Patience, please?" Darion asked politely.

"This is her." Patience answered cheerfully.

"Wha'sup sexy?" Darion asked.

"Excuse me?" Patience asked with an edge in her voice, copping an attitude instantly.

"I was just callin' to let you know that you left your panties over here last night." Darion said and then laughed.

"You are nasty." Teebaby said to Darion, laughing to herself.

"Teebaby? Who was that? Darion?" Patience asked her.

"Yeah girl."

"Don't call here playing on my phone boy." Patience warned. "If my mother was not in earshot I would curse you out."

"You ain't never said a cuss word in your life. I don't even think you know how to cuss." Darion commented.

"You wanna go to the show girl?" Teebaby asked before the two got to arguing between themselves.

"To see what?"

"Menace to Society."

"I do not want to go and watch some kind of gangster movie. I don't like that stuff." Patience replied with an emphasis on the word gangster.

"Atif is goin'."

"No he is not."

"Yes I am." I spoke for the first time.

"Atif?" Patience asked, slightly embarrassed. "I didn't know that you were on the phone. Why are you just now speaking?"

"Cause this the first time I got a chance to." I answered. "Are you goin'?"

"Yes." She replied humbly, smiling into the phone.

"Y'all make me sick to my stomach man. And you, Patience, you should be ashamed of yo-self. Your whole attitude changed when you realized Atif was on the phone. Y'all know y'all like each other, won't y'all gone and do the damn thing?" Darion asked.

"Shut up Darion." Patience answered.

"I don't know girl, he got a good point. I'm startin' to wonder what the hold up is myself." Teebaby commented. Patience inhaled sharply out of shock.

"Oh, so you are conspiring with *Darion* now? Against *me*?"

"I'm just sayin' girl, you know you *love* you some Atif." Teebaby answered, putting her friend on front street. This time it was me who was smiling into the phone.

"I can not believe you just said that!"

"Why don' t you and D-Mack gone and do the damn thing?" I asked Teebaby, coming to Patience's rescue. I was not going to sit back and let them gang up on her like that for too long. I liked Patience and I had her back.

There was silence on the line. All of a sudden no one had anything to say.

"Shut up Atif." Teebaby said. It was her turn to be slightly embarrassed, smiling into the phone.

"He has a good point." Patience pointed out. We all laughed at this.

*****

Hours later, I met up with Darion at the tilt. We both wore brand new outfits and the latest pair of Michael Jordan's basketball shoes. I wore a pair of white Dickie work pants with a black and white checkered flannel. Darion wore a pair of black Dickie work pants with a red and black checkered flannel work shirt.

The tilt was empty except for Malik and K-Red. Malik was in the kitchen, sitting at the table cutting up 9 ounces of crack cocaine. K-Red was in the infamous back bedroom taking a nap. Darion and I sat down at the table with Malik.

"Can I wear your herring bone?" I asked Malik.

"You got some money, buy your own necklace." Malik suggested, scraping crumbs from the crack he was cutting off to the side. We had been doing pretty well for ourselves financially lately by pocketing $25 off of every $100 we made for Malik and K-Red.

"Just for tonight. I will bring it right back to you." I pleaded.

"Where y'all goin'?" he asked, looking up at us. "What? Y'all supposed to be twins now?" he then asked, referring to the way we were dressed.

"We gone meet Patience and Teebaby up at the show." Darion answered.

"Y'all fucked them lil' bitches yet?" Malik asked. Before either one of us got the chance to answer, there was a knock at the front door.

"I will get it." Darion said, turning to walk out of the kitchen.

"A nigga!" Darion stopped in his tracks and turned around. "How many times I gotta tell you about answerin' that door without a pistol?" Malik asked with scorn.

"Aw, yeah. My bad." Darion apologized, reaching for Malik's .380 that was laying on the table. He picked it up, cocked it and left the kitchen holding it down at his side.

"What's wrong with yo boy, Atif? He got a death wish or somethin?"

"What is a death wish?"

"It's when you carry yo-self like you just *wanna* die." He answered. "What was Big Mama doin when you left?"

"Watchin' television."

"Kesha keep askin' me about you. What did you do, eat her pussy or somethin'?" Malik asked me with a smirk on his face.

"Hell naw!" I spat in disgust. This made Malik laugh. We all thought that it was something seriously wrong with performing oral sex on a woman at that time in our lives, which was unfair to the ladies. I think we all harbored secret fantasies of giving it a try though; at least *I* did.

"She keep askin' me if I think that you are still mad at her. I told her that I didn't even know that you was mad at her in the first place. Then I asked her why she thought you was mad and she wouldn't tell me. What did she do to you?"

"She called me a son of a bitch."

"Oh." Malik said, gathering the crack cocaine off of the table and placing it into clear plastic sandwich bags by the quarter ounce. "When somebody say that man it don't necessarily mean they talkin' about Mama. Why you be takin' everything so personal and literal?" Silence. "Don't hold no grudge with her over that Atif, she didn't mean it." He then stood up and went to the kitchen sink to wash his hands. "You miss Mama, don't you?" Malik asked me with his back turned.

"Yeah." I replied. The mere thought of my mother brought tears to my eyes.

"Me too. You can't keep trippin' with people like that over her man. Mama is dead Atif and Kesha ain't the one who killed her."

"Well who did then?" I asked my brother. I was getting upset. I was depending on Malik to find out who it was that killed Mama. Not only was he my only hope, but whoever did it was there in the first place looking for *him*, so I guess subconsciously I blamed him for her death. The police had given up a long time ago, dismissing her murder after a poor excuse for an investigation by chalking it up as another drive by shooting. Too much time was passing without us knowing much more than we knew in the beginning. I was beginning to lose confidence in my brother. For some reason I thought that he would be able to track the culprits down like Sherlock Holmes, but that had not been the case.

"I don't know yet. Don't trip though, we gone find out." Malik said, turning to face me. He then took off his necklace and handed it to me.

"Well I been dipped in a pile of shit and rolled in sugar!" Darion exclaimed from the front room. "Wha' cha know good, girl? Come on in why don't cha." He finished. Malik and I looked at each other, smiled and shook our heads.

Darion reentered the kitchen followed by a dark skinned girl wearing a red tennis skirt with a red halter top. She had extensions braided into her hair, tied back into a ponytail, revealing a very pretty face. She wore big gold plated earrings dangling from each ear.

"Hey Malik!" she greeted, kissing him on the check.

"Damn boa, what you got there?" Darion asked, staring at her behind while she hugged him.

"You know I like that red." Malik said to the girl, referring to her tennis skirt, ignoring Darion.

"I know, that's why I put it on." She replied with a smile on her face.

"Don't y'all got somewhere to be?" Malik asked Darion and I.

"Yeah, and we need you to take us there." I answered. Actually, we could have taken the bus, but Malik was driving a pearl white 1987 Chevy Caprice with 16 by 9 inch triple gold Daytons. I loved the looks I received from people when stepping out of such a vehicle.

"Do I look like a cab driver to y'all?"

"No, but you smell like one." I said. Darion laughed.

"Stop bein' so mean Malik." The girl said, turning around and leaning up against Malik. She then took his arms and wrapped them around her waist. Darion's attention shifted from her butt to her breasts.

"What's on your mind blood?" Malik asked Darion, noticing the undivided attention he was paying to the girl's breasts.

"Titties and nipples." Darion replied, licking his lips. This brought laughter from all of us. Malik then reached up and pulled the girl's halter top down, revealing two melon sized breasts with big black nipples that looked like two pacifiers. The girl screamed and playfully slapped Malik's hands away. She then fixed her top, giggling to herself.

"Whew, wee! That was a sight for sore eyes." Darion commented, wiping his brow.

"Come on y'all, lets go. I need to get me somethin' to eat anyway." Malik said. He then went and woke K-Red up so that he could lock the door behind us.

*****

Twenty-five minutes later Malik pulled into the Bannister Mall's large parking lot.   He then drove around to the theater entrance and we got out of the back seats.

"You gone come and pick us back up?" I asked my brother, leaning into the driver side window with my hands on the roof of the car.

"Call me."

"Gimme a joint, Malik." Darion said, leaning inside of the passenger side window. Malik handed the girl a joint and she in turn handed it to Darion. "Say baby, won't you let me get another peek for the road?" Darion asked the girl, trying to see down her top. She then looked at Malik and he nodded his head. She pulled her top down and shook her breasts. "Girl, you just don't know..." Darion commented, shaking his head.

As Malik pulled off, Darion and I headed towards the entrance. There was a crowd of teenagers standing out on the walkway. We recognized a few of them from the neighborhood, but the rest of them were strangers to us. After a few wha' sups, Darion and I made our way into the mall.

The movie theater was on the right. To the left of us was a string of small concession stands that encircled a wide area filled with white tables and chairs. The food courts were so packed with teenagers and adults that there seemed to be no place for us to sit.

"Atif, Darion! Over here!" A voice called from one of the tables. Patience and Teebaby were motioning for us.

"How long y'all been here?" I asked the girls, sitting next to Patience. She was looking real good. That girl never ceased to amaze me with how beautiful she was, naturally.

"Not long, we just got here a few minutes ago." Patience answered, smiling at me. I smiled back. We were happy to see each other.

Patience secretly admired the way I dressed. My style was neither boring nor flamboyant. She found my simple outfits and solid colors very attractive. Often times I caught her staring at me when she thought I wasn't looking.

"Why are you still standin' there like that?" Teebaby asked Darion, who had not yet taken a seat.

"I'm waitin' on you to pull my chair out for me." Darion answered, smiling chauvinistically down at Teebaby.

"Hold your breath." Teebaby said. Darion laughed and sat next to her. He actually liked that about her. She didn't bow down to his attitude like most females did.

"When do the movie start?" I asked Teebaby.

"In about an hour." She replied, looking at her watch.

"What are we supposed to do until then?" Patience asked Teebaby.

"Go smoke this." Darion answered for her, holding his joint in the air.

"What is that?" Patience asked Darion.

"A *joint* girl. What do it look like?"

"I don't do drugs Darion."

"Weed ain't no drug." Darion stated. "Wha' sup Atif, you ridin'?" Darion asked me, twirling the joint.

"Naw, I'm straight." I answered. The look I received from Patience greatly influenced my decision.

"I ain't finna get high by myself. Teebaby, come and smoke with your baby daddy." Darion said.

"You been smokin' too much of that stuff if you think you my baby daddy. I ain't got no kids."

"Come on girl." Darion said, grabbing Teebaby's hand and pulling her out of her seat. They then made their way out of the crowded food courts.

"Come on, I want to show you something." Patience said to me, taking me by the hand. Patience led me to an expensive jewelry store called Krigels. She then led me to a glass case full of diamond earrings. "Do you see those?" She asked me, pointing to a pair of diamond stud earrings.

"Yeah, what about them?"

"I was up here with my mother last week when I saw them. She just got engaged to some guy and she was getting her engagement ring fitted and I was looking at all of this beautiful jewelry when I spotted them." She said, spreading her arms wide, indicating all of the jewelry cases.

"I think they are so cute! I asked my mom if I could have them for my birthday next week and she told me no. She didn't even look to see how much they cost." Patience said. I glanced at the price tag myself.

"You didn't like that, did you?" I asked.

"What? My mom telling me no?" Patience asked. I nodded. "No, I didn't like that at all. It wasn't her telling me no that got to me, it was the fact that she didn't even pay me any attention. My mom never tells me no, I never really ask for much. Well, at least she didn't until she got so serious about this asshole who acts like he is my father. Ever since he started coming around everything has changed between me and Mom. We have always been the best of friends; all we had was each other. I could talk to her about anything, but now it's like I am not even there."

"What is so bad about him?" I asked as we walked out of the jewelry store. Patience grabbed a hold of my hand.

"He is nothing but an alcoholic, and I don't like the way he looks at me. I get the feeling that he is always trying to see through my clothes. He also is always finding some stupid and insignificant reason to come in my room when he knows that I am dressed down for bed." Patience said.

"Have you talked to her about it?" I asked Patience.

"No. She probably wouldn't believe me anyway. She is blind right now. I mean he has her so gone."

"What do you sleep in anyway?" I asked her as we sat down in front of a wishing fountain.

"A T-shirt and panties." Patience answered, digging into her pants pocket for some change. I automatically fantasized about seeing her like that in my mind.

"Damn, I would probably make up an excuse to see you in that myself!"

"That wasn't funny." Patience said, referring to the smirk I had on my face. "He is a grown man and it is not okay for him to be seeing me like that. Besides, he has my mother to look at." She threw a quarter into the fountain. "Make a wish." I looked into the water and wondered to myself who cleans out the fountains and what they did with all of the money people threw in them. "Did you make a wish?"

"Yeah." I lied, I didn't believe in such things. Fountains don't have the power to grant wishes. I was not going to spoil it for her though, so I played along.

"What did you wish for?" She asked me.

"It won't come true if I tell you, will it?"

"No."

"Then knowin' that, why did you ask me what I wished for?"

"Because I wanted to know if it had anything to do with me." Patience said, looking away.

"It did." I said smirking. She then turned and looked at me with a smile on her face.

"I know what it is!"

"No you don't."

"Yes I do!"

"If you know what I wished for, are you goin' to grant it to me?" I asked.

"Maybe." She answered, standing up. "Lets go and see if your boy is finished destroying what few brain cells he has left."

We got on the escalator and rode back up to the second level, still holding hands. When we reached the second floor, we saw Darion and Teebaby standing in front of the theaters. Darion had his arm around Teebaby's shoulders.

"Aw, would you looky there. That is so sweet." Darion said in a motherly voice, referring to our holding each other by the hand. Teebaby giggled.

"Shut up Darion." Patience said. "How much longer until the movie starts?" She then asked Teebaby.

"Huh?" Teebaby asked through eyes that looked as if they were closed.

"I said how mu...." Patience started. "Are you *high*?" She cut herself off, narrowing her eyes at Teebaby.

"High as a *mutha'* fucka'!" Darion answered for her, looking at Teebaby and shaking his head. "She been gigglin' since the first hit."

"Are y'all ready?" Teebaby asked us, still giggling.

"Girl what do you keep laughin' at?" Darion asked Teebaby.

"Your face, that's what," she answered. We then went and stood in line at the ticket counter. Teebaby burst out laughing again. "Why you starin' at me like that Patience? You act like I just picked up a piece of gum off the floor and ate it."

"I didn't know that you did drugs." Patience said, disgusted with her friend.

"I don't. Damn girl, it's just some weed! It ain't like I just smoked some *crack* or somethin'." Teebaby said.

"What is the difference?" Patience asked.

She was right, there really was no difference. We all used to rationalize with ourselves and each other in a similar fashion, attempting to make a distinction between what was cool to get high on and what was not. One drug may be more addictive and potent than the other, but they all are destructive to the community and society as a whole; even those which are "lawful"; like cigarettes and liquor.

"Can I help y'all?" A female asked from behind the counter. She was a black woman and sounded as if she was ready to go home.

"Yeah, uh, let me get two tickets for The Abyss." I answered.

"I thought that we were going to see Menace to Soc-*ouch*!" Patience yelped in pain, rubbing the back of her arm where Teebaby had pinched her. The lady behind the counter shook her head at us. Patience was *too* green.

"Eight fifty." The lady said, dishing out two tickets. I pulled out a wad of twenties and handed the lady one. Patience looked at me with her eyebrows raised, amazed at the amount of money I had just flashed. "What about y'all, y'all want the same thing?" the lady then asked Darion and Teebaby.

"Yeah." Teebaby replied.

"Eight fifty." The lady said, dishing out two more tickets. Teebaby looked at Darion.

"What you lookin' at *me* for?"

"Ain't you gone pay my way?"

"Hell naw girl, you should be payin' *my* way!" Darion answered. I burst out laughing and so did the older couple next in line. Teebaby rose her fist in the air as if she was going to strike Darion. "A'ight, a'ight . Girl you keep on actin' like you want to put your hands on me and one day I might just take you seriously and gone and knock you out." He said in resignation, pulling out his own wad of twenties. He handed the lady a twenty and she gave him the tickets and his change. "Women," Darion said to the older gentlemen standing next in line with a woman who appeared to be his date. "Can't live with them, can't kill them outside the state of Mississippi!" Darion finished, shaking his head. The older gentleman laughed at this and caught an elbow in the ribs from his date.

We then made our way to the concession stand. There were three high school students working behind the counter.

"I'm hungry. I want you to buy me some nachos and don't gimme no shit." Teebaby demanded, pointing her finger in Darion's face.

"Your hungry ass should've ate before you left your house." He commented, smacking her hand away.

"Can I please have some nachos with cheese and a large Sprite?" Teebaby asked one of the teenagers behind the counter, ignoring Darion.

"Hold up, wait a minute. How much is that gone cost?" Darion asked the teenager.

"Five-twenty-five." The teenager informed him after hitting a few keys on the cash register.

"Five-twenty-five! *Damn!*" D-Mack exclaimed in shock. "How much *without* the cheese on the nachos, and the ice in the pop?" He then asked the teenager. We all laughed at this. That boy was a nut.

"We will take it. With the cheese *and* ice. Put some jalapeno peppers on them too please." Teebaby told the high school student. "Why you so dang on cheap? You got all that money in your pocket."

"I ain't cheap. I ain't supposed to be trickin' my money off with the likes of *you* either." Darion replied.

"Will you add anoth-nah, I will just drink hers." The kid took the ten and gave Darion his change.

"Do you want somethin' to eat?" I asked Patience, stepping up to the counter for a better look at the menu.

"Some popcorn would be nice." She answered, standing on the tips of her toes.

"*Some popcorn would be nice.*" Darion mimicked, imitating Patience's voice and her proper English as well. "You females are somethin' else, boa I tell you." He finished, shaking his head from side to side.

"Shut up Darion." Patience and Teebaby said in unison.

"Dang, is them the only three words y'all can say?"

I bought some popcorn and soda; we then gathered our goods and headed up the walkway towards where the movies were being shown. When we got there, instead of going into the one labeled The Abyss, we looked to see if anyone was watching us and ran into the doorway labeled Menace to Society with Teebaby giggling the whole way.

"Girl, you almost got us caught with all that laughin' you was doin'." Darion scolded Teebaby.

"Where do you guys want to sit?" Patience asked us.

"Not with y'all." Darion answered, grabbing Teebaby by the hand. "I can't get my freak on with your hatin' ass breathin' down a nigga's neck Patience." He finished, pulling Teebaby.

"You ain't gone be freakin' nobody." Teebaby said to Darion, allowing herself to be led away.

Teebaby said things like that all of the time in front of Patience because she held Patience's opinion of her in high regard. When she was alone with Darion it was a different story altogether.

"Teebaby like that nigga for real, don't she?" I asked Patience.

"Yes, a *lot.* He is all she talks about. *Darion* said this, *Darion* said that." Patience said, mimicking Teebaby's small voice. "Ugh!" She took my hand and led me down to one of the front rows. The theater was packed and it took a while for us to find two empty seats next to each other.

I surveyed the theater to the best of my ability. I grew uneasy with every step I took. As I looked around, I saw numerous groups of Crips, Bloods, and G.D.'s. All these different organizations in the same room were like oil and water in the same container; they did not mix well. It was too dark to really see any faces, so there was no way for me to tell from which set anyone was from.

Movies and functions in general like that seemed to hype people up. Get them all excited and rowdy. It is true what the critics said about movies and some music to a certain extent. Movies and music *can* influence and motivate people. But what the critics failed to state was that if Menace To Society was so detrimental to the hopes for a peaceful society because of all the violence portrayed, then so were movies like Die Hard which was praised and given excellent reviews by these same individuals. To this day, such hypocrisy makes me sick.

"Do you ever talk about me?" I asked Patience, attempting to hide my uneasiness as we took our seats. When I came to that very theater to see Boys in the Hood a few years before then, Malik, Trigga and K-Red turned it into the OK Corral after being provoked by some crips from the south side of the city.

"A little bit." Patience lied, taking my right arm and placing it around her shoulders. She then laid her head in the crook of my neck.

This was the most affection that Patience had shown towards me up to that point. First wanting to hold my hand and then laying her head on me? I could see that she was growing more and more comfortable around me. I knew that Patience was not like the inner-city girls I was used to, she was different. Even though she was young, she carried herself like she was much older than she was. She was very mature, intelligent, and she had a lot of respect for herself. She was extremely cute and already had a nice body on her, but she was not conceited like the other kids at Central thought she was. In actuality, she was far from it. She just didn't feel the need to try and fit in with everyone.

80

I found myself liking Patience more and more with every day that passed. I had never been so interested in any girl before. I had yet to ask her to be my girl up to that point. I did not think that she would turn me down; I just knew that she would let me know when the time was right for us to take that step. That is how she was. All the peer pressure we received from Teebaby and Darion did not have an effect on her. She was very strong and an independent minded young lady.

"Have you ever smoked any marijuana?" Patience asked, looking up at me.

"Yeah, a few times. Well, more than a few."

"What does it feel like?"

"It feels...*good.*" I started, shrugging my shoulders. The effects of smoking weed were difficult for me to describe to someone who had never smoked any before. "I don't know. It makes things seem funnier and more interestin'. You could be sittin' in a room all day by yo-self with nothin' to do and if you was high, you wouldn't be bored at all."

"Hmph. What about all of that money in your pocket?" she asked. "Where did you get that from?" Uh-oh. Teebaby was not the only one who held the way Patience saw her in high regard. I knew how she felt about the lifestyle I was living, about drug dealers and gang-bangers.

"Do you really wanna know?" I asked in return. I was not going to lie to her. It was obvious anyway.

"No, maybe I don't. At least not right now. Then again, maybe I already know and just don't want to believe it." Patience answered. She then put a handful of popcorn into her mouth and I took a few sips of pop.

Patience remained silent throughout most of the movie. At times I thought she had fallen asleep until she would reach into her bucket of popcorn and put a handful of it into her mouth.

"Would you like some?" Patience offered, looking up at me again.

"Yeah." I replied. I was kind of hungry, I don't know why I didn't get me some nachos. Patience dug into

81

the bucket of popcorn and sat up, turning sideways in her seat to face me. She was even beautiful in the dark.

"Say ah." She said. I opened my mouth. Patience put some popcorn into my mouth, and thinking that she was finished, I bit her pinkie finger. "Ouch, Atif! Wait a second." Patience said, laughing and shaking her hand.

"My bad." I said, laughing also. Patience made herself a little more comfortable in her seat. Instead of just laying her head on my shoulder, she turned in her seat and leaned her whole upper body against me. She placed her bucket in between my legs. I could feel Patience's breasts through her shirt, laying against the right side of my chest and ribs. She then reached up and grabbed my chin, turning my face down towards her, and gave me a soft kiss on my lips. She pulled back, wiping lipstick off of my lips, looking into my eyes and smiling.

That was not my first kiss. It was not even a tongue kiss. It was a simple peck on the lips. Well, it might as well have been because none of the previous kisses I had received prior to that soft peck on the lips from Patience could compare.

"Is *that* what you wished for?" Patience asked me.

"Yeah, it is." I answered, grinning from ear to ear. Actually I didn't make a wish at all, but if I had, that would have been it.

"Will you be my boyfriend?"

"*Yeah!*." I answered, more stunned at the question than the kiss itself. I knew that she would let me know when she was ready to go there, but I never thought that she would be the one to ask.

Patience took her right hand and placed it on my opposite shoulder, laying her head back into the crook of my neck.

"*That* is what I wished for." Patience whispered softly into my ear. Maybe it *was* something to those fountains.

"I knew that." I said. I then began to rub her upper arm. Patience snuggled even closer to me.

"No you did not." She replied.

After a few minutes passed, Patience fell asleep. She never could remain awake for the duration of a movie, no matter how good it was. I didn't mind at all. I would have held her in my arms like that for the rest of the night if I could.

The movie was fascinating. I had fallen in love with the story line. I felt like I could identify with the lifestyles portrayed easily. Watching Menace to Society helped me realize that there were people all over the country traveling down the filthy route. There were people out there who felt my loss and my pain.

Commotion. Someone was fighting. I woke Patience with a shake.

"Come on, lets go." I said, grabbing Patience by the hand and pulling her out of her seat. The rest of her popcorn spilled from the bucket onto the floor.

"What is happening Atif?" She asked, looking around the theater. I didn't answer. When we made it out of the row and into the main aisle, I could see that there were many other people attempting to make their way out of the theatre at the same time. I didn't know who it was exactly that was fighting, but my instincts told me to get out of there as quick as possible. "Where is Teebaby and Darion?" Patience asked me.

"Hopefully they doin' the same thing *we* doin'."

At that moment, three gunshots echoed throughout the theater, followed by loud screams and panic. The entrance was crowded and people who had fallen were being trampled on. "Come on, this way!" I said, turning around and heading for the fire exit off to the side. My heart was racing and it seemed as if it was about to jump right out of my chest. Anybody was liable to get hit by a stray bullet in an area as packed and closed off as the movie theater was. All I wanted to do was get outside into the open.

Bursting through the fire exit, Patience and I spilled into the open air, breathing heavily. While bent over with my hands on my knees, I heard Patience standing behind me sniffling. When I turned around I saw that she was crying.

"You a'ight?" I asked her, placing my hand on her shoulder. She nodded. I could feel her body shaking like a scared little puppy.

Patience had never experienced anything like what had just happened. It frightened her. Patience hated violence, and thought it was senseless.

"Lets go find D-Mack and Teebaby." I said, wrapping my arm around her shivering shoulders. Together we walked off into the night.

*****

PERSONAL FRIEND

"I can see you with nothin' on
but a red bra with a matchin' thong,
erotic kissin' and touchin'
got your body twistin' and clutchin',
-mixed- with a little bit of lickin' and suckin',
don't play with my emotions;
I heard that you be strokin'
with that motion lotion.
Me?
I'm just hopin' for a shot.
We can stop by the block
and cop some pot after we shake the tilt; the spot.
-I got- a little proposition:
Can we be personal friends?
I understand you have a man,
but he don't play no role in my plan.
I'm real with it, if you have some problems
come on girl lets deal with it,
I'm still with it,
and no matter what we still gone kick it."
-*Soody Mak*

5

One week later, Darion and I approached Patience and Teebaby as they stood before Patience's locker, wearing our team jerseys like we did whenever there was a game to be played later on in the day.

So far, we were undefeated and were demolishing the teams we played, winning by at least a 21 point margin. Darion had proven his quarterbacking abilities and was put in the starting position.   Coach Turner thought it was amazing how Darion and I read each other out on the field. We had been playing together for our whole lives. Coach was taking things much more serious than we were. Kev was doing more than his share with the running game, making us seem unbeatable offensively. The only problem was that the three of us were beginning to miss practice too often.

"Happy birthday girl!" I greeted Patience, hugging her and kissing her on the cheek.

"Thank you Atif." Patience said, returning the hug.

"That's all you gone give your girlfriend for her birthday?" Teebaby asked me.

"That is more than enough for me."   Patience answered for me, grabbing my hand.

"Look in my locker and grab my history book for me, would you Patience?" I asked her. She then went to my locker and began to work the dial.

"You still can't open your locker?" Teebaby asked me. I stood there silently watching Patience with a smirk on my face, ignoring Teebaby. "What did you get Patience for her birthday?" She then asked, dismissing me and focusing her attention towards Darion.

"The same thing I got her last year."

"You didn't even know her last year."

"You catch on quick, don't you?"

"Forget you.   You are *wrong* Darion." Teebaby said, shaking her head in disbelief. There was a sharp click as Patience opened my locker. She reached onto the top shelf and grabbed my history book, the only book on the top shelf, and pulled it out. There was a small black box on top of the book and it fell on the floor.

"What is this?" Patience asked me, stooping to pick the box up from the ground. She then opened the box, revealing the two diamond stud earrings she had shown me at the jewelry store the week before. Patience let out a loud scream and covered her mouth with her other hand, forgetting about my history book for the moment, letting it fall to the floor. Some of the other kids in the hallway turned and gave Patience a questioning glance. Teebaby and Darion walked over to see what it was that she held.

"Oooh girl, those are *beautiful!*" Teebaby exclaimed, looking at the earrings.

"Aw man, no you *didn't*! You trick ass nigga!" Darion commented, doing the same with a shake of the head. "Wait till I tell Malik and them about *this*!"

"Oh, Atif." Patience said, speaking from behind the hand that covered her mouth. Her eyes watered and a tear spilled down her cheek. "I can't believe you actually went back and bought these for me." Tears were now covering both cheeks. It was the second time in a short period of time that I had seen Patience cry, and even though they were tears of joy, I still felt awkward. I had not anticipated such a reaction from her. Patience then ran over to me and wrapped her arms around my neck, knocking me backwards. "Thank you. Thank you so much."

"Aww, that was so sweet." Teebaby said, staring at us with a bright smile on her face.

"Don't be over there gettin' your hopes up." Darion said to Teebaby, smiling himself. He had to give it up to me, that was a slick move that even he knew nothing about.

"You ain't even *capable* of doin' somethin' like that." Teebaby said to Darion.

"You got that right." He responded. "Come on girl, lets leave the two lovebirds to themselves." Darion said as the two walked off. A bell then sounded throughout the halls.

"Come on Patience, we gone be late." I said, trying to pull away from her embrace.

"I don't care." She said, refusing to let me go.

"I can't get no more tardies." I said. Patience lifted her head off of my shoulder and looked at me through teary eyes.

"What are you doing to me Atif?" She whined in between sniffles. I laughed lightly.

"You said that like whatever it is, you don't like it."

"No, I like it a little *too* much. That is what I am afraid of." Patience said, letting go of me and bending over to pick up my history book. She had every right to be afraid. "You don't really need this, do you?" She asked, holding the history book up.

"Naw, you can put it back. It served its purpose." I answered, smirking. Patience put the book back into my locker and slammed it closed. She then took my right arm and wrapped it around her shoulders, sliding her left arm around my waist.

"You like them?" I asked Patience. I noticed that she was paying more attention to her new earrings than to where she was walking.

"I *love* them." She answered, giving my waist a squeeze.

"What is your mama gone say when she see you with them?"

"First she is going to ask me who I got them from. And when I tell her that you bought them for me, she is going to ask me who you are. Then, after I tell her that you are my boyfriend, she is going to ask me about a million questions about you. After she is through quizzing me, she is going to ask me if she can wear them." Patience said. We both laughed at that.

"What are you doin' for your birthday?" I asked as we turned into second hall.

"I'm going to watch you play football and scream my head off every time that you get the ball."

"Naw, seriously."

"I am serious Atif."

"You don't have nothin' planned?"

"No."

"Well, we gone have to do somethin' about that." I said as we walked into Mr. Williams' class.

89

The football game went well. We rode the team bus out to Excelsior Springs to play the Wildcats who were ranked number four in the state. The Wildcats were a bunch of preppy, arrogant white boys who underestimated us until they found themselves being annihilated 35-6 at half time. I was way too fast to be contained by any of the Wildcats' defenders, even with double coverage. And when the Wildcats would play their linebackers deep to try and contain me, Darion would hand the ball off to Kev who would run an average of ten yards or more before being tackled. We broke the spirit of the Wildcats and embarrassed them by a final score of 56-13. The fifty-six points scored set a district record for most points scored in a road game.

*****

"You wanna do *what?*" Darion asked me in disbelief. We were at the tilt with Malik, sitting at the table in the kitchen while helping him bag up crack cocaine.

"You heard me." I answered, rolling up a joint for Malik.

"I knew you was a trick ass nigga, but this here takes the cake! Patience done put some kind of spell on your ass. She done buried a pair of your boxers in her backyard or put some of her period blood in your spaghetti or somethin'." Darion said, shaking his head. This made Malik laugh.

"You gone go in with me or what?" I asked Darion.

"How much is it gone cost?"

"$350 for four hours." I answered. Darion whistled.

"Fuck it, I'm gee for that." Darion said, "I ain't never been in one anyway."
'

*****

90

Darion and I were missing in action during the first four hours of school the next day. Patience and Teebaby were sitting in the cafeteria eating their lunches when we all of a sudden appeared out of nowhere, pulling two chairs from the table and taking a seat.

"Where have you two been?" Patience asked us.

"Nowhere." I answered, smirking.

"Y'all leave y'all shit on the table and follow us." Darion said to the two young ladies as we stood up.

"I'm hungry boy, I ain't finna leave my food nowhere." Teebaby said. Patience was looking up at me, trying to figure out what we were up to.

"Come on girl, let's go." Darion said. We turned to leave. Patience and Teebaby looked at each other, shrugged their shoulders, and then got up and followed us. We then slipped undetected into the auditorium and hid behind the curtains on stage.

"What are we doin'?" Teebaby asked us.

"Shhh! Be quiet girl, with your big mouth." Darion hissed back.

"Skippin' class." I whispered, answering Teebaby's question.

"Why?" Patience asked me. Skipping class was something that she had never done before.

"It wouldn't be a surprise if I told you." I whispered back. "Come on y'all." The three followed me into the music hall and we quietly slipped out of a back door. We then ran around to the parking lot in front of the school.

"What the" Teebaby started, referring to the chauffeur holding open the rear door to a white Lincoln limousine with black tinted windows.

"Gone girl, get in. Hurry up!" Darion cut in, rushing Teebaby into the limousine. We tumbled in laughing after her and the chauffeur closed the door behind us. We were pulling out of the school parking lot when a large tinted partition, separating the back seats from the front, began to slide down.

"Where to little man?" The chauffeur asked, looking into the rearview mirror at me.

"Cool Crest." I answered.

As we rode in the limousine throughout the city streets, Darion and Teebaby made their presence known by hanging out of the sunroof for the onlookers to see. I sat back with my arm around Patience's shoulders, looking out of the window.

"My goodness, why is everything so rundown and abandoned around here?" Patience asked me, looking out of the window.

"Cause ain't nobody got no money, and the ones who do don't care."

"I don't see how you guys could take being raised down here."

"You would be surprised with what you could take when takin' it is the only choice you got."

Patience was from Grandview, Missouri. Grandview was a middle/upper class suburb located on the outskirts of south Kansas City. After her father left them and her mother was laid off from work, they had no choice but to migrate further down north. They now lived in southern Kansas City in a neighborhood that was not so bad but not what Patience was used to. Her mother went out of her way to enroll Patience into the brand new Central High School because she believed it had the best programs available for that particular district, and it resembled the type of school one would find in the suburbs.

Cool Crest was a recreational center located off of 40 Highway on the east side of town. We pulled into a small parking lot and the chauffeur let the four of us out of the back seats.

Behind the front counter stood a white man who looked to be in his forties. He was bald on the top of his head and he wore glasses on his face.

"Why aren't you kids in school?" The man asked, looking down at us suspiciously.

"We had a ½ day." I lied. The man grunted.

"Where are your mothers? Do they know where you are?" the man asked, folding his arms across his chest. A dark and stormy cloud passed across my face as it twisted into a mask of anger. Who did this dude think he was?

Darion then stepped in front of me in a jest that said "let me handle this."

"His mama got killed a few months ago. My mama is probably on her knees right now suckin' some nigga's dick for some dope. Now, where your mama at?"

"Hey, I don't want any trouble." The man answered, throwing his hands up in humility as if we were robbing the place.

The news had been full of adolescents such as us with a short temper and capable of committing murder. He didn't intend to find out for himself if whether the images portrayed by the media, concerning our generation of rebellious young black males, was indeed true or not.

"I see a couple of kids jumping out of a limousine during school hours and I have to ask questions, do you know what I am saying?" He was clearly shaken by the look on my face.

"Yeah, whatever." Darion answered, pulling Teebaby by her hand. "Punk peckerwood mutha' fucka'. If we was some white boys you wouldn't have had shit to say." He mumbled as the two walked off. I didn't make a move to follow, I stood still glaring at the man with my fist clenched at my sides. I wanted to go ahead and put some work in on him.

"I'm sorry son, I did not know." The man apologized, reaching over the counter and placing his hand on my shoulder. I knocked the man's hand away with more force than necessary.

"Don't touch me. I ain't your mutha' fuckin' son either." I said calmly. My tone made the threat twice as real.

"Come on Atif, lets go." Patience said, wrapping her arm around my shoulders and pulling me away. She could feel my body tense with anger and she had a feeling that if she didn't remove me from that man's presence, then something bad would happen.

A while later, Darion and Teebaby had forgotten the incident and were chasing each other around the track in go-carts. They were enjoying themselves immensely; their laughter could be heard over the go-cart's lawnmower engines. Patience led me to the miniature golf course and we sat down on the bleachers. I was swinging a miniature golf club lightly at the grass and Patience sat one row up behind me. I was between her legs with my back facing her. Patience wrapped her arms around my upper body and she just held me like that in silence until she felt my body loosen up.

"What was her name, Atif?" Patience asked.

"Rosanna." I answered, looking down at the ground, still swinging the golf club over the grass. "Everybody called her Rose."

"What was she like?"

I stopped swinging the golf club and looked up at the sky as some birds flew by overhead. "My mamma was pretty, *real* pretty. Every time we went out somewhere some dude was always tryin' to holler at her." I said. I then smiled to myself as my next thought surfaced. "She was crazy though, her and D-Mack used to go at it all the time. I remember once when D-Mack told Big Mama, with Mama sittin' right there, he said," I paused for a couple of seconds in recollection. "*You know Big Mama, I always thought that you called your daughter Rose because she is a beautiful woman, but now I see that her name didn't have nothin' to do with the flower itself. It was the thorns you was referrin' to.*" I began to laugh. "We all busted out laughin' till we was cryin'."

"That boy is so silly." Patience commented, laughing herself. I think that at that moment she saw my best friend in a different light. She turned her head in his direction; Teebaby was chasing him across the track. She had tricked him out of his go-cart somehow.

"Yeah," I started, watching Teebaby run him down. "She loved his crazy butt too. If a day rolled past without D-Mack knockin' at the door, she would ask about him."

"Does his mom really smoke crack? I mean, does she really participate in things like prostitution to get high?"

"Yeah, she out there bad."

"God, I have a lot to learn about the two of you, don't I?"

"Yeah, you do. And you will."

"What about your father? Where is he?" Patience asked.

"I don't know. My brotha' said that he sees him every once in a while. He out there somewhere. I ain't seen him in a long time. He didn't even come to Mama's funeral." I answered.

"I am sorry Atif."

"What you apologizin' for?" I asked, turning my head to look at her.

"Him, your father. And your mother." She answered, looking down at me.

"Don't." I hated when people did that for some reason. I didn't want pity.

"I have never seen you get so upset Atif. I mean, I can tell that you hold a lot of anger inside of you and it does not really scare me because you don't come off to me as the type that would ever hurt a girl. But you looked like you were about to *kill* that guy back there." Patience said. I didn't comment. I knew that if she had not removed me from his presence, then I sure would have tried to. "How did she die?" Patience then asked after a few moments of silence.

I really didn't want to go there. I wished that I could just forget about it, but I couldn't. I didn't want to keep reliving that night over and over again for everyone who was curious as to what happened. But with Patience it was different. Everything was. She just wanted to understand me and no one had ever really tried to do that before. So, I opened up.

"It was not your fault Atif." Patience said when I finished, hugging me from behind with tears falling from her own eyes. Something about the story set off an alarm somewhere in her brain. Whatever it was that was nagging at her would come to her later, she thought, so she dismissed it. "You can't go through life blaming yourself for your mother's death." She finished, sensing that I partially blamed myself for her death.

"I'm supposed to be takin' you out for your belated birthday and we done turned it into a therapy session."

95

"There is nothing wrong with opening up and talking about what happened. I think that you will begin to feel much better when you allow yourself to do so instead of holding it all inside. You do not ever talk about that night with anyone, do you?" Patience asked.

"No."

"Telling me about it wasn't so bad, now was it?"

"No." I admitted, smiling.

"You are not so upset anymore either, are you?"

"No."

"Can I have a kiss?" Patience asked, closing her eyes and perking her lips in preparation.

"No." I answered. Patience pushed me off of the bleachers. I laughed and stood up, turning to face Patience. I then took a hold of her waist and pulled her close to me, kissing her passionately. At that moment, Darion and Teebaby came around the corner and saw us kissing each other.

"Come on Teebaby, lets play monkey see monkey do." Darion said, grabbing Teebaby and kissing her much to her surprise. She wrapped her arms around his neck and kissed back.

*****

Later on that evening I was leaving the tilt and on my way home for the night. I had already practically made the money back I spent on the limousine after only a few hours or so of sitting at the tilt. Instead of the standard $25 dollars off of every $100 made, Darion and I were now selling our own dope, easily cutting close to $300 out of every 3 ½ grams of crack cocaine we purchased from Malik and K-Red. We were already fantasizing about opening up our own tilt.

The limousine ride and the trip to Cool Crest turned out even better than I had expected it to. Talking to Patience about my mother and how she was killed did make me feel better about the situation, but it did nothing to

96

quench the anger that I felt towards the ones responsible for her untimely death.

Walking down the alleyway behind 26th and Chestnut, I reflected on the question of how I could stand being raised in such an environment that Patience had asked me earlier in the limousine. I thought that I had answered correctly, I didn't have a choice. It was like asking Big Mama how she could have grown up during the times of segregation and Jim Crow laws. What did people expect? How could someone be brought up around all of that poverty, gang violence, drug abuse, and police brutality without becoming a victim or a victimizer him or herself? Looking around, I shook my head at my surroundings and vowed to find my way out of them real quick like.

"Atif."

My body tensed at the sound of the voice coming seemingly out of nowhere. Startled, I turned around. "Kesha?" I asked as a female figure emerged from the shadows. "Girl, what you doin' back here?"

"Waitin' on you to walk by." Kesha answered, walking up to me.

"How you know I was gone take the alley?" I asked, mentally telling my heart that everything was all right and it could stop beating so hard now. She had spooked me for real.

"Cause you and Malik *always* take the alley at night." Kesha answered. "Are you still mad at me?"

"No." I answered as we turned and began walking up the alley.

"I really didn't mean anything by it, Atif. When you caught me slippin' and started ticklin' me, I just said it in shock without thinkin'."

"I know."

"Malik told me that you had him rent a limo today. Why did you do that?" Kesha asked, changing the subject.

"Malik told you that I rented a limo and he didn't tell you why?" I asked in return, recognizing the trap Kesha was attempting to set for me. I was young but not dumb. Kesha remained silent. "You ain't gotta come at me like that girl, I ain't got no reason to lie to you."

97

"Aw, you recognize game huh? I like that in you." Kesha commented, looking sideways at me.

"Apology accepted." I replied sarcastically.

"I didn't know that you had a girlfriend."

"There is a lot you don't know about me."

"Come spend the night with me."   Kesha propositioned.

"What?" I asked, stopping in my tracks.

"You heard me."

"Girl, Big Mama ain't finna let me spend the night over your house."

"Tell her you over Darion's."

I didn't comment, thinking that it was not a bad idea to myself. Not a bad idea at all.

"Come on," Kesha started. "I'll make sure that you enjoy your self." She offered teasingly. That right there pretty much made my mind up for me. Kesha then grabbed my butt, giving it a hard squeeze like I used to do her, and then took off laughing and running up the alley. I took off after her.

Kesha lived in a yellow and white two story house. It was a little nicer than the rest on the block. Her mother took great pride in keeping their home presentable to the human eye.

"I don't know who you think you was foolin', I know you can run *way* faster than that," Kesha said, opening the front door. "Come on." She said, stepping aside and then shutting the door behind me.

"Where your mama at?" I asked, stepping into a spacious living room with nice carpet and matching furniture. I had been in Kesha's house once or twice before but it was a long time ago. Ms. Brown had been doing pretty good for herself over the years by the looks of things.

"She is over her boyfriend's for the night." Kesha answered, turning on the lights. "Are you hungry?" She asked, heading for the kitchen.

"Yeah."

"It's some chicken in the frigerator, want me to warm some up for you?"

"Yeah, but first I want you to go back in your room and strip down to yo panties and bra. Then you can warm some chicken up for me."

"Why you want me to do that?"

"Because that's what I want you to do."

"You expect me to walk around the house all night with nothin' but my bra and panties on?"

"Yeah."

"Who you think you are?" she asked, cutting her eyes at me.

"Atif."

"I know you are Atif, but what makes you think you got it like that?" Kesha asked with one hand on her hip, holding a plate of fried chicken in the other. Kesha liked me, I knew that. I also knew that she felt like she wanted or needed to make up for that night at the tilt. I wasn't upset with her over that anymore, I was being sincere when I told her so. She still wanted to make it up to me though, so why not play on that? I said nothing, I simply stood there leaning against the doorway. "Roll this up." Kesha said, setting down the plate of chicken on the kitchen counter. She reached in her pants pocket and pulled out a sack of weed and some papers, handing it to me on her way out of the kitchen.

Later on we sat in the living room watching television. I was laying across Kesha's lap, looking up at her as she took a hit from one of the joints I had rolled for her.

"Why you smoke so much weed?" I asked Kesha.

"Because I like the way it makes me feel."

"Did you have an orgasm when we did it a few weeks ago?"

"Two."

"*Two* of them?" Kesha nodded her head, smiling down at me. "Ha ha! I put it down like that?" Kesha nodded her head again, blowing marijuana smoke out of her mouth. "No wonder you was in the alley waitin' for a nigga to walk past!" I said.

"Forget you!" Kesha said, laughing.

"When did you...you know?"

"Well, I had the first one almost as soon as we started, then I came again when you did."

"Why you didn't tell me?"

"Because I couldn't believe that it was happenin'. I had sex before, but I ain't never had an orgasm durin' sex until we did it." Kesha said. So in a sense, our endeavor was a first for her also. We sat in silence for a while. "Can I ask you somethin'?"

"Yeah."

"Can we be personal friends?"

"Personal friends? I like that. What made you come up with that one?"

"I was thinkin' about the way I feel about you a-"

"Hold up, wait a minute! Stop the press!" I cut in. Kesha threw her head back and laughed at this. "You mean to tell me that you got feelins for me after we did it only once?" I asked, sitting up. I already knew all this for real, I was just playing that role. Kesha then switched positions and laid across my lap.

"I *always* had feelins for you. Ever since the first time I saw you walkin with Malik in the hood. Us doin' it just made it worse." Kesha answered.

"Hmph, I didn't know that. Finish what you was sayin'."

"Anyway, I was thinkin' about how I feel about you and I realized that I liked you a lot and I wanted you to be my-"

"I gotta girl." I cut in.

"Are you gone let me finish?"

"Yeah, my bad." I answered. "Go 'head." I said, slipping my right hand into Kesha's panties. Kesha opened her legs a little wider so that my fingers could find what they were looking for.

"I realized that I wanted you to be my man but I also didn't wanna....I didn't wanna have to ever worry about losin' you. So I.....I thought that you could be more than my friend but less than my boyfriend."

"If I was to get locked up, would you ride with me?" I asked, slipping my middle finger into Kesha's vagina.

100

Kesha moaned and began to move her lower body up and down on my finger.

"Yes." She whispered, looking up at me.

"What if I need somethin' you got, would you give it to me?"

"Yes." She whispered with a tear coming out of her eye.

"Why you cryin'?"

"Because you about to make me come." Kesha whispered, closing her eyes and arching her back. She grabbed me by my wrist and clamped down on my hand by squeezing her thighs together, crying out in pleasure. When the orgasm subsided, she released my wrist and looked up into my eyes. "I will do *anything* for you Atif."

"What if I have a fantasy that I want fulfilled?" I asked, waving my middle finger inches away from Kesha's lips with a smirk on my face.

"Then I will fulfill it." Kesha said, grabbing my hand and sucking her bodily juices from my middle finger.

"I think I better call Big Mama and tell her that I'm a spend the night over D-Mack's." I said. Kesha laughed.

*****

PUTTING IN WORK

"Who's in the wrong? It does not matter,
when it's on, then it's on!
Echoes of window shatter,
when I'm holdin' my own.
I'm hangin' up outta the sunroof, what you wanna do?
Yeah, you! Where you runnin' to?
You niggas is faggots,
we let the whole hood have it,
Grippin' automatics,
when we roll through."
-Soody Mak

"His future saggin' like Dickies,
off the ass of a banger.
His whole block is in danger,
bitch, I'm that South Side Mangler.
Ignore my feelins like I do a stranger,
when I bust.
Releasin' nothin' but anger,
retaliation's a must."
-Tazz Mania Devil

6

Darion and I were beginning to lose more interest in school by the day. We found ourselves skipping more classes than we were attending, spending the majority of our time at the tilt. Actually, we were making a little more money than we knew what to do with. We went from possessing a wardrobe that would be considered as fair, to not even wearing the same outfit twice. As freshmen, Darion and I were even out dressing the majority of the seniors. Big Mama didn't like it, but she didn't ask a lot of questions either.

One day we were at the tilt with K-Red and Trigga. Malik and Money Mike were out taking care of some business, as they put it. With those two together, there was no telling what that involved. Everything was going well. The tilt was *rolling*; I mean we were getting rid of at least two ounces a night in pieces alone. And the best part of it all was that it was Darion, Kesha and I who were there most of the time, especially at night. Malik, K-Red, Trigga, Money Mike, the whole clique (some of whom I have not mentioned yet), they were somewhat apprehensive about spending too much time at the tilt. They all knew from experience that it would not be long before the Task Force would be paying the tilt a visit. Darion and I didn't believe that fat meant greasy though. I guess we for some reason believed that we could go on like that forever; that they would leave us alone. That was way too good to be true. The tilt was hot. Some nights the police would roll by slowly and shine a spotlight into the house. At times they would even go as far as parking directly across the street, watching us for hours at a time. Malik cautioned us to only keep a few pieces of crack on us at a time and leave the rest hidden outside in the alley somewhere.

"Sell us your car." Darion said to K-Red. The four of us were sitting around the kitchen table smoking a joint. Business was kind of slow that day with it being the end of the month. Welfare checks had been spent up and all of the crack fiends that came by were short or trying to get some dope on credit until the checks were issued in a few days.

"Which one?" K-Red asked Darion.

"The Iroc."

"Yeah right." K-Red said, shaking his head. The Iroc was a candy apple red Chevy convertible with white leather interior and 15 inch speakers built into the trunk, sitting on some 17-by-9 inch triple gold Dayton standards. The stereo system with the wheels alone was worth over $8,000. We were doing good, but not that good; at least not yet.

"What about the bucket?" I asked. The bucket was a tan 1978 Impala that K-Red used to ride around in inconspicuously.

"How much money you niggas got?" K-Red asked in return.

"How much you want for it?" Darion asked.

"Where y'all gone keep it at?" K-Red asked. Right then I knew we had some action coming. K-red was money hungry. He would sell his own soul for the right price.

"Up here in the back." I answered.

"We ain't gone be here too much longer Atif, I keep tellin' y'all that. What y'all gone do with it when Task come closin' up shop?" K-Red asked.

"We will figure somethin' out." Darion answered.

"Gimme $1,200"

"*What?*" Darion and I cried out together in disbelief.

"Man you *crazy?* That car ain't worth no $1,200." Darion said, handing K-Red a joint.

"And y'all ain't supposed to be drivin'." K-Red said.

"And *you* ain't supposed to be sellin' dope." I said.

"A'ight, gimme $800."

"Man, come on man. Why you tryin' to juke us?" Darion asked.

"We will give you $300 a piece." I offered. Even that was too much, but I figured we needed some transportation. Especially if we were going to get our own tilt like we planned.

"Where the money at?" K-Red asked, holding out an open palm. Darion and I dug into our pockets and pulled out a wad of money. "Y'all be walkin' around with y'all money in y'all pockets like that?"

"Nope." Darion said, counting out $300. "We brought it with us just in case you went for the okie doke like you did." We both laid the money on the table and K-Red picked it up.

"Y'all just gave me $600 for the bucket and *y'all* think *I* went for the okie doke?" K-Red asked, smiling while adding the money to his own bankroll. "Whose name y'all gone put it in?" K-Red asked, throwing a set of keys on the table.

"We will find somebody." I answered, snatching the keys off of the table before D-Mack. "Where the title?"

"In the glove box." K-Red answered. Darion and I got up from our seats and turned to leave.

"Where y'all goin?" Trigga asked us.

"To go get some tags." I answered.

"What you know about gettin' some tags?" K-Red asked me.

"I know enough to only put $100 on the title so that the tags won't cost nothin' but $20 or so." I got that game from my mother. She always knew how to pay a little bit of nothing for something. I guess when one doesn't have a lot to work with in the first place they pick up these tricks of the trade along the way.

"Y'all can drop me off, shit. It's startin' to get a lil' too hot for me to be sittin' around here." Trigga said. He had every right to feel this way. The police were even beginning to harass the individuals they observed leaving the tilt.

"Here." K-Red said, tossing Darion another set of car keys. "Go around to my house and bring my other car down here."

"Let me have one of them joints." Darion said to K-Red, pointing to the numerous joints laying on the table.

"Naw nigga. Bring my car back first. You ain't finna get all high and wreck my shit. Don't touch nothin'

105

either, just get in the car and drive it over here. Don't touch my seats, my radio, nothin'." K-Red said.

"A'ight, a'ight. Yadda-yadda-yadda-yadda." Darion said, mocking K-Red. K-Red threatened him with his eyes.

"I ain't playin' with you nigga. If you wreck my shit I'mma wreck your *life*." K-Red warned. He was dead serious too. D-Mack knew when it was time to back off and take K-Red seriously. This was one of those times.

We left the tilt bound for K-Red's house on 28th and Benton after dropping Trigga off over some female's house on 24th and Norton. I followed Darion back to the tilt and we dropped K-Red's car off. Darion hopped into the passenger seat and we pulled off.

"Where you goin'?" Darion asked me as we headed north on Benton Avenue.

"To pick Kesha up so she can put the tags in her name."

"Drop me off at the house man, I gotta go somewhere with Mama." Darion said. I turned west on 25th street and headed for Montgal. A couple of minutes later we pulled in front of Darion's house. "You goin' to the Halloween dance tomorrow?"

"Yeah, you?"

"Yeah. A, won't you go by the Landin' and see if they got some Freddy Kruger masks for me?"

"A'ight, I'll holler." I said. We gave each other some dap and I pulled off. A few minutes later I pulled in front of Kesha's house. Turning off the engine, I made my way across her front lawn and knocked on the front door. I could still hear the bucket trying to shut off. After I took the keys out of the ignition, the engine was still sputtering. I remember thinking to myself that maybe we *did* go for the okie doke.

"Who is it?" Kesha asked from behind the door.

"Atif."   Kesha opened the front door, smiling brightly at me.

"Wha' sup?"

"Wha' sup personal friend?" Kesha greeted back, grabbing me by the hand and pulling me inside.

"Where your mama at?"

106

"Gettin' some dick." Kesha answered. I laughed. "Naw, I'm just playin'. She at work." Kesha said as she led me to her bedroom. I then took a seat on the edge of her bed.

"I remember the last time I was in here." I said, bouncing on the bed and looking around the room with a smirk on my face.

"Me too." Kesha said, pushing me down on the bed and climbing on top of me. "K-Red let you drive his car?"

"Naw, me and D-Mack bought it from him."

"Y'all ballin' ain't y'all?" Kesha asked. I only smirked in response. Kesha was getting her bread too. She spent almost as much time at the tilt as Darion and I. "Well, that's cool. Now you can take me to the hotel when my mama is at home." She said, smiling down at me.

"Girl is sex the only thing you think about?"

"No. I think about money too." Kesha answered, raising my sweatshirt up and kissing my stomach with little kisses.

"You wanna do somethin' for me?" I asked her, staring up at the ceiling.

"I wanna do a *lot* of things for you." Kesha answered in between kisses.

"I want you to put some tags for the bucket in your name."

"Okay." Kesha said, raising my shirt up further so that she could kiss on my chest.

"Lets go." I said, pulling my shirt down and sitting up.

"*Now?*" Kesha asked. I nodded. Kesha pouted and got up off of my lap. She then went over to her bedroom closet and grabbed a red T-shirt and a pair of black Guess jeans. Kesha slipped out of her sweat pants, revealing smooth and pretty thighs that disappeared into some white panties.

"When I come up and get my own spot, I want you to walk around my house just like that when you come over." I said, watching Kesha slip into her tight fitting jeans. I resisted the urge to put off the issue concerning the tags for a later date and time.

107

"And you say that *I'm* a real freak." Kesha commented, smiling at me.

*****

Kesha and I made our way to the state building downtown with her in the driver's seat. Kesha had to inform me that we needed to get an inspection slip in order to get some tags for the bucket. We stopped by a black owned repair shop and after slipping the mechanic a $20 bill for an inspection that usually only cost $7.00, the bucket passed the inspection with flying colors. After paying a little over $25 for some license plates, we then got on the Interstate I-70 turnpike heading east.

"Where to now?" Kesha asked me.

"Go out to The Landin'." I answered, trying to locate 103.3 on the radio dial.

Twenty minutes later, Kesha and I pulled into The Landing Mall's parking lot. The Landing was a smaller mall in comparison to the other malls in Kansas City. It was an orange one story building that sat at the intersection of 63rd street and Troost Avenue.

"Dang, you see them?" Kesha asked me, looking towards the front entrance. There were at least twelve Rolling 60's Crips standing in front of the main entrance smoking weed and staring at us as we rolled past.

"You still wanna go in there?"

"Yeah, just act like you leavin' and pull around to the other side. We will go in through the back." I answered. Kesha did as she was instructed and then parked the car. We then slipped into the mall through the rear entrance.

"Don't you have enough clothes and shoes?" Kesha asked me as we walked down the lobby.

"I ain't come up here to buy no clothes." I answered, turning into a Korean owned store called "Glamourama." We headed to the back of the store until we came upon an aisle containing Halloween masks. I found a Freddy Kruger mask for Darion and then selected a hockey mask for myself.

"Y'all a lil' too old to be bag snatchin' ain't y'all?" Kesha asked me as we headed up to the cashier. We used to go out south and snatch little kids Halloween bags from them back in the day.

"These are for the school's Halloween dance tomorrow." I answered. We approached the counter and I laid the masks down. There was a middle aged Korean man standing behind the counter accompanied by a middle aged Korean woman who appeared to be the man's wife.

"How you today?" the Korean man asked in broken English as he began to scan the merchandise.

"Fine." Kesha replied for the both of us, smiling at the man.

"$13.26" the man said while his wife put the Halloween masks into a black plastic shopping bag. I handed the man a $20 bill.

"Atif." Kesha said, looking out at the store entrance doors.

"Wha-?" I started. The group of Crips that were standing out in the parking lot were now crowded around the entrance to the store, waiting for us to come out. "Aw shit."

"What wrong?" the Korean man asked. "They you friend?"

"No." I answered.

"No violence in my store! I call security!" the Korean woman said, picking up a telephone.

"Here you change." The Korean man said, handing it to me along with the shopping bag. "You go now! Get out my store!"

"We ain't did nothin', why you puttin' us out like that? You see all them niggas out there." I responded.

"You go! No violence in my store! You go out there, they no come in here mess my store up." The Korean man replied.

"Come on Kesha." I said, grabbing Kesha by the hand.

"Hell naw!" Kesha spat in defiance, snatching her hand away from my grasp. "We ain't gotta go out there."

"Yes you do!" the Korean woman exclaimed.

"No I don't, bitch! You gone make me?" Kesha challenged, staring the woman down. The Korean woman faltered under Kesha's hostile gaze.

"Come on girl, fuck them." I said, grabbing Kesha by the hand again and leading her towards the entrance doors. For some reason I believed that there was a slight chance that maybe we could have made it out of the mall with only suffering a few insulting remarks from the Crips who were out there. "When we get out here, just keep on walkin'. Don't say nothin' no matter what they say."

I walked out of the door first, carrying the shopping bag in one hand and holding Kesha's hand with the other.

"Wha' sup cuz?" a brown skinned brother asked me. He stood about 5'9 and appeared to be in his late teens or early twenties, clearly older than I was. He wore a full blue Dickie suit and on his feet were a pair of blue and white sneakers.

I ignored him and kept on walking. I was nervous. I had never been jumped on before but I had heard numerous horror stories about the experience. I realized that I had been fooling myself. It would have taken an act of congress to prevent a can of whoop ass from being opened on us that day.

"Where the fuck you think you at lil' nigga?" a darker skinned brother asked, cutting our path off. The rest of the group began to surround us. I stopped and looked around, still holding Kesha's hand and my shopping bag, wondering to myself where the first punch would come from.

"Lil' slob ass bitch sure gotta fat ass on her." The brown skinned brother said, patting Kesha's buttocks. Kesha snapped. Letting go of my hand, she slapped the brown skinned brother across his face. He then took a step back and stared at Kesha in shock. A few giggles arose from the group.

110

Here we go. I thought to myself. The brown skinned brother's expression of shock turned into one of anger and embarrassment.

"You lil' punk ass bitch!" he spat, raising his right hand clenched into a fist in order to strike Kesha with.

At that moment I dropped the shopping bag I held and threw a right cross connecting with the brown skinned brother's chin, knocking him to the ground before he had the chance to hit Kesha. All hell broke loose. I began to feel punches coming from all directions. I swung wildly, only connecting a few punches here and there. A wild overhand right caught me in the left eye and everything went white. Unable to see anything but that blinding light, I covered up. The punches kept on coming endlessly. I could hear Kesha screaming in the background but her voice seemed to be coming from far away. Just when I felt as if I couldn't bear to take one more punch, I heard the sharp click-clack sound of a semi-automatic pistol being cocked. All the punches stopped. Kesha's screaming and cursing came to an abrupt halt. I remember thinking that I was about to be shot.

"Get up nigga." A deep voice said. I recognized the voice instantly and opened my eyes. I could feel my left eye swelling shut, but that bright white light no longer clouded my vision. I looked up and saw that Money Mike held a black .45 semi-automatic to one of the Crip's forehead. The other gang members were backing up as Kesha helped me off of the ground. "You gotta problem with the color my lil' hommie got on nigga?" Money Mike asked.

"Naw." The brown skinned brother replied shakily.

"Yeah, that' s what I thought." Money Mike said. "Y'all get the fuck up outta here before I shoot the shit outta one of you niggas." Money Mike lowered his pistol and the group of Crip's took off running down the lobby.

"Are you okay Atif?" Kesha asked, touching my left eye where I caught the worst.

"Ssss, ah shit girl!" I cringed in pain, slapping her hand away. "I'm cool."

111

"Yeah, you cool till I tell Malik and them about how them lil' crab niggas had your ass curled up like a fetus." Money Mike said.

"Fuck you. What you doin' up here anyway?"

"I had to holler at somebody. Lets walk, I'm surprised the police ain't came yet." Money Mike said. Kesha picked up my sack and we began to walk. "How y'all get up here?"

"We drove." Kesha answered.

"Drove what, a dope fiend rental? I told y'all about that joy ridin' and shit." Money Mike said. What was he talking about? He never told me nothing like that. I didn't even partake in renting dope fiends' cars.

"It ain't no dope fiend rental, me and D-Mack bought K-Red's car." I said.

"The Iroc?" Money Mike asked in surprise with his eyebrows raised.

"Naw, the bucket."

"I was about to say, shit. I know y'all ain't doin' it like that already. That nigga wouldn't even slang me that mutha' fucka' and I offered him $7,000. How much did he sell y'all the bucket for?"

"$600."

"What? $600? Man, that nigga should have gave y'all that raggedy ass car. I'mma tell that nigga about his-self." Money Mike said. By now we had made it to the entrance doors that Kesha and I had come in through. "What y'all finna do?" Money Mike asked us. Kesha shrugged her shoulders and looked at me.

"Head back to the hood." I answered.

"Y'all can take me around to my car and just follow me, I was about to head that way my damn self." Money Mike then looked at my face and shook his head. "Malik gone go smooth off when he see your eye."

He was right. Now if I just had a fight, one on one with someone my own age and lost, then he probably would not have tripped. But I got jumped, we got jumped. And what made it even worse was that they were older than me, they were like his age. If by reading these first six chapters you came to the conclusion that I had a pretty bad temper which I pretty much kept in check, or at least tried to, Malik's was ten times worse than mine was when he got upset.   And this was going to *PISS HIM OFF.* I got butterflies just imagining how he would react.

After driving Money Mike to his car around front, we followed him out of the parking lot.

"What are you starin' at?" I asked Kesha after a few minutes of silence between us. We had not spoken since Money Mike got out of the vehicle. I noticed that she kept staring at me when she could do so without running into someone.

"I don't know why you trippin' with me, *you* the one who wanted to come out here." Even though she was right, she had gotten under my skin with that comment. I was already upset. When I got like that, anything would irritate me.

"Yeah, but if you would have just did what I *told* you to do, they probably wouldn't have jumped me." I said, mis-directing my anger. I had that bad also.

"Hold up. First of all, *me?* What the fuck you mean *me?* You wasn't the *only* one fightin'. You wasn't by yo-self." Kesha pointed out. I looked at her and saw that her lip was busted for the first time. She was right there with me the whole time and I didn't really realize it until then. "They was gone jump us *regardless*, whenever you get through, and you *know* that." Kesha said, turning right on 63rd street.

Kesha followed Money Mike east on 63rd street. When we came to the 63rd and Prospect intersection, we followed Money Mike into the filling station on the corner. Money Mike proceeded to pull up to one of the gas pumps; got out of the car and stuck the pump into his gas tank. He then walked over to the bucket and leaned into the driver side window.

"I gotta run to make out south right quick. Get out and fill the tank up Atif, I want y'all to follow me out there. You need to get some ice for your eye anyway." Money Mike said. I got out of the car and placed one of the pumps into the bucket's gas tank. "You want somethin'?" Money Mike asked Kesha.

113

"Yeah, I want a Sprite and some Cool Ranch Dorritos."

A few minutes later Money Mike handed Kesha the pop and potato chips he had purchased for her.

"Thank you." Kesha said to Money Mike. I hung the gas pump back up onto the rack and then got inside of the bucket. Kesha then started the car and followed Money Mike out of the parking lot. We headed south on Prospect Avenue until we came to 75th street. We then went east of 75th street and got on the 71 South turnpike.

"Let me get some of them chips." I said to Kesha. Cool Ranch was the stuff and they were smelling good. I don't know why I didn't get anything for myself.

"No." Kesha said, keeping her eyes on the road. "Not unless you apologize to me."

"Apologize? Apologize for what?"

"For takin' your anger out on me." I was silent for a minute. I knew I owed her one. I was wrong for doing so.

"A'ight, I apologize."

"For what?" Kesha asked me. I looked at her and then snatched the bag of Dorritos out of her lap. She had received all that she was going to get. "A'ight, a'ight. That was good enough."

Fifteen minutes later, Kesha and I followed Money Mike as he merged from highway 71 South onto Interstate 435 East. Five more minutes later, we exited the Interstate onto Blue Ridge Boulevard. We then came to a stop light at a busy intersection. On the right hand side there stood a big brown brick building with a spacious parking lot which looked to be a church. Across the street there was a United Missouri Bank.

"Where we at? Grandview?" I asked Kesha.

"No, this is still south Kansas City. Grandview is still a few miles away."

"How do *you* know? Girl you ain't never been off of 27th street."

"Yes I have! My grand-daddy stay out here for your information."

"You know, you been gettin' smart with me ever since we left The Landin'."

"You gone gimme a whoopin'?" Kesha asked me, turning to face me. I laughed and shook my head.

When the light turned green, we trailed Money Mike up Blue Ridge until we came to Longview Road. We then turned east on Longview Road and made a right on Delmar after the second light.

"These some nice houses." I complimented, wondering to myself if we were anywhere near where Patience used to live.

In actuality, it was I who had never really been off of 27th street. I had only seen better neighborhoods on television. We just didn't go out there. For what? All of my family was in the inner city. 27th street was all I knew. From the dope fiends in the alleys to the little kids running around with no shoes on, the ghetto was my world. The houses we rolled by seemed to get nicer by the block. Clean sidewalks, white picket fences, sturdy staircases, two and sometimes even three car garages, to see things like that was a brand new experience for me. I sat in silence, staring out of my window in complete amazement. Kesha looked my way and smiled. If she knew me, then she knew that I was already plotting to own a house and live in a neighborhood such as the ones we were riding through.

Money Mike pulled into a circular driveway on the west side of the street. Kesha followed Money Mike onto the driveway leading up to a large three story house with a wide and spacious well kept front lawn. There was a big two car garage connected to the north end of the house and B.A.K.C.S.M. was stenciled across the garage doors in old English letters.

Money Mike exited his car and then motioned for us to do the same. We walked up to a large set of double doors and could hear dogs barking from the inside of the house.

"Who is it?" A female voice answered from within moments after Money Mike rang the doorbell.

"Mr. Mike."

The door cracked open and a very pretty light skinned face appeared. Her hair was long and black. She had pretty light brown eyes that were hard to turn away

115

from. She smiled, brightening up my whole day. She was *gorgeous*.

"Hello Michael!" she greeted. "Hold on while I let the dogs out back." She finished in proper English, shutting the door. Moments later she reopened one of the double doors and stepped aside, inviting us to walk in.

"Wha' sup Mrs. Thang?" Money Mike greeted as he stepped into the spacious foyer. We followed suit. "This is Kesha, my little home girl from the hood, and this is Malik's brother Atif." Money Mike said, introducing us.

"Hi! My name is not Mrs. Thang," she said, cutting her eyes at Money Mike. "It's Persistence, and it is nice to meet you both." Persistence shook both of our hands. "Atif? I know that name. It sounds familiar to me." Persistence said to me. "What happened to your eye?" She asked, reaching for my face.

"Nothin'." I answered, backing away from her touch and placing the bag of what formally was ice up to my eye.

"Here, let me get you some more ice." Persistence offered me. I then handed her the bag.

"I think he gone need a raw pork chop or steak or somethin' for that. Shit, that ice ain't cuttin it." Money Mike said.

"Stop Michael," Persistence scolded. "You guys have a seat in the front room, Smack Man will be down in a minute." She finished. I looked on in lust as Persistence walked away, heading for the kitchen.

"What you starin' at?" a voice said from behind me. I turned around and it was Smack Man standing there in a pair of black slacks with a black silk shirt. He had a gold Rolex watch on his left wrist and a diamond studded gold ring on each pinkie finger. I looked around and noticed that we were the only two standing in the foyer.

"I was just-"

"Lookin' at my wife's ass?" Smack Man cut in. Silence. "What happened to your eye?"

"I got jumped."

"Hmph. You got some work to put in then, don't you?" Smack Man asked. He then turned and walked away before I could respond to the rhetorical question. I reached up and tenderly touched the swollen area beneath my eye.

"Why are you still standing here?" Persistence asked me from behind. I turned, wondering to myself how it was that people kept sneaking up on me.

"Is that for me?" I asked Persistence, pointing to the bag of ice she held in her right hand.

"Oh, yes. Here you go." Persistence said, handing the renewed bag of ice to me.

"Thank you."

"Don't mention it. Follow me."

Persistence led the way to the front room with me in tow. We walked through a long circular hallway that opened up to a very large room equipped with a red brick fireplace, an aquarium built into the back wall, and a large 60' inch big screen television surrounded by an expensive entertainment system. The front room was furnished with a three piece black leather furniture set surrounding a coffee table which was a statue of a black panther fixed in a crouching position, with a large square shaped glass resting on its back.

Money Mike and Smack Man looked up at us as we entered. Kesha was over on the far side of the room admiring all of the colorful fish in the aquarium. Money Mike and Smack Man appeared to have been previously in conversation on the couches.

"Come here Atif." Money Mike said, motioning for me to sit next to him. I walked over and took my place on the couch. Persistence sat in the recliner on Smack Man's lap, with her arms wrapped around his neck. "You know this is Malik's brotha' right?" Money Mike asked Smack Man.

"Yeah, I know. I remember seein' him around a few times." Smack Man answered, looking at me. They were talking about me as if I was not even sitting there.

"Malik ain't seen his eye yet." Money Mike said, smirking.

"He ain't?" Smack Man asked, still looking at me.

"Nope." Money Mike answered. At that point, Smack Man, Money Mike and Persistence were looking at me. Smack Man shook his head.

"Man, that nigga gone go the fuck off. He got jumped too?" Smack Man asked in a rhetorical manner.

"A, and guess who it was?" Money Mike asked.

"Who?"

"Some Rollin' 60's niggas."

"Did they know who you were?" Smack Man asked me. I shrugged my shoulders. "Them niggas just don't know, they finna get *handled*. Malik and K been lookin' for a reason to get at them niggas." Everyone was quiet for a few seconds. "You be gettin' your hustle on?" Smack Man then asked me, changing the subject.

"A lil' bit."

"That your lil' girlfriend over there?" Smack Man asked me, nodding his head in Kesha's direction.

"No." I answered.

"Do you have a girlfriend?" Persistence asked me.

"Yeah."

"What is her name?" Persistence asked, sitting up.

"Patience."

"I knew your name sounded familiar! Patience is my sister! My name didn't ring any bells? Patience, Persistence?"

"I didn't know Patience was fuckin'." Smack Man cut in.

"She's not!" Persistence exclaimed, hitting Smack Man on his left shoulder. "Is she?" she then asked me, staring me down with those pretty brown eyes of hers.

"No, not that I know of. I mean, *we* ain't never did nothin'." Patience told me she was a virgin long ago.

"Y'all better not be." Persistence said, smiling at me. "So, you are the one who bought Patience those diamond earrings and took her to Cool Crest in a limousine for her birthday?"

"Naw, you got me mixed up with some other dude she must be messin' with on the side." I responded. Persistence inhaled sharply, covering her mouth in a gesture that said "un-oh." "Naw, I'm just playin'. That was me." I finished with a smirk on my face. I was feeling better all of a sudden. I had practically forgotten all about my eye.

118

"Boy! I was about to *say*. My sister is *not* like that."

"You trickin' at an early age ain't you?" Money Mike asked me.

"No, he was not *tricking*." Persistence stated in my defense. "You see? That is exactly what I be talking about. Mike you act like there is something wrong with doing something nice for a woman you care about." She said. "Don't listen to that jughead Atif, that was a very sweet thing to do."

"Jughead?" Smack Man and Money Mike said in unison. The two looked at each other and laughed. The two sisters were just alike: Square.

"Yes. Jughead." Persistence said, getting up from Smack Man's lap. "Can I get anyone anything to drink?"

"Got some yak?" Money Mike asked. Money Mike loved to drink and was known throughout the whole neighborhood for his ability to drink anyone under the table.

"Yak? What in the world is that? It sounds like something a camel would say." Persistence commented.

"Bring us some Remy and Coke." Smack Man said. Persistence nodded her head, kissed him on the check, and then walked out of the room.

"How is Pops?" Smack Man asked Money Mike.

"He cool. Him and his wife moved to St. Louis."

"Yeah, you told me. What you tryin' to get a hold of?"

"You still got some of that soft?"

"I got it however you want it."

"Can I get two for thirty-five?"

"You must have the money on the wood?"

"Money on the wood!"

"My dawg! That's why I call you Money Mike nigga. I see you gettin' your bread."

"Kesha, do me a favor." Money Mike said.

"Wha'sup?" Kesha asked, turning away from the aquarium.

"Go out to my car, look in the glove box and bring me that brown paper bag." Money Mike said, handing Kesha his car keys. Kesha took the keys and left the room.

"Atif, go help Persistence with the drinks. I need to holler at Mike." Smack Man said. I got up from the couch and left the room. Moments later I found Persistence in the kitchen with her back turned.

"Hey Atif." Persistence said with her back still turned. Patience sounded just like her big sister. It would have been hard to tell the two apart if one only had their voices to go on.

"How did you know it was me?" I asked with a smirk on my face.

"Well, I saw...Kita?"

"Kesha."

"Yes, *Kesha*. That's right. Anyway, I saw her go out of the front door and I figured that Smack Man would be sending you in here to help me with the drinks shortly so that him and Michael could do business." She said, turning to face me. "I know my man." She finished, smiling.

"Soooo, how do you feel about my sister?" Persistence asked me.

"I like her." I answered, blushing.

"She likes you too. She talks about you all of the time."

"Does she?"

"Yes."

"What do she be sayin'?"

"That would be a little too much information." Persistence answered. "Personally, I think you are a lot nicer than her last boyfriend."

"What was his name?" I asked. Patience had never said anything to me about this ex-boyfriend.

"Kevin, I think." Persistence answered. "You know him?" she asked in response to the look I had on my face. It was one of pure shock. Kevin? The first thought that popped up in my mind was the two of them talking to each other at her locker back on the first day of school. Right then I learned that Patience was not the type to just open up and give out information that was not pertinent.

"I think so." I answered. I was bothered by that revelation even though I truly had no right to be. I had never even asked Patience about any of her past

120

relationships, I didn't think that I cared.   Well, I did. Especially if it was Kev of all people. Maybe Persistence was referring to a different person.   After all, there was more than one Kevin in Kansas City.

"He needs his little ass kicked. He had this tuff guy attitude, I couldn't *stand* him."   Persistence said, as if reading my mind. It sounded like we were referring to the same person alright.   "Are you going to help with these drinks or stand there and look at my butt?"   Persistence asked me. She had turned back around and was placing ice into some glasses.

"I wasn't lookin' at your butt!"   I lied through my front teeth. She caught me off guard with that one. That was exactly what I was doing. How did she know?

"Yeah, right. Don't make me tell my sister on you." Persistence said, handing me a half gallon jug of Remy Martin and a two liter of coke.   "Carry this for me."   She said, grabbing the three glasses and leading the way back to the front room.

*****

Three hours later we said our good-byes and were getting into our vehicles.

"Hold up a minute."   I told Kesha. I got out of the bucket and walked over to Money Mike's car. I tapped on the driver side window and motioned for him to roll it down.

"Wha' sup?"   Money Mike asked, rolling his window down. I could smell alcohol on his breath. Mike was drunk and trying to fit one of his house keys into the ignition.

"You still comin' down to the hood?"

"Naw, I'm ridin' dirty. I'm about to go to the pad."

"Won't you let Kesha drive you to your house and I will follow y'all in the bucket."

"For what?"

"Cause you drunk."

"I ain't about to let that girl drive my car nigga, is you crazy?"   Money Mike was about to drive home drunk

121

with two keys of cocaine in his car and asked me if I was crazy.

"She got her license."

"Do she got about $15,000 to pay for my car if she wreck it?"

"No, but that is probably about how much your bond gone be when you get pulled over for swervin' and the police find all that dope you just bought. That is *if* you get a bond." Money Mike sat thoughtfully in silence for a couple of seconds. He was not too drunk to accept some good advice.

"Tell her to come on."

I followed Kesha as she drove Money Mike to his house. We helped him up his front steps and into the house. He practically passed out as soon as he laid across the bed. After letting ourselves out, we made our way back to the tilt.

*****

"Why y'all go in there after y'all saw all them niggas was there?" K-Red asked us. It was now after ten in the evening. Me, Kesha, K-Red, Malik, and a friend of Malik's that we called Small Balls because of his 5'3 frame, were in the front room of the tilt. I had just finished explaining what happened at The Landing a few hours earlier.

"We went in through the back; I didn't think they would see us go in." I answered. K-Red sighed and shook his head.

Malik? He was highly upset. We could almost see steam rising from his braids. He kept staring at me in silence. One would rather see him in a loud and obnoxious state when he was upset than in the cool, calm, and collective mood he was in. When he was calm like that, it meant that he was also planning dark plans in the back of his mind. Someone was going to pay dearly for what happened to us and everyone in the room knew it. Maybe they didn't know no better. I seriously doubt if they knew who I was, I didn't recognize any of them. It didn't matter though. It was on, regardless.

Malik continued to sit there staring at the wall deep in thought. He then got up and disappeared into the back bedroom. When he reappeared, he held a Mak-10 in one hand and a Calico in the other. He tossed the Mak-10 to K-Red.

"Where mine at?" Small Balls asked Malik.

"You drivin'."

"I wanna go." I said. Malik and K-Red, who were on their way out of the front door, stopped in their tracks. Kesha stared at me.

"A'ight nigga," my brother started, nodding his head. "Don't ride all the way out here with us and then nut up when it's time to get down." Malik finished. K-Red handed me his 9mm pistol. I took the gun and started out of the front door. "What are you doin'?" Malik asked me.

"What do you mean?"

"You ain't gone change your clothes? Put on a ski mask, a bandanna or nothin', huh?"

I turned around and headed for the back bedroom. When I told Malik I wanted to go, I didn't think that he would actually *let* me. Although I had never participated in something like what we were about to do before up to that point in my life, I didn't believe in turning the other cheek either. I would have been content with going out south with the hommies to fight fairly with the people who jumped us, but Malik and K-Red were on another level. Life in general was not fair anyway. If people knew in advance exactly what the consequences of their actions would be then they would not do 90% of the things they did in life. Or, they would at least go about them in a different way.

It was a new world order. The days of gang fights with knives and bats were long gone. Back in 1992 it was all about gunplay. You rarely saw a fight between two people. If you did so happen to witness a good old fashioned fist fight, it would be in your best interest to vacate the premises as soon as the fight was over because the loser would definitely be returning with a gun and whomever was unlucky enough to be in the line of fire would be catching a hot one.

When I reached the back bedroom, I changed into an all black sweat suit that Malik owned. I also changed into a different pair of shoes. When I came back into the front room, Kesha was the only one still there. Malik had instructed for her to stay behind.

"Atif." Kesha said to me as I opened the front door.

"Wha' sup?"

"Are you comin' back here after y'all put y'all's work in?"

"Yeah, probably."

"I will be here when you get back." I nodded my head and stepped outside. "Be careful." Kesha said, hugging me.

"Come on nigga!" Malik yelled from the passenger side of the car, reaching over and honking the horn when he saw us hugging on the porch.

I walked down the front stairs and got into the back seat of a four door Delta 88 as Kesha closed and boarded the front door to the tilt.

"Here." K-Red said to me, handing me a red bandanna. I took the bandanna and laid it across my lap.

We headed south on Prospect with music from Spice 1 blaring from the tape deck. There was no conversation. Small Balls kept his eyes on the road as he drove. The look on his face was impassive, it was hard to tell what he was thinking about.

Malik, on the other hand, was mad. There was no mistaking his emotions. He sat there staring out of the window with his weapon laying across his lap. The look on his face was a mask of pure resentment. The mere thought of me laying on the ground while being kicked and stomped infuriated him.

K-Red seemed more at ease than all of us. Based on his demeanor, you would think that he was merely on a trip to the grocery store. That is until you looked down and saw the foot long extended clip he was currently in the process of filling with bullets. He had a red bandanna wrapped around his hand and he was carefully wiping his fingerprints off of each bullet that he inserted into the clip, rapping along with Spice 1 as he worked.

When we reached 59th and Prospect, Malik directed Small Balls to make a right turn. We rode west on 59th street until we came upon Troost Avenue.

"Go up a block or two and pull into the car wash." Malik directed Small Balls.

When we reached the car wash, Small Balls pulled into one of the stalls. The car wash was deserted. Malik turned the radio off and pulled his ski mask down over his face. Small Balls did the same. K-Red and I proceeded to tie our bandannas around our faces.

"Some of these niggas usually be sittin' out in front of the house." Malik commented.

"Whose house is it?" Small Balls asked.

"I don't know."

"How do you know they are the ones who jumped Atif and Kesha?"

"Because I *do*."

"Do it be any kids in there?"

"I don't know nigga, do it *matter*?" Malik snapped. Small Balls sat in silence. "You ain't doin' shit but *drivin*'! If that's too much work for you to put in then let us know." Silence. "We will turn around, drop your ass off, and let *Kesha* do the drivin'." Malik finished. K-Red and I glanced at each other in the back seats. K-Red shook his head, laughing to himself.

Malik could be pretty cruel at times. He despised fear. As a matter of fact, ever since Mom's death Malik saw almost all emotions as a weakness with no basis in reality.

"You niggas ready to do this?" Malik asked us.

"Yeah, lets ride." K-Red answered. Malik turned around in his seat and looked at me for a second, then he turned back around in his seat.

Small Balls put the car in drive and drove out of the parking lot onto Troost Avenue. There wasn't much traffic so we shot across Troost without having to pause for any passing vehicles. Heading east, Small Balls made a right turn when we made it to a block labeled Tracy. Small Balls then turned off his headlights and crept up the street.

"Keep straight, it's one more block up." Malik said to Small Balls when we reached a stop sign.

I rolled my window down and made sure that the safety lock on the 9mm was in the off position. Butterflies filled my stomach as emotions of fear, anger, and anxiety mixed together into one.

"There them niggas go, slow down." Malik said, climbing halfway out of the passenger side window and sitting on the door. K-Red climbed out of his window and did the same, positioning himself so that he could shoot over the roof of the car. I stayed put with intentions of simply sticking my arm out of the window and shooting.

Three houses up, on the right side of the street, sat a two story building with what appeared to be seven or eight young men and three or four females standing in the front yard and on the porch, oblivious to the Delta creeping up the street carrying possibly death itself.

Malik opened fire, aiming at the front door, knowing that once people began to hear shots they would attempt to run into the house for protection. Screams began to erupt when K-Red and I began to shoot, transferring shock into panic. A young man was in the process of climbing a fence, trying to escape the hail of gunfire and I shot him two times in the back. He screamed as his upper body slumped over the fence. He laid there motionless. People were running and screaming and tripping and falling, K-Red attempted to put a bullet into everything that moved. At that moment, shots from a semi-automatic pistol rang out from one of the upstairs windows. I pointed my weapon at the small bursts of fire erupting from the gun being fired in the upstairs window and emptied the rest of the bullets from the clip. The window shattered and the gunfire ceased.

"Roll out nigga, roll out!" Malik said as he slid back into the front seat with his weapon empty. K-Red let off five more shots as Small Balls stepped on the gas.

Small Balls turned left at the end of the block and headed east. When we reached Swope Parkway, Small Balls turned left and headed north. We began to relax. Malik turned the radio back on and K-Red fired up a joint.

126

We had heard no police sirens, the police usually took forever and a day with responding to an emergency in the inner city, but I could still hear screams echoing in the back of my mind.

"You wanna hit this shit blood?" K-Red asked me in a strained voice, attempting to pass me the joint.

"Naw, I'm cool." I declined. I knew that I would throw up if I attempted to inhale anything. My stomach was queasy and it was hard enough to take in oxygen without vomiting.

Minutes later, Small Balls pulled in front of the tilt. I didn't know how to feel about what we had just done. At that time I thought that maybe we did what had to be done by those of us who were traveling down that filthy route. It was not wise to let something like what the Rolling 60's Crips had done to me go because it would come back to haunt me in the long run. We had to retaliate in some kind of way. True enough, the form of retaliation we took out was harsh, but so was their ganging up on me and Kesha like that. What it did do was relay the message that needed to be relayed. Mess with anybody from the neighborhood, serious consequences and repercussions would follow. If we would have let the situation go as was, it would eventually be known throughout the whole city that people from 27th street could be taken advantage of and done any old kind of way. No one would be able to possess anything of value. People from other neighborhoods would come through looting and robbing everything in sight because they would feel as if they could get away with it. Point being, on the filthy route you had to handle your business. Only the strong survived. The weak were preyed upon and made examples out of. When someone hit you, you hit them back twice in return. Such was life.

*****

RUNNING OUT THE CRACKHOUSE
"This filthy life
got me bailin' with my strap out.
I spend my time
slangin' 20's up outta the crackhouse.
-Ready to take that back route-
if I ever see that black van.
Or straight the fuck get smoked up,
it's no jail time, just blastin'!"
-*Tazz Mania Devil*

7

I woke up startled and breathing heavily. The clock on my night stand read 4:16 am. I had been dreaming about the night before, but in my dream we had all been captured and thrown in jail. After convincing myself that I was in my room and not incarcerated, I got up and walked to the bathroom down the hall. Turning on the bathroom light, I examined my eye in the mirror which was not only swollen shut but black and tender to the touch.

"Man, I ain't finna go to school with my eye lookin' like this." I said aloud to my self. Big Mama had thrown a fit when I walked in the front door the night before. She noticed my eye instantly despite the fact that I had tried to make it to my bedroom unnoticed. I told her that I had been in a fight and after at least twenty minutes of her suggesting numerous one-hundred-year-old remedies for keeping the swelling to a minimum, like holding a raw steak to my eye, something I refused to do, I went to my room and fell asleep wondering if I had taken another person's life.

Still standing in the mirror, asking myself if my eye was really as bad as it looked, that uncontrollable anger began to rise from the pit of my stomach, spreading throughout my chest, followed by a strong sense of accomplished retaliation that was as sweet as chocolate cake. I had never felt that feeling to that extent, but it seemed to swallow my anger whole and I liked it. Not that I enjoyed to hurt another person, for I was never one to start trouble, but the act of retaliation; the righting of a wrong that was done to me was exhilarating.

Turning off the bathroom light, I walked back to my room and laid back down. After 15 minutes of tossing and turning, I then got up and went into the front room and turned on the television. A few minutes later Big Mama strolled into the front room and sat down next to me.

"I'm sorry Big Mama, I didn't mean to wake you up." I apologized.

"Oh, that's okay baby. What are you doin' up?"

"I had a messed up dream and I couldn't get back to sleep."

"You wanna talk about it?"   Big Mama was assuming that I had been dreaming about Mama.

"No, not for real." I answered, wondering to myself how I could tell my grandmother about such a dream. I then picked up the remote and turned from the Christian program that was on the television.

"Why are you and your brotha' so quick to turn away from the Word of God?" Big Mama asked as I flicked through the channels.

"Aw, Big Mama." I groaned. She could be pretty compulsive with her beliefs at times and she often tried to impose them upon us. Especially me. My grandmother and I talked religion a lot. Even back then at such an early age, I never ceased to amaze her with my own insight and rationale. At times I inadvertently helped her to eradicate some unreasonable misconceptions she harbored, which were passed on down to her and accepted blindly without much consideration on her part.

"Oh you gone talk to me. You done woke me up out my sleep at four in the mornin' and think you ain't gone keep me company?" I smiled. "Now answer my question."

"Well, I wasn't turnin' away from the Word of God, I was turnin' away from the words of that *man*. It's not that I don't believe in God Big Mama, I know that everything that exists was created and didn't just come about by.....chance. I know that the way the earth spins and revolves around the sun so fast without missin' a beat that God designed it like that and maintains it, it don't just so happen to do that by accident." Big Mama nodded her head, smiling in agreement.

Now that I reflect, I understand why she used to provoke me like she did. Quiet as kept, she was encouraging me to think things through for myself instead of letting preachers, or any religiously learned people for that matter, do my thinking for me. I owe a lot of my spiritual development to her for that.

130

"It's just that everybody be sayin' that God is like this and God looks like that, God said this and didn't say that. All of that confusion is part of the reason why I am so quick to turn away from those kinds of programs."

"What is the rest of the reason?" I paused for a second, looking for the right words to explain how I felt.

"I guess I don't understand why He do the things He do. Like when Mama got killed like she did. She ain't never did nothin' to nobody. You got people walkin' around alive and well that be.....molestin' little kids for a livin', why is that? Why would He let somebody innocent like Mama get gunned down but let these freaky people not only live but.....*prosper*. Sometimes I wonder if God even care about what go on in our lives."

"God is very concerned with what happens in our lives, Atif. We are His *children* and he loves us. I loved your mother with all my heart and I miss her very much. I also know that she is in a better place. See baby, the Bib-" I rolled my eyes with the mentioning of the Bible. She knew how I felt about it. "Here me out now. The Bible says that the Lord works in mysterious ways and it is not for us to understand why He do the things He do."

"If we are God's children and He love us so much, how could He make a place for His children to go where they will burn forever just because of the way they was livin'? I wouldn't do that to my worst enemy, let alone my rebellious child. Why would he even allow some of His children to come into existence in the first place when He knew beforehand that they was gone end up in Hell? Why would He let them set themselves up for failure like that?"

"If you believe that Jesus died on the cross for your sins, then you don't have to worry about nothin' like that." Big Mama answered evasively. She was good at that.

Prophet Jesus dying on the cross for my sins? My rationale never did allow me to accept that along with the concept of original sin. Especially not after reading passages like Ezekiel 18:18-20 from the same collection of books that people claim to derive that concept from. Prophet Jesus dying for my sins was another subject

131

altogether. I cataloged it into a mental file for us to discuss another time.

"I don't mean no disrespect Big Mama, but that don't answer my questions."

"Well," Big Mama started, wrapping her arm around my shoulders. "I don't really have the answer to that question. But, like I said before, the Lord works in mysterious ways and to be honest, I don't understand why He would build such a place either." That was one thing I loved about talking religion with Big Mama, she would admit things like that. "I will tell you what though, why don't you come to church with me this Sunday like you used to and we will see if we can find the answers to all of your questions?" I remained silent, not wanting to commit myself while knowing that there were at least a couple of hundred dollars I would be missing out on by being at church instead of the tilt. Back then I, like the majority of us over here in America, put material things first on my life's priorities list. God was further down, at times *way* down. "Will you at least think about it?" Big Mama asked, nudging me.

"Yeah, I will think about it."

"Do you feel up to goin' to school this mornin'?" she asked, changing the subject. She was not aware of how much school I had been missing.

"No, not really." I answered, touching my swollen eye.

"You stay on home then. But I want you to clean this house from top to bottom before I get home and no company, ya' hear?" I nodded. "Especially that lil' fast girlfriend of yours."

"Who?"

"Kayla."

"You mean Kesha?"

"Whatever."

"She ain't my girlfriend."

"Who is that other lil' girl that be callin' here all the time for you with the cute lil' name?"

"Patience."

"Yeah, that's it. Is she fast too?"

132

"No."

"Is she white?"

"No. Why you say that?"

"Because she talk like a lil' white girl." Big Mama answered. "Is she your girlfriend?"

"Big Mama." I groaned, sheepishly.

"A'ight, a'ight." Big Mama said, raising her hands in resignation. "I don't mean no disrespect Atif, but you *did* answer my question." We both laughed at that. Man I miss the sweet sound of her laughter. I can still hear it sometimes in my head. "Well, I guess I will gone back to bed now." She said straining to get up from the couch. I helped her.

"Big Mama."

"Yeah baby?"

"Do you think God forgives people for killin' somebody?"

"Yeah, if they really mean it when they ask for forgiveness and turn away from that sin."

"Even the ones that killed Mama and shot Malik?"

"It don't matter who you are or what you done did. You can repent and accept Jesus Christ as your Lord and Savior before you die. In God's eyes all sin is the same."

"So you mean to tell me that if the devil himself asked for forgiveness, God would forgive him?"

"He wouldn't."

"You just said that it don't matter who you are or what you done did, God would fo-"

"I know, when I said he wouldn't, I was saying that the devil wouldn't ask for forgiveness. Not that God wouldn't forgive him if he did."

"What if he did though?"

"He wouldn't."

"Lets just say that he di-"

"He *wouldn't*, Atif. Good mornin'." Big Mama cut in and walked into her bedroom.

*****

133

Running out The
Crack House

I went back to sleep an hour or so later. I was awakened at ten minutes past ten that morning to the sound of the telephone ringing. When I opened my eyes, I noticed that Big Mama had gone to work, turning off the television I had fallen asleep in front of and covering me with a blanket. I then got up and answered the telephone.

"Hello?"

"Atif?" a female voice inquired from the other end.

"Wha' sup Patience?" I greeted, recognizing her voice. The sound of it was like splashing cold water on my face. She had that kind of effect on me. "Where you at?"

"I'm at school on the pay phone."

"What's wrong with you?" I asked, noticing the edge she had in her voice. She sounded like that whenever she had an attitude about something.

"Why didn't you call me yesterday or come to school today like you told me you would?"

"What if I was skippin'? What would you have did if Big Mama answered the phone?"

"I probably would have hung the phone up and taken off running." Patience answered. I laughed. She was afraid of my grandmother for some reason and could have sworn that Big Mama had something against her. "Your grandmother does not like me very well, does she?"

"What makes you think she don't like you?"

"I don't know, she is not very friendly towards me when I call." Patience answered. "Anyway, why didn't you call me?"

"I got jumped yesterday." I answered. Silence followed on the line.

"Are you hurt?" Patience asked with concern.

"No, I'm cool for real. My eye is black and my body is kind of sore though."

"Who jumped on you?"

"Some Crips."

"How many?"

"I don't know."

135

"Why did they jump on you?"

"Why do you think?" I asked sarcastically in return.

"I'm sorry Atif." There she go with that again, I thought to myself.

"I ain't trippin'." We both sat quietly on the line for a little while. "Patience?"

"I'm here." She answered in a far away voice.

"Why you ain't sayin' nothin'?"

"No reason."

"Girl, I know you ain't standin' there *cryin'* is you?"

"No, I'm not." Patience was lying.

"You better not be. *I'm* the one who got jumped."

"What if I were crying? What would you do about it?"

"I would get dressed and roll up to the school so that I could give you a hug and wipe the tears off your face."

"No you would not." Patience said, blushing and smiling into the phone. She then sniffled involuntarily.

"I heard that! I'm on my way!" I said, taking the phone away from my ear as if I was going to hang it up.

"Atif! Stop playing with me."

"You love me, don't you girl?" I asked, smiling into the phone.

"Excuse me?" Patience asked, surprised and being caught off guard.

"You heard me."

"Are you still going to the dance tonight?" She then asked me changing the subject.

"No."

"Why not?" Patience asked with that edge creeping back into her voice.

"I ain't goin' nowhere with my eye lookin' like this."

"Why not?"

"Because I *ain't*." Patience was beginning to get on my nerves.

"All that you have to do is keep your mask on."

"Naw, fo'get that. I ain't goin'."

136

"No, forget *you*. I am not going to stand here and beg you." Patience said. I could see her tilting her head from side to side in my mind as she spoke.

"Aw, you gotta attitude now?"

"I have to go."

"Yeah, whatev-" I was interrupted by the dial tone. I stood there staring at the receiver in disbelief for a few seconds before slowly hanging the phone up. I then picked it back up, intending on calling her back and letting her know how I felt about someone hanging the phone up in my face, but I put it back down remembering that Patience was at school on a pay phone and not at her house.

I spent the next hour or so cleaning the house like Big Mama had asked me to do. I then got dressed and left in route for the tilt. About halfway there, a car pulled up on the side of me. My heart seemed to have jumped right out of my chest as my mind raced. I immediately assumed that the car was full of Rolling 60's Crips looking for vengeance and retaliation for last night's dramatic episode. I scolded myself mentally for not staying in the house while striving to prevent urine from running down my pant leg. I was scared. I kept my head straight and continued walking as if I didn't notice the vehicle driving along beside me at my own pace.

"Whroop!" It was the sound of a police siren being turned on and then off instantaneously. Expecting the sound of a hail of gunfire instead, I almost took off running leaving my skin standing right there.

"Shit!" I exclaimed, coming to a stop and placing my right hand over my heart. I had never been so happy to see two members of the Kansas City Police Department in my life, even if it were those two.

The two officers were Detectives John Valentine and Bobby Vermil, both white males known throughout the neighborhood for planting dope and guns on people they were out to get.

"Hey youngblood." Detective Valentine said out of the driver side window. "Does your mother, oh, my bad. I forget. Does *Big Mama* know that you are playing hookie

137

from school today?" He asked, smiling at the intentional slip.

"Fuck you snowflake." I said. He knew how to get me riled up. But, I knew that right then was not the time to be losing control of my anger, so he could say whatever he wanted to say. "And for your information, big Mama *told* me I could stay home today." That didn't mean that I wasn't going to get off a few digs of my own.

"Yeah right, I'll just bet that she did. Got any dope on you?"

"I say no to drugs."

"Where you headed? To the tilt?"

"To mind my own business." I answered, wondering to myself how he knew to call the spot the tilt.

"Did that smart mouth of yours have anything to do with that black eye you have?" Detective Vermil asked, speaking up for the first time. I gave him the finger for a response.

"What about those Rolling 60's Crips that were shot last night? Know anything about that?" Detective Valentine asked.

"No." I answered and started to walk off. Detective Valentine threw the car into park and both detectives jumped out of the vehicle.

"Did we say we were finished with your ass?" Detective Valentine hissed, grabbing me and pushing me up against the car. "Put your fucking hands on the hood." I could hear the sound of bass coming up the street. I turned to see who it was. "Keep your head straight!" Detective Valentine instructed as he began to search me. "Where is your brother, Atif?"

"Probably over your mama's house gettin' his hair braided." I answered, laughing at my own joke.

"Look here you little shit!" Detective Valentine shot back, allowing his anger to get the best of him. He grabbed me aggressively by the back of my head and pressed my face down onto the hot hood of the car.

"A, pork bellies!   Y'all get off on harassin'
juveniles?" K-Red said, pulling up behind the detectives. K-
Red and Malik then got out of the Iroc.

"Well, well, well. If it isn't the infamous Malik and K-
Red.   We have been looking for you guys all morning."
Detective Vermil stated.

"Is my brotha' under arrest?" Detective Vermil
glanced at his partner.

"He's clean." Detective Valentine commented.

"I guess not, unfortunately. At least not right now."
Detective Vermil said in response to Malik's question.

"Get in the car Atif." Malik told me. I did as I was
told.

"Why don't you guys follow us down to the station,
we have a few questions for the two of you." Detective
Vermil said.

"Naw man, we got better things to do." K-Red said
as him and Malik got into the Iroc.

"You all can save us the trouble of putting a warrant
out for your arrests, or you all can come down on your own
free will. Which do you prefer?" Detective Valentine asked
as K-Red started the Iroc's engine.

"Personally, I would prefer *not* to save you any
trouble. What about you Malik?" K-Red asked.

"Roll out blood, fuck them." Malik answered. K-
Red put the stick shift into drive and peeled off, leaving the
two detectives in a cloud of smoke.

K-Red drove south on Prospect. The streets were
jam packed because of the lunch hour rush. I rode quietly
in the back seat lost in thought.

"Are they still followin' us?" Malik asked K-Red as
he prepared to turn onto 71 highway.

"Naw, they turned off a while back."   K-Red
answered, looking into the rearview mirror once again to be
sure. I was unaware of the fact that we were being
followed in the first place.

"Roll one up Atif." Malik said, handing me a sack of
marijuana and some EZ wider rolling papers. I took the
items from my brother's hand and went to work. "A," Malik

139

started, turning the music down and rolling the car windows up. "Did you see the news this mornin'?" I looked up into the rearview mirror and saw that both K-Red and Malik were looking at me in return.

"You talkin' to *me*?" I asked.

"Yeah nigga." Malik answered.

"No. Why?"

"One of them niggas is dead from last night." Malik answered. I paused for a moment with my tongue stuck on the adhesive part of the rolling paper, staring at Malik through the rearview mirror. I then looked away and went back to what I was doing. "One bitch got shot, three other niggas got hit, and the bitch on the news said that when the police got there, they found the nigga that died stuck on a fence, dead as a mutha' fucka'."

I dropped the joint I had just finished rolling onto the floor, my stomach seemed to have fallen right along with it. The person that was found dead on the fence was the one I had taken aim at and shot when I saw him attempting to get away.

Trying to act nonchalant about hearing the news, I discreetly picked up the joint I dropped and asked my brother for a lighter. I hadn't planned on getting high, but I think I felt as if I needed a little something to help me deal with the news. I then put the marijuana filled cigarette up to my lips with a shaky hand and lit it, unknowingly being watched by K-Red through the rearview mirror as I did so.

"Damn nigga, what the fuck is you shakin' for?" K-Red asked and started laughing. I took a couple of hits, inhaling deeply and then had a coughing fit as I tried to exhale.

"Gimme that man before you kill yo-self back there." Malik said, reaching for the joint. I handed it to him and sat back in my seat, welcoming the effects of the marijuana with open arms.

Deep down inside I had already known that I had killed someone the night before without my brother's confirmation. I knew it when I saw him slump over the fence like he did. I just refused to accept the gut feeling

that had been nagging at me ever since I let off those two
rounds. I no longer had a choice: I was a *murderer*. I had
killed someone's *son*. Someone's *brother*. I had done to
someone what was done to me some months back. I don't
possess the vocabulary needed to explain or describe how I
felt. I didn't know how I was *supposed* to feel. If there
was any grief, it was for his family members, not him. I
wondered to myself if that made me heartless? What if the
one I had killed was not even there at The Landing when
we were jumped on?

"-lkin about, Atif?" Malik asked.

"Huh?" I asked, snapping out of my trance.

"I *said*," Malik mocked, making sign language like
gestures with his hands as if he was talking to a deaf
person. "What was the po-po's talkin' about?" K-Red
laughed as he turned the car stereo down so that he could
hear my response.

"They asked me if I knew anything about them
niggas gettin' popped up last night."

"And what did you tell them?" K-Red asked, eyeing
me through the rearview mirror.

"Nothin'! What you think I told them?" I shot back
in defiance, offended by what I assumed K-Red may have
been insinuating.

"I'mma put you up on somethin'." Malik started. "If
the police was to pick you or any of us up for anything, you
already know not to say nothin' to them. Nothin'. Most
niggas that get locked up, especially for murder cases, they
get locked up either because they so called hommie told on
them or because they got down to the station with them
detectives and fucked themselves. I guess they be thinkin'
them detectives really give a fuck about them or somethin';
fallin' for that good cop bad cop shit you see on tv. I don't
give a fuck what a detective or anybody else might have to
say down at that station. They can't do *shit* for you. And
they wouldn't even if they could. They job is to try and trick
your ass into tellin' on yo-self like a dummy because they
usually ain't got shit on you. As long as you keep your
mouth shut; some down ass hommies that's willin' to ride

for you; and some ends for a halfway decent lawyer; you
don't have to worry about goin' to the pen."

Malik was smart. When he talked, people listened
because he usually knew what he was talking about. My
brother was just about the only one in the hood who could
whip out a thick book to read in the midst of the hommies
without having to worry about ridicule. When Malik talked
seriously, I was his most attentive listener. I never got the
feeling that I was being lectured or anything like it. My
brother was known to expound on many different subjects.
At times I could not help but wonder why my brother didn't
use his money to go to college or something.

We seemed to be heading towards Grandview. I
was feeling high off the weed, relaxing in the back seat
while letting the music take me away. My throat was dry
and my mouth felt like I was chewing on a ball of cotton.
The music sounded so good. I could feel the bass vibrating
throughout my entire body. I thought that there was
nothing in the world like rap music. Listening to it always
soothed me or encouraged me, whichever effect was
needed.

I could remember fantasizing about growing up to
play professional football in the N.F.L. But as I got older I
came to realize that the chances of my going to college
without a scholarship or hustling were slim to none. I was
already on the road to destroying my chances for a
scholarship by neglecting school like I was doing, and on
top of that, the money I was making? I wasn't
accumulating it with the goal of using it in such a
constructive way as paying my way through school. My
dreams seemed to be floating away at that time in my life.
The things I did want in life, I saw myself obtaining on the
filthy route. I no longer had the patience or the drive
needed to be successful in a legal way. Besides, it was
beginning to be difficult enough at that point in my life to
imagine seeing the next day. I wanted to take the shortcut
and I was willing to take my chances. At least I thought I
was. At that age, there was absolutely no way I could have

fully comprehended the serious nature of the consequences
that came along with such a way of life.

Back to the life I had taken. Was my black eye
really worth taking that brother's life like that? Of course
not. My eye didn't even hurt that much to tell the truth.
And what about the female that was shot? I didn't
remember any females with the ones who jumped us. It
was a little too late for feeling guilty. All of the guilt in the
world would not put that young Crip's life back into his
body. Nor my mother's in hers.

It felt like I had an angel whispering in my right ear
and a demon in my left simultaneously. The angel told me
that I needed to slow down; that I was moving too fast.
Ever since Mama died my life had taken off in warp speed.
I didn't even take time to sit down and think anymore like I
used to do. Thoughts of Mama's murder brought on the
demon's whispering. That voice asked me what was the
use in thinking positive with so much negativity around me?
I couldn't live in a den with wolves and be innocent and
playful like a puppy while expecting to survive at the same
time. It didn't work like that. Look at all of the teenagers I
knew who were not traveling down the filthy route. The
ones who went to school everyday and tried to stay away
from trouble. Trouble found them. They were the ones
who got picked on and harassed. They couldn't even have
a new pair of shoes without someone trying to take them.
No one wants to be the victim in an environment like that.
Everyday would be a living hell. Torture. I didn't want to
be the victimizer either, but I knew that if I was respected
by both the victimizers and the victims, then I didn't have a
whole lot to worry about. That kind of respect came with
retaliating when ones boundaries had been crossed and
violated.

K-Red exited 71 South onto 95th street. He turned
east on 95th until we reached the Banister Mall. K-Red then
turned into the spacious parking lot and drove around to the
JC Penny's exit on the upper level. After parking, we exited
the Iroc and made our way inside.

143

Man I was so high I didn't know what to do. I was hungry enough to eat a horse and I thought that I would die of thirst if I didn't get something to drink real quick like.

"A, Atif." K-Red said.

"Huh?"

"You got some more of them?" K-Red asked me as we made our way into the mall.

"Do I got some more of what?" I asked, perplexed.

"Don't tell me you done ate them all. You didn't save us none?" Malik cut in. I looked between the two suspiciously. I knew that I was being set up for something, no matter how good the marijuana was we were smoking.

"Save y'all none of what?" I asked in resignation, waiting for the punch line.

"Them powdered doughnuts you been eatin', nigga!" K-Red exclaimed as the two of them exploded in a fit of laughter. They then gave each other some dap.

"Fo-get y'all." I said, licking my dry parched lips. "Are they still white?"

"Naw, you cool." Malik answered.

We made our way through JC Penny's and were heading for the escalator. The mall was pretty empty. Everyone we did pass seemed to be watching our every move. Then again, maybe I was tripping.

"Where y'all finna go?" I asked the two as we approached the escalator.

"Down to the pager shop." Malik answered.

"I will meet y'all down there man, I'm finna get me somethin' to eat."

"A'ight." They said in unison as they got on the escalator. I turned and headed for the food courts.

While walking my mind began to wander. I saw a uniformed police officer patrolling near by. The marijuana I had smoked, mixed with the events that took place the night before, along with a teaspoon of the encounter with the detectives earlier that day, this combination gave me the notion that I was being followed by the officer. Did the police find out that I was directly involved with the shooting the night before? Was murderer written across my

144

forehead, so to speak? Or was I just high and tripping? I
had almost convinced myself of the latter before I witnessed
the officer whispering into his walkie-talkie and seemingly
looking at me simultaneously.

I picked up my pace.

I looked behind me and saw that the officer was
behind me. When I turned back around, I saw that another
policeman had appeared out of nowhere and was
attempting to cut me off. Thinking quickly, I ducked into
the spacious food courts. Unfortunately, the area was
pretty much desolate outside of the workers behind the
concession stands. With nowhere else to go and only a few
seconds before the two officers would reach the food courts
themselves, I jumped over the counter of a small
concession stand named One Potato Two Potato.

"What do you think you doin'?" A black woman in
her mid to late twenties asked me as I ducked down behind
the counter.

"Shhh!" I whispered frantically with my forefinger
pressed against my lips, pleading with my eyes.

"Get up off of that floor." The lady behind the
counter said to me. She was looking towards the main lobby
while wiping the counter at the same time. "They ain't even
trippin' on you." She finished.

"They ain't?" I asked in return, peering over the
counter. I began to rise slowly when I saw for myself that
the two officers were focused on some other individual. I
felt silly.

"Look at you." The lady said with amusement
showing on her face. "You so high you can't think straight."
She said, looking into my eyes. "That must have been
some *fire* you were smokin'. Climb back over that counter
and have a seat." I complied. "What you done did? You up
here stealin'?" she asked me as we both took a seat at one
of the tables in front of the concession stand.

"I don't steal."

"What you so spooked about then?" Silence. "Why
you ain't in school?" More Silence. "Let me get you

somethin' to drink, your lips lookin' like they about to crack
and bleed."

She then rose from her seat, returning minutes later
with some food and two large cups of sprite.

"I might as well take my lunch break now and you
might as well keep me company." She said, sitting.

"Thank you." I said, gladly accepting the
cheeseburger, small bucket of fries and Sprite. I then
hungrily bit into the cheeseburger and stuffed some fries
into my mouth, chasing it all with a large gulp of the cold
Sprite. I experienced a brain freeze, placing my drink on
the table and massaging my forehead.

"Better slow down. You gone turn your brain into a
big old ice cube." The lady warned, smiling. "What's your
name?"

"Atif." I answered between bites.

"You a Muslim?"

"No. Why do people keep askin' me that?"

"Atif is a Muslim name. It means compassionate."
She answered. "Did you know that?"

"Naw. I didn't." I always assumed that Mama had
made my name up. Black people do that a lot when naming
their children, which in my opinion is a good thing. Better
to do that than give them names like Dick or Peggy Sue.

"My uncle is a Muslim. That is how I knew that. My
name is Antoinette." I nodded.

We sat in silence for a few moments.

"I got jumped." I said, answering her question
before she had the chance to ask.

"Was I starin'?"

"Yeah." I answered, smirking. "You like this job?"

"No."

"Why you work here then?" I asked. I was curious
as to why people did that. I grew up watching my mother
work hard on a job she couldn't stand and I didn't
understand until later in my life why people did that. I
myself vowed not to live my life like that.

"I need the extra money." She answered, shrugging her shoulders. "I work down at the county jail, too. This job is only part-time."

"Why you need the extra money?" Anyone's claim that they needed extra money to a drug dealer was music to that drug dealer's ears.

"Bills."

"Your husband don't help you?"

"I don't have a husband, Atif.   At least not anymore."

"Why you still wearin' that ring?" she shrugged, twirling the wedding band around her finger. "What about your man?"

"I don't have one of *those* either."

"What? Why not?" I asked, genuinely perplexed. Antoinette was far from unattractive. Plus, the way her butt protruded from her apron? Someone *had* to be hitting that.

"Good question. Maybe I'm too busy." Antoinette offered. I curled up my lips in disbelief. Antoinette laughed at my facial expression. "People can't just tell you anything that they want you to hear, can they?" I shrugged my shoulders and finished off my cheeseburger. "I don't know. I went through a messy divorce and the relationship with my husband as a whole was so fucked up, maybe I'm a lil' scared of goin' through somethin' like that again."

"How long ago was that?"

"About four years ago."

"You ain't had a man in your life since then?" Antoinette shook her head. "How long you gone cheat yo-self like that?" Antoinette lowered her gaze and began to fiddle with her fries, which were more than likely cold by then.

"What   are   you,   some   kind   of   under aged.....*psychiatrist* or somethin'?" she asked me, watching me as I finished my pop.

"Naw, I just think that you are too fine, nice and smart to be thinkin' that you have to go through life without a good man to share it with because of the way some busta' treated you four years ago. That's *crazy.*" I said, rising up from the table and collecting my trash. "You finished?"

"Yeah, thank you." Antoinette answered, taken aback by the wisdom within my words. She watched me as I walked over to the trash can. "You are pitiful." She said aloud to herself, shaking her head.

"Was you talkin' to me?" I asked as I returned, sitting back down at the table. I heard her say something but couldn't make out what it was.

"No. I was talkin' to myself." She answered. I peered at her. "Do you have a brotha'?" She asked, looking past me.

"Yeah, why you ask that?"

"Because one of these dudes walkin' up behind you look just like you." She answered. I turned around and saw Malik and K-Red making their way over to where Antoinette and I sat.

"Wasn't you supposed to meet us downstairs?" Malik asked me, handing me a pager.

"I told you I was gone get me somethin' to eat." I answered. "What's this?"

"What do it look like?" my brother responded sarcastically. He hated it when people asked questions they already knew the answer to.

"This for me?"

"Yeah." Malik answered. With me and Darion purchasing the bucket, we would be hard to get a hold of at times. "Who is this?" he then asked me, indicating Antoinette.

"Aw, this is my new friend I was havin' lunch with Antoinette." I said, introducing her. "This is my brotha' Malik and the hommie K-Red."

"Wha'sup y'all?" Antoinette greeted, politely smiling at the two.

"Wha'sup?" they replied while offering a nod at the same time in unison.

"Well, I gotta get back to work Atif. It was nice meetin' y'all." Antoinette said, rising from her chair. "Bye." She turned to leave.

148

"Daaaammmnn." K-Red mumbled quietly out of her earshot, referring to her backside as she walked away. The both of them then looked at me.

"Man, she ain't gone gimme her number." I said in response to their looks.

"Go see." My brother suggested.

Damn. I didn't like rejection, especially not in front of the hommies like that. Antoinette not too long ago informed me that she had not been in a relationship with a man in four years, she wasn't going to all of a sudden make an exception for me. Not only that, but I never before even *approached* a woman who was so much older than I was. What was I supposed to say to her? By the time I reached her she was already back behind the counter I had climbed over.

"Don't tell me they done souped you up to come over here." Antoinette said, smiling.

"Yeah, kind of." I answered truthfully. "So wha' sup?"

"What do you mean?"

"You gone...... let me get your number?"

"No, I don't think so Atif." Antoinette answered, shaking her head.

"You thinkin' I'm too young for you?"

"Your *older* brotha' is too young for me."

"So, you just gone do me like this in front of my people, huh?" I asked her. "You could at least *fake* like you writtin' your number down for me." Antoinette looked at me and then reached up under the counter, grabbing a pen and a small notepad. She scribbled something on a piece of the paper, folded it and handed it to me. "I told you you was nice." I said, smirking as I walked away.

We made our way out of the mall. When we approached the Iroc, I climbed into the back seat, reaching into my pocket for the folded piece of paper Antoinette had given me and throwing it out of the car onto the pavement. K-Red started the Iroc's engine and was about to pull off.

"Hold up, wait a minute!" I said, thinking twice about the piece of paper and wondering to myself what

149

Antoinette had actually written on it. I then climbed out of
the car and picked the piece of paper I had just discarded
up from the ground. I climbed back into the car and
opened it as K-Red pulled off. On it, in very loopy, pretty
penmanship, it read:

    Meet me here for lunch again next week, I had fun!
Antoinette.

    "I be damned." I murmured to myself, smiling.

******

    Later that afternoon the three of us stood around in
Smack Man's backyard as he fed his dogs. There were six
cages paired off around the perimeter of his fenced in back
yard. Within these cages there were two Doberman
pinchers with short hair and smooth, dark coats, male and
female; two stocky Rottweilers with short black fur and tan
face markings, male and female; and lastly, a set of strong,
muscular, male and female American Staffordshire terriers,
otherwise known as "pit bulls" because of their dog-fighting
abilities.

    All six of the dogs were barking viciously at us
strangers and our presence in the back yard. They were
more concerned with guarding the territory than with
eating.

    Smack Man never fought his dogs, nor did he let
anyone around his dogs besides those who lived there; he
did not want his dogs getting used to anyone who did not
live in his house. He would allow a pair of his dogs out of
their cages to roam freely around the yard in order to
protect the property and get a little exercise. He would
alternate between the three sets each night, therefore any
potential trespassers would not be able to figure out which
dogs he let out of their cages on which nights. All six of
them were equally dangerous in their own way though, so
trying to decide which pair one would rather have to deal
with was kind of like choosing which weapon one would
prefer being killed with.

150

While attempting to feed the male pit bull, the task
was difficult because the dog was aggressively trying to
force his way out of his cage, a car horn was heard coming
from the circular driveway around front.

"A, somebody go see what she want." Smack Man
yelled over the barking dogs. Malik and K-Red looked at
me. I knew those looks like I knew the back of my own
hands. It was the looks I always received from them,
especially Malik, whenever my mother used to ask who
would like to cut her grass for her or help clean the
basement. Growing up, I was always the one helping my
mother do something. I didn't mind though. It was during
these times alone with my mother that we would have our
most memorable conversations.

My mother used to tell me about the unity blacks
had in the 60's and 70's. She would tell me about how
mesmerized she was by brothers like El Haj Malik Shabazz
(Malcolm X) and how devastated she was when he was
assassinated. She would talk about the Black Panthers and
the Black Liberation Army as well as many other black
organizations back in those days that I would not learn too
much about in school. She even spoke of how the C.I.A
flooded the ghetto streets with crack and how quickly it
destroyed the black community. She said that crack turned
my father into a whole different person than the man she
fell in love with long ago.

My mother never actually told me not to get off into
selling drugs with my brother. She believed that sometimes
a person needed to bump their own heads in order to learn
for themselves. What she would do was inform me of the
consequences of such actions and how it affected other
people's lives in ways that people usually didn't even realize.
She used to tell me that there is only two end results for the
life of a drug dealer; death or a life spent in and out of
prison. She said that the "game" was in actuality a trap,
but it was my decision to make if that was the type of life I
wanted for myself. Thinking back, I guess it was difficult
for my mother to convince us that all of the material things
to be gained by selling drugs was in fact an illusion and not

worth it. Especially when she was barely getting by herself. She simply warned me not to get off into anything in life if I did not think that I would be able to handle the repercussions that came along with it. The good and the bad; the highs and the lows.

Walking around to the front of the house, I saw Persistence getting out of a white Mercedes Benz. Her long hair flowed freely and she wore a pink Nike suit with white trim and a pair of white Nike Cross Trainers. Her pants clung to her hips and her top was partially unzipped, revealing a diamond studded heart shaped pendant that rested at the bottom of her small gold necklace, stopping just above her bosom. Persistence was a very beautiful woman. She didn't wear much make-up; she didn't need to. In fact, make-up would only take away from her beauty.

The trunk of the Mercedes was ajar. Persistence cheerfully greeted me as I approached. Grabbing a few plastic shopping bags, she asked me to carry what looked to be a new microwave into the house for her. Following behind her into the house, I could not help but stare at her behind as she walked. I seemed to have turned into a stalker of nice butts ever since breaking my virginity with Kesha. I shook my head and decided to pay more attention to where I was going. When we reached the kitchen, I placed the box I was carrying on the counter top.

"Where did you get a pager from?" Persistence asked me, noticing the new pager on my hip.

"My brotha' gave it to me." I answered. "You know, your sista be trippin'."

"What did she do?" Persistence asked me, washing her hands in the kitchen sink.

"First she called me with an attitude and then she hung the phone up in my face." Persistence laughed.

"Well, what did you do to her?"

"Nothin! I just said I didn't want to go to the Halloween dance tonight." Persistence stood there eyeing me with her hands on her hips. She knew that I had to be leaving something out because she knew her sister better than that. "Oh, yeah, I didn't call her yesterday or go to

school today like I told her I would, either." Persistence
nodded her head.

"When Patience is upset, she makes it known.
Word to the wise; do not ever tell my sister that you are
going to do something and then turn around and not do it."

"Yesterday was a long day for me, even you know
that."

"Why do you not want to go to the dance?"

"I don't want to go nowhere with my eye lookin' like
this."

"You are over *here*," she pointed out. I fell silent.
"Plus, it's a *Halloween* dance. All you have to do is keep
your mask on if you don't want for people to see your eye."

"That is the same thing she said."

"Great minds think alike." Persistence commented.
We stood there in silence for a few moments. "Patience
likes you and she just wants to see you. Spend time with
you, that's all." Persistence said, heading towards the
doorway. "Atif?" she paused. I looked up in her direction.
"Go to the dance with her." She then said, exiting the
kitchen.

*****

I joined Smack Man, Malik and K-Red who were
then sitting in the den watching music videos on the big
screen. I was more interested in the conversation my
brother was having with Smack Man than I was in the
videos. Malik was saying how he wanted to get his hands
on some liquid PCP. This was called "wet" or "dip" on the
streets. Wet was a strong drug, usually smoked with Moore
cigarettes, rumored to be the stuff that morticians pumped
into the bodies of the deceased. More and more people
were beginning to smoke dips and Malik wanted to spread
his hustle. I had no idea what would make someone want
to get high on something like that. It was too much for me.

I once asked my mother what was so bad about
smoking weed and she told me that weed usually led to

153

harsher drugs. She also told me that weed was what my
father started with.

"Hello?" Malik answered his ringing mobile phone.
After talking for a few moments he hung up. "Lets ride
y'all." Malik said to us, rising from the couch.

"Who was that?" K-Red asked Malik.

"Small Balls tryin' to cop some work."

After stopping by a small apartment where Malik
and K-Red stored their dope, money and guns, we headed
for the tilt. Parking the car, we got out of the Iroc and went
inside. I went around through the back in order to see if
Darion had taken the bucket. It was not there. Turning to
head inside, I thought I saw something move out of my
peripheral vision. I walked down the driveway and saw a
Caucasian man in the alley dressed in what appeared to be
some kind of city uniform. Further down the alleyway there
sat a large van. I could only see the front of the van and I
assumed, unable to see just how large the van was, that it
was what the city worker was driving. Dismissing the man
and the van, I went back inside and placed the board on the
door. I was making the same mistake I had made the night
my mother was killed.

Small Balls had pulled up also and Malik was in the
process of weighing two ounces of crack cocaine on a scale
in front of him so that Small Balls could see for himself what
he was buying.

K-Red was in the front room with Kesha, who had
never left the tilt since the night before, and they were
counting up the money she had made while everyone was
gone. The tilt was rarely left empty.

I went into the back room in search of the mask I
had purchased the day before. I found it and tried it on,
thinking that maybe it wouldn't be so bad if I did go to the
dance after all. I then headed to the bathroom to look at
myself in the mirror with the mask on. After urinating in the
toilet, I went to flush it but nothing happened when I
tugged on the lever.

"What the ...?" I started, directed to no one in particular. I then tried to turn on the faucet. Nothing. "Man, why they cut the damn w-"

"BOOM.... BOOM.... BOOM!" I was interrupted by the sound of something crashing against the back door.

"Kick in!" Malik yelled. Small Balls panicked. He tried to hand the dope back to Malik. "Nigga you bought the shit. What the fuck you tryin' to hand it to me for?" Malik countered. Small Balls ran towards the front of the house and came to a stop in the middle of the floor, looking around frantically for somewhere to hide the dope he had just purchased.

K-Red snatched up the dope Kesha had left over and jumped up off the couch, racing towards the bathroom behind Malik while pulling dope out of his pockets at the same time. Kesha just sat there stuck, not knowing what to do. Malik and K-Red rushed into the bathroom with me, dumping crack into the toilet.

"It ain't workin'!" I said.

"What?" Malik and K-Red asked in unison.

"The water! It ain't workin'!" I answered excitedly. At that moment the back door came crashing in.

"Kansas City Police Department! Everybody down on the fucking floor!" Numerous voices were yelling at the same time. K-Red ran out of the bathroom with the intent of placing some distance between him and all of the dope in the toilet. Malik opened up the bathroom window and climbed outside, being pursued by officers who were guarding the side of the house as soon as his feet touched the ground.

I looked out of the window and saw my brother being chased. I climbed out of it and ran faster than I had ever ran before. My heart was beating crazily and I was all of the way a few blocks over on the other side of Prospect before I looked behind me and realized that I was not being chased. Malik had carried all of the attention with him as he fled. After catching a breather, I began to jog back towards Big Mama's house. When I reached the block, I saw that police were everywhere. Not wanting to take a chance on

155

being apprehended, I headed for Darion's house. I spotted
the bucket sitting in front of his house and ran across the
front lawn until I reached the front door. I then knocked
hurriedly, looking around to make sure the coast was clear.

"Who is it?" Darion asked a few moments later from
within.

"Me man! Open the door!" I answered.   Darion
opened the door and I rushed inside.

Darion's house was not the nicest one in the
neighborhood. It was a small two bedroom house that sat
street level in between two larger homes on each side. It
looked as if someone built it in a haste, squeezing it
between the other two houses as an afterthought.   The
inside reflected the outer view. There was not much room
anywhere in the house and one got a crowded like
sensation when inside.   Especially in the bathroom and
kitchen. It was easy to see that the bulk of his mother's
welfare checks were spent elsewhere.

"Damn nigga, what's wrong with you?" Darion
asked, shutting the door behind me. "What happened to
your eye?"

"The tilt just got kicked in and I got jumped out at
the Landin' last night." I answered. "Where your mama at?"

"Ain't no tellin'." Darion answered. "Tell me what
happened man."

I told Darion the whole story starting from the point
where I dropped him off the day before. I began to calm
down as I talked. Darion sat there attentive, hanging on to
my every word. I told him everything. When I went into
details about the shooting, Darion fired up a joint.

"Man, you jumped over the counter?" Darion asked
in disbelief as I told him about my episode of paranoia with
the police. I nodded, taking a hit off of the joint. Darion
fell out of his chair onto the floor in a fit of laughter. I
began to laugh myself. I was feeling much better then
thanks to my best friend and a little bit of Mary Jane. I
looked at Darion, who was then up on one elbow wiping
tears from his eyes, and passed the joint back to him.
"Man, you crazier than a mutha' fucka'." I continued on.

156

"Where the note at?" he asked me. I dug into my pants pocket and tossed it to him. "That's my nigga, boa." Darion complimented, handing the note back to me. "You think they caught Malik?" Darion asked upon the completion of my narration.

"I don't know." I answered. "They was on him, and you know he can't run so fast no more.".

"Don't trip. Even if he did get caught, he got money to bond out." Darion said in consolation. Ignorance also. We didn't stop to think about what happens after bonding out, like the fact that Malik would still have to go to court eventually and deal with the situation.

"What you gone do about Patience?" Darion asked.

"What do you mean?"

"She highly upset with you dawg." Darion answered. "And you know Teebaby got her lil' snotty nose all up in y'all mix."

"Yeah, I 'm hip. You still goin' to the dance?"

"Yeah. I ain't got no mask now, thanks to the police, but I'mma go anyway. I'll just go as the pimp I be, ya dig?" Darion answered. "You ridin'?" I looked at him doubtfully. "Come on man, let's go get our freak on."

"Yeah, a'ight."

*****

We sat around the house for another hour or so, waiting for the police to clear out of the neighborhood. Once they did, we went and delivered the news about the raid to Big Mama and the only emotion she showed was a simple dismissive shake of her head. After waiting around for a while to see if Malik would call, we left enroute for the dance.

We rolled past the tilt and saw that a large black poster had been posted on the door with COMBAT DRUG ZONE written in big white letters across the front. Kesha, Malik, Small Balls or K-Red were nowhere in sight.

157

"Boa, them police really be thinkin' they done got
something off when they kick a spot in, don't they?" Darion
asked me as we rode down Benton.

"Yeah." I answered absentmindedly, staring out of
the window.

"I'mma miss sittin' up in there stackin' them ends
like that. Money was just comin' to a nigga. Damn. It
don't stop though. I was hollarin' at Fang-Fang just the
other day and she was talkin' about lettin' a nigga bust
some serves up outta her pad. What you think about that?"
Darion asked, looking again at me.

"Yeah, that a be cool. Gotta be strapped though.
She be on some skanless shit."

Fang-Fang was what everyone in the neighborhood
called a crack addict whose real name was Carla. She was
called such because four of her front teeth were missing.
When she smiled, all you could see was her two fang-like
incisors. Fang-Fang was also an alcoholic, bitten hard by
the bottle. Hard enough to draw blood. She would do just
about anything for some dope. Last year, Money Mike paid
her a $20 piece of crack to lick the penis of a neighborhood
mutt. Drunk off of some Bumpy Face Gin, she did it in front
of at least fifteen spectators with no shame.

The dance was packed. Once inside, I saw that
there were many "students" in attendance who did not even
attend Central. This was nothing new though, for I myself
had crashed a few school functions where I did not go also.
It was almost a tradition.

Making our way through the crowded auditorium,
Patience and Teebaby were not in sight. It was dark
though and very difficult to see. Mostly everyone wore
costumes of some sort, so if we had walked right passed
the two girls we probably would not have recognized them.
I made my way towards a dark corner, surveying the dance
floor while being obscured by the shadows. Whoever
looked my way would see nothing but a hockey mask
glowing in the dark, seeming to float in mid-air. Darion had
stopped in front of the stage and was dancing with a girl
dressed up as a witch. He was in no hurry to find Teebaby.

Everyone seemed to be having a good time. The disc jockey was playing all of the latest jams. Still high from the weed we smoked on the way, I fought the urge to go out on the floor and cut a rug myself. Come to think of it, I had been high all that day. I don't remember ever smoking as much weed in one day as I had, at least not up to that point in my life. Anyway, if I was to get out there on that floor, it would have had to have been a slow song. That way I would not have to do too much.

A teacher approached me. As she got closer I saw that it was Mrs. Ross, my math teacher.

"Is everything okay young man?" Mrs. Ross asked me over the music. The lights began to come back on as the song being played came to an end.

"Yeah, I'm just chillin'."

"Who are you? I can't tell with that mask on."

"It's me, Atif Grady."

"Oh! Our future wide receiver for the Kansas City Chiefs." She said, smiling. "Why have I not been seein' you in my class lately?"

"I be missin' my bus."

"Well, get it together. Don't let it happen again. Have fun." Mrs. Ross said as she turned to leave.

With the lights on I was able to see much better. I was even able to identify certain people despite their costumes by recognizing the shoes on their feet. Strolling across the dance floor, I spotted Patience conversing with three other females. She was wearing a long, white dress with fake blood all over it. Her long hair was down and she had some white make up on her face, giving her a ghostly appearance.

Heading towards her, I was beat to the punch by someone wearing a werewolf mask. I looked on as the werewolf crept up from behind Patience and wrapped his arms around her waist. Startled, she turned and pulled away from his embrace. He then took hold of her hand and she snatched it away. I smirked underneath my mask. The werewolf said something that I was unable to hear, whatever it was though, Patience did not like it. She

159

pushed him in his chest. I picked up my pace. As I approached, the werewolf was pointing his finger in her face.

"....punk ass bitch!" I heard the werewolf say as I appeared seemingly out of nowhere. I knocked the werewolf's hand out of Patience's face, stepping in front of her.

"Nigga put your finger in my face like that so I can break it for you." I threatened.

"You ain't gone break shit," the werewolf retorted, snatching off his mask and stepping up into my face. It was Kev. "Fuck you and this bitch. She ain't shit but sloppy seconds to me anyway nigga, I done been there and done that."

"Yeah, whatever." I answered. The reference to Kev's past relationship with Patience was diluted by the fact that I had already learned of it from Persistence. I was tempted to chin-check him for calling her out of her name like he did. Plus, he was speaking as if they had had some kind of sexual relations, at least that was how I took it. "You sure doin' a lot of rappin'. You wanna talk about who you used to go with or you wanna lockup?" I challenged. Malik taught me long ago not to do a lot of arguing, to go ahead and put my work in on someone if that was what the situation called for. Meanwhile, we were being encircled by onlookers. Mostly everyone had stopped dancing, focusing on the potential highly anticipated rematch between us. I noticed that Darion had slipped behind Kev undetected.

"You don't wanna see me, cuzz. Not again you don't." Kev answered, emphasizing the word "cuzz" with a shake of his head. He was trying to get further underneath my skin. It was considered disrespectful for a Crip to refer to a Blood using the title cuzz.

"Break it up, break it up you two." Coach Turner said, stepping in between us. "We got more games to win and we can't do so with you at each other's throats."

Patience grabbed me by the hand and pulled me away. She led me out of the auditorium, down the main hallway and out of the front doors. It was windy out. The wind blew Patience's hair everywhere.

"Let's go sit in the car." I suggested, noticing Patience trying to rub away the goose-bumps formulating on her arms. I led her to the bucket and we had a seat inside.

"Whose car is this?" Patience asked, looking around the interior.

"Me and D-Mack's." I answered. We sat in silence for a while, looking around at everything except each other.

"I'm sorry about hanging up on you like I did earlier." Patience apologized, looking at me.

"I ain't trippin'." I answered. A few more moments of silence. "Why you didn't tell me you used to mess wit Kev?"

"I didn't know that I had to inform you about everyone I had ever gone with." Patience answered. I stared at her, reprimanding her with my eyes. She looked away. "Why didn't you tell me that you and Kev had a fight?" she then asked me. More silence.

I had an idea. Reaching under the floor mat for the key to the ignition, I pulled it out and stuck it inside of the keyhole and turned it backwards so the radio would come on. R. Kelly's Honey Love drifted from the speakers. Turning the volume up, I then got out of the bucket and walked around to Patience's side, opening her door.

"You gone dance with me?" I asked, smirking behind my mask.

"Out here?"

"Yeah, out here." Patience smiled that pretty smile of hers and got out of the bucket.

"I didn't know you danced." Patience said to me as we swayed.

"I don't. Gangstas don't dance, we groove." Patience laughed.

"Whatever." We held each other in silence for a while. "Are we through bickering with each other now?" Patience asked, looking up at me.

"We have been goin' at it all day, ain't we?"

"Yes." She answered. "I would kiss you but I can't reach your lips with that mask on." I paused. Forget that mask, I wasn't going to pass up a chance to kiss Patience no matter how self-conscious I was feeling about my black eye. I then reached up and removed the hockey mask from my face. "It really is not that bad, Atif." she said, touching my eye gently. She then kissed my lips. "It makes you look like a .....raccoon!" Patience took off running around the bucket and screamed playfully when I began to chase her.

*****

Running out The
Crack House

DISCLOSURE

"She was a fool from the start,
lettin' him in after dark.
Knowin' that their relationship
had long since lost its spark.
-It was the —lust in his heart
that had her screamin' his name,
scratchin' his face and his back
as he forced himself upon her, mixin' pleasure with pain.
Now she got me askin' myself;
am I ready for this?
Stimulated and seduced
by her French kiss.
-Lost in a bliss-
holdin' her tight all night long.
Somethin' that feels so right,
can't be wrong.
Late night conversations
on the telephone.
Brought out the ugly confrontations
that went on at home.
After a certain altercation
that went way too deep.
Feeling violated, questioning her chastity,
She confided in me."
-Soody Mak

8

A couple of months later, Darion and I found ourselves out in south Kansas City at the Holiday Inn located off of Red Bridge. Malik and K-Red rented the ballroom, as well as five of the rooms upstairs including a suite, for the New Years Eve party they hosted. The party was in full swing. I had never been in the presence of so many beautiful women in my life. With an unlimited supply of alcohol and weed, there was not a sober soul in the party.

After Malik relinquished 10% of $25,000 for bail, he was released on bond after being apprehended by the police back in October. He was charged with illegal possession of firearms for the arsenal of weapons confiscated by the police during the raid.

K-Red was also charged for the weapons confiscated, but he was additionally charged with possession with the intent to distribute for the crack they found in the toilet. He too was able to post bail. A lawyer they had hired promised that neither of the two would have to do any jail time.

Kesha was detained in the Jackson County Detention Center. She was charged with illegal possession of a firearm after her fingerprints were discovered on Malik's .380 found underneath the couch in the front room. She was already on probation for an assault and the new case violated her probation. Her probation officer recommended that her probation be revoked, requesting that a seven year back up prison sentence be implemented.

Small Balls too bonded out. He was apprehended weeks later though by the authorities after being pulled over for a routine traffic stop. When the officer went to search his trunk, he found the Mack-10 that K-Red used during the drive-by. Apparently, instead of getting rid of the weapons along with his car, like Malik had instructed him to do, he decided to keep the Mac-10 for himself. He was always infatuated with that gun and on numerous occasions attempted to convince Malik into selling it to him. The groves on the barrel of the gun matched those found on the bullets retrieved by surgeons from one of the bodies of the people that were shot that night a couple of months back. He was then charged with one count of first degree murder, armed criminal action, and four counts of attempted murder to go along with his pending possession with the intent to distribute crack cocaine charge. During his arraignment hearing, the judge refused to set bail for him in accordance with the prosecuting attorney's wishes.

Detectives John Valentine and Bobby Vermil interrogated him for hours trying to get him to give up the names of the three people he was with that night. They tried taunting him, depriving him of sleep, the good cop/bad cop routine, they even tried promising him leniency. He refused to say anything.

We kept in touch with Small Balls through Antoinette. Malik not only kept money on his account to purchase items from the canteen, he also hired a more than competent defense lawyer for him and paid Antoinette to take weed to him on a weekly basis.

The tilt was reopened; but not as a place of business. It was more of a gathering place. Everyone in the hood would come by to shoot some craps or just chill. Darion actually spent more time there than anyone else. At night, instead of going home, he would sleep at the tilt if his mother was home. That way he didn't have to worry about fighting with her because of his refusals to supply her with dope or give her any money to purchase it from someone else. Malik and K-Red constantly found themselves warning him not to sell any dope to anyone out of the tilt. They began to notice customers seeming to all of a sudden knock on the door in the middle of the night after all of them were informed of the tilt no longer being in operation.

Me? I was not only getting money from opening up shop at Fang-Fang's house with Darion, I was also selling weed out of Antoinette's house out south. The two of us had really gotten to know each other well over the two months since we met. When Antoinette approached me about "making some money", I consulted my brother for some advice on the matter. Malik advised me to sell weed out of her house instead of anything else. He said that I should give her money to live in an apartment and use the house to serve out of. Antoinette agreed. She quit her second job at the mall and spent the day shift selling weed out of her old place of residence for me. I would hold it down while she was at work. The quality of the weed I was purchasing from Trigga surpassed anything that had been floating around out that way in a long time by far, so our clientele was plentiful. Within weeks Antoinette was moving a ½ pound of weed a night. She was very cautious and she didn't make many mistakes, if any at all. She never kept a lot of weed in the house and she was loved by all of her customers. She brought a lot of her own clientele to the table along with the people Malik and I would send her way.

I was beginning to find myself putting away thousands of dollars at a time; I was no longer into spending money carelessly on clothes and the like. I practically had everything I needed in those departments at the time. After putting a down payment on a 1992 Ford Mustang in Antoinette's name, Darion and I gave the bucket to two other young hustlers in the neighborhood who were selling dope for us out of Fang-Fang's. I still went to school on an average of three days out of the week. When I did go, I only went to Mr. Williams' class. After that I usually left only to come back and have lunch with Patience in the cafeteria.

Malik and K-Red were doing well for themselves also. In defiance of the raid, the two opened up four different tilts around the neighborhood. They sold $20 pieces of crack out of one, weight out of another, weed out of the third, and wet out of the fourth tilt. The weight house, weed house, and wet house attracted clientele from all over the city, whereas the piece house was more of a local thing. The thing about us as a clique was that we kept good quality product. Smack Man and Trigga's prices were high, but it was well worth the extra cash to get that kind of quality dope.

"Man, it's too many bitches up in here dawg!" Darion shouted to me over the loud music, holding a cup of liquor in his right hand. His eyes seemed to be closed; I wondered to myself how he could see out of them.

All of the women in the party were older than us, but with the type of money the two of us were making, age was nothing but a number. Everyone in the city it seemed was beginning to hear about us two youngsters coming up in the game. We were attracting a lot of harassment from the police, not only because of Darion, who was driving around town in a white 1988 Chevy Blazer equipped with a Phoenix Gold stereo system, but me and my new Mustang had a role to play in it also. We were too young to drive, let alone have such vehicles in our possession.

The party was full of drug dealers and gangsters. It surprised me how many people Malik and K-Red knew outside of the neighborhood from different sets.   There were people in attendance like Slicksta and Luv who were A.P.B.s from 56th, Antonio Nunn and his people from 68th, the Rountrees off of 33rd; everyone who wore red and had a reputation was there or passed through.

I was high from some weed Darion and I had smoked earlier. I was not into alcohol so I did not do any drinking. Women were hitting on me left and right. I even caught Niki, the female who insisted on escorting me to my third hour class on the first day of school, trying to slip her hand down my pants while whispering to me in my ear about how she wanted to perform oral sex on me.

The loud music was beginning to give me a headache. "I'll be back." I shouted to Darion as I made my way out of the ballroom. Once out in the corridor, I headed towards the elevators and rode one upstairs.

As I walked down the hallway, I heard music coming for one of the rooms. When I walked over to it, I realized that the door was partially ajar. Peering inside, I was somewhat taken aback by what I saw.

K-Red was laid back on the bed smoking a joint and Antoinette was stark naked on top of him. She was riding him backwards with her arched back towards K-Red. I felt a mixed pang of excitement and jealousy simultaneously. I looked on as Antoinette, with one hand placed on K-Red's chest for support while massaging her own breasts with the

168

other, moved her luscious hips in a slow figure eight like motion. She looked as if she really knew what she was doing. After another five minutes or so, Antoinette took her hands, placed them flat on the bed in front of her as she learned forward, and began to bounce up and down. I could see her buttocks clapping against each other.

"Daammmnn!" I mumbled to myself. I had no idea Antoinette could put it down like that. I guess that is where the jealousy came in at. I felt like she should have been on top of *me* like that instead. I was the one who introduced her to everybody. I wasn't a hater, I'm just being honest. I slowly backed away from the door and headed back downstairs.

A couple of minutes later, I was back upstairs. I was not alone. As I laid back smoking a joint on the bed, I watched as Niki disrobed in front of me. She then climbed into the bed on top of me.

"Naw, hun un." I said to her, shaking my head.
"What?"
"Turn around. I want you to ride me backwards."
"Aw yeah?"
"Yeah." She turned her body around while successfully keeping me inside her as she did so and went to work.

*****

A few weeks passed. Business out south was booming. Antoinette and I found ourselves running through over a pound of weed a day in $10 sacks alone. Beginning to worry about all of the traffic, she suggested that we stop selling $10 sacks. She said that we should start selling only ¼ ounces and up, nothing less. Doing so would slow traffic down by cutting out some of the clientele in my age bracket because $10 sacks was all they usually wanted. I was skeptical at first, but we did need to slow things down so I finally agreed. I just planned to open up another tilt and cater to them.

Antoinette and I were at the tilt out south, listening to DJ Quick's *Way 2 Funky* as we packaged up the weed I had brought over to her. Every time Antoinette looked up from what she was doing, she would see me looking at her with a smirk on my face.

"Why do you keep lookin' at me like that Atif?" Antoinette finally asked me.

"Like what?"

"I don't know.   Like you got somethin' on your mind."

"Honestly?"

"Yeah, honestly. We both grown, well, I'm grown and you might as well be. So, what'sup?"

"I saw you and K-Red that night at the Holiday Inn."

"What do you mean?"

"What I said, don't play crazy."

"I ain't playin' crazy. I mean, what did you see?"

"I saw you ridin' him backwards, playin' with your own titties, eyes rollin' in the back of your head, *all* that." I answered , smirking.

"And how long was you watchin' us?" she asked, placing some weed on a scale.

"About five or ten minutes." I admitted. She looked at me peculiarly. I wondered in my own mind if she felt violated or excited at the thought of my watching her have sex.

"So *that* is why you been given' me all these lil' looks of yours all this time, huh?" she asked me. I shrugged. "Okay, so you saw me havin' sex. And ? I like sex just like any other human being."

"*And?* You was *not* just havin' sex girl; you were puttin' it *down*!" Antoinette laughed at this. "You was ridin' that nigga's dick like you *invented* the position. Straight *pro-fession-al*. *And,* ain't you the *same* woman that was talkin' about... '*I just got out of a terrible relationship and I just don't know if and when I will ever be ready to be with another man?*'" I finished, mimicking her voice. She laughed again.

170

"That is *not* what I said and you *know* it ain't!" Antoinette said, rising from her seat and pointing playfully at me.

"Well, not them same exact words, but somethin' like that. All that *fakin'*!"

"I wasn't fakin', I meant what I said and I still do. That was just sex, that's all. We was both fucked up and horny, so we did it." Antoinette answered as she walked around the table and straddled my lap. I got excited instantly. "What I *did* say though was that my marriage was fucked up and I do not want to get hurt like that again. I didn't say nothin' about not havin' sex." She began tracing invisible lines softly on the base of my neck with her long polished and decorated fingernails. It used to drive me *crazy* when she did that. "Did it upset you in any way to see me and your boy havin' sex like that?" she asked, looking into my eyes.

"That sound like one of them women's questions. I don't know how I'm suppose to answer that one."

"Boy, what the hell is a woman's question?" she asked, laughing.

"You know what I'm talkin' about. One of them questions where I'm damned if I do, damned if I don't." We both laughed at this.

"Well, you ain't my man and I ain't Patience, so you can tell me the truth about how you feel."

"Naw girl, I ain't trippin' on that." I said, giving them my blessing.

"You better not be. You sure ain't gave me none."

"What?" I asked, genuinely surprised with a crease in my brow. She caught me slipping with that one. We had become good friends, I never really suspected that she wanted to go there with me.

"You heard me. Actin' all funny. I think you scared of me."

"Girl *please*! I ain't scared of you." The situation was getting a little heated. I chickened out and switched the focus. "A, you know what I did though after I saw you ridin' K-Red like that?" I then asked. Maybe I was a little afraid of Antoinette. Maybe I wasn't ready for her yet.

171

"What?"

"I went and had this female ride me like you were ridin' K-Red."

"You did that for real?" she asked me. I nodded. "You silly. Did she put it on you?"

"Naw, not for real. She did turn around on my dick though. Can you do that?"

"Yeah, I can do that if it ain't too small." Antoinette answered, wiggling her pinkie finger in the air. At that moment my pager went off. Antoinette reached for it. "767-1335. Who is that?"

"I don't know, hand me the phone." She got up from my lap and did what I asked her to do. Someone knocked on the front door as I dialed the number. "Handle that for me." I said, smacking her lightly on the backside.

Bluffing.

"Don't start nothin' you can't handle *or* finish." Antoinette warned as she walked out of the room.

It was Patience who had paged me; she was over at her sister's. Not wanting to go home, Patience asked me if I wanted to come over and keep her company while Persistence and Smack Man went out. After agreeing, I left Antoinette at the tilt and made my way over to Smack Man's. I pretty much knew that area by then and I made sure I took the back streets to avoid being pulled over in my Mustang by the police.

It always seemed to be so peaceful to me out south. I didn't see people hanging out on every street corner like I did in my own neighborhood. I didn't see any prostitutes, there was not a liquor store on every other block. As much as I enjoyed the peaceful surroundings out south, I could not help but feel a bit of animosity at the same time. Everyone was out there living in their own little world, oblivious to the people on the north end of the city who were living in hell. People like me who saw selling drugs as not the only way out of such living conditions, but as the only way that seemed realistic. That within itself showed just how bad things were because the dope game is not very appealing considering its drawbacks. Yet still,

172

many of us would rather take such chances than spend our lives struggling for crumbs.

Minutes later, I pulled in front of Smack Man's house and parked on the curb. I got out of the car and rang the doorbell.

"Wha'sup lil' hommie?" Smack Man greeted me, opening the door as he invited me in.

"Wha' sup Smack Man?"

"That's your Mustang out there?"

"Yeah, you like it?"

"It's cool. I liked the bucket better. You was more discreet with the bucket, you know?" I nodded. "You will learn though." I followed Smack Man into the den and had a seat on the couch. "Trigga say that you been runnin' through a lot of weed, wha'sup? Your tilt jumpin' like that?"

"Yeah, we been runnin' through about a pound a day."

"That's cool. What about down at Fang-Fang's? How you and the other lil' hommie doin' down there?"

"It's rollin'."

"Y'all gotta be careful down there youngblood. Y'all young and them geek monsters gone wanna try y'all; thinkin' that they can get somethin' off. Especially Fang-Fang, she ain't right. The only reason she ain't tried nothin' yet is because she know that Malik will tap that ass for her if she trip." I nodded. "Don't take that as a consolation though because you never know when it comes to them geek monsters. When that addiction get to callin' their name, they don't reason too good. They will mess around and try somethin' *anyway*, regardless of what the consequences of their actions may or may not be. In actuality, we ain't too different. When it comes to that dollar *we* be willin' to take chances. Chances that could lead to life in the pen or death itself, you know?" I nodded, hanging on to his every word. I was in sponge mode, soaking up every ounce of game that Smack Man threw at me.

"I got some plans for you and your brotha. I don't plan on doin' this shit until the day I get locked up or killed, you know? Shit, I want a family of my own, kids and all

173

that. Every step I take now is in preparation for the day I can lay back and my family will have nothin' to worry about."

"You say you got some plans for me and my brotha'?" I asked, Smack Man nodded. "Plans like what?" Smack Man laughed to himself.

"Don't concern yourself with that right now. You still got some maturin' in the game to do. I got some stuff in motion though. Just lay back and do what you do." Smack Man answered. "What you doin' with your money youngblood, you puttin' it up or trickin' it off?"

"Puttin' it up." I answered. Smack Man nodded in approval.

"Make sure you always got some ends put up. If you ever catch some kind of case, you ain't gone have no chance in that courtroom without some bread. It is bad enough to be black in front of the judge, but to be black *and* broke? Sh-i-i-i-t, they gone *lose* your ass." At that moment Persistence appeared in the doorway. "You ready to go?"

"Almost." Persistence then turned towards me and smiled. "Hi Atif! I didn't hear you come in."

"That's because I'm a smooth criminal." She laughed. "Where Patience?"

"Upstairs." I nodded, staying put. I didn't know if I should go up there or not. I had never been upstairs. "You can go up there, you are *family* boy." Persistence said to me, sensing my hesitancy. I got up from the couch and headed upstairs.

There were three bedrooms located on the third level of Smack Man's home. I found Patience located in the one at the end of the hallway. The door was open and she was laying across the spacious bed on her stomach, talking on the phone. She wore a pair of blue jeans and a red mock-neck sweater with her long black hair tied up into a ponytail. Her bare feet dangled off the edge of the bed.

I crept into the room undetected, sneaking up behind her. I then tickled the soles of her feet.

"My feet are not ticklish, you know that." Patience said, getting up from the bed. "Hi!" Patience greeted, followed by a kiss on my lips. She then took me by the hand and led me to the bed.

"Who you talkin' to?" I inquired.

"Teebaby."

"Tell her I said wha' sup."

"Atif says hi."

"That ain't what I said, I said *wha' sup*!"

"Same thing. Teebaby says hello."

"Let me talk to her right quick." I said, reaching for the phone. Patience handed the receiver to me. "Hello?....Nothin'...."

Patience leaned back onto the fluffy pillows, watching me as I talked to her best friend. She was far beyond the point of infatuation with me, and could not even begin to explain how deeply she was falling in love, nor could she begin to imagine not being with me.

"He probably down at the tilt.... Who said that?...... Yeah, *right.*" I listened to Teebaby for a moment. "Your home girl is retarded." I whispered to Patience, covering the mouthpiece with my hand. Patience pinched me on my thigh. "A, Patience gone have to call you back. She done started some funk." I hung the phone up and grabbed Patience before she had the chance to take off running like she was just about to do. She screamed as I picked her up and slammed her softly on the bed. Pinning her down, I began to nibble on her neck.

"That *tickles*!" Patience exclaimed, squirming and laughing.

"Atif! Patience!" Smack Man's voice thundered from downstairs. "Y'all come here!"

We got up from the bed and walked downstairs. Smack Man and Persistence were standing at the door, dressed to kill. Persistence was in the process of putting on a long black leather coat on top of a white body dress. Smack Man was dressed nicely as well. The two were destined to turn some heads, wherever they were going.

"Don't answer the door for *nobody*. I don't care if you look out that peephole and see Minister Louis Farrakhan. Tell him I said I will buy a bean pie and a Final Call paper when we get back." Smack Man said. We all laughed at this. "Whatever y'all do, don't open this door." We nodded in agreement. "Atif, you have to stay here until we get back man. Ain't no runnin' in and out of my house while we are gone."

"A'ight." I answered. Smack Man and Persistence opened the front doors and stepped outside.

"Aw, yeah. Don't be fuckin' in our bed either." Smack Man said as he slid inside of his black Mercedes Benz. Persistence gave him a slight shove. Pulling out of the circular driveway, Smack Man honked his horn and drove off.

*****

"Can I ask you a question?" I asked Patience hours later. We were in the den, curled up in each other's arms on the couch, watching Def Comedy Jam on the big screen. It was getting late and we were winding down as the excitement of having the house to ourselves began to wear off.

"Yes, you can ask me anything. You know that." Patience answered, looking up at me.

"You promise not to get mad?" Patience peered at me suspiciously.

"I promise. What is it?" Patience asked, sitting up and turning the volume down on the television.

"That night at the Halloween dance when Kev said that to him you ain't nothin' but sloppy seconds. What was he talkin' about?"

"What do you *mean*?" Patience asked. That slight edge of hers was creeping into her voice.

"Did y'all ever do it when y'all was to-" I was interrupted by Patience as she exhaled sharply and got up from the couch.

"I can *not* believe you just *asked* me that!" Patience shot at me, shaking her head as she stormed out of the den. I called after her, following her into the kitchen. She reached into the freezer and pulled out a ½ gallon carton of cookies and cream, slamming it down on the countertop.

176

"You promised you wasn't gone get mad." I reminded her.

"You did not inform me that your question would be a *stupid* ass question." She said, reaching into the cupboard for a bowl and then slamming it down next to the ice cream.

"Did you just *cuss* at me?" I asked, smirking. Patience ignored me as she retrieved an ice cream scoop from the utensil drawer. I walked around the counter and stood behind her, wrapping my arms around her waist.

"What is so stupid about my question?" Patience elbowed me in the stomach and turned around. I let go of her waist and wrapped my arms around myself.

"I seem to recall telling you early on that I was, *am*, still a virgin. Do you remember me telling you that?" Patience asked, pointing the ice cream scoop at me.

"Yeah, I remember." I answered, looking away. Patience turned back around and began to scoop ice cream out of the carton and into the bowl. "Why would he say somethin' like that then?"

"Probably the same reason why he kept on calling you *cuzz*. To upset you. Did such a notion even begin to formulate or manifest itself anywhere in that brain of yours?" Patience asked sarcastically as she turned her back to me and went back to what she was doing. Dismissing the insult on my intelligence, I wrapped my arms back around her waist.

"Can I have some?" I whispered in her ear.

"No. Make your own." She was *mad*. Patience then took her bowl of ice cream and walked out of my grasp, leaving me standing there in the kitchen alone. I stood there for a few seconds, then I reached into the utensil drawer and pulled out a spoon. After putting the ice cream back into the freezer and the scoop into the sink, I headed for the den.

"You forgot this."

"Thank you." Patience said, snatching the spoon from my hand. I stood there glaring at her.

"Yeah, a'ight. I'mma let that go." I said, taking a seat at the opposite end of the couch. I grabbed the remote and turned the volume up.

We sat in silence, ignoring each other. I pretended to be off into Def Comedy Jam, but I no longer found the comedians funny. My mind was actually elsewhere. All of sudden, "*SPLAT!*" I felt something cold and wet hit me on the side of my face. I reached up and wiped at the spot where I had felt the sensation at, seeing ice cream on the tips of my fingers.

"Why you do that?" I asked Patience, glaring at her. She ignored me with her eyes glued to the screen. "Don't do that again girl, I ain't playin' with you." I warned. She just didn't know. Anger was beginning to seep into my chest. I felt like she was testing me, and that was not a smart thing for her to be doing. A few minutes passed, "SPLAT!"

I lost my patience with Patience. She had gone too far. I rose from the couch and snatched my car keys off of the table. I then stormed out of the room and headed towards the front door, thinking to myself that Patience would be better off if I placed some distance between the two of us.

"Where do you think you are going?" Patience asked, following behind me.

"I'm *leavin'*."

"Rick said not to go anywhere."

"Smack Man ain't my daddy." Patience dipped in front of me and leaned against the front doors in protest. "*Move!*" She ignored me, placing a spoon of ice cream in her mouth. "What? You think I won't move you or somethin'?" Fiddling with the melting ice cream in her bowl, Patience began to speak.

"Kevin came over to my house unannounced one day when my mother was not home. I was still living in Grandview at the time and we had just broken up, well I had just dumped him because he was bragging to me about some things he did or had done which he thought would impress me." Patience paused for a second, looking at me. There was something else she wanted to say but she

178

changed her mind and continued. "Anyway, I let him inside so that he could supposedly use my telephone. Well, once I let him inside he would not leave. He started kissing me and the next thing I knew he was on top of me taking my shirt off. I was scared and I told him to stop. He wouldn't. He started pulling on my shorts and I began to cry, begging him to stop but he wouldn't. He kept going. He managed to pull my shorts and panties down to my ankles and ...." Patience paused for a second or two searching for the strength to continue on. "He held me down with his forearm at my throat while he took his thing out of his pants and tried to penetrate me. I kneed him in his testicles and took off running out of the house when he rolled over onto the floor. When I made it outside, I just ran and ran until I reached the house of a friend of mine. I stayed there until my mom came home. I wouldn't even walk back to the house; I made her come and pick me up." Still fiddling with her melted ice cream, tears were streaming from Patience's eyes.

"He did not penetrate me Atif, I swear he didn't." I grabbed her bowl from her with one hand and hugged her with the other as she buried her head into my chest. "I'm *still* a virgin, I'm still a virgin." She repeated over and over, crying.

Patience had never told anyone about the incident with Kevin. She couldn't really explain why. Part of it was fear, but most of it was simply wanting to forget about it. Telling me lifted a great burden from her shoulders. I understood that because I had done the same thing that day we spent at Cool Crest. There was still a lot of weight there though. She was still clinging on to something and she didn't know when or how to tell me the secret she had been holding inside for months. She wanted to. She didn't like withholding anything from me. Maybe she felt that there was a time for everything and that maybe she would tell me after some more time had passed, a *lot* more time.

I prophesied to myself mentally. It seemed that with every day that passed, my enmity towards Kev would increase in some shape or form. I just knew that a serious confrontation with him was somewhere in the near future.

And the confrontation would be on a whole new level than our last little scuffle on *The Battle Ground* a year earlier. I didn't know what the outcome would be. All I knew was it could not be avoided. I could almost feel the force and power of Someone greater than me in control of that situation whenever it was to occur. I didn't know if it would be a test for me or a test for Kev. Maybe it would be a test for the both of us. Whatever it was, it would be a life altering incident whenever it came to pass, changing the course of our lives forever.

Kev was dangerous. I had to admit that to myself. What made him so was not only his ignorance and his recklessness; Kev didn't care about anything or anyone outside of himself and his reputation. I sensed that Kev was very capable of killing someone, but so was I. The difference between us though was that I would do so out of retaliation or self preservation whereas Kev would be willing to go there at the drop of a hat for almost no reason at all. He could probably take someone's life just to prove that he possessed the courage to or, even worse, for a sick minded form of recreation.

After listening to Patience's revelation, I secretly vowed that I would make Kev *feel* it for that which he had done to Patience. His actions had left her with some issues that would take a lot of time as well as other things in order for her to deal with them. Something like that could change the way a woman sees men and the world in general. It could turn her into a reclusive, suspicious, bitter individual. It was one of the worst forms of robbery to forcefully deprive a woman of her chastity. Even though Kev was not successful in his indecent endeavor physically, he had succeeded in raping her *mentally* because Patience still found herself trying to convince herself that she was still a virgin. Regardless, Kev was still going to reap what he would have sown if he had succeeded in both aspects. I put that on my mother's grave; I put it on the hood. And to top it all off, I swore before the Creator Himself.

It was like that for him.

180

*****

FUGITIVE
"Lord help me,
I'm on the run again.
And as hard as I play the game,
I just can't seem to win.
My life is so corrupt
and filled with sin,
it seems with every step I take,
I'm closer to the pen.
I'm gone off a Backwood,
Lately I have been smokin' *way* too much weed for my own
good.
I know You see me
out here walkin' with my head down.
Runnin' and jumpin' fences
when the police come around.
-Shhh!- What was that sound?
I'm paranoid!
In my dreams they have red beams
on their plastic toys.
This nigga is tellin' on my brotha,
and when I get the chance I'm gone kill that mutha fucka!
Lord, take this anger from my heart.
Show me the Light and help me find my way home, -I'm
lost in the dark-
I want to change, and You *know* I do.
How else can I maintain, with what I'm goin through?"
-*Soody Mak*

9

"Man, Malcolm Little was a *traitor*!"

It was mid April and I was spending a rare morning hour in Mr. Williams' class, high as a kite. Rakim and I were engulfed in a heated debate about brother Malcolm X and the suspicious circumstances surrounding his untimely death.

Mr. Williams sparked our debate with the mentioning of brother Malcolm X and his affiliation with the Nation of Islam. The class had been studying the history of religious black cults in America. Mr. Williams, loving the experience of witnessing two young minds with contrary opinions collide on an intellectual level, observed us quietly, along with the rest of the class while seated at his usual position on the corner of his desk.

"Malcolm X was *far* from anything like a traitor!"

"Yes he was!"

"No he wasn't!"

"Keep it interesting. Rakim, you support your opinion of why you believe he was a traitor and how it was the C.I.A. who killed him instead of the Nation of Islam. Atif, you explain to us why you believe he was *not* a traitor and why you believe that it was a combination of both the Nation of Islam *and* the C.I.A. who were responsible for his murder. Rakim, you first." Mr. Williams said.

"As we all know, Malcolm Little used to be a cocaine snortin', petty hustlin', burglarizin', perm wearin' pimp, who was infatuated with white women. He was ashamed of his black skin and his kinky red hair. The Honorable Elijah Muhammad picked him up out of the gutter and transformed him into a strong, proud black man with the wisdom and knowledge of Almighty God Allah Himself, who appeared in the person of Master Fard Muhammad. After makin' some comments about the assassination of John F. Kennedy, in blatant defiance of the orders of the Honorable Elijah Muhammad, Malcolm Little was put on a mere 90-day suspension as a consequence of his actions. *Then*, while still servin' his suspension, he had the *nerve* to go on the pilgrimage to Makka, once again defyin' the Honorable Elijah

Muhammad's orders, whom had told him *not* to go because he was not ready."

"What you mean he wasn't ready?" I cut in. He was withholding pertinent information, plus I was getting a little hot under the collar with Rakim calling Malcolm, out of what I saw as disrespect, by the name he dropped because of how much he despised it.

"Let him finish, Atif. You will get your turn." Mr. Williams said.

"Thank you. *Anyway*, what I was tryin' to say before I was rudely interrupted was that upon Malcolm Little's return, he chose to abandon truth for falsehood. He called himself partin' with the Nation of Islam and founded a rival mosque. He told blacks to arm themselves and fight against white supremacy, and the C.I.A. saw him as a threat to national security so they dealt with him. He got exactly what he deserved, too." Rakim finished.

"Man that's some bullsh-"

"Atif." Mr. Williams warned.

"Not only is he leavin' stuff out, but he is tellin' half the truth and mixin' the rest up with some of that falsehood he was just talkin' about."

"If you spent more time studyin' than you did gettin' high, gang-bangin', and peddlin' the white man's poisons you would *know* that what I spoke was in fact the truth."

I stared at him for a moment, not appreciating him disclosing my business like that. The whole class focused on me. I looked at Patience and she smiled at me. She knew that thanks to my mother, there was not a student at Central High that knew more about brother Malcolm X than I did. She then nodded her head in approval, indicating for me to go ahead and break Rakim off a little something.

"It is your turn Atif."

"A'ight. Yeah, Malcolm X, or should I say El Haj Malik El Shabazz, *was* off into the streets back in his day and ashamed of his nappy hair, *all* that. And yea, Elijah di-"

"The *Honorable* Elijah Muhammad." Rakim cut in. I looked at Mr. Williams.

"You had your chance to say what you had to say, Rakim. Let him speak." I could practically feel Rakim's eyes

184

goring into the side of my face. He didn't want no problems with me though, we both knew that. He was one of the contributors to my undefeated record on *The Battle Ground*.

"Anyway, Elijah *Poole* did help shape him into the great man he was. But, before we get off into all that and why/how he was killed and by who, we gotta understand somethin' else.

"The C.I.A. implemented the Counter Intelligence Program which was all about the disruption and annihilation of *all* radical black organizations. The Nation of Islam was one of their primary targets.

"After Malcolm X was released from prison, he rose quickly through the ranks of the organization and because of him, people was joinin' the Nation of Islam left and right. Like Rakim said, after Malcolm said what he did about JFK, he was suspended. Which was funny to me because Elijah *Poole* had spent the last 30 years callin' the white man the devil and then all of a sudden he was concerned about hurtin' their feelins. Anyway, what Rakim *didn't* say was that people was hatin' on him within' the organization and was jealous of him. Elijah *Poole* used that incident as an excuse to do what he had been wantin' to do for a while anyway. Why? One reason was because Malcolm X was tired of sittin' on the sidelines and watchin', like Elijah *Poole* was tellin' him to do, while Martin Luther King and all the other civil rights leaders was puttin' in work. All the Nation was doin' was a bunch of *talkin'*. Plus, he had been hearin' rumors about some foul stuff that Elijah *Poole* had been doin' on the under. So, while he was suspended, he chose to investigate these rumors and see for himself if they were true or not. He met with some of the sistas in the Nation and they told him about how Elijah *Poole* was the father of the children they had, yeah, *out* of wedlock and there ain't nothin' *honorable* about that!

"Malcolm X decided that he was goin' to go on the pilgrimage to Makka. He asked his sista for some money and rolled out. When he got there, what he saw *shocked* him! See, Elijah *Poole* had taught Malcolm X that it was impossible for white people to be Muslims. That they were all devils and could not be righteous because it was not in

185

them. That God was a black man, and all kind of crazy stuff. There was all these blue-eyed, blonde haired white people who were Muslims just like he was, and he learned that none of the other 500,000,000 Muslims across the world believed this stuff *but* the followers of Elijah *Poole*. Malcolm X realized that everything Elijah *Poole* had taught him was a *lie*. These were some of the *real* reasons why he quit messin' with the Nation.

"As far as Malcolm X gettin' killed, everybody know it was some members of the Nation that pulled them triggas. The C.I.A. had they part to play in it too. Malcolm X wasn't a traitor, he was an *individual*. How could he have been a traitor? It was because of him that the Nation of Islam reached the level they did. He stood on what he believed in and *died* for it." I finished. Mr. Williams nodded his head. I then turned back to Rakim. "I might be all those things you said I am, but that don't make me no dummy."

I can remember the feeling I felt at that moment. Along with Patience, I could see that everyone in the class was surprised and impressed by my elaboration.   I felt good. Not just because I was high, but because I was able to speak my mind and know what I was talking about. Of course the weed *did* provide me with a little more courage than I usually had when being the object of a class full of people's attention. In the past, I tended to shy away from such things.

*****

"Guess what?" Patience asked me. We were sitting in the cafeteria having lunch later on that same afternoon. I had left school after Mr. Williams' class and was just not too long ago making it back.

"What?"

"I am *proud* of you!"

"For what?"

"For this morning in Mr. Williams' class."

"Aw yeah?" I was smiling sheepishly.

"Yes. I know that people probably think that because of the life you lead, the way you dress and the way you talk that there is not much more to you outside of what Rakim said about you. But *I* know that could not possibly be further from the truth. I believe in you even if no one else does." I kissed her on the forehead. "Ooooh, guess what else?"

"What?"

"Teebaby has been missing her period."

"*Ugh*! Why would I wanna know somethin' like that?" I thought a woman's menstruation was......nasty. I was so ignorant.

"Because, silly.   It *could* mean that she is pregnant." Patience said, laughing to herself. I sat there silently with my mouth wide open in a state of shock. Pregnant? Darion and Teebaby having a baby?

"Do D-Mack know?"

"No. Teebaby does not even know for sure yet. She bought a pregnancy test but was afraid to use it. She told me last night that she was going to make it her business to do so this morning. I am kind of worried about her too since she didn't come to school today." Patience then looked at me. "What is she going to do if she is pregnant?" I shrugged my shoulders. "Can I ask you something?" I nodded my head. "Have you ever felt pressured to attempt and have sex with me, you know, with knowing that Teebaby and Darion were sexually active with each other and all?" I hesitated for a few moments.

"Yeah at times. But not just because of them. I ain't used to seein' people goin' together for as long as we have been without doin' it, you know what I'm sayin?" Patience nodded. "Things tend to move fast like that in the hood. At the same time I know, especially with what Kev tried to do to you, that breakin' yo virginity ain't somethin' that you are in a rush to do. And I respect that." Patience smiled.

"I want to ask you something else, but I think that I am almost just as afraid of your answer as Teebaby is with the results of a pregnancy test." Patience said, looking at me. I looked back at her.

187

I knew what she wanted to ask me. I also knew that she had been hearing things about me. I grew up in an atmosphere where fornication and adultery were so prevalent that I honestly did not see a whole lot wrong with it. I even thought that a man was *supposed* to have a woman on the side. A personal friend. I didn't feel any guilt whatsoever about having sex with Kesha, Nikki, and many other women behind Patience's back. At least not until that moment. Not until I saw the inexplicable emotion in her eyes when she said that.

"I need to know something though Atif. What if we *were* to become sexually active with each other? Do you think that I could be the *only* woman you would be sleeping with? Hypothetically?"

"Naw, I don't think so. I *know* so." At that moment the bell rung. I gathered our trash from the table and walked her back to her fifth hour class.

"Are you leaving?" Patience asked me as we stood outside her science class.

"Yeah, I got somethin' to do." Antoinette was waiting for me to drop off 5 pounds of weed for her.

"Before you go, I want you to know that whenever I am ready," Patience started, wrapping her arms around my neck and looking me in my eyes. "I want it to be with *you*. I do not know how much that may or may not mean to you but-"

"Don't do that. You ain't gotta promise me nothin' like that to keep me interested in you Patience. What we got goin' ain't even about that. I would love to be your first and all, whenever that time may or may not come, you know what I'm sayin'? But I don't want it to happen because you feel like you *owe* it to me or because you might think that it is somethin' you *have* to do to keep us together." I cut in. Patience lowered her head. I took hold of her chin and lifted her face back up, kissing her on her soft lips. "A'ight?"

"Yes, alright." She said, kissing me again.

"I gotta go now." Patience leaned her forehead against mine.

"Noooo. I want to stand here like this forever."

"I got-"

"Okay, okay. Will you call me later?"

"Page me."

"Promise not to say anything to Darion?"

"Yeah, I promise."

"Bye." Patience kissed me again and turned to leave. "Atif." I stopped in my tracks and turned around. "Thank you." I nodded and headed up the hallway as she went into her class.

I was in the process of exiting stage right when I heard someone call my name. I turned and saw Mr. Williams motioning to me.

Damn! I stopped as he approached me. I usually tried not to let any of the teachers see me leaving before school was out.

"Going somewhere?"

"I was-"

"Why don't you follow me?" I looked out of the doors and contemplated ignoring him and leaving anyway. Mr. Williams was always cool with me though, so I decided against it. Had it been anyone else I would have done just that.

Mr. Williams turned and led me up the hallway. I could see that we were on our way to his classroom. I thought for a moment that he would try and lead me to the principal's office. He opened his classroom door, let me in and then shut it behind him. The classroom was empty; his fifth hour class was on their lunch break. He then took a seat behind his desk and I stood next to the chalk board.

"So, what's up Atif?"

"What you mean?" We sat in silence for a minute. My pager went off, breaking the silence. I looked to see who it was, thinking that it would probably be Antoinette wondering what the hold up was. If she was waiting on me then that meant that someone was waiting on her. It was not Antoinette, it was Darion.

"Business?"

"D-Mack."

"Mr. Nichols, how is he?" Darion had dropped out of school with the conclusion of the football season. We

189

went undefeated in the regular season but lost to a team out of St. Louis in the state championship title game.

"He cool." My pager went off again. It was Darion, this time 911 proceeded his usual code.

"The things Rakim said about you, are they true?" I shrugged my shoulders. "Hmph, I see." Mr. Williams got up from his seat and sat at the edge of his desk. "You know Atif, I keep my ear to the ground and I hear some of the things that the students whisper about in the hallways. I hear your's and Darion Nichols' names a lot. I reflect upon the first couple of weeks of the school year and I take into account how the two of you went from alternating between a few nice outfits to never wearing the same thing twice.

"I try not to interfere into my students' personal lives. But *you*? I see something within you Atif, something special. I get the feeling that your life has a significant role to play in the world, but I fear that the route you currently find yourself on may disrupt that purpose."

"By purpose I take it you mean that it is our Higher Power that decided to give me this purpose, right?"

"Hmmm, yes. I guess you could say that is what I meant."

"A'ight, so if I *did* have a purpose given to me by God Himself, then it wouldn't matter *what* route I was on because if God has ordained somethin' to happen then that is what is gone be, right?"

"You see, that right there is what I am talking about. It is when you say things like that that this aurora emits from your being. You have this.......insight. You see *into* things and I can't help but wonder how a person as gifted as you who is so good at seeing into things could be so *blind* as to the end results of such a way of life?"

"Maybe I'm not as blind as you think I am. Maybe I see clearly and just don't care. Maybe I ain't into breakin' my neck to fulfill any of God's so-called purposes for me." We sat in silence for awhile.

"You know Rose would have been proud to hear your synopsis on Malcolm X, don't you?" I smiled and nodded. I knew that he was right. I could almost see her smiling down on me right then. "Your outlook was more believable than Rakim's. And the beautiful thing about it was that the two of you went at it with your *minds* instead of your hands. Continue to use your mind in such a way Atif, think things through thoroughly before you do them. Weigh out the consequences of your actions.

"Honestly, the rest of the teachers in this school have long since given up on you. They don't care whether you show up for their classes or not. They see you as just another young black adolescent who is going to end up dead or in prison for the rest of his life. It does not have to be that way for you. You can prove them *all* wrong and prove *me* right. It's a choice, but it is a choice that *you* have to make for yourself. You have the power to decide right now if you want to continue living the way you are living or if you want to change. You look as if you are doing pretty good for yourself. You could decide to stop right now, keep all of the material things you have acquired and *still* avoid what everyone else sees in the future for you. All that you have to do is make the right decision, right now. Right here."

I understood what Mr. Williams was saying. I even contemplated taking his advice for a hot second. After all, I *did* have practically everything I wanted at that moment. I even had a little bit of money put away that I could probably use to go to college with. My thoughts were interrupted by my pager going off for the third time. I looked at the screen, this time it was Antoinette. I then looked at Mr. Williams.

"I gotta go man," I said. Without realizing it at the time, I had made my decision. I then walked out of the classroom.

*****

"Wha' sup?"
"Where you at?"
"Up at the scho-"
"Man get the fuck up outta there dawg!"
"What? Why?"

191

"Detective Valentine and them is on they way up there lookin' for you!"

"For what?"

"Man, just get up outta there dawg. Meet me out south at Antoi-naw, forget that. Meet me in front of the McDonald's in Hypermart and I will tell you wha'sup. You gotta get up outta there though man, they comin' for you."

"A'ight, I'm on my way." I hung up the phone in a state of panic and made my way to the front of the school. As I turned into the main hall, I saw Detectives Valentine and Vermil, accompanied by two more uniformed police officers, standing at the reception desk. They were more than likely trying to find out exactly which class I was supposed to be in. I ducked back around the corner and flattened myself against the lockers. My heart was racing and butterflies had filled my stomach. Why were they looking for me? Did they kick in one of the tilts? I doubt it, that didn't make sense. What was it then? I peeked around the corner and saw the small entourage, accompanied by the receptionist, making their way towards the swimming pools. I crept up the hallway and slipped out of the front doors.

My Mustang was parked in an empty lot next to the Aamco filling station across the street from the school. The police had all of my doors wide open and they had broken into the trunk. What were they looking for? I ducked down behind one of the teacher's cars and then decided to make a run for it. I sprinted out of the parking lot undetected and headed for some houses across the street. I kept running, hurdling fence after fence, trespassing through people's backyards. Dogs were barking, old ladies were shouting at me; I kept running. About 15 minutes later, I reached the Church's Chicken restaurant located on 39th and Indiana, darting inside. Just as the door was hitting me where the good Lord split me, I observed a police car slowly riding past. That was a very close call. I approached the counter breathing heavily and ordered a 5-piece meal with something to drink.

"Man, what the fuck is goin' on?" I asked myself. I was staring out of the window attempting to collect my thoughts. I needed to get away from the area, but how? I could call my brother or Antoinette or someone, but in order to do that I would have to go back outside. I didn't want to do that. Then again, I didn't have a choice.

Leaving my food untouched on the table, I got up from my seat, placing my charcoal gray hood over my head, and went outside to the pay phone. I called Malik's cell phone and I got no answer. I tried K-Red, again no answer. I then called Antoinette and she agreed to come and pick me up. I hung up the phone and went back into the restaurant.

A while later, Antoinette pulled up in her black Honda Accord. I watched her as she got out of the car and walked inside. She then sat directly across from me.

"Wha'sup Atif, what's goin' on?"   Antoinette whispered to me, leaning across the table.

"I don't know!" I answered. "Everything cool out south?"

"Yeah. Matter of fact, I got somebody out there waitin' on me now."

"They gone have to hold tight for a minute." I answered. We sat in silence for a minute or two. "A, check this out. Won't you ride down to Aamco and get on the pay phone, right?" Antoinette nodded. "You can call whoever is waitin' on you and tell them to give you about another hour or so. While you down there, I want you to see wha'sup with my car and if the police are still up at the school."

"A'ight." Antoinette said, rising from her seat. "You gone be okay?"

"Yeah, girl. I'm cool." I answered. She nodded and walked out of the restaurant.

Antoinette, that was my girl there. She had shown me so much within such a small amount of time. She had my back and I had hers in return. There was more to our relationship than business. We were friends too, and we talked about *everything*. I was beginning to see her as the older sister I never had.

Antoinette returned and told me that the coast was clear as far as she could tell. She also said that my Mustang was still parked in the vacant lot. I started to have her take me to my car, but I changed my mind. What if they were waiting on me to do just that? I decided that I would have Darion or someone pick it up for me later. We then made our way out south to Hypermart.

Hypermart was a supersized version of Walmart. Within it was a grocery store, a car repair shop, a string of small concession stands as well as many other things. Hypermart was open 24 hours and usually packed during the day.

Antoinette and I pulled into the large parking lot. After finding a place to park, we headed inside. I led Antoinette to the small McDonald's located at the other end of the main lobby. We spotted Darion seated at one of the tables in front of the concession stand, finishing off some fries. He wore a pair of creased red jeans, a white Stafford T-shirt and a red Cincinnati Reds jacket with the matching ball cap. On his feet were a pair of white Nike tennis shoes. Darion stood up as we approached.

"Wha'sup nigga?" Darion greeted me, followed with a slight hug.

"Wha'sup?" I returned the greeting, sitting down.

"I was startin' to think that they caught you for a minute there." Darion commented. He then turned to Antoinette. "Wha'sup Toni?" Darion greeted Antoinette, kissing her on the cheek. The two of them took a seat also. I knew right then that whatever the situation was, it was a serious one. I knew this because Darion was serious. He didn't have anything slick to say to Antoinette when he greeted her like he usually did. Darion and I looked into each other's eyes for a moment, he then lowered his gaze and shook his head. "Man, you ready for this?"

"I guess; wha'sup?" I pretty much had figured out what was going on while Antoinette and I were on the way to Hypermart. I was hoping that I was wrong, but it was the only thing that made sense.   Malik and K-Red not answering their cell phones fit right into the scenario also.

I was feeling an enormous amount of anxiety at that moment. It was kind of like back when my mother died. I *knew* that she was dead when I tripped over her body in the foyer. Yet still, I was hoping until the very last moment, that possibly I was wrong.

"*Small Balls*, man. He done turned state's evidence on ya'll." My heart sank as reality hit me like a Mike Tyson right hook. Darion continued on. "I was ridin' through the hood with Malik and K-Red. We got pulled over in front of Maxine's and the po-po's drew down on us. They was *deep* too man, had the helicopter on a nigga and *all* that. They made us get out of the car and snatched us up. They took us down to the station and ended up lettin' me go. They said you, Malik and K-Red had been indicted for that shit, you know what I'm sayin'?" I nodded. "When I was on my way out, I overheard Vermil and them talkin'. They said that they was goin' to go up to the school and see if you was up there, so I hurried up and paged you."

"They didn't question you?"

"Yeah, but not for long. I kept tellin' them that I didn't know what they was talkin' about and I hadn't seen you in days, so I didn't know where you were at." I laid my head down on the table. Antoinette must have thought that I was crying or something because she placed her hand on my back, massaging me softly, telling me that everything was going to be alright in my ear. I lifted my head and looked at her. There I was, on the run not only for one count of first degree murder and four counts of attempted murder, but I was on the run for these horrendous acts which I *knew* I was good for; guilty as sin. And here she was telling *me* that everything was going to be alright? I had always enjoyed Antoinette's company before, but I felt irritated by her presence right then. I suppressed it though, realizing that she meant no harm and that I was more than likely about to take my frustrations out on her, which she didn't deserve. She had been more than a friend to me. "Wha'sup man, what you wanna do?" Darion asked me after a long period of silence.

"Man...." I started shaking my head. I couldn't believe that Small Balls was snitching like that. He was supposed to be the hommie. It was *his* fault that he got caught in the first place. Not only that, but my brother was keeping it real with him despite all of that by paying all of

195

that money for an attorney and he wanted to turn his back on us like that? Forget that, I was not going to let that happen. As long as I was still out on the streets, my brother and K-Red had a chance. Small Balls had to be dealt with or intimidated, but how could I get my hands on him? I didn't care what it took, I was going to get us all out of that situation. I would kidnap his parents, his daughter, the *mother* of his daughter, whatever. I would kill them all one by one if that was what it took for him to recant.

That was a defining moment for me in my life. At that point, I felt that I had lost whatever sense of conscience I had remaining in my system. I was contemplating taking the life of an innocent *child* because I didn't want for my brother, K-Red and myself to deal with the consequences of our actions. I had lost complete control of myself. I was turning into a person only concerned with the pursuit of fulfilling my own carnal desires.

I was turning into my brother.

"Antoinette, you gone have to run down north and pick that weed up on yo own." I said. She nodded.

"What you gone do?" Antoinette asked me as I handed her a set of apartment keys.

"I'mma catch the bus and meet up with you a lil' later." I answered.

"Well, I better leave now then because I gotta get to work here in a little bit." Antoinette then said, looking at her watch while rising from the table. "Be careful, okay?" Antoinette said, placing her hand on my shoulder. I nodded. "Bye D-Mack."

"I'll holla." Darion replied. Antoinette left us sitting there.

"You know this is gone have to be the last time you see me for a while, don't you?" I started after a few moments of silence. Darion looked at me. We had never went for more than a day or two without seeing each other for as long as I could remember. "The detectives might start followin' you around, hopin' that you will lead them to wherever I'm at. So, until I ta-"

196

"I know." Darion cut in, shaking his head. "That's a *bitch* ass nigga man, damn!" I nodded my head in agreement. "This is *fucked* up." Darion's pager went off. He checked the screen and looked up at me. "Teebaby."

"Wha'sup with her?"

"She pregnant, *that's* wha'sup with her."

"Pregnant?" Darion nodded. "Is she sure?"

"She took a home pregnancy test this mornin' and it came out positive."

"What ya'll gone do?"

"Shit, I don't know. I told her to get an abortion, but she wasn't tryin' to hear that."

"Abortion?"

"Yeah, man I ain't tryin' to have no kids right now."

"You should've thought about that when you went up in her without a rubber on." Yeah, just like I should have thought about going to prison before I pulled that trigger back in October. We sat in silence.

"You know I got your back, Atif. Whatever you wanna do, whatever it take to get ya'll up outta this man I'm gee for that. I know the rest of the hommies gone feel the same way. But at the same time, as much love we got for Malik *and* K-Red, don't nobody got more love for that nigga Malik than you do. Ain't nobody gone get his back for him like you will. So, as much......experience niggas like Trigga, Money Mike, Lay-Low, and all of the rest of them niggas might have in dealin' with shit like this, I think *you* need to take control of the situation man and do whatever gotta be done. You gotta be your brotha's keeper, you know?"

"Yeah, I know."

"I'mma slide by Teebaby's house, see what she want. She said she was gone tell her mama about her bein' pregnant and *knowin'* her mama, Teebaby probably gone be sittin' on the curb with her bags packed." Darion said, rising from his chair. I stood up also. "You know if you need somethin' man, all you gotta do is holla'. I nodded, hugging my best friend. "Want me to holla at Big Mama for you?"

"Yeah, just tell her that I'm cool and that I'mma stay on the low for a minute. Pick my car up too man and

197

put it up for me. It is parked across the street from the school." I handed him my car keys.

"A'ight."

"A'ight then, I'll holla'." Darion walked off without looking back.

He was right. I had to be my brother's keeper.

*****

MY BROTHER'S KEEPER

"Wha'sup bro'? How are you doin'?
Me? I'm holdin' mine,
I have a lot on my mind
so I thought I'd drop you some lines.
I'm doin' bad at this point in time,
I can't seem to stay sober.
I'm ready to get it over,
tired of lookin' over my shoulder.
Did you know they called Big Mama up and told her:
I'm a dead man walkin'?
I ain't buyin' that ole bullshit that they sold her,
fuck what they talkin'!
I hear that y'all are in there representin', you know it's all
good.
I bet them niggas get to flinchin' when you mention *our*
hood.
-On the news- they say that I am comin' your way:
are they too blind to see?
Multiple life sentences without parole?
That is too much *time* for me!
I'm sorry bro, I couldn't intimidate that witness like you
expected.
Plus, I hear the mutha'fuckin' pigs got him protected.
I know that ya'll are probably feelin' neglected,
just hold on tight.
Because no matter what happens to us,
we are brothas for *life*."
-*Soody Mak*

10

June 6, 1993.

On this day a year ago my mother was slain and there I was with a flathead screwdriver attempting to pick to lock on a small basement window discreetly without shattering the glass.

I did it.

Slowly I began to slide the window open. I then looked around to see if anyone had seen me, shedding a black book bag I wore containing duct tape and women's stockings, making my way through the window.

What was I thinking? Was I really going to go through with it? Yes! I *had* to. It was crazy, but at that time in my mind it was even more ludicrous for me to surrender without even trying to force Small Balls into not testifying. Grabbing my book bag while gripping a 9mm in my other hand, I made my way through the house.

It was empty.

Looking around for a good hiding place, one where I could possibly spend a long period of time in if necessary, I passed by some photographs sitting on top of the fireplace. At that moment the telephone rang and I paused in my tracks, startled. I stood still for a minute until the phone stopped ringing. I started to keep on walking but the pictures caught my eye.

There was a photo of an older couple, more than likely Tawanna's parents. Next to it was another photograph of Small Balls, Tawanna and their then five year-old daughter Tayshawnna. It was a beautiful picture. Staring at it brought on second thoughts of my reasons for being where I was. Those thoughts were suppressed and replaced by visions of Malik sitting in a jail cell. My brother needed me, so I continued on. I knew the house pretty well, I had been there before on countless occasions.

I had been on the run for almost two months by then.   I was living with Smack Man and Persistence out south for the most part, on the low. My face was all over the news. Earlier that week I had made it to the number two slot on the Kansas City's Most Wanted list.   I was stressed out; I hadn't seen my grandmother and didn't talk to her often. Whenever I did she pleaded with me to turn myself in because she knew like I did that the police would probably kill me on sight, telling the public that I reached for some kind of weapon or something. The media already had colored me bad, labeling me armed and dangerous. I hated to worry Big Mama, but there was no way I was going to just give up like that. I knew that once I did, it was all over with.

I *had* to try.

Walking down the hallway I noticed a small closet Tawanna used to store their winter coats in. I opened it up and peered inside.   Perfect. I could see no reason why Tawanna or Tayshawnna would be interested in the closet whenever they made it home. I stepped inside and pulled the door closed behind me, engulfing myself in darkness. I pulled out my ski mask and put it on, gripping my pistol. All I had to do now was wait.

*****

"Man fuck that shit man, I ain't been out for no hour!" Small Balls said to the guard, hanging up the phone. He had been trying to call Tawanna but got no answer. Little did he know that I was the only soul in their house, harboring some seriously ill ulterior motives.   "Why you lockin' me down so early dawg?"

"You can lock down now so that you can be escorted to medical here in a few minutes, *or* you can refuse to go to your cell and get restrained and shackled to your bunk. Your choice Reynolds, we wouldn't mind the exercise at all." Sergeant Owens said over the speaker.

Small Balls, having been shackled to his bunk the week before for six hours, did not like the thought of experiencing that again so he willfully complied.

Twenty-five minutes later, Small Balls' cell door slid open. He stepped out into the small module and made his way out of the sliding doors into the hallway. Sergeant Owens escorted him to the elevator.

"Toni, I need a favor. Will you please escort Reynolds down to medical? I need to go and count the dinner trays." Sergeant Owens said to Antoinette when the elevator doors opened, revealing her standing inside. Smalls Balls stepped into the elevator.

"Yeah Sarge, I got yo back."

"I need for you to pass out the trays also when you return."

"A'ight."

"Wha'sup beautiful?" Small Balls greeted Antoinette as soon as they were alone.

Small Balls was skeptical and suspicious upon first seeing Antoinette after he turned state's evidence on us. Slowly but surely she was able to convince him that she no longer was affiliated with us. She told him that me and Darion had robbed her and looted her house.

Antoinette also pretended to be attracted to Small Balls. With him being so lonely and vulnerable it was not difficult for her to do so at all. She would bring him food from the outside and a little bit of weed here and there to soften him up. She also requested to be transferred to the sixth floor, which was where the disciplinary segregation module was located along with the protective custody module, allowing Small Balls to believe that she had done so in order to be close to him.

He was just as wrong as he was right.

"Hey Smalls, wha'sup?" Antoinette answered, smiling at him. She then pushed one of the buttons on the elevator panel. He crept up behind her and wrapped his arms around her waist, grinding his mid-section against her buttocks.

"You got somethin' for me?"

"No, I was runnin' late today." Small Balls began to kiss her neck. She was repulsed by the sensation of his lips touching her and the erection she felt through his jumpsuit, but she withstood it for the home team. "Stop boy, you see that camera up there? You gone get me hot."

"Hot as in your superiors gone start askin' questions hot, or *hot* hot?" Small Balls asked, releasing her and backing up against the rear elevator wall. Antoinette cut her eyes at him with a smirk on her face.

"*Both.*"

*****

Someone was home.

I had been cooped up in that hot closet for at least three hours by then. Now that the time was approaching for me to act, I was *really* beginning to have second thoughts. I heard the front door open and Tayshawnna running inside, asking her mother if she could have some ice cream. Something was up though because I could have sworn that I heard a male voice. I wasn't tripping, there was a man with them. Who could that be? I was expecting for the two to be alone. This threw me for a loop. I had not made plans for anyone outside of Tawanna and her child.

I was sweating profusely. Who was he? A family member? I calmed myself down by commanding patience. I would simply sit tight and try to figure things out. Meanwhile, Tayshawnna was sent pouting to her room as Tawanna and the mystery man made their way to Tawanna's bedroom, walking right past me.

Another couple of hours passed; it was getting late. Tayshawnna had long since been put to bed and I caught myself nodding on and off. The mystery man was *still* there. Whatever questions I still had concerning his relationship to Tawanna were answered by the soft moans I heard through the back wall of the closet which was adjacent to her bedroom. They were having *sex*! I was wide awoke then. I pressed my ear up to the wall and was able to hear everything. He was hitting it alright, asking her questions while doing so and everything. Tawanna was answering them too with her freaky self. I couldn't identify who he was because he was talking quietly. I could have swore that I knew the voice, but it couldn't be the person I was thinking of, could it? Nah. I listened on, straining to identify his voice *if* he was from the hood, whoever he was.

The phone rang.

"Wait a minute, stop. Stop." I heard Tawanna say. "Hello?" She paused for a while. "Shhhh! It's Small Balls!" I heard her whisper. More silence ensued. "Hi daddy." Her voice was different now, she was faking like she was sleep. "Layin' here about to go to   sleep……….You know it's past her bedtime, she is sleep……..What you doin' out of yo cell so late?………"

Tawanna was out of control! She was laid up with some other man while the father of her child was incarcerated. Not only that, but she was talking to him on the phone like she was doing nothing wrong. *Scandalous*! I learned right then that women could be nickel slick. Tawanna told whoever she was with that Small Balls was on the phone like whoever he was knew of him. I took that into account and surmised that he was someone from the hood.

I listened on.

"Boy I ain't finna be lookin' all over my shoulder. I ain't worried about nobody doin' nothin' to me or my baby." Tawanna said. I guess she underestimated the severity of the situation. She was taking for granted how much love I had for my brother and how I was willing to do whatever it took to get him out of jail. Hearing her utter those words in such a nonchalant and dismissive manner made me want to burst out of the closet and murder everyone in the house in front of her just to see the look on her face. Before I finished off I would ask her, *Are you worried yet*?

"Daddy I'm tired, I gotta get up early in the mornin'. Will you call me back tomorrow so that I can get some sleep?…………Okay………I love you………Bye bye." I heard her hang up the phone. The man she was with said something that I couldn't make out. "Fuck that nigga, shit. He ain't finna get out no time soon. What I'm supposed to do; *wait* on him? He should of thought about all that before he did what he did." Aw man, she was *too* scandalous. I heard the man chuckle. That laugh, I *knew* that laugh. What was going on? I listened in as the two went back to having sex.

An hour or so later I no longer heard any voices from Tawanna's bedroom. I assumed that they were asleep. That was cool, but she and her daughter were still not alone and I was not 100% *sure* of the mystery man's identity. Telling myself that it was now or never, I crept silently out of the closet and made my way across the short distance to her bedroom with my gun drawn. My feet had fallen asleep but I walked it off. The floor boards creaked underneath me but still I pushed on. Opening her bedroom door slowly, I crept into the bedroom. My plan was to install fear into the man she was with first since he was the one I was more likely to have problems with. I planned to leave him tied up and duct taped behind though, I didn't want to take him with me. Dead or alive? I had not decided yet. I would leave that up to him and how difficult he wanted to be.

As I approached the bed, I saw Tawanna on her right side. I walked around silently to the other side of the bed. Even though I had already figured that I knew the sound of this individual's laugh, I was still taken aback by what I saw. It was Darion laying there asleep by her side. It had been him the whole time. What was he *doing* there? Well, I clearly heard what he was doing there, but what was he *up* to? Was this his way of keeping tabs on Small Balls? Maybe so. I decided to give my hommie the benefit of the doubt. I hadn't seen him since that day at Hypermart, so I didn't know what he had been up to. Then again, maybe this was his little way of getting back at Small Balls. Darion was not really a killer, so I didn't too much expect for him to do what I was plotting myself, so I wasn't mad at him. Whatever he was doing there though was at the same time interfering with my plans. Him and K-Red was probably working on a plan of action of their own.

206

I improvised. I told myself that I would kidnap Tayshawnna alone, leaving a note behind warning Tawanna of contacting the authorities.   I would even make Tayshawnna write the note herself, if she could. It would take a while but at least the police wouldn't be able to trace it back to me if Tawanna did contact them anyway. I made my way out of the room and headed down the hallway. I had to hurry because I knew Darion was not into spending the night over no female's house. I didn't want him or anyone to know what I was up to. He usually didn't stay long after he had gotten what he came for. I slipped into Tayshawnna's small bedroom as she was asleep in her bed. She was laying on her back just as peaceful as could be. As I approached her bed, I thought I heard a noise and turned around. When I turned back around I saw Tayshawnna's little eyes staring up at me in the darkness.   I was paralyzed, I couldn't move. I stared back down at her. We did this for at least a full minute, one of the longest minutes I had ever experienced in my life.

What was I thinking of? Look at her, she was so cute and innocent. She had absolutely nothing to do with what was going on.   Why should she have to suffer anymore than she already had with her father's incarceration? What surprised me the most was that she didn't look afraid despite my wearing a ski mask. This testified to the fact that Tawanna was allowing too many strange men around her daughter. I can't explain what I saw in little Tayshawnna's eyes but whatever it was, there was no way I was going to do anything to that sweet little girl. I know how much I have been trying to describe my love for Malik and how I would do whatever it took to get him out of prison, but right then I found that there was something that I did not have the heart to do. I thought that I had lost all my conscience; I thought that I was hopeless and capable of doing anything. Well, I wasn't. And that in itself was a positive sign for me. I wasn't *all* of the way gone into the deep end just yet.

I *wasn't* my brother.

I sat down next to Tayshawnna on her bed and held my index finger up to my lips, signaling for her to be quiet. She didn't make a sound. I then reached down and cleared a stray braid from her forehead. God, what was I thinking? How could I have entertained such thoughts? I placed my hands together and laid my head against them, signaling for her to go back to sleep. She nodded and closed her eyes, laying on her side with her back towards me.

"That's a good girl." I said quietly, rubbing her small little back as she went back to sleep. I was either going to have to find another way to get us all out of this situation or just give up and turn myself in. There was absolutely no way that Tayshawnna was going to be done any bodily harm by me or anyone for that matter, not even threatened with it. I would deal with Small Balls personally somehow or not at all.

*****

"Why you just now tellin' me about this?" I asked Antoinette. A day had passed and we were at a hotel room located in Grandview. I had her rent the room, way in the back, over three days before. I was in the process of writing a letter to Malik when she knocked on the room door.

"Because I didn't want to get yo hopes up for nothin'." Antoinette answered, counting money she had separated in stacks of $500 across the bed. I was sitting at a small desk rolling up a joint. "Plus, I thought I would tell you now so that you wouldn't do nothin' else crazy like you was about to do yesterday."

Antoinette had just finished telling me about how she had been working on the sixth floor lately in the county jail, which was where Small Balls was at, and how she had been able to get close to him and earn his trust. He had been trying to justify his actions with lies of how *we* were the ones who got him caught in the first place. He also fabricated some nonsense about how one of us had supposedly made a statement against him which was a lie because *none* of us had ever been arrested or formally

208

questioned until *after* he was already incarcerated for over six months! Hearing these false accusations *infuriated* me. Not only was Small Balls snitching, but he was also trying to slander our names.

"Wha'sup Toni? What you up to?" I asked Antoinette, turning around to look at her.

"I think I gotta idea Atif. I mean, I think we might be able to get Malik and K-Red up outta there." My interest was piqued. I knew that she worked down at the county jail and all, I just never entertained the thought of getting her involved in such a thing.

"Like how?" After failing with being able to bring myself to kidnap and possibly murder Tawanna and Tayshawnna the night before, I was beginning to feel like there was nothing I could do. I was even in the process of writing to Malik and telling him so. I hate to say this, but I know that if the roads were reversed, Malik would have been more than capable of killing both Tawanna and Tayshawnna.

"They got Small Balls in the protective custody unit and I be passing out the dinner trays. Now, if we could get our hands on some type of top notch binary poison or somethin' that I could slip him in his food, then......" Antoinette let me finish the sentence in my own mind.

It was a good idea.

"What about *you* though? Ain't they gone be a lil' bit supicious about him comin' up poisoned like that? They gone come straight for you!" I cared about Antoinette and as much as I wanted out of those circumstances, I was not willing to leave her hanging out to dry like that.

"That's why I said *top notch* poison, somethin' that wouldn't show up durin' an autopsy."

"Where the hell could we get some stuff like tha....." I cut myself off mid-sentence. *Smack Man*. If I knew anyone who could get their hands on something like that it was him. Antoinette and I stared at each other for a moment in silence. "You willin' to do that?" I asked Antoinette. She tilted her head and shrugged her shoulders.

209

"I don't like seein' you all stressed out and shit like this, Atif. I want it to go back to the way things were when we was gettin' money *together*, you know what I'm sayin'? I miss that. Before you came into my life, I was strugglin' with my bills, depressed and lonely. We started kickin' it and I started *livin'* again. Smilin' and laughin', getting money. I wasn't trippin' off of Rob no more or none of that. And now that this shit been goin' on, lately I been feelin' myself slippin' back into that state of loneliness and depression. I don't wanna go back to that Atif." She touched me with that one. I didn't realize how she felt.

"Have you ever even *thought* about killin' somebody girl?" She shook her head no. "It ain't somethin' that you gone just be able to forget about. And the dreams, man they be comin' back to you in yo dreams." Antoinette seemed to be deep in thought.

"You know, I thought about killin' my ex-husband now that I think about it. Him and that white bitch he was cheatin' on me with."

"Aw yeah?"

"*Hell* yeah! I didn't think I could bring myself to do it though. I guess I was wrong about myself. After we put this down, maybe I will look both of their asses up next." We both laughed at that. "That lil nigga really think that I'm gone give him some of this pussy too."

"Good, let him keep on thinking that."

*****

"I got three and a possible." Malik said. He was in E-module on the fourth floor of the Jackson County Detention Center playing a game of spades with three other prisoners.

"Can you get four?" a man who was on Malik's team from 33rd street by the name of Little John asked him.

"Naw blood, I doubt it. It's a weak possible."

"Damn nigga, might as well just show him yo hand. Y'all board talkin' like a mutha'fucka'." One of their opponents spoke up.

"Aw yeah? Give us *ten* then nigga. How you like them apples?" Little John said. He then cocked his hand back and smacked an ace of spade on the table surface, causing the other prisoners in the module to look their way. The card hitting the table sounded like someone getting slapped. At that moment a small square slot so called the "chuck hole" located in the center of a panel at the front area of the module, used for the purpose of passing out food, medicine, clean laundry, canteen and mail to the prisoners, swung open. The majority of the prisoners flocked to the chuck hole.

"Where you goin' nigga?" Malik asked one of their opponents as he laid his cards face down on the table and headed for the chuck hole.

"Mail call!"

"These niggas fucks me up." Little John commented, watching the other prisoners shuffle towards the chuck hole. "Half these niggas *know* damn well ain't nobody even thinkin' about writin' they funny lookin' asses, but they be the *first* ones up at the chuck hole when mail come." Malik laughed, turning towards the small television.

"Malik! You got some mail dawg." One of the prisoners said. Malik got up and made his way through the crowd to the chuck hole. The guard handed him three letters and Malik turned and walked away, heading for his cell on the top walk.

"Wha'sup man, you through?" Little John asked Malik as he walked passed the card table. Malik nodded, walking up the stairs. "Nigga get some mail and now he don't wanna be bothered with us."

"One of these is from Atif nigga, *fuck* that card game." Malik responded. His hearing was always keen.

Malik hadn't heard from me since him and K-Red were apprehended. I sent him and K-Red money on a weekly basis and would have Antoinette take them some weed when she could, but it was my first time writing to him. A couple of days had passed since that night at Days

211

Inn with Antoinette. I had her mail the letter to him for me anyway even though things were not looking hopeless as they were when I had written the words I did before she told me about her plan.

Malik walked into his cell and sat on his bunk. The other two letters were from Kesha, who was currently beginning a 7 year sentence in the Vandalia women's penitentiary, and the other from his lawyer. He took my letter anxiously from the stack and laid the other two on his desk.

Malik read my letter over and over again. He was happy to hear from me but he was concerned about me at the same time. He knew where I was staying and to prevent bringing any heat my way he refused to call over to Smack Man's house. After finishing the other two letters, Malik stood up on his bunk and looked out of his cell window onto the city streets below, lost in thought. Little John appeared at Malik's cell door.

"Wha'sup with lil' Atif man, he cool?" Little John asked, removing his sandals and climbing up onto the bunk, joining Malik at the window.

"Yeah, he cool. Sound like he might be gettin' himself a lil in over his head by tryin' to get me and K up outta here, you know what I'm sayin'?"

"Yeah. I like that lil' nigga man, he a *rider*." Malik nodded. They sat in silence for a while, watching people go in and out of the state building downtown. "I'mma leave you to your thoughts blood, holla' at you later or somethin'." Little John said, climbing down and slipping on his sandals. Malik nodded and went back into his zone.

*****

"Kick off yo shoes... and relax yo feet. Party on down to the Xscape beat! Just kick it! *Juuuuuuust kiiiiiick iiit! Juuuuuuust kiiiiiick iiit!*" Small Balls crooned aloud, singing along with the recently released hit single by Xscape. He too was standing up in his bunk, looking out of the window with his headphones on, ironically directly two

212

floors above Malik. "I want you to...kick off yoursho-" Small Balls was interrupted by his cell light flicking on and off. He turned around, removing the headphones from his head.

"Boy, you want this food or not?" Antoinette asked him, standing in his cell doorway with a cart full of trays. Small Balls walked over to her. "Soundin' like a sick dog."

"What is it?"

"Beef stew."

"Naw, I ain't fuckin' with that shit." Antoinette's heart sank.

"I'm pullin' a double shift tonight so I'm gone be up here by myself after one in the mornin'." Antoinette said quietly, smiling at Small Balls, thinking quickly.

"Aw yeah?" Antoinette nodded, handing him a tray as if she did not hear his refusal. "You gone come see me?" Antoinette looked around to see if she could be seen. She then took a hold of Small Balls by the chin and licked his lips seductively, finishing off with a light peck.

"Eat your food, you gone need your energy." Antoinette said. Small Balls smiled and took the tray excitedly from her grasp as she shut his cell door. He then turned the tray into a happy plate, eating everything on it.

*****

"This is Ann Peterson reporting live on the scene in front of the Jackson County Detention Center located at 1300 Cherry Street in downtown Kansas City Missouri. Early this morning, prisoner Steven Reynolds was found dead lying on his bed......"

"*Ha Ha!* You *bitch ass nigga! Fuck* you *nigga!*" K-Red exclaimed, jumping from his seat and pointing at the television screen as a mug shot of Small Balls appeared on it. He was down the hall from Malik in C-module watching the noon edition of the news. People were emerging from their cells and gathering in front of the television. "We *out* this mutha fucka! *Hell* yeah!" K-Red exclaimed. He then grabbed his testicles and began to sway from side to side.

213

"RATHEADS GET NOTHIN' BUT CHEESE Y'ALL!" he chanted loudly, quoting lyrics from an E-40 song.

"THE NIGGA THAT TALKED, HE'S A *BITCH!*" the other prisoners completed the bar in unison, swaying back and forth along with him. K-Red jumped up on a table and led the module in the chant again.

"RATHEADS GET NOTHIN' BUT CHEESE Y'ALL!"

"THE NIGGA THAT TALKED, HE'S A *BITCH!*" This time even the white boys joined in.

"RATHEADS GET NOTHIN' BUT CHEESE Y'ALL!"

"THE NIGGA THAT TALKED, HE'S A *BITCH!*"

*****

"....sometime around four-thirty this morning. Investigators are very suspicious of his untimely death but as of yet have been unable to find traces of any toxins within his system that they believe may have been responsible for his apparent cardiac arrest.

"Mr. Reynolds was arrested for the drive-by shooting of some Rolling 60's Crips late last year and was a vital material witness against the others allegedly involved in that shooting. Once again..." I turned the volume down on the big screen. Me and Persistence looked at each other.

"Is that Small Balls they are talking about?" Persistence asked me. I nodded, smiling. "So they are going to have to dismiss the case then aren't they? I mean his statement is all that they have, right?" I nodded again, smiling even harder. Persistence screamed and we both jumped up from our seats, hugging each other.

Smack man came into the room while we were celebrating, followed by a Caucasian man wearing an expensive suit.

"Atif, this is my lawyer Gary Jaco."

"Wha'sup?" I greeted him, smiling brightly and breathing heavily from jumping around the room with Persistence.

214

"Nice to meet you Atif." Gary Jaco said, shaking my hand firmly.

"I got a surprise for you." Smack Man said to me. At that moment Big Mama entered the room. I lit up like a Christmas tree.

"*Big Mama!*" I yelled, running over to her and hugging her tightly. I had not seen her in two months and I missed her dearly.

"Hey baby, I was so worried about you!"

"Come on y'all, lets ride." Smack Man said to us. We all got into his Mercedes Benz and rode downtown to the police headquarters. I then found myself in a small room with Detectives Valentine and Vermil. I was not alone. Smack Man stayed in the car, so I was accompanied by Mr. Jaco and Big Mama. The detectives were seething with anger. It was written all over their faces.

"No use in playing any games here, Atif. Where were you on the night of October 30, 1992?" Detective Vermil asked me. I looked at Big Mama and then at Gary Jaco, the latter nodded his head.

"On the advice of counsel I wish to exercise my right to remain silent."

*****

215

HARDHEADED DECISIONS

"Who's gonna save *me*?
I take my pistol off safety when I roll.
Jealous niggas be out to break me; why they hatin' me?
I don't know —so here we go-
Hardheaded decisions
puts my pedal down to the flo'.
I don't really wanna be in this situation,
Knowin' that I just might go —but I *still* roll-"
                    -*Tazz Mania Devil*

"Ridin' down the filthy route
With my Glock clocked back.
Ready for the burnin' bullet
if I drop like that.
-If I don't pop like that-
I get caught slippin.'
Man, drivin' down this road
Is like crashin' while you dippin'."
                    -*Tazz Mania Devil*

11

Everything was everything.

Malik and K-Red were out of jail, on probation for the incident at the tilt, but free nonetheless. What me and Antoinette had done initiated her into the clique and put me up on a pedestal. I loved every minute of it. When people passed me in traffic they went out of their way to acknowledge me. Our clientele quadrupled and money was coming in *unceasingly*. And the women? One night stands were almost an everyday occurrence. I really enjoyed my time in the spotlight; too bad it was short lived.

It was the second of August, my fifteenth birthday. Smack Man was barbequing and we all were invited. Me, Darion, Patience, and Teebaby were all riding through the city streets in Darion's Blazer. It was a beautiful day out. Teebaby sat in the passenger seat up front with Darion, arguing with him because she wanted to listen to some slow music instead of the rap that was currently in the tape deck. Darion hated for people to mess with his tape deck.

"So how does it feel to be fifteen, birthday boy?" Patience asked me during the small intermission.

"I don't know, it feel like any other day to me."

Actually that was not the truth. I had this strange feeling that day, one that I could not describe. It had nothing to do with my birthday. I guess the closest thing to it would be the feeling of déjà vu, but it wasn't that. Déjà vu, roughly defined is a feeling (more like an illusion) of having already experienced something actually being experienced for the first time. That does not define the feeling I woke up with that day. It was more like I was watching the events of that day from outside of my own body. Not only that, but everything and everyone seemed to be moving in slow motion but *my* perception was still operating at a normal pace. I was not high, I stopped smoking so much weed once Malik and K-Red were released, so that feeling had nothing to do with the effects of drugs. Was it a premonition? In a way, but somehow I *knew* that I was not about to die. What I did not know

217

though was that my whole life was about to change drastically.

"Who is that?" I asked Patience. Her pager went off and she was checking the screen to see who it was.

"It's my sister. Darion let me use your phone." Patience said, reaching for the car phone Darion kept between the two front seats.

"Whoa, you crossin' my boundaries girl, you crossin' my boundaries!" Darion said, reaching back and confiscating the phone from her hand. "See, looky there. It's a *pay* phone right up on the corner and you can call whoever you want and talk for as long as you want and it will only cost you a quarter instead of them chargin' *me* for every single minute."

"Ooooooh, boy you are so *cheap* it's *pitiful*. You would rather make her stand outside than use your phone?" Teebaby asked Darion.

"Here we go Patience, Teebaby ain't talkin' about nothin'." Darion said, pulling up to a pay phone on the corner of 35th and Prospect.

"I swear to *God* it embarrasses me to be with you sometimes." Patience slid out of the Blazer and got on the pay phone. I remember a time when she would be too frightened to stand out on the corner of 35th and Prospect. She had grown more comfortable with me and my people over the past year, realizing that we were regular humans like everyone else, in a sense. Darion pulled out a joint and fired it up. "Don't smoke that around me while I'm pregnant boy, what's wrong with you?"

"Get out then, somethin' wrong with yo door or somethin'?"

"I don't *feel* like gettin' out, *you* get out!"

"It's my car, *you* get out."

"D-Mack, smoke it outside man." I interjected. It used to amuse me to witness the two go at it but sometimes things only remain funny for so long, after that those same things would begin to annoy you.

"Man why you be sidin' with her all the time like that dawg?" Darion asked me, turning around in his seat.

"I ain't sidin' with nobody. She got your baby in her stomach nigga, you act like that don't mean nothin' to you." Darion and I were together all the time and it seemed to me that he would treat females that he didn't even know better than he did the future mother of his child. Darion got out of the Blazer, slamming the door. I leaned up against the back of Teebaby's seat, wrapping my arms around the headrest. "You cool?"

"Yeah, Atif, I'm cool." Teebaby said, wiping a tear from her face. "That nigga just be getting on my damn nerves. What is *wrong* with him? He treat me like he don't even *like* me; like I am a burden on him or somethin'. I know he be fuckin' around on me too."

"He do care about you, and between me and you he always be talkin' about how he can't wait for you to have that baby." I said in consolation. I wasn't going to touch that subject of his infidelities. We both were guilty of that so I had no right to speak on it. I was more discreet though. Teebaby was always catching Darion with females numbers, etc. All that Patience had on me were rumors.

"Do he for real?" Teebaby asked, turning sideways in her seat. We both looked at Darion who looked back at us and shook his head.

"Yeah, he do. You have to understand that D-Mack ain't used to showin' stuff like that towards a female. You know we be thinkin' it's somethin' wrong with that in the hood."

"Yeah, I know. Y'all are crazy. Where do y'all be gettin' that crap from?"

"I don't know." At that moment Patience hung up the pay phone and got back into the Blazer.

"What's up girl, you in here pushing up on my man?" Patience asked Teebaby, smiling.

"Girl please." Teebaby responded, reaching for the tape deck. She removed the Deep Cover soundtrack and replaced it with a Rude Boys tape. "Ooooh girl, you remember this?" Teebaby asked Patience, turning up the volume as a song entitled *Written All Over Your Face* drifted from the Phoenix Gold system. I was surprised that Darion

did not go off with hearing the change of music.   He
seemed to be off in his own world when I looked out at him.
Meanwhile, Patience and Teebaby were singing along with
the music.

"What did Persistence say?"   I asked Patience,
talking over the music.

"What?"

"Teebaby, turn it down some." Teebaby complied.
"I said, what was Persistence talkin' about?"

"Oh she wants us to pick up some chicken and
some more lighter fluid for the grill on the way out there."

"Let me out." Patience moved her legs and I made
my way out of the Blazer. I walked over to where Darion
was finishing off his joint. "Wha'sup man? I know you ain't
standin' out here with no attitude, is you?"

"Man, I ain't trippin' on that girl." Darion answered,
looking towards the Blazer. "This lil splif got me high as a
*mutha'*fucka' though, I know that much."

"Lets walk."

We made our way across the street to the Piggly
Wiggly grocery store.   The parking lot was full of cars
presumably belonging to Sunday shoppers restocking their
refrigerators for the week.

"You think that baby in Teebaby's stomach don't
mean nothin' to me?" Darion asked me, opening one of the
doors to the store. We walked inside.

"Naw, I *know* that baby mean somethin' to you.
You just be *actin'* like it don't."

"Man.....that girl be *startin'* stuff! She be seemin' all
innocent around y'all, but she be doin' or sayin' lil shit on
purpose because she *know* it fuck with me." We turned
down one of the aisles and made our way to the back of the
store. "What you lookin' for?"

"Some chicken and some lighter fluid."

After retrieving the items we were looking for, we
made our way back up to the front of the store where the
cashiers were located.   Darion was in the process of
grabbing a couple of Nestle Crunch candy bars when
Tawanna appeared out of nowhere and pushed me in the

220

back of my head. I turned around instinctively, stopping
myself from throwing the right cross I had cocked and ready
when I saw that it was her.

"Come on! I ain't scared of you pussies!" Tawanna
said, putting her dukes up. She had amped herself up
alright.

"Girl you put your hands on me again and I'mma
fuck you up." I threatened. An older gentleman appeared
amongst us resembling the man I saw in one of the
photographs sitting on her fireplace back in June. He was
holding Tayshawnna's little hand.

"Girl, what is wrong with you?" he asked his
daughter. Tawanna screamed and lunged at me, her father
held her back with his right arm. I swear if she would have
made it about one more foot I would have knocked her out
cold.

"Let me go! Let me go!" Tawanna yelled, struggling
to free herself. Her father was a powerful old man.
Tayshawnna began to cry. "They killed Steve!" Her father
looked at us.

"I wasn't even *in* the county when that happened
girl, what you talkin' about?" I asked in response to his
glare.

"So *what!* I *know* you had somethin' to do with it!"
A security guard pulled up on the scene.

"Oh no, we can't have this up in here. Y'all two",
the security guard said to me and Darion, "come with me.
Y'all gotta get up outta here."

"Man we ain't did nothin' *she* the one trippin'."
Darion said. The security guard reached for Darion's arm.
"Don't *touch* me man." Darion warned.

"Come on man, let's go." I said, dropping the
chicken and the lighter fluid and turning to leave.

"Punk ass bitch. You wasn't trippin on Small Balls
when I was all off in them *guts*, was you?" Darion taunted,
laughing. Tawanna went wild. We ignored her idle threats
and walked out of the store.

It didn't feel good knowing that I played a part in
the death of little Tayshawnna's father. I did feel a little

remorseful about that because of her. I knew what it felt
like to grow up without having a father around. I
rationalized with myself saying that it was better him than
us, or better yet, better him than Tawanna and
Tayshawnna.

"What, was you too *cheap* to pay for the chicken
and stuff too?" Teebaby asked Darion as we got in the
Blazer. Darion looked up at me in the rearview mirror and I
shook my head, indicating for him not to feed. He didn't.
Darion simply pushed the eject button on his tape deck,
removed the Rude Boys tape and replaced it this time with
Dr. Dre's *The Chronic*. He then started the Blazer's engine
and made his way onto Prospect heading south.

"What happened Atif? Where is the chicken and
lighter fluid?" Patience asked me.

"We will get it from somewhere else." Patience
looked up at me. She could feel it whenever I was
withholding something from her. She also knew that
whatever it was was more than likely something she didn't
want to know about anyway so she laid her head on my
shoulder without asking anymore questions.

*****

"Wha'sup Atif, you ain't ridin?" K-Red asked me.
The barbeque had wound down and mostly everyone who
was in attendance had already left. Smack Man,
Persistence, K-Red, Antoinette, Patience, myself, Malik and
the woman he was with for the night were the only ones
remaining. They all were about to go out somewhere.

"No Kenyatta, Atif is staying here with *me.*"
Patience answered for me, wrapping her arms around my
waist from behind with a smile.

"Damn, like that? My bad." K-Red said, raising his
hands in resignation. "A'ight then, I will holla." K-Red said
to us, walking out of the front doors followed by Antoinette.

"Bye. Y'all be good.   Happy birthday Atif."
Antoinette said as she trailed K-Red. Malik walked up to me

222

and hit me hard in the chest. The blow caught me by
surprise, knocking the wind out of me.

"Happy birthday nigga. I will get the other fourteen
in tomorrow." Malik said to me, escorting his date out of
the front doors.

"Y'all clean all this stuff up for us before we make it
back since y'all ain't fuckin' with us tonight." Smack Man
said to us. We nodded our heads in agreement. "Don't be
fuc-"

"Come *on*, lets go." Persistence cut him off, pulling
him outside. We locked the doors behind everyone and
went to work.

Hours later I was in the den lounging on the couch
in front of the big screen, wearing some red Nike shorts and
house slippers. I was feeling good. I had just taken a
shower not too long before, I was full and relaxed. I heard
Patience coming down the stairs and when she entered the
den she instantly commanded my attention.

She paused in the doorway, standing there with
nothing on but a towel wrapped around her body and her
long black hair, still damp and curly from the bath she took,
was down. She then dimmed the den lights and walked
slowly over to me, straddling my lap. She took the remote
control from my hand and turned off the big screen. We
stared at each other for a moment.

"You know, we have been together all day,"
Patience started, wrapping her arms around my neck.
"Aren't you curious as to what *I* may have gotten you for
your birthday?"

"I thought your presence was a present within
itself." Patience smiled. "Well, I got you something
anyway." Patience reached into the top portion of the towel
and pulled out a Lifestyles contraceptive. My eyes widened
in surprise. Had that time really come?

"You been carryin' that thing around all day?"
Patience nodded. I reached for the condom.

"Wait a minute, waaaiiit a minute! Down boy,
dooowwwn boy!" Patience said, denying me access to the
condom. "Do you remember the conversation we had the

last time you walked me to my class after having lunch with
me? You know, the day you found out the police were
looking for you?"

"Yeah, I remember."

"Did you mean it?"

I thought for a moment. Was I really serious when
I told her that? I mean *no* more sex with all of the females
who were throwing themselves at me? Darion would drive
me until I could be driven no more, so would the rest of the
hommies. But you know what? Deep down, I really wanted
to be with Patience and Patience alone. She was all I
needed. The rest of those girls, their only purpose really
was to help me maintain my status in the hood. I thought
that I was *supposed* to be with those women. It all came
with that way of life. I must have been thinking for a little
too long because Patience started to get up from my lap.

"Wait, wait." I said, grabbing her. She sat back
down, the smile had disappeared from her face. "I meant it
then and I mean it *now.*"

"Why did it take you so long to answer?"

"It wasn't because of what you thinkin', I was just
not expectin' nothin' like this tonight."

"Well, it wouldn't have been a surprise if I would
have told you, now would it?" I shook my head,
remembering me saying those same words to her when we
went to Cool Crest for her birthday last year. "You know,
you and Malik sure do have an awful strange way of
showing your love for each other." Patience said, rubbing
my chest where Malik had bruised me with his blow. "It
used to bother me when I would tell you that I love you and
not hear you say the same in response. But after watching
how you and your brother act towards each other when you
guys are together, I started to understand why that was. It
is not that you don't love me like I do you, it is just that
maybe you are uncomfortable with saying those three
simple words. Maybe Rose raised you guys *showing* you
that she loved you without telling you every chance she
got." I smiled. That girl was right on the money. Patience
then removed her towel from her body and discarded it
224

onto the floor. "So, it is just *me* and *you* now, right?"
Patience whispered softly into my ear, nibbling on my
earlobe.

"Yeah", I started closing my eyes. "It's just me and
you."

*****

"I can't *believe* this!" Patience said, shaking her
head. We were upstairs in the guest room. She was lying
in the bed and I was standing near it, putting my pants on.
I had got a page from one of the hommies from the hood
whom we called Lay-Low; he was looking to purchase two
ounces of crack.

"What?"

"You are leaving, *that's* what."

"I'm comin' right back." Patience was silent. I
walked over to her and sat on the edge of the bed.

"I don't see why you can't just stay here with me
for the night, *without* making any runs, *without* answering
your pager, *none* of that."

"I will be right back Patience; I won't be gone
longer than twenty-five minutes."

"I don't want you to go. Please? Just *stay* here,
with me." I exhaled sharply. $1,600 for twenty-minutes of
my time? Should I pass it up, call Darion and let him get
that money? Naw, ain't no telling what he was into.

I had never been able to shake the feeling I woke
up with that day. It was still present in my system and I
was forcing myself to ignore it. Patience's pleas seemed to
be dousing that feeling with a flammable liquid, intensifying
it. I suppressed it nonetheless.

"I am goin' to make this quick run and then I am
goin' to come back here, turn my pager off and just chill
with you for the rest of the night. I promise." I said,
kissing her on the lips. Patience looked into my eyes.

"You are coming *right* back?"

225

"*Right* back."

"Okay, but if you are not back in twenty-five minutes I am going to put my clothes back on and *keep* them on; catch my drift?"

"Yeah, I caught it. You have only had sex *one* time and *already* you are exercisin' the powers of the pussy." Patience laughed. I grabbed my car keys.

"I love you Atif." Patience said to me as I was on my way out of the room. I paused in my tracks and turned to her.

"I believe you."

"That will suffice: for now." Patience said, smiling at me. That smile, that *moment*. I can close my eyes right now and still visualize her laying in that bed, clenching the sheet around her naked torso, smiling up at me. I smiled back at her and walked out of the room.

Hard-headed decision number one.

*****

I climbed into my Mustang and hit the road. I was riding to a song by The College Boys called *Victim of the Ghetto*. There was a Glock 9 semi-automatic in my glove compartment. I reached over and retrieved it. I liked Lay-Low and did not think that he would try to rob me or anything but Malik had always taught us to stay strapped when we were doing business, no matter who with. I glanced at my gas gauge and decided that I would go ahead and fill my tank up then so that I could just handle my business down north and shoot straight back out south.

Riding south on Blue Ridge, I pulled into a small filling station. There was a small nightclub across the street next door to a liquor store and a Chinese restaurant. I had just crossed into the city limits of Grandview, down the street from the Truman Corners Shopping Center. The club was packed and so were the pumps at the gas station. There were lines of cars. I pulled into the shortest line

which consisted of about four cars ahead of me waiting for
the same thing I was waiting for.

*...if you are not back in twenty-five minutes I am
going to put my clothes back on and keep them on; catch
my drift?* Patience's words echoed in my mind. I changed
my mind and decided that I would go ahead and handle my
business first and then stop and get some gas on the way
back out south. I looked behind me in my rearview mirror
and to my dismay a car full of people had blocked me in. I
honked my horn trying to get the driver's attention. When
he looked up, I saw him squinting his eyes at me.

I recognized him right off the bat.

His name was LaRon Killabrew and he was from
24th street. LaRon was Malik's age and probably one of the
rowdiest young gangsters from that particular
neighborhood. My brother once knocked him unconscious
with a right hook to the chin. They were at the Skateland
skating ring in Grandview when Malik embarrassed him in
front of everyone there. That didn't make him a punk
though, he was far from that. LaRon was known for putting
in work.

I noticed LaRon getting the attention of the
individual seated next to him in the passenger seat. Kev
looked my way and our eyes locked in my rearview mirror.
I shook my head, looking to see if there was any way that I
could squeeze my way up out of the gas station by moving
forward. There wasn't; I was stuck. At that moment I felt
my Mustang jerk forward; LaRon was ramming my back
bumper! I looked up into the rearview and observed
everyone in the car laughing as if it was funny.

LaRon did it again. This time I turned around in my
seat and mugged LaRon and his crew. If looks could kill
they would have dropped dead on the spot. All four doors
of the dark gray Ford Taurus opened simultaneously as the
four occupants exited the vehicle.

Damn.

Gripping my pistol, I got out of the Mustang
shielding it with my body. I was not about to let them walk

227

up on me while seated in the car like that. They were liable to leave me sitting there dead.

"I see you by yo-self, huh nigga?" LaRon asked me. I ignored him. Kev was grinning ear to ear, making his way around the front of the Taurus in order to join LaRon and another person, whom I had seen around but never really knew, that had gotten out of the back seat on the driver's side. I watched the fourth person out of my peripheral vision advancing alongside the opposite side of my car.

They were trying to surround me.

"This a nice lil' ride you got here, Atif."

"What you niggas want, man?"

"You ain't know that nigga was gettin' money like that?" Kev asked LaRon, looking at me.

"Naw cuzz, not like *this*. 92 Mustang," LaRon was saying, running his finger across the trunk of my car. "Graphics, nice lil system. I *like* it, I *like* it."

I could clearly see that LaRon was trying to divert my attention for some reason. The brother on the other side of my car was slowly but surely easing his way up. If I allowed him to come too much further, he was going to see my pistol. I heard a gun cock. I had tripped and took my eyes off the brother who had gotten out on LaRon's side of the car. He was pointing a 357 Magnum at my chest.

"Gimme the mutha'fuckin' keys nigga, *and* empty your mutha'fuckin' pockets! Wha'sup Kev cuzz? You want this nigga's ca-" This time *he* tripped and took *his* eyes off *me*, talking to Kev.

My adrenaline was racing. My first mind told me to just let them have the car; let them get their rocks off and I would simply make sure that I got the last laugh in the end, on the rebound. That would have been the smart thing to do. There were a lot of people out, a lot of witnesses and they were just showing off. I didn't think that they would take my car *and* murder me in cold blood in front of all those people. This was the route I started to take.

That is until I looked at Kev and saw the smirk on his face.

This was the person who had tried to rape my girl, my *only* girl. I had been plotting on getting at him *anyway* because of what he had done to her. And there he was smiling like he didn't have a care in the world.

I raised my pistol and fired at the brother pointing the Magnum at me, hitting him in the chest. The force of the bullet knocked him backwards, dropping the gun as he fell to the ground. I heard women beginning to scream and could see people panicking around the parking lot.

The brother on the other side of the car pulled out a gun and fired it at me. I ducked beside the Mustang, feeling a bullet whiz by my head. The brother let off a few more rounds as I was ducking down, shattering my passenger and driver side windows. Meanwhile, Kev was trying to make his way over to where the brother had dropped the Magnum. I pointed my pistol at him and let off two shots. Kev grabbed his right bicep, changing his mind about retrieving the Magnum and his direction. He took off running across the street behind LaRon, leaving their friend behind. I wanted to chase them but the brother on the other side of my car held me at bay. I then looked up and realized that I was seated not too far from a gas pump and panicked. People were ramming theirs cars into each other trying to force their way out of harms way.

I peeked underneath my car and did not see any feet. I slowly rose up, peeking through the car to the other side and saw that the brother had taken off running along with Kev and LaRon. I got up and walked over to the brother I had shot in the chest. His T-shirt was soaked with blood and he was staring up at me with wide eyes, gasping for air. I stood over him, pointing my pistol at his forehead.

I didn't start out looking for any trouble that night. All I wanted to do was meet with Lay-Low, get that money and come back to Patience. But no, *they* wanted to start trouble with me. *Me*! Hadn't they heard about me and my people? Hadn't they heard about us beating the murder rap on those Rolling 60's? What about what we had put down on Small Balls? Hadn't they heard about that? I was feeling untouchable. I was feeling like we couldn't be locked up and held for long because we had money and some riders on our team. Isn't that all that my brother told me I needed? Who did they think they were messing with? Especially Kev, I was not the same little dude that he was able to wrestle down on *The Battle Ground*. I had risen in the ranks of my set and commanded respect.

All I had to do was leave well enough alone. At the most I would have had to face weapons charges, because my shooting that brother in the chest was clearly done so in self defense. They were trying to rob me! I did what I *had* to do. It wasn't enough though.

I pulled the trigger, splattering brain matter all over the pavement.

Hardheaded decision number two.

All of a sudden the rest of the world caught back up to real speed. Things were no longer moving in slow motion. I heard sirens. With my heart racing, I climbed into the Mustang and sped out of the gas station, darting across Blue Ridge and onto 71 North.

Lights! There was a police car behind me. Where did he come from so fast? I floored it, panicking. I *couldn't* get caught, it was *impossible;* wasn't it? This couldn't be happening.

I don't want you to go. Please? Just stay here, with me. Patience's voice echoed through my mind once again. Patience. Since Malik and K-Red's being released from the county, I had not wanted anything like I wanted to be back at Smack Man's house curled up with Patience in the guest room. Things were going too good for me, I *couldn't* get locked up right then.

"*Damn* man! God *please* don't let these mutha'fuckas catch me! *Please?*" I pleaded, beating on my steering wheel while looking into my rearview mirror. *Now* I wanted to talk to our Creator. *Now* I was asking *Him* for a favor. Yes, the same One I was referring to in Mr. Williams' class when I said that I wasn't into fulfilling any of His purposes for me.

It is funny how we as human beings tend to ignore the existence of our Creator with our actions until we find

230

ourselves in a "tight spot". *Then* we want to call out to Him. I didn't know Him when I was doing my thing. I was too preoccupied with hustling for Him then. But *now*? Oh I wasn't so busy anymore.

There were even more police cars behind me then, like ten to twelve of them. Not only that, but a helicopter was above me, shining a spotlight down on my car. Where did I think I was going? College Boys was getting on my last nerve. I snapped the tape-deck off, breaking the button in the process. What was I going to do? How was I going to get away? I could *not* go to jail for murder. I was speeding at well over one hundred miles per hour. Other cars on the highway were pulling over to the shoulder for the police just like the good citizens they were.

I exited the highway on 75th street. Three more Kansas City police cars were waiting for me there. They joined in on the chase. I was being chased by *both* police departments. Making a left, I floored it once again west on 75th street. My pager went off. I just *knew* that it was Patience. She probably couldn't even begin to imagine what I was in the middle of. Approaching Troost Avenue, I saw that the light was yellow. There was no way that I was about to stop. I pressed harder on the gas pedal even though there was no more room for it to go. My foot was to the floor. As I came upon Troost Avenue, all I remember is seeing some high beams shining on the right side of my face for a millisecond.

After that, darkness.

*****

231

PART 2:

<u>FOOTPRINTS IN THE SAND</u>

Or think you that you will enter
Paradise without such (trials) as came
to those who passed away before you?
They were afflicted with severe poverty
and ailments and were so shaken that
even the Messenger and those who believed
along with him said: "When (will come)
The Help of Allah?" Yes!
Certainly, the Help of Allah is near!
-Noble Qur'an 2:214

CERTIFICATION

"Conversatin' with my conscience;
is it real as it seems?
Or have I slipped unconscious;
trippin' off of some fucked up dream?"
-*Soody Mak*

12

"Rise and shine, for this is a day that the Lord has made!" A male staff member shouted. His voice echoed throughout the corridors. This was followed by the loud metal clanking sounds of our cell doors being opened using a metal box full of levers located at the beginning of each corridor. The particular sounds spoken of above, along with the sound of keys jingling, are two of the most irritating sounds I have ever heard in my life. "Get y'all bad asses *up*! Let's go!"

I opened my eyes, silently hoping to myself that the past two weeks had all just been another one of my horrible nightmares. I wasn't dreaming. Once again I was surrounded by cemented blocks in a cold dark cell laying on a slab of metal atop a poor excuse for a mattress. I laid there for a few more moments after my cell door popped open, routinely asking myself why I didn't stay back with Patience that night. Every time I laid down and closed my eyes for the night, I did so praying that I would wake up next to her in Smack Man's guest room.

I slowly began to rise to a sitting position, grimacing in pain and exhaling heavily as I rose. The stitches in my head were throbbing from where I had banged it against my car window during the accident. My ribs were bruised and my chest hurt with every single breath that I took. I began to put on a two piece navy blue uniform. The top piece they had issued me was too small and it usually took a couple of minutes for me to put it on and take it off.

"Get *up* y'all, let's go! Y'all got five minutes to get yourselves together and if you ain't on that elevator when I am ready to go then you gone spend the day locked down in that cell." The staff member warned. I quit procrastinating and got up. Locked in that cell was the last place I wanted to be.

I made my way out of my cell and closed the door behind me. Others were doing the same. There were four different "team" areas located upstairs in the Juvenile Justice Center. Each team had two corridors lined with about sixteen cells each. At the end of each corridor was a shower, a sink, a water fountain and two latrines.   I retrieved my hygiene bag from a desk where the staff member was seated at, which consisted of a three inch toothbrush, a small hair brush, a bar of generic hotel soap and a small tube of generic toothpaste enclosed in a Ziplock bag, and stood in line for my turn at one of the sinks. After getting ourselves together, all but one of us packed ourselves into the elevator along with the staff member and made our way down to the second floor. Someone had refused to get out of the bed.

On this floor was where we spent our long and boring days. It consisted of the kitchen, two restrooms, the orientation room, a classroom, and four team areas sectioned off by wooden partitions. These team areas were labeled with one of the last four letters of the alphabet and in each area there was a color television mounted up from the ceiling, tables and chairs, a small desk and floor to ceiling windows looking over the small yard down on the first floor. That was where we went for an hour or so a day to have recreation, if the weather was nice and the staff was in a good mood. There was also an indoor gymnasium down there.

I was on the Y team which was closest to the kitchen so we usually got to get our trays first. There were girls in JJC also. Their area, B team, was located downstairs on the first floor but they usually spent their time up on the second floor also in the classroom. Y team was right next to the classroom so we were the closest to them also.

"Wha'sup man?" One of the detainees greeted me, sitting down at the table with me. His name was Jamil, but he went by the nickname of Lil' Ham. Lil' Ham was an A.P.B. (Athens Park Blood) from further out south and he was practically the only person I had been associating with up to that point in time since my arrival at JJC. He was locked up for escaping from a ½ way house and had been in JJC for a little over a month.

"Wha'sup?" I returned the greeting. We had just got our breakfast trays.

"When you gone start eatin' man?" Lil' Ham asked me. I had made no attempt to eat the food on my tray and had been giving the majority of my food away to whomever wanted it.

"I don't know. I just don't be hungry for real." I answered.

"Let me get them toast then, shit. I'm hungry than a mutha'fucka'." I slid my tray over to him. "You don't want none of it?" I shook my head. Lil' Ham went to work.

"Wha'sup y'all?" Another detainee greeted as he joined us at the table. His name was Demitrius and he was locked up for auto theft. Demitrius didn't claim any set but surrounded himself with other bloods. Lil' Ham greeted him in return and I simply nodded my head.

"Damn, Ham. Let me get some of that shit." Demitrius said, referring to the extra tray Lil' Ham had sitting before him. Lil' Ham gave him a packet of grape jelly. Demitrius threw it back at him.

"You see how the crip niggas on Z team was muggin' you when you got off the elevators?" Lil' Ham asked me moments later with a mouth full of food. I nodded my head. "Them niggas up to somethin' man, they probably gone try to get at you again."

On my second day at JJC, I was in the orientation room waiting to go to court. There was about thirteen of us in there all together, including three girls. All of the other detainees were playing cards and dominoes, laughing and joking, and I was sitting at a table by myself staring off into space. I remember feeling the whole atmosphere seeming to change around me all of sudden. It was like the whole room fell silent and I could *feel* someone's presence approaching me from behind. By the time I turned around there was a fist coming at me. I ducked just in time making him miss but was unable to dodge the next three punches that followed. Somehow I made my way out of that chair and pushed him up off of me; we squared off. I couldn't really put any power behind my punches because my bruised ribs and chest wouldn't allow me to do so. I did catch him with a three punch combination that knocked him backwards. At that time four staff members ran up and grabbed us. I yelled out in pain as one of the staff members called himself restraining me, ignoring my injuries.

The orientation officer, Mrs. Henderson, came to my rescue and told the staff member to release me because I was only defending myself. They led the other detainee off with him trying to free himself, vowing to avenge the death of his cousin, whom I killed that night at the gas station.

"You think so?" I asked Lil' Ham.

"Yeah. I know I ain't knew you for long, but you cool with me so I ain't about to just let them niggas run up on you again or nothin' with you bein all fucked up and shit. Fuck them niggas, it's *whatever.*" Lil' Ham said, offering his services. He was getting riled up, too.

"Me neither. What y'all niggas wanna do?" Demitrius asked us.

"What you mean?" I asked in return.

"Lets get them niggas man, shit, I'm bored anyway. I could use a little action in my day. Wha'sup?" Lil' Ham and Demitrius looked at me.

"Wha'sup Atif? You feeling good enough to slide up under the partitions and put some work in?" Lil' Ham asked me, chewing our food.

"Y'all serious?" I asked in return. They nodded their heads in confirmation. To tell the truth, I was in no shape to do such a thing. But at the same time I wanted to get back at Terrell (the one who had run up on me in the orientation room) and finish what he had started. "Yeah, I'm straight. When y'all wanna do it?"

"Now! Wha'sup?" Demitrius offered, jumping up from his seat excitedly. He began to pound his right fist into his open left palm.

"Naw man, not right now. Chill out." Lil' Ham said, shaking his head. The staff member looked questioningly at us. "Let me finish eatin' first, at least. I ain't tryin' to be sittin' in the hole hungry."

Jamil finished eating as Demitrius and I drew out a plan of action. Z team was all the way on the other side of the floor and in order to get there we would have to run through W team. It was a good plan because of the element of surprise that came along with it. No one was expecting for any of us to attempt anything as daring as that. It had never been done before. All I had to do was figure out how I could keep up with the two without hurting myself anymore than I already was.

"Y'all ready?" Demitrius asked us after we had all taken our trays back. We nodded.

Demitrius took off running and slid underneath the first partition, we followed suit. The staff member yelled out in protest but we ignored him. We ran on through W team to the surprise of everyone on that team and slid underneath the third partition, reaching our destination. I sought out Terrell, spotting him at a table in the far corner of the team area and ran up on him as he tried to rise from his chair. He wore a look of surprise and shock on his face, being caught off guard, as I connected a short but powerful right hook to his temple, ignoring the pain in my ribs. He fell over the table and rolled onto the floor. Demitrius ran up to my side and we began stomping him with our feet. Lil' Ham was in the process of slamming one of Terrell's associates on top of the staff member's desk. Moments later, every staff member on the floor rushed into the team area and restrained us, leading us out of Z team. The floor was in an uproar. The other detainees, females included, were shouting and cheering at us as the staff members led us away.

Down by the rest rooms were the isolation tanks. There was only two of them and one was occupied. The staff members put Demitrius into the vacant one and slammed the door locking him inside. I got a peek of the room and was glad that they hadn't put me in it. There was nothing but a small, thin mattress on the floor of the isolation tank, nothing else. Lil' Ham and I were led through a door and into the processing area. The lady in there informed the other staff members that they would have to take us upstairs because the cells in the processing unit were filled with kids waiting to be processed in. We were taken upstairs and locked into our cells.

"A, Atif!" Lil' Ham shouted to me through the small space underneath his cell door about two cells down the corridor from me.

"Wha'sup?" I shouted back. It hurt for me to yell like that.

239

"A, we *fucked* them niggas up, didn't we?" Lil' Ham shouted, laughing as he finished his sentence.

"Yeah!" I shouted back.

"I can barely hear you dawg! Put yo mattress on the floor and talk through the slit!" I complied. "A, did you see me slam that nigga flat on his shit?"

"Yeah, I saw that! Did you see me drop that nigga?"

"Yeah! I saw that shit! You hit that nigga hard as a mutha'fucka'!"

"Ham?" a third voice inquired.

"Soody Mak?" Lil' Ham inquired in return.

"Yeah!" Soody Mak shouted. He was in the cell next door to me. Soody Mak was also an A.P.B. He was locked up on a CCW (carrying a concealed weapon) charge. Him and Lil' Ham went back like car seats.

"Why you didn't come downstairs nigga?" Lil' Ham asked Soody Mak.

"Man I was *tired* than a mutha'fucka', *fuck* that shit!"

"Ole lazy ass nigga! You missed out too, dawg!"

"What happened?"

"Me, Demitrius and Atif ran up on the crip niggas on Z team and tapped danced on their asses!"

"Man, why y'all didn't tell me y'all was gone do that?"

"A, we didn't even know! A, it was a spur of the moment thing! Them niggas was muggin' Atif and shit when we got off the elevators this mornin' so Demitrius was like lets run up on them niggas, so we did!"

I listened in silence as the two talked to each other. They strayed from the subject of what we had put down and was doing some reminiscing about some things they had done on the street. I lost interest in their conversation and my own mind began to wander. I thought about Big Mama. It was Sunday morning, so she was more than likely at church. Possibly praying for me. I wondered what Darion and the hommies were up to. My thoughts then switched to my predicament. What was going to happen to me? When I went to court a week or so ago, I was only in the courtroom for a few moments. I didn't understand

240

nothing that was said. Big Mama was there though and I was content with seeing her. It took everything I had to walk out of that courtroom, leaving her behind. Big Mama needed me out there, I knew that and I felt like I had let her down.

"A, Atif!" Lil' Ham yelled.

"Wha'sup?"

"Why you so quiet?"

"No reason!"

"What's on your mind?"

"I was wonderin' what they gone be talkin' about when I go back to court!"

"What you charged with?" Soody Mak asked me. Everyone in the detention center knew what I was charged with. I was hesitant to answer at first until it dawned on me that he may have meant "exactly" what charges did I have altogether.

"Second degree murder and armed criminal action!"

"That's it? Nothin' else?"

Wasn't that enough?

"Yeah!"

"Did the prosecutor recommend that they put you up for certification?"

"I think so, I remember him sayin' somethin' like that!"

"Did they ask you if you understood?"

"Yeah!"

"What did you say?"

"I just said yeah!"

"Do you know what certification is?"

"No!"

"Then why did you say yeah?" That was a *very* good question. Why did I say yeah to something I didn't understand? That was unlike me. I guess I was a little intimidated in that courtroom. I had never been before a judge before then.

"I don't know!"

"A, fuck that Atif man! I don't know you and I ain't tryin' to tell you what to do or nothin', but don't be doin' that! The last time I agreed to some shit I didn't

241

understand I ended up doin' ten months in McCune for some shit I didn't even do!"

"Nigga you did that shit!"   Lil' Ham cut in.

"No I didn't!   Anyway, don't be scared to ask the judge or *whoever* what is goin' on!   That's *your* life and *your* freedom that they talkin' about!"

"What do certification mean?"   I asked.   I understood what he had said and from that point on I took that advice and always remembered that.

"It means that they wanna try you as an adult! They sayin' that they wanna send you down to the county and let *them* deal with you down there!   The juvenile system can only lock you up until you are eighteen, no matter *what* you done did, and what they are sayin' is they want for you to do more time than that!   They tryin' to lose you dawg!"   His revelation hit me hard.   I had no idea that that was what the prosecutor was referring to.   I didn't even know that such a thing was possible.

I had come to grips with the realization that I was more than likely going to have to do some time, but I was thinking more along the lines of a year in McCune or some other juvenile facility.   But they were contemplating something else.   They wanted to send me to the *penitentiary!* The big house.   The slammer.   And for how long? Ten years? Twenty years? For the rest of my life? I couldn't even begin to comprehend that.

"Do you got a lawyer?"   Soody Mak cut into my thoughts.

"I'm gettin' one!"

"What you need to be focusin' on now is tryin' to fight your certification! Whether you guilty or innocent don't even matter right now!"

"My lawyer ain't goin' to be able to holler at them and make sure that I don't get a whole lot of time?"

"Naw man, you ain't listenin!   It ain't even goin' to come down to that right now, they not even goin' to go off into none of that!   They don't wanna deal with you Atif, they wanna send you to the *adult* courts and let *them* take care of all that!   The only thing a lawyer gone be able to do for you right now is try to fight your certification so they will have to deal with you in the juvenile system instead of the adult courts!" I was beginning to understand, and with this new understanding I wanted to do some thinking to myself.

"A!"

"Wha'sup?" Both Lil' Ham and Soody Mak asked in unison.

"I'mma lay back for a minute and holler at y'all later!"

"A'ight!" they both answered.

I picked my mattress up from the ground and laid it back onto the slab of metal. I laid down, staring up at the ceiling. Certification? Jamil began to beat rhythmically on the door with this fist and a hair brush as Soody Mak recited some of his newest material. I liked to listen to Soody Mak rap, I thought that he was pretty tight. I liked his style, his lyrical content and the fact that he had developed such skills at an early age astonished me. As much as I liked to listen to him, I was not in the mood. I wanted some peace and quiet. I didn't comprehend yet at that time that peace and quiet was another luxury I had given up when I decided to pull that trigger.

I had killed *again*. That made it two people who were no longer alive because of me. My dreams were haunted by them both. I would wake up in the middle of the night swinging at the air. I often stayed up for the majority of the night and would only go to sleep when I could no longer hold my eyes open.

I got up from my bunk and paced my cell, reading the graffiti written on the walls and the door. How long was I going to be on lock down? After a fight, the staff usually would put one of us in an isolation pod for a few hours and then let us back out. When they locked one of us in our cell upstairs though it was a different story. They had a tendency to "forget" about us and not let us out until the next day. I set my mind for the possibility of the worst case scenario, that way if they didn't let us out before the next day my anxiety wouldn't drive me crazy. After another hour or so, I laid back down on my bunk and dozed off.

*****

"Atif."   I opened my eyes.   There was a man
standing at my cell door, I hadn't even heard the door come
open. I squinted my eyes, sitting slowly up. It was Mr.
Thomas, one of the staff members.   "You got a visit
youngsta', get up." I stood up and began to slowly put my
shirt back on, grimacing as I pulled it down over my body.

"A Mr. Thomas man, when y'all gone let us out?"
Lil' Ham shouted through his cell door as the two of us
made our way up the corridor.

"Y'all stuck up here until tomorrow Jamil.   Y'all
pissed the supervisor off with that shit y'all pulled. You lil'
niggas was lookin' like some generic ass commandos, slidin'
all up under the partitions and shit like y'all ain't got no
home trainin'." Mr. Thomas said, laughing at his own simile.
"Where you lil' niggas think y'all at?"

"Man holler at him for us Mr. Thomas man, see if
you can get us up outta here!"

"Yeah, a'ight. I'll see what I can do." Mr. Thomas
led me to the elevator and turned to me when the doors
closed. "How you doin' man? Your ribs a'ight?"

"I'm cool."

"What's wrong with you lil' niggas man? Whose
bright idea was that, Demitrius'?" Silence. "Y'all watchin' a
lil' too much television up in here." More silence. "Ain't
Terrell the one who ran up on you from behind a couple of
weeks ago in the orientation room?" I nodded my head.
"Aw, shit. I don't blame y'all then. I would've went Rambo
on that nigga's ass myself. Sneakin' up on a mutha'fucka'
from behind, that's some cowardly shit right there." We
reached the second floor and exited the elevator.
"Everybody talkin' about that shit too, you lil' niggas almost
kicked a young riot off in here this mornin'."

We made our way to the orientation room where
there were rows of plastic chairs lined up facing each other
for the visits. The room was packed and the noise level was
loud. I spotted Big Mama and Malik seated in the last row
and walked over to them.

"Hi Big Mama!" I greeted, hugging her when I approached.

"Hey baby!" Big Mama said squeezing me.

"Ssss, ahhh." I complained involuntarily as pain shot through my ribs with her embrace.

"Ooooh baby, I'm sorry. I forgot." Big Mama apologized , pulling away from me. "How have you been feelin'? You gettin' any better?"

"Yeah, I feel better." I answered her. "Wha'sup punk?" I routinely greeted my brother, sitting down and grabbing my ribs. He didn't rise from his seat like Big Mama had done when I walked in the room.

"Wha'sup fag?" Malik greeted me in return. We were happy to see each other, don't let our strange way of greeting each other fool you. "What took them so long to bring you in here?"

"I was upstairs on lock down."

"For what?"

"Me, this dude name Jamil and Demitrius ran up on ole boy that snuck up on me a couple of weeks ago."

"Man you can't be in here fightin' with your ribs all fuc.....*messed* up like they is." I nodded.

"Do y'all go to church in here?" Big Mama asked me.

"Yeah. The preacher dude that be comin' up though ain't got it all. He told us last week that he saw Jesus Christ ridin' down Holmes on a Harley Davidson." We all laughed at that. "And he be smellin' like liquor when he come up in here."

"What church does he preach at?" Big Mama asked me, wiping a happy tear from her eye brought about by her fit of laughter.

"He said he preaches from a Quick Trip parkin' lot." We erupted in laughter again. It felt good to laugh like that. For those few seconds I forgot that I was facing certification. I forgot that I was a murderer because in my grandmother's eyes I was *still* her favorite grandson.

"Lord Willin', I'mma talk with Pastor Jenkins and see if we can get somebody with some doggone sense who will volunteer to come up here and preach the Word to y'all." Big Mama said. I nodded my head.

"Y'all know they tryin' to certify me, don't y'all?" I asked them after a few moments of silence.

"Aw yeah?" Malik asked me. I nodded. He shook his head.

"What does that mean?" Big Mama asked me.

"It mean they wanna try him as an adult." Malik answered for me.

"An adult? The boy *just* turned fifteen years old! What they mean they wanna try him as an adult? What about that fast talkin' lawyer, what he say?" Big Mama asked Malik.

"He said he gone take on the case."

"What lawyer?" I asked.

"Gary Jaco."

"Aw, y'all got him?" Malik nodded. "How much he want?"

"That's irrelevant." Malik answered.

"*Irrelevant?* Can you even *spell* irrelevant?" My brother was far from illiterate. Questioning his intelligence was just my way of messing with him.

"Can you spell *right cross*?" My brother countered.

"So what's gone happen when we go to court next week?" Big Mama asked me.

"From what I hear, they just gone set me another court date for my certification hearin'."

"You mean I'mma be takin' off from work just so that they can set another court date?" Big Mama asked me. I nodded. "How long will they set the other court date for?"

"About four months." Malik answered.

"*Four months*? Lord have mercy."

We talked for a few more minutes until Mr. Thomas came in and told all of the visitors that the visiting hours were over. I don't know why they called it visiting "hours", they only lasted for twenty minutes. I hugged my grandmother and watched them both walk out of the visiting room. It really felt good to see them and doing so lifted my spirits.

Mr. Thomas led me back to the elevators. I peered into Z team on the way and didn't see Terrell. While waiting for the elevator doors to open, Mr. Thomas nudged me with his elbow.

"You got some fans." Mr. Thomas said, tilting his head over towards the classroom. Five or six girls were standing in the window trying to get my attention. I looked their way and they all waved at me, smiling. I waved back. One of them in particular, a tall and slim dark-skinned girl with a very pretty face, motioned with her hands that she was going to write me a letter. I nodded. The elevator doors opened and we stepped inside. I looked back over towards the dark-skinned girl and she smiled at me, I smiled back. Mr. Thomas chuckled to himself.

"All of them used to be infatuated with Terrell. Well, except for the one who just said that she is goin' to write you a letter. She can't stand him. Every time he writes her a letter she will throw it away without even readin' it. Anyway, you done put it on *him* and they want *you* now. Females are somethin' else."

"What's her name?"

"Fatimah. Let her tell it, she's a Muslimah."

"A Muslimah? What is that?"

"I guess it's the term you use when referrin' to a *female* Muslim." I nodded. "She be prayin' five times a day and everything, fucks me up too. What is a female *raised* by Muslim parents doin' in *here*?"

"Maybe she is innocent."

"Yeah, *right.*"

We rode in silence for the rest of the trip back to my lonely cell. By the time we made it up there, they were passing out trays. Good, I was hungry this time.

Fatimah. I thought she had a pretty name. Antoinette informed me that Muslim names had a meaning, I wondered what hers meant. I had never met a Muslimah before or ever seen how a Muslim prayed. I was curious about her. I was not infatuated on first glance from a physical standpoint like I was when I saw Patience for the first time on the first day of my freshman school year. Fatimah was pretty and her height was almost intimidating.

247

I couldn't see her hair because she had a white garment wrapped around her head and neck. I couldn't make out her body either because her uniform was too big and loose fitting for me to make anything out. I was more *intrigued* than anything else. I accepted my tray, which consisted mainly of some roast beef and potatoes, sat on my bunk and ate a nutritious full course meal for the first time in weeks. As I ate, I found myself highly anticipating a letter from her, almost as much as I was waiting to hear back from Patience.

*****

"I come through with my Glock cocked,
strapped with enough heat to make yo heart stop.
North side, player, dime block,
I'm sayin', we be clockin' fat knots slangin' fat rocks....."

Four months had gone by to the day. It was early in the morning and all of us on Y team were having co-ed with the girls on B team. We had gone the whole month without any violations and for this we were treated with some barbeque from a local restaurant chain by the name of Gates Barbeque. An hour in the gymnasium with the girls was also a reward for a month of such good behavior. There was a full court five-on-five game of basketball being played, detainees against staff, and the game was being watched by most of the people in the gym. The rest of us however were observing a rap contest between a recent arrival by the name of Chris and Soody Mak.

The whole detention center had long since flipped over time and time again. The only detainees remaining who were there when I got there were Soody Mak and Fatimah, both of which were taking their cases to trial. Jamil and Terrell was sent to the McCune School For Boys and Demitrius went home on house arrest.

248

The past four months had passed by long and slow without much incident. I spent my days teetering somewhere between boredom and depression. Patience wrote to me on a regular basis and our correspondence kept me motivated. Kesha and I wrote to each other also, I would even receive an occasional letter from Persistence and Antoinette, so I usually went no longer than a couple of days without a letter from one of the four. I missed everyone, especially Patience. When she wrote I could see the ink on the paper smeared here and there from tears that had fallen onto the paper as she wrote.

As much as I hated to be there, I adjusted nonetheless. I was adored by all of the staff members and they all would come and get me for odd jobs here and there to get my mind off of the up and coming certification hearing. Well, the day had come. In a couple of hours they would be calling me to the orientation room to go to court.

It was a cold December day out, we were given gray sweatshirts to wear over our short sleeve uniform tops. Even though we were not outside, it was a little chilly in the gymnasium for those of us who were not running up and down the court. The majority of the girls from B team were present, watching the rap contest between Soody Mak and Chris. Chris had a nice slow rap style but his lyrical content was not as deep as Soody Mak's. Chris had begun to get personal with his lyrics, slipping in an occasional disrespectful gang slur here and there. Soody Mak however simply nodded his head in humility as Chris rapped. Soody Mak and I had gotten to know each other pretty well over the past four months and if I knew him at all, he was going to bring some of his lyrics out of the bag that would crush Chris and end the contest instantaneously. He liked to bait his opponent in by allowing him to build up his confidence, giving him a false sense of hope and security, then he would annihilate him.

Fatimah was not in the crowd. She was walking laps around the gymnasium by herself with her customary garment wrapped around her head. Watching her would give one the impression that she was depressed, but I didn't get that vibe from her. Fatimah was a strong person and

249

she had a lot of faith in her religion. She told me in a letter that she was innocent of the assault charges that she was awaiting trial for because she felt like she was defending herself against what she called a "Kafir" (non-believer) whom had tried to snatch her head piece off one day when she was on the Metro bus.

I thought Fatimah was kind of strange. She didn't allow herself to indulge in the typical everyday conversations that boys usually had with girls at that age. She was distant and preferred solitude. It seemed to me like after I responded to her first letter, she withdrew from me as if she had all of a sudden lost interest. Her letter was full of Arabic writing and Islamic terms that I was unfamiliar with. She informed me that when she had heard my name for the first time she assumed that I too was a Muslim and thought that I was someone she could relate to. This was why she wanted to write me in the first place. After finding out differently though, she almost ceased our correspondence altogether. All of this just made me that much more interested in her.

Meanwhile, Chris had gone a little too far and Soody Mak had heard enough. He cut Chris off in the middle of a bar and attacked.....

"Who said this nigga was bad like Soody Mak?
Bitch I'm the shit!
Thug-bred, Bloodhound, strapped
with a Mak and two clips.
Oh so raw when I spit,
dusty ass crip niggas fall if I trip.
When I hit 'em up, I split 'em up
from their hips to their lips.
My enemies get dealt with,
buried so they don't get smelled quick.
I got this nigga feelin' sick
all because of the wrath of my felt tip
-I represent- out the south nigga,
cross that T.
And if you come out south nigga,
don't cross me!
-Soody- the lyrical uzi,

250

raw like a big plate of sushi.
Hell naw!
This busta will never do me!
He saw!
But he couldn't see through me!
From the womb to the tomb
I'll live the life of a thug.
I ride shotgun wit' a shotgun
when it's time to spill blood."

It was over. I don't know if Soody Mak meant to continue or not but whatever the case he was cut off by the audience's cheers. Everyone was patting him on his back and giving him dap.

"A Jay man, spit somethin'. Get on this nigga." Chris urged one of his companions.

"Shiiiit, I can't fuck with that nigga. He ain't about to embarrass me. Fuck that!" Jay said in response to Chris' statement and the challenging look Soody Mak gave him.

"Spit some more of that shit, Soody." Someone in the crowd said.

Soody Mak went off into one of his songs. I noticed Fatimah making her way past us and I left the crowd to join her.

"Wha'sup Fatimah, can I walk with you for a minute?"

"I kind of wanna be alone, Atif."

"Just put up with me for *five* laps then and after that I will leave you alone." Fatimah stopped and shook her head.

"I will give you *two*." I nodded and we began to walk side by side.

"Have you been gettin' my letters?"

"Yeah."

"Do you read them?"

"Sometimes."

"Well why you don't be writin' me back? You found out I wasn't a Muslim and started actin' like I wasn't worthy of your conversation or somethin'."

"No, Atif, it isn't that." I looked at her with my lips curled up in disbelief. "Really, it isn't. I'm not like that."

251

Fatimah said humbly, smiling. She had the cutest little gap between her two front teeth.

"What is it then?"

"I have to be very careful with who I allow myself to associate with. *Especially* in here." I nodded. I felt her on that one. "Why do you be gettin' all of that mail from the outside? Do you have a girlfriend?"

"Yeah."

"What's her name?"

"Patience."

"Patience? That is a pretty name. In Arabic her name would be Sabirah."

"What about you? Do you have a boyfriend?"

"No, Atif. Muslims don't do the boyfriend/girlfriend thing. At least not the ones that strive hard to do what Allah says."

"What about male friends? Can you have them?" Fatimah stopped and turned to me.

"What do you *want* from me Atif? What are your intentions behind persistently trying to associate with me?"

That was a good question. What *did* I want? I had a girlfriend that I loved. Why did I keep on going out of my way to communicate with Fatimah? Did I harbor any ill ulterior motives? I thought Patience was "different" from the rest of the girls I had come across in my life but Fatimah took the cake.

"I ain't tryin' to get nothin' off on you or nothin' like that. I just....I don't know. You seem like a nice person, somebody I would like to get to know and maybe even *learn* a few things from." Fatimah smiled and we started walking again.

"All praise is due to Allah, He knows best what you reveal *and* what you conceal." My brow creased with curiosity as I thought about what she said. "Don't you go up for certification today, inshaa Allah?" I nodded my head in affirmation. "I mentioned you earlier in my morning prayer."

"Aw yeah?" I asked, smiling. Fatimah nodded. I was touched. "As much as I appreciate that, I don't think God is fuc....I mean is *messin'* with me right now."

252

"When I said that I mentioned you I did not mean that I was asking Allah not to let these people certify you or nothin' like that. From what I've heard the girls sayin' about you and your reputation, it may be *good* for you in the end. Allah says in the Qur'an that He will never place a burden on our shoulders that we can't handle so whatever the outcome of your certification hearin' may be, insha' Allah, it is a matter already decreed for you by *Him*."

"See, I don't get that. Since all this that I'm goin' through has already been decreed for me, before I was even *born*, then what is the point of you mentionin' me in your prayer in the first place? What's the point in prayin' about something that's already been written and ain't goin' to change? Why pray *period*?"

"*Atif!* It is a *serious* mistake to allow Satan to cause you to doubt the significance of prayer. To do so is to destroy the importance of prayer from your heart, and with such doubt even if you *did* pray, your prayer would be *soulless.*

"The Qur'an, Allah's Word revealed to Prophet Muhammad (peace be upon him), roughly translated says: 'Call upon me: I will answer your prayers. Those that disdain My worship on account of pride shall certainly enter Hell, disgraced.' This verse answers your question in two ways: First, it proves that fate or destiny is not somethin' which, Allah forbid, might have tied the hands of Allah Himself also, and the power to answer prayers might have been withdrawn from *Him*. We have no power to change the decrees of Allah; but Allah Himself certainly has the power to change His decrees and decisions on hearin' you cry out to Him. Prophet Muhammad, peace be upon him, said: 'Nothin' can avert destiny *but* the prayer.' And secondly, know that prayer is *never* without advantage, which is this: When you humble yourself by praying to Allah, you acknowledge His Lordship and Supremacy and admit your own servitude and helplessness before Him, an act that you won't in no case be deprived for performin', whether you are granted *specifically* what you prayed for or not."

253

"If I don't get specifically what I asked for, then how am I *not* deprived?"

"If you believe in Allah and follow His messenger, when you pray, *unless* it be a prayer for a sin or for severing ties of kinship, Allah grants it in one of three ways: Either your prayer is granted in this world, or it is preserved for rewarding you in the Hereafter, or a...calamity of the same degree is *prevented* from befallin' you."

"So if I ask God to let me out of here, and believe in Him, and for whatever reason He allows me to get certified and go to the pen, then He will look out for me somewhere down the line?"

"*Yes*! And when you pray, don't say stuff like: 'O God, show me mercy *if* it be your will,' etc- You should say *definitely*: 'O God, fulfill my such and such need!' Pray to Allah with a *certainty* that He will answer it. Don't be hasty, meanin' that you think your prayer is not bein' answered and give up. You should ask for your every need from Allah, even if your *shoelace* breaks, you should pray for it to Allah."

"I'mma take you up on that."

"I really hope you do, Atif."

We walked in silence for a while with me inspired to do a whole lot more praying now that I saw it in a different light. I had lost what control I did have of my life and my future was not in my hands, which in itself without a strong faith and trust in the Creator's wisdom is a frightening position to be in.

I looked at her as we strolled, yearning for more time to get to know her, feeling almost honored to be walking by her side carrying on a conversation with her, for she wouldn't allow any of the other dudes to do so. They weren't allowed in her radius and the majority of them, those who had any sense whatsoever, didn't even *try*. They let her be, thinking that she was weird. Even I did initially, but the more I listened to her, the more I realized that she was only strange in the sense that she was going in the complete opposite direction as the rest of the world, which was good and testified to her strength and individuality. She didn't *want* to fit in with those who didn't share

254

pleasing the Creator and striving for a good position for their souls in the Hereafter as the primary objective of their lives and what they put the bulk of their energy into and this limits her association to a small body of "strange" people.

"What are you thinkin' about?" I asked her, breaking the silence. My time with her was short and I didn't wish to spend it without talking.

"You got me thinking about Allah's decree. The Qur'an roughly translated says: 'Glorify the name of your Lord, the Most-High. Who has *created* everything and then *proportioned* it. And who has *measured* and then *guided*.' Elsewhere the Qur'an says which is roughly translated as: 'Surely, your Lord is Allah who created the heavens and the earth in six days and then *rose* over the throne, disposin' the affair of all things.' See, Allah is so great that when He created all things He not only arranged it with *harmony* and *balance*, but he gave everyone and everything all that it needs to function and protect itself. The birds have their wings; the sharks their razor sharp teeth; the chameleon has its colors; the porcupine has its spikes. And then He *guided*-"

"What's that mean, He *guided*? I don't mean to cut you off but break that down for me a little before you move on." Fatimah smiled at me, a smile filled with compassion and patience, appreciating my inquiries.

"That's okay, we can digress for a while. And since I referred to some animals I'll use them to answer your question, insha' Allah. Allah's guiding the animals is what scientists refer to as instincts, but they fail to explain *how* instinctive behavior arose in the first place. For instance, bees build *extraordinary* and *mathematically* precise regular six-sided combs. Since these animals don't have the intellect to acquire these superior features but were *born* with them; where did they get it from?"

"Mother Nature?" I offered with a shrug.

"That's the thing! People reach that point in reflection and stop there without really thinkin' about what that implies- Mother Nature consists of rocks; soil, water, trees, and plants...right?"

255

"Yeah."

"Which of these elements could *possibly* make animals behave in a rational, conscious manner? Which part of nature has the intellect or ability to *program* living creatures? The atlas moth caterpillar will present predators with decoys like dry leaves. Who told it to do that not long after being hatched? These are survival tactics that a *human* would resort to! And the caterpillar is clearly incapable of *reasonin'* like that. And to say that Mother Nature did it is like seein' a beautiful paintin' and sayin', 'Wow! Those *colors* can draw'!"

I laughed at that.

"It is *Allah* who inspires in them their seemingly intelligent behavior; He *guided* them at the moment of their inception, encodin' most of the instructions that they need within their genes."

"Dang, that's kinda deep. You know, I always *wondered* that! Like how a newborn baby already knows how to suck his mama's..." I caught myself, afraid of being disrespectful to her.

"Nipples for milk? I think we're mature enough to say such things, don't you?"

We shared an amusing smile.

"Okay, so back to..."

"Yeah, yeah; how, you know, so on and so forth."

"You are somethin' else Atif. Anyway, Allah created, proportioned, measured, guided, and then rose above it all. Everything is goin' to unfold in the way that He wills it, because He is the All-Knowin', All-Wise, and returns to Him in the end. Even with us having the will to choose."

"He's *that* good, huh?"

"*Better*!"

"When you mentioned me in your prayer, what did you ask on my behalf?"

"I'll only tell you a part of it...for now."

"And the rest when?"

"On a day that Allah alone knows of."

What?

256

" Will you settle for...when the time is right as a response?" Fatimah asked in response to the look of perplexity on my face.

"Yeah, I'll settle for that. So wha'sup? What is *some* of what you asked?"

"I prayed that Allah will guide you, increase you in knowledge that benefits you, beautifies faith in your heart, and...well, that's enough."

"Fatimah!" She laughed, refusing to disclose any more. "A'ight then, what does insha' Allah mean?"

"It is Arabic for if Allah Wills it."

"Why do you call God Allah instead of just sayin' God?"

"Because Allah is the name that *He* called *Himself* by in the Qur'an. He never approved the name God as befittin' for Him in *any* of the revelations He sent to mankind. God is just an English *translation* of one or some of His names contained in what's left of *some* of the previous revelations before the Qur'an. Allah says in the Qur'an that to Him *alone* belongs the most beautiful names, so when we call upon Him we should do so by a name that He has approved of. One that is *only* used when referring to Him and not some deity, past or present. I know that I wouldn't want for people to just be calling me by whatever *they* wanted to call me.

You see, the term God in the English language is used too *loosely*. When I say Allah I am referrin' to the Originator of *everything* in existence, no one else. Not Prophet Jesus peace be upon him, not the Holy Spirit peace be upon him, not Mary may Allah be pleased with her, Osiris or any of the other false deities that people take for worship besides Allah. The word God is watered down and people use it in reference to the most strangest, evil and vile things sometimes."

Interesting. Actually I was amazed. This sixteen year old girl was deep. I could see that she enjoyed talking about such things and she came out of her shell a little bit while doing so, even becoming animated in a sense. We had something in common after all. I noticed something about her too. She was not confused about her beliefs, she

257

understood what she believed in. I could sense that. She was unlike anyone I had ever discussed religion with before, meaning that there was more than likely not a whole lot of questions I could ask her that would confuse or trip her up. She would not only be able to answer them, she would also be able to elaborate and break things down in such a way as to where I *too* could understand. I was impressed by this and humbled before her at the same time. In other words, I was not so quick to attempt to draw her out by attacking the rationality of her faith. Why? Because deep inside I knew that I had met my match; that she would shut me down if I tried to go there with her. I wanted to talk to her some more but she stopped and informed me that my two laps were up.

"Fee amaan Allah!" she said, turning around and walking in the reverse direction.

"What does *that* mean?" I asked her as she walked away.

"It means I leave you in Allah's protection." Fatimah answered, turning to face me momentarily while smiling at the same time. She then giggled softly and went back to her walking. I watched her as she faded from my view.

*****

Two weeks later I found myself sitting on my bunk, locked in my cell. I held a letter from the judge who heard my certification hearing I had just received in the mail and all I kept focusing on was the last few words contained within it:

......certified, to be tried as an adult.

*****

258

NO WAY OUT

"Flashes of badges
and evil racist faces,
presenting me
with cases after cases.
Accusations of association
with a combination of thugs,
gang affiliation
smokin bud and slangin' drugs.
I offer no cooperation
for your investigation,
I put it on my mama;
always death before dishonor!"
-*Soody Mak*

13

"Tap-tap-tap-!"

Someone was tapping on the door, I decided to ignore them. I was in the middle of my 5th set of push-ups, sweating profusely and smelling like all outdoors attempting to exhaust myself so that I could go to sleep. I had been on lock-down status for 3 days waiting for the Jackson County Sheriff's Department to come and pick me up. Now that I was waiting to be tried as an adult, the supervisor would not allow me to have any contact with the other "juveniles". At first I found it funny how my transition from adolescence to adulthood was brought about overnight by a simple stroke of the pen. But upon deeper reflection my transition was actually brought about long before I received a letter from the judge.

"Tap-tap.....tap-tap-tap!"

Not wanting to be bothered, I rose from the floor in an irritated manner. I wanted to be left alone. Ever since news of my certification hit the wire a couple of days back, staff members had been showing up at the cell door of the isolation tank I was in with their eyes full of pity expressing how sorry they were. I knew they meant well, but an individual could only take so much of others condolences. So, who was it this time?

"*What* man? Won't y'all leave me alo-" I cut myself off as I approached the small plexi-glass window. My irritation melted away quickly like a stick of butter in a pot of hot grits.

"I'm sorry Atif, were you sleep?" Fatimah asked me in a low voice through the cell door. She was holding a dust mop with her hands clad in latex gloves, dressed in her traditional tan two-piece uniform with a white garment wrapped stylishly around her head and neck, looking down at the floor. I had been thinking of her and hoping that I would somehow get the chance to see her at least one more time before I left.

"What if I was? How long would you have knocked?"

"Prophet Muhammad said that we should only knock on someone's door three times and if they don't answer then we should turn away and leave; so I would have knocked one more time."

"Naw, I'm up. I just thought you was somebody else." I answered, looking at her. She refused to lift her head. "Wha'sup?"

"All is well considerin' all, the praise is Allah's. How are you feelin'?"

"I'm cool; I guess."

"Are you scared?"

"Yeah," I started after a slight pause. I was afraid, afraid of the unknown. "A lil' bit."

"At least you are honest about it. Allah knows best, but I think the rest of these brothas would have had too much pride to admit somethin' like that to a female."

"I ain't like the rest of these brothas."

"Yeah," Fatimah started smiling. "I noticed that." She then began twisting the handle of the dust mop she held as a few seconds of silence passed between us. "Don't be afraid Atif, Allah is with you."

"I can't tell." I replied, looking around the isolation tank. "It feels to me like I am by myself up in here."

"I don't mean that in a *physical* sense Atif. Allah is with you through His knowledge, He could *never* be encompassed by manmade walls." I nodded. At least she didn't go against my own rationale by trying to convince me that some ghostly presence *was* in that isolation tank with me.

"Why you lookin' down at the floor like that Fatimah?"

"Are you decent?"

"*Yeah* girl. You been in here enough times to know that they ain't got me up in here butt naked." Fatimah lifted her head.

"Subhan Allah!" She exclaimed, looking back down at the floor.

"What?"

262

"Will you please put the *bird* back into its cage?" I laughed for the first time in days as I bent over to retrieve my uniform top.

"My bad," I respectfully apologized, pulling my uniform top over my head. "And I ain't got no bird chest either girl, whenever you get through."

"Can I look up now?"

"Yeah."

Fatimah lifted her head smiling that wonderful smile of hers that should be marketed as an anti-depressant. You know, I believe that as I gazed upon Fatimah's pretty black face, no, better yet my encounter with her as a whole taught me where true beauty in a woman actually lay. I grew up believing that beauty was to be found in thick hips and a nice butt with a pretty face. I was *so* wrong. These physical attributes are superficial and pass away with age. Some of your most attractive women whom you see prancing half-naked around on your television screen are truly some of the ugliest women in the world at the same time. God consciousness, self-respect, integrity, kindness, humility, honesty, etc., these are some of the things which really makes a woman "beautiful".

"Can I ask you a question?" I asked Fatimah. She nodded. "Is your hair long or short or what?"

"Not too long, not too short."

"Do you gotta perm in it?"

"No Atif. My father taught me at a young age to be content with the kinky hair Allah chose for me." I nodded. "I keep it braided. I am even thinkin' about lettin' it lock up."

"*Dreadlocks.*"

"Yeah." Fatimah looked at me. "You don't know the history behind the locks, do you?" Fatimah asked in response to the look I had on my face. I was always told that dreadlocks stank.

"No."

"Well, if our paths ever cross again then I will tell you."

"Inta Allah?" I tried. Fatimah grinned from ear to ear.

263

"Insha Allah," she corrected, giggling.

"Yeah, in*sha* Allah. See? I told you that I could learn somethin' from you."

"All praise is due to Allah."   Fatimah suddenly turned away from me and began dust mopping the floor as a female staff member by the name of Mrs. Harris rounded the corner. Mrs. Harris was a Caucasian woman but one could tell by her dialect, attitude and style that she had been raised around a lot of blacks.

"Oh *please*, girl you think I don't know you over here talkin' to Atif?" Mrs. Harris asked Fatimah. The latter smiled. "Hey, Atif, how are you doin' in there?"

"I'm straight."

"Whew boy! Is that you smellin' like that?" Mrs. Harris asked me, backing up from the cell door and pinching her nose.

"They won't let me have my deodorant!" I said, slightly embarrassed. Fatimah had been all of the way up on the door; had she smelled me also? If so, she didn't say anything. That was just like her too.

"Girl we gone have to disinfect the *walls* and everything whenever they let him up outta here." Mrs. Harris said jokingly to Fatimah.

"Forget you Mrs. Harris!" I said, laughing myself.

"In there smellin' like a grown ass man."

"What's that you got?" I asked Mrs. Harris, noticing a letter in her hand for the first time. I could have sworn I recognized the small handwriting on the face of the envelope from a distance.

"Oh, yeah. *That's* why I came over here. Got a whiff of you boy and my mind went blank on me." I let that one slide. "Anyway, this is for you. You ain't supposed to have anything up in there with you but I'm gone give this to you and come back and pick it back up after you done had some time to read it. Don't let the supervisor come by here and see you with it." Mrs. Harris then slid a thick white envelope underneath the cell door. The sweet scent of Patience's favorite perfume instantly followed. I grabbed the letter and tore it open.

Enclosed were some photos and at least a 10 page letter. It felt *so* good to hear from her. I read on as she wrote about how sorry she was to hear about my certification but at the same time was exhilarated behind the fact that she would finally get to visit me once I made it down to the county after being forbidden to do so by detention center policy (which only allowed my direct family members to see me) for over 4 months.

Patience wrote about how much she missed me and how things were not the same without my being out there. School was not the same without our daily lunches together to look forward to. She told me that Teebaby was due next month and was having a little girl. She then ended the letter with promises of how she would always be there for me no matter what the outcome of my situation was. I pressed the pages up to my face inhaling her scent and softly kissed the imprint left behind by her lipstick from where she had done the same.

All of a sudden it dawned on me: With receiving a letter from Patience I had forgotten all about Fatimah. I jumped up and rushed to the window; she was gone. While cursing myself for my stupidity as I turned away, I accidentally kicked a small folded piece of paper that had also been slid underneath my door. I picked it up and opened it:

In the Name of Allah, the Most Gracious, the Most Merciful.

Greetings Atif! I know that things are not looking too good for you right now. Despite all of that, I can see that you are a good person and you have a good heart; that you are not the person the courts are trying to make you out to be, and Allah knows best. You just need some understanding and I pray that Allah blesses you with it, Ameen! Whatever happens, stay strong. I believe that Allah has a plan for you and all of this is a part of it. Man plans but Allah is the Best Planner. Below is one of my personal favorite verses from the Qur'an (2:286). I want you to put it in your heart so that you can take it with you wherever you go, insha Allah:

Allah burdens not a person beyond his scope. He gets reward for that (good) which he has earned, and he is punished for that (evil) which he has earned. "Our Lord! Punish us not if we forget or fall into error, our Lord! Lay not a burden on us like that which you did lay on those before us; our Lord! Put not on us a burden greater than we have the strength to bear. Pardon us and grant us forgiveness. Have mercy on us. You are our Protector and give us victory over the disbelieving people."

I pray that it be Allah's will for us to see each other again someday.
Fee Aman Allah!
Fatimah

Fatimah had the most eloquent penmanship! Smiling to myself, feeling motivated and inspired by her words, I read the passage over and over until I had it memorized. I had never before even *seen* a Noble Qur'an let alone heard any passages from it before meeting her.

*****

Later that night the Sheriff's Department showed up. I was dressed out and led handcuffed and shackled to a sheriff's patrol unit waiting in front of the detention center. I got into the back of the vehicle and rode downtown to the city jail in silence. Once there, I was taken in through the garage and rode an elevator upstairs. The first thing that hit me when those elevator doors opened was the smell. It was a repugnant, stale, musty smell; the scent of thugs, drug addicts, alcoholics, and the homeless all mixed together (if you can imagine that). It reeked! The sheriff then led me to the front desk and

266

removed his cuffs from my wrist. A Kansas City police officer directed me to a small room where he took my mugshots. I was fingerprinted and locked in a cell across from where the rest of the people in custody were. Even though I had been certified, I was still considered underage and they wouldn't allow me in the same tank around the others in custody. I remember wishing that they would make up their minds; was I an adult or a juvenile?

"A lil Mo', you ain't gone eat that bologna sandwich?" One of the brothers in the bullpen asked me, standing up at the bars. The police officers were passing out sandwiches and I had just denied mine. There was no way that I was going to be able to keep some bologna down while inhaling the stench of that place at the same time. I shook my head. "A let me get his sandwich man!" The brother then shouted to the officer. The officer gave it to him. "Wha'sup lil Mo? You ain't hungry?"

"No!" I lied, shouting over the rest of the people in custody. I was *starving*.

"How old are you? You look a lil' young to be in here!"

"I'm 15, I just got certified!" The brother looked at me and shook his head.

"I'm 36 years old! I got certified when I was 16 and I am *just* now makin' it outta prison!" He had my undivided attention with that revelation. I found his purpose for telling me such a thing at that point in time enigmatic.

"That's *20* years!" The brother nodded his head, chewing a mouth full of food. "Why did you get certified?"

"2nd degree murder!" My heart sank into my thighs. 20 years? I couldn't even imagine doing that much time. "Don't worry lil' Mo', I doubt if you will have to do that much time! You got certified for the same thing?" I nodded my head. "I was with a partner of mine and the police killed him so they charge *me* with his death along with the person I had killed! That is why I had to do so much time! They gave me two consecutive 20 year sentences and made me do one flat before I made parole!"

"And you *right* back in jail?"

267

"Naw, I got out this mornin' but these peckerwoods put a detainer on me and came to pick me up because of some 20 year old traffic tickets! Can you *believe* that?" I shook my head. "I'll get out in the mornin' though! Ain't no judge in his right mind gone even wanna deal wit'em, they gone dismiss 'em!"

Our conversation was cut short when an officer came and escorted me downstairs. He led me to a small interrogation room, stepping inside I had a seat. About a 1/2 hour later, Detective Vermil stepped inside the room, smiling. He shut the door behind him.

"Well, well, well.   What do we have here?" Detective Vermil asked with a rhetorical question, sitting at the small table in front of me. "*Whoa*! 2nd degree murder and armed criminal action." he exclaimed, feigning shock while flipping through a vanilla file folder he had brought in with him. "Hmm, *execution* style too.   Your goose is *cooked*! They're going to fry your young ass. You will *never* see the light of day again."

"Ain't you supposed to be readin' me my rights or somethin'?" I asked, trying to hide the fact that I was indeed shaken up by his words.

"*Rights*? You know your rights from the last time we went through this. What was it about 6 or 7 months ago? *Come on*, you remember! You had your big fancy lawyer with you, Big Mama, not to mention a shitload of arrogance. Besides," Detective Vermil started, pulling out a pack of Malboro cigarettes. He offered me one, I declined. He then slid a cold Pepsi across the table to me; I slid it back to him. As thirsty as I was, and to tell you the truth my mouth actually *salivated* and began to tingle when he slid that ice cold Pepsi towards me, I was not about to allow myself to get comfortable. If I would have taken anything from him he would have expected some kind of information from me in return. "You don't want to exercise your right to remain silent. You want to talk to me about a.....Ms. Antoinette Henderson and how she killed Small Balls so that we can get your future prison sentence reduced before the Feds get involved. That way you just *might* make it out of prison before your granny kicks the bucket."

He almost buckled me with that one. Watching television would give one the misconception that it was *easy* to remain silent under such circumstances. I beg to differ. Detectives are crafty and very good at what they do. I used to wonder how a person could possibly allow a detective to convince him to tell on *himself?* With experiencing an interrogation firsthand I understood. They can break you down and make you feel as hopeless as a one-legged man in a butt kicking contest; deceiving you and making you feel like *they* are your only friends in the world whom you can trust and depend on with divide-and-conquer tactics. If they can so much as get you to try and distort the story or contrive one in an attempt to out-smart them then it usually plays out in their favor. Once they get you to *talking* period the battle is already half won. After that they begin implementing certain gestures proven to encourage you to open up. They are so conniving that at times they can even convince people who are innocent and know absolutely nothing about what they are being questioned for into believing that they are guilty of the crime and admit to it!

As much as my walls of defense had been penetrated with his comment about Big Mama, it turned into a double-edged sword for him because after the shock wore off from being hit below the belt like that, I got angry. It was this sudden rush of anger that revived me and made me even stronger than before. I was tired, hungry, thirsty, scared, confused, cold and now upset also? I was far from feeling cooperative. Antoinette was my homegirl and I got even angrier at the very thought of siding with Detective Vermil against her.

"I don't know nobody by that name and I want to talk to my lawyer." Detective Vermil extracted some photos from the file and slid them over to me, ignoring my request.

"*You* are telling *me* that this is not *your* car parked in front of her house? That this is not *you* and *your* brother getting out of the car? *Goddamnit Atif*! I'm trying to help you out here! So quit this tou-"

"*Fuck* you! You don't give a *fuck* about me *or* what happens to me! I *said* I want to talk to my lawyer!" I cut him off mid-sentence. Silence ensued. My heart was racing; tears filled with fear of the unknown mixed with fury soaked my face. I just sat there seething almost to the point of hyperventilation. I wanted to go home. Detective Vermil gathered the photos from the table.

"This is not television Atif, nor is it a game. These are some *serious* charges you are facing. Now is not the time for being loyal or whatever to anyone because it will only make things worse for you." Detective Vermil said in a soft tone. I was then in the presence of Mr. Good Cop: Mr. Bad Cop had left the building. "We both know you are guilty as sin, they caught you with your hands in the cookie jar for Christ's sake. All the fancy lawyers in the world can't change that. You need to think about *yourself*. You need to think about your grandmother and how much she needs you out there with her as she continues to get up in age. Your brother is not going to be around to look after her Atif, I can promise you that. I've seen his kind come and go time and time again. The little organization you guys have is going to crumble. Rick, Antoinette, Kenyatta, Darion, Michael, Travis and the rest of them are going down, eventually. You're still young and you still have a chance. All you have to do is cooperate with me and I can assure you that I will make something happen for you. Now, for the last time, are you going to answer my questions or not?"

I looked at him, reached for the cold can of Pepsi and opened it up. I then took a good long sip, enjoying the feeling of the pop tingling in my throat. I finished it off and sat the empty can back on the table.

"Are you ready to talk now?" Detective Vermil asked me softly, grabbing the tape recorder with a smile. I belched loudly.

"Fuck you snowflake." I answered, smirking in return. Detective Vermil's face flushed. He gathered his file and rose from his seat.

"Okay, it's *your* grandmother's *lonely* funeral, not mine." Detective Vermil said as he headed for the door. "You guys aren't going to be able to *poison* the eyewitnesses and get away with it this time. Lets see you

270

slither your way up out of *this* one." He said, slamming the door closed behind him.

*****

The next day was New Year's Eve. The last year and a ½ had been something like a roller coaster ride for me. In that short time period I experienced some of the best times I could remember, strangely mixed at the same time with some of the worst. I had reached the highest of heights obtainable for someone my age from 27th and Benton; getting money, cars, clothes, women, clout. But all of a sudden, seemingly when things were going so good that it felt as if nothing could go wrong, as if it was meant for me to live my life prospering in such a way as recompense for the loss of my mother, it all came to an abrupt end. Just like that.

And that is how our Creator catches us. He gives us respite and allows us to do our thing for a while and then catches us slipping, humbling us with a reality check and breaking us down to our knees. Whole ancient civilizations were done in the same manner. The people of these civilizations had reached the level of what we call today a "super power" and were all of a sudden dealt with because of their arrogance, disobedience, stubbornness, and transgressions (according to the scriptures). If we travel throughout the world we will witness their ruins, and if we are wise this will encourage us to take heed and understand that the same thing that befell them will happen to us if we don't get it together.

The ancient civilizations spoken of above were sent prophets and messengers to warn them of the impending destruction awaiting in the near future, but they refused to take heed. Me? I had my signs and symbols too. I knew a lot of people from the hood who were dead or doing life in prison for living the same way of life I was. I was also warned by Mr. Williams back in April of that same year. He tried to convince me to turn away before it was too late and

271

avert the sure end result. But I too refused to take heed and now it was time to deal with the consequences.

After my 20 hour investigation was up I was transported to the Jackson County Detention Center. It took almost 6 hours for them to process me in. I brought January 1, 1994 in by standing on my bunk, gazing out of my window down onto the downtown Kansas City streets and wondering if I would ever see them again. While in juvenile I kept telling myself that I would find a way out of this. That I would come up with some plan to put forth to my brother and the hommies that they could execute and force the authorities to release me like Antoinette and I had done for Malik and K-Red. I just knew that I could escape the inescapable. It wasn't until that very moment did I finally accept reality. Detective Vermil was right; there really was no way out. Sometimes, and in some situations, all of the "down hommies" and "money" in the world could be of no avail.

*****

<u>FACE 2 FACE WITH DEVIL</u>

"I'm in the county jail
playin' card games wit' killas,
thought the judge was insane
when he called me nigga.
85%
since they labeled me a violent offender,
and my so called defender
wants to surrender?"
-Soody Mak

"It ain't no doubt,
that he
saw the crook in me,
when he
took a good look at me,
because he
threw the book at me.....
I'M FACE 2 FACE WIT' THE DEVIL HIMSELF!"
-Soody Mak

14

July 4, 1995.

I had been rotting in the county jail for over 18 months. I made the necessary adjustments and fell into a daily routine of lifting weights, writing letters, reading Donald Goines books, sleeping and playing cards. There was a television in the module but it was always too loud in the module to hear it so I never paid it much attention. I spent that past 18 months staying out of trouble, following my attorney's advice. The prosecuting attorney assigned to my case had not been very willing to agree with my lawyer on a sentencing agreement in exchange for my guilty plea. This was why I had been there for so long, trying to wait things out. I was offered a sentence of life without parole when the bargaining began, which meant that I would be held in prison until the day I died, of which we of course refused. It went back and forth like that for months on end, up to that point the bidding was stalled at 25 years.

A new law had passed called the "Violent Offender Act" which I had no knowledge of prior to my incarceration. This law stated that all persons convicted of a violent crime would have to do a mandatory minimum of 85% of their prison sentence before they could be released on parole. News of this law crushed me. It meant that even if my lawyer *could* get my sentence down to 10 years like he was trying to do, I would have to do 8 ½ years flat before I could make parole. I had been witnessing people come back from court with lengthy sentences and the looks on their faces were depressing for all of us in the module because we knew that one day some of us would make a similar entrance. Some came back bawling like babies, looking as if they had been crying for the *whole* ride from the courthouse all of the way back to the module, whereas others would hold it in until they found the solitude of their cells.

People went through a lot of phases in the county. I would sit back and watch them come in and keep quietly to themselves for the first week or so before they became

275

comfortable enough to come out of their shells. They would begin doing so by asking a lot of questions concerning sentencing guidelines and lawyers, most would try and convince *you* of their innocence as if what you thought really mattered. I surmised that these types were searching for any kind of hope they could get their hands on, and it was these very ones who were usually the guiltiest of them all. I observed how they would get filled up with all of this false hope by jailhouse lawyers and others who were just as ignorant concerning the legal system as they were, go to trial and get *lost* in the shuffle. When, *knowing* they were guilty as sin, they could have snatched out on a plea bargain instead of ending up with a number that was impossible for them to do in a couple of lifetimes.

You also had what I labeled your "all of a sudden want to get religious types" who would spend their time reading the Bible, praying, etc. until they lost their trial. They would deceive themselves into believing that our Creator was simply going to release them back into society so that they could go right back out there and continue acting a fool just because they professed belief with their tongues. Those who fell into this category always amused me when they came back from court found guilty on all counts, especially the child molesters. Feeling forsaken, they would throw their Bibles in the trash, along with their faith, giving up all hope in their religion.

There is another type of individual who comes through the county that I will mention here. This was the kind of person who realized just how much they were in love with their girlfriends *after* they got locked up. They did their time in the county on an emotional roller coaster, more depressed with the thought of losing their girlfriends than spending the rest of their lives in prison. They always wanted to talk about the women in their lives. They didn't have time to spend with them on the streets. But now? Now you couldn't pull these people off of the phone. They *fought* over use of the phone. I would watch on as they went from calling their girlfriends 20 times a day to not being able to get their girlfriends to accept the charges of *one* collect call, all within a few months time. These people amused me also, second only to the "all of a sudden want to get religious" types. I swore that what Patience and I had was in some way deeper than what these people had with their girlfriends and I just knew in my heart that Patience would *never* roll out on me like that, especially not for another man. Not me; not her *first*!

I thought I knew a lot of things when in fact I knew not much of anything at all.

Big Mama was doing pretty good. Malik brought her down to see me once or twice a month. Patience, Darion and Teebaby came to visit a lot. Darion and Teebaby had the prettiest little girl who they named "Destiny Ayanna Nichols." They fought a lot. Teebaby wrote me once informing me that Darion had ceased having sex with her altogether for some reason she had yet to figure out. All he did was come around their apartment every once in a while to check on his daughter and then she would not see him for days at a time. I hardly *ever* saw the two together anymore. One usually came without the other.

Antoinette no longer worked in the county. She was "laid off" after her supervisor got tired of receiving numerous notes from unanimous senders about her bringing marijuana to me, not to mention suspicions they already harbored concerning the death of Small Balls. They were unable to catch her bringing anything in to me but they still let her go nonetheless.

As for everyone else: Smack Man, Money Mike, K-Red, Trigga and Persistence, everything was kosher. I warned Smack Man about Detective Vermil and he laughed it off, saying that he was not on his level. That if he needed to worry about anyone it was the Feds.

It was late in the morning, sometime near noon. Me and 3 other people were sitting at a table playing spades, hoping they would have something eatable for lunch. My partner was an immigrant from Bangladesh named "Ngueyn". None of us could pronounce his name so

277

we gave him the nickname "Two-Fifty". We called him this
because he didn't weigh anymore than 115 pounds soaking
wet but would talk slick to you and even attack you as if he
weighed *250*. I liked Two-Fifty and was practically the only
one who had the patience to try and understand his broken
English. Come to find out, the brother was *very* intelligent.

"When I come country," Two-Fifty started, "I get
off......fly?" I looked up as he spread his arms out like
wings.

"Airplane?" I offered, shuffling the cards.

"Yeah, airplane. I get off airplane and day later get
on.....you know, it big.....it blue, it white..........drive?"

"The bus? The metro bus?"

"I get on Metro." Two-Fifty said, nodding his head.
"We ride, I see my sister house, I no know how speak
English! How I say stop Metro? I ride, ride, ride," I laughed
as I pictured him in my mind sitting on the bus and riding
right past his house not knowing how to signal the driver to
stop. "I hear *ding*! Metro stop, someone get off. I look
around; how make *ding* sound? I ride, ride, ride, we pass
my sister house, I look around nobody make *ding*! I ride,
ride, ride, I see someone touch wall I hear *ding!* They get
off. I ride, ride, ride, we pass my sister house I touch wall,
no *ding*! Later I *last* one on Metro. He say, driver say,
come. I go. He ask I speak English? I shake head no. He
say sit, touch him shoulder when I want him stop Metro.
We ride, ride, ride, I see my sister house and touch him
shoulder he stop Metro I get off."

"How long was you on the bus Two-Fifty man?" I
asked.

"*Six* mutter futter hour!" he answered. We all
exploded in a fit of laughter. He still didn't know much
English but he sure tried to pronounce every curse word in
the language.

"How many times did you ride past your house?" I
asked in between laughs.

"At least *20* mutter futter time!" I fell out of my
chair and laughed until my stomach cramped up. Two-Fifty
had been making me laugh like that since the day I met

278

him. I got up from the ground and dealt the cards, still laughing.

We played two more games of spades, ate our lunches and then the majority of us retreated to our cells to nap, reflect, or whatever. I was in my cell listening to my walkman when my neighbor appeared at my doorway informing me that I had a visit. I got up, freshened up and made my way to the sallyport. A guard by the name of "Smitty" escorted me down the hallway to the visiting booths. As I entered, I spotted Malik and Patience in the only booth that was vacant. The small room was noisy and crowded. I took a seat and picked up the receiver.

"Wha'sup punk?" I greeted my brother first with a traditional insult, smirking.

"Nothin', fag."

"Why do you guys *greet* each other like that?" Patience asked the two of us.

"Because he's a fag." Malik answered.

"And *he's a* punk." I added. Patience shook her head. "Wha'sup with you?"

"Oh, I'm just happy to have made it here in one piece. Malik almost drove us off of a bridge on the way." Patience answered, eyeing my brother. "I think I am going to ride the Metro back."

"You need some bus fare?" Malik asked her, digging into his jeans' pocket.

"Anyway, how are *you* doing Atif?"

"I'm chillin'", I answered. "Why come I didn't get a letter from you yesterday?"

"I wrote you, I just haven't sent it yet."

"That's some bullshit right there Atif." Malik cut in.

"I did so!" she said, nudging my brother. I had to side with Malik on that one. I was beginning to not hear from her as much as I used to when mail call came.

"I ain't trippin'."

"You said that like you don't believe me or something."

"I ain't say all that; I just said I ain't trippin'."
Patience looked at me. "Did you pop some firecrackers
today?" I then asked her, changing the subject.

"Don't you even fix your mouth like you wanna lie
and say yeah." Malik warned Patience just as she was
about to answer my question.

"*Yes,* I did. One or two." Patience answered,
ignoring him. Malik curled up his lips in disbelief.

"What he talkin' about then?" I asked. Patience
looked at Malik.

"Go ahead, tell'em about this *firecracker* or two you
popped." Malik said.

"I po-"

"She lit a mutha'fuckin' *Sparkle* man, that's it!"
Malik cut her off. "Patience is so scary it don't make no
sense."

"That is *not* the only thing I lit Malik and you *know*
it!" Patience exclaimed. I laughed.

"What else did you light?" I asked.

"One of those.....I don't know what they're called.
One of those black things."

"A Black Cat firecracker?" I offered.

"*Hell* naw! She talkin' about one of them lil' black
snakes that come out of the wrapper or whatever when you
light'em. Some shit we bought for Destiny." I laughed
again.

"Why you hate firecrackers so much?" I asked her.
The summer I caught my case I could not persuade her to
light a firecracker for the life of me.

"I don't know, they sound too much like guns." We
all sat silently for a few moments.

"You still workin' out?" Malik asked me.

"I haven't been lately."

"Don't stop workin' out Atif. It's a jungle where you
headed. Juvenile and this county shit ain't nothin'. Don't
pull chain thinkin' that the pen gone be laid back like this
county."

"It ain't laid back in here."

"It is compared to *prison*. These niggas ain't talkin' about nothin' for real in here. A nigga might get his head busted with the coffee pot or get his ass whooped or somethin', but the penitentiary is a whole different world. Stay on your square man and workout consistently, don't let yo-self get too comfortable. You need to stay in *top* condition. With the case you goin' down on you never know when you gone have to get a nigga, or a *few* niggas, up off of you. You can't out box *everybody*. It's some niggas that will get a hold of your ass and your boxin' skills ain't gone do you no good if you ain't got no strength. Shit, if they send you to the right place, niggas ain't gone wanna fight anyway. They gone be on another level; stabbin' mutha'fuckas and shit."

My brother was not trying to scare me, he was just keeping it real with me. He was however scaring Patience though, I could see it in her eyes. Her idea of prison life was what she saw in the movies.

"Let me quit man before Patience get to cryin' and shit." Malik said.

"I am *not* going to cry today." Patience said, beaming with confidence. She had never before came to visit me without crying.

"Whatever," Malik started, rising from his seat. "I'm gone let y'all get the last few minutes alone so y'all can get some of y'all lovey-dovey mush-talk in. I ain't tryin' to hear that shit."

"A'ight then." I said.

"Stay up nigga, remember what I told you. Aw, and write Big Mama too." Malik said. He pressed his right fist against the glass and I did the same. He then turned and left, leaving the two of us alone together. We spent a while staring lovingly into each other's eyes, smiling.

"What's on your mind?"

"Missing you." Silence. "Are you *absolutely, positively* sure that 6 ½ more years is the *best* it can get?"

"Yeah Patience," I answered for the 100th time.

"That is such a long time,"

"Is it *too* long for *us*?"

281

"Atif, even if they refuse to go any lower than the 25 years they are talking about, then 25 years from now I will *still* be here standing by your side. I will *never* leave you, I *promise*. You are the only one for me and I just know that we are going to pull through all of this." Patience vowed.

It sounded good, sounded *real* good. I honestly believe she meant what she said at that time. But with the passage of time things change. Emotions are forgotten or transferred. Promises that were once so binding become not such a big deal. "That is, insha Allah." Patience added. I smiled. *"What?* I like to say that. When I do, people are like: Girl what does *that* mean?" I laughed. "Where did you learn that anyway?"

I hesitated before I answered. The two of us talked about everything but for some reason I felt uneasy about mentioning Fatimah to her. True enough, I was more *attracted* to Patience than I ever had been to anyone before her physically and even emotionally, but I had never been so *intrigued* by a girl before like I was by Fatimah, not even by Patience.

"Somebody back in detention taught me that."

Fatimah. I wondered to myself what she was up to. I had heard that she beat her case, that the prosecutor dropped it the day before they were scheduled to go to trial. I also wondered to myself if she ever thought of me.

"What are you thinking about?" Patience asked me. I had spaced off, thinking of Fatimah.

"Nothin' for real," I answered in dismissal.

"It was a pleasant thought, whatever it was."

"So are you havin' a nice 4th of July?"

"It's okay, I guess. It would be better if you were out here to spend it with me. Everyone is over Rick's house; swimming, eating, popping firecrackers, *smoking* and *drinking*, listening to music. It's a beautiful day out too.

"You know, every time I find myself even *beginning* to have any fun I will think of how you are locked up in a cell and it depresses me." Patience said, her eyes were

282

brimming with tears. At that moment the door behind me opened.

"Say your good-byes gentlemen, visits are over." Smitty said, stepping into the room. I looked at Patience and smiled. Tears were falling from her eyes despite her efforts to hold them back.

"We gone be a'ight Patience." I consoled.

"I know," Patience started sniffling. "I just......why couldn't you have just *stayed* with me that night Atif? Huh?"

"Every time I close my eyes to go to sleep I ask myself that same question. But you know what? I think that if it wasn't *that* night it would have probably been the *next* one. I was on my way regardless."

"Lets go Atif." Smitty said. I was the only one remaining, all the others were already outside in the hall waiting to return to the module.

"I got to go." I said, rising. Patience did the same. "Send me my letter."

"Okay," Patience kissed the tips of her fingers and pressed them against the glass. I did the same. "I love you Atif, see you again soon."

"Insha Allah,"

"Insha Allah." Patience said, smiling. She then turned to leave, waving at me when she reached the door. She looked above me and shook her head. I followed her gaze and saw someone in the module located right across from the visiting room standing up on the table signaling to Patience with his hands. The plexi-glass was lined with others gesturing towards her. I mugged every last one of them on my way out.

"That was your girl Atif?" An older brother asked me on our way back to the module. I nodded. "That's a *bad* young mutha'fucka' there boa." He was right, Patience *was* blossoming into an even more attractive woman. He was also well into his forties, way too old for her. Old enough to be her father. I started to ask him how he would feel about a man his age lusting after *his* 17 year old daughter; but I changed my mind and ignored him.

"A, you want another one of those lunch trays?" Smitty asked me as he let the rest of the people back into the module.

"Yeah," I answered. Barbeque chicken, ice cream, chips, potato salad? We only ate like that once or twice a year!

"Clean something up for me upstairs and I will see what I can do."

"A'ight."

I followed the guard to a small closet where we took out a mop bucket, a mop, a broom and a towel. We then got on the elevator and rode it to the next floor. On the way it was explained that a guard dropped a bunch of lunch trays onto the floor down in front of D-module. Getting off of the elevator, we headed down the corridor. When we reached D-module, I went to cleaning the mess up. Minutes later when I finished, I rose from the floor and there stood Kev, along with five other people, standing at the plexi–glass window staring at me. I heard that he had been arrested on an attempted murder charge, but this was my first time seeing him.

"When I get my hands on you nigga, it's *curtains!*" Kev said to me through the chuckhole.

"Whatever. Last time I saw you nigga, you was all ass and elbows." I responded with a smirk, referring to his running away after I shot him in his arm that night at the gas station.

"Aw yeah? You think that's funny cuzz?" Kev asked, glaring at me. I had touched a sensitive nerve with my remark.

"I think it's hilarious."

"A'ight, lets just say we *even* then nigga." he said, smiling. My smirk disappeared, it was *my* turn to glare at *him*.

Even? What did he mean, *even?* He didn't mean what I thought he meant; did he? I had killed his friend, someone had killed my mother. I shot him, someone had shot my brother. Rage seeped into my chest. I dropped the mop and just stood there stiff with anger.

"Come on Atif, lets go." Smitty said, pulling me
away. "Whatever y'all got going on there is nothing you will
be able to do about it with all of that steel and plexi-glass
between the two of you."
"Do you think *that's* funny cuzz?" Kev taunted,
"You find that hilarious? Laugh at *that* you *bitch* ass nigga!"

*****

A month later I was on the first floor locked in a
holding cell handcuffed to a bench. I was waiting to go to
court to get sentenced and had been waiting for hours. I
was frustrated and very uncomfortable, not to mention
afraid. My lawyer had talked the prosecutor down to 15
years for each count, but the agreement was that I would
have to plead guilty in what is called an "open plea". This
was because the two could not agree on a recommendation
for a concurrent sentence. The prosecutor wanted me to
receive 15 years for 2nd degree murder and another 15
years for armed criminal action and wanted them to be run
consecutive to each other, sort of like what had been done
to the brother I talked to back at the city jail. Even back
when he was shooting for life without parole, he meant 2
lives without parole; and when that was negotiated down to
25 years instead, he actually meant 50 years because he
wanted 25 years for both counts. He wanted to make an
example out of me.
I was hesitant to agree to the 15 years because
there was too much of a chance that I would actually end
up with a 30 year sentence. My lawyer persuaded me to
trust him, which was something I was not good at, with the
help of Smack Man. An open plea meant that the
prosecutor would put forth his argument as to why he felt
my sentences should be run consecutive and my lawyer
would in turn put forth his argument as to why he felt my
sentences should be run concurrently and then it would be
up to the judge to decide.

285

There was no predicting how things would play out.
15 years was a long time, especially with knowing that I
would have to do close to 13 years flat before I could get
out. I would be 27 by then! Moments before I witnessed a
couple of bailiffs literally carrying a brother out of the
courtroom while referring to the judge as a "devil". He too
went in front of the judge and pled guilty in an open plea.
Things looked as if they didn't go as he had planned. Not
only that, but now the judge was in a bad mood and I still
had to go before him. I gave myself confidence by saying
that the brother had a public defender, of which was known
for dealing with people's futures in a half-hearted way, and
I at least had a paid for attorney.

I wanted to *kill* Kev. No, that wasn't good enough.
I wanted to torture him. For the last month I had been
fantasizing about ways that I could torture him for months
on end and keep him alive just so that I could continue
doing so. I thought about some horrendous acts; burning
the tip of his penis with a welder's torch; making small
incisions all over his body and then drop him into a tub filled
with alcohol and salt, reopen his wounds and then do it
again; then I would take a pair of vise grips, pull out his
teeth, fingernails and toenails all one by one, and that
would only be day number one.

It had been Kev the *whole* time. All of those funny
little looks he used to give me, as if he knew something I
didn't. Who was he with? It took every ounce of discipline I
had not to begin "acting up" so that they would move me
up to the next floor. I had to lay back though, my lawyer
warned me not to give the prosecutor any more ammunition
than he already had. I wanted to tell Malik but at the same
time I didn't because my brother would slaughter everything
Kev loved. I heard that a girl we went to school with whose
name was "Ranita" had given birth to his child. I always
liked Ranita and I knew that if I told Malik then she and the
baby would be the first ones to go. They had nothing to do
with this. Kev had taken something from me that could
never be replaced. I would get some "get back"; I didn't
care if it was 13 years into the future.

"You ready to go youngsta?" the bailiff asked me as he entered the holding tank. I nodded. He then released me from the bench, took hold of my right arm and led me into the courtroom.

The courtroom itself was almost empty. My lawyer informed me later that he had orchestrated it that way. None of the victim's family members were even present. I wondered to myself how he pulled that one off. I was led up to the front of the courtroom and left standing between my lawyer and the prosecutor before the judge.

The judge was an elderly balding white man with glasses. After asking me if I had agreed to plead guilty in exchange for a 15 year sentence on both counts without coercion, I was informed that it was his decision if the sentences were to be run concurrent or consecutive. I then was instructed to recount the events that had taken place on the August night in question back in 1993. When I finished, the judge asked me a few more questions and then accepted my guilty plea. The prosecutor explained why he felt my sentences should be run consecutive and my lawyer put forth his opinions as to why they shouldn't be. The judge took a long deep look off into my eyes and then rendered his decision. 15 years for 2nd degree murder and 15 years for armed criminal action, both of which to be served consecutive to each other within the Missouri Department of Corrections.

I was sick. I felt faint. My knees got weak and I suddenly had to use the rest-room. 30 years? I looked towards the prosecutor and envisioned myself wrapping my cuffs around his neck and choking him. The judge rose from the bench and exited the courtroom without even giving me a second look. Just another day at work. My lawyer placed his hand on my shoulder and when I looked up at him I noticed that even he was genuinely upset with the turn of events.

"It's not over Atif. I asked you to trust me and I need for you to continue doing so, don't give up. When you get to where they send you, lay low and I will pull some strings. I took that *personally*, and believe me when it's all

287

said and done his judgment will be reversed and your
sentences will be run concurrent."

The bailiff then led me out of the courtroom. I
remember walking out of there feeling as if I had just left
the presence of the devil himself.

*****

<u>FROM ELEMENTARY TO THE PENITENTIARY</u>

"I went on a school trip,
been ridin' the same bus since elementary.
Blind, not knowin' that I'm
on my way to doin' time in the penitentiary.
-I have to stop this misery!-"
-Soody Mak

15

Stepping off of the elevator I, like many of those who went before me, made my entrance into the module in a daze. It was like I wasn't even walking, as if I was *floating* with my head straight and my eyes fixed forward staring at something no one else could see but me. All eyes were on me as I made my way to my cell. No one said *anything,* all conversations were on hold indefinitely.

When I reached my cell I floated across the threshold and had a seat on my bunk. I then slumped over and placed my face in my hands. I wanted to cry, but I didn't. What was the point? I could have cried a river and when it all dried up I would have *still* been on my way to prison with a 30 year sentence on my shoulders.

30 years? I couldn't even begin to imagine being incarcerated for such a period of time. I had *hardly* been in *existence* for 17 years and I couldn't even remember back *that* far!

I spent the next few days in a state of depression and solitude. I stayed in my cell and slept in anticipation of the one time I would wake up from that which I was experiencing. It didn't work. Every time I opened my eyes the first thought was how much time I had been sentenced to. I didn't eat. I didn't go to the gym or the library. No one came to visit me, not even Malik. My brother and everyone else knew me well enough to know that I did not want to be bothered by *anyone.* That I had my own way of dealing with things and I needed to be left alone in order to do so. I received letters but they all sat unread on my desk. My nightmares even seemed to respect my wishes.

I tried to rationalize with myself; maybe I *deserved* it. After all, I was responsible for the deaths of 2 people directly and another indirectly by the age of 15. I had only been caught and charged with one of them. Even that didn't work because I would then tell myself that I would trade places with any one of those 3 in a heartbeat; that I would rather be dead than spend so much of my life in prison. At least that was how I felt at the time.

A week later while waiting to pull chain I decided that I would give my grandmother a call. I knew that she must have been worried sick about me. I went and told one of the "I realize just how much I love my girlfriend now that I am locked up" types who was then using the only working phone in the module (and had been *all* day) that I needed to use it. He respectfully got off of it without incident. I then called Big Mama's house.

"Hey baby!" Big Mama exclaimed after accepting the charges.

"Hi Big Mama." I greeted solemnly.

"Aw, listen at you. You sound so *depressed*!"

"I don't even know how to explain how I feel right now. How are you doin'?"

"Oh, I'm still breathin' so I praise the Lord for that. I haven't been feelin' too well lately, my suga' is really kickin' my butt." A slight pause. "Well, I'm glad you called. Everyone's *so* worried about you. We all heard about what happened and Malik say tha-"

"Big Mama?" I cut in.

"Yeah baby?"

"I....I can't do this. 30 years," I started, shaking my head. "I can't do that much time."

"Now you listen here Atif," my grandmother began in a stern tone, "Don't you dare let them white folk break you down; you hear me boy?" I nodded. "I didn't hear you...?"

"Yes ma'am."

"You are a warrior, much stronger than you even know. You come from a strong and *mighty* race of people and you got their blood flowin' through your veins. We have been through *countless* trials and tribulations. Some we brought on ourselves, most we didn't. And durin' these times we too felt like we wasn't gone make it; like we couldn't take one more of our own bein' lynched and hung; like we couldn't take one more of our baby girls gettin' raped; like we couldn't stand bein' called a *nigger* not one more time. But you know what?"

"What?"

292

"We *persevered*. We kept our faith in God and we made it even though we thought we couldn't at times. Let me tell you a story grandbaby:

"One night this man had a dream. He dreamed he was walkin' along the beach with the Lord. Across the sky flashed scenes from his life. For each scene, he noticed two sets of footprints in the sand; one belongin' to him, and the other to the Lord.

"When the last scene of his life flashed before him, he looked back at the footprints in the sand. He noticed that many times along the path of his life there was only one set of footprints. He also noticed that it happened at the very lowest and saddest times in his life.

"This really bothered him and he questioned the Lord about it: 'Lord, you said that once I decided to follow you, you'd walk with me all the way. But I have noticed that durin' the most troublesome times in my life, there is only one set of footprints. I don't understand why when I needed you most you would leave me.'

"The Lord replied: 'My precious, precious child, I love you and I would never leave you. Durin' your times of trial and sufferin', when you see only one set of footprints, it was then that I *carried* you.'"

I smiled to myself, feeling a new sense of motivation. Calling Big Mama was a smart thing to do, something I should have done *days* before. Throughout my childhood she always did have that effect on me. It was her, along with my best friend that helped me cope with my mother's death without going completely nuts.

"Did you get the point of that story?" Big Mama asked.

"Yeah, I think so."

"What does it mean to you Atif?"

"It means that God is there to help us get through life even when it seems like we are alone and can't make it."

"That's right. And you know what else?"

"What?"

293

"You wouldn't have all of this weight on your shoulders if you wasn't strong enough to carry it." I smiled again, thinking of the Qur'anic verse Fatimah had taught me, calling it to mind for the first time in months. To my surprise it was still etched into my heart word for word. I would *never* forget that verse. "Sometimes God will allow us to go through some changes in life that we don't *want* to go through even though it will be better for us in the long run. And the things that we *do* want are **not** in our best interests. Believe me baby, everything that happens does so accordin' to God's plan. You understand what I am sayin'?"

"Yes Ma'am." And I did. I just didn't see how 30 years in prison was going to be better for me *personally* in the long run. At that moment a recording cut in informing us that we had one minute remaining to talk.

"Sounds like we runnin' outta time," Big Mama said. "Wanna hang up and call me right back?"

"Naw, that's okay Big Mama. I don't want to keep you." Big Mama didn't like to talk on the phone for long periods of time, even though she would have made an exception for me if I needed her to. "Besides, I think I'm...I'm feelin' a lil' better now." I was too.

"That's good, I'm happy to hear you say that. I love you and I want you to be strong now, ya' hear?"

"Yes ma'am."

"Remember, God is with you every step of the way. Even when you are at your lowest, darkest points in your life and you look down and see only one set of footprints in the sand."

"Okay,"

"Bye grandbaby."

"Bye Big Mama."

*****

Early the next morning I woke to the sound of my door sliding open a little earlier than usual. I rose from my bunk and peered outside of the cell. A guard opened the chuck hole and told me to pack my things, I was pulling chain.

The time had come.

I didn't know where to start, I had so much stuff! Letters, cards, pictures, drawings, magazines, legal work, the list went on and on. I retrieved a list of things we could enter the Department of Corrections with, which wasn't much of anything at all, and was dismayed at the fact that I would have to either leave most of my possessions behind or take them with me and send them home when I got to the Fulton Reception and Diagnostic Correctional Center. I decided to leave the things I couldn't take with me behind. What was the point in sending them home to a place I wouldn't be seeing for at least another 25 years?

I started first with the few things I *could* take with me and put them into a small box: a Bible, stamps, legal work, 10 photos, and a calendar. I had so many photos I couldn't decide which ones I wanted to take with me and which to leave behind. I gathered them all and threw them into the box along with the letters and cards. Maybe I *would* send them home but everything else I would give away.

I grabbed my walkman, food, and pornographic magazines and took them upstairs to Two-Fifty, sliding what I could beneath his cell door and leaving the rest just outside of it. He heard me doing so and woke up.

"You go?" Two-Fifty asked me.

"Yeah,"

"Write me you get there."

"For what? You can't read English you illiterate ass, funny lookin' wanna be Chink you." I said, lightening the somber mood.

"Fuh' you you ugly blah' mutter futter you." We both laughed, trading insults for the last time. Two-Fifty then flexed his right biceps indicating for me to stay strong. I nodded.

"Don't be swingin' on people twice your size while I'm gone man."

"I no start! I beat mutter futter ass *he* fuh' with *me*." Two-Fifty said, showing me numerous scars on his knuckles. I smiled, turning to leave. "Atif!" I turned back around. "Thank you man!" Two-Fifty, holding up the walkman and girly magazines. I threw up my fist and went back downstairs.

I distributed the rest of my things throughout the module, said my good-byes and walked into the sallyport carrying what I had left in the small cardboard box I held in front of me. I was then led downstairs to the first floor and locked into a holding cell with 12 others who were also pulling chain. I recognized two people in the holding cell, one a 24th Street Crip by the name of "Alonzo" who had been standing in the window next to Kev upstairs that day back in July. We mugged each other briefly and he turned his head away as I sat.

The other was someone from the neighborhood whom we called "Knock-out". He was 29 years old and built like a world champion body builder. His muscles appeared as if they were going to rip holes in his jumpsuit. He earned his nickname by having a reputation for knocking drug dealers unconscious and taking their product from them. He didn't smoke a lot of crack, but when he did one would be wise to practice extreme caution when doing business with Knockout, especially if he didn't know you and didn't have any money.

He had never tried anything with anyone from our clique, whenever he used to come by the tilt I would serve him while holding a pistol in my other hand when Darion, Kesha and I were there alone. That way if he even acted as if he wanted to make me one of his victims I could blow his heart right out of his back before the mere thought had the chance to manifest itself.

"Wha'sup lil' nigga?" Knockout greeted, picking me up and squeezing the very life out of me with his embrace. That brother had too much strength for his own good. "This my mutha' fuckin' *dawg* right here, shit."

"Wha' sup Knockout?" I returned the greeting as he released me.

296

"Nothin' man, I'm on my way back for a funky ass parole violation. I heard about what happened in court man; how you holdin' up?" I shrugged my shoulders. "Yeah, that's fucked up. A, you gone be cool though man. Appeal that shit. Plus, you know I got your back nigga. Anyone of your so-called enemies wanna trip they gone have to trip with me too." Knockout finished, loud enough for Alonzo to hear.

Moments later we were given our breakfast trays and then two hours after that 6 or 7 guards came in, handcuffing and shackling us all together with chains. It was then that I understood why being transported to prison was called "pulling chain".

Black History buffs would get an eerie sense of déjà vu while observing the parading of blacks to the penitentiary because of how closely the process mirrors the experience of our ancestors being trafficked to the "Americas" by way of the Middle Passage. They fastened these iron black boxes over our cuffs which prevented *any* wrist movement whatsoever. One of the guards informed us that it was in fact an inmate who designed the black boxes when we expressed our displeasure. I shook my head with disgust. Whoever the prisoner was that designed that contraption needed to be dealt with. That was like a slave designing a whip in order for the slave master to whip the slaves with, himself included. And just like back in those days, I suspect that the inmate did not profit off of his invention at all like our ancestors did not profit from the things *they* invented.

The four hour ride to Fulton, Missouri was so uncomfortable that it is indescribable. I didn't sleep a wink. I was seated next to Knockout and we spent the trip talking and staring out of the window. I looked on as motorists passed us by on the highway, wondering to myself how it felt to be riding in a car worry free, for I no longer remembered. I saw people talking on cellular phones, singing along with their car stereos, eating, disciplining their children and talking nonchalantly to one another while driving at the same time. They had no idea that I even

297

existed, let alone was on my way to prison for a lifetime. I remember peering down upon a red Toyota, inside was a white woman and an infant strapped into a car seat on the passenger side. I thought about how by the time I made it out of prison that child would more than likely be married with a child of his or her own and turned away.

I had never been so far away from Kansas City. I appreciated the passing landscape as we traveled through county after county. The small towns, the pastures, the woods, etc. All these things I took for granted and never really paid much attention to.

Especially the restaurants. At that time I would have killed for a McBLT with cheese from McDonalds. It didn't help none at all when the guards stopped at a Wendy's restaurant, ate the rich smelling, mouth watering food in the van with us and then passed out some thick choke sandwiches (peanut butter) for us to eat. If I wasn't so hungry I would have thrown mine back at them. Knockout and I joked about committing a strong armed robbery for food. I never was a thief or one to rob anyone for anything, but if Knockout and I were not shackled down like we were, those guards would have relinquished that Wendy's food willingly or unwillingly.

Pulling up to the Fulton Reception and Diagnostic Correctional Center was an experience within itself. Don't let the name fool you, Fulton was also a maximum security prison equipped with rows of electric fences and razor wire. It was very intimidating. We were not alone. There were numerous buses and vans in line ahead of us bursting at the seams with prisoners. So many of them were blacks! They had come from different counties and prisons all over the state.

When our turn finally came we were ushered stumbling and struggling to maintain our balance off of the van and into the reception area. Our shackles and cuffs were removed, we were stripped searched and then locked in a small, cold room with nothing but a small white towel to cover ourselves with. I was *so* cold. I thought of Kesha and wondered to myself if she had went through such a

298

degrading experience when she entered the penitentiary. Kesha could be very uncooperative, I just knew that she gave them a mouthful if she did. What if *Fatimah* would've had to be subjected to that? There was no way she would have disrobed in front of so many people.

They began calling us out 3 at a time. When they reached me I made my way out into the long, cold corridor. My towel was confiscated and I was asked what size clothes I wore. I was then directed to a shower area and instructed to raise my hands above my head and close my eyes. A guard sprayed me with something cold that smelled like some type of pesticide. It was horrible. When I finished I rushed to the shower to rinse it off. The water was scalding hot but I withstood it. Three minutes later the water was shut off and I was given some green shorts, a pair of socks, a white T-shirt, a comb, a toothbrush, toothpaste, a bar of lye soap, some boxer shorts, a razor, and a roll of cheap rough toilet paper. I got dressed and then went and stood in line to have an identification card made. Here my whole sense of identity was taken from me and replaced with a 6 digit number.

I spent the next few hours being directed from one office to another, answering question after question. I saw caseworkers, nurses, a psychiatrist, etc. After there was nothing left for me to do, I found a spot on the floor at the opposite end of the crowded corridor and had a seat. Knockout joined me an hour or so later.

"I hate this shit, I'll be glad when it's all over with."

"That wasn't all?"

"Hell naw, shit, we just gettin' started." I shook my head. I was tired and I just wanted to lay down and go to sleep. "That's it for today though. Let me see your paperwork, see where they put you at." I gave him all of the papers I had been given. "Let's see.....aw, shit. We in the same wing. That's cool." Knockout handed my paperwork back to me. "I'm gone put you up on some game before they put us in our housin' unit.

"I know I ain't got to tell you this but I will anyway. If anyone of these fags, booty bandits, Crips, G.D.'s, St.

Louis niggas, *whoever* try to get *anything* off on you lil'
dawg, I don't care *how* minor it may be, you *act.* You hear
me?" I nodded. "Don't do no talkin', no arguin', none of
that. Just haul off and try to knock his mutha' fuckin' head
off. If he's bigger than you, so what. 2 or 3 of'em, so
what. Lose the best part of your *mind* on a nigga's ass and
don't stop til the mutha' fuckin' *cows* come home, or the
c.o.'s pull you up off of him, whichever one comes first.
You ain't gone get through this bit without *somebody* tryin'
you in *some* way. Whenever this situation presents itself,
whether it be today or 10 years from now, make an
example out of him. You do that, surround yo-self with *real*
niggas, mind your business, let your word be your bond and
you ain't gone have a whole lot of shit to worry about; you
know?"

"Yeah,"

"Hold my spot man; I'm gone hustle up somethin'
to smoke." Knockout got up and retreated down the
corridor.

A homosexual pulled up moments later.

"Is there anyone sitting here?" he asked, gesturing
towards the empty spot next to me.

"Yeah." I answered concisely. Was he trying to get
something off on me? Was I being tested in some way?

"Okay." He said, turning to leave. I watched him
as he searched for a place to sit. I told myself that I should
get a deeper understanding of exactly what it meant for
someone to try and get something off on me. I had been
ready to snap on someone who probably meant me no
harm. Knockout came back and sat down clutching a lit
cigarette.

"What that punk want?" he asked me offering me
the cigarette. I declined.

"Lookin' for somewhere to sit."

"Lookin' for somewhere to sit my ass. You told him
to kick rocks?" Knockout asked, suspiciously eyeing the
homosexual who was still searching for a place to sit.

"Yeah."

"You know that nigga from the city don't you?" I shook my head. "Yeah, put in a lot of work out there too. He one of them out south niggas. Got to the Walls though and them wolves brought the freak out in him, turned him smooth out.

"You gone see a lot of niggas from the hood that you ain't seen in a long time in this system. Don't be so quick to clique up wit'em when you come across them because you never know what the fuck they been off into. Prison *changes* niggas Atif man, a lot of them ain't gone be the same way you remember them to be. Some of them gay now, some of them conscious and some done even went religious or crazy. Niggas take all kinds of twists and turns in these places. But niggas like me? Thugs for life, you know? From elementary to the penitentiary."

I liked the sound of that at the time. Now I think it was one of the most ignorant slogans I have ever heard anyone utter. There is nothing "cool" about being a misfit from the school yard all of the way to the prison yard, or even worse, the *graveyard*. I used to pattern my way of life after such sayings, such misguidance.

My generation, many of us walked selfishly through life as if no one was affected by our actions (or the consequences of them) outside of ourselves, not realizing that in actuality they pervaded shock waves throughout the whole community in countless aspects.

The rest of the day passed without incident. I was put in a cell with an older brother from St. Louis who was on his way to begin a 7 year bit. All through juvenile and the county I had grown accustomed to one-man cells. Being locked in a cell the size of an average bathroom with a total stranger was something I was not ever able to get used to. As uncomfortable as I was, I went to sleep and slept through the rest of the evening and night nonetheless. I didn't realize just how many people were in the wing with me until they called us for breakfast.

Stepping out of my cell the next morning, I was amazed at the sight of so many people emerging from their cells. There were 4 wings to a housing unit. Each wing

301

housed over 150 inmates, all scurrying to the dining hall in droves. I spotted Knockout waiting for me by the wing door, motioning for me to pick up my pace. When I reached him we waited for the majority of the people to make their way outside before we followed suit.

"Be careful of crowds in the penitentiary Atif." Knockout warned. There seemed to be a lesson to be learned somewhere within every step we took. "You get some shut-eye?"

"Yeah man, I slept like a baby." I answered as we stepped briskly outside. It wasn't even 7 o'clock in the morning and already the humidity was thick.

"It's gone be hot as a mutha' fucka' today. Them cells gone turn into young ovens."

"They ain't got no air conditionin'?"

"Hell naw!" Knockout exclaimed with a chuckle, "Nigga where you think you at, the Holiday Inn? It was cold in the reception area yesterday because they got air conditionin' for *them*, not us."

We entered the small, crowded and noisy dining hall after standing in a long line for a while. We then collected our trays which consisted of eggs, oatmeal, toast, butter, sugar, jelly, and some salt and pepper. I was hungry enough to eat a *couple* of servings. We found a table with two open seats and sat down. Knockout went directly to work as did everyone else at the table. I called myself taking the time to season my eggs, butter my toast and put sugar in my oatmeal. Knockout looked up at me.

"You ain't got time for all that lil' dawg." Knockout said, chewing. I continued doing what I was doing. After I had finished buttering my toast, seasoning my eggs and putting sugar into my oatmeal, I picked up my spoon and scooped up a spoonful of eggs.

"Time's *up*! Let's go!" a guard shouted before I even got the chance to place the eggs into my mouth. All of the inmates began to rise from their seats.

"I see you like to learn shit the hard way, huh?" Knockout asked, rising from his chair. I did the same,

stuffing food into my mouth while doing so.   Knockout
shook his head, laughing to himself.

Later that morning we were called out of our cells,
those of us who had just arrived the day before that is, in
order to complete our processing. I was given a test to see
how far along I had gone in school, asked a million more
questions, my eyesight checked along with my hearing,
given a physical, and then last but certainly not least I
found myself standing in a line in order to have my blood
drawn for an AIDS test.

AIDS test? Before that moment I had never given
the disease much thought. I knew I wasn't HIV positive;
didn't I? I wasn't sick. I wasn't getting all skinny and losing
weight. Nor had I ever had a homosexual encounter. The
only people that I had heard about being HIV positive were
either gay or had some type of blood transfusion. I had
never had one of those either or shared a needle with
anyone.

Well why was I so terrified?

Magic Johnson, he wasn't gay.   How had he
contracted the disease? Sex.   Sex with a woman and
without a condom.   I began to get butterflies in my
stomach. How many girls had I been with without using
protection?

I backtracked mentally: Patience? Did I use a
condom with her? Yes, plus she was a virgin anyway.
Sharita? Yes.   Aishah? Yes. Marquita? Yes. Toi? Yes.
Cassandra? Yes. Kendra? Yes. Kesha? Yes. Lets see...DiDi?
Yes. Naomi?

Un-oh, no rubber.   Alexis? No rubber.   Aw man,
Latrice! How could I have not used a condom with *her*? Her
legs stayed open like a 24 hour laundromat.

I had reached the level of being petrified. I didn't
even want to take the test. If I *had* contracted the virus I
didn't want to know about it. Many of us would rather
remain in a state of denial than face reality when it came to
such a thing as a terminal disease which there was
(allegedly) no cure for.

"Next!" I heard what I thought was a woman's voice. I stepped into the office and saw that the voice belonged to an overweight homosexual white male nurse.

I had a seat thinking to myself that a homosexual male working in a men's prison had to be like a 9 year old kid working at Toys R Us. Blood was taken from a vein in my arm. "How long do it take y'all to test it?" I asked.

"Oh, about 2 weeks." *2 weeks!* The nurse then pricked me with a small needle.

"What was that for?"

"Tuberculosis. *Don't* mess with that!" he warned as I went to scratch the area he had stuck me in.

"It itches." If I would have had any knowledge concerning the Tuskegee Experiment there was no way I would have allowed that nurse to shoot that substance into my body. To this day I suspect that they experiment on convicted felons in a similar fashion.

"If you scratch it, it will give off a false reading and you will have to take it again." The nurse said, placing a band-aid over it. I left it alone and left the building in route for my cell after I was informed that I was finished.

Knockout was right, it was hot. Stepping into my cell was like stepping into a bonfire. I climbed into my bunk and tried to remain still. It was all I could do. I dozed off here and there for no longer than a few minutes at a time. It was *torture.* We were only allowed out of our cells for an hour a day. I spent the next 3 weeks roasting in that inferno.

When the month of September came so did my ride out of Fulton. I said my good-byes to Knockout and was handcuffed and shackled once again in route for the Moberly Correctional Center located in Moberly, Missouri. We stopped over at Missouri State Prison in Jefferson City to switch busses and use the restrooms. After doing so, I was on the road again.

This journey was just as uncomfortable as the one to Fulton. I didn't know anyone on the bus so not having anyone to talk to made it even worse. I made the trip in silence, contemplating as I gazed out of the window.

What would it be like in Moberly? Were there going to be Crips from 24th Street waiting on me? What about some Rolling 60's? Did I know anyone there? I hoped the cells weren't hot boxes like the ones back at Fulton, I couldn't take too much more of that. Whatever awaited me, I was ready to get it started and over with.

The Moberly Correctional Center was not as intimidating in appearance as Fulton. It was a big camp and I got a good look at the yard as we pulled around to the back and then made our way across it. I saw handball courts, basketball courts, a softball field encircled by a track, a miniature golf course and a weight pile.

The yard was packed with inmates. I saw people in all shapes, sizes, colors and creeds as they moved about. Our bus ride across the yard distracted the majority of them from their recreational activities and they all crowded around the walkway we eventually found ourselves walking on.

Each one of us was scrutinized as we stepped off of the bus. Gang-bangers searched for friends or foes, booty bandits looked for potential targets, revolutionaries for fellow comrades and the others who were not expecting anyone were simply being aware of their surroundings. I surveyed the onlookers as I made my way down the pavement. I could see no one that I recognized but it was hard to conduct such a search with there being so many faces. I heard insults, threats and cat calls, none of which were directed towards me, I figured.

We followed the guards to one of the housing units. After being assigned to our cells, we were called to meet at the card tables within the wing. We were given thick packets filled with rules, regulations, directions and other information. One thing I came to realize later on was that the rule packet was insufficient; the *unwritten* rules of prison life had to be learned by trial and error.

"Any questions?" an inmate asked. He had been giving us a rough outline of the ins and outs of life in Moberly, what to expect and what to stay away from. No one had a question. "Alright, they are not going to let y'all

305

go out on the yard until tomorrow. Y'all have to stay in the
wing after ya'll get settled in. Also, y'all get to eat first and
if y'all ain't back in the wing within 15 minutes they will
write you a conduct violation. They do this to avoid
altercations in the chow hall."

"Altercations like what?" a Caucasian newcomer
asked.

"Prison is still segregated in a sense. The whites sit
on one side of the chow hall and stand in their own line as
do the blacks. Then every organization has their own
places where they all like to sit together. The Bloods, Crips,
Vicelords, Muslims, Aryans, Mexicans, Cubans, Rastafarians,
all of them. They are *very* sensitive about who they sit with
and where they sit. Some have been sitting in the same
spots for over a decade and the last thing they will stand for
is an R&O sitting in their spot. People have lost their lives
in that very chow hall for not paying attention to where they
were seated." He finished.

"*Those* types of altercations." we laughed nervously
at that.

"When do we go to the store?" another R&O asked.
"Tomorrow."

The store was in actuality a small concession stand
called the canteen. On the inside it resembled the way the
liquor stores back in the neighborhood were set up. All
things from snacks to color televisions could be purchased.
The prices were inflated; the state made a *killing* off of the
families of prisoners. I myself had left the county with a
nice chunk of change on my account and couldn't wait to
spend it up. A 13-inch color television, cassette player,
crock-pot, fan, clock, I planned to purchase all of those
things on my first trip along with filling my locker up with
snacks. Maybe the going was not going to be as ruff as I
thought it was.

The cell I was assigned to was a 4 man cell. 3 of us
were R&O's and the fourth was a brother from St. Joseph,
Missouri. He had all of his appliances and positioned his
television so that we all could see. We spent the next few

hours watching television and playing spades until it was time to eat.

"Atif!"

We had not too long before made it back from the evening meal and I was down at the sinks brushing my teeth. I turned and saw that it was my cellie from St. Joseph who was approaching me. I rinsed the toothpaste out of my mouth, turning to face him.

"Wha' sup?"

"I just came back from medical and I bumped into 2 different people, both of them asking me about you." I nodded. Maybe I did know someone in Moberly after all. "They came at me from different directions; one of them on the up and up, the other kind of sideways. Which one you want to hear about first?" I thought to myself silently for a moment. That was an articulate way of asking whether I wanted the good news or the bad news first.

"Tell me about the one who came at you sideways."

"A'ight, come on. Lets walk. The phone is off the hook in here." We left the latrine area and began to pace the wing. "Now I don't know you man but you seem like a cool person to me so I don't want to see nothing bad happen to you, especially without you seeing it coming. This Crip dude named Static Addict p-"

"Name what?" I cut in.

"Static Addict, at least that is what they call him. I don't know his real name. Most people in prison go by nicknames." I nodded, signaling for him to continue. "He pulled up on me with about 3 other Crips and asked me if a young dude named Atif was in R&O. I could sense that they wasn't looking for somebody they was cool with, you know what I'm saying?" I nodded. "So I told them that I didn't know who they were talking about or if you were here."

"You know what set he claim?"

"Rolling 60's, all 4 of them."

"Is there a whole lot of them up here?"

307

"Yeah man, they are pretty deep. Some out of Kansas City, most from St. Louis. There is even a couple from California."

What was I going to do? I hadn't been on the camp a full day yet and it was on *already*. Malik and Kenyatta were not there to ride with me this time. I had to take care of myself. There were only two options: I could stand up to them like a soldier and face my problems head on, or I could run from them by "checking in" and go to protective custody.

I thought about what Knockout said and the latter was not even an option. I was not going to do my time cooped up in protective custody like a coward. Once you made a move like that it would follow you *wherever* you went. In prison this was called a "jacket". Once you put such a jacket on you wore it at all times. No matter what prison you went to everyone would know that you had made such a cowardly move and they would treat you as such.

I was far from a coward. I had built a reputation for myself out in society and the time had come to do it again. Whatever became of me it would be recorded that I stood up for myself and that alone commanded at least some level of respect.

"You want to hear about the other dude?" my cellie asked me. I had forgotten all about the other person. Maybe I was not alone after all. I nodded in response. "Now he just told me to give you this." Looking around, he handed me something. It was a piece of paper folded and taped shut. "Be careful with that, you are riding dirty now." I nodded, cuffing the paper. "You straight?"

"Yeah, good lookin' out."

"No problem. You gone be a'ight." My cellie left the wing and went back outside on the yard.

I went back up to my cell and found it empty. I turned down the television and pulled the door closed. Positioning myself so that I could see anyone coming from both directions, I carefully undid the tape on the paper and opened it up. Inside was a tight ball of marijuana wrapped

308

in plastic sealed shut by fire. On the paper was written a small note:

What's up little hommie?! Malik told me to be on the look out for you. You got some funk out here that needs to be handled, you know? So don't go to breakfast in the morning and don't come out on the yard until I send somebody in for you. You and your brother, y'all my peoples nigga so your enemies are my enemies. Here is a little something to put your mind at ease. I'll holler at you in the morning blood.
1-Luv
P.S. Smoke something with St. Joseph man, he good peoples.
Skooter-B

*****

ROCK-A-BYE BABY

"I'm doin' hard time;
they confiscated my life!
I'm writin' hard rhymes;
Tryin' to make it through one more night!
And it's a long line;
of killas tryin' to get at me!
And I will stand on mine;
when they decide to attack me!"
-*Soody Mak*

16

I woke up the next morning feeling sluggish and hung over from the weed I had received from Skooter-B. It was some good stuff. St. Joseph rolled up 8 what he called "sticks", rightfully so because the joints he rolled were thin as needles, and the 4 of us smoked 4 of them in rotation. We spent the night laughing, listening to music, and watching television. It had been well over a year since I had smoked any weed and by doing so I was taken away from my anxiety, problems and reality, which felt good to me.

Skooter-B was a friend of Malik's from the neighborhood. I remembered him and reading his name at the end of that note was cause to exhale. He had been incarcerated for 6 years by then on a conspiracy charge. I didn't know that he was at Moberly, the last time I spoke to him over the phone he was in another institution.

The situation with Static Addict didn't cross my mind not once after receiving Skooter-B's letter until I opened my eyes the following morning from the deep sleep I was in. It was count time. Everyone in the wing was instructed to stand outside of our cells as two guards walked past, counting us like cattle. When count cleared I grabbed my cosmetics and rushed to catch a clean sink.

"You going to breakfast?" St. Joseph asked me when breakfast was called about 30 minutes later.

"Naw, I'm gone chill." St. Joseph nodded and walked out of the cell.

I didn't know how the day would turn out. If my situation was the weather, a good meteorologist would have predicted a hurricane in his forecast for me. I reached into my stash and pulled out a stick. Whatever the case would be I planned to weather the storm flying high as a kite on cloud nine. I checked the scenery, opened the windows and took one to the face. I had forgotten how good it felt to wake up and start the day off with a fire "splif" for a picker-upper.

My mind wandered as I surveyed the front walk, watching all of the inmates making their way to breakfast.

Static Addict? For someone to walk around prison with a nickname like that probably meant that he was the type of person who walked around starting trouble. I wondered if he was one of the ones who had jumped me and Kesha at the Landing Mall back in '92? Whoever he was, I wasn't afraid of him. I was pretty sure that there was nothing he could do to me that I couldn't also do to him.

Not wanting to waste my high thinking about Static Addict, I turned away from the window and decided to listen to some music. St. Joseph had the new D-Shot compilation, I had fallen in love with every track on it the night before. I put it in the tape deck and laid back, bobbing my head to the music. I told myself that later on I would spend some time on the phone. I would call Big Mama, Malik, Darion, and Patience. Yeah, that's what I would do. Would it be safe for me to go to the store? I sure could have used some "vittles". Chips, pop, cakes, candy bars...

"Good thing you *didn't* go to breakfast Atif man, Static Addict and them was *deep* up in there this morning." St. Joseph said, cutting into my thoughts as he walked into the cell.

"Did you see Skooter-B?"

"Naw, I didn't see none of them." St. Joseph then sniffed at the air. "I see you got your mind right early this morning on the solo tip." I smiled. "Ain't nothing wrong with that, ain't nothing wrong with that at all." I was beginning to like St. Joseph.

We spent the next hour or so listening to the radio waiting for the yard to open up at 8:30 am. There was a track on the compilation that I couldn't get enough of. It was called "Straight Killa" by C-Bo and on it he rapped about being sentenced to do time in the penitentiary and the mentality he had while serving it. I played that song over and over again.

"You going to the canteen this morning?" St. Joseph asked me when the yard opened. My other 2 cellies made a dash for the store as soon as recreational movement was announced.

"I don't know man." I replied.

"A'ight, let me know if you need some help carrying your groceries and stuff back if you do go. I'll be in the gym." St. Joseph said, exiting the cell.

Whatever the day held for me would begin in just a little while. I stood up at one of the cell windows surveying the front walk. There were a lot of people incarcerated at Moberly. I looked trying to see if I recognized anyone. No luck. After about 15 minutes of watching the walk, I saw a group of about 10 Crips making their way down the front walk towards the housing unit I was in. They stopped by the All Faiths Chapel, which was located next to the housing unit I was in, and looked up seemingly in my direction as someone who had been standing there the whole time shook his head in the negative. He had been watching the housing unit, waiting for me to come outside. I noticed that it was a tall skinny brother that led the Crips down to where they were. This individual was also the one who questioned the person who was already standing there, and he was the first one to look up in my direction. My instinct told me that this person was the one who had inquired about me to my cellie: He was more than likely whom they called "Static Addict".

They all wore blue and gold. They had bandannas on their heads, some of them, and others had them wrapped around their knuckles. Man, they were ready to put some work in on me! I don't know what I would have done if I didn't know anyone at the prison. I looked on as they stayed there posted, waiting patiently.

Movement caught my eye. I looked beyond Static Addict and his clique and saw a long line of brothers in red making their way through the gangway from the back part of the yard. The line was unending! There were at least 25 of them. I recognized Skooter-B instantly because of the way he walked. He had what had to have been the coolest walk in the world. The group made their way past the Crips as if they didn't even notice them. I could tell by the look on the face of Static Addict that this was unexpected and not a part of his plan. Skooter-B led the brothers down the pavement all of the way to the front of the housing unit where it split off into 3 different directions.

Skooter-B shouted a war cry, throwing his hands up in the air. I smiled and made my way out of the cell. Stopping by the sinks, I checked my game face in my reflection from the slab of steel and then I walked outside. Skooter-B smiled as I approached them, light from the sun made the golds in his mouth glisten.

"Wha'sup blood? I ain't seen you in *hella*!" Skooter-B greeted, hugging me.

"Wha' sup Skooter B?" I returned the greeting and the hug. Skooter-B had been working out during his incarceration I saw.

"Damn nigga, you done got tall as a mutha' fucka'." I smiled. "Lets ride y'all." The entourage surrounded us, engulfing us in the middle as we headed for the back yard.

What Skooter-B and the brothers had done was a sign of strength and support for me. It was also a warning. It said that if something happened to me then whoever was responsible for it would have to deal with all of the Bloods. The attention from the inmates and guards as well were focused on us as we walked. Everyone was trying to get a good look at me to see who it was that deserved such a show of love and protection.

"You recognize that tall nigga with the jersey on?" Skooter-B asked me as we walked past the group of Crips.

"I think so," I answered after looking in his direction. Our eyes locked briefly. He *did* look familiar to me.

"That's Static Addict, he was one of them niggas that jumped on you at the Landin'."

"Aw yeah?" I asked, taking a second look. If my memory served me correctly, he was the one whom Kesha had slapped; the one I dropped with a right cross. "How did you know about that?"

"I keep in touch with what's goin on in the hood."

"You know Kesha was with me when they did that don't you?"

"Yeah, I heard. Anyway, I know Static ain't gone let that shit ride, that was his father's house that got shot up that night." Small world, I thought to myself.

314

"My cry. 2 tears in a bucket, fuck it." I commented without compunction, mimicking a line from the movie "House Party" that we all used to go and see. Skooter-B chuckled. "That nigga should have thought about that before they jumped on us like they did."

"I'm hip." Skooter-B said. As we made our way through the gangway, a group of about 6 brothers were also coming through from the backyard, headed in the opposite direction.

"Islam, how you brothers be this morning?" A tall dark one whom I instantly labeled as their leader greeted us. He stood about 6'4 with a thin build. On his face he wore some glasses with tinted circular lenses. Others from amongst us uttered greetings in return. I gathered that whoever this brother was, he had a lot of respect. "We was just coming around to check with you young brothers. There's tension in the air and I saw your brothers moving as a unit and that made my spidey senses go off. Wha' sup? Y'all peaceful?" Skooter-B paused, smirking a guilty smirk. "I see. Who's the new young brother?" he asked, focusing on me.

"My name is Atif." I answered. The brother nodded.

"I see you don't have no problem with speaking up for yourself, do you?" he asked me, extending his right hand out to me with a smile on his face. I shook his hand. "I like that in you. I'm brother Cook-El."

"He got some funk with Static Addict from the bricks and they was about to move on him." Skooter-B informed him.

"Yeah, I knew it was something." Cook-El said, looking back at the brothers he was with. They all nodded their heads knowingly. "Y'all know what time it is when it comes to *all* things which are counter-productive to the struggle. Brothers at each other's throats, it's time out for that. It's too much-"

"I don't mean to cut you off Cook-El man, but I *understand* all that. But at the same time them niggas ain't *near* about to move on my peoples like that." Skooter-B cut in.

315

"Right, right, I'm saying though, check this out. Why don't *y'all* let *me* step in and mediate the situation, whatever the situation may be, that way if this can't come to a peaceful solution then let us at least seek one that keeps the violence between you brothers at a *minimum*. It's always helpful for brothers to open up some form of dialog before things escalate to a level that probably could have been avoided with some *understanding*." Cook-El said. Skooter-B looked at me.

"You cool with that Atif?" Everyone looked at me.

"Yeah, I'm cool with that."

"Yeah, that's what I'm talking about. A good, reasonable young brother. Where y'all headed?" Cook-El asked.

"To the softball field."

"A'ight, I will tell you what. We are going to go and speak with Static and then we all will meet up on the field."

"A'ight."

"Peace brothers." Cook-El and the brothers he was with made their way around front.

"Who was he?" I asked Skooter-B as we made our way around back.

"He is the Shiek of the Moorish Science Temple of America." The *what?* I had no idea what that was. "Him and the dudes he was with; they all Moors." I still was at a loss. "Did you smoke some of that shit I sent you?"

"Yeah, that was good lookin' out."

"I'm goin' to give you some more after we see wha' sup with these niggas." Skooter-B then took the time out to introduce me formally to everyone in attendance. I shook hands with every last one of them, grateful for all of their support despite the fact that they didn't know me from a hole in the wall. "This is only like 1/2 of us."

"Where is everybody else at?"

"They around, posted with the knives just in case it pop off." I looked around the yard. "If you lookin' for red, you ain't gone find them like that." I gave up the search. "This ain't the first time we been into it with Static and them."

"Aw yeah?"

316

"We stay into it with them hatin' ass cats." A brother introduced to me by the nickname of "Concrete" from St. Louis spoke up. "Gotta give it to them though, they don't be fakin'. When it's on them cats *will* slang that iron, you hear me? Scraight up."

"Wha' sup with Kesha? When she get out?" Skooter-B asked me.

"Next year."

"Yeah, I need to holler at her. See if we can get somethin' workin'."

"Wha' sup dirty, you in touch with some of them gals from the city?" Concrete asked me.

"Yeah...I'm in touch with a few of them."

"I heard that Persistence's lil' sister got you sprung like that worn out mattress we used to flip on in the hood back in the day." Skooter-B commented.

"Forget you nigga," I countered, throwing up my dukes at him with a chuckle. "Get off my girl dawg." Skooter-B laughed.

"I got a picture of y'all in the cell. She done grew up, lookin' just like Persistence." I silently wondered to myself how Skooter-B got ahold of a picture of us. There was no telling, Patience and I had taken probably a thousand photos. "Wha' sup with K-Red man? Who is this female he messin' with that I keep hearin' so much about?"

"Antoinette? She cool."

"Yeah, I heard she about her bread." I nodded. "What about lil' Darion, y'all still tight?"

"Yeah, that's my dawg for life."

"He still think he somethin' like a pimp?" I laughed, nodding my head. "Y'all should hear this lil' nigga blood. When it come to them ho's he's a mutha' fucka'! I used to make it my business to go swoop that nigga when we had some ho's at the crib. He kept me laughin'." Skooter-B said, directed towards the brothers. "Ole D-Mack. That lil' nigga fucks me up."

Our reminiscing was cut short when we saw a crowd of brothers making their way through the gangway. The group was led by Cook-El, Static Addict, and some other brother I was just then seeing for the first time. He was older, probably around Cook-El's age, and he was built like he was no stranger to the weight room.

This time there were just as many Rolling 60's, or Crips in general, as there were of us. As they made their way past the basketball courts, the Moors that were with Cook-El stopped there as the rest of the group advanced.

"This the nigga you been talking about?" the older brother asked Static Addict when they approached us.

"Yeah." Static Addict answered, glaring at me. I returned his glare with one of my own. He was definitely who I suspected he was.

"5-0 y'all." Concrete alerted us. We turned as a vehicle resembling a golf cart made its way across the yard towards us. Four prison guards stepped out of it, one a sergeant wearing a white uniform shirt instead of the traditional blue that the others were wearing.

"How's it going gentlemen?" the sergeant asked. Everyone remained silent. "Search him, him, and him." He then said, singling out Skooter-B, Static Addict and Cook-El. I thanked the Creator that he didn't choose me. I still had 3 sticks left from what Skooter-B had given me in my sock.

"Man why y'all fuckin' with us-"

"Don't feed brother, that is what they want us to do." Cook-El said, cutting Static Addict off as they were searched.

"What you got going on here? A gang summit? Pep rally?" the sergeant asked us. Silence. "Well, whatever it is has to cease. You know you can't assemble on the yard like this." He finished. Cook-El grunted.

"If ya'll draw off of it," Cook-El started, talking to both the Crips and the Bloods in attendance.   "Our ancestors was not allowed to *assemble* on the *plantations*, either." He said, turning to face the sergeant. "Ain't that right, Sarge?" Cook-El asked, fixing his clothes as the guard finished his search.

"I don't know what in the hell you are talking about guy, this isn't no goddam plantation and I am not a slave owner. Those days are long gone; when are you going to get that through your thick skull?"

318

"Nothing is over *Sarge*. The institution of slavery was *never* abolished, it was simply *transferred* from society to these institutions. It is being perpetuated and you know that just as much as I do." Cook-El said. The sergeant's face reddened.

"I will tell you what, Cook." The sergeant started, reaching behind his back and retrieving a set of handcuffs from his belt. "Anymore of that black revolutionary shit out of you and I'm going to escort you to the hole for inciting a riot." Cook-El and the sergeant glared at each other for a moment. Cook-El then smiled.

"It ain't strange Sarge, it ain't strange at all." Cook-El said, placing his hand on my shoulder. "Come on little brother, let's get a lap or 2 in. Get some fresh air." He said to me, following it with some Swahili that I didn't understand. Skooter-B, the older brother, and Static Addict joined us. "Don't let them give us a reason y'all." Cook-El said to the rest as we walked off in route for the track. All of the brothers began to disperse.

Witnessing the confrontation between Cook-El and that sergeant was something I will not be quick to forget. From that point on I took an extreme liking to Cook-El. I saw within him the attitude that my mother used to tell me was prevalent during the 60's and 70's. In time I learned a lot from that brother. His never being hesitant to take the time out to sit down and talk with me despite being busy working with the members of his own organization was very instrumental to my awakening. He taught me who I was and from whence I had come.

"I told the brother Static not to feed and damn near set a double standard by losing my own patience with that Europe, you hear me?" Cook-El said as we all walked. Skooter-B was on my left, Cook-El to my right and then Static Addict and the older brother were to my far right.

"What language was that you was speakin' in?" I asked Cook-El.

"Swahili. I said that it will not be fun when the rabbit gets the gun." We all laughed except for Static Addict. "I see the brother is not in the mood for small talk so let's get down to business."

"In what way has this young brother wronged you Static? Let's start at the beginning." Cook-El said. All attention was on Static Addict.

"This nigga and his brotha' and them came through the block set trippin'. They shot up my pop's house and left my hommie layin' dead on a fence. Not to mention everybody else they shot."

"Atif?" Cook-El asked, looking down at me.

"Man this nigga can't say that was *us*, he don't even *know* me. He ain't seen me a day in his life before they jumped on me."

"Oh, wait a minute. Wait a minute. Hold on." Cook-El said.

"I'm hip, I didn't know nothing about anyone getting jumped." The older brother said, eyeing Static Addict.

"Aw, you didn't tell your peoples about all that did you Static?" Skooter-B inserted.

"I said lets start at the beginning and you skipped over ½ the story. We are trying to get some understanding here and we are not going to get anywhere like that. Lets hear some more about this. Go ahead Atif, I see Static don't want to tell the whole story for some reason. What happened?" Cook-El asked.

"Me and my home girl Kesha went to the Landin' to buy some Halloween masks and this nigga and about 8 of his boys *jumped* on us."

"Both of y'all? The *sister* too?" Cook-El asked.

"Yeah, her too." I answered. I could see that both Cook-El and the older brother did not like the sound of that at all.

"Why y'all do that Static?" the older brother asked.

"They was out of bounds."

"Naw nigga, *y'all* was out of *law*! Since when is the mutha' fuckin' *Landing* out of bounds?"

Silence.

"How old are you Atif?" Cook-El asked, peering down at me.

"I just turned 17."

"And when did this happen?"

320

"About 3 years ago."

"*What?*" the older brother exclaimed in shock.

"Hold on Jay Smooth, lets break this down." Cook-El said. The brother was seething. "Now how old are you Static?"

"23."

"So you mean to tell me that a *20* year old man and 8 of his *grown* homeboys jumped on a *14* year old adolescent *and* his old gal at a mall; and you are upset because this *adolescent* and his people *may* have came back, of which you ain't even in *fact* of, and retaliated?" Cook-El asked Static Addict. Cook-El had a knack for breaking things down to their simplest components so that everyone could see and understand the whole picture.

"Man don't you *ever* pull me up out of my sleep for no little boy shit like this cuzz. You got us out here riled up with a *teenager* about some shit that you brought on yourself. I wish some grown ass niggas would jump down on my little brother. I would have taken the whole mutha' fucking block out." Jay Smooth said. I came to learn later on that he was an "original" from Cali.

"I'm hip." Cook-El added. We all walked in silence for a while. "You know what you need to do, don't you Static?" Static Addict looked up at Cook-El. "You need to let this ride and establish peace between you and this good young brother. I say so for at least 2 valid reasons.

"*You* and *your* people started this. You are 6 years his senior. What kind of stripes is there to gain by doing what y'all did?"

Silence.

"And most importantly, you can't even say for sure that it was *him* that hit y'all block. I can tell by the way you move in here that you must have at least 1,000 *other* enemies out there on them bricks.

"You got 50 brothers out here ready to go to war over something that don't even make sense. Why get all of these brothers involved in something like this? I mean if we are going to put some work in, let it be against those who are *oppressing* us, holding us hostage from our loved ones, not on each other. Let's take all of that anger and animosity and point it in the *right* direction where it belongs."

Static Addict was quiet for a minute.   He then looked at me. "Naw, fuck that shit. I ain't lettin' that ride. I *know* it was him, I ain't crazy."   Static Addict said, confirming my assumptions concerning the reasons why he was called by such a nickname.

"I see, you just want to be difficult." Cook-El said.

It wasn't just him being difficult, Static Addict was a predator of sorts. He was the type of person who was a bully in kindergarten.   He saw me as someone he could intimidate and use as a stepping stone in order to maintain his reputation. I couldn't blame him though for not being reasonable because at that point in my life if it had been *Kev* and I that Cook-El was trying to establish peace between I would have been "difficult" also.

"No I don't." Static Addict denied, "My cutty ain't goin' out like that. Everybody ain't even got to get involved. I will just beat the nigga's ass and leave it at that."

"You will just beat *whose* ass?" I wanted to know, speaking directly to Static Addict for the first time. I hated it when people talked around me like that, I saw it as cowardly.

"*Yours* nigga!"

"Nigga you can't fuck with me one on one and you *know* that from when I knocked you on your ass! That's why y'all jumped me in the *first* place. That's why you had all your partnas out there waitin' on me to come out on the yard nigga, you need all of the help you can get!" Cook-El grunted, smirking. Skooter-B laughed. I was getting upset.

"What you want to do then cuzz?" Static Addict challenged.

"It's *whatever* blood!" I answered, attempting to step around Cook-El.

"No, not here." Cook-El said, barring my passage. "We been at this all morning and they have taken us all of the way back to the drawing board that quick." He then said to Jay Smooth.

"Not for real, we will just let them take it to the handball courts and handle their business one on one like men." Jay Smooth said.

"I don't know Smooth," Cook-El started, looking down at me. "I think Static needs to be fighting with someone his *own* age, the brother is kind of young."

"My age don't mean nothin', it didn't when they gave me all of this time so why should it matter now?" Static Addict glared at me; I glared back. My refusal to back down was throwing him off and I knew it.

"Youngster got some heart in his chest, don't he?" Cook-El asked Jay Smooth.

"A lot of people *talk* like they got heart; let him stand on it." Jay Smooth answered.

"I know a soldier when I see one." Cook-El said, looking at me. He too had taken a liking to me in return.

"Y'all know that the *only* way them goin' one on one is gone squash this is if Static win." Skooter-B pointed out, speaking up for the first time in a while. "Static can't take no ass whoopin' with dignity."

"*When* I win," Static Addict added.

I silently vowed to make him eat those words.

"Wha' sup Static? Whatever the outcome, win, lose or draw, do we have your word that it will be over and done with?" Cook-El asked. Static Addict nodded. Cook-El then turned to me and I did the same. "Okay, it's on then. Y'all should wait until the evening yard though, let the guards change shifts. They are waiting for something to kick off right now." We parted in different directions.

"After you whoop this nigga," Skooter-B started as we walked, "you gone have to stay on your toes. That nigga's word ain't shit, I *know* how he is. It's not gone end on the handball courts; mark my words. He ain't had a fair fight since he been in the penitentiary. All he want to do is slang iron. The nigga probably can't even fight for real." I nodded. "You got some ends on your books?"

"Yeah."

"You goin' to the store?"

"Yeah, I might as well."

323

"You might want to go now man and get it out of the way." Skooter-B then placed his fist up to his mouth and then spit something into it. He then took this same hand and offered it to me. I caught on to what he was doing as we gave each other the 27th Street handshake. As his fingers locked onto mine he passed me another ball of marijuana. "You can move around freely for now. They ain't gone try nothin' with y'all havin' an agreement to go one on one, that would be some bitch ass shit right there. I got some business to handle so I'm goin' to catch up with you in a lil' bit damu."

"A'ight." Skooter-B turned to leave. "A, what does damu mean?" I asked him as he turned to face me.

"It means blood in Swahili." Skooter-B answered. I nodded. "Put that shit under your tongue man so if the police run up on you, you can swallow it. These guards is crazy man, they'll choke your ass out if they know you tryin to swallow somethin'."

As much as I hated the thought of placing that ball of marijuana under my tongue after it had been under his, I complied. I then told myself that I would go on a quick tour of the camp before I went inside the housing unit to fill out a canteen purchase list, starting with the handball courts. After doing so, I made my way inside.

I felt pretty good actually, considering all. I was content with the way things turned out. Fighting had never been a thing I was afraid of, whomever my opponent. I was no tuff guy, I just knew that I would give it my all and if I lost then so be it; I would at least get my rocks off in the process. I didn't plan on losing though. Static Addict had a weak chin and I planned to exploit it once again.

*****

The yard closed on me while I was in the cell being indecisive about exactly what I wanted to get from the canteen. I could only spend $62.50 a week, appliances excluded, and there was *so* much I wanted to get. I told myself that I would start with my cosmetic necessities and go on from there.

St. Joseph suggested that we whip up what he called a "pimp meal", smoke some weed and watch "Bad Boys" to be shown later on that evening on the movie channel. I agreed; it sounded like a good idea to me. All I had to do was get the thing with Static Addict out of the way and then I could relax. I spent the next 2 ½ hours watching television and talking to my cellies.

The yard opened at 1:30 pm. I had to go to the property room for a voucher so that I could get my appliances. The population seemed to have doubled. Apparently all of the inmates who I had seen on the yard that morning in actuality only amounted to about ½ of all the prisoners who were there.

I stood in a line at the property room window watching the yard. There was so much going on. Everyone it seemed was busy doing something, looking for somebody for some reason with a million other things to do as well. They resembled a colony of ants.

I witnessed transactions of all kinds. It didn't take very long for me to realize how many homosexuals were there; they were everywhere. Some of them following in their man's footsteps wherever he went, others standing around in small groups. The penitentiary was a sick place. What had I gotten myself into?

"Brother Atif!" Cook-El called out to me from the walk. "Can I get an ice cream sandwich out of you?" I pulled out my canteen list and began to add the requested item to it. "I am just jeffin' brother, don't worry about it. You would have purchased one for me for real, wouldn't you?" I nodded. "Come here, let me put a bug in your ear."

I asked the individual behind me in line to hold my spot for me. I then made my way towards Cook-El who was standing just off of the front walk in some rocks. He was accompanied by 3 other Moors. I hadn't seen Skooter-B yet and was curious as to where he was at.

"Wha' sup?" I greeted the brothers as I approached.
"How you be?" Cook-El asked.
"I'm cool."
"You about to get you some appliances?"
"Yeah."

"That's cool, a lot of young brothers come to the joint and trick their money off instead of sacrificing and getting the things they *need* to get instead of their *wants*.

"As much as I hate to see 2 brothers fighting with each other, I will be pulling up a front row seat to watch the 2 of you go at it. You see, brothers like Static *hinder* the struggle because they choose to wallow in their ignorance. This type of brother needs to be taught a lesson. He could have been more reasonable than he was but he sees you as someone he can get something off on. Only a *fool* underestimates the one he sees as his enemy, you dig?" I nodded. "When they call yard this evening, you come out to that handball court and you be about your work, you hear me? Don't hold anything back. I want you to *humble* that brother out there. The way you handle yourself this evening will shape the way the rest of your bit will be for you." Cook-El said, driving home his point with his index finger in my chest.

"I know Static probably *better* than Skooter-B does because I know his type. After you *smash* him, he is going to come back at you. But the thing is he will have to do so on his *own* because he will be moving out of law and them 60's are not going to back him in such cowardice. I know what I am talking about brother, I have been doing this for 14 years now. I made him give us his word for a *reason*. I know his word is not worth the funky breath it slid out with, but the point is he *gave* it and one of his OG's *witnessed* it. In prison your word is all you have, once you forfeit that, you don't have *anything*.

"You handle your business and stay on your toes afterwards. And if Static so much as lift a *finger* towards you we will drop down on him like cold rain, you dig? You won't even have to retaliate, *we* will handle that and take it to another level. Once you step off of that handball court this evening, your job is done. Let *us* worry about the rest. You stand on yours like I know you will and you got my up most, you hear me?"

"Yeah," I answered, nodding. For some reason gaining his respect meant a whole lot to me. With his respect also came the respect of those he was affiliated with.

"Don't let me keep you any longer my brother, I know that you have other things to do besides standing here and letting me talk your ear off." Cook-El then said, smiling. Right then I realized that Cook-El had complete control of his moods and changed them instantaneously with a mental push of a button, bringing forth whichever type of mood that best suited the circumstances he was under. His smile reminded me of my brother's; meaning that just because they were smiling did not mean that they were happy or pleased. Malik could kill you with a smile on his face.

After receiving all of the vouchers I needed, I went to the store and spent what we called back in those days a "knot". I bought a 13 inch television, a double cassette Panasonic radio, an electric alarm clock, a Crock pot, a walkman, a stinger, a fan, and an ice chest along with $62 worth of cosmetics and food for my locker. St. Joseph and I had to enlist the help of a third person to help carry all of my things back to the housing unit.

One of my cellies was in the cell when we got there. I found it peculiar at the time how he all of a sudden preferred being cooped up in the cell instead of outside on such a nice day. I found out not too long afterwards that a few of the booty bandits had targeted him and he was afraid to go out on the yard. Within a year's time they had him walking the yard wearing a pony tail with Kool-Aid on his lips. What a shame.

I spent the rest of the afternoon shooting the breeze with Skooter-B and a few more of the fellas while they worked out on the back yard. I could sense that the brothers were anxious to see me in action. Concrete stuffed a Black & Mild cigar with some weed and I hit it a couple of times, not wanting to do too much, and enjoyed my buzz along with some music, laughter and good weather without a worry in the world. I saw Static Addict walking the track with a couple of his people but I paid him no never mind. I had already done all of the mean mugging and dished out all of the threats I felt were necessary so there was nothing left for me to do besides put my work in on him.

"You are something else Atif," St. Joseph said as he poured chili into my crock pot. A few hours had gone by and evening yard was just announced over the intercom. Showtime. "You about to go and fight that nigga for real man?"

"Damn right, you comin'?" I asked in return.

"Nah, there is a fight to see everyday on the yard if that's your fancy. I'm going to whip this pimp meal up man and chill, wait for you to come back."

"A'ight, I won't be long. I'm goin' to go out here, whoop this nigga's ass, come back in, eat some nachos, wash it down with an ice cold pop, smoke some weed, watch Bad Boys and call it a night." I said, St. Joseph laughed. "Here," I started, spitting a ball of weed into my fist. "Hold this for me until I get back." I finished, tossing it to him.

"Oh! The *gunja* mon!" St. Joseph exclaimed with a Jamaican accent. "Mmmm, zee light green. We kick it tonight esse'!" He finished with a Mexican accent as he examined the product. I laughed and walked out of the cell.

I stepped out on the yard full of confidence. I was running a little late on purpose. I preferred for Static Addict to be there on the handball court waiting for me than the other way around. My mind was made up; I was going to *embarrass* him. I was going to ruin whatever the reputation was he had going for himself and build one of my own at the price of his.

He should have let it ride. He should have given me the benefit of the doubt when sizing me up instead of dismissing me as some youngster he could have his way with. I was not upset anymore; just *focused*. I was all about business, suppressing all emotions like Malik would have done.

I made my way through the gangway oblivious to my surroundings. My attention was on where I was headed and where I was headed only. In my mind I was the champion of *The Battle Ground*, maybe not the *undisputed* champion thanks to Kev, but a champion in my own right and I planned to uphold my status. Going from *The Battle Ground* to prison's new arena was like stepping up from the Golden Gloves tournaments and into the pros.

Emerging from the gangway, I walked across the basketball courts and onto the grass. I saw Skooter-B and 3 of the hommies playing a mock game of handball. I also saw about the same amount of Crips doing the same on the adjacent court. Cook-El was leaning against the fence, *alone*. That was the first and only time I would ever see him on the yard without being surrounded by other Moors.

"Handle   your   business   blood."   Skooter-B encouraged as I walked by. I almost didn't even hear him. Cook-El nodded as I walked by him, I nodded in return. Static Addict put his dukes up as I rounded the corner. I advanced.

"Wha' sup with all that shit you was talkin' now c-"

"Sss! Sss!" I cut him off by serving him with a quick 2-piece extra crispy chicken dinner with a jalapeno pepper on the side to the grill. Connecting with both shots, his head snapped back as he fell on his behind. I was a lot stronger than even I thought and hitting harder than a lot of grown men thanks to all of the push-ups and weight lifting I had done during my stint in the county. I didn't come to talk; I had things to do and people to see.

"Oh, shit! That's gotta be a new fuckin' world record blood!" I heard Skooter-B exclaim. Concrete laughed. "That was quicker than Tyson-Spinks!"

Static Addict wasn't hurt, just caught off guard. The first thing I noticed when I rounded that corner was that his feet were not set so he was off balance. He rose from the ground wiping blood from his mouth. Seeing the blood on his fingertips enraged him. Good, I thought to myself. Just what I wanted; an emotional opponent.

Baring blood filmed teeth, he then charged at me throwing a wild hook. I ducked underneath his long arm and caught him with a short but powerful Jean Claude Van Dam like right hook to the ribs, knocking the wind from his lungs.

Static Addict folded into a ball of pain, gasping hungrily for air.

"Aw I'm fucked up behind this shit here!" Skooter-B said. "The 3 knockdown rule is not in effect ladies and gentlemen. I repeat, the 3 kn-"

"Skooter!" Cook-El spat.   He then smiled disarmingly. "That is not necessary brother." He was right. Skooter-B was instigating and doing so could have easily fueled the already burning fire.

One would probably say that if I was really "about my work" then I would have finished him off instead of giving him so many chances to recuperate. But, like I said earlier, I wanted to *embarrass* him. Him and his hommies had embarrassed me by having me walking around town with a black eye; even Patience had said that I looked like a raccoon. Oh yeah, he was going to reap what he had sown. I planned to dot *both* of his eyes for that alone. Right back ain't *never* been cheating.

Static Addict rose, grimacing in pain as he did so. This time it was me who took the initiative. I advanced on him once again, faked with my left, and then put everything I had into an overhand right that I shot straight down the chimney as if it was Santa with a bag full of gifts on Christmas Eve. I heard the bone in his nose snap when I connected. This time the ground seemed to leap up and catch him.

It was over...or was it? Static Addict climbed shakily to his feet but fell again as his knees buckled, unable to carry his own weight. There was so much blood protruding from his nose that his face and white tank top was covered in it. The Crips then gathered their fallen comrade and escorted him to medical.

"Man, I ain't never seen nobody knock a nigga out twice with one punch dirty." Concrete said, congratulating me.

"I'm hip! Fuck Tyson-Spinks, nigga that was some Foreman-Frazier shit there. You was lookin' like Malik out there nigga." Skooter-B said.

I took my emotions off of suspension and basked in the glow of victory. By the morning the whole camp would

330

hear about what the new youngster had done to Static Addict. The story would change though as it got tossed around. Animated storytellers would exaggerate and turn the four knockdowns into eight. Whatever the case, I had done what I came to do. Respect was won. My victory would make things easier for me at Moberly like Cook-El had insinuated. By making an example out of Static Addict I had eliminated many of the potential problems someone young and new to the penitentiary would come to face in time.

The praise I received from the hommies was the same thing that motivated a lot of us misguided young blacks in the streets. We sacrificed so much for the approval of others, whether we wanted to admit it or not. We weren't the only ones though, even the most law abiding citizens in society are guilty of the same thing. They also dedicate their lives to the pursuit of financial gain in order to be looked at and treated in a certain way. To be able to enjoy the finer things in life.

They want the treatment of the privileged. They want to fly first class, not coach. There is a difference in the way one is treated when they fly coach when compared to flying first class. We wanted the same thing: respect. We wanted to be treated like we were somebody instead of everyone turning their noses up at us. We just sought it in a different manner, one that is difficult for another to understand who is on the outside looking in.

The way a person is treated because of the way others view that individual, especially from a financial standpoint, is one of the world's oldest forms of oppression. We will never rid the world of crime until we first rid the world of *classism*; until we learn to make the *whole* airplane "first class". But we aren't willing to make such a sacrifice, are we? We are just not too long ago removing some of the "white only" signs (the *physical* ones at least), but the invisible *class* signs are not going anywhere anytime soon. Those who fly first class don't want to be in the same section as those who fly coach, or treated as such. In their mind they are *better* than them. If the whole plane being first class was the case, people would have no *reason* to treat one who had better than one who had not. Where would the much needed praise come from?

I digress. My point is, from that point on I flew first class in Moberly and was treated as such. My celly (the one who the booty bandits had targeted)? He was flying coach and being treated as such, dealing with the things that people flying coach had to deal with.

I remember looking over in the direction where Cook-El had been leaning against the fence. I of course wanted *his* praise too: He was not there.

*****

I was moved from four house to one house days later and given a job picking up cigarette butts, along with other discarded things, on the yard early in the mornings. I didn't mind getting up so early, I utilized my time on the job with reflection. I thought about a little bit of everything during those early morning hours. They paid me $7.50 a *month*! I kept money on my account so it didn't bother me; I enjoyed the serenity of the empty yard. Any other time there was always someone 10 feet away from me.

One of the first things I noticed about flying "first class" was that everywhere I went people I didn't even know began to greet me when we passed each other in traffic. Cook-El had told me to be very selective with who I associated with because a lot of people in prison get to know people solely for the purpose of getting something out of them.

I was given a key to my cell door, a *key*! This was real strange to me. I was in a wing with an older brother that I knew from the county and he had a collection of Malcolm X's speeches on tape. I was fascinated with them. On one of them Malcolm X predicted that by the turn of the century, prison guards will have trained the inmates to lock *themselves* into their cells. He was right. When it was time to lock down all that the guards had to do was announce it over the intercom and all of us would go to our cells and close the doors behind us on *ourselves*.

Skooter-B and Concrete were in 1 house so that was the good thing about my being placed there. The bad thing however was that I was not in the same wing they were in, I was in B wing along with Static Addict. I filled out a cell move pass the day after I was moved over there but the caseworker told me that I had to wait for 4 months before I could move to another cell or check in to protective custody if I felt uncomfortable with my living arrangements. This was not good at all. Static Addict looked as if he wanted to kill me when our eyes locked. I thought that the only thing holding him back from trying something sneaky with me was his tender nose. All I would have to do was blow at it and he would probably scamper away in pain yelping like a scalded dog.

There was a concept in prison and if you fell victim to this particular demonstration then you were what was called "rocked to sleep". This process was called such because it could be likened to the way a mother holds an infant in her arms and slowly rocks an alert child to a state of unconsciousness.

As the months rolled passed, Skooter-B and Cook-El cautioned me not to let Static Addict do this to me by acting as if he had moved on from our bout on the handball court and was not looking to retaliate. The patience one learns to practice in prison is *phenomenal*. Despite all of their warnings, I had gotten too comfortable flying in the first class section and I allowed myself to be fooled. Static Addict went from glaring at me when our paths crossed, to not acknowledging me at all, and then finally to even greeting me: all within the time period of 4 months.

I don't remember much about this day. Not much was different about it from the beginning. I spent the morning working out with the hommies, came in for a shower and then called myself taking a nap until they opened the yard at 1:30. I was scheduled to move in the wing with Concrete and Skooter-B that very weekend. My cellie had left for work and I was worn out. I turned my television off and put a SWV tape in my radio. I laid there for a while drifting in and out of a light slumber until I heard a key being inserted into the lock on the cell door.

I was facing the wall and feeling lazy, so lazy that I didn't even want to turn over to see if it was my celly or a guard like I usually did when my cell door was being opened. I didn't have any weed or crack on me at the time so I was not worried about a surprise cell search. I rationalized with myself by thinking that maybe my celly had forgotten his pouch of nicotine and was returning to retrieve it or something along those lines.

Something ain't right I thought when the door did open. You see, my celly worked in the kitchen and when he came in from work he would come into the cell smelling like the food in the kitchen. He also treated the showers as if there were alligators, crocodiles and anacondas in the water so I always smelled him the instant he appeared at the door. I didn't smell him so it was someone else.

A guard? The guards carried a ring full of keys and they could be heard jingling as they walked along with the correspondence on their walkie-talkies. Even at the times when they would turn them down and grip their keys, trying to sneak up on the cell undetected, I could smell their bodily scents because their aromas were foreign and not of the penitentiary. Especially the female guards. It was not a guard at my door either.

If it wasn't a guard or my celly, the only 2 with a key to the cell, then who was it? I thought to myself while turning over. When I did so I saw something bearing down on me. Whatever it was was *solid* and it hit me right in the forehead. The pain was excruciating. My head split instantly and blood squirted from the wound.

I jumped off of my bunk dizzily and saw Static Addict gripping a sock with some canned goods stuffed down at the bottom of it tied around his right hand. I rushed him, blinded with rage and blood in my eyes. Static Addict side stepped and hit me once again on the top of my head. I actually saw *stars* with that one and lost touch with where I was at and what was going on. Multi-colored pinwheels spun behind my eyes and I clung to consciousness.

Static Addict didn't stop. He swung and hit me a third time, knocking me unconscious.

Rock-a-bye baby.

*****

OUT OF SIGHT AND MIND

"My memories are foggy,
clouded by scenes from prison.
It is difficult for me to conceive of life
other than the penal one that I am livin'.
Even in my *dreams* I'm no longer free;
Institutionalized!
Traumatized,
by being certified.
She swore that she would ride,
vowed to stand by my side.
But with time?
Her empty promises transformed into lies.
I COULD HAVE CRIED!
Will I ever love like that again?
Or put my trust in
the same one I bust in?
I'm so lonely,
my people are out there dyin' on me.
If it was me,
would there be anyone cryin' for me?
I got me locked down
in this 4 cornered cell.
Out of sight and mind
feelin' like I failed.
I put in work for so long,
ended up alone,
away from home,
wonderin' if the world even notices that I'm gone."
-Soody Mak

17

March 8, 1996.

I had been in the infirmary for over a month recovering from a rare type of temporary amnesia brought about by the injuries I suffered to my head. As it turned out, after knocking me unconscious Static Addict continued delivering crushing blows to my skull with his makeshift weapon. Ironically, it was some of his fellow Crips whom had finally pulled him away. He had tried to kill me, there was no doubt about it, and if it wasn't for his own hommies he probably would have. The guards found me laying on the floor of my cell face down in a puddle of blood.

My condition was strange because of the way in which my memory bank was affected. I remembered how to walk, talk, what happened to me, where I was, how to add, subtract, etc. Though I remembered all of these things, there was this *wall* in my mind that I couldn't breach. I remembered who all the people were in my life but at the same time I couldn't remember *how* I felt about some of them and *why* I felt the way I did.

It was very peculiar. My grandmother had slipped into a diabetic coma following a stroke of which had paralyzed the whole left side of her body. When I received the news I felt sorry for her because I understood that she was my mother's mother, but it did not affect me like it would have if I could have remembered at the time how much *love* I had for this woman. Instead of her being Big Mama, my favorite person in the whole world, she was like a distant relative to me and hearing about her condition was like hearing such about a family member I had met but never really *knew*.

I also could not remember all of the hatred I once harbored in my heart. I remembered my whole altercation with Static Addict from the beginning to the end, but the *emotion* was no longer there. Kev? I remembered knowing what he had done to my mother and Malik, I just could not remember hating him or the burning desire to retaliate.

337

I was not devoid of emotions; I was more than capable of feeling them. It was more like I had to start all of the way over with learning how to apply them in the right places and situations. Sometimes when I laughed it felt like I was doing so for the first time.

I couldn't even remember how much I missed my mother.

My comprehension was at a very low level also. I could express myself but I had a difficult time understanding other people when trying to express themselves to me. People had to talk slowly to me and give me time to think about what it was they were trying to say to me, what was meant by the way they said certain things. Things like innuendoes and oxymoronic statements confused me. People had to be very direct and to the point when talking to me, saying exactly what they meant. I could remember how to read but I couldn't comprehend what I was reading well at all.

I spent my days working on my comprehension skills with the help of one of the nurses in the medical unit. She was a Caucasian woman in her mid-thirties by the name of Rebecca.

Rebecca was a very kind, down to earth woman and we clicked instantly. Unlike the other inmates she had grown used to dealing with, I always treated her with respect instead of barraging her with unending come-ons.

She was attractive in a mature way. Short, with her long red hair kept in a bun and rimmed glasses on her face, she was the type of attractive woman that men usually didn't notice on the streets. We had fun together, so much so that she had begun to come in on her off days to work with me. She was married but unable to bear any children. So that, along with the fact that her husband despised her for it and never paid her much attention, left her at home with a lot of time on her hands wishing she were somewhere else and living another life. We really enjoyed each other's company.

"Hi Atif!" Rebecca greeted cheerfully as she entered the room. It was a little after three in the afternoon and

she was just beginning her shift by making rounds. "How is
my favorite patient doing today?"

"I'm doin' good." I answered, smiling. I was happy
so see her.

"There is that smile I have been looking forward to
seeing all morning." Rebecca said, approaching my bedside.
"Speaking of your smile, I was thinking about you while
cooking dinner last night. Now, I'm not a doctor or
anything, but I think that your injuries may have removed
everything from your system that may have hindered it in
any way so that *now* when you smile it is pure and you hold
nothing back."

"You think so?"

"Yes, but it is just a thought." At that moment the
nurse Rebecca was replacing appeared in the doorway.

"Rebecca?"

Rebecca turned to her. "Hi Diane," she greeted.
"How are you?"

"Tired." Diane answered. She then turned to me.
"Hey Atif, you're up?"

"Yeah."

"Atkins is calling for you Rebecca." Diane then said.
Rebecca rolled her dark blue eyes. "Tell me about it. I
have been putting up with that guy all day. I think he may
have gotten ahold of some aphrodisiac or something
because he has got it *bad* today sister. They should pay us
time and ½ just for dealing with him. Anyway, don't forget
to turn your force field on before you go down there, good
luck!" Diane then left.

"You know," Rebecca started as she wrote
something on my chart. "It is people like Atkins that makes
me really want to quit this job."

"Why? Wha' sup with him?"

"He is a creep! I mean in every sense of the word.
He is probably a child molester. In fact, I am going to look
it up to be sure."

"What he be doin'?"

"This guy calls me into the room, strikes up some
stupid conversation attempting to hold me in there while he
339

masturbates underneath his blanket; like I don't know what
he's doing. Maybe he knows that I know and that makes it
even better for him." I shook my head. "Oh, you have not
heard anything yet. Let me tell you *why* I make my
presence known before I enter one of these rooms. I just
so happened to walk in on this...*freakazoid* one day and he
had moved his chair over to the water fountain positioning
himself up over it, butt naked mind you, running the cold
water *up* his ass while performing *oral sex* on *himself* at
the-"

  "Ugh!" I exclaimed with disgust, sticking my fingers
into my ears. "I don't want to hear no more. Stop! Please!
For all of *humanity!*"

  "Okay, okay," Rebecca said, laughing as she pried
my fingers from my ears. Her hands were so soft. "Do you
see why I spend the majority of my shift in here working
with you now?" I nodded. I noticed that Rebecca had not
released my wrists just yet. "If I was to tell Atkins what I
told you about your smile he would swear to God that I
wanted to have sex with him. Why do men think like that?"

  Good question.

  "I don't know, probably because we know that if it
was *us* that said somethin' like that then that is *exactly* why
we would have said it." I answered. Rebecca giggled.
"Some of us at least. Can I ask you a question?"

  "Sure."

  "Did you change your perfume, if you don't mind
my askin'?"

  "Of course I don't mind. And *yes*, I did! This is the
new Bora Bora by Liz Claiborne that I picked up over the
weekend. What do you think?" Rebecca asked, tilting her
head as she leaned over closer to me. I sat up and drew
my face in close to the crook of her neck, softly inhaling her
scent.

  "Mmm, that smells *good!* I mean, the other stuff
you usually wear is cool too, but that right there is *fire!*"
Rebecca laughed. She loved the way I talked.

  "Why *thank* you! Too bad my husband didn't notice
like you did." Rebecca said.

Not only was she still holding my wrists, but she also had made no attempt to pull herself away from me. As she leaned over, her uniform top was hanging pretty low and I couldn't help but notice her 2 voluptuous white breasts disappearing into a white bra from my peripheral vision. From what I could tell, they looked soft and creamy like thick homogenized whole milk.

Rebecca had told me once before that women *always* noticed it when men's eyes dropped from their faces to their chest area and out of respect for her it took every bit of the self-discipline that my body contained in order to prevent my eyes from dropping to get an eye full.

"You are very mature for your age. Has anyone ever told you that?" Rebecca asked. I shrugged my shoulders, still struggling to keep my eyes where they belonged. "If I didn't have access to your file I would have never believed that you are only 17 ½ years old." I didn't respond. "You should meet my husband, maybe he could learn a thing or 2 from you."

"Or 3 or 4."

"Or 5 or 6." We laughed. She then rose, gathering her chart. "Well, I guess I'll go and see how many sexual misconduct violations Mr. Atkins wishes to earn today. I'll see you a little later Mister." Rebecca finished, leaving the room.

I had never been attracted to a Caucasian woman before in my life. Not that I had anything against them, I just never had gotten the chance to ever get to know one. Rebecca? I liked her, she was cool. Being incarcerated can broaden one's horizons and have him paying attention to things he used to not even notice.

White women were different than what I was used to. They were more touchy-feely and they got attached quickly. They also put up with a lot of things that most sisters wouldn't stand for. I was of course basing my synopsis off of Rebecca which was an over generalization, something that I couldn't stand to be done to me.

I was receiving mixed signals from Rebecca. I couldn't figure out if she was *attracted* to me or simply

341

comfortable with me. There was a big difference between the 2 but a thin line separating them at the same time.

The penitentiary was filled with people like "Atkins". Taking away so many men's God given right to reproduce and packing them into an enclosed area like sardines creates an unnatural environment which in turn breeds unnatural desires and behaviors. Some would say that we forfeited certain rights when we broke the law, but in actuality there is no such thing as forfeiting a God given right. Such a right remains with a person as long as he is a human being and cannot be revoked because of a certain unlawful act he has committed without God's approval. No matter how many people a serial killer kills or what have you, he is still entitled to the right to be clothed and fed during his incarceration because he is still a *human*. He must be allowed an hour of recreation and exercise out of his cell because he is still a human. The right to reproduce is just as vital as the right to sustain life, in fact the 2 are synonymous with each other because to not reproduce pretty much nullifies one of our purposes for *existing*, not to mention defies a direct commandment from the Originator. Certain states in America understand this and allow conjugal visits for the incarcerated.

During my stint in prison I witnessed how that particular atmosphere could take a perfectly sane human being who had never before had a lets say...homosexual thought before their incarceration and turn them into a *raging* homosexual in a matter of time. Some of them could turn those impure desires off like a light switch the moment they were released and carry themselves in society like they had never taken such a turn, passing on the diseases they acquired while in prison.

I also witnessed how that unnatural environment could take a man who was respectful towards women prior to their incarceration but had allowed themselves to be reduced to sexual predators and stalkers of women. Stalking the female administrative members was the thing to do in prison. When a ½ decent looking woman made her way across the yard you would see a line of inmates following behind her, *stalking* her with their hands in their pants doing what they do in front of everyone. They made it a living hell for the women who worked there. It was not always the inmates themselves who were *sick*, so were some of the female guards. Some of them enjoyed the attention and brought such things on themselves. A lot of them were country girls who harbored secret fantasies of being with a real "bad boy".

The stereotype Rebecca had labeled Atkins with, as far as *why* he was in prison, was probably not even true. He *could* have been there for ditching Sunday school for all we knew, point being that it was possible that prison life had turned him into the individual who sexually harassed Rebecca on a regular basis. But then again, maybe it *was* true. Maybe it did fit him.

I was working out of a book Rebecca had purchased for me by an author who had an extraordinary memory. He could shake hands and greet a room full of people and remember all of their names. His book was full of exercises to help strengthen one's memory and comprehension. It worked too. In some areas my short term memory was crystal clear because of it, even better than before the incident. I read as much of it as I could before experiencing a migraine. I then put it to the side and dozed off.

*****

"Wake up and keep me company sleepy head." I woke up to Rebecca's hand on my shoulder. "You can sleep on the other nurses' shifts." I smiled and sat up. "Your lips are dry. Would you like some water?" I nodded. Rebecca took a paper cup and headed for the water fountain.

"Aw naw, hell naw! I will die of thirst before I drink a sip of Atkin's *booty* water out of one of these water fountains." I said. Rebecca laughed out loud.

"I'll go and get you some spring water from the nurse's station." Rebecca said. She then exited the room. Watching her leave made me think to myself how white

343

women seemed to have their own little way of walking. They more than likely said the same thing about sisters.

I had a letter tucked under the edge of my mattress. Mail had been passed out and apparently whoever it was that did mail call didn't want to wake me. As I retrieved the envelope, I was overwhelmed by the emotional onslaught I experienced upon recognizing the handwriting on it. A small hole had been punctured through the wall in my mind and the love I felt for the sender came rushing through.

It was from Patience. I felt excited, I had not received many letters from her since I had left the county. The latest being a few months back. All of a sudden I remembered how I felt about her. I also remembered all of the anxiety I had been feeling because of her being so slow to respond to my letters to her.

"Someone loves you today, eh?" Rebecca asked as she walked into the room referring to the letter I held in my hand. I was staring off into space with a smile on my face, lost in reflection.

"I *remember*!" I said as she handed me the cup of water.

"Really?"

I nodded, sipping the fresh cold water. "This is from my girlfriend Patience." I started, holding the letter up in the air. "When I saw her handwriting it all came back to me."

"That's great! You are really coming along! The doctor said that it is going to take such things to stimulate those feelings you can't remember." Rebecca said, smiling brightly. She was happy for me. "Soooo...are you going to read it or what?"

"I can't right now. My head is still hurtin' from doin' the exercises in that book all day."

"Would you like for me to read it to you?"

"Would you?"

"Sure I would." I handed the letter to her. "Are you sure it's not too personal?" I nodded. Rebecca took a seat on the edge of my bunk. She then extracted the letter from the envelope.

The first thing I noticed was that the letter was short, only a page and a ½ long. I had not received a letter from her in a few months and all she had was a page and ½ worth of things to say to me? Patience had gone from writing me 12 to 15 page letters 2 or 3 times a week all of the way down to 3 or 4 pages every couple of months; now she was down to a page and a ½?

When I brought this up during our conversations on the phone it always triggered an argument.   I tried countless times to convey to her how much it meant for me to receive a letter from her and she would in turn attribute her lack of writing to being busy with school and a part-time job she had. Lately it had been difficult for me to catch up with Patience, even on her days off she was never at home. She had her own car and yet she had only been to visit once. She would tell me she was coming and then never show up. When I would question Teebaby about Patience and why she was never around when I called, I sensed that Teebaby was withholding information from me. There were even times when I suspected that Patience was right there with Teebaby when she claimed she wasn't and hadn't even seen her.

"Aww, she was crying when she wrote this." Rebecca commented as she unfolded the letter. She then cleared her throat. "*Atif,*"

Whoa, wait a minute.   Atif? What happened to salutations like "To my dearest" and "*To the love of my life*"? Since when was I just Atif? I usually didn't catch on to things like that due to my injury but like Rebecca had said, I was really coming along.   My comprehension was getting better. Rebecca continued on, reading slowly.

"Hi! How are you doing? Fine I hope. As for me I can remember better days. I know that it has been a while since I wrote last and I apologize for that. I know how you feel about my slacking up on our correspondence. I have just been so busy Atif and for some reason it is difficult for me to make you understand that. I can't seem to find the

345

*time for much of anything with work, graduation, studying
for the S.A.T.'s and all. Not to mention trying to decide
which college I wish to attend. I am engrossed!*

   *"I really do miss you Atif, even if it has not seemed
like it lately. I have something to tell you. I know that I
told you I didn't want to go to Senior Prom because you
were not out here to go with me, but that was not the truth.
I wanted to go so bad! All of my friends were going and
Senior Prom is a once in a lifetime experience that you don't
just pass up. So I went. There is this guy at work and his
name is Monsieur. He is really nice and he is who I went
with.*

   *"Speaking of Monsieur. I think I need to get to the
point of my writing this particular letter. I know that with
your grandmother being in the condition she is in, this has
to be the worst time for me to be telling you this, but
Monsieur and I have been getting to know each other real
well and I am beginning to develop feelings for him. The
only way I can possibly pursue them is to let you go."*

   Rebecca paused and looked up at me. She then
continued.

   *"I think we just need to be friends. I can't do this
anymore Atif, I tried but I can't. I need to move on with my
life. I can't continue living like I am incarcerated because of
the decision that you made. I promised that I would always
be there for you and I will, this is not my way of telling you
that you will no longer play a significant role in my life. We
can still write to each other. I will never stop loving you Atif
and-"*

   Rebecca stopped there and sighed in sorrow as she
saw me no longer paying attention to her recital. I had
zoned off and was gazing in the opposite direction, looking
out of the window. I couldn't believe what I had heard.
The smile Rebecca was so used to seeing on my face had
vanished without a trace.

   "Maybe this was not such a good idea after all."
Rebecca said, folding the letter and placing it back into the
envelope. "I don't understand why she would send you a
Dear John letter right now considering all that you are going

through." Silence. "I'm pulling a double tonight, Lisa called in sick. If you want to talk or if there is anything I can do for you let me know, okay?" More silence. Sensing my desire for solitude Rebecca then exited the room without another word.

Not too many things in this world can compare to being forced to swallow a mouthful of bitter reality once all the avenues of denial have been exhausted. Whoever this Monsieur character was might as well of sat down and wrote that letter to me himself because I sensed his presence all throughout it. Most of those words did not belong to Patience; they belonged to him.

I was hurt. All of the joy I experienced when my memories of my emotions for Patience came flooding back upon the recognition of her handwriting plummeted at such a high rate of speed that I almost felt dizzy. I was no longer so amused about those brothers back in the county jail whose girlfriends had left them. I loved Patience, I had come to that realization *before* I was incarcerated even though I never told her so, and she was the only one I had *ever* felt so strongly about. And now it was over? I was not experienced in matters of the heart but I knew that it was going to be very difficult for me to get over her if I could. She was not just some fling I had fornicated with like the other females that had long since ceased writing me. All except for Kesha.

I began to console myself with fantasies of winning her back whenever I made it out of prison. I was not going to just give her up that easily. We had been through too much together. And what did she *mean* "we can still write to each other"? Now that she had dropped me like a bad habit I really was not going to hear from her. She was hardly writing to me when she was still my girlfriend. How could she do that to me? She promised me she would never do that to me! It had only been 3 years, I was just getting started! What was the point in having a name like Patience if she didn't have any?

I learned a valuable lesson from Patience's departure that I still cling on to this very day. A promise is something that we as human beings have no right to give to another. I say so because we do not possess the power and authority to make *sure* it does not get broken. You can *promise* to fly home and spend Christmas Day with your child but what are you going to do if when you reach the airport, all of the planes are snowed in and the flights have been canceled? You *intended* to be there and tried, but you still broke your promise because of circumstances that were out of your control.

Only the one in whose hand the "control" rests possesses the right to make promises. He alone has the authority to make a promise with a surety that it will not be broken because what He promises *must* come to pass. When I came to this realization, I also understood why Fatimah and Big Mama would always say "insha Allah" or "Lord willing" when speaking of something to occur sometime in the future whether it be near or far. They were acknowledging the fact that they had no control over such things or even the power to be able to say that they would even live to wake up the next morning, let alone do something they intended to do. Our Creator has promised us that we will all be resurrected after we die and will be judged, this and promises like it from *Him* are the ones I put my faith in. Everything else is up for grabs.

I remember glancing over at the letter, tempted to read it for myself. Maybe Rebecca had misunderstood what she was reading? Yeah right. I grabbed the letter and put it up. I was going to begin getting over her by taking it along with the rest of her letters, cards and pictures, and sending them all back to her in one big envelope.

"Let's see how you like *them* apples you *bitch*." I said to myself just before I drifted off to sleep.

*****

What was that noise? Someone was moaning. The voice was feminine. A *woman*? I opened my eyes and sat up with my ears perked at attention like a dog's ears. I was not in the infirmary, I was in my cell on the hill in population

348

laying in my old bunk. It was *very* hot in the cell for some reason. The moaning was coming from beneath me. I just *knew* that whoever my celly was wasn't freaking with some homosexual down on his bunk while I was in the cell sleeping.   There would be *grievous* consequences and repercussions for such an act of disrespect; I mean, and in the words of Bernie Mack, there was going to be some *furniture* moving up in there if so!

I leaned over the edge of my bunk and peered down onto the bottom bunk which for some reason was oddly a good 10 feet down. What was even stranger than that was there appeared to be an actual woman laying down there.

I climbed over the edge, dangling myself from my bunk, and let go. The drop was even more than I expected. I landed on the floor in a crouched position.   It was *Patience*! She was laying on her back with the blanket pulled up to her chest area. Her eyes were closed and she was gripping the end of the bunk behind her head with both hands as she moaned in ecstasy, licking her lips. There was someone in the bed with her. I snatched the blanket away, discarding it on the floor, and my facial expression twisted in a mask of horror and fury.   Patience was naked underneath and Small Ball's face was in between her wide spread legs literally *eating* the flesh of her vagina. He looked up at me and snarled a bloody snarl.

"Yo bitch ain't your bitch no more nigga!" Small Balls hissed at me, laughing.

He looked demonic.   Blood from Patience was smeared all over his face and bits of her flesh was stuck in his teeth. The once white bed sheets were soaked with blood. I swung at him and fell onto the bed because of my momentum. He was no longer there. I looked at Patience, her body was covered by a sheen of perspiration and her eyes were open, looking at me in return. The look she had in her eyes was one I had never seen. Whenever Patience used to look at me I could see her affection towards me in her eyes. This affection was no longer there.   I saw mockery.   Her hands had found their way down to her

349

mangled vagina and she began to fondle what was left of herself.

"Nanny-nanny-boo-boo," Patience chanted, waving her bloody fingers in my face. "You-can't-have-none."

I reached for her hand and she removed it from my face, placing her fingers into her mouth, giggling as she sucked her own blood from them. I sat there staring at her, disgusted. She then exploded in a fit of rage all of a sudden.

"You stupid *motherfucker*! I *told* you to *stay* there with me you *fucking asshole!*' she screamed, clawing at my face. She then kicked me off of the bunk.

The floor was gone! I kept on plunging deeper and deeper into the complete impenetrable darkness of what seemed to be a bottomless pit. I panicked and began to scream, flaying my arms and legs wildly. It was so hot I couldn't take it.

"Atif! Stop it!"

"Heellp!"

"Atif! Calm down!" I began to recognize my surroundings. I was safe on the floor back in the infirmary and no longer falling. Four guards were on top of me trying to restrain me. My head was throbbing. "It was just a dream!" I recognized Rebecca's voice saying to me. I slowly stopped struggling. I was panting, out of breath, and my heart was racing. "It was just a dream, you are okay now." Rebecca coaxed softly as I began to calm down. "That's right, take it easy. Breathe."

"Jesus!" One of the guards exclaimed, wiping sweat from his brow and breathing heavily. "What is God's name is wrong with him?"

"He is okay, you can let him up now." Rebecca said. The guard looked down at me.

"You okay big guy?" I nodded.   "You got some serious demons in you brother." The guard then rose and the others did the same.

"Okay people, the show is over." Rebecca said, shooing the guards, nurses and inmates standing in the doorway from the room. I sat up, took a deep breath, and rose shakily to my feet.

"*Whoa*, take your time." Rebecca said, catching me as I lost my balance. "Here, let me help you." She said, guiding me to a seat on my bunk.

"You okay Rebecca, want me to stay?" One of the guards asked her, reappearing in the doorway.

"No, I have it from here. Thank you." Rebecca answered. The guard nodded and left the room. I reached for a fresh wound in my head and cringed in pain as I touched it. "Don't do that." Rebecca said, grabbing my hand. There was blood on my fingers. "Sss, ouch. Looks like you hit your head when you fell." She then reached for some cotton balls and a bottle of peroxide. "Look at your shirt, it is soaked with sweat! Take if off." I complied. "I had no idea you were that strong."

Rebecca must have forgotten what she told me about how women noticed it when men were taking inventory of their goods. I am not a woman but I sure noticed that her eyes lingered on my upper torso a little longer than necessary. Maybe she *was* a little more than comfortable with me after all.

"You almost punched my lights out." Rebecca said, applying pressure to my head wound to stop the bleeding.

"What you mean?"

"I came in to check on you and when I went to wipe some sweat from your forehead you swung at me so hard that you fell on the floor."

"Did I?"

"Um-hmm."

"My bad, I didn't mean to. I was trippin'."

"Oh, I know." Rebecca said, discarding the bloody cotton ball in the biohazard bin. "Besides, my husband has thrown more than a few punches my way, enough for me to develop a knack for dodging one. Bend your head down please."

"He be hittin' on you?" I asked. Rebecca stood on her toes and examined my head. I could see straight down her top then, the only way around it was to close my eyes; I kept them open.

"He never has been one who could hold his liquor and when he gets drunk he starts...*trippin'*." Rebecca answered, attempting to mimic my slang. I remember thinking to myself how it took a real coward to put their hands on a woman as nice as Rebecca. I wouldn't have minded putting my hands on someone like that. "You want to tell me about your dream?"

"You don't want to hear about it."

"Was it *that* bad?" I nodded. "I'm worried about you." Rebecca said, removing her rubber gloves as she finished up, throwing them into the biohazard bin.

"Why you say that?"

"While you were sleeping I was thinking about how excited you were when you remembered the way you felt about your girlfriend, pardon me, ex-girlfriend, and then how *sad* you had become all of a sudden when I read her letter to you. Not knowing your father, your mother being dead, you must be very close to your grandmother and I am afraid that whenever you remember this it is going to be too much for you to handle."

"Allah burdens not a person beyond his scope." I said, reciting the first line from the Qur'anic verse Fatimah had taught me. I then smiled as another hole was punctured through the wall in my mind, remembering how intrigued by Fatimah I had been.

"Hey, there's that smile again!" Rebecca exclaimed, smiling herself.

"I remember."

"Really?" Rebecca said, placing her hands on my knees. If this woman was not attracted to me, I was sure that I would have been able to look up the phrase "touchy-feely" in the dictionary and find a big picture of her next to it as the definition. "Who?"

"This Muslim girl named Fatimah that I met back in juvenile. When I got certified she wrote a verse from the Qur'an down for me and told me to put it in my heart so that I could take it with me everywhere I went."

"How does the rest of it go?" I recited the whole verse for her. "Wow, she must be a very interesting young lady. Tell me about her."

I did. I didn't stop there though. I also told her about a lot of other things. We talked for hours, pausing only to let her make her rounds. She was fascinated by my past and the way of life I was living on the streets. I told her about the things that she had only seen on television. We talked about my mother, my neighborhood, school, the hommies, we went on and on and on. We even went off into the drug trade in the penitentiary and how much money there was to be made. As much as she tried to hide it, she was very curious about it. So much so that I believed I could convince her to meet up with my brother and bring some drugs in to me.

I then went off into stories of Patience and our times together. She just loved hearing about the trip to Cool Crest, the diamond earrings I purchased for her, and many other occurrences. I really got a lot of weight off of my shoulders and I was feeling a lot better after talking to her.

"Well, I guess I ain't got to worry about standin' in my cell doorway like a hungry dog at mail call no more hopin' to get a letter from her." I said, finishing up my synopsis on our relationship.

"You'll be okay. It is going to be hard, especially under such circumstances, but time heals all wounds." Rebecca said, patting my thigh. "Out of sight, out of mind." My brow creased in concentration as I struggled to figure out what was meant by that phrase. "Oh, I'm sorry. What that means is tha-"

"I get it." I cut in with a smile.

"Look at *you*! That wall in your mind is going to come tumbling down in no time." Rebecca said. "I don't see how she could have let a young man like you go, you truly are one of the good ones."

"I don't see how a woman like you could put up with a man like your husband."

"And what is a woman like me?"

353

"One who could find a better man."

"I wouldn't be so sure about that Atif. Not too many men out there want anything to do with a woman past her prime that can't bear children."

I had her figured out upon hearing her utter those words. She was still married to her husband because he had convinced her that he was the only one who wanted her. Since he had established that he was free to treat her however he wanted to because she would more than likely, out of her fear of dying old and alone, not leave him.

Rebecca reminded me of Antoinette in a sense. She was a little worse off than Antoinette though. I felt for her and I wanted to change the way she viewed herself. I wanted to make her feel good for once. Wanted and desired. She deserved to be treated better than she had grown accustomed to. My intentions were sincere at first, I did not wish to take advantage of what was going on in her life and play on it.

"What are you talkin' about past yo prime? You *still* look good." I complimented her.

"I would be flattered if that didn't just come from a man doing 30 years in prison."

"I don't lie Rebecca. I will either tell you how I honestly feel about somethin' or I won't, either way I ain't gone lie about it." Silence. "You said that like I'm one of these dudes that ain't been with a woman in 20 years! I just got locked up in '93. It ain't been *that* long for me, you know what I'm sayin'?"

"Yeah, I know."

"Stand up." Rebecca stood, facing me. "Can I?" I asked respectfully, reaching for the glasses on her face. She answered my request by tilting her face towards my hands. I gently removed her glasses, folded them, and set them onto her cart. "You got some pretty eyes."

"Yeah, *right.*"

"I'm *serious*! Lookin' into them is like...lookin' into the ocean's water at nighttime." I said, looking deeply into them.

"Oh you are *good*, a regular Casanova."

"Do you always wear your hair up like that or do you do it just for work?"

"I keep it up."

"Can I see it?"

"Why?" Rebecca asked, reaching up for the pin holding her hair in place.

I ignored her question. I didn't believe she actually expected an answer. If so, she would not have been so quick to comply. She *wanted* to show it to me. Her long, curly red hair fell onto her shoulders as she released it. It was even longer than I thought. I gently took a hand full of it into my right palm, caressing it. It was the first time I had ever felt a white person's hair. It was so thin!

"Rebecca you are *trippin'*, you are *sexy*! Why you be holdin' out like this?"

"Would you stop it? Enough already. I am going to need a pair of boots in a minute here."

"I'm for real, you got some pretty eyes, long beautiful hair," I started. I then leaned close to her, sniffing her new perfume. "You smell like the potential subject of a man's wet dream." Rebecca laughed at that. "Turn around." She complied, turning in a 360 degree circle with a roll of her eyes. "You got a nice body on you too."

"Do you want some Ibuprofen for your head?" she asked, turning away from me with an attempt to change the subject. I took her hand and pulled her back towards me.

"How long has it been since you went out?"

"God, ages."

"You know what I think you should do?"

"What?"

"You should go and buy you a nice new dress, get you some open toe high heeled shoes, let your hair down, doll yourself up with some red lipstick and don't forget the Bora Bora," Rebecca laughed out loud. "Leave your glasses at home along with your husband. Then you should hit the club. I bet you would have every man in there tryin' to holler at you."

"This is *Moberly* Atif, not Kansas City. There aren't many night clubs in a small town like this; more like bars."

"Well go to the bar then! Have you a few drinks, get tipsy, tease a couple of these country white hillbillies for a while and then call it a night."

"I doubt if even the country white hillbillies would get excited on account of me."

"I don't see why not, you got *me* excited." I gambled. Rebecca peered at me.

"I don't believe that." I took her hand and placed it in my crotch area. Rebecca gasped, looking around to make sure no one had seen. "You are too young to be walking around with a-" I interrupted her by kissing her softly on the lips. My kiss was tentative, asking. "Stop, don't Atif."

I probably would have if her hand had not still been gripping my manhood. "But you don't *want* me to." I said, kissing her again.

"I could lose my job."

"*If* we got caught." I said kissing her. She knew just like I did that it was late and on the graveyard shift no one ever paid much attention to what was going on. Some of the nurses and guards even went off to a secluded area and slept.

"My husband would *kill* me."

"*If* you told him." I said, kissing her once more. This time she responded.

"This is...*crazy*," Rebecca started in between kisses. I slid my hand down the front of her white slacks and into her panties. She was soaking wet and had been the whole time. "I can't believe I'm doing this." She said as she slipped her own hand down into my prison grays, taking a hold of me. "*Man*, you are excited! Wait," Rebecca then started, pulling away from me. "Let me go and make *sure* the coast is clear." Rebecca put her glasses back on and began to tie her hair back up into a bun. "For years I have been coming to work," she began with her hair pin in her mouth as she worked, "and leaving here feeling like a piece of meat because of the way the other inmates treat me. Then I would go home to my husband and *he* would make me feel worthless and unattractive." Rebecca finished her transformation back into the old Rebecca, taking my face into her hands.   "And *you*, a man ½ my age almost, convicted of *murder* for God's sake have miraculously convinced me that I just might still have it; all within a matter of minutes." Rebecca then kissed me, smiling.   "I'll be right back."

I watched her as she headed for the door. Her little hips even had an added swagger to them as she walked. I smirked to myself. I was the one who couldn't believe it was happening. I was in the penitentiary and about to have sex with a *woman*!   I felt like the luckiest inmate in the Department of Corrections.

"By the way," Rebecca started in a hushed tone, pausing just before the doorway. "Since you took your HIV test back in September, have you had any se-"

"No-I-never-no!" I cut her off, mimicking Tisha Campbell in the movie "House Party". I wasn't offended. Considering that environment and all of the AIDS patients she dealt with on a daily basis, she had every right to ask.

"Just checking." Rebecca smiled and left the room.

I see no point in going into details as far as what transpired when she made it back. I hate that I did so with Kesha, Antoinette and Niki back in part one. I wanted to display our being astray and I believe that has been accomplished; the need for sharing illicit endeavors with the women of my life has been exhausted. From here on out I will be sparing you the sexual explicit scenes. With all of that said, lets just say that Rebecca and I gave each other some much needed attention.

*****

JUSTICE OR JUST US?
"I'm feelin' like I have a purpose;
I'm not blind no more!
Smokin' weed is a worthless
high that I don't try to find no more!
-I- no longer love illusions,
give me reality.
Show me my enemy
and I will turn him into a casualty.
My anger is mis-directed,
I have to harness it and check it.
Only then will I be ready to go to war
for the justice we've been neglected."
-Soody Mak

"Is it justice;
or just us?
Are you ridin' with the Black fist;
or the Klu Klux?
-Klan- man do you need another fix;
or have you had enough?
Can you see through the mist;
or are you still stuck?"
-Soody Mak

18

    I was released from the infirmary a month or so later. Rebecca had pulled all of the strings she could for as long as possible, as it turned out she had been doing so the whole time. I was not supposed to have been in there for as long as I was. Within a week after my initial admittance they had been ready to kick me back out into population. Rebecca explained to them that it would be dangerous for me to be on the yard while in the condition I was in at that time and the administration propositioned to put me in protective custody. Rebecca then, knowing how I felt about protective custody, persuaded them to allow me to stay and that she would take it upon herself to work with me like she did.

    Eventually I convinced Rebecca to meet with Malik and bring drugs in to me. She finally agreed on the condition that my brother was the only person she would meet up with and that I had to get a job in the infirmary so that we could "continue spending time together." She didn't want any of the money I made, didn't need it. She just wanted for me to keep on making her feel the way I did. After a few practice runs her fears were suppressed and we were in business.

    I hit the yard flying first class all of the way in a window seat with slippers on my feet and a pillow behind my head. I had the most reliable horse on the camp as far as moving drugs went *and* I was having sex with a woman on a regular basis in the penitentiary. I received a warm welcome from everyone I had gotten to know before I was admitted.

    It was not the same though.

    Skooter-B was in administrative segregation under investigation and Cook-El had been transferred to another prison. Static Addict had been found laying comatose on the restroom floor in the gymnasium with so many holes in him that if he had regained consciousness from the deep coma he was in, he would not have known from which hole to urinate out of. The prison officials lacked the evidence they needed in order to seek prosecution for what happened to Static Addict. All they had were the statements of a few prison rats, none of which had actually witnessed the stabbing, and even though it wasn't much to go on, it was enough to get rid of Cook-El.

His type was not welcome in Moberly. People like him threw a monkey wrench into their well oiled machine, igniting rebellious attitudes that the administration worked hard to suppress. I had even heard that the guards had given him the nickname "The Nat Turner of Moberly" when referring to him amongst themselves behind his back.

With Skooter-B being in the hole, the Bloods had fallen to the bottom of the totem pole in the underground drug trafficking industry. The hommies were in bad condition. Unity was diminishing. Some of the hommies were becoming affiliated with other cliques and crews trying to associate with those who were getting money in order to scrape up whatever crumbs they could that fell from the table. I was disgusted. Seeing them on the yard made me think of moths and how they all are attracted to porch lights. Concrete and a few more of the hommies had been trying to get something going but was unsuccessful. When they were able to make something happen it was not enough to keep everyone satisfied. Not only that, but it was not the same level of quality that Skooter-B had been flooding the camp with so people chose to spend their money elsewhere.

"So how is your memory and comprehension comin' along?" Smack Man asked. A few weeks had gone by and he surprised me with a visit.

"Good, matter of fact, even better than before I got into it with ole boy in some areas." I answered. "Where is Persistence at?"

"She ain't feelin' too good today so she stayed behind."

"What's goin' on with everybody else?"

"Well, you know, everything is everything. Antoinette and K-Red is talkin' about gettin'married. Actually *she* is doin' more talkin' than he is but I think they gone do it eventually.

"The rest of the brothers is still doin' what they do. Lil' Darion be disappearin' on everybody man, don't nobody be knowin' where he at. I think somethin' is up with him; somethin' he don't want to tell us."

"Somethin' like what?"

"I ain't gone speculate youngblood, I'm just gone get to the bottom of it." We sat in silence for a few moments. What was going on with my best friend? Even I hadn't been hearing too much from him. "Patience is thinkin' about goin' to law school down in Georgia. They offered her an academic scholarship."

I tried to act nonchalant with his mentioning her name. I didn't do very well, I think that he could clearly see that I still had feelings for her. It was written all over my face.

"Aw yeah?" Smack Man nodded. "That's cool."

"Why you won't talk to her?"

"What is there to talk about?"

"Where did you come up with the idea to send all of her letters and stuff back to her like that?" I shrugged my shoulders.

"I don't know. All I *do* know is that they were full of her lies and empty promises and I didn't want them anymore."

"You hit her hard with that one; she was *sick.*"

"Well, now she can *almost* understand how I felt when she sent me that dumb ass letter."

"Persistence *told* her not to send you that letter she wrote. I think the youngsta' she kickin' it with convinced her to do that."

"Yeah, I kind of figured that. Who is this dude anyway? Wha' sup with him?"

"I don't trust him to tell you the truth." I nodded. "Patience say she wrote you and apologized for bein' so inconsiderate but you never wrote her back." Smack Man said, taking us back to the original topic.

"Man I ain't finna take myself down through there again so that she can clear her conscience. Fuck that."

"She want to come and see how you doin' but she scared that you might have taken her off of your list."

361

"I see they ain't givin' her that scholarship for nothin'." Smack Man laughed.

"Y'all ain't got to be enemies Atif." I shrugged in dismissal. Honestly I didn't want to be enemies with her but my ego wouldn't allow me to forgive her. "Anyway, I heard about this white woman you got puttin' in work for you. What do Malik be callin' her?"

"Snowflake." Smack Man laughed.

"You are ahead of your time man, you know that?" I smirked. "How is things lookin' in here on that end?"

"Man I been ridin' solo on the hustlin' tip. Ever since Skooter-B went to the hole everybody done split up so I ju-"

"Atif, you are not on the streets, you are in prison and the penitentiary is not a place where you can really get money on your own." Smack Man cut in.

"Why not?"

"Because you got people around you that ain't never comin' home, they don't have people on the outside to look out for them like you do. After so many years even *family* members have forgotten where they are at. And if they see you gettin' paper and clutchin' it to your chest they gone hate on you.

"The dope game in prison is a *dirty* game. You got to spread some love, make it so everybody can get a little bit, *you* just get the *majority* of it, you know?" I nodded. "Bein' greedy and stingy is not the smart thing to do.

"Now, I ain't talkin' about everybody *literally*, some niggas just gone have that to do and would hate *anyway* regardless of what type of doors you open for them. What I'm sayin is, get you a few real niggas and y'all put it down. When you take it upon yourself to put a real nigga on his feet his loyalty is something you will be able to depend on. If you try to do it by yourself then you gone have to do all of your dirty work too, the things that draw attention to you, and you don't want that. You want somebody *else* doin' that.

"What you need to do is take control of the situation like your brotha' did in the hood. *You* have the horse, *you* have the plug, so *you* need to be orchestratin'

362

shit. We got you faded, whatever you need whenever you need it, you got that comin'. You got leadership in you, and just need to let it come out. Just be careful because like I said..."

"It's a dirty game." I finished for him.

"That's right." Smack Man stood up. "I was just stoppin' through, I got a plane to catch."

"A'ight, thanks for comin'."

"I will start swingin' by a little more often, I didn't know that nobody had been comin' up here to see you. Everybody that would, can't. Well, except for Darion. I don't know what his trip is. I will check on Big Mama for you too when I get back in town. Keep your head up and know that when you ain't hearin' from Jaco then it means he is puttin' his work in for you. That's what I like about him, he don't talk. He just do what needs to be done; *if* you keep him paid." I nodded. "You want me to tell Patience anything?"

YES! Tell her that I miss her; that I can't stop thinking about her! Tell her that I do want to see her. Tell her that I'm sorry about sending all of her letters back to her like that and I meant to respond but I was hurting and...

"No, I don't want you to tell her nothin'."

*****

I remember the walk back to my housing unit after that visit with Smack Man. Before I went to prison I used to be so into things he said to me and I took all of it to heart. I used to find our conversations so motivating and inspirational. But as I walked back pondering over the things he had said to me during our visit, I was not so affected by his words and opinions like I was in the past. The only part that even came close was when he said that Patience and I didn't have to be enemies.

I was maturing, there was no doubt about it. While in the infirmary I had been thinking about other things besides hustling for the first time in years. A lot of the things Cook-El had broken down for me made a lot of sense and I found myself more interested in reading the books he recommended for me to read than standing around on the yard all day talking irrelevance with the hommies. I felt like I was wasting time when doing so, time that could be spent doing something more constructive.

Some of the hommies were in their 30's but still adolescents in the mind. I didn't want to be 30 years old, playing the dozens and running around pinching each other's behinds like children, not knowing enough to know that I didn't know. I was just beginning to feel like there was more to life and that there were some things going on in the world that I had been blind to while growing up; things that I was developing a desire to open my eyes to. A lot of unanswered questions that I wanted the answers to.

That night I laid awake in my bunk unable to sleep, not because of a fear of bad dreams, but because I was wondering what was going on with me and why? I started to liken it to my injuries but that was not it. There was a struggle being initiated within me. I sensed the presence of another side of me striving to emerge and take over. A side of me that had been suppressed for years, only coming up to the surface for air every once in a while. I thought about what this would mean for me and those who knew me. I was not going to spend the rest of my life being the same old person that everyone had come to know.

With all of the above said, just because I was harboring thoughts other than hustling didn't mean that the urge and inclination to get money was not still present. At that period in my life, and in the words of a good Christian brother I would come to know, I was still too in love with the dark.

*****

A week later I was standing out on the back part of the yard with about 8 of the brothers waiting for the rest of them to show up for a meeting I had taken it upon myself to call. I didn't expect for everyone to show. Some probably felt like I didn't possess the authority to do such a thing. Whoever felt that way, it would be their loss because those who didn't show would not play a part in my plans.

"Why everybody call you Concrete?" I asked. A couple of the hommies laughed.

"You got jokes Atif?" Concrete asked in return.

"Naw man, I'm serious." Concrete looked at me.

"Me and this clown was drivin' each other one day and he told me that my grill looked like I tripped and fell face first into some concrete with a smile on my face." I busted out laughing along with the other hommies as the old joke gained new life on account of my hearing it for the first time.   Concrete was missing his front right tooth. "Niggas been callin' me that shit ever since."

At that moment I decided that I was not going to allow anyone to up and give *me* a name like that. People were not going to call me by what they wanted to. Besides, my mother had given me my name and after entering the penitentiary and being stripped of all my belongings, it was the only thing I still possessed that she had left me with.

Only 17 people actually showed up for the meeting, which was fine by me. I began informing the hommies why I had summoned them and we discussed how things were falling apart since Skooter-B was placed under investigation. I then revealed to them the fact that I had a horse and a plug so we could do our own thing instead of looking to the other organizations for a handout.   They were happy to hear this and gave me their undivided attention as I broke down a plan I had sketched out.   It was simple and I stressed how if we all adhered to it then we would be raking in thousands of dollars at a time and gain control of the drug trade in Moberly.

"You got a *solid* plug?" One of the hommies by the name of Vern asked me.

"Yeah, it's solid.   Whatever we want, I can get that." I answered.   "Hard, soft, snotty, meth, wet, pills, ecstasy, whatever."

"We should flood this camp with *all* of that shit, sew it up for *real*." Another one of the hommies by the name of Jihad suggested.

"I was thinkin' that we should concentrate more on the powder and snotty; where all the major money is at, and leave the rest of that stuff to the other people tryin' to get money. We just want to take control, not cut off everybody else's life lines like that." I said.

"Man *fuck* these niggas Atif," Vern started, "Ain't none of *them* been doin' nothin' for *us* for real while *we* been doin' bad. They only been thinkin' of themselves." He finished. The rest of the hommies murmured in agreement.

"Yeah, I know. But if we go that route then we gone be funkin' with these niggas more than anything. Every time we look up we gone be over in ad-seg under investigation right along with Skooter-B because they gone be hatin', droppin' kites and sickin' the administration on us."

"They gone do that regardless Atif." Vern said.

"Yeah, but we should leave some avenues open for them, that way they will be preoccupied with doin' their own little thing instead of trippin' off of us. It will keep the whole camp happy. Let the white boys have the meth and the ecstasy, we gone have our hands in their pockets anyway because all of them like that powder. All the Crips, G.D.'s and the rest of them want to do is sell some crack, weed and wet to each other so we will let them have that. And the St. Louis niggas, no offense to those present," I paused with a grin, "but they like to move that snotty, which we gone take control of, but they be gettin' it through visits and shit only a few grams at a time so they ain't steppin' on *our* toes. Let them do that. They be runnin' out before they even get started. Us though? We gone *keep* that shit. And ours gone be so *fire* we gone knock them out the box anyway."

"Your people got some heat like that?" Vern asked.

"All the fire shit Skooter-B used to have?" I started. Vern and the rest of the hommies nodded. "Same source." Vern smiled that closed lip smile of his.

"All that is cool, I agree with all that except for the part about us only fuckin' with powder and snotty." Jihad spoke up.

"Why?" I asked.

"Because, some of us is doin' bids that we can't do, you know what I'm sayin'?" I nodded. "And that bitch Mary Jane, she like my...she like my mutha' fuckin' *psychiatrist* blood." We all laughed at this. "A, I ain't bullshittin'. I love gettin' money but at the same time doin' so don't take my mind off this time like me and Mary Jane's *therapy* sessions." We laughed again. "You see what I'm sayin'?" I nodded. "Plus, that weed game got a lot of money in it too."

"It do, I know that. But it's too bulky to be sittin' on. And when I said we should concentrate on the powder and snotty, I didn't mean that *we* ain't gone move a little weed of our own. We just ain't gone *sell* it, it will just be for us to smoke on." I commented.

The hommmies *really* liked the sound of that one. The meeting was concluded minutes later with the agreement that we would all continue to meet in such a fashion once a week.

Meanwhile, I went to work and in no time we were back in business. Our product was top of the line, deals were sweet and we kept our goods in stock. Rebecca was routinely making her trips to Kansas City biweekly. I personally did more orchestrating than anything else. I rarely participated in any actual transactions. A lot of the hommies didn't have anyone they could call when they needed a 3-way to check on funds being sent so I had Niki install a blow up line in her apartment that we all could use. Not just to check on money, but also to call family members that had blocks on their phones because of high phone bills resulting from numerous collect calls. As the months rolled by the money rolled in. The depression was over; everyone was content.

That is everyone except me.

*****

August 10, 1998.

Big Mama was no longer with us. She died a couple of months before. As far as I had come along in recovering from my injuries, Big Mama was the only one remaining

367

whom I could not "remember". I learned of her death through the Chaplain whom had called me in from the library and into her office one day. When I got there she had Malik on the phone.

I already knew in my heart what was wrong but he told me anyway. I felt sorry for him more than anything because that left him alone out there in the streets. He was a grown man and could take care of himself like he had been doing since he was a teenager, that wasn't what concerned me. Big Mama was all that remained of his *sanity*. With her gone and me incarcerated, he no longer had much to care about outside of the hommies. He needed a woman in his life that he could trust and love, but let him tell it no such woman existed.

Kesha was out of prison, making parole over a year before, and she was doing very well for herself. While in prison she had gained a little weight but slimmed back down soon afterwards. She was trying to get her cosmetology license with dreams of opening her own beauty salon in the hood. I was happy for her and appreciated how she kept in touch after her release from prison. I couldn't wait to see her. Since she was on parole they would not allow her on my visiting list.

Skooter-B was out of the hole. He emerged in humility, taking a seat on the passenger side of the car and allowing me to continue driving. Prison officials were upset with not being able to prosecute him or anyone else for that matter in the stabbing death of Static Addict. They kept a close watch on him, harassing him whenever the opportunity presented itself. He called himself staying low key but if you knew Skooter-B like I did, such a feat was almost impossible for him with his personality.

As for me the previous 2 years were spent deep off into my studies. The conflict I spoke of earlier within myself had matured into an all out war. I had a deeper understanding of my history and the detrimental effects of such things as selling drugs. I understood that I was taking part in perpetuating "The mugging of Black America", as Earl Ofari Hutchinson so eloquently put it in a book of his I had studied, and it was becoming more difficult by the day for me to continue flooding that camp with narcotics.

I moved out of the cell with one of the hommies and into a cell with a brother in the Nation of Islam by the name of DeAnthony X. I did so because I wanted to be around someone whose conversational content was heavier and more versatile than how sexy Ananda Lewis was.

Me and DeAnthony X got along very well. We were the same age and like minded on most issues, all except for the topics of Malcolm X and the religious teachings of the doctrine DeAnthony X followed. We had many heated debates but always laid down to go to sleep on a good note afterwards. We did a lot of growing together.

DeAnthony X had a nice collection of books. His family was pretty well off and he used the money they sent to him to purchase these books. I lost myself digging off into his books authored by people like: Dr. Na'im Akbar, Ph.D., Stokely Carmichael, Chancellor Williams, Amos Wilson, Bobby Seale, George Jackson, Carter G. Woodson, Dr. Frances Welsing, the list goes on and on. We studied *together* and discussed what we had learned and how to *apply* it. He was persistent in trying to bring me away from the drug trade and, knowing how much I despised hypocrisy, explained how it was hypocritical of me to say some of the things I would say while still *doing* the things I was doing. Sometimes he would say something so powerful and realistic that I would be left dumbfounded at a loss for words. He, like brother Cook-El, helped me open my eyes to a lot of things.

I was changing. My mannerisms were different, my conversation was positive. I began to watch my language and deleted a lot of the slang from my vocabulary, replacing them with words that helped me do a better job with expressing myself. I even watched television in a different way. I was no longer interested in the music videos on BET or hoping that a movie with some sex scenes within it was played for us on the movie channel. I watched CNN and other news channels, seething with anger as I saw right through the crap they (politicians and the like) were feeding Americans.

Yes, this period of my life was very tumultuous yet interesting at the same time. Revolutionaries all gave me a knowing smile when I came around, understanding exactly what I was going through.

"Wha' sup blood?" Skooter-B greeted as the two of us walked unannounced into the cell Concrete was currently in. It was a hot August day and Concrete had been spending an awful lot of time cooped up in the cell with the white homosexual he had for a cellie.

"Hey, what's up Skooter-B?" Concrete's *boy* greeted. Skooter-B nodded his head in response, too friendly for his own good. The homosexual didn't even bother to greet me, he knew how I felt about him without a doubt.

"Get up, let me get that spot." I said, instructing him to get up from his *own* chair so that I could sit down as if I had more right to sit there than he did. He complied without a word, having a seat Indian style on the opposite end of Concrete's bunk. The dude was scared to death of me and was very uneasy when I did come around.

"Wha' sup man?" Skooter-B began. "You know it's that time and everybody done contri...con-"

"Contributed?" I offered.

"Yeah, contributed. I was gone get it right. Anyway, everybody done contributed to the pot except for *you*. What's the hold up?" he asked Concrete. We were ready to re-cop and for the second time in a row Concrete had not paid his dues.

"Aw man, I uh, I...things been kind of slow dirty. I'm still waitin' on some ends to hit and I don't want to get nothin' out until I get what er-body owe." Concrete said, sniffling. Not only was he lying but he was high as a kite and we knew it.

"Why you keep snifflin' like that brotha'? You got a cold?" I asked Concrete.

"Aw naw Atif man, it's just my allergies." He answered. I stared at him. "Damn damu, you lookin' at me like I'm lyin' or somethin'."

370

"I didn't say you were lyin' brotha', I just don't *believe* you." The homosexual looked nervously between us sensing tension in the atmosphere.

"I'm going to go and see what is on the menu." The homosexual said, rising.

"Beans and cornbread." Skooter-B informed him without taking his eyes off of Concrete. "Sit your ass down." He sat down slowly. "So, you say you ain't set nothin' out yet?" Skooter-B then asked Concrete.

"Naw dirty, not yet." He answered, scratching his forearm.

"So that mean you still sittin' on a ½ ounce of cocaine, 7 grams of tar and an ounce of weed?" Skooter-B asked him. Concrete nodded, entrapping himself with no other alternative. "Let me get it, I will dump it for you."

Concrete and the homosexual looked at each other. "It's put up right now blood, I will give it to you a little la-"

"What the *fuck*, is you deaf now?" Skooter-B exploded at the homosexual, cutting Concrete off. "I *said* let me get that shit! Get up, dig in that loose booty-hole of yours and pull that shit up out of your ass before I have you touchin' everything up in this mutha' fucka'!"

"Skooter-B, why you trippin' dirty? I thought we wa-" Concrete's chin dropped into his chest as he nodded off in mid-sentence. Skooter-B looked at me and I shook my head. He then looked at the homosexual who by then was so scared that if he did have anything stuffed in his anus he would not have had to pull it out; it would slide out on its own free will on account of his nervousness.

Skooter-B then bent over and picked up an empty cup from beside the desk. "Here," he said, handing it to the homosexual. "Go to the rest room and fill this cup up with water from the toilet." The homosexual took the cup and looked in my direction, afraid to walk past.

"Go ahead, I ain't gone do nothin' to you." I reassured him. He then slipped out of the cell keeping as far away from me as possible, inching his way along the left wall of the cell.

"Why these punks around here so scared of you Atif? You ain't never whooped on one of them that I know

of." Skooter-B asked me. I shrugged my shoulders. "Look
at this nigga man, he ought to be ashamed of himself."

Concrete was out like a light. It *was* a pitiful sight.
Talk about a fall from grace, I used to have a lot of respect
for him. Place any man under the right circumstances for
the right amount of time and his weaknesses will surface. I
was beginning to feel disgusted with myself for trafficking in
something which broke a grown man down to his knees like
that. Like my father.

Moments later the homosexual returned with the
cup and handed it to Skooter-B. "You got this from the
toilet?" he nodded. "A'ight, you can go look and see what is
on the menu now." Skooter-B didn't have to tell him twice,
he got the point.

Skooter-B threw the water into Concrete's face,
waking him with a start. "A man! What the fuck you do that
shit for Skooter-B?" Concrete exclaimed, wiping the water
from his face with his T-shirt.

"Was better than that." Skooter-B said. Concrete
peered at him.

"What?"

"You thought we was better than that. I was
finishin' your sentence for you," Skooter-B said, "didn't they
teach you in your G.E.D. class about how you should finish
your sentence first before you start another one?"

"Fuck you nigga," Concrete said, insulted. He had
been trying to get his G.E.D. for over three years by then.

"Naw, fuck with me nigga! That's what you do!"
Skooter-B challenged.

Concrete had fallen off, reducing himself to a level
that I despised true enough, but that didn't make him an
easy win. If Skooter-B and I were forced to go to extreme
measures Concrete would have still given the both of us a
run for our money up in that cell.

"So, this how it's gone be? You mean to tell me we
gone fall out over some punk ass dope?" Concrete asked us.

"It ain't even about the dope, Concrete. My days of
funkin' with my people over some drugs are long gone. It's
about you goin' left on us like this, man, trickin' with these
homosexuals. What's wrong with you? For the last year or

372

so you been on some other stuff. What made you want to start bakin' cakes with these.... fags?" I asked him. "Where did all of that come from?"

"I don't be bakin' no mutha' fuckin' cakes, nigga, you can get that shit off your mind. I might let him knock me down hurr and thurr, but that don't make *me* gay," he answered. He, like many people in prison, had fooled himself into actually believing that was true.

"First of all, I ain't nobody's nigga. I done asked y'all a million times to stop callin' me that," I started. "Secondly, where you get that line of rationale from?   Let me tell you somethin' brotha', whether you're pitchin' or catchin' don't matter because you *still* playin' baseball."

Silence.

"What did you throw on me Skooter-B?" Concrete asked, smelling his T-shirt. "This shit stink." He then tasted his fingertips, "Taste...metallic." I laughed at that, I couldn't help myself.

"You got to get yourself together Concrete, man, this ain't for us blood." Skooter-B said.

"Yeah, dirty, I know. I'm trippin'."

"We ain't gone give you nothin' out of this next package," I said.

"What? Y'all just gone cut my water off like that?"

"You cut your own water off," I said, rising from my seat.

"Naw, man, on my old bird y'all ain't finna just do me like that," Concrete said, as I made my way out of the cell. Skooter-B followed behind me. "Atif!" I ignored him. "Atif! Come here man!"

We made our way outside. Vern and Jihad were standing by the gymnasium entrance and we made our way in that direction. "I don't see why you be puttin' up with Concrete, Skooter-B," I said, as we walked.

"You got to understand somethin' Atif. You got 30 years to do and that is a lot of time but if these people was to make you do everyday of it you would still make it out one day. Concrete? He could die of old age and come back reincarnated to *continue* doin' his bit and still wouldn't make it out. You know what I'm sayin'?" I nodded. "It is hard for somebody to stay focused when in that kind of predicament, one that you yourself would have to be in to understand."

I pondered that for a moment. "As much sense as that which you just said makes, at the same time, it ain't a valid excuse for him to be doin' what he be doin', especially since he put *himself* in such a predicament." I commented as we approached the hommies.

"Wha'sup my nig-," Jihad caught himself. "Aw, my bad. I got to greet you in your own way, you the *brotha* now." He then said to me, respectfully correcting himself.

"Wha'sup Jihad?" I returned the greeting, giving him my fist for some dap. "What's the play, Money Vee?"

"You know me, calculatin' figures, doin' big things," Vern answered. I laughed. I liked Vern, he was cool.

"Y'all might want to be on your toes around here. Since Concrete can't get nothin' from us he might be on some junkie shit, you know what I'm sayin'?" Skooter-B cautioned us. "When a nigga get to gettin' sick ain't no tellin' what type of shit he will pull." We all nodded.

"Ain't your birthday next week, Atif?" Jihad asked me. I nodded.

"What you turnin', 20?" Vern asked me.

"Yeah."

"We gone kick it, blood, have some fun around this mutha' fucka'," Jihad said. I shook my head.

"It ain't no such thing as havin' fun in prison."

"What you mean by that?" Vern asked me. I looked around the yard thoughtfully for a second.

"I'm just sayin' man, in my eyes ain't *none* of this stuff fun. Playin' ball, getting high, crackin' jokes.... I mean the closest we can get to actually havin' fun is to find somethin' to do that temporarily takes our minds off of how much *time* we doin', or the fact that we may never go to sleep holdin' a beautiful sista in our arms again; or....or how we locked up in here while our kids is growin' up without us in their lives for real, becomin' strangers to our own seeds. You know what I'm sayin'?" All of the brothers nodded in agreement as my words hit close to home. A few more had even joined the group. "But it ain't never fun because as

374

soon as you get through doin' what you doin', or when that high come down, you still in the same condition and ain't nothin' changed. Still got to deal with reality, man, and it ain't *nothin'* fun about that."

The hommies tripped off of what I said for a brief moment and then the conversation went elsewhere. I tuned them out, looking towards the horizon. I was turning 20 years old and had been incarcerated for 5 of those years. As much as things around me remained the same day in and day out, I was in my own little cocoon going through a metamorphosis. I had not smoked any weed in 9 months and the incident with Concrete had made my mind up as far as dealing drugs was concerned. I wanted to quit cold turkey.

"What's on your mind, man?" Skooter-B asked me, cutting into my thoughts. I figured that then was the time to tell him something that I had been wanting to for a while.

"I was readin' somethin' earlier and this author was talkin' about growth. He said that once someone *knows* better then it is incumbent upon that individual to *do* better." Skooter-B nodded. "I don't know, Skooter-B, man, this dope game? I feel like I know better now and it's time for me to let it go because my heart ain't in it no more." Skooter-B smiled.

"I been wonderin' to myself how much longer it was gone take for you to make that decision."

"Ah, yeah?"

"Yeah. I been peepin' you out ever since I got out of ad-seg and a blind man could see that you are changin'. Ain't nothin' wrong with change man, not when you are serious about it and it's for the better. All that shit you be readin' is cool, blood, because it's puttin' some fat on your head. Maybe I need to start readin' some of that shit.

"And I know why it has been so hard for you to let the game go, too. When I went to ad-seg, you got out of the infirmary, and put the hommies back on their feet and you feelin' like you got to keep on because you don't want to see them fallin' off again. But you know what?"

"What?"

"You ain't got no kids, Atif. Especially not no grown ones. You can only do so much for somebody; they have to do the rest on their own. Whoever ain't sittin' on somethin' fat right now, then it's because they don't deserve it." I nodded. "It is not safe for you to keep hustlin' when your heart ain't in it no more, because you are gone start makin' mistakes that could put us all in jeopardy. You see what I'm sayin'?"

"Yeah."

"And don't be worryin' about what the hommies gone think, because this is somethin' you doin' for you. After puttin' so much energy into helpin' everybody else out, it is time for you to focus on yourself. Whoever can't understand that, fuck 'em. All that means is that they don't care about you for real, anyway. The hommies will be cool. I think the coast is clear enough for me to get some things workin', so we'll be straight. Do your thing, playboy, I ain't mad at you."

'Thugs' like Skooter-B are misunderstood. Those on the outside looking in would not expect anything positive to come from one who is capable of such negativity because the negativity is all that they wish to see. It is kind of like Delores Tucker and her attitude concerning rap music. All she hears is the curse words. She doesn't hear those brothers rapping about police brutality, about stress, about yearning for a better way of life and their pleas for guidance.

Positivity exists within us all. It just needs to be nurtured. It needs to be convinced of its purpose. Positiveness within a young misguided adolescent is like a flammable liquid sitting dormant; all it needs is a spark to ignite. Each individual is unique so all of the reading I personally had been doing was my spark, but at the same time it is possible for Skooter-B to have read the exact same literature and not been affected in the same way. Some people have to be approached in a different manner than others. Words can't relay how much his support meant to me.

"It is too late for me to reverse what is already in motion," I started. Skooter-B nodded. "But this will be my last move. I will get it, put it in your hands and then you can do what you do. I'm through."

And just like that I never sold another piece of dope again in my life.

*****

Six days later I was in the chapel attending a Nation of Islam meeting. DeAnthony X was scheduled to speak and I wanted to offer my support. There were oversized photos of both Elijah and Fard Muhammad, along with one of Minister Louis Farrakhan, hanging up on the walls. There was also a red flag on the wall with a white star and crescent. I noticed that the crescent moon was facing in the opposite direction than in the usual star and crescent symbols I had come across and I took a mental note, telling myself that I would ask DeAnthony X why that was.

"Who's the greatest?"

"Allah is the greatest!"

"Who's the greatest?"

"Allah is the greatest!"

Members of the Nation and supporters from the crowd chanted as DeAnthony X made his way to the podium. He spent the next 30 minutes speaking about the way blacks were treated during slavery by the slave masters and then comparing this to the way we were treated in America's prisons by prison officials. He held my attention, as well as everyone else's in the room, and I was amazed by the way he broke things down, making them real to us all.

My favorite parts of his elaboration were when he took something from the times of slavery, such as how in the informal slave courts, the guilt or innocence of a slave rested upon the word of the slave master, alone, and compared it to how we were treated when written up and brought before a team of caseworkers. Most times being for charges that the guards had fabricated out of spite, and these caseworkers would automatically find us guilty and

377

sanction us "...based on the officer's written report", to put it in their words.

He also spoke about how the rare black on black violence during these times was treated with a slap on the wrist, whereas any violence towards whites carried extremely harsh and excessive punishments. It was the same in prison. For instance, when one inmate struck or assaulted another, they would go to the hole for 10 days at most. But if an inmate struck a guard, he would be prosecuted in a court of law, sentenced to even more time, to be served consecutive to the sentence he was already serving, and would spend a good 2 years in ad-seg!

DeAnthony X concluded his speech with a question. "After listening and being exposed to the truth, do you actually believe that slavery was abolished in the 1800's?"

Silence. I assumed that his question was a rhetorical one, so I didn't answer and to tell the truth, I was still a little skeptical. There were similarities, but according to my studies our ancestors had things much worse than we did. Sensing this, he put me on the spot.

"What about you brother Atif? Are you still a slave?"

"Naw brotha', I ain't nobody's slave."

"Hmph," DeAnthony X grunted. "So I take that to mean that you do believe that slavery was abolished over a century ago, correct?"

"Yeah, it was."

"Brother Bryan X," he started, " would you mind taking over for me?"

"No Sir! I wouldn't mind that at all." Bryan X said, approaching the podium.

"There is something I wish to show you in the library, Atif. Do you mind?"

I stood up and followed my celly from the chapel. "Why you put me on the spot like that, man?" I asked him.

"Because I saw that I had everyone else convinced except for you. Convince the skeptic and you will have a stronger ally in the future," DeAnthony X answered as we entered the library. "Can I see the 13th Amendment of the Constitution of the United States, please?" he asked the law clerk who was seated behind the counter.   The clerk retrieved the requested text and handed it to DeAnthony X in exchange for his identification card.   We then found an empty table and had a seat.

"Turn to Article 13, Section 1," DeAnthony X said to me as he slid the book over to me. I couldn't help but think of a specific scene from Spike Lee's Malcolm X movie as I complied. "You find it?"

"Yeah."

"Read it out loud."

"Neither slavery nor involuntary servitude, except as a punishment for crime whereof the party shall have been duly convicted, shall exist within the United States nor any place subject to their jurisdiction." I paused, looking up at him.   I was shocked? 'Except'?   What did they mean 'except'?

"Read Section 2."

"Congress shall have power to enforce this article by appropriate legislation."

"Did they tell you in school that if you were to break the law, then they reserve the right to enslave you?" DeAnthony X asked me. I shook my head, unable to even speak. "Yeah, me neither. You see, this is why they have these boot-licking negroes busting their feet down in the laundry plant for 10 hours a day and only paying them a measly $30 a month.   It is legal for them to do this according to their laws written by their own hands.   The astonishing thing is that according to these same very laws it is illegal for anyone to pay an employed U.S. citizen anything under $5.25 an hour."

"Minimum wage."

"Right, now, how much do they pay you for working up in the infirmary?"

"$22.50 a month."

"Mathematics is truth and according to truth they are paying you $.75 a day." DeAnthony X said, calculating this figure in his head surprisingly fast. "Now, if the law says that a U.S. citizen must be paid at least $5.25 an hour but these devils are only *legally* paying you $.75 a day, then

379

what is it exactly that they are conveying to those of us with eyes to see?"

"That we ain't U.S. citizens," I replied musingly.

"And when one is living in the United States as a non-citizen, then when it comes to the laws of equal protection, equal opportunity under the law, the right to vote, the right to bear arms and protect oneself and one's family, etc., they…."

"Don't apply to us."

"You see how this conniving demon operates? What type of individual do you know of that was born and raised in America but couldn't vote, couldn't bear arms, and was forced to work for crumbs?"

"Our ancestors and others who were slaves."

"There is not a whole lot of differences between the slaves of old and us convicted felons in this day and age. It is difficult to even say that we are considered humans because our ancestors were considered as 3/5 a human and they were allowed to reproduce. We can't even do that!

"The United *Snakes* of America has been oppressing us for over 400 years and to think that all of a sudden within a matter of a few decades this problem has been rectified is to fool oneself. When the white man wrote those laws in the Constitution he did not have us in mind. It would take at least another 400 years worth of reparations and reciprocity to fix what was put down on us and the white man is too greedy, selfish, heartless and content to ever do what it takes for real to bring that about. This is why the Honorable Elijah Muhammad teaches us that we need to do for *self* because when it comes to this mentality that we are up against there is no justice; it's just *us.*"

*****

380

AD-SEG
"Lookin' out my cellblock window,
just like the stars,
my out date seems *so* close,
but it's oh so far!
I spend a lot of time in a little room,
watchin' the sunset.
I swear I'll lose my mind if I don't get out soon,
but I'm not done yet.
My transgressions manifested,
come for me in the night;
-chanting-
I'm deeply contemplatin' changin' my life.
I have a lot of bad dreams;
I CAN'T SLEEP!
I wake up chokin' on my screams;
I CAN'T SPEAK!
Livin' with so many sins on me;
I DON'T THINK YOU UNDERSTAND!
I wear the blood of a dead man
on my hands."
-Soody *Mak*

19

"I received your letter," Rebecca said, closing the door behind her. She then wrapped her arms around my neck and kissed me on the lips. We had been corresponding for a year and a ½ by way of a post office box she had rented specifically for that purpose.

It was my 20th birthday and we were in a linen closet, labeled by us as "our spot" in the infirmary. Rebecca had undergone a remarkable transformation. She was no longer the self-conscious, middle-aged nurse, lacking self-esteem, with librarian glasses on her face and her red hair in a bun atop her head. She had rid herself of the glasses, replacing them with contacts which accentuated her dark blue eyes. Her pretty freshly-permed hair hung loosely down upon her shoulders. Her smile was bright and full of confidence.

Rebecca had gotten her groove back.

"To tell you the truth, I was not surprised by one single word of it," Rebecca said, staring deep into my eyes. I explained to her in my letter that the package she had recently retrieved from Malik would be the last one because I was turning away from selling drugs.

"Is that right?"

Rebecca nodded, "Atif, I have watched you grow and mature more in the past 2 years than most men do in 20. You are evolving into the most beautiful man I have ever met in my life, physically and mentally. Look at you; look at what you have done to me! I have been a brand new woman ever since the moment they carried you into my life. You just have this effect on the people you come across and the impact you have on them and their lives is something like a *phenomenon*. I just can't thank you enough for what you have done for me. For the way you make me *feel*." she finished.

She wanted me to make love to her so naturally I gave her what she wanted. It differed from the wham-bam-thank-you-ma'am style that we usually practiced out of caution. This time we almost forgot where we were at and what we were doing was forbidden. We took our time. My penetration was deep, slow and rhythmic. Rebecca stuffed a mouthful of my T-shirt into her mouth in order to stifle her cries of pleasure while I was strokin' like Clarence Carter.

"Girl what you done did to my back?" I asked Rebecca after we were finished, gently pulling my shirt down over my torso. Rebecca had scraped whelps into the sensitive skin of my back with her long fingernails.

"I'm sorry, I couldn't help it!" she whispered, fixing her uniform. "I felt you all of the way up in my rib cage for God's sake." I laughed. "I just had the absolute best sex I have ever had in my life in a linen closet. You brought me to more orgasms in 40 minutes than my husband has done throughout the duration of our whole marriage. I think we just set a world record."

"How many?"

"You would not believe me if I told you," I looked at her, "three."

"*Three*, you came 3 times?" Rebecca nodded, smiling. "Forget that, I only did once so you still owe me 2," I commented, grabbing her from behind.

"Stop," Rebecca started, giggling softly. "I have to make my rounds and we've already been missing in action for too long."

"Yeah, you right," I said, releasing her. "I want my two, though, I ain't playin' either."

"Maybe later," Rebecca said, kissing me, "Happy Birthday!" She then exited the closet and I went back to folding the clean linen like I was supposed to be doing the whole time.

After slipping into the housing unit for a quick shower during lunch, I returned to work noticing the presence of more guards than usual. I no longer ignored my instincts and my instincts told me that the prison authorities had been alerted to the fact I was anticipating a package.

How? Irrelevant. I was not going to be outsmarted by a bunch of chain-smoking country hicks in uniform. Even Rebecca told me to be careful when she handed the package off to me. She too sensed that the guards were up to something, informing me that there had been no altercations in the infirmary during my absence so their presence made her suspicious as well. Watching them attempting to watch me without me knowing that I was being observed tickled my funny-bone because they were so obvious! I remember thinking that their training sessions must be a joke.

I slipped into a rest room located in the hallway, unnoticed, and turned on the cold water lever in the sink. This way I could hear it if the water was shut off. Even though I doubted that they actually would do that, considering that the infirmary was full of sick patients that needed it, I had learned my lesson from experiencing the kick in back at the tilt. I then put some "slippery when wet" caution signs around the doorway and spent the rest of my shift in earshot of the running faucet. I harbored thoughts of getting rid of the drugs just in case, ahead of time, but the hommies were depending on that last package to hold them over until another avenue was opened up so I decided to wait things out.

My shift was over and it was evident that the guards were lying in ambush, anticipating my attempt to exit the infirmary. A couple of them had even eased their way into the hallway I was mopping for the third time. I set the mop down and headed for the rest room.

"Hey!" One of the guards exclaimed as he saw where I was headed. "You, come here!" I ignored him, acting as if I had no idea who he was talking to, and stepped inside of the rest room and shut the door.

I only had seconds to do what needed to be done. I lowered my trousers and had a seat on the latrine dumping drugs in the toilet that had a penitentiary value of over $20,000. My legs were stretched out with my feet on the door making it difficult for it to be opened from the outside.

"Open this goddamn door!" I heard a guard shout. I then felt one of them trying to force it open with his body weight.

"I'm usin' it, man!" I shouted, flushing the toilet. I could hear other guards running up the hallway. Standing up, the guards barged into the rest room. While doing so I noticed that the sandwich bag in which the drugs were formerly contained did not go down with the rest of the dope. Not only that, but residue that the water had rinsed from the sandwich bag was still in the stool water. I turned and reached for the button.

"Don't you fl-"

WHOOSH!

My flushing the toilet in defiance like that really ticked them off. "Mace him!" A white shirt said in cowardice to the guard standing in front of me after my hands were cuffed behind my back. With no way to shield myself, the guard sprayed mace into my face. It felt as if my eyes had been set on fire while still in their sockets. I went off. With my hands still cuffed behind my back and my inability to see a thing, it did not take long before I found myself subdued on the restroom floor.

When guards restrain an inmate they rush him to the hole. Me? They purposely took their sweet time allowing me to suffer. I vowed to retaliate against the guard in particular who had sprayed the mace in my face while I was in such a defenseless position.

When we reached 2 house, I was thrown into a cell on the top walk. The guards walked off, leaving me with my hands cuffed behind my back so that I was unable to flush my eyes out. I felt like I was being tortured. I began to contemplate sticking my face into the toilet, that's how much agony I was in. I dismissed the notion; thinking to myself how they probably did this to brothers on a regular basis, and I wouldn't have put it past them if they were all standing outside my cell door, snickering amongst themselves as they gambled with each other trying to predict how long it would be before I broke down and put my face in the toilet. Since I couldn't see, there was probably even urine and feces floating around in it waiting for me to do so.

The cuffs were not removed until 30 minutes later, when two of the guards came in order to read my violation off to me. After squatting down to the level of the chuckhole while they were removed, I rushed to the sink to rinse my face, ignoring the reading of the conduct violation. When the water hit my face it seemed to only renew the burning sensation. It took almost 2 more days for the effects of the mace to wear off.

Time passed by slowly for me. The guards in 2 house quickly developed feelings of animosity towards me. They played little games with me such as nonchalantly walking right past my cell when they were handing out trays. I would throw a fit, beating and kicking on the door until I was fed. Sometimes it worked, most times it didn't.

I went before the team members a week later and they placed me under investigation, which was an indefinite status. As it turned out, the sandwich bag I had been trying to flush never did go down and the guards retrieved it, sending it out to be tested. I knew that if there was any residue remaining on it, then it would not be enough for them to test.

Two months later, I was on my way back to my cell after being interviewed by the investigator. There was a guard walking in front of me and another one behind me. My hands were cuffed behind my back and I had not eaten at all that day.

"Y'all need to quit playin' these childish ass games and start givin' me my food you mutha' fuckin' pink-toe-incest-babies."

The guard walking in front of me stopped abruptly, causing me to bump into him. "Did you just attempt to push me down?"

"What the fuck you talkin' about, man?"

"Did you see that, Mel?"

"Yep, sure did."

"I'm going to have to write you a conduct violation for that. #2 major assault on staff."

"You do that and you might as well make it *2* of them because I'm gone fuck you up for real as soon as the opportunity presents itself!"

"Oops, did you hear that, Mel?"

"Yep, sure did."

387

"I'm going to have to write you up for that one too, buddy, #12 threat."

"Why y'all playin' with me, man?" I asked.

"Huh?"

"Huh you can hear!"

"Did you just say that you want to commit suicide?"

"*What?*"

"Did you hear that, Mel?"

"Yep, sure did," he answered, smiling. He then spoke something I couldn't understand into his walkie talkie. I turned and saw that guards were running into the wing, appearing seemingly out of nowhere like cockroaches. "You're so young and you got your whole life ahead of you."

"Yeah, now why you want to go and kill yourself for?"

"Man, ya'll know I ain't said no shit like that!" I spat. Five guards and a white shirt ran up on the scene, out of shape and breathing heavily as they crowded into the caged walkway.

"What is going on here?" the white shirt asked.

"This offender here tries to push me down, threatened to ... what was it again?" he asked me. I looked at him with indignation. "Oh yeah, *fuck me up* whenever the opportunity presents itself." The white shirt he was talking to looked at me. "And then he refuses to take another step, saying that if we put him back into that cell he was going to hang himself."

"He's lyin' man, I didn't eit-"

"Take him to the strip cell," the white shirt said, cutting me off.

I was restrained and carried downstairs to a small scarcely ventilated cell no larger than a housing project closet with a slab of concrete for a bunk, a sink attached to a toilet and a camera mounted up on the ceiling. The small cell had a set of bars reinforcing the cell door and after being closed in by the bars, my cuffs were removed.

"I need for you to strip down to your birthday suit and throw all of your clothes out here on the floor," the white shirt said to me for the second time.

"You got me fucked up," I said. I was in a state of fury. "You want my clothes you gone have to come in here and *take* them. I ain't givin' you shit!" At that moment a guard appeared holding a hand held video camera, filming the altercation. The white shirt stepped up closer to the bars.

"Sir, for the *last* time, I need you to take off your clothes and throw them out here on the floor." I refused.

I watched as the white shirt extracted a large spray can from his back pocket and butterflies filled my stomach. The can was as large as a spray paint can full of what the inmates on the yard called "that hot shit!"

I had heard numerous horror stories about being sprayed with its contents. This was not your average everyday can of mace, by far, more like tear-gas-pepper-spray. My experience of being sprayed in the face by the small can of mace that all of the guards carried on their persons was a picnic compared to what I was about to go through.

Not wanting to be caught in the face, I turned my back as the white shirt waged chemical warfare on me. The stuff was powerful, shooting out of the can in a jet stream with tremendous force like water from a fireman's hose. My breath was instantly taken away. The white shirt, after emptying the contents of the can, then closed the cell door on me and they all vacated the premises. Even they couldn't stand the secondhand exposure, so you can only imagine what I was going through.

My whole body was ignited with a burning sensation that was more like actual pain. I went into convulsions as my body involuntarily attempted to reject the intake of the potent unnatural chemical. Mucus clogged my nostrils and a thick spittle formed within my throat as my glands began to swell. I broke out into a serious uncontrollable coughing fit with my ears making a popping sound from the strain. I couldn't take it, I needed air. I needed to breathe.

These crackers is tryin' to kill me! I screamed in my mind just before passing out.

******

"*Inna jahannama kaanat mir-saadaa!*"
I opened my eyes and bolted upright in consternation, startled by the dreadful face hovering so close to mine. The cold eyes of which were like those of a serpent, staring unblinkingly at me. My heart filled with fear upon recognizing him as being the person I had killed the night I caught my case. Blood oozed from a bullet hole in his forehead.

He then stood up and turned around, walking towards the bars at the front of the strip cell uttering a wordless snarl of horror. Queasiness settled in my stomach and my mouth filled with sour saliva. I began dry heaving when I saw maggots feasting on what remained of the back of his skull.

"*Llitta-geena ma-aabaa!*" he chanted, rocking back and forth with his head banging against the bars. "*Laa-batheena feehaa ahqaa-baa! Laa-yathu-quna feeha bardan wa laa sharaabaa! Illaa hameeman wa gassaa-qaa! Jazzan wi faaqaa!*" His head was now splitting with the force of it hitting the bars as his chanting grew louder and louder. Blood squirted all over the walls. "*Innahum kaanu laa yarjuna hisaabaa! Wa kath-thabu bi-ayaatinaa kith-thaa baa!*"

Of all my nightmares, this was in fact the worst one yet. His chant was melodic and the foreign words seemed to penetrate the depths of my very soul. What was he saying? Had I died? Was I to be forever locked in that hot strip cell being tormented by my manifested transgressions?

"*Kalla saya-'alamun!*" There was someone else in the cell. Even though in my heart I knew who it was, still I was too afraid to look in the direction where I had heard the voice from; but my head turned anyway in disobedience to my desires.

The voice had come from someone sitting on the toilet. I recognized him as the Rolling 60's Crip who was found hanging dead over a fence back in '92.

I was trembling. My knees were drawn up to my chest and I was whimpering. Backed into a corner, there was nowhere for me to run. The one who had been beating

390

his head against the bars opened his jaws and voiced a shriek that combined the worst aspects of a siren, steam valve and the howl of a dying dog, running towards me with lightning speed, grabbing me by the throat with an amazing grip then lifting me high into the air. I was choking and couldn't breathe. My head felt like it was going to explode from the pressure.   Gagging, I clawed at his fingers crushing flesh, tendon and cartilage into bone. The skin of his hands was coming off into my hands like wet newspaper.

"*THUMMAKALLAA   SAYA'A-LAMUN!*" he shouted, shaking me violently. More frightened than at anytime in my life; feeling as if I were trapped in a hideous, ongoing nightmare I slid slowly into a state of unconsciousness.

When I came to, my body was in the most uncomfortable and unorthodox position it had ever been in before in my life.   There was an extremely heavy 5-inch thick iron collar fastened around my neck. My hands and feet were hog-tied behind my back with heavy iron chains. Something had a powerful hold of my right leg and another was holding my left leg, dragging me on my face. It felt as if my limbs were in the grip of mighty steel talons.

The heat was suffocating and intense; mixed with the humidity in the air seeming to get a degree hotter with each step my captors took. I could hear a fierce roaring in the distance, the sound one would probably hear as he approached the sun.

It was a fire.

I could tell that is was unlike any kind of fire I had ever known or even could have imagined. It sounded like the whole earth had been set ablaze. Even more terrifying were the moans and cries I heard coming from the direction we were headed in.

"*STOP!*" I heard a deep voice command.   My captors halted.

"Kai?" the one holding my right leg inquired. I then felt the both of them as their hands began to tremble. Whoever this "Kai" was for some reason instilled a lot of fear within them.

So Far From Paradise / LANE   Ad-Seg

"Upon whose orders are you acting?" Kai asked the two. Silence ensued. "RELEASE HIM!" The rest of my body fell hard to the rocky turf as I was released. "The Trumpet has not been blown and if it had this is not your duty." I then heard footsteps running off into the distance. My collar was removed and the chains around my hands and feet broken.

"Where am I?" I managed hoarsely.

"Maubiq."

"What is that?" I asked. No answer. I no longer felt the presence there with me. Forging my inner fiber into an iron strength and implacable stoicism, I staggered to my feet, breath clogging in my throat. There were numerous cuts on my face from being dragged on it like I had been; dirt, rocks and blood clouded my eyesight. My mouth was dirt dry, I felt feverish and nausea was a clawed beast trying to tear its way out of my stomach. My legs cramped and gave out on me.

"I got you, Atif," a feminine voice said, reassuring me as two soft yet firm hands pulled me up to my feet. I recognized the voice instantly.

"Mama?"

"Aw, look at your face baby. Lookin' like a mile of bad road," another feminine voice said as two more familiar hands began to pick the dirt and rocks from my eyelids.

"Big Mama?"

Opening my eyes I saw my deceased mother and grandmother standing before me, smiling. They were so beautiful! The both of them looked as if they were not too much older than I was at the time, looking more like sisters than mother and daughter. With my fascination pushing away my aches, pains, and worries, I hugged them both.

"Come now, grandbaby, we have to go. Can you walk?" Big Mama asked me. I nodded, wiping a tear from my eye. Both my grandmother and mother took a hold of each hand of mine and we began to walk in the opposite direction.

"They will not come to you anymore son."

"And they are not who you have been thinkin' they were. None of them are the people they have been
392

appearin' to you in the person of," Big Mama said. "You see, grandbaby, once somebody is dead they can't communicate with the livin' like that. Even if it was possible for them to try, you wouldn't be able to hear them through the barrier."

"How come I am communicatin' with y'all then?" My mother laughed softly.

"Your inquisitiveness and the prayers of a special person may rescue you from where you were headed," my mother said, stopping in her tracks. My grandmother and I did the same. "This is as far as we can lead you, you have to go the rest of the way by yourself."

"But I don't know my way, Mama. I don't know where I'm goin'."

"You are headed in the right direction. You will come upon a path that is straight and narrow, ain't no crookedness within it. If you choose to get on this path, Atif, you take off runnin' as fast as you can, you understand?" I nodded. "Don't look back because if you do you will stray from the path and find yourself lost again. It will get hard at times and you might slip and fall every once in a while, but you get back up, dust yourself off and you keep on runnin'."

"Where do the path lead to?"

"Paradise," the both of them replied in unison, smiling at me. Something was strange about them, something I couldn't put my finger on.

"Will y'all be there when I get there?"

"Only God knows that, grandbaby."

"Why can't I just go wi-"

"Shhh," my mother cut in, gently putting her finger to my lips. "Go ahead now, it is time. I am so proud of you, Atif."

My mother and Big Mama took each other by the hand, turned and walked away. I cried out to them, begging them not to leave me. They only waved in response. I blinked and they were gone. I was alone again. I looked in the direction they had instructed for me to go in and I took off running as fast as I could without looking back, searching for the path.

******

There was no telling how long I would be stuck in ad-seg. Since I was under investigation, I was in a one man cell and as much as I hated being locked down 24 hours a day like that, I at the same time enjoyed the solitude. In prison they threw any and everyone in a cell together and there are not many things worse than being stuck with a cellmate that you can't stand in a room small enough to where if one of you were moving then the other had to remain still.

"Brother Atif?"

I was lying on my bunk staring at the ceiling. It was a Wednesday afternoon and my stomach was touching my back. I got up from my bunk and saw that a Christian brother who went by the name "Pastor Cool Breeze" was at my cell door. He was called such because he used to spend every Sunday afternoon in the summer preaching on the front yard from the time that yard opened at 1:30 in the afternoon until it closed at 3:45 and his sermons were likened to a cool breeze blowing on a hot and muggy summer day by the inmates who were inspired by them.

"Wha'sup, Pastor Cool Breeze?" I greeted as I approached the cell door.

"I'm blessed my brother," he stated, sliding some candy bars underneath my cell door. "Just in case they don't want to feed you, you'll have a little something for the hunger pains."

"Good lookin' out man, I appreciate that," I thanked him, scooping them up from the floor. "You got any literature for me today?"

"No, all I have are some calendars. You want one?"

"Yeah." Pastor Cool Breeze slid a small palm sized calendar underneath my door.

"Let me ask you a question," Pastor Cool Breeze said. Every time he had the chance, he would drop some wisdom on me before we parted company; something for me to think about. I intrigued him because everything he came at me with I was able to decipher and figure out. "In this type of environment, an individual is either a thermometer or a thermostat. Which is the best one to be, and why?" My brow creased in thought as I tried first to understand what he was saying and then what the best answer would be. "Take your time, brother, take your time," he said, smiling. "I think I got you on this one, Atif."

"It is best to be a *thermostat*," I said after a few minutes spent in silent contemplation. His knowing smile disappeared from his face, causing me to laugh out loud.

"And why is that?"

"Well, a *thermometer* is regulated by the atmosphere or environment of which it is present in, whereas a *thermostat* actually does the opposite; it is *not* controlled by the atmosphere of its surrounding, it *controls* the atmosphere of its surrounding." Pastor Cool Breeze nodded in approval. "So, in essence, it is better for a person to be a thermostat because as this type of an individual he will not let the way things work in prison dictate how he lives his own life or succumb to the evils of the atmosphere he is forced to live in. Instead, he will command the respect of those in his surroundings and force them to adjust to the way he moves, or, possibly even change the condition of those around him," I finished, smirking.

"I have been posing that question to brothers for the last 2 days, and you are the first to hit the nail on the head." We stood in silence for a while. "Well, I am going to pass out the rest of these calendars while I still have a little time left. Next time I see you I will hit you with something that will make your head spin." I laughed at that. "I expect for you to be that thermostat whenever they let you out of ad-seg, you hear me?" I nodded.

Pastor Cool Breeze walked off and I tossed the calendar he gave me onto my bunk. While in the air it flipped over onto its backside, revealing some words on the back. I picked it back up and began to read them.

At the top of it was the word 'footprints' and there was a poem below. As I read on I realized that it was the poetic form of the story Big Mama had told me over the phone back in the county.

I sat down on my bunk and read on. I was only halfway through it when the last portion of the wall remaining in my mind came crashing down. All of the love I felt for my grandmother washed over me like the tide and I smiled, closing my eyes as it hit me. It felt so good to remember her.

I then got up from my bunk and grabbed a pencil and paper; I wanted to write her and tell her that I remembered! As soon as I wrote her name down, followed by a salutation, it dawned on me that she had passed. My being so used to her being there for me, coupled with my injuries, had left me in a state of denial. Subconsciously I had not yet fully accepted her death; not even with seeing her and my mother during my dream while in the strip cell a week or so before. Once again, this time even worse, my emotions spiraled down to the lowest of lows as my heart sank bearing the heavy weight of my sadness. I began to cry softly to myself, silently at first with hot and involuntary tears descending from my eyes. Then I lost control of the tears; I cried hard and I cried long until I cried myself to sleep. Before I dozed I remember thinking that with my grandmother and my mother gone, locked down in ad-seg for only our Creator knew how long, things couldn't get too much more worse than they already were. If our Creator really was walking with me like Big Mama had told me over the phone in the county then the time had arrived for Him to pick me up and carry me because I was hurting so much and I was so sick with the way my life had turned out that I was far too exhausted to take another step. I never before had felt such a sense of remoteness. I felt alone, insignificant, helpless and to top it off I felt like a failure.

Part 3:

THE PATH

"Whoever treads a path searching for knowledge,
Allah will make the path to Paradise easy for him."
-Prophet Muhammad
(may Allah mention him amongst the angels)

<u>SIDDIQ</u>

There is no compulsion in
religion. Verily the Right Path has
become distinct from the wrong path.
Whoever disbelieves in false deities and
believes in Allah, then he has grasped
the most trustworthy handhold that will
never break. And Allah is All-Hearer,
All Knower.
Allah is the Wali (Protector or Guardian)
of those who believe. He brings them out
from darkness into light. But as for those
who disbelieve, their supporters are false Deities,
they bring them out from light into darkness.
Those are the dwellers of the Fire, and they
will abide therein forever.
-Noble Qur'an 2:256-257

"3 down, 15 to go," I mumbled to myself, standing at my cell window watching the sunset. After being written up for a major assault on a guard and a threat, I was then written up for disobeying a direct order for refusing to disrobe and creating a disturbance because my "actions disturbed institutional staff causing them to deviate from their assigned stations." I appeared before the team of caseworkers, better defined as the informal slave court in the words of DeAnthony X, and was found guilty on all counts (based solely on the reporting officer's written statement of course). They released me from under investigation and gave me 12 months for major assault; 90 days for threat; 30 days for disobeying a direct order and 60 days for creating a disturbance. 18 months in total, all to be spent locked down in ad-seg. The 3 months I had spent down there already while under investigation was not calculated, thus it was dead time and didn't even count.

Since I was no longer under investigation it meant that I would be receiving a cellmate which was something I was not looking forward to at all. I wanted to be alone with my thoughts.

I couldn't stop thinking about the dream I had while unconscious in the strip cell. I was even starting to believe that it was more like a vision or an experience than a mere dream. It felt too real to be just a dream. The heat, the fear, the pain, I felt every bit of it. And if it was a vision, what did it mean? Why was it that every night since then when I went to sleep I dreamed of being back on that plain searching for the path my mother spoke of? Where was this path? In my dreams I began to feel as if maybe I had lost my sense of direction and was headed in the wrong one. Why was this path so difficult for me to find?

Slowly, a hypothesis began to crystallize. Maybe my mother was not speaking in a literal sense. Maybe my wandering about in my dreams of late was symbolic.

I began to break down the things she said to me using the comprehension skills I had developed by working with Rebecca. Some of the incidents that took place were too strange for me to even begin to understand (like the foreign chants of the 2 who were dragging me on my face for instance) so I started with what I could make sense of.

A path is something like a track or a way made by footsteps. Whose footsteps? Maybe it was ironed out by the Creator of the path or those who had trod it before me. A path can *also* be defined as a course of action or conduct. Since I was trying to come away from a physical interpretation, I rolled with the latter definition.

She also said that this path was straight and narrow. When something is straight then it extends continuously without curving in a certain direction. It could also mean that this path is direct and un-candid, unbroken, accurate, unmodified or undiluted. When spelled S-T-R-A-I-T it could mean strict. Once again I rolled with the latter but kept the former in mind since she said that it had no curves, twists or turns in it.

Now, narrow meant that it is of limited width. It can also mean being rigid in views or ideas; limited in outlook. I chose to keep both definitions because if it was of limited width then there would not be room for people, ideas or things that didn't fit into its rigid views and its limited outlook; it didn't compromise for materialistic things such as fame, fortune, etc.

So, I had a course of action or conduct treaded by those before me that led in one specific direction without being modified or diluted. It was accurate and strict being of limited width, rigid views, limited in scope or outlook.

My mother cautioned me not to look back; to stay focused on where I was heading and not to worry about from whence I had come. I was to leave those things behind which had no place on this path of limited width. I read in the Bible about Prophet Lot's (Peace be on him) wife who was told the same thing and when she did look back she was turned into a pillar of salt.

I got the point.

She warned that if I was to look back I would stray from this path and find myself lost again, which had to mean that while on the path I would be found. I had been feeling lost all of my life. She said that this path would become difficult for me at times, that I would slip and fall. But since there was enough room for me to get up and keep on moving then the One who designed this way must be merciful, forgiving and understanding. Lord knows I was far from perfect.

I was also told that I was already headed in the right direction. Maybe that was because of the changes I was beginning to make in my life. I stopped getting high, gave up selling drugs, I was striving to stop cursing (though my dealings with those guards was causing me to backslide a bit), and I had become very studious. My whole way of thinking was changing and this transformation was from the heart, not because I wanted to impress someone else but because I wanted it for myself.

I understood what Mama meant about the path, all I had to do was find it.

I couldn't remember specifically when the last time I prayed was. I remember crying out the night the police were chasing me before the accident, but that was about the closest I had come to prayer in a long time. I didn't even know *how* to pray! Was there a certain thing I was supposed to say or a particular action that needed to be carried out? If I shouldn't just refer to our Creator with any old kind of name like Fatimah had said, well then didn't He want me to pray to Him in a certain fashion?

Closing my eyes and bowing my head like Big Mama used to, I silently asked our Creator to guide me to this path. My plea was short, simple and to the point. I didn't ask to be miraculously released from prison, to win a million dollars, or anything else in vain. I asked for guidance, wisdom and understanding.

I drifted off to sleep with a smile on my face, thinking of how beautiful my mother and grandmother were. How good it felt to wrap my arms around them. I really missed them and would've given anything just to close my eyes and see them once more. But in my heart I knew that, like my nightmares, they would not be coming for me again.

****

January, 1999.   It was so cold in my cell that I could see my own breath when it came out of my mouth. I just knew that one of those nights I would fall asleep and freeze to death before I woke up. I had run through 4 cellies within the last 60 days, the last of whom had left me his blanket, which was very kind of him I might add, but it did nothing to shield my body from the cold arctic like wind blowing unceasingly through my window.

The last 2 of my cellies I got along with pretty well. Both of them were decent brothers who didn't mind bathing and cleaning up after themselves. The second one was a Thorazine patient who spent 5 days in the cell with me lost in some other dimension detached from time. And the first one? We were not cutout for each other. Not only did he like to lay around the cell passing gas and reeking of body odor all day, but he also had a bad habit of defecating in the toilet without "courtesy flushes" while he did so, as if I wanted to smell his feces until he was finished.   After threatening to beat him to a pulp and leave him hog tied underneath my bunk, he got some act-right real quick like.

I missed Rebecca and thought of her often. Honestly it was the sex that I missed the most. I had not heard from her since the day I went to ad-seg back in August, but I understood why. She was probably paranoid, thinking that our correspondence could be traced back to her, so I didn't take it personally when I wrote to the post office box, and my letter came back to me with "return to sender, addressee unknown" stamped on the face of the envelope.

It didn't take long for me to figure out that it was Concrete who sent the police my way that day in medical. He didn't know exactly who my horse was, neither did Skooter-B or anyone else, but he knew when we were scheduled to touch down and that I had someone putting in work for me that worked in the infirmary. That explained why things unfolded in the manner that they did. A part of me wanted to retaliate when I got out of ad-seg, but then again I was on another level and far above harboring such thoughts. My mind was on other things and thinking about Concrete was not worth the brain cells it took to do so. Besides, I was informed that Skooter-B and the hommies had put 2 and 2 together and dealt with the situation in the best way that they saw fit.

Kesha wrote to me faithfully and anticipating her letters helped the time pass by. She was pretty busy out there, but never too busy to take some time out of her week to sit down and write to her "personal friend". I loved her for that. She understood how good it felt for the guard to pause by my cell during mail call. To tell the truth, I think she would have done the same even if she didn't.

Her letters were filled with ideas for the beauty parlor that she had convinced Malik to help her fund. She had purchased an empty lot in the hood and was currently negotiating with a contractor and an architect to construct a building for her. My brother allowed her to put everything in her name. He said that he suspected he was under surveillance and didn't want her to have to worry about the business being shut down if the Feds came for him one day.

My letters in turn were filled with motivation and support. I never got tired of telling her how proud of her I was and how happy I was to see how she had taken control of her life and was really getting it together.

Kesha was also proud of me. She said that keeping in touch with me made it extremely difficult for her to even pay attention to the men that approached her because she kept on comparing them to me and the type of man I had become over the past 5 years. Since there was rarely anything even close to a comparison, she was still single. Her compliments felt good, but my humility refused to allow me to really believe I was worthy of them. I felt she was exaggerating to say the least.

I had come a long way but I still had so far to go. Rebecca told me once before that I was becoming the best man she had ever met on a physical and mental level, which was cool, but I was still missing something. I once read that man exists on 3 different spheres that must be balanced out in order to reach full potential. These are the physical, mental, and spiritual. The physical and mental were the only 2 planes I had been focusing on and this was why I was feeling so incomplete and out of whack. I had been neglecting the spiritual, which I would later come to realize is the most important of the 3.

"A, cell 259!" someone shouted, interrupting my thoughts. There never was much hope for peace and quiet during the day time.

"Wha'sup?" presumably cell number 259. Over in ad-seg, people went by whatever cell they were in instead of their names.

"Y'all got a dictionary down there?"

"Nope! What you tryin' to spell?"

"Embarrass!"

"What?"

"Em-bar-rass!"

"I can't understand you cuz, use it in a sentence!"

"I got a sentence for that nigga!" cell number 250 cut in, "The fact that I am a grown ass 37-year old man and still dumb as a box of rocks *embarrasses* me!" The whole wing erupted in laughter. It was contagious, I even found myself chuckling underneath my blanket.

"Man, *fuck* y'all, *all* of y'all!" More laughter. "A, cell 266!" I rolled my eyes, 266 was the number on the cell door occupied by yours truly. It was too cold to be getting up. "266!"

"Wha'sup?" I shouted through the cell door pane when I reached it.

"A, how you spell embarrass?"

"E-M-B-A-R-R-A-S-S!"

"Good lookin' out dirty," a slight pause as he wrote the correct spelling down, "I should have asked you in the first place!"

"Naw, nigga, you should have went to school in the first place. That's what you should have did ole retarded ass nigga!" Cell number 250 shouted. Laughter ensued.

I had heard the door to the wing opening up and saw that they were bringing someone in. After stopping briefly at the correctional officer's desk, the guards escorted him in the direction of the cell I was in. Why couldn't they just let me do my time in ad-seg alone?

When the party of 3 reached my cell one of the guards asked me if I would accept a celly. They asked me this because 2 days before they tried to put a homosexual in the cell with me and I threatened to harm him if they did. I didn't mean it, I was above hurting people for no reason, I just wanted to be alone. Since I had had almost a week to myself I took a look at the bearded brother they had handcuffed and agreed to accept him. I was instructed to "cuff up" through the chuckhole and they made sure that I was secured before they opened my cell door.

The first thing I noticed about this brother when they ushered him into the cell was that he was highly upset about whatever he was in ad-seg for. His body was tense and he walked stiffly to the cell window with his fists clenched down at his sides without saying a word. I had seen him around the camp but we never acknowledged each other. Usually when a person came to ad-seg the first thing they did when reaching a cell was fix the sheets on their bunk. I stood by the door out of his way waiting for him to do this; he just stood there.

"Prophet Muhammad, may Allah's peace be upon him, observed some of his companions wrestling with each other one day," the brother began, still looking out of the window with his back towards me. Even though we were alone in the cell, I wondered to myself if he was talking to me and who this Muhammad was. Elijah? I listened nonetheless. "When they finished he told them that the strong one is not the one who overcomes people with his strength, but the strong is the one who controls himself while in anger."

The brother stood in contemplative silence for a few moments and I did the same as my mind processed what he had said. He then turned away from the window with a smile on his face. All of a sudden there seemed to be no trace of the anger he entered the cell with.

"My name is Siddiq," he said to me, offering his hand. I shook it.

"I'm Atif," I said. He peered at me.

"You Muslim?" I shook my head in the negative without disguising how tired I was of people asking me that question. He picked up on my body language. "You get asked that a lot?"

"Yeah!"

"You have a Muslim name, Atif means-"

"Compassionate," I cut in. "I know what my name means." Siddiq nodded.

"Forgive my condescension, I meant no harm."

"No harm done," I said. "What about you, you a Muslim?"

"Yes, all praise is due to Allah," Siddiq answered, smiling. He seemed proud of it as well.

Siddiq took a look around the cell as if seeing the condition it was in for the first time. He then sniffed at the air, looking at the toilet and sink, nodding his head in approval as if he was some kind of a health inspector.

"I see you keep a clean cell," Siddiq complimented as he began fixing his sheets on his bunk.

"I try to."

"All praise is due to Allah." After getting his bunk together, Siddiq looked out of the window at the position of the sun in the sky. "It is time for me to offer Salah. Do you mind if I have this area over here for a while?"

"Man, you ain't got to ask me if you can pray."

Siddiq chuckled softly. "No, brother, you misunderstood. What I am asking is do you need to come over here for any reason that can't wait for about 10 minutes?"

"Aw, no brotha', I'm straight."

"You don't have to use the rest room or anything like that?"

"No man, do your thing."

It seemed as if from that very second, all of the way until he finished praying, I ceased to exist. Siddiq went into a zone. I observed him as he went to the sink. "*Bismillah*," I heard him utter softly underneath his breath as he turned on the warm water of the faucet. He then rinsed his right hand 3 times, mumbling something foreign incoherently as he did so, and then the left. Cupping his hands underneath the faucet, he allowed the water to fill up the space provided in his hands and then rinsed his mouth out 3 times. With his right hand he sniffed water up into his nostrils 3 times, blowing the water out of his nose with his left hand after each time. He then rinsed his face 3 times and both forearms 3 times each beginning at the wrist and stopping around the elbow area. Wetting the tips of his fingers, he brushed his scalp lightly from the scalp to the nape and wiped each ear all in one swift stroke. Lastly, he removed his shoes and socks, and rinsed each foot 3 times beginning with the right one first.

Turning away from the sink with water dripping from his beard and limbs, he took a face cloth from his bag of cosmetics and positioned it strategically on the floor. He then stood with his feet shoulder length apart and his hands hanging loosely down at his sides, facing away from the toilet. Raising both hands just above his shoulders, he said, "Allahu akbar," and folded his arms across his chest.

I had never witnessed a Muslim's prayer before in person. I tried not to stare, but I couldn't help it. The way he slowly shifted positions with fluidity; bowing, rising, prostrating with his forehead and the tip of his nose touching the face cloth, sitting with all of his weight balanced on his left foot which was tucked underneath his body and the right foot up on its toes, all of this intrigued me. I found myself wondering if this was the way Fatima prayed and why I had never seen DeAnthony X praying like that. What was he saying?

After going through all of his positions, starting over and going through them again about 4 times in all, he turned his head to the right as if he was peering over his shoulder and said "As-salaamu alaykum wa rahmatul-lah," and then turned his head to the left and did the same. I then heard him repeating something over and over again that I couldn't make out as he appeared to be keeping track of how many times he said whatever he was saying by using his thumb to count the natural spaces on each finger inside the palm of his right hand.

"It's cold in here," Siddiq said, rising from the ground and scooping up his face cloth as he climbed into the top bunk. He covered himself with his blanket and within a matter of minutes I heard his breathing even out as he drifted off to sleep. I got into my bunk and followed suit.

******

"It amazes me how these brothers will exercise their minds in such an inventive manner when they want to," Siddiq said thoughtfully as he looked out of the cell door. "The brother down in cell number 153 folded a piece of notebook paper in half, slid it through the crack of his cell door by the lock and the walk man is pouring some scalding hot coffee through the closed cell door by using the piece of notebook paper as somewhat of a funnel in order to get the liquid to travel around the corner."

Three weeks had gone by since they first put Siddiq in the cell with me. We did more than get along, we had become friends. We spent practically every waking hour discussing matters of religion, most times staying up from the time of the sunset until they passed out the breakfast trays in the morning, which they then did every morning, noon and evening without passing the cell up like they used to do thanks to some paperwork Siddiq had filed on the ad-seg guards.

I liked Siddiq and was amazed by his understanding of the scriptures, not only Qur'anic but Biblical as well. I loved to hear him relay to me the stories of the lives of the prophets. He helped me understand why I found the Bible so confusing by educating me about the history and process of the compilation of the books contained within it and its numerous revisions. He supported his claims with established facts instead of biased opinions. I was appalled with the knowledge of the Council of Nicea held in 325 A.D. and how they not only declared the doctrine of the Trinity to be the official doctrine of the Church, but out of 300 or so Gospels extant at that time, 4 were chosen (written almost a century after the advent of Prophet Jesus by people who had never even met him) as the official Gospels of the

Church. The remaining Gospels, including those written by actual companions of Prophet Jesus, were ordered to be destroyed completely with an edict issued stating that anyone found in possession of an "unauthorized" Gospel would be put to death.

Out of it all, the above was the most shocking I must say, though there is much more. I am merely scratching the surface. Siddiq told me the life story of Prophet Muhammad, making it clear that he was not referring to Elijah, co-founder of the Nation of Islam, but a man who had died over 1400 years ago. I had never heard anything about him and was fascinated with Siddiq's narration, almost shedding a tear when hearing of his death and how he forgave the Jewess who poisoned him.

Like Big Mama had told me years before, Siddiq proved to me how our Creator was very concerned with what goes on in our lives. This helped me see the tragic events of my life in a different light. He taught me that it was my lack of knowledge and understanding of our Creator that caused me to be so weak in faith. We then went to work on rectifying this problem. Within a matter of time I understood that our Creator was far above anything we could conceive of with our own minds; that there was nothing like unto Him. I understood what was meant by His being One and that He has no partners in His Divinity. To this day I believe that the way I learned to perceive our Creator while locked down in that cell with Siddiq is the most important thing I have ever learned in my life.

"You through?" I asked Siddiq, rising from the floor. We had been taking turns doing push-ups in sets of 50 for exercise and to stay warm.

"Yes, brother, I'm pretty tight," he said, wiggling his arms. "How many was that?"

"550," I answered. I then dropped down and did one more set to make it an even 600. "Answer me this," I paused afterwards, catching my breath. "Why would Allah create a place for people to burn for eternity if He loves us so much? There is no way I could do such a thing to my child or my worst enemy for that matter. Why would He do that?"

"Allah is the Best Knower, but I think that in order to understand that you must first understand two things."

"What?"

"First of all, Allah says in the Qur'an that He does not beget, nor was He begotten. So, we are not Allah's children, we are His *creation*. One of the many things Allah is far above is siring children. With that said, and with as many similarities there may seem to be between our relationship with Allah and a parent's relationship with his child, the nature of our relationship with Allah should not be looked at in such a way. The way you may treat your child is really irrelevant in comparison to what Allah may do to us, His creation. Allah does as He wills.

"The Qur'an also says that Allah created us for no other reason but to worship Him so our relationship with Allah is more like a servant repaying a debt owed to his or her master."

"A debt?" Siddiq nodded. "A debt owed for *what*?" I asked, taking a sip of water from the sink.

"That sip of water you just took is merely one of infinite reasons." I nodded. "When we show ingratitude and step outside of the reason for which we were created in the first place, Allah punishes us for that."

"What's the other thing?"

"The second thing you must understand is that Allah is a just Lord. People don't realize that the laws of nature *He* wrote operate in accordance with a well defined pattern, and that premises lead to their natural conclusions, actions receive their just reward. Every action is recorded and we will taste the consequences of them either in this life or the next, or both, no matter how rich, powerful, or slick one may be, for He has full knowledge of everything we all have done in open and in secret, along with the shockwaves that emit from them, and Allah's law of requital will not be suspended to appease *anyone*.

"Allah does not inflict too severe a punishment on mankind. Instead, it is their *own* misdeeds that are severe, and it is these they have to endure the natural consequences of. The Qur'an says: 'It was not Allah who wronged them, but it was they who wronged themselves. The evil consequences of their misdeeds overtook them, and they were overwhelmed by the very thing they used to deride.' So, people are not punished with anything other than the natural consequences of their own actions. These are the very things which sink them to a degree lower than that of human beings. So, they are punished with something lower than what is fitting for humans. They endure a humiliating abode and painful suffering. With our limited scope of vision we don't realize at times the full impact our actions have on our societies and others, we regard things with indifference that we think are light, but in reality are heavy and serious in ways we cannot see, considering all. Allah is gracious, kind and forgiving for those who repent, believe in Him and follow up their wrong actions with good ones, but at the same time His wrath is severe for those who don't. What I mean by that in this sense is that as much mercy and beneficence that Allah bestows upon His creation, His anger and wrath is almost just as intense. There is balance. His graciousness is incomprehensible, but at the same time, so is His punishment."

"So the Creator is not all love like they used to teach me in Bible school?"

"They taught you that in Bible school?" I nodded. "Well, they must have skipped over the numerous verses contained within the Bible where Allah demonstrates the opposite. For instance, in Ezekiel 25:16, the bible says: 'Therefore, says the Sovereign Lord, I will raise my fist of judgment against the land of the Philistines. I will wipe out the Kerethites and utterly destroy the people who live by the sea. I will execute terrible vengeance against them to rebuke them for what they have done. And when I have inflicted my revenge, then they will know that I am the Lord.'" I didn't know what to say. "Or how about in ISamuel 15:1-3, 'Now listen to the Lord's words. This is what the Lord of Armies says: I will *punish* Amalek for what they did to Israel. They blocked Israel's way after the Israelites came from Egypt. Now go and *attack* Amalek.

413

Claim *everything* they have for God by *destroying* it. *Don't spare them, but kill men and women, infants and children, cows and sheep, camels and donkeys...*' Does *that* sound like the words of One who is all *love*?" I shook my head. "Since He possessed the level of love it took in order to create a place like Paradise for His righteous servants to spend eternity in; then why would He not possess what it takes in order to create the Hellfire for the disobedient ingrates to spend eternity in?"

I had no answer to his question. That was why I loved talking to Siddiq, he didn't do too much speaking on things that he didn't know or understand. If I asked him a question that he couldn't answer, instead of just telling me anything he would simply say "Allah is the best knower," in humility.

"A'ight, answer me this then," I said, cocking the pistol in my mind.   The proceeding question always stumped everyone I had ever asked.   "Why does Allah, knowing before He allows anyone to come into existence that he is going to Hell, allow the one who is destined to go to Hell to be conceived?   Why not only allow the ones destined for Paradise to come into existence; that way no one would have to worry about going to the Fire?"

"In order that Allah may distinguish the wicked from the good."

"Huh?"

Siddiq chuckled softly. "Your question is in a way similar to the one the angels posed to Allah when He made it known that He was about to create us. The angels asked Him why He would create something that was going to cause so much mischief and bloodshed in the land. And you know what Allah told them?"

"What?"

"I know that which you know not." Siddiq left the area near the front of the cell and walked over to his usual spot, sitting on the desk. I had a seat on my bunk. "Allah is All-Mighty, All-Wise. He does what He wills with wisdom and purpose. It was His will to create us with a soul that is susceptible to both good and evil. He gave us the freedom of thought and choice. He has not only shown us all His

414

signs placed in the universe around us and within our own souls, but He has also sent numerous Prophets and Messengers with revealed Books distinguishing right from wrong and warning us against the consequences of our actions.   He leaves us to choose, and to bear the consequences of our own doings in accordance with His laws.   Our fate is a case of action rebounding on the perpetrator.

"Those who choose the steep path of righteousness, gratitude, obedience and sacrifice, selling the life of the world in return for Paradise in the Hereafter, usually suffer injustice, harm, ridicule, humiliation, poverty, and at times torture and death along the way. These will be rewarded with peace, overlooking of their faults, and will in the end enjoy Allah's mercy by residing for eternity in Gardens underneath which rivers flow, and as for those whom He knows before-hand will choose the path of satisfying all lusts and desires, neglectful ingratitude, arrogant defiance, purchasing the life of this world at the price of the Hereafter, ending up in Hell as a consequence; to not allow them to come into existence does not coincide with His will to give us freedom of choice and thought. And to do such a thing would not be fair to those whom He *did* allow to come into existence that is destined for Paradise because of all that they had to suffer and go through with unyielding hope for the positive consequences of their choices in order to obtain entrance in Paradise. The Qur'an says: 'Shall we treat those who believe and work deeds of righteousness the same as those who do mischief on earth? Shall we treat those who guard against evil the same as those who turn aside from the right?'"

"But if Allah only allowed these individuals to come into existence then they wouldn't have to suffer because the world would be full of good."

"That is not necessarily true brother. Just because one is destined for Paradise does not make him perfect and sinless. Some of the people destined for Paradise have led sinful lives but repented before it was too late, living upright thereafterwards.

"Allah is just for giving us the *chance*. Allah knows which route we will take but He still lets it come to pass in order to be fair. I would say that it is like if you had a set of twin kid brothers, right?" I nodded, "And you know your kid brothers like you know the back of your own hand. So you take two candy bars and lay them on the table and you tell them not to eat them until after dinner. You also promise to take the one who obeys you to the Worlds of Fun theme park and spank the one who disobeys you, leaving him behind, confined to his room. Now you know that one of them is destined to be punished, not only that, you even know which one will do what. Would it be fair to tell the one who will disobey you; 'No, never mind. I know you are not going to act right. I am just going to punish you right off the bat and you can't go to Worlds of Fun?'"

"No, that wouldn't be fair."

"Why not?"

"Because I still should give him that chance."

"What about if you took him to Worlds of Fun anyway with his brother; would that be fair?"

"No. His brother practiced self-restraint and patience, *earnin'* the trip to Worlds of Fun whereas the other one disobeyed and forfeited it. He preferred the candy bar before dinner, trading it for the trip to Worlds of Fun. And I can't be wrong because I made both the rewards and repercussions clear to him from the beginnin'," I said, smiling. Understanding is a beautiful feeling.

"All praise is due to Allah. The Qur'an teaches us that we too tend to purchase or trade the life of this world at the price of Paradise in the Hereafter in a similar fashion."

Siddiq then began to gaze out of the window, watching the sun as it dipped below the horizon. I followed his gaze. Before then I had never really watched it with the understanding that I was doing so with just then. I was witnessing evidence of not only our Creator's existence, but His concern for His creatures and omnipotence as well.

"Atif, whenever things get rough for you brother and you begin to harbor doubt in your heart because of the way things may be happening in your life of which you don't understand," Siddiq began, still staring out of the window. "All you have to do is...open your eyes. Allah tells us to study His creation because within it are signs and proofs for those of us who have eyes to see. Allah is the Greatest."

Siddiq rose from his seat on the desk and went over to the sink, tuning me out of his world as he began to make ablution. By then I had this ritual memorized, even though I had never actually performed it myself, but nevertheless I still enjoyed watching him do his thing. I had observed him so much over the preceding three weeks that I even knew how many times he was going to rise, bow, prostrate and sit for each prayer.

Some of the times when he prayed he would recite what he informed me were verses from the Qur'an out loud, whereas other times he did so silently. When I inquired about why this was, he said that even he didn't know. That he did so because it was the way Prophet Muhammad prayed. He recited these verses in Arabic and to hear him do so actually shook me up a little. This was because the way he chanted and held certain vowels and consonants eerily reminded me of the two who had come for me in my vision while in the strip cell back in the fall.

Speaking of which, I remember the proceeding events vividly. I was sitting quietly and respectfully on my bunk as Siddiq offered Salah. He was reciting out loud and I remember wondering to myself why he prayed with his eyes open, taking a mental note to ask him when he was finished, just before I heard him chant: "Kalla saya'alamun!" I felt a palpitation of terror in my solar plexus.

"Thumma kalla saya 'alamun!"

I covered my ears and began to shake my head, rocking slightly back and forth. I wanted him to stop! I didn't know Arabic and up to that point it had been practically impossible for me to accurately recall what my captors had been chanting. I panicked. What if Siddiq was one of them and had been the whole time? I didn't want to go back to that place! I didn't want for my body to be forced back into that uncomfortable position. I didn't want that thick iron collar fastened around my neck along with those heavy chains, being dragged on my face.

"Atif?" I felt a hand on my shoulder. At least 10 minutes had gone by and Siddiq had concluded his prayer finding me in the state I was in. "Are you alrigh-"

Siddiq was cut off by my pushing him violently in his chest. Caught off balance, he flew across the room slamming his body hard against the cold cement wall.

"I ain't goin' back there!" I shouted storming over to him. "I will *die* first, y'all gone have to *kill* me this time!" I noticed Siddiq's fist clenched into balls and his feet set in a fighter's stance.

"Going back where?" Siddiq asked me. "What are you talking about little brother?"

Our faces were separated only by inches of thin air. Looking into his eyes I saw no fear, nor did I see any malicious intent. What I saw was genuine curiosity, concern and confusion. At that moment I remembered what my mother had said about how those ...demons were not going to come for me anymore. Maybe I was trippin' after all.

"Siddiq?"

"Yes, it's me. Siddiq." He answered, smiling as he sensed my return from Never Never Land. "Back up Atif," he said, gently placing his left palm on my chest. I took a couple of steps back, removing myself from his personal space. His hands relaxed as I did so.

"I apologize brotha', I was... I'm sorry, man." I apologized, backing away. "I shouldn't have put my hands on you like that."

"It's alright brother, I'm not hurt," Siddiq replied as I walked over to the window. Touching the back of his head, he winced and pulled his hand away with blood on his fingertips. "But your apology should be accompanied by an explanation. What was all of that about? What place is it that you are so afraid of returning to?"

Siddiq was right. I did owe him an explanation. The brother had just finished praying to the Almighty and was practically attacked by me. Maybe it was me who was the demon instead of him. "For the last 5 years or so, man, I've been havin' these dreams..."

I told him everything, practically my whole life story. I told him about my mother's death; my life on the

418

filthy route; I talked about Malik, Patience, Big Mama, the hommies, Kev, Mr. Williams; I really confided in him. He would smile and nod at some points in my narration whereas he would grunt and scowl during others. When we reached my arrival at Moberly I began to tell him about my dreams in detail. He was infuriated by the way the guards had played me and by the time I reached my experience in the strip cell he had begun pacing the cell.

"Are you sure that you have never, ever read the Qur'an?" Siddiq asked me after I finished telling him about my search for the path.

"No brotha', I haven't. I told you that already."

Siddiq stared at me for at least a full minute. "Some of what you experienced is in total accordance with the Qur'an."

"What do you mean?"

Siddiq retrieved his Qur'an and handed it to me. "Turn to chapter 36, and then read verse number 8." I found the chapter and began to read.

"Verily, we have put on their necks iron col....iron collars reaching to the chins, so that their heads are raised up." Words can not describe the fear I felt in the depths of my heart when reading those words.

"Go to chapter 40 and read verses 70 through 72."

I complied. "Those who deny the Book and that which We sent Our Messengers, they will come to know. When iron collars will be rounded over their necks, and the chains, they shall be dragged along, in the boiling water, then they will be burned in the Fire."

"17:97"

My hands were trembling as I turned the pages. "And he whom Allah guides, he is led aright; but he whom He sends astray, for such you will find no...A-ul-"

"Auliyaa," Siddiq corrected. "It is Arabic for helpers or protectors."

"...Auliyaa besides Him, and We shall gather them together on the Day of Resurrection on their faces, blind, dumb and deaf; their abode will be Hell; whenever it abates, We shall increase for them the fierceness of the Fire."

419

"You see what I mean, now?" Siddiq asked me. I nodded. He then grabbed a pencil and paper, handing them to me. "I am going to recite that particular chapter from the Qur'an that I did during the sunset prayer, insha Allah, and I want you to stop me whenever you hear something that sounds like what those demons chanted and write down what I tell you to write down, okay?"

"Yeah, a'ight."

"You are not going to trip out on me again are you?"

I smiled. "No brotha', I'm cool. You ain't gone let me forget that are you?"

Siddiq only smiled in response and then began reciting. By the time we were finished I had 10 numbers written down. Everything the demons had chanted was contained in the Qur'anic chapter, out of order, but in the Recitation. After putting the numbers in the correct order of which I had heard them in the strip cell, Siddiq took a look at the sheet of paper.

"Turn the Qur'an to chapter 78 and read the verses in the order we put them in."

I found the chapter titled "The Great News" and started reading at verse number 21. "Truly, Hell is a place of ambush, a dwelling place for (those who transgress the boundary limits set by Allah). They will abide therein for ages. Nothing cool shall they taste therein, nor any drink. Except boiling water, and dirty wound discharges. An exact recompense. For verily, they used not to look for a reckoning. But they denied Our verses completely." I paused for a second, stopping at verse 28, and then went to verses 4 and 5. "Nay, they will come to know! Again, nay, they will come to know!"

Siddiq and I stared at each other for what seemed like a long period of time. I could feel cold nausea leap-frog in my belly, chilled fingers tapping out a ditty of dread up and down the buttons of my spine.

"What did the being say when you asked him where you were?"

"Maubiq, or somethin' like that."

"Allah has blessed you brother. Maubiq is a valley in...those demons were dragging you to the Hellfire." Siddiq said. "It is close to midnight, I should pray before then." Siddiq then got up and made his way over to the faucet.

"Siddiq?" He looked up in my direction as he turned on the water. "Excuse me for interruptin' you, but um…. do you think that you could teach me how to pray like that?"

******

I spent the next 4 weeks learning how to offer the Salah, how to give the call to prayer; along with numerous supplications as well as things I needed to know concerning the 5 daily prayers. We prayed together day in and day out with me standing on his right side while he led. I learned the prayer first in English and then in Arabic.

We also discussed Islam and deciphered my experience in the suicide cell. Siddiq told me that he believed the being whose name was "Kai" is an angel. He showed me in the Qur'an about the blowing of the Trumpet and the Day. He then explained why Kai forced those demons to release me saying that theirs was not the decision to do such a thing, the decision belonged to Allah alone.

"A Siddiq," I said, rising to a sitting position on my bunk. It was late, and I had no idea what time it was or how long I had been asleep.

"What's up brother?" Siddiq asked, closing his Qur'an. He was standing by the window using the light reflected from the moon to read by.

"I had another dream."

"A nightmare?"

"No, not a nightmare. I dreamed I was back on the plain still searchin' for the path." Siddiq nodded. "But this time I *found* it."

"Straight up?" he asked. I smiled. "Did you get on it?"

"No."

"Why not?"

421

"As soon as I came upon it I woke up." Siddiq sat in silence for a while with his brow creased in thought. "What do you think about that brotha'?"

"You know, Atif, when these people told me that my urine analyses test had come back diluted, cuffing me up and escorting me over here, I didn't understand why. I have not smoked any weed in at least 14 years, so of course I have no reason to try and flush my system out. All I drink is water throughout the day, so why wouldn't my system have a lot of water in it?

"The Muslim community, we were scheduled to have a feast. Some sisters from a Masjid on the streets had cooked up a bunch of good food for us and everything. I was really looking forward to this when they came and locked me up so you can imagine why I was so upset when I first came in here.

"But like young Fatimah told you back in juvenile; everything happens for a reason and Allah is the Best Planner. All praise is due to Allah, for I believe that I now understand that which has been wrecking my brain for the last two months. I know why I am over here locked down in this cell with you and I must say that I am overwhelmed that our Lord chose me for this task.."

I was confused, what task?

"Who is Allah?" Siddiq asked me.

"Allah is the Cherisher and Sustainer of all that exists. He is One, with no equals or partners. He is far exalted above His creation and Laa ilaha ill Allah; there is nothing worthy of worship except Him. It is upon Him that all creatures depend and He is rich and free from all wants and needs. To Him belongs the dominion of the heavens and the earth."

"Who is Muhammad?"

"Prophet Muhammad, peace be upon him, is Allah's servant and Messenger sent by Him to the whole world. He was born over 1400 years ago in the Holy city of Makkah from the Quraysh tribe, descendant of Prophet Isma'il, Allah's peace be upon him, the seal of the prophets."

"What is Iman?"

"Iman is Arabic for faith and faith is to believe in the Oneness of Allah. To believe that the angels and jinn are a part of His creation, just as real as we are. To believe in the prophets; from Prophet Adam all of the way down through Prophet Jesus and lastly Prophet Muhammad, Allah's peace be upon them all, including those we have no knowledge of making no distinction between them. Faith is to believe in the whole of the Qur'an which was revealed to Prophet Muhammad, and that Allah also similarly revealed scriptures to Prophets Jesus, Moses, David, etc. as well. Faith is believin' that we will be resurrected physically and literally after we die, judged and sent to either the Hellfire or Paradise. And lastly, faith is to believe in the Divine Decree."

"What is Islam?"

"Islam means submission and it is a way of life which is submissive to Allah. One practices Islam by believin' in Allah and in His Messenger, prayin' 5 times a day, fastin' durin' the month of Ramadan, given' charity and goin' on the pilgrimage to Makkah at least once if he or she is able."

"And a Muslim?"

"A Muslim is one who is in a state of submission to Allah in Islam."

"Ihsan?"

"Ihsan is the highest level of deeds and worship. Ihsan is to fear Allah like He should be feared in all that we do. It is to worship Allah as if you see Him, though you see Him not, knowing full well that Allah sees you."

"Do you believe in those things you spoke of?"

"Yeah, I believe in them."

"Do you want to turn in repentance to your Creator and submit to His will?"

"Yeah, I do, but it's still some things I'm not understandin'."

"Things like what?"

"I was readin' your Qur'an and came across a verse that says, '...whoever seeks a religion other than Islam, it will never be accepted from him, and in the hereafter he will be one of the losers'. I also saw one that reads, 'Abraham

423

was neither a Jew nor a Christian, but he was a true Muslim Hanifa and he was not of the polytheists'. My question is why do I have to choose Islam if I want Allah's mercy in the Hereafter over all of these other religions? Why can't I just, you know, treat people right, believe in God and pray in my own way instead of makin' Salah; why won't this be accepted from me? And how was Abraham a Muslim if he lived long before Muhammad?"

"You never cease to amaze me with your questions little brother. They're *always* valid and poignant. When talking to you, one had better make sure he has done his research and speaks nothing but truth. You put a brother to *work*!" I laughed out loud at that.

"What most people don't understand is that the term "Islam" is not a title that man attached to this way of life, nor is it named (by men) after Muhammad like 'Christianity' is named after 'Jesus the Christ' or 'Judaism' after 'Judah' or 'Buddhism' after 'Buddha'. *Allah* chose the term 'Islam' from the language He revealed the Qur'an in for the name of the message he sent His Prophets with and 'Muslim' for the true followers of it because of what these terms actually *mean*. Islam means the way of self-submission to the Creator of all that exists, and a Muslim is one who is in a state of self-submission to Allah by way of the message He sent down. This message, in essence, has *always* been consistent and the same. The Qur'an says, 'And We did not send any messenger before you (Muhammad) but We revealed to him saying: none has the right to be worshipped but I, so worship Me'. Allah didn't reveal or send His Prophets with a bunch of different religions or contradictive, inconsistent scriptures. The Qur'an says, 'Those who were given the Scripture did not differ except out of mutual jealousy, after knowledge had come to them,' and elsewhere it says, 'But they have broken their religion into sects, each group rejoicing in what is with them.'

"Abraham was neither a Jew nor a Christian because the Laws of Moses and the teachings of Jesus Christ were not only revealed *after* he was long dead, but because the condition they are in today, after centuries of oppression, corruption, and tampering, are *alien* to what Abraham himself brought and what these two great men actually taught. Abraham didn't believe in a Trinity; the Father, the Son, and the Holy Ghost, he believed in one God alone without associating partners with him and was not of the polytheists. This is the message that all of the prophets brought. And he submitted to the Creator, *this* is why Allah said he was a Muslim because that is what a Muslim is, past, present, or future; one who submits to the message He reveals.

"The Qur'an says, 'And seek the means of approach to your Lord.' Allah is Exalted and Glorified, Great and Sublime. You must humble yourself before Him. The reason why you can't believe and worship Him in your own way is because it is *Him* that accepts worship, therefore it is *Him* who decides *how* He wants to be worshipped, perceived, and shown gratitude, not *you*. Your own way of worshipping Him is insufficient and your own way of believing in Him is off base. Think of Patience: You couldn't just love her in your own little way, you had to get to know her and learn what *she* likes and then gain her affection by approaching her how *she* wanted to be approached. Think of the President: Because of his position and authority, you can't just barge in on him in the white house when and however *you* feel like it. Allah is the Creator and Lord of all that exsists, His position is far greater than that! This is why before you stand before Him in salah, you purify yourself with ablution, dress how He orders you to dress, bow and put your *face* on the floor before Him, addressing Him with humility in the manner He wants to be addressed based upon what He taught you by way of His Messenger. It is arrogant for one to disregard the instructions Allah sent down regarding how He is to be worshipped and try to do so in one's own way, and foolish for him to think that for one second this will be accepted from him.

"Dear brother, Islam is the only religion acceptable to Allah because it is the religion of self-submission, the religion of Abraham, Moses, Jesus, and the rest of them, and their followers were Muslims because they were in a state of submission. The way of self-submission to Him is the only way He has ever authorized, the only one that gives Him what is His due; the only one He'll accept."

"But what about those that don't *know* the correct way to approach Allah?"

"They have to make it a priority and *seek* it with the time, intellect and energy that Allah provides them with. If they do this, with the intention to accept and act upon what they learn, then Allah will guide them to the right path and make things clear for them.

"But you'll find that most people don't know only because they have their priorities mixed up and their goal is relaxation and entertainment. They overindulge in these things and they devote their time and energy to satisfying desires, trying to obtain and maintain materialistic things in excess. They let someone hand them a book saying 'This is from God', and instead of utilizing their time, intellect and energy to delve into understanding or verifying it as such, they accept it blindly, allowing themselves to be misled. Allah, because of their own lack of initiative, leaves them to wander blindly right into the Hellfire and they have none to blame but themselves."

"But there have been sincere people, like my Grandmother, who never even *heard* of Islam and tried to follow the best of what they knew. What will happen to *them*?"

"The Qur'an says 'That was a nation who passed away. They shall receive the reward of what they earned, and you of what you earn. And you will not be asked about what they used to do.' Don't fret yourself. Allah is just and will deal with everyone who ever lived with justice, fairly considering all they had to deal with. Concern yourself with you and what you are going to do, for Allah will raise you up as an individual soul." I nodded.

"Have those things you were confused about been made clear?"

"Clear as a *bell*!"

"The Qur'an says, 'Verily, the right path has become distinct from the wrong path.' Brother, you have discovered

426

the path you have been seeking. All you have to do now is step onto it. What are you waiting for?"

I lowered my gaze, looking down at the floor. "I ain't ready yet brotha', I'm still.... I just ain't right yet. I be lustin' in my heart, harborin' thoughts of killin' people still, all kinds of crazy stuff."

"Atif, you don't have to perfect yourself before you step foot on the path. All you have to do is believe with the intent to strive for perfection. This is what the path is for! Once you reach this point it is time to take that step. Everything else comes afterwards; you are not going to be able to come away from certain things overnight brother. You will spend the rest of your life fighting against the Shaytan, insha Allah. When you get on the path all that remains is for you to do what Allah says, He will show you how to do the rest."

"How do I take that step?"

"You take what is called the Shahadah by openly bearing witness that there is nothing worthy or worship except Allah and you bear witness that Muhammad is His Messenger."

"Right now, right here?" I asked. It couldn't be that simple, could it?

"Allah witnesses all things."

"*Ash-hadu an laa ilaha ill Allah, wa ash-hadu anna Muhammadar-rasulullah.*"

Siddiq   smiled   brightly,   hugging   me. "Congratulations my young Muslim brother; you just stepped foot on the path."

"That's it, just like that?"

"Well, when they come and get us for showers in a minute here, insha Allah, you have to bathe a certain way and then pray; but yes, just like that. All of those things you mentioned such as the Salah have become an obligatory duty upon you." I nodded, accepting these responsibilities. "Welcome to the path which leads to Paradise."

*****

After coming back from the shower and offering Salah on my own for the first time, I laid awake in my bunk. It was time and I knew it in my heart. I had been leaning towards change for the past couple of years slowly but surely, but it wasn't until that particular night that I actually committed. I had accepted a whole new way of life.

"Atif?"

"Wha'sup?" I asked. I thought Siddiq had fallen asleep by then.

"Prophet Muhammad said that if a person embraces Islam sincerely, then Allah shall forgive all his past sins, and after that starts the settlement of accounts; the reward of his good deeds will be 10 times to 700 times for each good deed, and an evil deed will be recorded as it is unless Allah forgives it."

I smiled in the darkness, "Aw yeah?"

"It is what the Prophet said."

"You know what I have been wonderin'?"

"What is that?"

"I wonder why my mother and Big Mama couldn't take me any further once they reached a certain point durin' my dream."

"That was not your mother or your grandmother, Atif."

"You don't think so?"

"No, she was on point when she told you that the dead can't communicate with the living. Not even Muhammad. He too is dead, waiting to be resurrected right along with everyone else who has passed away and there is a barrier between us and them. I think she was trying to tell you that."

"Well, who were they then?"

"Allah is the Best Knower. They could have been 2 angels or 2 of the jinn. Not all of the jinn are evil, some of them are righteous servants of Allah. As for Kai, if he is who I think he is, then he was sent to your mother's womb with your soul 3 months after you were conceived and has been with you ever since."

428

"Why would they come to me fakin' like they were Mama and Big Mama?"

"Well, the angels and the jinn are 2 parts of Allah's creation totally different from us. Allah says in the Qur'an that the angels He created from light, the jinn from a smokeless flame and us from clay. When angels do appear to us like when Angel Gabriel did to Maryam, the mother of Prophet Jesus, in order to announce to her news of the upcoming miraculous birth of a son, they do so taking the form of a well made man, something we are familiar with. Only Muhammad has seen the angel Gabriel in his original form. So whoever they were, maybe they didn't want to frighten you with their appearance which would have been foreign to you. Maybe they wanted you to be comfortable considering what you had went through. We tend to fear things we see that we don't understand.

"To answer your first question, they stopped and were unable to take you any further because Allah says in the Qur'an that there is to be no compulsion in accepting religion. That the right path has become distinct from the wrong path. All they, or anyone else, could have done is point you in the right direction. The rest you had to do on your own. Only Allah can open one's breast to Islam." I laid there silently for a moment. "I have a question for you."

"Wha'sup?"

"You were told that it was the prayers of a special person that was one of the reasons why you were being rescued. Who is this special person?"

"Allah is the best Knower," I answered.

"Salaamun alaykum, Atif."

"Wa alaykum as-salaam."

Siddiq turned over and was fast asleep in minutes. I myself drifted off feeling clean and pure. It was a cleanliness that I had never felt before in my life. I slept peacefully that night for the first time in close to 7 years.

*****

429

ELEVATION

And certainly, We shall test you
with something of fear, hunger, loss of
wealth, lives and fruits, but give glad
tidings to As-Saabiruun (the patient).
Who, when afflicted with calamity,
say: "Truly, to Allah we belong and
truly, to Him we shall return."
They are those on whom are the
Salawat (i.e. who are blessed and will
be forgiven) from their Lord, and (they
are those who) receive His Mercy, and
it is they who are the guided ones.
----*Noble Qur'an 2:155-157*

"When an individual is sent to prison he or she
will do 1 of 2 things: they will either take it upon
themselves to rise above their surroundings
or they will succumb to them. Whichever the case,
they will never be the same again, there is no
in between. The weak? They are broken down to the level
of a beast, despised and rejected. But as for the strong
it's all about elevation."
--Atif

21

"Hey Miss Lynn!" someone shouted. I was standing at my cell door looking out at nothing in particular as a female guard entered the wing. "Hey Miss Lynn, come to cell number 1-4-7!"

My instincts told me that the Caucasian in cell 147 was up to something because he always was. It was just after breakfast time and it was dark so I couldn't see anyone standing at his cell window. I looked on as Miss Lynn approached his cell door. She recoiled in shock when she looked into his cell, turned and ran out of the wing. I could see a substance running slowly down his cell window. It didn't dawn on me what he had done until I saw all of the guards rushing to his cell in order to subdue him and take him to the strip cell to be maced, stripped naked and spend 72 hours shivering and suffocating. *"Lick it off you fucking whore! Taste my cum you cunt!"* he shouted as they dragged him away.

What he had done was called Miss Lynn to his cell door, standing up on his sink and masturbating as she approached. Timing himself just right, he ejaculated all over the cell window just as she peered in it, which in her mind probably carried just as much of an impact as if he had done so on her face, literally.

There was a name for what he had done to Miss Lynn. It was called "stoning" and every female guard who worked for the Department of Corrections had more than likely fallen victim to being stoned at least once in her career in some way, maybe more, depending on how attractive she was. Something like that took a lot of practice, honestly there was a *science* to it.

"Subhan Allah," I mumbled, shaking my head in renunciation. As disgusted as I was about what he had done, I was just as disgusted with the guards for misusing their authority and using that suicide cell as a tool for punishment instead of what it was supposed to be used for: suicide prevention. It was okay for them to bend the rules of their own policies but when it came to us it was a different story. Hypocrisy.

"Bismillah," I uttered softly, zoning out my surroundings as I began to make ablution. After doing so I offered the morning prayer. I recited out loud but did so quietly in order to not disturb my celly, who was sleeping.

It was the morning of September 28th. Siddiq was released from ad-seg back in March. Allah knows I hated to see him go. I grew to love that brother during the two months we spent locked in the cell together. He left his Qur'an with me and his advice to me while on his way out was: "Keep up the Salat and establish regular prayer. Don't be of those who are neglectful of their duties to Allah. Seek help in your prayers and practice patience, for our Lord is with the patient. You do this, study diligently and strive hard against your vices, then, insha Allah; you will achieve the Greatest Achievement."

He hadn't been gone a full 24 hours before Pastor Cool Breeze appeared at my door with a legal binder full of materials for me to study. When I finished with the material I would send them back out and Pastor Cool Breeze would bring me more of what Siddiq had sent for me.

I once read where statisticians wrote that when a prisoner is locked down for at least 23 hours of the day in a cell, then an average of 17 of those hours are spent sleeping. This was not the case with me; I reversed it and did the opposite. I spent 17 hours of my day studying, praying and contemplating the things I had studied, sleeping for the other 6. Sleeping for more than that felt like a waste of valuable time.

Ever since meeting Siddiq back in January of that year it was like I had gotten on an elevator, pushed the button marked "perpetual elevation status" and had been rising in understanding and wisdom from that point on whereas before I had been laboriously taking the stairs slowly one step at a time.

I studied Ibn Kathir's collection of Tafsir on the Qur'an which is a 10 volume set; I studied the authentic narrations of Prophet Muhammad and his life; I was learning to read and write Arabic so that I could study the Qur'an in its essence instead of having to depend so much on someone else's translation of the Arabic Recitation which had not been tampered with in over 1,400 years, not one single letter.

I was learning so much that at times I felt as if the days did not contain enough hours for me. I went through a string of cellies but hardly even noticed their coming or going. I paid no attention to the guards and I had become a complete stranger to the other inmates locked up in ad-seg.

"Excuse me, sir, would you like a Medical Service Request form?"

It was a little after 7:00 am and I was standing at the window watching the birds as they abandoned their nests in order to seek the bounties Allah provided them with, a habit I had developed over the past 6 months. An hour or so had passed by since the incident with cell number 147. I was waiting for either my cellie to wake up so that I could turn the light on or for the sun to provide the cell with it so that I could see clearly enough to begin my studies. I once read where Malcolm X said that his eyes got bad from studying in poor light when he was in prison and I didn't want for that to happen to me.

"Sir?"

I smelled perfume, not just any perfume but the familiar scent of Bora Bora. I turned and saw that it was Rebecca accompanied by a guard standing at my cell door. I walked over to the front of the cell. "Hey nurse, how are you doin' this mornin'?"

"I'm fine, and you?" she inquired, smiling her bright new smile.

"I'm good, all praise is due to Allah," I smiled in return. It was nice to see her. Rebecca slid an M.S.R. form through the crack of my door and winked her eye at me.

"Have a nice day," she said as she left. The guard glared at me as he passed by, trying to kick something off before his shift even got into full swing. I ignored him, grabbing the M.S.R. form. I could see that it was full of writing on its flip side.

Her writing was full of apologies for what transpired 13 months ago and for the way the guards had maced me up there. She explained why she closed the post office box and had not written to me. Rebecca also wrote that she missed me and would do everything that she could to get my job in the infirmary back whenever I made it out.

I didn't think that would be a good idea. I had read the whole Qur'an 6 times cover to cover by then and could recall numerous verses that warned of a grievous chastisement prepared for those who participated in fornication and adultery. But then again, what if she was no longer married to her husband? Then we could.... nah, forget that. Other inmates with a 30 year sentence would under no circumstances forfeit such privileges, but I was no longer an inmate.

*****

"Cuff up, you have a visit," a guard said later that afternoon, tapping rudely on my cell door with a set of handcuffs.

"Who?" I asked. After all, there were 2 of us in the cell.

"*You!* Let's *go*, will ya? I don't have all freaking day; I got better things to do."

I ignored his smart mouth. They hated to see me receive a *letter* from the outside, let alone a visit. I rose from the desk and thrust my hands through the chuckhole. The guard slapped the cuffs on me tight enough to not only cut off the blood circulation in my hands, but also tight enough to leave whelps behind on my wrists. I didn't complain, to do so would have been a waste of breath. Once out on the walk a chain was fastened around my waist and cuffs were attached to it. I was then led to the visiting room wondering who it was that decided to drop by.

The visiting room was pretty spacious. I hated going up there while in ad-seg because my visits had to be non-contact and I was paraded through the visiting room cuffed and chained like a wild animal while kids and other visitors visiting inmates in population stared at me like I was a black Charles Manson. While enroute for the non-contact booths in the far corner I saw Concrete hugged up with an overweight Caucasian woman he was taking advantage of, feeding her hot & spicy wings.   Our eyes locked momentarily; I smirked and turned away.

There was only one visiting booth still open. Looking in that direction I saw a little girl climbing up to grab one of the phones. I didn't recognize her from that distance. Whoever had brought her up there must have told her to sit down because she looked behind her and then sat. It took a couple of seconds for my brain to process the image fed to it by my optic nerves once I rounded the corner.

It was *Darion*! He wore a Kansas City Chief's football jersey with a platinum necklace around his neck that had a diamond encrusted emblem hanging at the bottom of it just between the 2 numbers on his chest. I hadn't seen my best friend in over 3 years and to say he looked different was an understatement. He was so thin! His head looked too big for his body and I could actually see traces of his facial bones just beneath his skin. The eyes of his gaunt face were sunken and he just looked weary and tired.

The little girl was his daughter Destiny. She had diamond earrings in her ears with pink overalls on and a white turtleneck. Her hair was neatly braided with pink and white beads hanging in the front and rear. She was the cutest little thing and had really gotten big since I saw her last. I smiled at her as I took a seat, grabbing the phone from its stand. She was too busy staring at my restraints to notice me doing so.

"Wha'sup Darion, man? How you doin'?"

"I... lets just say this is one of my good days, you know?" Actually I didn't, but I nodded anyway. I had a feeling that it wouldn't be too long before I found out. "Ain't you gone speak?" Darion asked Destiny, looking down at her.

Destiny smiled shyly at me, "Hi Atif," she greeted me. My heart turned into mush. "When are you get-ting

435

out of jail?" I smiled at her. I could see that Destiny, like her mother, didn't waste a lot of time with small talk; she got right to the point.

"I don't know," I replied. "One day though, insha Allah."

"What does in-shaa Allah mean?" Destiny asked me.

"It means if the Lord wants it to happen."

"Aw," her response.

"You lookin' good man, I see you done got your swole on," Darion complimented.

"All praise is due to Allah."

"I heard about the Muslim thing too, man, that's cool Atif. Whatever it takes, blood, I'm for that." I nodded. "When you gettin' out of the hole?"

"March of 2000, insha Allah." Destiny giggled with the second mentioning of the foreign expression.

"Kesha told me to tell you to send her a visiting application because they lettin' her off parole early."

"Aw, yeah?" Darion nodded. "How is everything goin' for her out there?"

"She is doin' good, man, waitin' on her shop to be finished. She already got all kinds of clientele from doin' hair out of Ms. Brown's basement so she really gone do her thizzle when she open her place up."

"All praise is due to Allah."

"She be talkin' about you and your letters all of the time, too. I be takin' Destiny down there to get her wig done and she always pullin' out your pictures and letters, showin' them to us. Man you are gone have a beauty salon full of women waitin' for you to get out so that they can shoot their shot at you." I laughed. "You heard from Patience?"

"No." Silence. "You go to Big Mama's funeral?"

"Yeah," Darion started, sighing. "It was ruff, too, man. I mean it was a nice service and the morticians did a good job on her but, I don't know. I just didn't handle it very well. None of us did, really. Malik? That dude is *weird* man, he didn't shed one tear." What Darion said about Malik was true. Even I couldn't remember ever seeing him

436

cry.   Thinking about him made me space off for a second until Destiny brought me back to reality.

"Atif,"

"Wha'sup?" I looked down at her, smiling.

"My da-ddy said that *you* got to be my daddy when you get out of jail be-cause he is dy-ing." My smile disappeared from my face.   My sudden change of expression caused her to look up at her father wondering if she had done something wrong. I too looked at my best friend.

"It's a'ight, baby girl," Darion started.   He then wrapped his arm around her small shoulders and tickled her armpit.   Destiny screamed, laughing as she attempted to protect her armpit from being tickled again.   "She is smart, man, and she understands what is happenin' to me." Darion said to me.   "Go ahead, Suga Bear, and tell Atif what is wrong with Daddy."

Destiny looked up at me, pleased with the opportunity to prove just how smart she was.   "My da-ddy had H-I-V, but *now* he has AIDS."

I shook my head in denial, pleading with my eyes for Darion to tell me that it wasn't true. In my heart I had suspected something like this for the last couple of years because only such a thing could keep him from knocking down that visiting room door on a regular basis. I was tired of death; it seemed like everyone I loved was dying.

"What does AIDS stand for?" Darion asked his daughter.

"Um....   Aqui-red...Im-mune....De-fi-ci-ency......Syn-drome," she answered. I was truly amazed at this 5 and a ½ year old girl's intelligence. "It is a sex-ually trans-mitted dis-ease," she then informed me as an afterthought.   I smiled at her while trying to hold back the tears I felt welling up inside of me.

"That's *good*, girl! You *are* smart, ain't you?" I complimented. Destiny blushed. I focused my attention on Darion.

"I been wantin' to tell you this for the longest man, but I guess I had to come to grips with it myself first and that took a long time. I told everybody when it came out not to tell you because I wanted to myself." I nodded, understanding.

"How long have you known?"

"I found out about the virus not long after you got locked up. I started gettin' sick, man, catchin' colds and stuff that just wouldn't go away; you know what I'm sayin'?" I nodded. "I took a blood test and it came back HIV positive. I don't know who I got it from or how many females I might have given it to. I started trippin', contemplatin' suicide and everything. I even thought about infectin' girls on purpose just because one of them gave it to me. I just couldn't believe it was happenin' to me. I didn't want to take any medicine, none of that."

"Why not?"

"Because, man, like now they got me takin' 24 pills a day. 24! I got to take certain ones at certain times; some with food, others on an empty stomach. Some make me nauseous; some give me the runs; some be makin' my head hurt; man I'm..." Darion paused, shaking his head. Destiny took a hold of her father's free hand and I wondered to myself if the child understood the significance of her action. Darion smiled at his daughter. "If it wasn't for Suga Bear, I don't know *what* I would do. It ain't strange that God gave me, of all people a little girl, you know? She changed my whole attitude towards females. It's all about her now. On my good days I spend them with her, don't nothin' else matter to me. I take her to see her grandmother, man, and we just kick it, together."

"How is she doin'?"

"Moms?" I nodded. "Aw, she cool, man. She be goin' to NA and she is really tryin' to get it together. She uh....when I told her about my bein' HIV positive, man, she got some get right. I got to give it to her because for the first time in as far back as I can remember she is actually bein' there for me. I can depend on her now and she loves her some Destiny."

"What about TeeBaby? Wha'sup with her?"

"TeeBaby is out of control. I ain't mad at her though because I took her through a lot of changes. She is a grown woman and she can do what she want to do. I just don't like these bustas she be havin' around my daughter. That's why I have her with me every chance I get."

We spent the next hour reminiscing. I then took some time to talk to Destiny. She was good at holding a conversation and she asked me a million questions. We talked about her kindergarten classmates, her teacher, her favorite cartoons, everything. I taught her how to play paper, rock, scissors and lost every game to her once she got the hang of it. It didn't take long at all for her to win me over.

"We tryin' to get your time ran concurrent man, so when you get out I want you to take care of my little girl, Atif, treat her like she is yours. She need somebody like you in her life, somebody that's on somethin' positive and that will keep her away from the streets. I be readin' your letters man and I want you to breathe some of that religious knowledge and real talk on her when she is ready for it. I don't want her to be confused about God or herself as a black girl, you know what I'm sayin'?" I nodded. "Teach her how to love herself and school her about these dudes that be movin' like I was when we were growin' up."

"I got your back, brotha', all of that goes unsaid. You are in a serious situation, one that we *all* must face; and that is approaching death. You have to turn to Allah in repentance and submit seekin' His forgiveness before it's too late. We've put out a lot of negativity, did a lot of dirt and spread some corruption; the total effects of which we can't *begin* to comprehend with our limited scope of vision and knowledge. But Allah sees and knows all, and He will send us to the hell fire on the day that we're raised up if we don't seek His mercy. So whatever time you have remaining should be spent doin' just that."

Darion smiled. "Yeah, I know," He started dismissively. He was my friend and I loved him, but it was only my duty to warn him and not force him to take me seriously. "A, I almost forgot. I bought Rose's old house from the bank, they didn't even want 10 grand for it. It's in bad shape, though. Somebody was usin' it for a tilt. I really ain't got the energy to fix it up for you but I will leave it to you in your name so that you will have your own place to come home to. I also got some ends put up that I want you to give to Destiny when she is old enough and has figured out what she wants to do with her life. I would like for her to go to college for real."

"A'ight," I said, rising. Visits were concluding. "I appreciate you comin' up and bringin' Destiny up here. It feels good to see y'all man, you know?"

Darion nodded. "You too, man. I will have Persistence or someone start bringin' Destiny up on a regular. That way y'all can really get to know each other."

"A'ight."

"Much love and respect, blood, you hear me?" Darion said, pressing his right fist against the glass. I did the same. "Stay focused. Say 'bye' Destiny."

"Bye-bye, Atif."

"Bye Destiny."

Darion took his daughter by the hand and walked away. Destiny looked back over her shoulder at me and waved. I smiled and waved back. Ole D-Mack, that was the last time I saw my childhood friend alive.

*****

After offering the last prayer of the day, I relived our visit in my mind. Darion had matured a lot also in his own right. Life was no longer such a joke to him anymore. And that precious little girl! She was truly a blessing. I didn't notice until then that Darion had not uttered so much as one curse word in front of his daughter. He didn't say the word 'nigga', nor did he call a woman a 'bitch', or a 'hoe'. All of us were growing up; and apart.

Seeing my friend emaciated by the AIDS virus was difficult for me to handle. I must admit that my faith was a little shaken after my visit with Destiny and her father. I kept asking myself why the people I loved were still being taken away from me. After all, I had gotten on the path and committed to change. I guess in my own mind I had been expecting for life to be peaches and cream from the moment I became a Muslim until the day I died, which was in fact far from reality.

I wrote to brother Siddiq and expressed these thoughts to him; he in turn wrote me back a lengthy letter explaining that Allah tests those who believe in countless ways. That many people profess belief with their tongues but when affliction is lifted from them they forget their faith. Thus Allah trains Muslims to remember Him during trials and calamities as well as times of prosperity and practice patience and gratitude instead of turning back on our heels. He included some relevant supplications for me to learn and told me to stay strong. I came to realize that, like me, my friend was dealing with the consequences of his way of life.

*****

FOR THE SAKE OF ALLAH

And hold fast, all of you together,
to the Rope of Allah and be not
divided among yourselves, and remember
Allah's Favour on you, for you were
enemies one to another, so that, by
His Grace, you became brethren, and
you were on the brink of a pit of Fire,
and He saved you from it. Thus Allah makes
His signs clear to you, that you may be guided.
--Noble Qur'an 3:103

22

I spent the next seven months going downhill on cruise control. I was so deep into my studies that whole weeks passed by like days. Persistence brought Destiny up to see me twice a month and we had become really attached to each other. Every few days, I received a picture that Destiny had drawn for me in the mail. Some were cute and brought a smile to my face while others were sad expressions of the way she was feeling about Darion's declining health. She put her thoughts to paper very well.

The prison authorities refused to approve Kesha's visiting application because of her prison record. They told her that she had to be out of prison for at least 5 years before she could be considered. I am pretty sure that they heard every insult and curse word known to man when telling her this over the phone. I, too, was disappointed; I was really looking forward to seeing her after all those years.

Still no word from Patience. I can't say that I didn't think of her. I wondered how she was doing, what she was thinking and if I still crossed her mind every once in a while. Persistence told me that she inquired about me often but I couldn't tell if it was the truth or her trying to make me feel good. Patience was still with Monsieur and probably just as into her studies as I was into mine. I was no longer upset with her and I always told Persistence to extend my greetings and well wishes to her.

"You just made bond bud, you ready to go?" a guard asked me. The smile on his face almost convinced me for a hot second that he was actually happy to see me being released from ad-seg. I thought to myself that his smile probably had more to do with the fact that I would be stepping out of that cell for the first time without my wrists wearing restraints and he wanted to remind me that he was not one of the many guards who attempted to make my stay a living hell on earth.

"Yeah." I answered, grabbing my things. If it wasn't for Islam, he would have definitely had a whole lot to worry about. I didn't discriminate, whoever wore their uniform was a part of the same system I had grown to loathe, only my fear of Allah kept me from going upside his head.

"Stay up, Atif," my neighbor "Midnight" said as I walked by his cell. They called him such because the brother was so dark that if he was to stand next to a building at night passersby would mistake him for a dark alley. I slid some things I would no longer need underneath his cell door. "Right on, good lookin' out, bro."

"All praise is due to Allah," I told him. A lot of others; black, white and of other ethnic backgrounds shouted their well wishes to me as I made my way down the walk. I had been down in ad-seg for a long time, 20 months in all counting the time I spent under investigation and on bed space, 4 months shy of 2 years. They were going to miss me over there because whenever someone needed anything they could always depend on the young Muslim brother up in cell 266.

I paused briefly at the rotunda in 2 house to receive my new living arrangements along with a key so that I could lock myself into my cell every night. I stepped outside carrying a fan in one hand and a pillowcase full of my belongings in the other. I had lost some weight; the gray pants I got locked up wearing were a little too big for me in the waist. My T-shirt was dingy and my tennis shoes felt funny, but I was out of the hole at last. The feeling I felt while stepping out into that beautiful spring day was about the closest I would get to the feeling of actually being released from prison for still a while to come, but it was pretty close.

News of my being released from ad-seg had reached everyone I knew who was still at Moberly. There was a small crowd awaiting me on the front walk. I saw people in red; people wearing kufis; a couple of people in all state grays with red bow ties; there was such diversity that I didn't know who to greet first. All of them had bright smiles on their faces, happy to see me after so long.

"*Collect calls to the tilt, sayin' how you changed! Oh you a Muslim now? No more dope game!*" Skooter-B rapped as I approached, quoting lyrics belonging to Tupac

Shakur. "Wha'sup, blood?" he greeted as he hugged me tightly.

"Wha'sup Skooter-B, man?   Wha'sup y'all?"   I greeted him and the hommies in return. It felt good to see them. "How y'all been doin'?"

"Aw man, we been chillin', passin' time," I nodded. "A, I know you a Muslim now, and I respect that, but if you need us blood all you got to do is holler and it's like that, you hear me?"

"Wha'sup? What you talkin' about?" I asked, perplexed. He was hinting at something, and I knew it.

"We all promised Siddiq that we was gone let him talk to you first so he'll let you know wha'sup." I peered at him and he smiled his gold smile at me. "We'll holler at you, man, go ahead and get yourself together."

At that moment I was approached by DeAnthony X and two other members of the Nation.   "As-salaamu alaykum, brother Atif!" DeAnthony X greeted, hugging me.

"Wa alaykum!" I returned the greeting and the hug.

"I must say that I was elated upon hearing the news of your submission to All Mighty God Allah. I missed you out here brother. Where did they put you at?"

"3 house."

"All praise is due to Allah. Can I get a few minutes of your time when you get a chance brother?"

"No doubt, insha Allah." I turned and headed down the walk towards Siddiq and five other Muslim brothers from the community who had been waiting patiently for their turn.

"As-salaamu alaykum Atif!" Siddiq greeted, hugging me. I returned both the greeting and the hug. "This here is brother Taj Malik, Rafeeq, Sabir, Abdullah and Muhsin." We all exchanged greetings and introductions. We then headed towards 3 house as a group.

"Feels good stepping out of the old dungeon, huh?" Taj Malik asked me.

"Yeah man, it does."

"All praise is due to Allah."

"Atif, there is-" Siddiq started but was cut off by Pastor Cool Breeze shouting from across the yard.

"Brother Atif!"

"Excuse me Siddiq," I then turned towards Pastor Cool Breeze. "Wha'sup Pastor Cool Breeze?"

"Same old soup, just warmed over!" Pastor Cool Breeze responded. I laughed softly. "You see all of these thermometers out here?" he asked, spreading his arms. I nodded. "I expect you to be that *thermostat*, you hear me?"

"Yeah!" Pastor Cool Breeze threw up his right hand and I did the same. "What was you sayin' brother?" I asked Siddiq, pausing at the beginning of 3 house's walkway.

"When I was in ad-seg with you, you told me about an individual who claimed responsibility for the death of your mother. Well....he's here."

"*Kev*? Kev is up here?"

"His name is Khalid."

"*KHALID*?"

Siddiq nodded, looking into my eyes. "He too is a Muslim now."

*****

Kev. If it wasn't one thing it was another. I allowed Siddiq to talk me into agreeing to a temporary truce agreement until after Jumu'ah, the Friday Muslim prayer service the following day. I was hesitant, but gave my word before parting the brothers' company. I then went into 3 house and put my things away.

My new celly was an older brother who was not at Moberly when I went to the hole back in '98. He ran a store and I purchased the ingredients I needed from him on credit in order to make myself a big plate of the nachos I had been fantasizing about while in ad-seg. I did so in part celebrating my release from the hole; but also wanted to eat at least one nice meal because there as a good chance that I would be going right back.

I didn't know what to think honestly. I knew that I was being tested and up to that point in my Deen (religion) I had been passing every test taken through. I didn't feel

446

so confident about this one though. I had come a long way and the last thing I wanted to do was backslide. I had developed humility and the ability to control my anger; to overlook things.

But at the same time this was not some smart remark coming from one of the guards. This dude killed my mother! Killed her, took her from me and almost my only brother in the process. How was I *supposed* to feel about that? I had been yearning for the day our paths would cross again but I had not been anticipating Islam. Not only that, but *his* being a Muslim definitely played no role in my pre-Islamic plans of torturing him. And according to my studies, his being Muslim introduced a set of rules into the situation that once were not there.   Especially since all of this transpired *before* our acceptance.

I woke up the next morning actually feeling good. I had never been to Al-Jumu'ah services and I was anxious to experience it for the first time. After praying I sat in the darkness letting my mind wander until breakfast was called. When I made my way from 3 house to the main walk, I joined Siddiq and Muhsin who were waiting for me.

"You ain't never been to Jumu'ah have you?" Muhsin asked me after we all exchanged greetings.

"No, I've read about it though."

The three of us made our way into the cafeteria and stood in line. I greeted a few brothers that I didn't see out on the yard when I got out of the hole the day before as we slowly made our way to the serving line. I found myself surveying the cafeteria for my childhood nemesis; I didn't see him. I saw Skooter-B and some of the hommies, they all nodded at me. I hadn't seen Concrete since that day in the visiting room and I was preoccupied with a quick search for him when I heard Siddiq.

"As-salaamu alaykum brother."

I looked up to see who it was that he was greeting and almost didn't recognize him. It was Kev, standing on the serving line putting pancakes on the trays. He wore a black T-shirt and his muscular forearms were full of tattoos. His trademark scowl was no longer there on his face and I could see that he had spent a lot of time pumping iron over the last 5 years or so.

"Wa alaykum as-salaam," Kev returned, placing four pancakes instead of two on Siddiq's tray. "How you brothas be this mornin'?" he then asked, placing four pancakes on Muhsin's tray as well. His words were muffled by the beard guard he was wearing but I could hear that his voice had acquired some bass in it over time.

"All praise is due to Allah. Thank you and may He reward you with the good." Muhsin said, pleased with the extras.

I was next in line. We looked into each other's eyes for a second; a second that felt like minutes. I actually contemplated jumping over the serving line and going to work on him. Out of fear of Allah, I restrained myself. I slid my tray across the open space between us and he placed four pancakes on my tray like he had done for the brothers before me. I nodded in acknowledgment of his action and moved on down the line. That was the best I could offer at the time, considering all. There were no Islamic greetings of peace and paradise between us but his giving me those extra pancakes and my nod alone spoke volumes.

Kev had grown up as well. Seeing him for the first time since the county was strange because I didn't feel that old sense of rage seep into my chest that I had grown so accustomed to over the years. My thoughts of jumping over that counter at him were more instinctive than anything else.

I sat down at a table with Siddiq, Muhsin and another Muslim brother by the name of "Bashir" that I was just then meeting for the first time. After greetings and introductions I went to work buttering my pancakes. Siddiq looked at the extra pancakes on my tray and smiled to himself.

"Alhamdu lillah."

*****

When the yard opened later on that morning at 8:30, I spent the majority of it standing in a long line at the property room, along with others who were recently released from ad-seg, waiting to get my property. By the time my name was called only 45 minutes or so remained before the yard was to be shut down so I decided to go in and get myself and all of my belongings situated in the cell before my celly came in. After this I spent a couple of hours reading my Qur'an, skipped the mystery meat they were serving for lunch, and then went over some material I had concerning Al-Jumu'ah service and how one was to conduct himself during it. I then took a shower and by the time the yard opened again at 1:30, I was ready.

Stepping out of the housing unit I saw more Muslims than I thought were in Moberly as they made their way to the All Faiths Chapel coming from all directions. The atmosphere within it was one of serenity. There were no crucifixes or any images for that matter hanging anywhere on the walls. The set up was very simple. There were four rows of prayer rugs laid out next to each other facing the east, a wooden podium, and seats in the back for guest.

I found myself an open rug on the right end of the front row and prayed a quick prayer in respect of the Masjid (house of worship). I then sat back and listened to one of the brothers as he gave the call to prayer in Arabic. His voice was beautiful and I took a mental note to compliment him as soon as I got the chance. I was too self-conscious about my voice to do so in front of the whole prison yard like he did.

I spent the next 15 minutes sitting quietly taking in my surroundings as the rugs filled up to capacity. There were so many Muslims! A fifth row had to be added in order to accommodate them all. They came in all shapes and sizes; white, black, Cuban, Mexicano, you name it. No one spoke, they all came in, removed their shoes and prayed as I did before having a seat. Everyone wore their best clothing and smelled of men's cologne. I saw people that I knew were serving so much time that their parole officers had not even been born yet, but still they came turning in repentance to the Creator and seeking His forgiveness and His forgiveness alone. Society would *never* forgive them no matter how much time they did.

I saw Kev come in with his hair in two thick, neat cornrows. He took off his shoes and found an empty rug somewhere behind me. I could see that he too was focused solely on the worship of Allah and I doubted if he even noticed me watching him. I must admit, he looked....mature and I surmised that this was far from his first Jumu'ah service. I couldn't help but wonder if he was begging Allah to forgive him for what he had done to my mother and Malik in the prayer he was offering. But then again, if he had come to the Deen wholeheartedly then maybe he had already been forgiven like the Prophet said.

Siddiq approached the podium and the brother who gave the first call to prayer did so again. Standing behind the podium, Siddiq greeted the Muslim ranks and then the guests in the back. He then began his sermon with praising Allah and asking Him to bless His Messenger Muhammad. He read a few verses from the Qur'an and then warned the community about innovating within the Deen of Islam and the punishment for doing so.

His sermon was a powerful one about brotherhood and forgiveness. So much so that I felt butterflies in my stomach by the time he concluded the first part of the sermon, kneeling behind the podium to beg Allah's forgiveness for any mistakes he may have made in the duration of it, and then rising to begin the second part.

This portion of his sermon blew me away. At times I felt afraid, ashamed, guilty, stubborn, and ungrateful; then I felt blessed, chosen, guided, confident, and pure elation. The brother took me on a *ride*. I was not the only one, the brother to my left had a tear or two coming from his eyes. I honestly had to put forth an effort to control my own. Siddiq summed up his sermon with a question that I could have sworn was directed solely at me and Kev:

"The Muslim Ummah (community) is a *Brotherhood*. Prophet Muhammad said that a Muslim is the *brother* of another Muslim. Will you not then love your brother and show forgiveness to him solely for the sake of Allah?"

After a few announcements Siddiq requested for me, Kev and the security personnel to remain behind after the congregational Salah. The brother gave a shortened version of the harmonic call to prayer and the Muslims stood, squeezing tightly together shoulder to shoulder, heel to heel with our hands down to our sides forming the prayer ranks. Siddiq walked through the ranks examining them, making adjustments here and there.

"Step up to the front brother," Siddiq instructed someone behind me. There was room for one more person on my right side. The brother was hesitant. "Go ahead akhee (my brother), it's alright. Prophet Muhammad said that there are blessings in the front row."

Kev stepped up beside me on the front row. My body tensed unconsciously as he anchored his left heel to my right heel and our shoulders touched. I suspected that Siddiq had done that on purpose and to tell the truth I didn't like it very much at all. I was not going to let it bother me, at least not right then. I had come with the intent to worship Allah; all other emotions and the like would have to wait until later. On that note, I went into my zone.

Siddiq led the community with his slow melodic recitation. I could see that he had memorized some more chapters from the Qur'an because I was unfamiliar with the ones he recited. I remained seated after the prayer was over and said: All praise is due to Allah and glorified is Allah 33 times each, and then Allah is the greatest 34 times. I then rose, seeing that Kev was still supplicating and approached the brother who had given the calls to prayer.

"As-salaamu alaykum!" I greeted the brother.

"Wa-alaykum as-salaam brother!" he answered, smiling. "You are Atif, right?"

"Yeah," I answered, nodding. "You give a real nice athaan man. I ain't never heard nobody chant it like that before."

"The praise belongs to Allah."

Someone was tapping me on my shoulder. I turned and saw that Siddiq was trying to get my attention. He waved me over and I excused myself, heading in his direction.

"Did you enjoy your first Jumu'ah service?" Siddiq asked me after we embraced each other.

"Yeah man, I loved it. I was feelin' that Khutbah (sermon) too."

"Alhamdu-lillah." Siddiq then wrapped his arm around my shoulders. "I would like to introduce you to the community, do you mind?" Actually I did, but I played along, not wanting to be difficult. "As-salaamu Alaykum!" Siddiq said in an elevated voice. The room fell silent as over 100 people's attention focused on us. "This brother here is a young *beautiful* brother who accepted this Deen while over in ad-seg. Many of you have heard about him on account of my inability to stop talking about him," he paused as some of the brothers laughed. "As for those who have not, his name is Atif and I want you to give this good brother your warmest welcome to this community, insha Allah."

I was amazed by what happened next. The brothers assembled themselves in a line before me that curved all the way around the chapel. They then approached me one by one, embracing me and introducing themselves. I was so lost in the moment that before I knew it Kev was standing before me.

"As-salaamu alaykum," he greeted. We shook hands and embraced in a loose and uncomfortable fashion. Mostly on my part. "May Allah accept your prayers." He whispered in my ear while doing so. He then turned and left my presence without another word. It was then that I noticed I had not returned his greeting and I felt a little bit guilty about it. The Qur'an specifically commands for us to return a greeting with one that is better or at least its equal.

Within 30 more minutes the chapel was clear of all except for those of us Siddiq asked to remain behind. It was a beautiful day outside and members from the Nation began to trickle in to set up for their own services, so Siddiq suggested that we all walk the track. It was me, Kev, Siddiq, and four members of the security staff. Once we reached the basketball courts Siddiq stopped.

"Brothers, I really don't have much more to say outside of what was said during the khutbah. I pray that the both of you will at least consider some of the things uttered because it was your situation that inspired the sermon I gave.

"From what I have heard thus far, you brothers have some *serious* issues that needs to be dealt with. I want you to think about something though: neither of you are no longer the individuals you used to be. I can't tell you what to do because I have never been in your shoes, but Prophet Muhammad forbade for two Muslims to go for three days without speaking to each other. So you have three days to deal with this and if the both of you are still standing when the smoke clears then you will have to be *brothers*; no longer enemies. And if one of you wishes to remain the aggressor after the other has sought peace then it is *obligatory* for the whole community to side with the peace seeker. I can't say that it is *forbidden* for the two of you to seek retribution for your losses, but what I will say is that it would be nearer to piety for you to *forgive*.

"I will be glad to mediate between you but there will be no rocking each other to sleep. Whatever you decide on is what you will *stand* on. Understood?" Me and Kev nodded. "Let's walk."

We hit the track. Me and Kev made up the first row, Siddiq and the chief of security the second, so on and so forth. Other inmates on the yard peered at us, curious as to what was going on. I saw Skooter-B and a few of the hommies working out and Concrete was walking the track in the opposite direction listening to his headphones. We walked in silence for two whole laps, neither of us knowing where to begin.

"Wa alaykum as-salaam." I said, breaking the silence. Kev looked at me. "I was returnin' your greetin' from earlier, I didn't mean to be rude. It was just that the last time we stood before each other without anything between us like that was-"

"When we was about to fight at the school dance back in'92; I remember. I was tauntin' Patience." Kev cut

453

in. He then shook his head. "I was somethin' else, always tryin' to start somethin'. Is she still ridin'?"

"No, she jumped out of the car on me a few years or so ago."

"Yeah, it be like that sometimes."

"What about Ranita, what happened with you and her?" I asked.

"Time." We both chuckled softly, understanding. His one word reply pretty much said it all for the both of our past relationships.

"What did y'all have?" I asked him.

"A boy, his name is Ke'von." Kev answered. "I ain't never seen him though. She moved away to Greensboro North Carolina with some old head before I even got sentenced. She used to write here and there but that ceased not too long after. She never did get around to sendin' me no pictures of him." Kev was silent for a few steps, probably thinking about his son. "Is it true what I heard about your hommie D-Mack?"

"Yeah." I answered with a sigh.

"That's messed up."

We went on with small talk for a while longer. I was trying to feel him out and see where he was at; if he had really changed from the Kev I once knew. I studied his conversation and could find no trace of the old immature troublesome adolescent that I grew up at odds with. I heard no cursing, no gang slurs or bragging, none of that. From what I could tell so far, his transformation was genuine. After coming to this conclusion I thought that it was time to get some answers. I didn't dress it up or sugar coat it; I came right out with it.

"Why did you kill my mama Kev? Why her?"

Kev looked at me. "*Khalid*, Atif. My name is Khalid." We stared at each other for a moment. He was right. I had no right refusing to recognize his Muslim attribute which in essence was like not acknowledging his *Islam*. From that moment forward I never referred to Khalid as "Kev" again. "I didn't mean to shoot her Atif, I didn't even *see* her. I was tryin' to hit *you* and I thought that I did because I could have sworn that you fell. I didn't

454

know that I had hit your mother instead until I saw the news the next day. And as much as I tried to hide it, as *heartless* as I tried to act about it in front of everybody else, I was never able to...I don't know man. I can't even begin to express how sorry I am about what I did, about how stupid that was."

"But *why* man? Why was y'all there in the *first* place? What did we do to y'all that was so bad?"

"I was bein' initiated. I was supposed to kill Malik but when he survived they went on and let me in since your mother died. He said that was even better."

Rage seeped into my chest.

"Who?"

"La'Ron. He was drivin'. I think it was all about Malik knockin' him out like he did at Skate Land in front of all them people."

"Is La'Ron a Muslim too now?"

"No." Khalid answered shortly, looking at me. I believe he understood that he had just signed La'Ron's death warrant. "Wherever you want to take this Atif, I understand. I know that all you have to do is tell Malik what I just told you and then La'Ron, along with everything that we both love, will die a slow death. If you want to knife up and get down like that, I will understand that too. I know that you are a rider and to be honest I always respected that about you. But like I said man, it's up to you and however you want to handle this. I just felt like you should know the truth, you *deserve* that. Whatever it costs me, La'Ron or whoever else then so be it. No harm will come to me that has not already been decreed by Allah. I just want to let the truth be told and turn my face towards Him in repentance because I believe that's what He wants me to do."

I let some time pass before I said anything. Really there was not a whole lot left for me to consider because I had made my mind up before the conclusion of Siddiq's khutbah. I knew my options and I knew what I could have done with a mere phone call. But what would that solve? I was not going to tell my brother about Khalid because he would not be able to accept or even comprehend what I was about to do. But La'Ron? He could kiss the baby.

In Islam there are four steps to repentance: Step #1 is to give up the sin itself. Step #2 is to feel remorseful over what has been done. Step #3 is to have a firm resolve not to repeat it again. Step #4 is to compensate. This is how a Muslim obtains forgiveness and Khalid had already shown me that he had taken the first 3 steps. The fourth step was one to be worked out later. La'Ron? He hadn't even began to *think* about any of the steps listed above and because of that Malik would be over to holler at him. Forgiveness comes only with sincere repentance to the Creator and since Khalid was earnestly striving for that, who was I not to acknowledge it?

"Look at all these spectators," I began, looking around the yard. I then looked at Khalid. "They don't even know what's goin' on with us but we have their undivided attention. They just want to see somebody get hurt; somethin' they can run around the camp gossipin' about like old women."

"Yeah, I'm hip."

"I'm tired man. I'll be 22 this year, insha Allah, and I'm just...tired." I started, shaking my head. "How long we been feudin'?"

Khalid whistled. "At least 13 years, ever since *elementary* school."

"And for what? Because I grew up on 27th street and you on 24th?" I shook my head. "That don't make no sense man." We walked in thoughtful silence. "It ain't nothin' you can do that's gone bring my mama back or take away my brother's limp. Nor is it anything I can do that's gone bring your hommie back to life and remove that bullet hole I put in your arm." Khalid instinctively grabbed his arm where I had shot him.

"Man that bullet hurt like a mug too." Khalid said, caressing his wound. He then began to chuckle softly. I joined in, unable to contain myself.

"I apologize for that brotha'." I said, smiling at him.

"It's cool Atif man, I ain't trippin'."

456

"Like I was sayin' though, goin' to war ain't gone change nothin'. It got to stop somewhere. I ain't gone tell Malik that you was with La'Ron that night but as for La'Ron..."

"I understand."

"I don't want to go there with you Khalid. I know that you are a rider too and I have always respected that about you as well. But, I ain't into funkin' no more if it ain't in Allah's cause. Us stabbin' each other up or whatever ain't gone change what we did to each other so why not forgive each other? That's all that remains in my mind! Plus, like Siddiq was sayin', now that we both are Muslims man that makes us *brothers*, not enemies. Islam nullifies all that enmity we been harborin' over the years. So whatever emotions, ill feelins and whatever else that needs to be sacrificed in order to bring Allah's will into manifestation then I'm for that."

"Do you mean that, Atif?" Siddiq asked me from behind, speaking up for the first time. I had almost forgotten the brothers were even back there.

"Yeah, I mean that."

"What about you Khalid? Do you feel the same way? Are you willing to do what it takes to forgive your brother for his transgressions against you?" Siddiq asked.

"Yeah, I'm willin' to do that."

"I asked that for a reason," Siddiq started. We stopped and turned to face him. "May Allah reward you for your intentions, but what you two young brothers have just established is actually far from forgiveness. An *armistice* of sorts, but not forgiveness." Me and Khalid looked at each other. "Now if you really wish to *forgive* each other you must wipe the slate clean and start all over, rebuilding a new relationship between the both of you on top of a new and pure foundation. You have to get to know each other as *Muslims* for the sake of Allah. That is how you become *brethren*."

"You know this dude Atif?" Khalid asked me as Concrete passed on the far end of the pavement. Concrete began to bob his head in exaggeration to whatever he was listening to, mugging me. He had been doing so every time he walked by us since we first got on the track but I had been ignoring him.

"Yeah, I know him." I answered.

"Why he keep lookin' at you like he got somethin' on his mind?" Khalid asked me after staring him down. I saw that old scowl that I once knew on his face for the first time in a long time. I smiled because this time it was not directed at me but in defense of me. We were becoming brothers already.

"I'll tell you about that later, insha Allah." Khalid looked at me, so did Siddiq as well. I only smirked in response. Siddiq shook his head.

"Anyway, what I was saying is that if you brothers want to learn how to forgive each other I can show you how."

"How?" Both Khalid and I asked in unison. Siddiq paused for a moment before answering.

"You can begin by moving into a cell with each other, insha Allah."

*****

9/11

"I hear missiles whistle through the sky,
get off of the floor!
When they hit we all will die,
so what are you runnin' for?
I see a one world religion
underway,
headed by the government
they don't want to see us pray
-and across the way- They're fightin' an oil based war,
only the blind can't see,
what you're *really* over there for.
Does it have to be
So many people cryin' and bleedin'
Because they stood up
For what they believe in?"
            -*Soody Mak*

23

"Inmate number 5-3-0-3-1-7, report to the rotunda; you have a visit!" I heard the rotunda officer say over the intercom for the third time. Khalid and I were in the middle of offering the late afternoon prayer together so the c.o. and my visitor(s) would have to wait just a couple of more minutes.

A year had gone by since Khalid and I agreed to move into a cell together for the sake of Allah. To say that we got along is an understatement, we had become brothers. Growing up, we never gave each other a chance to get to know each other on any level and come to find out we had been missing out on something wonderful that should have been established almost a decade and a ½ ago.

Of course it was a little awkward at first but once we really began to open up to each other and feel comfortable in each other's presence we became the best of friends quickly. So much so that we did everything together. We prayed together, ate together, worked out together, studied together, played handball together, everything we did and everywhere we went people hardly saw one of us without the other.

Darion passed on from complications of the AIDS virus and it devastated me. But at the same time it felt as if Allah was taking my best friend away from me but out of His infinite mercy providing me with another one. It was amazing to discover how much the two of us had in common. We even had the same favorite movie: Harlem Nights.

Khalid had been doing hard time. He was not in touch with any of his family members or so-called friends from the streets. He didn't get visits and had absolutely no money coming in to him from the outside so he survived off of the food served in the cafeteria and the $15.00 a month he made working in the kitchen. Out of fear of Allah and piety he stayed away from "hustling" and made due with that which Allah ordained for him to have.

His only appliance was a fan that he had saved up a couple of his "state tips" to purchase. This didn't bother him though, he told me that many of those things were a distraction to him anyway and that he would rather spend his time studying than glued to a television set.

When we moved into the cell together it took a while for him to feel welcome enough to treat my appliances as if they were his. The man would literally ask me if he could turn the radio on! After a couple of weeks I was able to convince him that he didn't need to *ask* me for anything; that what I had was his and he had free access to everything in between.

When two people are in prison living in a cell together that are compatible with each other they become close and learn more about each other in a matter of months than most people do in *years*. This is because you are forced to spend more time together than a lot of married couples do. You learn personal things about your celly that others probably wouldn't know. Everything from what foods he enjoys and what makes him laugh to whether or not he clips his toenails.

"Have a nice visit man, insha Allah." Khalid said, rolling up our prayer rugs after we concluded Salah. I nodded, putting my shoes on.

The visiting room was pretty empty. There were a few couples spread out here and there and only one person from ad-seg using the non-contact booths.

"*ATIF!*" Destiny shouted in glee, jumping from her seat and running over to me. I stooped down and caught her in my arms.

"Hey Suga Bear!" I said, hugging her tightly. She was so tiny, even for her age.

"Hi!" she said as I released her.

"As-salaamu alaykum!"

"Wa a-lay-kum as-salaam!" Destiny said, returning the greeting I had taught her. "Guess what?" she said as we headed over to where Malik was seated.

"What?"

"I went to Worlds of Fun!"

"Really?" Destiny nodded, smiling up at me. "Did you have fun?"

"Yes."

The prison officials would not allow Malik on my visiting list until 24 months after he was released from the supervision of his probation. He began to show up accompanied by Destiny on a weekly basis not too long afterwards, which was right around Darion's passing. Before then I had not seen my brother in 6 years, ever since I left the county jail back in August of 1995.

He looked pretty much the same outside of a few extra pounds and facial hair. He still had braids in his hair which by then were crawling down to his solar plexus area. His hair was so long! He wore an expensive platinum necklace with his standard black jeans and white T-shirt with a white wife-beater beneath it.

"Wha'sup lil' bro?" Malik greeted me with a smile revealing the $10,000 worth of platinum and diamonds he had done on his upper row of teeth.

"Wha'sup?" I returned.   There was no hugging Malik, he wasn't too much for demonstrations of affection. And this was strange because I hugged Muslims in the joint on a regular basis. At least we no longer greeted each other using offensive nicknames. I then sat down opposite of him and Destiny.

"Destiny got some good news for you."   Malik looked down at Destiny giving her permission to tell me.

"Wha'sup?" I asked her.

"Mis-ter Jaco got your sen-ten-ces ran con-cur-rent-ly so now you don't have to be in jail for too long." Destiny said smiling at me. My stomach dropped. I looked at my brother and he smirked.

"For real?" I asked. Destiny looked up at Malik and he nodded. I wanted to *scream*! I wanted to jump up into the air and click my heels together like Dorothy from the Wizard of Oz! I had long ago given up hope on such and had actually accepted my predicament. Finally, some *good* news for once. I bottled up my excitement for the moment. "All praise is due to Allah."

"You should be gettin' somethin' in the mail sayin' the same thing but Destiny wanted to tell you herself first. You should be out by 2005-2006." Malik said. Destiny got up and came over to my side of the table. I wrapped my arm around her shoulders and kissed her on the forehead.

"Insha Allah." I said.

"In-shaa A-llah." Destiny repeated.

"Yeah, all that. If you want anybody else to know then *you* tell them." Malik said. "Anyway, I saw your girl the other day."

"Patience?"

"Who else?" he asked sarcastically in return. Ole Malik hadn't changed a bit.

"What was she talkin' about?"

"*You.*"

"Aw yeah?" I asked smiling.

"Is Pa-tience real-lly your girl-friend?" Destiny asked me.

"No Destiny, she isn't. She used to be though." I answered.

"Aw," her only response.

"She can't picture you bein' a Muslim, strivin' for...*righteousness* like you be doin' now. Man the broad asked me 50 questions in a row." Malik said.

"Questions like what?"

"What are you like? Do you still *talk* the same? Do you ever ask about her? Are you *mad* at her still? Do you *look* the same? *Damn*! I went on and shook her man, she was gettin' on my nerves." Malik said. Destiny giggled.

"Wha'sup with that Monsieur dude; she still with him?"

"Monsieur is....missin'."

"*Missin*?" Malik nodded.

"She mad at Smack Man about that too because she think that he done put some work in on him."

"Why would he do somethin' to him?"

"Man, Smack Man been leery of that dude for the longest. I kind of saw why for myself when *I* met him. I got a sense that the dude is *older* than he claim to be. His eyes is too *intelligent.* He is too aware of his surroundins for somebody who ain't never been to prison and ain't ridin' down the filthy route. Which in my mind, and Smack Man's, only leads to one last conclusion."

"He the *police*." I said. Malik nodded.

"When I met him it felt like I was bein' sized up by him when he shook my hand, you know what I'm sayin'?" I nodded. "Like he was takin' mental note of everything from the color of my eyes all of the way down to my shoe size. I bet the dude could probably tell if I was strapped or not. I didn't think he was to be trusted either but Patience wasn't tryin' to hear nothin'."

"Smack Man had him checked out and he came up clean, *too* clean. He ain't even got a *traffic* ticket on his record. So then Smack Man had his house swept and come to find out *somebody* been plantin' bugs all over his crib."

"Whaaat?"

"They comin' for us Atif, I *know* they are. I can *feel* it. K-Red and them think I'm bein' paranoid but I ain't crazy blood. I think he was an undercover Federal agent and If I'm right then the *fit* is finna hit the shan." Malik said, mixing up the letters for the purpose of watching his language around Destiny. I noticed that he had just referred to Monsieur in the past tense. If I knew my brother he had a lot to do with Monsieur's disappearance. "I'm finna roll out lil' bro."

I looked at him. "What do you mean?"

"What I said."

"I mean, where to?" Malik paused for a second.

"I was thinkin' maybe Haiti or Libya."

"What you gone do then?"

"Disappear in the chaos they got goin' on over there." I shook my head in disbelief. He was all of the family I had left and now even *he* was talking about leaving me.

"Why don't you just *quit*?"

"It is probably too late for that." Malik then smiled soothingly. "I would rather be there than in the Feds. I would have *been* gone but I was hangin' around to fix Mama's house up for you and make sure you didn't have to do all of that time. But now it's time for me to bounce. You are a man now and you can take care of yourself. You livin' your new way of life and all that, which is cool, so all you have to do is stay focused and you will be straight." I nodded. "I'll be in touch, some way, and if you want to come and holler at me when you get out then that will be cool. But I don't know if I am ever comin' back man."

"I'm hun-gry Atif." Destiny said. I rose from my chair, taking her by the hand.

"You need to talk to her while you are at it man because she be talkin' bad to Teebaby, which is who she get it from. You are the only person she will listen to since..." Malik trailed off, catching himself.

I allowed Destiny to lead me to the vending machines. We got her a candy bar, some chips and a Sprite. After which I kneeled down before her.

"What is this Malik is talkin' about Suga Bear? Why are you bein' disrespectful towards your mother?" Destiny's bottom lip protruded from her face instantly as she lowered her gaze. My friend's daughter was a very sensitive little girl.

"Be-cause, she is...she is *mean* to me! And, and...she be get-ting on my *nerves*!" Destiny spat, tears shining in her eyes. That little girl was Teebaby all over again.

"Look at me Destiny," I started, gently lifting her chin with my finger. I then looked her in the eyes; Darion's eyes. "That does not give you the right to be mean to her in return. Allah don't like it when you talk back to your mother like that. Do you want to hear what Allah says?" Destiny nodded her head as a tear slid slowly down her cheek. She was fascinated with the verses of the Qur'an.

"And your Lord has decreed that you worship none but Him. And that you be *dutiful* to your parents. If one of them or both of them attain old age in your life, say not to them a *word* of disrespect, nor *shout* at them but address them in terms of *honor*. And lower unto them thy wing of submission and humility through mercy, and say: My Lord! Bestow on them your Mercy as they did bring me up when I was young." I then wiped the tear from her face. "Now, do you want to hear what Allah says about those who do this?" Destiny nodded once again. "They are those from whom We shall accept the best of their deeds and overlook their evil deeds. (They shall be) among the dwellers of Paradise-a promise of truth, which they have been promised." Destiny grinned. "Do you want to go to Paradise after you die?"

"Yes."

"Well then do what Allah says and treat your mother with respect, okay?"

"Okay."

"I love you Suga Bear." I said smiling.

"I love you too Atif."

"Can I have a hug?" Destiny nodded, wrapping her small arms around my neck.

"Atif?" she started, squeezing me tightly.

"Wha'sup?"

"Is my da-ddy in Pa-ra-dise?"

*****

"Atif!" I opened my eyes, startled a bit. It was the morning of September 11, 2001. "Atif, wake up man!"

"Wha'sup?" I asked, rising to a sitting position.

"Look man, look!" Khalid said, pointing at the television.

The first thing I saw was what looked like the tail end of an airplane protruding from one of the World Trade Center Twin Towers. Billows of smoke were rising in the air. I turned off the caption and turned the volume up.

"How do you accidentally run into one of the tallest buildings in New York?" I asked Khalid after listening to the reporters for a few minutes.

"That wasn't an accident brotha'." Khalid commented, looking at me.

"You don't think so?" I asked, looking at the screen. "Look! There go *another* one!" I exclaimed, seeing yet another airplane come flying into view. It was not a small airplane either. These were big passenger planes. We looked on as the airplane seemed to be turning in a wide arch heading directly for the other Twin Tower building *deliberately*. The plane then crashed into the upper portion of the building, engulfing it along with the structure in flames. My first thought was trying to estimate how many people I had just witnessed lose their lives on national television.

We spent some time watching the television in silence. The whole wing was doing the same. The noise level within the housing unit was usually deafening, even at that time of morning, but that day a mouse could be heard urinating on cotton.

I felt confused at first, baffled and wondering what was going on. I saw so many people running, screaming and crying with terrified looks on their faces. People of all races and genders. They were covered in a gray like substance and to me resembled a bunch of ghosts, all with cellular phones held up to their ears.

There was another emotion I felt that didn't come into play until after the hijacking suspects were being pasted all over the television screen. This feeling was similar to the way I felt when me and Kesha were at the Landing Mall back in '92 and I looked out of the store seeing all of those Crips waiting for us to come out; when I was about to be pounced on for no real apparent reason. I just knew in my heart that I was not going to make it out of that building unscathed.

But this time the Glamourama store doors were prison gates and the Rolling 60's was society waiting for me to walk out so that they could take their pain out on me. I think that every Muslim in America probably felt the same way. Discrimination, stereotypes, prejudices, you name it. But for the Black Muslims in America this was going to be nothing new to us because we of course had been experiencing such for centuries and we were more than familiar with it.

The fit was about to hit the shan.

*****

My brother was gone. The 9/11 attacks was just what Malik needed in order for him, along with K-Red and Antoinette, to slip out of the country amidst all of the

468

confusion. Afterwards a handful of indictments came down and the Feds snatched Smack Man, Persistence, Money Mike, Trigga, and 30 others (most of whom I didn't even know) up off of the streets from different cities and states across America. My brother and Smack Man had been right all along, Monsieur *was* an undercover Federal agent and his whole relationship with Patience was a set up, all pre-planned from the beginning. He was playing her the whole time.

    Monsieur's body had still not been found.

    Malik was wanted not only by the feds, but the state police wanted to question him in the bizarre torture/murder of La'Ron. Reading in the Kansas City Star about the condition La'Ron's mangled corpse was discovered in made me wonder if my brother had lost the best part of his mind. It took someone with a few sandwiches short of a picnic basket to do what was done to La'Ron, even if it was in retaliation for his role in my mother's death.

    I assumed that Persistence would get out because I had never known her to get her hands dirty. But then again, why had they snatched her up in the first place? Was it possible for her to go to prison because her *husband* was a drug dealer? Sure the lap of luxury she enjoyed was furnished with blood money but so was every single red cent that the rich continent of the United States possessed.

    I wrote to Patience. I felt for her because I just knew that she felt like everything was her fault for ever letting Monsieur get up on her like she did. I didn't blame her though, the man was a professional and Patience never stood a chance. He used her and I could only imagine how the situation was affecting her. She genuinely loved the dude and I am sure that her heart was broken by his betrayal, let alone everything else. Patience did not respond to my letter.

    I had been pretty much on skid row since everything began. With my brother gone and the hommies locked up, I no longer had any money coming in. I was content though and didn't let it bother me. I could have asked Kesha to look out for me but I couldn't bring myself to.

I missed Destiny dearly. I wrote to her weekly in high hopes that Teebaby would bring her up to visit. She didn't. I took comfort in me and Destiny's little secret: I wouldn't be doing as much time as everyone thought.

"Wha'sup brotha'? What were they talkin' about?"

Khalid had just left a meeting with the institutional parole officer. He went up to see the parole board just months before 9/11 and he was given an out date. His being summoned again all of a sudden worried him because it could only mean bad news.

"They didn't take my date but they might as well had because they are talkin' about since I don't have a home plan I have to go to the Honor Center and the waitin' list is so long that it could be another year or so after my parole date before they get to me."

"A *year*? What do they mean another year?" I was very disappointed. I had been looking forward to seeing the brother get out of prison. Khalid only shrugged his shoulders in response. His face was flushed and I could see that he was struggling to restrain his anger. "Do you *have* to go to the Honor Center?"

"Yeah Atif, I don't have anywhere else to go."

We walked in silence for a while, heading towards the canteen. I smiled as an idea took shape in my mind and then cursed myself for not thinking of it earlier.

"If you had the chance to be a reason why the angels record a good deed in my favor, would you jump at that chance?"

"Of course man, you know that."

"Why don't you go and live in *my* house?" Khalid stopped in his tracks, searching my face.

"Are you serious?" I nodded. "Your *mother's* house?" I smiled in response. "No man, I can't do that. I can't live there."

"You mean to tell me that you would rather stay here for an extra year?"

470

"With you? Yeah. I'm not in no hurry to part ways with you brotha'."

I was touched. We had become closer than we or anyone else ever could have imagined. "That's cool man, and honestly I feel the same way. But it would be selfish of me to allow you to stay here when Allah has provided you with an opportunity to get out. Take *advantage* of that. Plus, it ain't no tellin' what could transpire within a year's time in this unpredictable and explosive environment brotha', you know that. You could mess around and catch a fresh life sentence behind one of these infidels."

"Yeah, I know."

"Accept my act of kindness so that the angels will record it as a good deed in my favor, insha Allah. We both know that my scales are lackin' and I got a lot of catchin' up to do." Khalid laughed.

"Me too man, me too."

"Malik told me he fixed it up, but knowin' him he was probably bein' modest. It ain't no tellin' what he done did to that house. Anyway, all you have to do is get the utilities turned on and hold the fort down until I get out, insha Allah. Ain't neither one of us got any family out there for real so we can stay there together. What's mine is yours brotha', me cassa tu-cassa."

"I think you are mispronouncin' that phrase Atif."

"You know what I'm tryin' to say!" I said, pushing him lightly and throwing my dukes up. Khalid laughed. He then looked at me seriously.

"I appreciate this brotha', may Allah reward you with that which is good."

That is forgiveness.

The canteen area was packed. It was state tip week, the time of the month when everyone in the penitentiary had at least $7.50 to work with. All of the workers were issued their money this week also, usually around the fifteenth of every month.

Khalid and I found us a spot where we could place our backs against the wall. I had been leery of crowds in prison ever since Knockout warned me about them back in Fulton. Not only that, but I had witnessed a few incidents with my own eyes that took place under the cover of a crowded area myself.

There was tension in the atmosphere after the 9/11 attacks. Siddiq cautioned us to be on our toes because there was no telling what one of the white supremacist groups or some other individuals who had all of a sudden become "patriotic" might try. Up to then we as Muslims had not experienced nothing much more than some questioning glances and disrespectful comments on the sly. The most severe being a few attempted set-ups where some cowards had slid some knives under a few of the Muslims' cell doors and then dropped a kite on them sending the guards their way. The brothers always discovered the contraband first on their own before the guards were able to search their cells in response of the numerous kites, thwarting their frivolous attempts. I made it a point to search my cell thoroughly every time I stepped foot in it before closing the door and so did Khalid.

"I was watchin' that kafir on the 700 Club this mornin' and you know what he said?" Khalid asked me as we waited for my number to be called.

"What?"

"He said that Islam is an enemy that threatens freedom, democracy, and the American way of life." Khalid answered. I shook my head.

"I don't know why you be watchin' that show. It ain't gone do nothin' but upset you."

"Yeah, it does that. But it also exposes some of the citizens' mentalities to me who are like him that I will be dealing with when I am released from prison here shortly, insha Allah. Those with a disease in their hearts who are ignorant to our Deen. He be playin' on this and fillin' his followers' minds up with these ½ truths, takin' verses from the Qur'an and misinterpretin' them. He ain't the only one though. I will tell you why people like him are doin' this.

"Oppressive elements who want to have control over society paint a false picture of Islam because they are afraid of losin' their influence over the people at large. When people accept *Islam* as the source of guidance and influence in their lives, they free themselves from subservience to *any* human bein' and they *refuse* to be oppressed, exploited or dictated by those who desire misguidance over guidance, and prefer falsehood to truth.

"So what these so-called political leaders and monopolizers of industry, media and resources have to do is depict *Islam* as their enemy toward freedom and democracy and the American way of life. The only people threatened by Islam are those who would pull the wool over the eyes of the public and the thing is the Muslims ain't goin' for it! So for someone who has always had ill-intentions and evil designs on fairness, justice and equality, this is a dangerous attitude-fundamentalist, subversive they say. Watch what I tell you, insha Allah! They are gone label us as all these things and much more! But you know what? This attitude only subverts a *bully*.

"The only people who don't want to see Islam take root in so-called western society, or anywhere else for real, are those who don't want to lose what does not belong to them in the first place: hypnotic control of people's lives, people who have become slaves to fashion and passion, and have become blind to reality.

"So many people are livin' in a fantasy world.....eclipsed from the fact that this life is temporary, and full of attractions and distractions from the mission of the human being, which we both know is to fulfill his and her purpose for bein' created in the first place: to obey the Creator by worshippin' Him alone, not allowin' any *human* bein', any *concept*, any...style or anything else to enslave him or misguide him from the path to success in this temporary life, and the permanent, eternal life of the Hereafter.

"Man Islam is only an enemy to the enemies of Allah. The oppressive, exploitive, greedy, uncarin' misers who don't wish to see themselves as equal to people like me and you, people who want *true* liberty and *justice* for all, not just those with enough money to *pay* for it."

Khalid was riled up and his voice elevated as he drew people's attention to his words. Conversations ceased around us and people of all colors began to gather around.

"And the 9/11 attacks is gone give President Bush the excuse he needed to finish what his father started, believe that. Their money is in oil, so they gone go gain control of it under the guise of fightin' terrorism...."

My name was called and I made my way into the store, smiling as I went. I was proud of Khalid and he too had come a long way. I couldn't think of too many things that we didn't have in common or too many levels we couldn't relate to each other on.

I stepped up to the window in order to receive the small $4 bottle of cologne I had placed on my list along with a pint of ice cream each for me and Khalid. The cashier was a white woman in her fifties and she usually had a bad attitude. There was a small 13" color television on the shelf behind her and she was trying to do 2 things at once: watch the latest on the news concerning the 9/11 attacks and her job. I retrieved my items, signed and fingerprinted her copy of my receipt and exited the store area.

Khalid was finished with his speech, waiting for me on the sidewalk away from the crowded area in front of the canteen. I handed him a pint of ice cream as I approached.

"Thank you brotha'."

"Thank Allah."

"Alhamdu lillah."

"Man you was spittin'." I complimented, opening my own ice cream.

"More like ventin'." Khalid answered. Something was nagging at me. I retrieved my receipt from my pocket and examined it. "What's wrong?" Khalid asked me when my brow creased. I then held up the bottle of cologne.

"She didn't charge me for this."

"Her bad." Khalid commented. "Maybe it is a small blessin' from Allah."

I thought silently to myself for a moment, looking back at the canteen. Maybe Khalid was right, I sure could have used that 4 extra dollars. It was chump change in society but in prison an individual who knew what he was doing could eat for 3 days off of $4. But then again, maybe it was more like a small test from Allah. I then asked myself what everyone standing in front of the canteen would have done about the situation and decided to do the exact opposite; for I was to be not of that world.

"I'll be back, insha Allah." I turned and headed back to the store with my receipt and the bottle of cologne in my left hand. Once inside, I waited patiently for the cashier to finish with her current customer and then slipped up to the window before she had the chance to call another name. "Excuse me ma'am, can I talk to you for just a moment before you get started on someone else?"

The woman did everything but roll her eyes at me. "What is the problem?" She asked with an edge in her voice. I was tempted to turn and walk back out of there but I dismissed the thought. I held up the bottle of cologne.

"The problem is that I bought this bottle of cologne-"

"I don't see anything wrong with it." She cut me off rudely.

"Let me know when *I* can talk," Silence. I continued on. "What I was sayin' is that I bought this bottle of cologne," I started, setting the cologne down on the counter. Her eyes followed my every move as if I was attempting to pull a "switch-a-roo" on her. I then held up my receipt. "But you didn't charge me for it." She looked at me for 5 seconds.

"Let me *see* that." She said, sticking her hand out for my receipt without her eyes leaving mine. I handed it to her. She studied it for a moment and then looked up at me with a different look in her eyes; one that she probably gave to her co-workers and all of the other *humans* she encountered on a daily basis out in society. "This is a first." She then turned her head to the left. "Hey Barbara, come here a sec will ya'? You are not going to *believe* this!" She then turned back to me with a smile on her face. By Allah, I would have never thought that her lips were able to do such a thing. "Please forgive me for being rude. I have been through a lot within the past few weeks. I lost a son in one of the towers and I have been a real bitch lately."

You were one of those long before 9/11 lady, I thought to myself. "I ain't trippin'." I said. Actually I felt for her. I understood how it felt to lose and take from my own experiences.

"What is it?" Barbara asked, pulling up on the scene looking between us.

"This guy here purchases a \$4 bottle of cologne with the \$7.50 he has on his account. 5 minutes later he brings the bottle of cologne back, along with his receipt mind you, in order to inform me of the fact that I forgot to scan it."

Barbara looked at me, smiling. "Wow," was all she said. The cashier then grabbed the bottle of cologne and then handed it back to me.

"I'll tell you what, since you are so honest I want for you to keep it free of charge Mr..." she paused, looking on the receipt for my name. "Atif, is it?" I nodded.

"What kind of name is that?" Barbara asked me.

So it begins, I thought to myself.

"Atif is a Muslim name, it means compassionate."

"Are you a Moslem?" the cashier asked.

"A *Muslim*, yes I am."

All of the previous times in my life that I had been asked that question it used to irk me. But for the first time I was proud to answer it in the affirmative. Honestly, I expected for the smiles to disappear, especially from the face of the one who had lost her son; the smiles remained.

"Is there a difference between a Moslem and a Muslim?" the cashier asked.

"Moslem is just a mispronunciation, kind of like someone mispronouncin' your name." I answered, grabbing the bottle of cologne and my receipt. "Would it be too much to ask for a couple of spoons? I forgot to get some the first time." The cashier took a look at my ice cream which by then had melted. She then disappeared and returned seconds later with 2 spoons and a new frozen pint of ice cream.

"No, that's okay. I'm coo-"

"I *insist*." The cashier said, thrusting the items at me. I took them and handed her the old one.

"Thank you."

476

"No, thank you." The cashier said, leaning over the counter. "Thank you for reminding me that we should never take a few people who may misrepresent a certain religion and take them as an example of what that religion actually teaches and is about.

"Over the past 3 weeks I have grown to hate a group of people who represent a religion that I honestly don't know a thing about." She then shook her head and sighed. Barbara patted her on the back softly. "Losing my son has just been....ruff to say the least. But from now on I will not let what the television says about your religion mis-educate me because there is no way that your religion could be one that instructed those guys to do what they did and do something like what you just did with that bottle of cologne at the same time. It may not seem like a real significant act but it showed me a lot. I don't know a handful of God fearing Christians, myself included, that would have done the same. Especially considering the few dollars you have on your account. God bless you Atif."

"May Allah bless you too, with His guidance and His mercy. You ladies have a nice day." I said, turning to leave. I walked out of the canteen and handed Khalid a spoon.

"What happened?" he asked, digging into his ice cream.

"She told me to keep it."

Khalid chuckled. "See," he started, pointing his spoon in the direction of the canteen. "That right there is one of the reasons why I am in no hurry to part ways with you Atif, man you are somethin' else! I ain't never had a friend like you brotha'."

"Alhamdu lillah." We started walking, eating our ice creams. "You know what I just learned?" I asked Khalid.

"What?"

"The best way to combat these *false* images of Islam is to exemplify the true one."

"You think it's that simple?"

"Allah is the Best Knower, but yeah, I do."

*****

477

HE BOARD
"Why was my heart filled with anger
towards strangers you ask?
Why did I walk around with my smile upside down;
was I mad?
Why did I do the things I did
and think what I was thinkin'?
Was it Mary Jane messin' with my brain
mixed with some of that drinkin'?
NO! You can't peep a young black male like me
from a book,
or by referrin' to some kind of
psychology class that you took.
-Look- you already have me stereotyped
but you have me faded,
thinkin' that for the rest of *my* life
I will be incarcerated.
You hate it that I learned a way of life
submissive *only* to Jah.
I refuse to be your *slave* or your *nigger*,
The praise belongs to Allah!"
-Soody Mak

24

When I was a child my mother would take me, Darion, K-Red and my brother to an enormous theme park filled with rides, games and endless other activities called Worlds of Fun. While there I can recall wishing that time would stand still or at least pass by more slowly. I always knew that the park would be closing down within a matter of hours and all of the fun would come to an end. I dreaded that moment and no matter how much of my will power I exerted in order to make the earth start spinning backwards like Superman so that I could rewind time back to our first entering the theme park and relive it all over again, it never worked. Closing time always seemed to rush up on us so fast!

"It's okay Atif, we will come back soon, okay?" my mother would kneel before me and say, attempting to coax my young arms into releasing some pole that I had attached myself to in protest. I didn't want to leave, I wanted to stay there forever. "I promise."

I could not be convinced. I knew that "soon" meant next summer and my little eyes could not see that far into the future.   Next   summer   was   just   too   far   away.

"Let go of the pole Atif," my mother would then say, her patience wearing thin. "You are not gone embarrass me out here tonight. We go through this same shit every year."

Let go of the pole? I could do no such thing! I had become *one* with the pole! I *was* the pole! I was Malcolm X; I would die for what I believed.

My revolutionary thoughts would be cut into with the shocking sensation of my exposed armpits being tickled by Darion as my arms involuntarily released the pole. K-Red and Malik would then grab me and carry me kicking and screaming all of the way to the car with my mother in tow predicting how she was going to wear my butt out when we made it home.

Darion and Kenyatta, to hell with them both! Not to mention Malik, my own flesh and blood, that...Benedict Arnold! How could they? Didn't they understand what my mission consisted of?

Khalid's last year of incarceration seemed to fly by in the same fashion. As much as I wanted to see the brother get out of prison, I at the same time just wished that time would slow down and stop moving so fast. But, like closing time at Worlds of Fun, there we stood at the steps of the administration building experiencing the moment I looked forward to yet dreaded at the same time.

We both did.

"Man I can't thank you enough for allowin' me to go and live at your mother's old house Atif. Without your charity I don't know what I would have done for a place to lay my head." Khalid said. I nodded. "Do you remember the khutbah Siddiq gave back in 2000 about forgiveness?"

"Yeah, I remember. That was the day after I got out of the hole and we hit the track." Khalid nodded.

"He mentioned 4 steps to repentance, 3 of which we both had already taken. But the fourth step, compensation, is a step that we have yet to talk about."

He was right, but where was he taking this?

"Well, I accept what you are doin' for me, providin' me with a place to stay for compensation for what happened at that gas station back in '93. So with Allah as my witness brotha' you have completed all 4 steps. Allah alone is the Forgiver of sins but you have obtained every aspect of forgiveness that I know how to give."

Khalid and I then embraced, ending it with a handshake. We had accomplished so much, removing 13 years worth of enmity between us and replacing it with that which is better: love.

"I want to do somethin' for you." Khalid said.

"No man, you don't have to do nothin' for me. You don't owe me anything."

"Yes I do, I owe you a lot. And I think I know a way to compensate you for what I took away from y'all. It is a long shot but by Allah all things are possible."

I regarded him quizzically. "What are you talkin' about?

"I'm not gone talk about it, I will *be* about it. You'll see, insha Allah."

"A'ight." I said in dismissal. I had no idea what he was talking about and I was not about to wreck my brain trying to figure it out.

"As-salamu alaykum Atif."

"Wa alaykum as-salaam Khalid."

"Fee aman Allah." Khalid said with a smirk, turning to leave. Just like that he was gone.

Closing time.

Fee aman Allah, in Allah's protection. I had not heard the phrase since Fatimah used to say it back in detention and hearing him say it made me think of her. I wondered what she was up to? Probably married, I thought to myself as I headed back to the housing unit and eventually my lonely cell.

*****

I was scheduled to appear before the Board of Probation and Parole in April of 2003, seven months after Khalid's departure. By then I had been incarcerated for a little over 10 years flat on a 15 year sentence without even so much as hearing from the parole board until then.

No matter how good (or bad) of an impression I made on the board members, by law I would still be ineligible for release until November of 2005; a measly 2 ½ years shy of my 12/12 date. I really saw no point in going before the board after doing so much time flat. At the time I could care less if they paroled me in 2005 or held me until my 15 years was up in 2007. But I *wanted* to go before them. I wanted to go and speak my mind unlike others were able to do because of fear of not making parole. I harbored no such fear so there would be no boot-licking, butt-kissing or biting my tongue, no sir! I was going to let it all hang out, with the best of manners I could muster of course.

I spent that seven months corresponding with Khalid, Destiny and Kesha. I referred Khalid to Kesha's salon in order to get his hair braided and ever since her first encounter with the new "Kev", her letters were filled with praises of him and the way he conducted himself. Khalid

481

was the talk of the shop and I suspected that Kesha's customers were not the only ones who had a thing for him.

Khalid first wrote to me in shock of what Malik had done to my mother's house. He told me that I would not recognize it as the humble abode I grew up in. He said that Malik had purchased the house next door and the lot on the other side of the house, had the old abandoned home torn down and utilized the space by adding on to my mother's old house. Khalid said that it was like a miniature mansion in the hood. I refused to allow him to tell me any more, I wanted to get out and see for myself. The fact that whatever he had done to the house was financed with drug money bothered me and I couldn't shake it for the life of me.

Khalid had a job at Gates Barbeque but quit after his supervisor tried to get him to barbeque some pork ribs. He also had met Destiny and whenever they saw each other she would brighten up his whole day by greeting him with the Islamic greeting she had learned from me. Khalid told me about the Masjid he attended and how the atmosphere differed from the ones in prison.

April 11, 2003. I will never forget this day. It was my first real experience of speaking truth to power, or pretty close to it. Most people had a bad experience with the board and left upset or feeling like trash. Me? I had a good time. I didn't allow those judgmental hypocrites to put me down. I knew that I had elevated far above the type of person I used to be and I refused to let them take away from that.

"You may be seated." Krashonda Higgins, an extremely overweight African American woman said to me. She introduced herself to me as the chairperson of the board. There were 2 others besides her: a fairly attractive Caucasian woman and an older Caucasian male.

The room was small and empty for the most part. There were none of the victim's family members from my case present. The walls were blank and the board members sat behind a long table with stacks of files situated neatly on top.

"Thank you but I would rather stand." I said, standing my ground with my hands behind my back. My refusal to sit was symbolic for what was to come. Krashonda Higgins glared at me, I could hear her wheezing from where I stood.

"Suit yourself," Krashonda Higgins started. She then spent the next few seconds looking at me and I held her gaze, refusing to be intimidated by her. "What do you bring to the table?"

Let's get ready to rumble, I thought to myself.

"My struggle to submit the whole of my bein' to the Cherisher and Sustainer of the worlds, associatin' no partners with that Deity, enjoinin' good and forbiddin' evil. That's what I bring to the table." I responded. The board members looked between themselves and Krashonda Higgins smirked as if I had told a joke or something.

"Looking through your files I saw absolutely no recommendations, no G.E.D. or high school diploma, no certificates or any other proof of your successfully completing any institutional programs whatsoever. So how are we to know that you have been rehabilitated into one who..." she paused, throwing up quotation marks with her meaty stubs she had for fingers. "Enjoins good and forbids evil?" she finished with a chuckle that made all of her rolls shake.

I didn't like this woman. Actually, I was disgusted by her. If she wanted to mock me, I had no problem with that. I would walk out of there still possessing every shred of self-confidence that I had entered the room with, which in my mind was also having the last laugh.

"I don't do things for show, therefore I am not concerned with what you know. My rehabilitation, better defined as my *repentance* is not for you, your pleasure, your approval, or some parole date. My change is from the *heart*, my Creator *knows* and that is all that matters to me.

"Your institutional programs are a *joke*. They are full of homosexual activities and drug trafficking, coordinated by half-hearted underpaid instructors that would rather be outside havin' a nicotine...pow wow, talkin' irrelevance with their own co-workers. I could have been

483

one of these inmates who fakes their way through all of your programs in pursuit of some frivolous piece of paper but I don't do no fakin' on no level. What I needed was somethin' stronger and more dynamic than what your programs have to offer. Besides, them generic certificates ain't gone do me, *you*, or anyone else any good on the Day of Decision. My reward is with my Lord."

"Do you have any remorse for the crime you committed?" the white man whose name was Donald Gruff asked me, speaking up for the first time. I welcomed the opportunity to take my eyes off of Krashonda Higgins and hoped that Donald had some sense.

"Yeah."

"Care to elaborate?"

"My feelings of remorse is threefold. At first the only reason I felt any remorse for the life I had taken was because I was no longer on the streets." Donald nodded. I continued. "Then as time passed and I began to mature, I honestly began to feel sorry for my victim's family because I know first hand how it feels to lose a loved one in such a way. But thirdly, as I began to come into knowledge, I felt bad for takin' part in the ...muggin' of Black America so eloquently put by Dr. Earl Hutchinson."

"Did you have anything to do with the stabbing death of a Mr...James Patterson?" Krashonda Higgins asked me.

"Who?" I asked, genuinely perturbed.

"Also known as Static Addict?"

"No."

Where did *that* come from?

"What about this #2 major assault you caught on staff back in '98? What do you have to say about such violent behavior?"

"Violent behavior? There was no violent behavior on *my* part."

"Are you insinuating that this guard lied on you?"

"Yeah he lied on me! Is that hard for you to believe?"

"Actually, *yes* it is."

484

"If you find it hard to believe for a white man to tell a lie then you can look forward to a lot of betrayal, let downs and broken promises in your future sista'."

Krashonda's eyes widened and she looked at her co-workers. She was clearly the only one who took offense to my statement. Maybe she was the only one remaining in the room who was still mis-educated concerning the European's history of savagery, lies and betrayal. *Some of my people are in bad shape*, I thought to myself.

"Have you ever been in a gang?" Gloria Stevens, the white lady, asked me speaking for the first time. I threw my head back and laughed out loud, I couldn't help myself.

"That is irrelevant. If I was, why would I stand here and admit to something which you have no evidence concerning? Doin' so could only hurt me and be of no benefit to me."

"If we were to stipulate you to complete a drug program if you were to make parole, would you be willing to do that?" Krashonda Higgins asked me. She had her nerve. When I shook her hand all I smelled was cheap perfume and cigarette smoke and she wanted to stipulate me to a drug program?

"For *what?* I'm not a drug addict. You don't have the results of a single positive urine analysis test in my file, let alone any drug convictions. So why would you stipulate me to complete a drug program post release? That would be like stipulatin' a college graduate to pass the G.E.D. test; it don't make sense! *Unless* I consider the fact that I would have to pay an arm and a leg for these classes and in order for y'all to continue misappropriatin' all these funds, you have to keep shovin' people like me who don't need any drug rehabilitatin' into these programs. Now that makes all of the sense in the world.

"*And*, on top of all that, you are sittin' there *reekin'* of an addiction to tobacco and you want to stipulate me to a drug program? You are more of a drug addict than I ever was! Maybe *you* need to consider stipulatin' *yourself* to a drug program before you finish committin' *suicide*." I

485

finished, showing mercy by deciding to leave her addiction to food alone.

Krashonda Higgins did not like that; she did not like that at all.

"First of all," she began. I could see that I had gotten underneath her skin. *It ain't fun when the rabbit got the gun*, I thought to myself. "I'am not a convicted *murderer.* Secondly, I'am not the one going up for parole, you are. *Thirdly,* tobacco is *not* an illegal drug and it is not against the law, okay, for me to smoke all of the cigarettes my soul may desire."

I chuckled softly. Being a convicted murderer was something I would always be in her mind. "Just because it ain't against your law does not make it right. It's *still* addictive and detrimental to the health and one of the leading causes of death in this country. Your *addiction* to that tobacco plant is not different than a convicted murderer's addiction to the marijuana plant, coca plant, poppy plant or any other plant; an addiction is an addiction is an *addiction.*

"Let me inform you about the *law* you spoke of while I am at it. It was against the law for you to be considered any more than 3/5 of a human bein'; it was against the *law* for you to even drink a sip of water from the same fountains as your co-workers here. What is illegal and legal in your mind is whatever your desires call for. The *law* ain't nothin' but somethin' y'all write with your own hands."

"Sir?" Gloria Stevens spoke up. I focused my attention on her after a brief staring contest with Krashonda Higgins. "If we were to grant you parole, will you be a productive citizen in society?"

"I will be a productive member of my *community*, which we both know is a totally different world than *society*. Being productive in society as an ex-con really means servant, cursed to a life of flippin' burgers and takin' your order in the drive through window. I intend to live more of a fulfillin' life than that."

"Do you really expect for us to simply take your word for it that you have changed and recommend an early release for you?"

"All that I *expect* from the 3 of you is for you to do your jobs without prejudice, nothin' more or less. You can find no justifiable reason anywhere in my file to so much as stipulate me for any type of drug program, let alone continue my incarceration."

"Well, considering the serious nature of your crime is all of the justification we need to continue your incarceration." Krashonda said. That woman just couldn't get enough.

"Don't feed me that 'due to the serious nature of my crime' crap because I don't eat it. I don't eat *swine* and I don't eat *crap*. The serious nature of my crime ain't gone *ever* change. You will *have* to release me in 4 ½ more years *despite* the serious nature of my crime, which by then will still not have changed one bit, so what's the point in denying my parole now because of it?"

Silence.

"May I be excused? To continue on in this manner is redundant. I suspect that your decisions of whether or not to recommend parole for me were made long before I stepped foot in this room anyway.   The final decision though of if I will make parole or not is actually in the control of our Creator, though you may perceive it not." The board members looked between themselves.

"Yeah, sure.   You can be excused." Donald said, smiling.   "Have   a   nice   day.   This   meeting   has been….interesting, to say the least." I nodded, smiling back. I then looked at Krashonda Higgins.

"May Allah guide you and rectify your condition." I said, turning to leave with a smirk on my face. I walked out of that room in that which I came: Allah's protection.

*****

"Brother, will you *please* open that envelope before you drive me crazy?" Bashir, my latest celly asked me. They had just did mail call and I received a letter from the parole board, which undoubtedly contained my answer. I had been staring at the envelope for at least 20 minutes.

A few weeks had gone by since my parole hearing and until receiving that letter I hadn't given it much thought. Up until then I didn't care if they paroled me or not. I knew that the worst case scenario was me doing another 4 ½ years and after doing 10 ½, the 4 ½ was something I could do standing on my head.

All of that changed the moment I was handed that letter.

I wanted out of prison and as soon as possible. This was how I really felt. All of that talk about not caring one way or the other was just me steeling myself in preparation for the worst. I *hated* that place; I hated the guards; I hated the food; I hated the small cramped cells. I was tired of taking showers out in the open with water that was always either too hot or too cold. I yearned for a bath! I was sick of all the noise and smelling other people's feces and urine. I no longer could stand the lack of privacy, strip searches, counts, uncomfortable bunks, metallic tasting water, cold winter nights and brutally hot suffocating summer days, and most of all: I was sick of being *lonely*. I wanted a woman, a *wife*. Some femininity for Allah's sake!

"Here man, you open it." I said, handing the letter to Bashir.

"Alrighty then," he said, taking the letter and opening it. "Lets see what The Bestower has ordained for you brother."

"Not so fast!"

"Huh?"

"Slow your roll brotha', take your *time*. You trying to give me a heart attack?" Bashir laughed. He then slowly extracted the letter from the envelope and began to read it. I studied his facial expression but it remained stoic, void of any emotion. His eyes darted from left to right, speed reading. After an eternity (it seemed) of this, Bashir sighed. "I should of known better than to think for even one *second* that those *kafirun* woul-"

"You have been scheduled to be released on November 23rd, 2005." Bashir cut in with a smile on his face.

"That is what it says?"

"Yes, that is what is says."

"Don't be playin' with my emotions man."

"Prophet Muhammad said that he guarantees a home in the middle of Paradise for a person who gives up lying, even while joking. I wouldn't play with you like that Atif. Here," Bashir said, handing me the letter. "Be what you know and not what you are told."

I grabbed the letter and read it. Sure enough, I had been given an out date, a two year out date but still an out date. Of course I was happy to read that I would be getting out within the next 24 months, it was just that after 10 years of prison life, it was hard for me to comprehend life in the free world, especially with my having experienced so little before I was incarcerated. I forgot what it felt like to answer a ringing telephone or even drive a car.

Envisioning my release to me was like trying to imagine how deep into space I would be after traveling at the speed of light for 10 million years. I knew that I would get out one day, it just did not seem real to me. My reality was routine, day in and day out. Not having to worry about such things as bills and other responsibilities.

I was *afraid*; I would be a 27 year old black man with absolutely no job training or even a G.E.D., being released into society with not much more than the deed to a home purchased and furnished with drug money. I had never even had a job out in society and the only thing I was good at while in society was selling drugs and catching a football. What was I going to do? I had been so focused on bettering myself as an individual that I didn't stop to realize that piety alone would not keep the lights on and food in the refrigerator.

As volatile as prison was, it at the same time had *security*. I didn't have to worry about these things. We were treated and cared for like children to be honest. Our food was prepared for us 3 times a day without missing a beat, our clothes and sheets washed for us; we never had to worry about sleeping outside without a roof over our heads. (The system was our daddy and he supported all of his kids. The system was more of a provider for me than my real father ever was.) But in the free world things were not that simple. In the free world my toilet paper and soap wouldn't be passed out to me once a week, I had to get up, get out, and get my own.

For the first time in a long time I began to doubt myself. I had matured a lot during the course of my incarceration, but I had not been supporting myself like an adult does, which is one of the key components of adulthood. So had I truly become a *man* or was I in reality still just some overaged adolescent who was now kind, respectful and God fearing?

*****

November 23, 2005. I opened my eyes, awakened by Bashir standing in the middle of the cell giving the call to prayer. The day had finally come. My heart began to pulsate rapidly. I took a deep breath and sat up. Listening to the brother soothed me. I waited patiently until he was finished and then left the cell enroute for the sinks so that I could get myself together and make ablution.

Moberly didn't have much to offer in the trade department but I spent the preceding 2 years taking advantage of what little they did. I took up welding and passed the G.E.D. test. After successfully completing these courses there wasn't much left for me to do but count the days down.

I didn't tell Kesha I was coming home, I wanted to surprise her. She had absolutely no idea about my sentences being ran concurrent like they were. She was going to go off on me after the shock wore off, I knew, but it would be worth it. Destiny had an idea but did not know the exact date. Khalid was the only one in the free world who knew exactly when I was to be released and I was depending on him to come and pick me up.

"What's wrong brotha'?" I asked Bashir. I had returned to the cell and we were about to begin the prayer with me taking the lead. I noticed that his attention was on me instead of where he was going to prostrate.

490

"This will be our last Salah in congregation together." Bashir pointed out. I smiled at him, I was really going to miss the brother. He was serving 2 consecutive life sentences so chances were he would never walk out of prison alive.

"No it won't," I started. "As long as you continue to offer the daily prayers at their earliest fixated times then we will *always* be prayin' together. These walls, these gates, the distance between us; none of it means nothing, you know?" Bashir nodded, smiling in return.

"I didn't think to look at it like that...humph. I still would like to cherish this moment so recite 2 of the longest Surat (chapters) that you know, insha Allah."

After offering the Morning Prayer we broke our usual routine of Qur'anic reading until breakfast and decided to pass the time with some early morning conversation. When chow was called we strolled to the dining hall, picked up our trays and sat at our usual table with Siddiq and Muhsin.

"How do you feel?" Muhsin asked me.

"Good, alhamdu lillah."

"How long has it been?"

"13 years almost." Muhsin whistled.

"A lot of things change with the passage of so much time." I nodded. "Are you ready?"

"Yeah, I think so."

"I remember being in your shoes. I *thought* I was ready too. After 5 years of incarceration, coming into the fold of Islam, I just *knew* I was ready."

"What happened?"

"Well brother, to make a long story short, I pretty much walked out of prison and left my Islam behind. I wasn't out for 6 whole months before I caught a murder case and came right back with a fresh 25 year sentence."

I was silent for a while. Was it possible for me to do the same? Walk out of prison and abandon everything I had learned? Was my Islam a way of life or just something I got into in order to pass the time?

No. I was a *believer* and I knew with a surety that Allah had intervened in my life, blessing me with His mercy and guidance. I was grateful for that and there was no way I would allow myself to become an ingrate. However, I still could use some advice on taking precautions which would help me stay focused.

"Where did you go wrong Muhsin?" I asked.

Muhsin chuckled softly. "I went wrong in *numerous* areas little brother. I take it though that you mean where did it all begin?" I nodded. Muhsin thought silently to himself for a few moments. "I began to go astray the *moment* I became so preoccupied that I began to neglect the 5 daily prayers. That is where I went wrong Atif.

"I don't know what is in your heart, and I of course pray that you will stay on the path once you walk out of here. But I am going to say this: No matter what you may or may not find yourself off into or no matter how many women you may or may not be fornicating with or whatever, you know, I'm just keeping it real, whatever the case is don't ever feel too ashamed to stand before your Lord in prayer. Cling to the Salah because I don't care how dirty your life may be, for at least a few moments at a time 5 times a day you will be on point. Prophet Muhammad said that in the later days Islam will be like a hot piece of coal in the palm of your hand, which of course is difficult to hold on to. The moment you walk out of these gates, Islam just may become that hot piece of coal in your palm considering all of the temptations you will be facing. Hold on to your Islam though Atif, hold on for dear life you hear me?"

"Yeah, I hear you." I answered, examining the breakfast meat patty on my tray. I was glad that I would no longer be party to such mystery meat.

"It is almost a three hour drive back to the city Atif, you might want to eat breakfast." Siddiq said.

"Man I have exercised 4 out of my 5 senses and I still have no idea what kind of meat this is. I looked at it, touched it, smelled it and tasted it. I'm afraid that if I put it up to my ear and listen to it I might hear it growl at me or somethin'." I said. The whole table erupted in laughter. "I'll wait."

"We are really going to miss your presence at this table Atif, believe that." Bashir said. The rest of the brothers murmured in agreement.

I could see that they were genuinely happy for me. There was no envy or jealousy. Bashir and Muhsin were both doing bits that they could barely handle, *if* they could. Siddiq still had four more years to pull. It is hard to part with someone you have done a significant amount of time with, even on the individual's part that is being released.

"I will be at work when they call you, insha Allah, so I can't walk you up to the front," Siddiq began as we all exited the kitchen. He along with a lot of the Muslims worked down in the sign shop and had to report to work directly after breakfast. "You truly are a remarkable person Atif and honestly I feel blessed to have known you. I will always remember our experience while in ad-seg together and it is a story that I will not be quick to tire of telling." Siddiq then smiled his full toothed smile at me. "Allah is with you brother, so keep Him first in all that you do and you will be successful."

"Let's go gentlemen, keep it moving." A guard said to us.

"As-salaamu alaykum little brother." Siddiq said.

"Wa alaykum as-salaam." We then embraced.

"Extend my greetings to brother Khalid, insha Allah." I nodded. Siddiq turned and walked off. I sighed and did the same.

*****

Two hours later my inmate identification number was being called over the loud speaker. Being identified by the 6 digit number had long ago begun to feel like the word "nigger" to me and I was happy to no longer be forced to answer to it. I took one last look at my cell and walked out to the rotunda area. I was walked up to the front by DeAnthony X and Pastor Cool Breeze. Skooter-B was back in ad-seg. I saw Concrete and he threw his head back at

493

me in acknowledgment.   After saying our good byes, I walked into the administration building.

As I walked by medical I thought of Rebecca and wondered how she was doing. She had quit not long after my emergence from ad-seg back in 2000.   I was then buzzed through an iron gate and I approached the reception area. I could see the parking lot from where I stood. So close to freedom! My anxiety was intense and I had butterflies in the pit of my stomach like I used to get as a teenager.   The lady seated behind the desk gave me an envelope containing my release papers and $100. After 13 years they were sending me out into a materialistic world with $100?

"Hey Mel!" the lady called out.

"Yeah!"

"I got one to go!" she said smiling at me.   "Don't come back now."

"You don't mean that. If I didn't come back then you would not have a job." I commented. Mel, one of the guards who had free cased me back in '98, then appeared.

Ain't this a...

"Hey big fel-" Mel cut himself off in mid-sentence upon seeing my face. "Don't I know you?" I only glared at him in response.

"Will you please escort this gentleman out to the front?" the lady behind the reception desk asked Mel after looking questioningly between us. Mel nodded and led the way. We walked in silence for the first few steps. Mel then snapped his fingers.

"That is where I know you from! You were the guy back in ad-seg, right?" I didn't answer.   Lord knows we couldn't make it to the front doors fast enough. "You didn't take that personal did you? We were just kidding around man."

Kidding around? I did an extra 17 months in the hole and I wasn't supposed to take it personal? What was wrong with those people? Was it something in the water? Goodness! It was all a game to them.   Playing with our freedom, our lives, it was all in fun.

When we reached the front doors I could see Khalid out in the parking lot leaning up against a white rental car. Mel pulled out a set of keys and unlocked the doors. "For what it's worth big fella, I apologize for any harm that me and my co-workers may have caused you in ad-seg." Mel said, offering me his hand with a smile on his face. I looked at his open hand, I guess he was expecting for me to give him "five" or something. What I wanted to do was spit in it. I then looked up into his eyes, seeing within him the demon that lurked beneath the surface.

"May Allah guide you and rectify your condition." I said. I could have made it my business to come back and slaughter him, his family and a few more of his counterparts for all of the injustices I had suffered at their hands.

Their system had almost bred a serial killer.

Dismissing the urge to retaliate in such a horrible fashion, I turned on my heels and stepped out into the free world without looking back, putting my faith in Allah to deal with the likes of him. Islam, the very thing he and people like him hate, is their only hope...if they but knew.

*****

PART 4:

THROUGH THE FIRE

"I don't remember where I came from,
and yet after all these years it is still
difficult for me to accept where I am at.
With all of that said, I just hope to end up
where I want to be."
-Atif

"Perhaps, then I have learned that even the most negative
of circumstances can yield positive consequences."
-unknown

NO WAYS TIRED

Have We not opened your breast for you?
And removed from you your burden which
weighed down your back?
And have We not raised high your fame?
Along with every hardship is relief.
Verily, along with every hardship is relief.
So when you have finished, devote yourself
to Allah's worship. And to your Lord turn
intentions and hopes.
-Noble Qur'an 95:1-8

25

Stepping out of that lobby and into the brisk November air was like stepping into a whole new dimension. There were no shackles around my ankles, no handcuffs on my wrists. I didn't see any signs that read "out of bounds" or any guards stationed at check points waiting to frisk me before allowing my passage. I was leaving the world of such violations behind.

"As-salaamu alaykum brotha'!" Khalid greeted me cheerfully as I approached. He wore a black leather jacket with some creased blue jeans and black Jordan boots. He had traded in his traditional two cornrows for a small natural with a crisp lining.

"Wa alaykum as-salaam!" I returned the greeting as we embraced. Khalid was solid, hugging him was like hugging a stone pillar. "Dang brotha'," I began as we released each other, poking my finger into his chest. "How you get so solid man?"

"Bally's ain't got nothin' on the gym Malik had installed in the basement, I'm *tellin'* you!"

"Free weights?" I asked as I walked around to the passenger side of the car.

"Yeah, free weights. Them universal weights is cool, but free weights will have you *right.*" He answered, sliding into the driver's seat.

"What you been doin', *eatin'* the weights instead of liftin' them?" Khalid laughed. "Man you done left me in the dust." I complimented, opening the passenger side door. I noticed for the first time that someone was seated in the back seat.

"Subhan Allah! I ain't workin' with nothin' for real, I'm still tryin' to cut up like you." Khalid said in humility. "Oh yeah, I'm trippin'. Atif this is my son Ke'von and Ke'von, this is Atif."

"Wha'sup lil' brotha'? It's nice to meet you man." I said, turning in my seat and offering him my hand. Ke'von was the spitting image of his father and looking into his face was strange because to do so took me back in time to when Khalid was my nemesis.

"It is nice to meet you too." Ke'von said in his North Carolina drawl, shaking my hand. He was looking at me in amazement; Khalid must had been telling him some good things about me.

"You down here to stay?" I asked him.

"No, just for Thanksgiving."

"All the changes he been down there takin' his mama and step-father through, they are liable to leave him behind." Khalid said. He then started the car. "Take a good look at this place Ke'von because if you keep on trippin' you just may end up in one just like it; probably worse."

"You don't want to go to prison Ke'von, you hear me?" I said, looking at Khalid's son. Ke'von nodded, looking at the Moberly Correctional Center. "You don't want to go there at all. It is the institution of slavery all over again behind those gates." I finished, shivering inwardly.

"You ready brotha'?" Khalid asked me. I took a deep breath and nodded. He then put the transmission into drive. "Head'em up! Move'em out!" he shouted, stepping on the gas.

I got a brief and boring look at the small town of Moberly as we found our way to the highway. It had been a long time since I had been in a car. I kept looking around the interior and fiddling with knobs, buttons, and switches that seemed to do everything but drive the car. I played with my seat, my window, the rearview mirror, the vents, everything! It didn't take long however for me to figure everything out and run out of things to experiment with. I made small talk with Ke'von and spent a lot of time staring out of my window.

The ride to Kansas City was long. No wonder people hadn't been in a rush to make the trip to Moberly and back in order to visit me on a consistent basis throughout my internment. It didn't bother me though, I was anxiously anticipating my return to my old neighborhood but at the same time I enjoyed taking in all of the sights along the way. I was hungry but my mind was made up: I was not settling for anything less than some home cooked food.

"I have to stop by this shop real quick," Khalid said, exiting the highway onto Truman Road. "After that y'all can drop me back off at work."

Within an hour me and Ke'von were riding in the car by ourselves. I didn't have anything remotely close to a license, never had, but I drove as if I didn't have a worry in the world.

"What do you want to do?" I asked Ke'von. He shrugged his shoulders. "Well, I am hungry and I want to see what my brotha' did to my mother's house." I said, heading for my neighborhood.

Driving up Benton gave me goose bumps. A lot had changed since my departure back in '93. I could see that an honest effort was being made to make the old drug ridden neighborhood more presentable, outwardly, but what was that supposed to change? Recently built low income homes jumped out at me here and there. The liquor store on the corner of 27th and Benton was no longer in operation and I got the feeling that 27th and Benton was no longer the hangout spot it once was.

If driving up Benton alone gave me goose bumps, pulling up to the house I grew up in sent me into a state of shock. I couldn't believe my eyes. Malik had really stuck his foot in renovating our childhood home. It stood out on the block like a sore thumb. Painted red with white trim and surrounded by a black iron gate that could be opened by remote control, it resembled one of the homes I used to long for when riding through Smack Man's neck of the woods.

The car was not good and set in park before I jumped out of it. I was awestruck. Everything was so nice and the house was so big! I couldn't wait to see the inside. After a search for the right key to the front door, I stepped into my home followed by Ke'von.

The interior was coordinated and well put together I saw as I rushed from room to room. Malik had even turned one room into a study. Inside of it was a large desk with a comfortable leather swivel chair behind it and the walls were lined with books resting on wooden bookshelves. Even these were consciously grouped together in their perspective places. One of the shelves was filled with nothing but Islamic literature, not just anything but important collections of Hadith, Qur'ans and numerous books that were hard to find in the English language.

Adjacent to this study was a small room with no windows or anything in it besides a long ivory basin attached to the far wall filled with clear water. Directly in the middle of the room were three rows of prayer rugs built into the floor with one positioned on a row of its own in front of the rest, all of them facing the east! How did he *know*?

Which reminded me, it was time to offer the noon prayer. My first Salah in the free world. I removed my shoes and walked over to the basin to begin the process of purifying myself. The water was lukewarm and very comfortable.

"You about to pray?" Ke'von asked, stepping inside of the room.

"Yeah."

"Can I pray with you?" I paused, looking up at him.

"You know how to make Salah?" I inquired. Ke'von nodded.

"My father taught me how. I don't have it quite down in Arabic yet, but I'm learning." Ke'von said as he walked over next to me at the basin. I watched him as he made ablution and could see that it was an exercise that he had been doing a lot of. He did so with confidence and fluidity.

"Don't tell me you know how to give the call to prayer too?" I said after we had made ablution and situated ourselves on two of the prayer rugs on the first row. Ke'von smiled at me and stood up, cupping his hands behind his ears with his elbows extended as he gave the athaan. His pronunciation of the Arabic terms was a little off and his changing voice cracked here and there, butchering the call. Listening to him was kind of like listening to a werewolf howl at the moon, but he knew it for the most part and the rest would come with practice and time. "Alhamdu lillah." I said as he concluded the call. "Did Khalid teach you what to say after the athaan is given?"

"No." Ke'von answered, shaking his head. I sensed that he was searching my face for disappointment in him, which in itself gave me a small clue as to how things were for him back in his North Carolina home. Maybe he had grown up feeling as if nothing he did was good enough and no matter what he did *someone* (I couldn't pinpoint who exactly) always found some reason to be disappointed in him.

"This is what you say," I started, smiling up at him. My smile relaxed him and convinced him to give up his search as a pointless exercise. Ke'von didn't have to worry about such a thing under *my* roof. "Oh Allah, Lord of this perfect invitation and established Salah. Endow Muhammad with favor, merit and exalted rank. Raise him to the good position you have promised; for you never break Your promises."

"You are going to have to write all of that down for me or something." Ke'von said. I chuckled. Ke'von then gave the shortened version and we aligned ourselves and prayed together.

"Now, let's get our grub on; shall we?" I said after we finished praying, walking into the spacious kitchen. I then spent a few seconds searching the stainless steel refrigerator for a way to open it up. Ke'von laughed at me.

"I don't know why you are trying to open that thing up anyway, there is no food in there."

"It isn't?" I asked, finally opening it up. "*Goodness*! What do y'all be eatin'?" The inside of the refrigerator was empty except for some Arm and Hammer baking soda and two pitchers, one empty and the other filled with cold water.

"Pops been procrastinating about going grocery shopping, he don't like to do it."

"Why not?"

"Something about the women, probably. My father acts like he is scared of girls or something."

"Your father does not fear women Ke'von, he fears Allah." I said. "We'll just have to do it ourselves. You ridin'?" Ke'von nodded. "Lets roll."

We locked the house up and got back into the rental car. Pulling out of the gate, I looked over at Old Lady Jenkins' house and wondered if she was still alive. I would make time to go and knock on her door and find out either that day or the next, I thought to myself. I then drove off, heading south on Benton.

"I wonder if the school district has started Thanksgiving vacation yet?" I said, thinking aloud as I drove.

"Today is the last day." Ke'von answered. I looked at the clock; if my memory served me correctly Central let out in just a short period of time. "We gone make a pit stop real quick." I said, heading towards my old school.

I remembered my last day at Central. I remembered debating with Rakim, having lunch with Patience, my talk with Mr. Williams, and most of all, my phone call to Darion. Central still looked pretty much the same to me as I pulled into the parking lot. The gas station bearing a different name was still located directly across the street. The front of the school was lined with buses waiting for the bell to ring.

"Isn't this where you guys went to school?" Ke'von asked me.

"I guess you could say that."

"It is nice." Ke'von said. "Are we going inside?"

"Nah, I just want to pick someone up."

"Who?" Ke'von asked after hearing the bell ring. Students began to flood the front walk, emerging noisily from all doors. I was amazed at the way they all were dressed. Everyone wore black designer clothes: Sean John, Fubu, Ecko, Enyce, Rock-a-Wear, etc. When I was going to school only the drug dealers dressed so nice.

"Her name is Destiny," I said, opening my door. "Come on." We got out of the car and walked over to the front walk. I could see that all of the girls were eyeing Ke'von as we passed them. I smiled to myself. Ke'von acted as if he didn't notice all of the attention.

"What does she look like?" he asked, searching the crowd.

504

"She skipped the eighth grade and went straight to the ninth, so she is younger than everybody else. Look for the shortest girl you can find. That will probably be her." We spent a couple of more minutes looking for her.

"Is that her?" Ke'von asked, pointing at four girls standing in a group to our right. Sure enough, Destiny was amongst them, the shortest one of the four. She wore a red and white Baby Phat hooded sweat suit with some white Baby Phat sneakers. She was holding some school books in one hand, trying to put on a red wind parka with a fur lined hood without setting them down. I hadn't seen Destiny in four years and the sight of her gave me a warming sensation in my heart.

"Yeah, that's her. Go get her for me Ke'von." Ke'von started off in their direction. He then paused and turned towards me.

"What is her name again?"

"Destiny, but call her Suga Bear."

Ke'von nodded and approached the four girls. Like his father at his age, he was not shy at all when it came to females. I saw Destiny's head snap around when Ke'von called to her. Her pretty face scrunched up at the sight of Ke'von and I could see her mouthing the question of who was he and how he knew her nickname. Ke'von said something and pointed in my direction. All four of the girls' sets of eyes followed. I smirked as me and Destiny's eyes locked.

"*ATIF!*" Destiny screamed, dropping her coat and her books on the ground. She then took off running towards me, breaking down crying on the way. That girl ran into my arms hitting me at 100 miles per hour. I picked her up, spinning her in the air, redirecting her momentum so that we wouldn't fall.

"As-salaamu alaykum!" I greeted, squeezing her in my arms. She had to be the tiniest freshman in the country.

"Wa alaykum as-salaam!" she returned tearfully.

"I missed you!"

"I missed you too!" Destiny said, wiping her eyes. "When did you get out?"

"This mornin'."

"Why didn't you tell me? By Allah you almost made me pass out! Got me out here crying in front of everyone like this."

"Look at you girl," I started, stepping back. "You are lookin' good Suga Bear!" I finished, mimicking a photographer taking snapshots with my index fingers.

"Quit Atif!" Destiny exclaimed, looking around. "Come on, I want you to meet my friends." She said, grabbing me by the hand and pulling me in their direction. "Are you out for good? I mean, you don't have to go back or anything do you?"

"No, I'm out for good, insha Allah." I answered with a chuckle as we walked. Approaching her classmates, Destiny introduced me to them. One of them, her cousin Sparkle, stared at me with her mouth gaping wide open. "You a'ight Sparkle? You gettin' enough oxygen?" I asked Destiny's cousin. Sparkle nodded, making no attempt to take her eyes off of me or close her mouth. "You better close your mouth sista' before a bug flies into it." I joked, everyone laughed at that.

"What is your name?" Destiny asked Ke'von. All of the young ladies' attention focused on him. They were all at least a year to three years older than him (except for Destiny who was about his age) and nice looking young girls. When I was his age I would have broken out in a cold sweat under the pressure of four Kansas City teenage girls scrutinizing me.

"My Name is Ke'von." He answered, just as calm, cool and collective as could be.

"Where you from?" Destiny's friend Leah asked Ke'von upon hearing his accent.

"I'm from Greensboro North Carolina." The young ladies nodded.

"What grade are you in?" Destiny's other friend Shay asked.

"I'm in the eighth."

"Age ain't nothing but a number girl." Leah said to Shay, looking at Ke'von.

506

"I'm hip!" Shay said, doing the same.   Ke'von smiled, not taking them seriously.

It was time for us to leave.

"It is nice to meet you beautiful young sistas and all, but I will die of starvation if I stand here too much longer," I started, rubbing my stomach. "You ridin' with us Destiny?"

"Can my cousin come with us?"

"Yeah, she can come. Shay, Leah, y'all need a ride home? I don't have a license and we might end up in jail on the way, but I'll drive y'all if y'all want to roll."

"No thank you, we will catch the bus." Leah answered for the both of them. "Bye Ke'von." She then said, smiling at him.

"Looking like Genuine, *gone* boy!" Shay said, the ladies laughed. Destiny took both me and Ke'von by our elbows and began to lead us away. "Quit hatin' girl!"

"I am not hatin', we have to go!" Destiny called back behind her. "I'll call y'all later."

"Make sure you got Terrrance Dashon Howard there on 3 way when you do!" Shay said. Destiny rolled her eyes.

Getting into the driver's side of the car, I noticed that Ke'von had opened the back door for the young ladies before opening his own, allowing them to slide in from his side of the car and gently closing it behind them. Both Destiny and Sparkle smiled at him while doing so, giggling to themselves. I smiled at him myself when he finally climbed into the passenger seat.

"What?" Ke'von asked me.

"I didn't say nothin' lil' brotha', I didn't say nothin' at all." I said, shaking my head. I had to tip my hat to him, that was a smooth move for an eighth grader. I was really taking a liking to Khalid's son. "Can y'all cook?" I asked Destiny and Sparkle, turning down the radio as I pulled out of Central's parking lot.

"I can." Destiny answered.

"Girl *please*, you can't boil water. Now *I* can cook." Sparkle said, speaking up for the first time since we all were introduced.

"What do you think?" I asked Ke'von. He turned around in his seat and sized Sparkle up.

"I don't know," he started, turning back around in his seat. "She does not look like a chef to me." I laughed.

"Forget you Ke'von, my cousin can cook for your *information,*" Destiny spoke up in her cousin's defense, eyeing Ke'von through the rearview mirror. "She can cook spaghetti, hamburgers and French fries, chili, she can fry chicken-"

"Wait, wait a minute," I cut in, slowing the car down and pulling over on the side of the road. I then turned around in my seat, facing Sparkle. "Girl you know how to fry chicken for real?"

"Yes, frying is easy."

"Smothered potatoes?"

"Easy."

"Onions, bell peppers?"

"All that."

"I have not had a home cooked meal in 13 years," I started, pulling back into traffic. "I will *pay* you to cook my first one for me; what do you think about that?"

"You don't have to pay me, I'll cook for you." Sparkle answered.

"You can pay *me* to help her though." Destiny said. I laughed out loud. Destiny, just like her father, wasn't going to turn down anything but her collar.

I thought of Darion as I drove enroute for the supermarket and how nice it would have been to come home to his smiling face. I missed him. Taking a quick peek through my rearview mirror at his daughter, I couldn't help but reminisce about when we both were about her age. We never imagined our lives taking the turns they did just a couple of years later. I loved Destiny and I would make sure that she had the chance to enjoy her adolescence without rushing through those precious years in any way that resembled the way me and her father had done. He would have been so proud of her and the way she had been persevering without him.

"Atif?"

"Wha'sup?"

"Sparkle wants to know if you will make a muscle for her?" Destiny said, laughing.

"What?" I said, turning the radio down.

"Nothing! I didn't say anything!" Sparkle spoke up, pushing Destiny.

"You make me sick girl." Moments later..."Ke'von, Destiny wants to know if you-"

"Nothing! I don't want to know anything!" Destiny cut her off, covering her cousin's mouth with her hand. Ke'von looked at me briefly with a smile on his face and then went back into his own little world, staring out of the window. I wondered what he was thinking about as I turned the radio back up.

Within minutes we pulled into the Thriftway parking lot located at 31st and Prospect. Exiting the vehicle, I smelled the aroma of Popeye's Chicken and my stomach actually began to cramp up. I resisted the urge to run over there and devour a 10-piece extra crispy with an extra large order of red beans and rice, something I used to love to eat as a teenager.

Thriftway was pretty packed. Once inside, I instructed Destiny and Sparkle to take a basket and fetch all of the ingredients they would need to prepare dinner with. Me and Ke'von headed in the opposite direction with the intent to put some food into the refrigerator and cupboards.

"Can I ask you a question Ke'von?"

"Shoot."

"How did it feel to meet your father after growin' up without him in your life?" Ke'von thought silently to himself for a moment.

"I don't know, strange I guess. Kind of hard to explain."

"Were you upset with him?"

"Growing up?" he asked, looking up at me. I nodded. "Sometimes. All my mother ever told me about him was that he was locked up and probably wouldn't make it out of prison until I was a grown man. I used to wonder why he didn't write to me or send me a card or something on my birthdays; why he didn't want anything to do with me. But come to find out my mother had never given him our change of address when we moved for the second time in Greensboro.

"When I first met him I acted real funny towards him, like I was upset with him but to tell the truth I wasn't. I was actually glad that he had tracked us down. I made things difficult but he was real patient and understanding with me so it didn't take long for me to open up to him and be myself. Plus, I *liked* him and was impressed by the way he was able to answer all of my questions and explain things to me."

"How do you feel about him now?"

"I love him. It's almost like he has been there the whole time. Him and my mother are talking about allowing me to stay down here with you guys."

"Is that what you want?"

"Yeah! I like it down here in Kansas City."

"Well, if she decides to let you stay you are more than welcome."

"Really?" I nodded, smiling.

We made our way from aisle to aisle throwing items into the basket. I had to be careful because all I had was $100 to play with and I still needed to put some gas in the tank. I filled the shopping cart with all kinds of fruits, ice cream, condiments and seasonings, milk, cereal, eggs, sausage, etc. We then met up with Sparkle and Destiny in the back of the store. Destiny was trying to lift a sack of potatoes from a shelf.

"Here, let me get that." Ke'von said, taking the burden from her arms. He then effortlessly slid the bag of potatoes on the lower section underneath the shopping cart.

"I got my eye on the two of you." I said, looking suspiciously between Destiny and Ke'von with a smirk.

By the time I paid for the groceries and stopped across the street to put some gas in the tank, my $100 was pretty much gone. I gave what little I had left to Destiny. On the way back home I decided to stop by Kesha's shop and say hello.

Kesha's salon was a nice one story building painted white with a big glowing neon sign that read "KESHA'S HAIR & NAILS" in red. Pulling into the parking lot I could see that

510

business was good even at that time of day. The place was full of sisters getting their hair done for the holidays. The four of us got out of the vehicle and went inside.

There were women all over the place; black women. Some underneath hairdryers reading magazines and others getting their nails done. I missed my sisters! I only saw them on television and the few I did encounter while incarcerated were so far removed from the African American culture that the only thing black about them was their skin.

With all of the above said, I regretted my decision to stop by Kesha's shop the moment I crossed the threshold. All of the women looked in our direction with the sound of a small bell's ding positioned on top of the door. It wasn't really all that bad. I was just more than a little uncomfortable. I told myself that if Ke'von could hold his own so could I. Clearing my throat, I asked an attractive sister to my right who was curling a woman's hair with a curling iron if Kesha was in.

"Who are you?" she asked me.

"An old friend."

The sister looked me up and down and then smiled as (what looked to me as) recognition became apparent on her face. She then tilted her head towards the back of the shop. "She is going to pass out! That's her," the sister began, gesturing with the curling iron in the same direction she had tilted her head in. "Back there on the phone."

I thanked her and walked across the room. It was a short distance but a long walk for me. All eyes were on me as I made my way to the back. It felt to me like I was walking deeper and deeper into a den of lionesses. Perspiration beaded up under my armpits and I wondered to myself if any was visible on my forehead.

Approaching the counter, I saw my friend seated behind it talking on the phone and scribbling something in an appointment book. There was a small attention bell on top of the counter and I tapped it twice. Without looking up, Kesha cradled the receiver in between her shoulder and her ear, signaling for me to "wait a minute". I reached over the counter and pushed in the button on the phone, hanging up on whoever she was talking to. Kesha's head snapped up sharply in rage, eyes flashing in anger, which almost instantaneously changed into shock when she saw me standing there.

"Atif?" Kesha asked in disbelief. I smirked. "*ATIF!*" Kesha let out a shriek so loud that it tickled my eardrums. She then jumped up and carefully ran (if you can call what a woman does in heeled shoes "running") around the corner of the counter as fast as she could without twisting an ankle, screaming the whole time. I caught her in my arms, hugging her. The elegant feminine scent of Classique tickled my nostrils.

Then came the tears.

After that, a right fist to my stomach that doubled me over.

"Why you didn't *tell* me you was getting out, huh?" Kesha asked me as I grabbed her wrists so that she couldn't punch me again. I heard laughter from the women in the salon.

"I wanted to surprise you," I answered, gasping for air. Kesha still packed a nice punch. Movement caught her eye. She looked beyond me and saw Destiny tip-toeing towards the door we had come in.

"Grab her Di Di girl!" Kesha exclaimed to the woman who had pointed Kesha out to me when we first entered. Di Di put down the curlers and Destiny took off running full speed, slipping just by Di Di's grasp and out of the door, laughing all the way. "You can run but you can't hide Destiny! I knew you was holdin' out on me girl!" Kesha called out to the open door. More laughter from the women in the salon. "And *you*," Kesha started, focusing once again on me while pointing her finger in my chest. "I am *so* mad at you. How could you *do* this to me? I thought you still had at least another 12 more years to do! How did you...what...?"

"My sentences were ran concurrent, all praise is due to Allah." I said, answering the question she could not voice.

"It's *so* good to see you," Kesha said, hugging me again. Crying again.

"It's good to see you too. You was there for me every step of the way and I will *always* remember that."

"No, *we* was there for each other." Kesha said as we let go. "I see you took good care of yourself. God Atif," Kesha said, squeezing my shoulders and biceps with her fingertips. "Where did you get all of this from? What happened to the tall and skinny personal friend I once knew?"

"He grew up." I said, removing Kesha's probing fingers from my person. "I see you doin' big things out here."

Kesha smiled. "I'm doin' a'ight."

"I am proud of you, you know that?" Kesha nodded, wiping Mascara filled tears from her face.

It was time for me to go.

"I was just stoppin' by to see you, I have some runs to make."

"Atif I have not seen you in 14 years, what do you mean just stoppin' by?"

"Girl, I got milk, meat, and all kinds of other stuff in the trunk, I have to go and see my p.o., *and* I have to pick Khalid up from work. I'll tell you what," I said in response to the look on her face. "Why don't you come and eat an early dinner with all of us at my house in a couple of hours?"

"Ok. Oh, wait." Kesha sighed. "I have to pick my grandmother up from the airport at 4:45." She said, looking at her watch. I walked around the counter and retrieved a pen, along with a piece of paper, and wrote my telephone number down for her.

"Here, call me later on tonight once you get your grandmother settled in and we'll do some catchin' up." I said, handing her the number.

"That will work, for now." Kesha said, grabbing the piece of paper. "Well, I will let you do what you have to do and talk to you later."

"Insha Allah."

"I'm happy that you are home Atif."

"Me too."

513

"Be careful, I know that you don't have a license." I smiled at her and turned around, walking back down the green mile. I wasn't as uneasy going as I had been coming. "Ke'von, Sparkle, y'all can't speak?"

"Hi Kesha, bye Kesha." The two of them said in unison, laughing at the coincidence.

I drove back home with a bright smile on my face. Seeing Kesha had made my day all over again. She was doing so well for herself; after dropping the young ladies off at the house and stopping by the parole office briefly, Ke'von and I went to pick his father up from work.

"You looked a little nervous around all of those girls in the salon Atif." Ke'von said to me as I drove.

"Nervous? I was *petrified*!" I said, biting into a plum I had brought along for the trip. Ke'von laughed aloud.

"You and my father are two weird people man."

Khalid worked at a factory down on Front Street in North Kansas City. We rode the rest of the way in silence, listening to the radio. It was a few minutes after 4 by the time we pulled into the parking lot, right on time because Khalid was emerging from the building before we had the chance to park. I got out of the car.

"As-salaamu alaykum, how are you feelin' workin' man?" I greeted as Khalid approached.

"Wa alaykum as-salaam! Tired and hungry." He answered. "How was y'all's day?"

"Good, alhamdu lillah." I said, climbing into the back seat.

The 3 of us spent the trip back home laughing and joking about the day's events. When we were about halfway there Destiny's phone went off. I had taken it along with me just in case the girls needed to get in touch with me while I was gone. I was apprehensive about leaving them behind alone but allowed myself to be convinced that they were "not little girls" and would not burn the house down. I handed the phone to Ke'von, unable to open the thing let alone work it. The little contraption had a thousand tiny buttons on it, far more advanced than the Mobile Phones in circulation back when I left the streets.

"These teenagers out here walkin' around with little computers on their hips, ain't they brotha'?" Khalid asked me.

"Yeah," I said, watching Ke'von expertly operate the mechanism. "Makes me feel...left behind."

"The food is almost ready." Ke'von announced. "Is it true that you and my father had a fight when you were my age?" Ke'von then asked me.

"He told you about that?" I asked.

"Yeah."

"Did he tell you that I kicked his butt?"

"Noooo, actually the version I heard said otherwise." I reached up and put Khalid in a choke hold.

"A man! You gone make me wreck!" Khalid exclaimed. "This is something like the move I put on *him* back in the day Ke'von."

"Yeah," I started, releasing him. "After I ran off about a 6 punch combination. I would have grabbed me too." Khalid laughed.

How can I put into words how good the house smelled when I opened the back door after Khalid parked in the back driveway? *Impossible*! The scent of Popeye's Chicken I had smelled earlier could not compare. Sparkle and Destiny had the whole house smelling like my mother used to when I would come in after hearing her call me inside for dinner, hoping that I would be able to finish my food before the street lights came on so that I could go back outside and finish playing. My mother's food was always so good that I would forget about the game and take my time. Plus, Mama would smack me across the head if she caught me eating fast.

Sparkle was standing in the kitchen at the stove finishing up the last batch of chicken. "The food smells good Sparkle, you are ahead of your time girl." I complimented her. She turned from the stove, smiling. "Did you cook enough for 6?"

"6?"

"Yeah, 6. If it taste anywhere near as good as it smells then I'm eatin' *two* servins." I said, walking out of the kitchen. Sparkle laughed, shaking her head.

515

Destiny was in the dining room setting up the table. In the middle of the table there was a big plate filled with crispy golden chicken legs, wings, thighs and breasts; a big mixing bowl filled with smothered potatoes; another mixing bowl filled with garden salad; 2 big pitchers, 1 filled with Kool-Aid and the other with ice water; a basket of rolls; and a bottle of Louisiana hot sauce, ranch dressing, and catsup. I was very impressed.

"Hey Suga Bear, wha'sup?"

"Hi, Atif, did you get my text?" Destiny asked, placing plates on the table.

"Yeah, I got it. Y'all hooked it up, didn't y'all?" I asked. Destiny grabbed a piece of chicken and tore off a small portion of meat and crust.

"Here, taste." She said, placing it into my mouth. My taste buds tingled as I chewed and I could have sworn that I felt tears welling up in my eyes. "Good ain't it?" Destiny asked me. I nodded. "Told y'all my cousin can cook." I reached for a piece of my own and Destiny slapped my hand. "Huh-unh Atif. You waited 13 years, you can wait a few more minutes." Destiny giggled, licking chicken grease and crumbs from her finger tips.

"Have you still been goin' to the Masjid?"

"Every week. I am learning a lot too. I know the 99 attributes of Allah, the 6 articles of faith, the 5 pillars, um...I know the titles to all 114 chapters in the Qur'an in order, the Arabic alphabet and vowel sounds, and some other stuff. I'm the youngest girl there and I'm like the star of the class."

"Alhamdu lillah!" I said, proudly hugging her. "Your father would have been proud of you Destiny, he wanted for you to understand Allah and His Deen." Destiny smiled up at me. "Have you learned the prayer yet?"

"I know the positions but I have not memorized everything that we are supposed to say yet."

"Can you make ablution?"

"Yes."

"Come with me then, it's time to pray."

*****

After me, Destiny, Khalid and Ke'von all offered the late afternoon prayer together, we filed into the dining room and found Sparkle seated at the table waiting patiently for us to finish. We all pulled up a chair, sat down and went to work! I myself had a monstrous appetite.

"How old are you Sparkle?" Khalid asked.

"I'm 14."

"Who taught you how to cook like this?"

"My mother. I cook for her and my brother Anthony all of the time."

"Ole *Ifae*, how is she?" I inquired.

"Fine." A few minutes passed with no one doing anything but chewing.

"Don't you run track Ke'von?" I asked. Ke'von nodded. "Are you fast?"

"Faster than *you*."

"*Blasphemy* which thou utter!"   I exclaimed, slamming my fist down onto the table. Khalid, who was drinking from his glass, spit red Kool-Aid all over his son's face as he exploded in laughter. The look that Ke'von gave his father made the rest of us follow suit. Ke'von, partly being a good sport and the rest not being able to fight off the contagious laughter filling the atmosphere, joined in. I was on the floor, laughing so hard with tears in my eyes that I thought I was going to throw up all of the good food I had just eaten.

"That was messed up Pops." Ke'von said.

"My bad son, it was an accident." Khalid said, still laughing as he grabbed a table cloth and tried to wipe his son's face with it. Ke'von pulled away, grabbing the cloth.

"I'm not a child Dad. I can wipe my *own* face man."

"What about you Khalid? You don't really think that your son wants to see me do you?" I asked. Khalid shrugged his shoulders.

517

"I don't know Atif; he is incredibly fast to be his age. At least as fast as you were back in the day, if not faster."

"Aw naw, see," I started, shaking my head and sliding my chair off from underneath the table. "Y'all done kicked somethin' off. It's *on*!" I said, sucking chicken grease from my fingertips. "I want *you*!" I said, mimicking Apollo Creed in the movie Rocky, pointing across the table at Ke'von. "I want you!" I stood up and stormed from the room. Destiny and Sparkle laughed. When the 4 found me I was outside in the middle of the street stretching my legs.

"You are not seriously challenging me to a race are you Atif?" Ke'von asked.

"Don't try to cop deuces with me now." I replied. "Go up to the corner Sparkle and Destiny and see who wins." I then instructed the girls. They took off running up the street. Ke'von took his place on the street without making any effort to stretch one muscle in his body. Was he underestimating me? "You know you done messed up now, don't you?" I asked, looking up at him as I finished my stretches. Ke'von looked down at me in pity and shook his head.

"Whatever man."

I lined up next to him as Khalid stood out in front of us with his arms raised. After a couple of seconds he dropped them to his sides and Ke'von and I took off. The boy *was* fast! He left the starting point like a bolt of lightning, beating me from the jump! Halfway to the corner I noticed that Ke'von began to slow down just a bit. My pride told me that he was a short distance sprinter and was running out of gas; whereas my heart said that he was slowing down on purpose. My heart always told the unadulterated truth. I caught up to him just before we crossed the stop sign on the corner. It was a tie.

Ke'von walked up to me afterwards. "Just so you know old head," he started, whispering in my ear. "I let you catch up. I didn't want to embarrass you in front of Destiny. And to think, I wasn't even running my *fastest*." He finished with a smirk, patting me on my back before walking off. He wasn't even breathing hard!

Ke'von had to have been just joking, right? I mean, that *was* his fastest wasn't it? I sure had given it all I had! Did he *really* slow down on purpose? And what was that "old head" business? I was only 28, I wasn't getting old yet, was I? *Was* I?

*****

I have a lot of adjusting to do, I thought to myself after looking at the radio clock and wondering if night rec would be canceled or not. I was still thinking *inside* of the box, literally. I wondered how long it would take for me to get used to not being in prison.

I had just dropped Sparkle off where she lived on 39th and Wabash. It was dark out and I wanted to get the girls home before too late. I enjoyed their company and planned to spend more time with them. I stayed there at Sparkle's house for a little while and talked to Sparkle's mother, Ifae, who used to babysit me, Darion, Darion's cousin "Pipsqueek", and a few more of us rug-rats when we were younger. We all had crushes on her back then. After all those years, trials and tribulations she was still a very beautiful woman.

As Destiny and I rode through the city streets, it seemed to me like all of the people driving alongside of me were in such a hurry. But to do what? Maybe to just get home after a hard day's work.

"What?" I asked Destiny who had been staring at me for I don't know how long.

"Nothing," she started, smiling. "I just can't *believe* you are home, finally. I keep thinking that I am going to go to sleep tonight and when I wake up you will still be in jail and today will have been just a dream." We rode in silence for a few blocks. "So what are you going to do?"

I chuckled softly. "Get a job, insha Allah. Hopefully a decent one. I am thinkin' of trying to locate my father, see if I can find him if he is still alive. Maybe do some volunteer work down at the Don Bosco Center or somethin'

519

like that. Spend a lot of time with *you*," I paused, reaching to tickle her. Destiny shrank her body against the passenger door, giggling. "Of course I am going to continue strivin' to perfect my worship of Allah, but besides all of that not much else really matters to me anymore."

"What about a girl?"

"You *are* my girl." I answered smiling.

"I know that! I mean...don't you want a woman?"

"A *wife*, yeah. But not right now, I *just* got out. I don't think I'm ready for a woman in my life yet."

"Why not?"

"Well, I wasn't too much older than you are now when I was sent to prison Destiny, so I have yet to experience a lot. Honestly, after doin' so much time I don't have a *clue* when it comes to women. I have to get *used* to them again. You remember when we went to Kesha's earlier?" Destiny nodded. "I was so... I can't even explain it. Bein' in the same room alone with all of those sistas, girl it just felt *strange*."

"Atif you are *scared* of girls!" Destiny exclaimed, throwing her head back in laughter. "Daddy would have a *whole* lot to say about that." She was right. Darion would have done a whole hour of stand up ridiculing me if he had even suspected such a thing.

Another block or 2 in silence.

"I miss your father."

"Yeah, me too. I can't remember every single thing we used to do together or all of our conversations and stuff like I used to be able to do. That kind of scares me because what if I end up not being able to remember him at all?"

"Girl, forgettin' someone like your father is next to *impossible*. I don't believe you have to worry about that." I said, pulling in front of a two story house that Teebaby was renting to own. It was fairly nice, considering all. An out of place cherry red Lincoln Navigator was parked in the driveway.

"You're not coming in?" Destiny asked with her door ajar.

"Nah, I better get back to the house."

"Aw man," she pouted, closing the door. "I don't want to go in there if you aren't coming in. Why can't I just stay with you?"

"Teebaby ain't goin' for that!"

"She wouldn't even notice."

"Go on in Suga Bear and call me as soon as you wake up in the mornin', insha Allah. Khalid gave me some money and I want you to go shoppin' with me and pick some clothes out for me."

"For real?" Destiny asked smiling.   I nodded. Destiny then leaned over and kissed me on the cheek. "Okay, I will call you early too."

"Insha Allah."

"Insha Allah." Destiny got out of the car and headed towards the front door. When she reached the steps she paused and turned back around, jogging back to the car. "I can't believe I almost forgot to tell you!"

"Tell me what?"

"Malik told me that when y'all were growing up you had this hiding place that you swore up and down no one knew about but you. Well he said he left something there for you."

"You mean to tell me that dirty rotten scoundrel been knowin' about my secret hidin' spot all this time?" Destiny laughed. "A'ight, I'll look when I get home. Whose Navigator is that?" I asked, looking past her. It was new and very nice.

"That is Auntie Patience's truck." I felt a flutter in my chest. *Patience?*

"Patience is in there?"

"It's her truck, she must be. Why don't you come on in and say hello? Mama and Auntie Patience will be happy to see you."

"I don't think so, maybe some other time." I said, starting the car.

"Oh my goodness, don't tell me you are *scared* Atif."

"Destiny, I am *not* afraid of women, okay?" Destiny only looked at me in response, challenging me with a smirk on her face. I exhaled and turned off the car's engine. "I don't know *who* you got me mixed up with," I said, exiting the vehicle. "But I ain't scared of no once-a-month-bleedin-"

"*Atif!*" Destiny exclaimed in shock. I laughed. "Subhan Allah."

"I was just seein' if you was on your toes." I said. "Ladies first."

Destiny took me by the hand and led the way. I hadn't seen or heard from Patience in over 10 years so what was the big deal? I long ago stopped yearning for her, though I was not able to cease thinking of her here and there. The only woman I had ever loved was just on the other side of the door, I thought as Destiny inserted her key into the lock. If it wasn't such a big deal then why was my heart going crazy like a gorilla who was trapped in my rib cage? I involuntarily took a deep breath as Destiny twisted the door knob.

"I heard that, fraidy cat." Destiny said, smiling up at me as she opened the door. Stepping inside what appeared to be the living room, I could see directly into the kitchen. The furniture was nice and there was a large plasma flat screen television hanging on the wall. "Lucy! I'm home!" Destiny said, shutting the door behind us.

"Girl where have you been all day? I was just asking about you." I heard a voice say. I recognized it as belonging to Patience. Besides some evident maturity, she sounded the same. I signaled for Destiny to be quiet and crept into the kitchen. Patience was bent over looking into the refrigerator. "Since when is it okay for you not to check in with your mother directly after school?"

"Since I decided to pick her up and take her with me." I said. Patience stood straight up and turned around at the sound of my voice. The incredulous look she had on her face told me that she had not forgotten my voice either.

She was the embodiment of an independent professional woman, letting the world know she was playing to win with a pricey designer suit and a smart-wedge-cut hairstyle that just brushed the top of her shoulders, framing her face with thick black waves and highlighting her light brown eyes. She had matured into a striking woman that could dress herself in a sackcloth and still be as lovely as ever.

"Wha'sup stranger, remember me?"

"Oh...my...*God!*" Patience exclaimed in shock, covering her mouth with hands that looked as if they had possibly been manicured at Kesha's.

Then came the tears.

"Girl don't cry, don't! People been cryin' all day, I don't want to see no more tears."

"I can't help it! I can't help it!" Patience said, jumping up and down while fanning her eyes with her fingertips.

"Mama!" Destiny called out, leaving the two of us alone in the kitchen. "Auntie Patience is crying again!" I heard her finish as she made her way down the hall.

"You gone give me a hug or stand there and cry?"

"I don't know! *Can* I?"

"Girl come here." I answered, holding my arms out. I couldn't deny the fact that I was actually happy to see her. Patience collapsed into my embrace. I could hear her whimpering on my shoulder, soaking my shirt with her tears. I didn't understand her reaction, I mean if she missed me like that then why no visits or letters? I had not spent the last 10 years buried 6 feet deep out of her reach.

"I'm so sorry Atif. I'm so sorry about *everything!* I didn't *know*, I swear I didn't *know!*"

"I know you didn't."

"They *used* me!"

"I know they did."

"It's all my fault!"

"No it ain't girl," I started, pulling away from her. "Don't be sayin' that to yourself. Here, sit down." I guided her to a stool at the end of the kitchen counter. "You need some water or somethin'?" I asked looking through the cupboards for a cup.

"Yes, please? I think I'm going into hyper-ventilation." Patience answered, dabbing at her eyes. "How did you get out?"

"Allah's mercy." I answered tersely, handing her a cup of water. She took it with a trembling hand and sipped at it. I had almost forgotten how attractive this woman was. Teebaby entered the kitchen trailed by her daughter.

"Hey, Atif! *Look* at you!" Teebaby said, smiling ear to ear as she approached me with her arms out. I hugged her. "When did you get out?"

"This mornin'." I answered, pulling away. "You ain't gone cry is you?"

"No, I'm not gone cry." Teebaby answered, laughing.

"*Good.*" I said, sitting at the kitchen table. Teebaby and Destiny followed suit.

"Did you know Atif was getting out?" Patience asked Destiny. She smiled.

"If that girl is good for anything it's keepin' a secret from everybody else." Teebaby said, looking at her daughter. Destiny lowered her gaze. Seeing her feelings hurt infuriated me. I felt anger seeping into my chest.

"I'll get it." Destiny said, storming from the room upon hearing the telephone ring.

"So, how does it feel to get out after all of this time?" Teebaby asked me, smiling.

I wasn't.

"Why would you say somethin' like that to your daughter?" I asked, answering her question with one of my own.

"Somethin' like what?'

"You told her she was good for nothin'."

"She knows I don't mean that."

"No she doesn't. Do you remember the day I got locked up? You were pregnant and it was my birthday and we was all ridin' around kickin' it, you remember?" I asked Teebaby. She nodded. "We stopped by the pay phone so that Patience could use it?"

"Yeah, I remember. Darion wouldn't let her use his car phone with his cheap ass."

"Me and you were in the car by ourselves for a couple of minutes and do you remember what you said to me?"

"No, not really."

"Let me refresh your memory. You told me how Darion made you feel as if you were a burden on him, like he didn't even *like* you, you remember now?" Teebaby nodded.   "Do you remember how you felt?" Teebaby nodded once again.   "Well, that is how you just made Destiny feel." I admonished. Teebaby's full lips pursed at the mild rebuke.

Destiny appeared seemingly out of thin air, smiling. She had let go of her mother's comment and her mind was elsewhere. "Atif, Sparkle wants to know if you are going to let her cook for you again someday?"

I smiled at my friend's daughter. "Tell Sparkle that I would be honored and blessed to eat her cookin' again, insha Allah." Destiny nodded, smiling as she vacated the room.

"Insha Allah," Patience started, smiling at me. "Every time I heard Destiny say that phrase it made me think of you."

Silence.

"Sparkle cooked for you?" Teebaby asked me.

"Yeah, my first home cooked meal too."

"That girl can throw down, can't she?" Teebaby asked. I nodded, rubbing my stomach. I noticed that Patience's eyes followed my hand to my torso; I put it back on the table. "It don't make no sense for a 14-year old girl to be able to cook everything under the sun like that."

"You should have given *me* a call, I would have loved to cook your first homemade meal for you." Patience said, looking me in my eyes.

It was time for me to go.

"Well, I better be goin'," I started, rising from the table. "I just wanted to come in and speak."

"You're leaving already?" Patience asked, standing also. When I nodded it was as if someone let all of the air out of her.

"Do you mind if I go and say goodnight to Destiny?" I respectfully asked Teebaby.

"No, go ahead. Last room on your left."

I smiled at both of them and left the kitchen, heading down the hall once I passed through the living

525

room.   There were pictures on the wall in the hall and I paused by one of Darion, Teebaby and Destiny when she was 6 months old.   It was a very nice picture but D-Mack looked as if he had been coerced to be there, taking part in the photo under duress. After that I continued on down the hall until I reached Destiny's room. Her walls were covered with hundreds of photos. I even saw some that I had sent to her from Moberly.

"I'm about to go Suga Bear. Insha Allah I will see you in the mornin', okay?"

"Okay." She answered, removing the mouthpiece from her mouth.

"Make Salah before you go to sleep. And not in here with all these photos, the Angels won't come around these images."

"I will, and when I do I'm going to ask Allah to bless you with a wife."

I laughed. "I can' just marry any-old-body Destiny, she has to be special."

"So I'll ask for a special person." I smiled down on her. Destiny was such a sweet girl.

"You do that.   Allah says in the Qur'an that He answers the invocations of those who believe and do righteous good deeds." Destiny smiled.

"I love you Atif."

"I love you too. Goodnight." I left Destiny to her phone conversation. Walking back down the hallway, I saw that Patience was standing at the front door and I didn't find it strange at all. "A'ight then Teebaby, it was nice seein' you again." I called out to her as she sat at the kitchen table.

"You too Atif, don't be no stranger. I'm glad that you are out." She answered. I then headed for the door.

"Do you have to leave now? Why don't you stay for a while? I want to talk to you." Patience said as I approached.

"It has been a long day Patience, I'm tired and I want to take a hot bath for the first time in a *long* time."

"I understand." She answered with a sigh.

"That is a nice truck you have."

"You like it?" I nodded. "It likes you too." I chuckled.

"Bye Patience." I said, stepping out of the house.

"When will I see you again?"

My world stopped revolving around you a long time ago Patience, I thought to myself silently. *How does another 10 years sound? Maybe I could let my life become so busy that I would not be able to make time for such a thing; how would you like that?*

"I ain't hard to find. I wasn't while I was in prison and I ain't now." I answered as I turned and left. I could feel her eyes boring into my retreating back.

What a day, I thought as I walked to the car. Running into Patience like I did was the last thing I had expected to take place. I wasn't really prepared for our encounter but I believed I handled myself well and maintained a fear of Allah in all that I did. I needed to learn how to handle being in the presence of women again, I had been tucking tail and running all day the moment I suspected things were venturing into an area where temptation lay in wait. I knew doing so was not something I could spend the rest of my life doing.

As I pulled off I saw Patience standing on the front porch, watching me. I honked the horn and she waved at me, smiling. 13-years ago we had a bond between us that I naively thought could not be broken, we were living a fairy tale that I thought would never end. But that was a lifetime ago. I no longer believed in such fairy tales because in reality things don't always happen like we believe they are supposed to.

"I-i-i-i....don't....feel....no....ways ti-i-red. I've come too fa-a-ar from where, I sta-a-a-rted from-m-m. Nobody to-o-old me....that the road.... Would be ea-a-a-s-s-y-y. I don't beli-i-ieve He brought me this far, to leave m-e-e-e." I crooned aloud as I drove, singing a Christian song that I used to love hearing Big Mama humming early in the mornings. I had told Patience that I was tired and that was why I was leaving so abruptly, but honestly, and like in one of my grandmother's all time favorite songs, I didn't feel no ways tired at all.

*****

COMPENSATION
And there is no sin on you if you
make a hint of betrothal or conceal it
in yourself, Allah knows that you will
remember them, but do not make a promise
of contract with them in secret except
that you speak an honorable saying
according to the Islamic law. And do
not consummate the marriage until
the term prescribed is fulfilled. And
know that Allah knows what is in
your minds, so fear Him. And know that
Allah is Oft-Forgiving, Most Forbearing.
-Noble Qur'an 2:235

26

On December 25th, millions of Christians around the world celebrate this day commemorating the birth of Prophet Jesus. I have read where there are some Muslims in the Middle East who have attributed a day out of the year to celebrate the birth of Prophet Muhammad in a similar fashion. The truth is both of these dates are moot, no one is positively sure of exactly which day either Prophet Jesus or Prophet Muhammad was born; nor has it ever been recorded anywhere that the 2 celebrated their own days of birth or instructed for their followers to do so.

In Islam this is called "Bid'ah" or *innovation*. We believe that when our Creator sent prophets to a people they taught them their religion and didn't forget or leave anything out except for that which didn't belong and had no place. (Practices, customs, etc.) To invent or add something to a way of life taught by one of the prophets after their death (or what have you) is to say that the prophet sent by the Creator did not do his job very well and was unsuccessful in completing his mission and duty. Or, even more outrageous, it says that the Creator Himself made a mistake in His judging of character by choosing someone to fulfill a duty that wasn't qualified to do the job.

Subhan Allah!

In actuality, Prophet Muhammad only instructed for the Muslims to celebrate 3 occasions: The breaking of the annual monthly fasting of Ramadam ('Idul-Fitr), the sacrifice ('Idul-Adha), and every Friday (Jumu'ah). Any "holidays" other than these, as far as *within* the religion of Islam is concerned, is rightfully considered as "bid'ah", such aberration is a thing that the Muslim who clings to the teachings and practices of Prophet Muhammad stays far away from.

"Come on Atif, we are going to be late!" Destiny said, wrapping her arms around my neck from behind. I was seated behind the desk in my study finishing up a letter I was writing to brother Cook-El who was still incarcerated. I had already written Skooter-B, Pastor Cool Breeze, and DeAnthony X (whose name was now legally changed to

"Amiri-Taalib Rubanza", which means courageous prince and seeker of knowledge) earlier that morning after returning from the 'Id prayer. I intended to write to brothers Siddiq and Muhsin after the celebration so that I could tell them about it.

It was January of the year 2006. I had been out of prison for three months and was about to attend my first 'Idul-Adha in the free world. Things had been going really well for me since the day I walked out of the penitentiary. I had my driver's license, a job at Payless Cashways working nights and a savings account. I spent my days off helping Old Lady Jenkins (who was still ticking) around her house, studying and kicking it with Destiny.

My brother had left a significant amount of money in my secret hiding spot I had as a child. The money that Darion told me he was leaving behind for his daughter was there also. I hadn't spent one single dollar of the $250,000 Malik had stashed for me because my conscience wouldn't allow me. I left it safely where it was at, believing that Allah would reveal to me which route was best for me to take. Whatever He put in my heart was what I would do; whether it was giving it to the relatives of the people I had killed or setting it on fire.

As for Destiny's money, I planned to put it in her hands when she reached a certain age and let her decide for herself what to do with it. I didn't feel as if I could make the decision for her based on how I felt about it's origins.

"Here, seal this one for me." I said, handing her the letter. In prison we were not allowed to seal our envelopes when we wanted to send our letters out. Ever since my release, licking the adhesive on an envelope always made me sick to my stomach.

"Can we go now?" Destiny asked me after sealing the envelope.

"Yeah," I answered, peering at her as she turned and headed for the front of the house. Why was she in such a hurry? I looked around the study making sure that I wasn't forgetting anything and then I walked out of my favorite room. Climbing into the passenger's seat of Khalid's car, I turned the heat up and honked the horn.

"You know Atif, I have never seen Khalid use the front door of the house. He goes out of his way to go in and out through the back." Destiny pointed out as Khalid came from around the back of the house. I too had noticed this and I knew why. However, I didn't comment on it. Insha Allah he would get over his transgression in time. Like me, Khalid had his own way of dealing with things; a method that no one understood but him.

"Y'all ready to get y'all's grub on?" Khalid asked us, sliding into the driver's seat. The both of us nodded. "'Id Mubarak! (Blessed 'Id!)"

"'Id Mubarak!" We responded in unison as Khalid pulled off.

It was cold out and the streets were covered with a late snowfall from the night before which was quickly turning into slush and ice. We moved along at a snail's pace, Khalid was the most careful, traffic law abiding individual I had ever known. He stopped at all stop signs, always used his blinker, never went over the speed limit and didn't tailgate other cars.

"When is Ke'von coming back to Kansas City?" Destiny asked Khalid.

"When school is out, insha Allah."

"Why?" I asked Destiny.

"I was just curious."

"Mm-hmm, curiosity killed the cat; you know that don't you?" I asked.

"Can you say over-protective?" Destiny countered. Khalid chuckled. I threw an M&M at her.

"Speakin' of *Flash Gordon*," I started, talking to Khalid. "I got the impression that he be dealin' with a lot down there in Greensboro."

"He does, yet his mother can't seem to understand why he down there actin' up. They don't support the boy in nothin' positive that he do! Everybody in the city goes to his track meets just to see *him* run except for his....guardians. Anytime you don't pay your child any attention at home he is gone seek it in the streets and we both know how such a story plays out.

"When I tell his mother these things all she does is throw my incarceration up in my face and how I wasn't there." Khalid shook his head. "That's cool, because since he is comin' to stay with us he won't have to trip on that. I got his back."

"Ke'von is *moving* down here?" Destiny asked in elation, sounding as if Nelly was coming to town. I looked peevishly at her. "*Okay, okay!*" Destiny said in response to that look, sitting back in her seat.

"Where you goin' brotha'? The Masjid is in the opposite direction." I said to Khalid as he turned west on 47th street instead of east.

"We ain't goin' to Masjid Omar for the 'Id feast. We are goin' to a Masjid out south, insha Allah."

"Why?"

Khalid smiled. "Do you remember when you walked me to the front on the day I was released from prison?" I nodded. "I told you that I was accepting your act of kindness as compensation for your transgression and that I wanted to do something in return to compensate you for mine. Well, with the help of Allah I was able to make it happen."

"Make what happen?" I asked, regarding him suspiciously.

"You'll see in a few minutes, insha Allah." Khalid then looked into his rearview mirror. "Won't he Destiny?"

"Yes." Destiny answered, smiling knowingly at me. I looked first at Khalid and then I turned around in my seat facing Destiny. I *knew* that she was in a hurry for a reason!

"I thought you was my girl, Suga Bear."

"*What?* I am your girl Atif!"

"Then tell me wha'sup, you know that we tell each other everything. Keepin' secrets ain't even for us, not me and you."

"Don't you fall for that Destiny! Stay strong, hold your water girl!" Khalid interrupted just as Destiny was about to give in. Khalid knew that I was the only person in the world capable of prying some confidential information out of Destiny.

"Yeah, you are not slick. Trying to play on *my* soft spot. You will get over it." Destiny said, regaining her composure.

Dangnabit, I had lost her.

I didn't have the slightest idea what the two were up to. Back in early '93 I remember feeling it in my heart that me and Khalid would have a life altering confrontation. The next thing I knew I was 15-years old and sitting in the county jail awaiting to be prosecuted for second degree murder. This feeling was back with a vengeance. Once again something that I was not expecting was about to take place that would have a monumental effect on my life. And just like the morning of the night I caught my case, I woke up with this feeling in the pit of my stomach.

A short while later we pulled into a wide parking lot filled with automobiles. The building itself was large and I wondered to myself if it was there before I got locked up. "This is a Masjid?" I asked Khalid. He nodded, parking the car and we all exited the vehicle.

"Now *I* done did my part," Khalid said, holding the doors open for me and Destiny. "The rest is up to *you*."

Stepping into the atmosphere of the Masjid was like being at a family reunion. Not only was the inside of the building very nice but even better than that was the sight of so many Muslims congregating from all nationalities and walks of life. There was food *everywhere*! I saw lamb, chicken, fish, roast beef, broccoli and cheese, cake, all kinds of different pies, rice; I mean everything and so much of it that one would not know where to start. We were greeted by smiling Muslims that I had never seen before a day in my life.

It didn't take long at all for me to become a part of the festivities. Destiny was missing in action but I was not concerned about her whereabouts with there being a room full of Muslims and all. I had forgotten all about whatever it was that her and Khalid were up to and I found myself deep into a conversation with a group of brothers about how imperative it is for the Muslims out in society to show more support for the ones who are incarcerated.

"Excuse me Atif, but someone wants to see you." Destiny said. I wondered to myself how long she had been standing there unnoticed on my right side. Excusing myself, I followed Destiny over to one of the serving areas where the Muslim women were. As we headed in that direction, I didn't feel uncomfortable like I did at Kesha's or Teebaby's because I knew that in the presence of a group of God fearing women wearing head coverings, there was no need for me to feel uneasy at all. Especially considering the fact that most of them were probably married.

Destiny knew exactly where we were heading. We approached a table where a sister was facing us and another was turned in the opposite direction, reaching for what looked to me like a roll. The sister who was facing us had a very pretty face drawn tight over a smoothly curving bone structure, decorated by a multitude of small red freckles across her nose and cheeks. Her complexion was a very pale gold with roses and milk for an accent and her almond shaped eyes glinted with innocence that was almost childlike. She smiled as we approached, touching the sister she stood beside on the shoulder and gently turning her around with her hand.

When she faced me it was like Allah pushed a mute button silencing every single sound in that place just so that I could hear no one else's voice but hers.

"As-salaamu alaykum Atif!" Fatimah greeted, smiling her unforgettable smile at me.

*****

Love is a bold emotion. It can barge rudely into the door of your heart without knocking first, and once it makes itself at home there really is no denying it. It becomes one with your whole being, selfishly forcing itself to be paramount in every waking conception as if it has a spoiled, only-child like mind of its own.

Sometimes love is unwanted and confusing, no matter how much you try to shake it by occupying your mind with other things or transferring it, it lingers nonetheless. Yet at other times when you *are* yearning for

536

it, crying for it, praying for, *paying* for it even; love is nowhere to be found. Love also can *hurt*! And it is the pain which often accompanies love that makes people run from it. But with all of its side effects, when love is good, oh how good love is!

I could not stop thinking about Fatimah. Everything I did, everywhere I went, she was on my mind. At times I found myself spacing off and thinking about her when I should have been focused on other things. Every once in a while she would even invade my prayers and I would have to catch myself, redirecting my thoughts to where they belonged.

13 years! I had not seen or heard from that woman in over 13 years and even then I hardly knew her. 6 months had gone by since I saw her at the 'Id feast. Not long after that blessed day I received an unexpected phone call from Aminah (the sister who was with Fatimah with the freckles) asking if I was interested in (get this!) escorting the two of them to dinner at one of Fatimah's favorite restaurants. Of course I agreed, allowing Destiny to pick out every part of my attire from my socks to the Black by Kenneth Cole Cologne I wore and everything in between. I then went out and had the time of my life.

Aminah was 25-years old and at first her constant presence was strange, but once the evening got into full swing I welcomed her company. Fatimah would not allow herself to go anywhere with me without a third person present. She related a narration of Prophet Muhammad to me where he said that when an unmarried man and woman are alone together, Satan is the third party. So out of piety and fear of Allah, Aminah accompanied us wherever we went. Aminah was so shy! I had no idea that it was possible for a grown woman, a beautiful woman at that, to be so bashful.

Fatimah and I connected on levels that I never thought possible. I was so comfortable around her and each time she smiled at me I fell in love with her all over again. Which of course meant that it was time for me to propose. This was the topic of my everyday conversations with Destiny, my underaged confidant.

"So, have you figured out what you want to say yet?" Destiny asked me, sitting on my bed. I was scheduled to rendezvous with Fatimah and Aminah at the Reverse Bar and Grill on the Plaza in less than an hour where I intended to pop the big question.

"Will you marry me?"

"No! That's what *everyone* says."

"How would *you* know?"

"Atif I have seen every single love story known to man."

"Well what should I say then?" I asked her. Destiny fell silent for a moment.

"Say this," she started, smiling. "You know Fatimah, if a man were to marry a woman like you he would be very happy."

"That is *corny*!"

"No it isn't! You don't want to come straight out and ask a woman like Fatimah to marry you, you want to hint at it."

Why was I seeking counsel from a 14-year old teenage girl concerning how I should propose to the woman I loved? "Hand me the phone, I am goin' to call Kesha and ask her what I should say." At that moment the telephone rang as if on cue.

"Hello?" Destiny answered it. "Hi Auntie Patience!" *Patience*? "Here he is right here, hold on." Destiny handed me the phone.

Patience and I talked on the phone every once in a while since my release. One time I was at Teebaby's when she came over and the two of us went for a walk together talking about everything from our very first day at Central to how things were going for her at the law firm she worked for. We agreed that we would just be friends in respect of my Deen and not expect anything more from each other *unless* we both were willing to make our relationship lawful in Islam with marriage.

"Hello?"

"Hi Atif! What are you doing?" Patience asked cheerily.

"I was about to walk out of the door."

"Got a hot date?" Patience asked, she was joking but had hit the nail on the head.

"Actually, yeah, I do. In a way, I guess you could call it that."

"Oh...um, well I guess that this is a bad time then. Maybe I will call you back some other time or something."

"Insha Allah." I heard a dial tone for a response which, if I remembered her characteristics correctly, meant that she was upset. What was her problem? Was I supposed to lie or cancel my plans to sit home and talk to her or something? My clock did not stop ticking when she came around, life was not all about her, no, not in my mind. "Here," I said, handing the phone back to Destiny. "I don't have time to call Kesha, I am runnin' late as it is." I put my shoes on and gave myself a quick inspection in the mirror.

"How are you going to propose then?"

"I don't know, I will think of somethin' along the way. Walk me to my bike Suga Bear." Destiny got up and strolled with me out of the house to the front where a yellow and black Suzuki Gsxr900 motorcycle I was making monthly payments on sat. "Do you think she will say yes?" I asked her, putting my helmet on. Destiny smiled.

"In Allahu 'alim (Truly Allah is the Best Knower)."

I enjoyed riding my bike through the streets and the solitude that came along with it, especially late on week nights when the streets were fairly empty. I had a full black helmet with a tinted shield through which I was able to look at everyone around me as I rode by without them knowing it. I only opened my bike up on long, flat stretches of highway, racing at speeds of over 115-125 miles per hour. It was exhilarating. I liked the power, the noise, the speed, I liked everything about my bike and purchasing a car was one of the furthest things from my mind.

The Plaza area was a nice one, lined with expensive retail chains and sports bars as well as other things, it sat in the heart of the city frequented mostly by those who were a little or a *lot* better off than others, financially that is of course. I found the restaurant I was looking for after riding past it at least three times. I was still 10 minutes early, which was late by my standards, but upon my entry I saw that I had beat the ladies there.

Going places with Fatimah and Aminah provided me with the opportunities to experience other tastes and cultures that I never even before had given much thought about. Sometimes I went shopping with them down at the City Market whereas other times we found ourselves meeting up in the nicest restaurants. Fatimah appreciated the simple things in life as well as the rest. An evening out with her and Aminah was always unpredictable, the only thing I could predict was going somewhere I had never been or doing something that would have been boring to me if it were not for their company. The seemingly most insignificant things and places always attracted Fatimah's attention and presence, and she would bring the light of her winsome personality to shine on the dim surroundings. From the first time I met her back in detention, I was affected by the energy Fatimah radiated, a force intangible, yet one that now triggered a longing in my soul.

Looking at my watch 10 minutes after being escorted to our reserved table I saw that it was one minute after 8 and sure enough, when I lifted my eyes I saw Fatimah and Aminah heading in my direction. My heart skipped a beat and then began to thud frantically as it always did upon laying eyes on her.

Fatimah was tall and willowy, her waist slender and taught. Long in the leg, her athletic physique reflected an unusual strength without detracting from her undeniable femininity. Despite her height, she had an almost supernatural agility. Her deep brown eyes sparkled with wisdom but they held a proud glint like that of a fierce young eagle. The corners of Fatimah's mouth quirked in a mirthful smile as she strode purposely across the restaurant with Aminah in tow. The women *commanded* respect whether the purpose and reasons why were comprehended or not. I smiled boyishly in return, standing as the two approached.

"As-salaamu alaykum!" I greeted the two ladies, pulling out their chairs for them.

"Wa alaykum as-salaam!" they returned in unison.

"Have you been here long?" Fatimah asked me, still showing her pearly whites.

"No, not long at all." I answered, taking note as to how Fatimah's head-scarf coordinated with the rest of her outfit as always. Allah knows I was happy to see her.

"Isn't that your motorcycle out in the parking lot? The yellow and black one?" Fatimah asked me. Taking a look over the menu. I noticed a while back that Fatimah had added the ending "g's" to the words in her vocabulary and no longer butchered the English language with slang.

"I'm still payin' for it, but yeah, alhamdu lillah it is mine." I answered, sipping from a glass of water.

"When are you going to take me for a ride on it?" Fatimah asked. I choked on the water I was drinking as the image of the both of us on my bike flashed briefly in my mind. *Subhan Allah*! I scolded myself; where did that come from? The two ladies laughed softly. "I am just *kidding* Atif. Allah knows I am scared to death of those things. I think the colors are cute though."

We lost ourselves in conversation after giving the waitress our orders.   Fatimah was the Administrative Director for Sprint PCS with a lot of people working under her, her days were usually very busy and stressful. She liked her job but was contemplating going back to school. As it often did, our conversation journeyed back to juvenile. Aminah just loved to hear about our experiences while there in detention.

"You should have seen him trying to show me his chest in that isolation tank Aminah." I laughed out loud.

"No I wasn't!" I exclaimed in my own defense. "I had my shirt off and was doin' push-ups *long* before you came to that door."

"Mm-hmm," both ladies hummed in disbelief.

"Did y'all know each other back then?" I asked.

"Yes, we have been best friends since the sixth grade." Fatimah answered.

"I was with her when she was arrested." Aminah offered.

"Why was Fatimah the only one in detention then?"

541

"Because I didn't do as much…*damage* as Fatimah. She went off! There was blood and everything. That poor boy didn't stand a chance; Fatimah had him touching everything on the bus. Me? I did more screaming and scratching than anything else." Aminah answered. I laughed at that.

We talked about old times for a few more minutes. I kept on trying to find the right words to propose within the back of my mind the whole time but was unsuccessful. I was so nervous! What if she turned me down? I would be *too* embarrassed. Finally, with grim determination replacing the anxiety in my mind, I waited for the next conversational break and decided to go out on the limb. I was tired of hearing Destiny's voice echoing in my mind calling me a "fraidy cat". I was *not* scared of women!

"You know Fatimah," I started, disappointed with myself for not being able to come up with anything on my own. "If a man was to marry a woman like you he would be *very* happy."

Silence.

Aminah gaped at me wide-eyed, shocked into speechlessness. Her and Fatimah then looked at each other, giving me the uncomfortable feeling that I had over stepped my boundaries and disrespected a God fearing woman in some way. *I'm going to get Destiny for this*, I thought to myself. Fatimah looked into my eyes, searching.

"Atif, was that like a hint at *betrothal*? Are you asking me to marry you in a round about way?"

I could have backed out right then and there and saved face. But I *had* to go all of the way, there was no use in stopping then. I loved her; I *longed* for her and I just had to take my chances. "Yeah, I am." Fatimah paused, but otherwise did a good job of seeming unaffected by my answer. This time the silence seemed infinitely, tortuously long.

"You should find out what a Muslim woman's dowry is before you make a hint of betrothal like that." Fatimah responded smoothly. Was that a yes? Maybe? Remember, I was Mr. does-not-have-a-clue when it came to women.

"What is your dowry?"

542

"I don't know Atif, I *could* ask for your house,"
And I would give it to you.
"I *could* request $10, 000,"
And I would give that to you.

Fatimah held my eyes, smiling. I was a nervous wreck and I wondered to myself if her smile had anything to do with what she was doing to me. "What do you think Aminah?" Fatimah asked, turning to her best friend. Aminah shrugged her shoulders. "Sister you are sitting over there looking like Atif was talking to *you* or something. You *were* talking to me weren't you Atif?"

"Yeah!"

"I can't help it," Aminah said, unshed tears glimmering in her eyes. "That was so sweet!" she finished with an admiring smile tugging at the corners of her mouth.

"Yes, it *was* sweet, wasn't it?" Fatimah asked rhetorically, smiling at me. "And original." She added. *Maybe Destiny was on to something*, I thought to myself. "When you were in that isolation tank back in detention the day you left I slid a note under your door. Did you get it?" Fatimah then asked me, her face becoming serious.

"Yeah, I got it." I answered as the waiter brought us our food.

"On it I wrote down a verse from the Qur'an and I told you to put it in your *heart* so that you could take it with you wherever you went. Well, if you can not only remember *which* verse it was that I wrote down for you but *recite* it to me *in* Arabic.... I will accept *that* as dowry and insha Allah, I will marry you."

Relief spread throughout my entire body in waves. This was one of the million things I loved about Fatimah the most. A lot of women wanted a big fat diamond ring or what have you as an engagement gift, and though Fatimah dressed very nice, liked nice things and carried herself with a lot of class, she was far from your average materialistic woman. As far as she knew, all I had was my mother's house and a job working at Payless Cashways trying to stay afloat, yet none of this mattered to her.

She was not concerned with what I had or what I didn't have and did not want to make things difficult for me financially. She knew all about my past and didn't hold it against me. Fatimah even liked it that I was so inexperienced with women and found it amusing in a fun way. She was willing to work with me and teach me how to love her and treat her like she wanted to be treated.

"Fatimah that was *14* years ago! You expect for me to remember what you wrote on a piece of paper way back then?"

"That is what I want for my dowry. I asked you to put it in your heart Atif so that you *would* remember it. If you can't-"

I cut her off by reciting the verse in question, *in* Arabic. Of course I remembered it! It was the first verse of the Qur'an I had ever read. Not only that, but it had always been very motivational for me during the most trying times of my imprisonment.

"Is that the verse you were referrin' to?" I asked her with a smirk upon completion of my recitation.

"Yes, it is." Fatimah said, smiling in return. A tear slid down Aminah's cheek.

"So are we....?"

"Engaged?" Fatimah finished for me. I nodded. "Alhamdu lillah, yes we are. What took you so *long* to propose my future husband?" She then asked me, smiling. Hearing her call me that was like a drop of ice cold water on the tip of the tongue of a dehydrated man dying of thirst.

"Actually, I was waitin' for *you* to ask *me*!" I joked. Both ladies laughed out loud. *That one was for you D-Mack*, I thought to myself in remembrance of my friend.

"Allahu Akbar! I am so happy for the both of you!" Aminah said, hugging Fatimah.

"Shall we eat now?" Fatimah asked me.

"Yeah, let's do that." We dug in. I thought the food was delicious. Allah knows how much of an appetite I had worked up with all of that anxiety. Something was not right though. I noticed that Aminah had a funny expression on her face as she chewed and she was beginning to pick through her food with her fork, examining the meat. "What's wrong with your food sista'?" I asked her.

544

"I don't think this is what I ordered." She managed. Suspicion swelled in my mind.

"Let me see that," I said, gesturing towards her plate. She nodded and I picked it up, smelling the meat. "This is...man this is *pork*!" Aminah upchucked, catching the vomit in her mouth by sealing it shut with her hand. She then rose from the table and all but ran towards the bathrooms in the back.

Ever since becoming a Muslim I had conditioned myself to be slow to genuine anger because, like my brother, when I was provoked my destructive ruthlessness could be frightening. Well, I did everything but turn green and rip my clothes from my person up in that restaurant. I slapped the plate filled with the forbidden meat onto the floor, shattering it. All conversations ceased with the sudden sound of the plate breaking and all eyes were on me.

Yes! The only black man in that restaurant was about to get real *niggerish*. I just knew in my heart that someone had slipped the sister some pork on purpose. Many people don't know much about Islam and the Muslims, but what *everyone* did know was how we felt about pork. Maybe one of the cooks and the waitress thought it was some kind of joke or something. Well, they picked the wrong one. I was about to lose my mind and catch an assault/attempted murder case up in there.

"Is there a problem?" a tall man in a suit asked me as he approached our table with the waitress who had served us our food in tow. I stood up, so angry that I could hardly even speak.

"That plate of *pork*," I spat in disgust, gesturing towards the broken plate on the floor. "Is *not* what she ordered!"

"Get someone out here to clean up this mess and bring them whatever it was they *did* order." The man said to the waitress, fluttering a dismissive hand through the air. The waitress, without so much as an apology, turned on her heels and walked off.

I felt a hot flash of anger and started towards the man. My gait was menacing and ominous; I had every intent on trimming the man's chin with a well placed right hook. It would be an adequate penalty for the both of their inconsiderate dismissive gestures. Fatimah, seeing me coming even though the man had no clue what was about to transpire, gracefully slid in front of him, shielding the man with her body.

"Atif, why don't you go and see if Aminah is okay? Please?" Fatimah asked, her firm tone held no hope of debate. I nodded reluctantly and left the scene in the same direction that Aminah had gone in.

When I reached the ladies' room I tapped on the door. "Aminah?"

"Yes?" I heard her answer in her soft voice.

"Are you a'ight?" I heard the toilet flush and a second or two later the faucet turn on.

"I will be out in a second, insha Allah." A little while later Aminah emerged from the rest room. Looking up at me, she gave me a wan, jittery smile. "I am sorry Atif, I hate to ruin your evening like this but I am not feeling very well and I want to leave this place. This is why it is not good to eat at the kuffar restaurants."

I understood and agreed. Leading Aminah out of the restaurant, I took her over to Fatimah's pewter 2005 Infinity. As I reached for the door handle on the passenger side I heard the chirp of the alarm being turned off and the doors unlock. Turning, I saw Fatimah heading across the parking lot in our direction with the small remote control on her key chain pointed at the vehicle. I then opened the door for Aminah and shut it behind her when she climbed in. Walking around the car I did the same for Fatimah.

"Thank you." Fatimah said, smiling up at me as I closed her door. "Call me when you make it home, insha Allah." I nodded.

"As-salaamu alaykum sistas." I offered, detached.

"Wa alaykum as-salaam." They returned. Fatimah eyed me as she started the car's engine. I turned and walked off, heading unconsciously in the direction of the restaurant entrance doors. I heard a car horn and stopped in my tracks.

"Come here Atif," Fatimah said.   I walked back towards the car, leaning over with my elbows on the door. "That man was very rude and inconsiderate, I know. But Allah says in the Qur'an to show forgiveness, enjoin what is good, and turn away from the foolish. The Qur'an also says that whosoever shows patience and forgives that would truly be from the things recommended by Allah." Fatimah then placed her hand on my forearm.

Her touch! It was so soft, so gentle and it seemed to magically force the tension in my body to abate. She had never touched me before for any reason and my arm almost shivered in delight as it bore the welcomed weight of her hand. By degrees, the twin flares of rage glittering in my eyes guttered out.

"Allah is the Best Knower, but I believe what happened was an honest mistake. Even if it wasn't, you can't be so *physical* Atif, unless it is in the way of Allah. You still have that prison mentality and you have to shed it if we are going to build something together. I can help you if you will let me," Fatimah said soothingly. She then looked me in the face, pleading with her eyes. "Don't go back in there, please don't. The matter is settled and over with, okay?"

I sagged my shoulders and bowed my head in resignation.   My whispered "A'ight" was barely audible. Who gave this woman such power over me?

"Besides," she began, putting her car in drive and removing her hand from my forearms. My arm could have cried.   "It would be difficult for us to...consummate our union if you were to go back in there, violate your parole and end up in prison." Fatimah offered as an inducement. She smiled at me and drove off.

I stared after her numbly, struck speechless by astonishment. Either my understanding of "consummating" a union was a little off or she had just made an indirect referral to having sex with me the night of our wedding. Maybe I was tripping, maybe my mind was in the gutter like it seemed to have been all evening long.

I picked my chin up from the pavement and walked over to my bike. Putting on my helmet I told myself that I would look the term up when I made it home. Starting my motorcycle, I looked in the direction of the restaurant entrance and shook my head. I would begin my life with Fatimah by accepting her counsel and keeping my word. Plus, she made all of the sense in the world with what she said.

"It's almost time for me to pray." I mumbled to myself just before riding off into the night.

*****

A SPECIAL PERSON

And beside them will be Qaasiraat-at-Tarf
(chaste wives, restraining their glances,
desiring none except their husbands), with
wide and lovely eyes. (Delicate and pure)
as if they were (hidden) eggs (well) preserved.
-Noble Qur'an 37:48-49

27

October, 2006. Hundreds of millions of Muslims around the world were celebrating the breaking of the Ramadan fasting. It was the last day of the 3 day festivities of 'Id-ul-Fitr, one of the 3 Muslim holidays. Fatimah and I were scheduled to have a simple Muslim wedding the next day, 3 months after my proposal. Fatimah wanted to wait until *after* Ramadan to get married. This way we would not be tempted to do what newlyweds do during the daylight hours of the month of Ramadan while we were to be fully occupied with the remembrance of Allah. I had not been with a woman in over 14 years by then so I had a lot of lost time to make up for. Fatimah understood this and planned ahead.

Persistence was released from the Feds and Patience was having a get together over her house. Me and Destiny were invited but I was not sure if I was going to be able to make it. After the festival I promised my old history teacher Mr. Williams that I would let him have one of the two tickets I had for an Enrico Lane boxing match to take place that day.

Enrico Lane was a Jr. Middleweight from Kansas City with a devastating right cross that could end the fight at any time. I was not quick to pass up on seeing the brother do his thing. I intended to drop by the get together before the night was over. I wanted to see Persistence after all of the time that had gone by since I saw her last.

"As-salaamu alaykum!" I greeted Fatimah later that day. I had just parted with Mr. Williams and decided to drop in on the homeless shelter where Fatimah was volunteering. The fights lasted longer than I expected and Persistence was long gone, the get together was over with and I saw no reason to go out that way just then. I talked to Persistence on the phone though and promised to go and see her soon.

"Hey you, wa alaykum as-salaam!" Fatimah returned the greeting, smiling brightly. "I was just standing here thinking about you."

"Thinkin' about *me* or thinkin' about tomorrow?"

551

"Hmm, a little of both. What are you doing down here? I thought you were going..."

"To the get together?" Fatimah nodded. "Persistence ain't even there no more so I thought that I would come and see you instead. Where is Aminah?" I asked, looking around the shelter.

"She is around here somewhere." At that moment my cellular phone rang and I retrieved it, reading the text message. "Something wrong?" Fatimah inquired in response to the look on my face.

"This is Patience and, for one, how did she get the number to my phone? And for two, why does she want me to stop by her house even though the get together is over with and Persistence ain't even there no more?"

Fatimah's eyebrows knitted at the edge of her nose. "Does she know that we are getting married tomorrow, insha Allah?"

"Yeah, she knows." I answered. Fatimah thought silently to herself for a moment. "I will just tell her I am busy." I said as I began to key the numbers on my phone.

"No, don't tell her that. I think you should meet with her, not over her house of course, but somewhere else out in the public." Fatimah suggested.

"Why?"

Fatimah smiled. "That woman still loves you Atif."

"Fatimah! That was a *long* time ago."

"Yes, it was, *but* you were not only her first, you were also her first love. A woman never forgets her first love and she is not going to just sit back and let her first love marry some other woman without putting up a fight. Trust me, I am a woman and I know how we are."

I thought silently for a short period of time. "Okay, just for argument's sake lets say that is true. *Knowin'* this, why would you suggest that I go and meet with her? I don't understand that."

Fatimah gazed into my eyes. "I love you Atif and I am giving my heart to you. I desire you and you only, I am opening myself up to you without holding anything back and I need for you to do the same. In order to do so you must first close that old chapter of you and Patience once and for all. Allah is the Best Knower, but I think she is going to try and convince you to marry *her* instead of me and I need for you to either...take her up on her offer or tell her to her face that you are choosing me, this way there will be no more room for denial. Without which she or you will never truly move on."

"I moved on when she sent me that Dear John letter while I was in the infirmary back in '96." I said, knowing it was a ½ truth the moment the last word came off of my tongue.

"If that is the case then I don't have anything to worry about."

"You don't have nothin' to worry about either way."

Fatimah smiled. "Meet with her Atif, and if our getting married is Allah's will then you will withstand everything she throws at you for our sake. I trust you but at the same time I want you to go with your heart and if your heart does not lead you back to me than I would rather deal with that than settle for anything less than what I deserve."

Fatimah was right and I knew it. I had butterflies in my stomach and I really didn't want to go and meet with Patience because she was not the only one who was still harboring these feelings. I myself had been in a state of denial and sensing this, Fatimah was asking for me to face reality and deal with it instead of avoiding the matter like I had been doing ever since my release.

I guess I was thinking that what I did still feel for Patience would go away with time. Fatimah saw it in a different light. She felt like that seed which was burrowed deep in the fertile soil of my heart needed to be uprooted because as long as it still lingered there then there was still a chance for it to grow and mature if watered with enough temptation under the right circumstances. She trusted me true enough, but she also knew that man was created weak in this area of his nature. Fatimah was willing to lay all that she had on the table for the sake of pursuing a life with me and she needed for me to do the same. She *deserved* it.

Looking into Fatimah's eyes, I just knew that she was the woman for me and there was no way I could hurt her. But why was my stomach doing flip-flops as if in reality I didn't have a whole lot of confidence in my ability to turn away the very woman I spent so many years yearning for?

"A'ight, I will go." I said peremptorily.

"I won't be here much longer, insha Allah Aminah and I are going to my place when we leave here. It shouldn't take you long so drop by afterwards if-"

"Don't go there Fatimah, no ifs, I'm comin' back." I cut in with more confidence than I truly had.

"Insha Allah." Fatimah said. She then made shooing gestures with her fingers. "Go, and be careful on the motorcycle. It is supposed to rain some more later."

"As-salaamu alaykum."

"Wa alaykum as-salaam."

*****

"Why did you want to meet me here instead of my house?" Patience asked me an hour or so later. We were at a McDonald's restaurant located at Blue Ridge Blvd and Grandview Road. The first thing I happened to notice was that she was wearing the diamond stud earrings I purchased for her 15th birthday.

I didn't want to meet you at all, I thought to myself. "I've already explained that to you, it's improper." I said, maintaining my mask of non-interest as if I didn't even notice them.

Patience shrugged. "It makes no difference to me Atif." She said, dipping a French fry into some catsup.

Why did you ask then?

"How was the get together?"

"It was nice, I am *so* glad that Sis' is home. You should see her," Patience then lowered her voice to a whisper, "She has gained at least 20 to 25 pounds."

"Straight up?" Patience nodded. "Wha'sup with her and Smack Man? They still together?"

"Yes, if there is such a thing as being with a man in prison who will more than likely never make it out alive." I cast her an irritated glance and shook my head. "What?"

554

"Is that how you felt about me when I got sentenced?" I asked in a flat voice. Patience glared at me. Our eyes momentarily clashed.

"What are you talking about? I was there for you when you were sentenced."

I laughed without mirth. "What? *How*? By fillin' my head up with a bunch of empty promises? You call *that* bein' there for me?" Patience's face turned so red it could have been mistaken for a stop sign.

"It is not *my* fault that you did what you did to go to prison! It was no one's fault but *yours*, a decision that *you* made! You decided that you would rather pull that trigger than stay out here with me!" Patience declared. "You were out here selling all of that dope, sleeping with God knows how many women, and driving around in your fancy little Mustang like you were a grown man but when the time came for you to deal with the consequences of your lifestyle it was a different story."

I pursed my lips, attempting to curb my anger: I failed miserably. "I *did* deal with the consequences of my lifestyle like a man, no, scratch that. Like a *warrior*! I couldn't shake you when everything was all good, fun and games but when things got ruff you disappeared on me without a trace."

Patience rolled her eyes in exasperation, touching her forehead in disbelief. "I was a *teenager* Atif! *God*, what did you expect? 30 years Atif, they gave you 30 *years*!"

"I *expected* the love you spent our whole freshman year trying to convince me you had for me; I *expected* for you to be there for me when Big Mama and Darion died; I *expected* for you to be there for me when I was laid up in that infirmary barely able to even remember who I was! Or when I was in the hole! That is what I *expected*! Not that you deprive yourself of a life because of me, I didn't *expect* that. I needed you to be a friend to me like you said you would be in that letter you wrote. But you just cut me completely out of your life and treated me like I was dead or somethin'." Silence ensued. Patience frowned and nibbled at her underlip. I then looked at her and smiled. "*Man* that felt good!"

Patience threw her head back in laughter. "Yes, it *did* feel really, really good I must admit."

"I feel like a 100 pound weight has just been lifted off of my chest."

"Me too." Patience smiled at me. She looked so good! She needed to be on someone's runway instead of sitting in that restaurant with me. "So, what now?"

"What do you mean?" I asked, my throat going dry all at once.

I knew doggone well what she meant.

"Look," she began, wiping salt from her fingertips with a napkin. I took a sip of my chocolate milkshake, hoping that my nervousness could not be detected with my slightly trembling hand. "I am just going to come right out and say this Atif....I don't think that you should marry Fatimah tomorrow."

"Why would you say somethin' like that Patience? You don't even *know* Fatimah."

"No, I don't. But what I do know is that you should be marrying *me* instead."

I stared at her for a full minute, at a loss for words. I don't know if I was searching her eyes for sincerity or punch drunk on account of her words. For some reason the Gap Band's "Stop Running" began to play in my head.

"How do you figure that?"

"Because Atif," Patience said, taking ahold of my free hand. "*We* are *meant* to be together, it is supposed to be *me* and *you*. It is supposed to be us. I know that I made some mistakes and did some things I should not have done, we *both* did. But I am dealing with them like you did and with time I just know that we can get past all of that. I know that I hurt you but if you give me another chance I will make it up to you; I will *never* hurt you again. I still love you, I *always* have and even though I acted as if I didn't I was never able to *stop* loving you. If you were able to forgive Kevin for what he did then *surely* you can forgive me, can't you?"

I rescued my hand from her grasp. "You knew who killed my mama the whole time, didn't you? That is what he was bragging to you about, wasn't it? That is why you broke up with him, isn't it?" Patience looked down at the table and nodded her head. "How could you keep somethin' like that from me? Why didn't you *tell* me?"

"I *tried*!" Patience exclaimed, lifting her eyes which were now glistening with tears. "But it wouldn't come out! How was I supposed to tell you such a thing?"

She was right, I couldn't fault her for that. She knew what me and my brother were capable of and she didn't want to play a part in a potential blood bath. Hearing some thunder, I turned in my chair and looked outside just as the rain began pattering down, first in a lazy drizzle then in a sheet. I sighed, I had been there far longer than I had expected to be. I had a mind to call Fatimah so that she wouldn't be thinking that I decided to leave her for Patience but thought against it. Why? Because honestly I wasn't even sure that my decision had been made. My conscience was sympathizing with Patience and as much as I wanted to deny it, I was actually giving marriage with Patience some thought.

Were we *really* meant to be?

"I have been out of prison for a whole year now Patience, why are you just now tellin' me this?"

"You have been avoiding me since the day you were released," she answered, looking at me. "I also didn't want to come on too strong too soon since you said that you weren't looking for anything less than marriage. I wanted to give you some space so that you could get yourself together. Your getting engaged all of a sudden shocked me! I knew that I loved you and I tried convincing myself that I just wanted for you to be happy but I am not content with that. I called you up today because I just had to tell you how I felt before it was too late."

"It is all about *you*, huh Patience? It always has been. That is so selfish. And what do you mean before it is too late? It *is* too late! I am gettin' married *tomorrow* girl!"

"No it is not! It is not too late until the 2 of you say I do and that has not taken place yet!"

Then came the tears.

"Please Atif, just think about it okay?" Patience asked, reaching for my hand.

"I don't have *time* to think about it!" I retorted, pulling my hand away from her grasp. I then shook my head, releasing a sigh.

You can't keep runnin', in and out of my li-i-i-fe...

"It does not work like that Patience. Where were you when I *needed* you? You can't just come back into my life like this *after* the storm is over and expect for everything to be peaches and cream. It is too late for that, not only because I am getting married tomorrow, insha Allah, but because with the passage of so much time I fell *out* of love with you and accepted the possibility that I may never even have seen you again. I got *used* to not being with you and learned how to do my time without depending on your letters. I never stopped thinkin' about you and I *still* care for you but it is too late because my heart is with Fatimah now." I said, devastating her. She looked more hurt than angry, but she gave no hint that she was going to cry again or say anything else.

It was time for me to go.

"What we had is over with. When you wrote me that letter after Big Mama's first stroke, you chose Monsieur and a life without me in it. Now you need to deal with the consequences of that decision, only *then* will you really be doing so like I did with the consequences of mine." I said, rising. "I am goin' to marry Fatimah and move on in the process. I'm choosing *her*. I suggest that you do the same."

With that, I walked out of McDonald's and into the pouring rain. I didn't want to ride my bike home in the rain like that but I needed to get away from there. I climbed onto my bike and put my helmet on.

"*ATIF!*" I turned and saw Patience standing out in the rain. "Don't go! Stay here, with me! Please?"

Patience was hitting below the belt, picking at an old scab. The last time she mouthed those same exact words, I made a hard-headed decision and ended up killing a man which in turn led to me doing close to 13 years in prison. But what she failed to realize was that even though I made a terrible decision that night, some *positive* consequences ensued along with the negative.   I met Fatimah, found Islam and forgave Khalid.

I lifted the tinted shield on my helmet and looked at her, feeling an incredible amount of nothing and something at the same time.   Like I got all ready to feel something forgotten but changed my mind.

Patience was successful, independent and an attractive woman, everything I wanted in a girl before I went to prison.   But I was no longer 14 years old or the type of individual I was at that age: Patience was no longer my type of woman.

You can't keep runnin', in and out of my li-i-i-ife, dun, dun-dun-dun....

"Bye Patience," I said, I then pulled down my shield and started my bike, pulling slowly and carefully out of the parking lot without looking back.

*****

Two hours later I found myself walking along the shoulder of 71 Highway in the rain.   I had fallen off of my bike when I hit a submerged part of the pavement, causing my motorcycle to hydroplane.   Not wishing to be led to where the mindless current was taking me, I leaned over, dropped my bike and rolled to safety.   The engine had been submerged as well and to my dismay flooded by the water. I then pushed it off to the side of the road and left it behind, not having the patience to stand still in the pouring rain and wait for it to start acting right.

I sent a text to Destiny asking her to call Kesha for me and have her come and pick me up.   My phone had broken when I fell and sending a text message was the only thing it would allow me to do.   Khalid was at work and I doubted if he would be able to up and leave his job like Kesha could.   Fatimah? She would have probably panicked, thinking that I had been hurt.   I didn't want to startle her like that, even if for only a moment.

559

"I am so sorry Atif," Kesha apologized as I slid into the passenger seat. "Destiny told me you were on 470 and I have been drivin' that stretch back and forth from Kansas to Lee's Summit lookin' for you."

"I *was* on 470, an hour ago." I informed her, putting my seat belt on. I was drenched.

"When Destiny called me I was in the middle of putting a perm on someone's head and everybody else was busy with clients so I had to finish her up before-"

"I ain't trippin' Kesha, I understand." I cut her off. "Thank you for comin'." Kesha smiled, pulling back into traffic.

"Why are you out here ridin' that motorcycle in the rain anyway like you ain't got no sense?"

"I went to Grandview to meet with Patience and it started rainin' on me while I was out there."

"Patience? You are gettin' married tomorrow, what are you meetin' with her for?" Kesha asked, looking over at me.

"We sat down and got some things off of our chests, had a conversation that was long overdue."

"Some things like what?" Kesha prodded.

"Patience doesn't think that I should marry Fatimah. She said that I should marry *her* instead."

"*What?* Huh-unh, *hell* naw. The *bitch!* What makes her think she can just pop back up after 10 years-"

"Kesha?"

"And expect you to mess with her after rollin' out on you like-"

"Kesha,"

"She did? Where was *she* when Big Mama died? Where was *she* when Darion died? Where was *she* when you did all of that time in the hole? Spoiled ass-"

"Ke-e-e-sha?"

"Bitch, forget her. I'll tell you where she was at, laid up somewhere with that federal agent's *dick* in her mou-"

"*KESHA!*" I shouted, silencing her. We rode in silence for a few moments, the windshield wipers making

560

the only sound. Kesha never was too fond of Patience. "I didn't go for it, insha Allah I'm still marryin' Fatimah."

"She just...*ugh*! I can't *stand* that woman. How could she even *think* about interferin' with what you and Fatimah have together? If it wasn't for her K-Red and Malik wouldn't have had to leave and everybody else wouldn't have went to jail."

"That is not true Kesha, don't put all of that weight on her shoulders. It wasn't her fault. We all brought that down on ourselves. If they had not infiltrated through her it would have been someone else, possibly even *you*." Kesha thought about that for a moment.

"Yeah, I guess you're right." She said, sighing. "But I *still* don't like the bitch. I swear to God I would love to just kick her ass one good time for the way she left you hangin' like that."

I chuckled softly as we reached the 75th street exit. A lot had changed with the passage of all that time as far as the landscape and scenery was concerned, but every time I used that exit vivid memories of the almost fatal highspeed chase I took the police on back in August of '93 flooded my mind. So much had transpired in my life since that night. Even though it felt like it was just yesterday, it at the same time felt like a lifetime ago.

"Kesha, while you were locked up did you ever...you know, get down with any of them females?"

"Once." I lifted my brows with surprise. "Most women who go to prison do. I let this Puerto Rican girl go down on me when I was in the hole one time. Afterwards I got so disgusted with myself that I lashed out and beat her up."

"Why did you beat her up?"

"I don't know! She didn't deserve that and I wish I could take it back. From that moment on I knew that there was nothin' a woman could ever do for me, regardless of my circumstances. I needed some beef summer sausage with my Ramen Noodle Soups." I threw my head back and laughed out loud at the sexual innuendo. "I am *serious*! The hot and spicy kind too, not the regular."

"Girl you are crazy." I commented, wiping a tear from my eye.

"What about you? Did you ever let one of them dudes...?" I glared at her. "*What?*" She asked in response to that look, laughing. "You asked *me*, so why can't I ask *you?*"

"No, I never messed around. Never even came close. I don't know how but for some reason it was like they just *knew* that I wasn't the one, even before I came to Islam. The homosexuals in prison didn't even like to be in the same area I was in. It was kind of weird now that I reflect."

"So let me get this straight," Kesha started as she stopped at the very same light where I crashed at. "You have not had any sexual encounter whatsoever since bein' with that nurse back in '98?" I shook my head, smiling. "Oh my God, poor Fatimah. You are goin' to hurt that girl Atif."

"No I am not. I am more afraid of what she may do to me."

"Does it still *work?*" I laughed. "My goodness! That is over 8 years. I can't seem to go 8 days without a shot. You never cease to amaze me man, your self-discipline and self-control is unparalleled. You have really come a long way and I feel damn near *honored* to have been able to witness how you changed and matured so fast. Patience does not even *deserve* a man like you. You and Fatimah are like a match made in Paradise."

We rode in silence for the rest of the way. Arriving at Fatimah's apartment complex a short while later, I looked at my watch and saw that I was at least 4 hours late. Seeing her Infinity parked in her parking space, I scolded myself for not calling her.

"I didn't tell you I wanted to come over here," I started as Kesha parked. "What made you drive to Fatimah's?"

"I don't know," she answered detached. Kesha then looked at me. "Do you remember a long time ago when you spent the night over my house? We made a pact sayin' that we was goin' to be-"

562

"Personal friends," I cut in, smiling. "Yeah, I remember."

"I promised to always be there for you, as well as a few other things. Did I hold up to them, my promises I mean?"

"Every last one of them. I can't even begin to explain how vital your support was to me over the years. Our correspondence kept me goin' even through the worst times of my incarceration. When I felt like I was all alone in the world and left for dead in that hole I could *always* depend on your encouragin' words, pictures and cards to lift my spirits without bein' disappointed." Kesha smiled from ear to ear.

"Well, with you and Fatimah gettin' married and all, I think that we *still* can be personal friends, without sex of course, but you know what I mean."

"No we can't." I said, shaking my head. Kesha stared at me with a hurt look on her face. "That was cool when we were teenagers, but now that title does not describe the nature of our relationship. It is not *befittin'*. We are so much *more* than personal friends. Girl you are like my sista'." With her eyes brimming' with tears, Kesha leaned over and kissed me on the cheek.

"Go to your wife boy." I smiled, grabbing my helmet and opening the door, causing the interior light to come on. "Atif! Wait!" Kesha exclaimed, reaching in her console for a napkin. She then wet the tip of it with her tongue and wiped her lipstick off of my cheek. "Fatimah would have assumed that lipstick was Patience's and beat her ½ to death."

"You think Fatimah would put hands on Patience or some other woman behind me?"

"Boy Fatimah would *kill* somethin' behind you. That woman is head over heels in love with you Atif. When I twist her locks for her you are all we talk about. She loves to hear stories about you back in the day, especially about you and Khalid and how y'all used to feud with each other.

"I am goin' to tell you somethin' about the woman you are marryin', Atif. She is real laid back and humble but don't let that fool you. Now *me*? I will fuck a bitch up, you know that.   But Fatimah? She ain't to be played with. Especially when it comes to *you*."

"Do you think you could handle her if y'all was to get into it?"

"Mmmm...lets just say she has my respect. What is that you be sayin' all the time?"

"In Allahu 'alim, truly Allah is the Best Knower?"

"Yeah, truly Allah is the Best Knower."

"Be safe Kesha," I started, getting out of the car. "And put your seat belt on girl, I told you about drivin' around like that a million times before."

"You said I am your sista', not your *daughter*." Kesha said as she complied. I stood there in the rain for a moment, watching her as she pulled away. I then skipped up the apartment stairs and knocked on Fatimah's door. Moments later she opened it, holding a stem of green grapes in her hand.

"As-salaamu alaykum." I greeted.

"Wa   alaykum   as-salaam."   Fatimah   returned, stepping outside of her apartment.   "Atif you are soaking wet!" She disappeared into her apartment and came back with a dry beach towel. Placing the grape stem in between her teeth, she took it upon herself to dry me off with it. Her scent was embedded within the towel and I closed my eyes, relishing it every time I inhaled. "You are going to get sick if you don't come up out of these wet clothes."

"I will be a'ight, thank you." I said, looking at her as she drooped the towel around my shoulders. It wasn't until then that the significance of her eating green grapes dawned on me. "You been *cryin'*," I pointed out. Fatimah looked at me. "You told me that when you cry you develop a cravin' for green grapes."

Fatimah threw a grape at me, hitting me smack dead in the middle of my forehead. "You are four hours late! Do you have any idea what I was thinking?" I told her about my motorcycle acting up on me.   "You and that motorcycle are going to be the death of me."

"Are you a'ight?" I asked.

"Yes, it wasn't the first time that I cried on account of you."

"What are you talkin' about? I ain't never made you cry." Fatimah held up three fingers. I looked at her in bewilderment.

"I cried when I heard you were getting certified," she began, counting down with them. "I cried the night you left detention, and then I cried again when I saw on the news how much time you were sentenced to."

I was shocked! She had me fooled.   Back in detention Fatimah presented a dour, closed and private persona, rarely showing much more emotion than her smile. I understood though why she hid this from me back then, she was fearing Allah.

"Earlier at the homeless shelter," I started, changing the subject. "You told me that a woman never forgets her first love." Fatimah nodded. "Well who is this first love that you are still clingin' to?"

Fatimah smiled, placing a grape in her mouth. She then looked into my eyes. "*You.*"

"*Me?*" I asked. Fatimah offered me a grape, I nodded and she fed one to me. She then leaned back against her apartment door.

"I remember back when I was in middle school, I read in the Qur'an where Allah says that beside the righteous men in Paradise there will be Qasirat-at-Tarf, or chaste wives with wide and beautiful eyes. He said that they will be *delicate* and *pure* as if they were hidden eggs well preserved. I knew right then that I wanted to be *pure* like a hidden egg well preserved for my future husband."

"You are a *virgin* Fatimah?" She smiled proudly and nodded. I smiled in return, proud of her for she had every right to feel proud of herself. A beautiful 30 ½ year old virgin is rare in the U.S. The woman never ceased to amaze me.

"To proceed, when I met you in detention and you began to write me all of those letters, only Allah comprehends how much I loved reading them over and again. Not only do I *still* possess every single one of them to this day, but I even used to sleep with them underneath my pillow."

"*Wha-a-a-t?*"

"It's true! I did!"

"Why?"

"Not only were they written in a respectful manner without all of the sexual references, bad grammar, chicken-scratch-like handwriting, and irrelevance like the other boys used to write to me, but I loved the way you shared your thoughts with me. Men don't do that. Some of them were very dark and borderline psychotic, but I really got to know you through your letters and I couldn't shake the feeling that I was saving myself for *you*."

I stared at her. "But I didn't have an Islamic bone in my body back then." I finally managed.

"Yes you did, they were just hiding behind the *flesh*. Reading your letters helped me see *within* you and gave me some insight on the type of person you really were on the inside. I saw Islam within you and I began to pray for you every time I prayed, for hours at a time sometimes, asking Allah to help you conquer the flesh and for Him to guide you to the path which leads to Paradise. I think I remember telling you that back them."

"No, you told me that you *mentioned* me in the mornin' prayer that you offered on the day of my certification hearin'. You didn't say nothin' about prayin' for me *constantly*, 5 times a day *everyday*. You mean to tell me you been *stalkin'* me for the last 13 years or so?" Fatimah hit me with another grape. I smiled ruefully. "I'm just playin'. But seriously though, why save yourself for someone on his way to prison for murder for no tellin' how long?"

"My faith in Allah was nowhere near as strong as it is now back then, but I still had it. I really can't explain it Atif, but it was like I just knew that we were joined by the hands of fate, our destinies linked somehow within Allah's pre-ordainment. I began to believe that my sole reason for being locked up like that was just so that I could meet you.

"I asked Allah not to make my mission too difficult for me and continued to have faith even when you were sentenced to 30 years, I understood that to Allah belongs the final decision. And when Khalid got out and hunted me down like he was a private eye or something, he told me

566

that you were a Muslim, a *good* Muslim at that and your sentences had been ran concurrent and you would be getting out soon. He also told me about how much you used to talk about me." Fatimah paused, smiling at me. She then continued on. "I prayed hard that night, praising Allah for I knew He had answered my prayers. And since Khalid said that you had established regular prayer and was adamant about making them at their earliest fixated times, I always prayed on time imagining that we were praying together."

Something about her revelation was nagging at me. It was connected somehow to something I had been trying to understand for *years*. I just couldn't grasp it right then with all of the guilt and anxiety I was feeling. How could I have even allowed myself to *begin* contemplating leaving Fatimah for Patience? Fatimah was there with me during the whole time of my incarceration in mind and spirit where it *counts,* without me even realizing it. Not through letters and visits, no, her form of support was much more meaningful than that.

"Why are we standin' out here?" I asked her.

"Because my wali (protector, guardian) is not here." Which meant that we were for the first time alone together.

"I think that if you were to let me inside I can keep my hands off of you for at least 24 more hours."

"Don't be Fitnah (trial, temptation) for me Atif. Besides, maybe my fear is that I won't be able to keep *my* hands off of *you* if I were to let you in." Fatimah said, smiling alluringly at me. She then fed me another grape. "What did Patience have to say?"

"Everything you said she would." I acknowledged. Fatimah nodded knowingly. "Did you *really* think that I had chosen Patience over you?"

"What was I *supposed* to think Atif? You were late, you didn't call..."

"Yeah, I tripped. I apologize for that." Fatimah fed me another grape. "You know," I started, chewing. "The Qur'an says that I can have up to 4 wives so I could have just married *both* of y'all." I said jokingly.

"One is better for you if you only but knew."

567

A moment of comfortable silence.

"Let me see your hair Fatimah."

"No."

"Why not?"

"Because you are not my husband yet."

"You know I *could* have Destiny come over here and examine you for me before the wedding to make sure I would be pleased."

Fatimah looked at me. "You *would* know something like that, wouldn't you Atif?" I smiled mischievously. "I think that you know in your heart such a thing is not necessary." She was right. Fatimah covered herself well but I couldn't help but "notice" that Allah had truly blessed her in all of the areas where Black men loved for a woman to be blessed at. Fatimah then handed me what remained of the stem of grapes and reached underneath her head-scarf. "I will show you *one* lock, but that is *it*."

She then extracted one lock. It was about 18-inches in length with the circumference equaling that of a jumbo drinking straw, stopping just at the heart of her chest. Un-dyed by the sun, it was solid black and neatly matted all of the way through. I saw no lint or anything else trapped within it. It had to be the most beautiful lock of hair I had ever seen.

"Can I feel it?" I asked. She gave an acquiescent nod and I caressed it. It was surprisingly softer than what I had imagined a lock to feel like. I leaned over and smelled it, it smelled *good*. It didn't stink of chemicals or anything like that, it had a natural and organic-fruit-like-smell to it.

"Are you pleased?" Fatimah asked me.

"No, not yet. Now I want to see yo-"

"Subhan Allah! Huh-unh, see?" Fatimah cut in, putting her lock back in concealment. I laughed out loud. "It is time for you to leave Atif."

"Girl you are somethin' else, you know that?"

"No, *you* are something else." She said, grabbing the grapes. "I will be right back, insha Allah."

While Fatimah was gone I allowed my train of thought to take me where my emotions were hindering them to go just minutes earlier. It was not until that point that I understood who the being that had appeared to me in the person of my deceased mother was referring to when she told me that it was the prayers of a "special person" along with my inquisitive nature that was rescuing me from the Hellfire. This special person was the same individual that Destiny had supplicated for on my behalf the night of my release.

"Here take my car." Fatimah said as she stepped out of her apartment, handing me her car keys. I took them.

"You ready to do this Fatimah?" I asked her seriously.

"Get married?" I nodded. "I am a nervous wreck and I don't think that I will be able to sleep tonight, but yes, I am ready. I have been dreaming about this day for a long, long time Atif." I stared at my soon to be wife, smiling at her. "What?" she asked, smiling back.

"You are that special person, it has been you the whole time."

"What are you talking about?"

"I will tell you some other time, insha Allah." I said. Fatimah nodded, practicing patience. "I don't ever want to make you cry like that again Fatimah."

"It is okay to make me cry Atif, just make sure that from this moment on they are happy tears."

"As-salaamu alaykum, my dear Muslimah."

Fatimah smiled lovingly at the pet name. "Wa alaykum as-salaam, my dear Muslim." She answered, ascribing to me one of her own.

"Fee aman Allah." I said as I turned and walked back out into the rain.

*****

A TASTE OF PARADISE
"It feels like I have lived my whole life
for this moment we are experiencin'.
Caressin',
kissin',
reflectin',
reminiscin'.
So many years of yearnin'
for that which I could not have.
Reapin' the repercussions
for travelin' on a filthy path.
I never thought that I would love again,
but that changed,
when you came,
provin' that what I sought exists on a higher plane.
There is music in your name,
poetry in your touches.
Ecstasy within the warmth
of your contractin' clutches.
The night spent, holdin' you tight,
dear wife,
will suffice,
as the closest I will ever get to paradise in this life."
            -Soody Mak

28

I'm *married*, I thought to myself as I lay with my wife in my arms the following night, playing with one of her locks. And the wedding! It was a simple Muslim wedding but it seemed as if every Muslim in Kansas City attended or dropped by to meet this man whom Fatimah, after turning down countless proposals, was giving herself to. I had no idea my wife was so well known and respected in the Muslim community.

I had a mother and a father-in-law who accepted me as one of their own, a whole Muslim *family* that welcomed me with arms wide open into the fold. It was almost like I was being given a whole new sense of identity along with a support system that totally eliminated the feeling of being alone in the world, a feeling that took root with Malik's exile. We were showered with gifts, money and smiles. My only wish was that my mother and Big Mama could have been around to meet Fatimah, they would have absolutely adored the woman. My wife was the type of person that you liked right away.

"My dear Muslim?"

"Wha'sup?"

"I have another revelation for you. Remember the day you left detention when I came to your cell?"

I nodded. "The day I pray we will never tire of talkin' about?"

"Yes, *that* one! It was not my turn to be on the clean up crew that night. I paid one of the girls who *was* scheduled to be on the crew that night 8 toasts, 5 juices, 3 sausages, 2 chocolate milks, *and* promised to give her my *whole* tray the next time we had cheeseburgers and French fries, just so that I could take her place on the crew and see you one last time before you left."

"I had no idea Fatimah."

"I know you didn't."

"Was it *worth* it?"

"Every bit of it. It was Ramadan and I was fasting anyway though so don't get the big head." Fatimah added, giggling.

"My Muslimah?"

"Yes?"

"That same night you promised to tell me the history of the locks if our paths were to ever cross again," I said, twisting one of her locks around my finger. Fatimah lifted her head from my chest and looked up at me, smiling her smile. It was *always* real. And always measured. People either got the combination or they didn't. The ones who did were charmed by it into helplessness. The ones who didn't thought her calculating and shrewd. In the predominantly male world she operated in, the split was close to even.

I got the smile completely.

"You *remember* that?" she asked me. I nodded with a smile of my own. "By Allah, you have an elephant's memory Atif."

Back when we were in detention as teenagers I would ask her certain questions, not just out of curiosity, but also to penetrate what little was possible of the wall she kept up around me. It was the only way I could get her to talk with me at length and I loved how animated she became when breaking things down for me.

"The locks were originally a part of an African tradition of the Nazarites and other African tribes. Along with a vow to Allah (Jah), the Nazarites were commanded not to eat pork or any other forbidden food and not drink wine or any intoxicants and not cut their hair; to let the locks of their hair grow. The Bible speaks of this rite in the book of Numbers, chapter...6, verse 5 I believe, in Allahu 'alim. Also if you read the story of Samson in Judges starting in chapter 13 you will see that Samson's strength was in his *locks*." Fatimah sat up. "Would you like for me to retrieve a Bible from the study so that you can check for yourself?" she asked me.

"I will take your word for it." Fatimah rested her head back onto my chest and continued on.

"It is *said* that the locks represented *antennas* which were energy transmitters and receptors to communicate with Jah." Fatimah paused and giggled softly. "Of course I believe this was all symbolic. The tradition of the locks is, perhaps, *thousands* of years old.

"During the Trans-Atlantic slave trade the first African slaves were brought to South America and the Caribbean Islands (Haiti, Jamaica, Panama, etc.). Amongst these Africans were some tribal people who still practiced the tradition of the Nazarites and locked hair.   The European slave holders felt that the Africans' locks gave them a *dreaded* look that kind of spooked the slave holders so they forced all of the slaves to cut their locks off and made it forbidden to ever wear locks again.

"But as time went on our ancestors would organize, time after time again, against the slave holders and rebel against them and slavery. Every time our ancestors rose up they would grow their locks back as a sign of rebellion. These rebellions were initially put down in their first efforts, but then of course our ancestors in Haiti and Jamaica were eventually successful in winning their liberation and running the slave holders and colonizers off of the islands and became the first independent ex-slave countries or Black Republics.

"From that point on, the locks (or *dreadlocks* as the Europeans termed them) became not only a religious ritual but was now also a sign of unity amongst the freed Africans. In the Rastafarian teachings the locks also now represent the lion's mane. So you see, the locks didn't start in Jamaica or Haiti or Panama, but was initially an African Nazarite tradition." Fatimah finished. She then lifted her head. "I get the feeling that you already knew that and just wanted to get me started."

"You should listen to your feelins, they be tellin' you the truth."

"I have been falling for that for *years*." Fatimah said, shaking her head. I chuckled. "Now I want *you* to break something down for *me*."

"What is that?"

"My dear Muslim, in the Qur'an Allah says that in Paradise there will be Gardens underneath which *rivers* flow. In your humble opinion, based on your portion of understanding, what are these Gardens and what does it *mean* for rivers to be flowing beneath them?"

"Oooh, that is a *good* one!" I exclaimed, rubbing my hands together and licking my lips. Fatimah laughed. "That is gone cost you though."

"Cost me what?"

"I think a seductive kiss on the lips will be an adequate down payment." Fatimah reached up and pulled my head down, kissing my lips, her own lips slightly parted, our mouths lingered together a moment before she pulled back, the taste of her remaining with me a good deal longer. Fatimah was an honest woman but it was very difficult to believe that I was the only man she had ever kissed. "Mmm, why don't I break that down for you a little later and we-"

"Atif!"

"A'ight, a'ight," I said, smiling. Fatimah snuggled closer to me, tracing invisible lines around the muscles of my abdomen with her head on my chest, of which she had already labeled as her favorite place. I took ahold of another one of her "energy transmitters" and began twisting it. "Gardens underneath which rivers flow..." I began. My gaze seemed at once there and apart, distant and tightly focused, as if telescoped onto some horizon that lay far outside the walls of our bedroom.

"A garden, in this life, is a plot of land used for growing flowers, vegetables, or fruits, and we as humans *depend* on these things that a garden produces as sustenance vital for our own survival. A garden in turn depends on rain water and light/heat from the sun in order to sustain its life. Without sufficient water and light, the gardens of this life shrivel up and cease to bear fruit.

"But imagine a *Garden* where its source of light is an *eternal* one, the Light, Allah, instead of a star that will not only one day go supernova, insha Allah, but is not always in close enough proximity with the earth to sustain the life of a garden. Imagine, my dear Muslimah, a *Garden* where its source of water is a *river* flowing directly beneath it instead of having to depend on an *occasional* rainy season that may not even come! Such a Garden will *perpetually* bear fruits and the like of what we need, want, and desire. The inhabitants of such a Garden will never go hungry or be without, we will have everything our purified souls may desire in abundance.

"A garden in this life is also a place of tranquility filled with sweet aromas and colorful flowers which are pleasing to the human senses. Come to think of it, as we grow older and closer to the grave, especially women, we tend to find solace in a garden. An elderly woman can always be found tending to her small garden in her front yard or wherever. And if you draw off of it, this is not strange at all. I believe that this within itself is evidence of the fact that we once dwelled in such Gardens underneath which rivers flow and we are innately yearning to come back home like an ingrate adolescent who has been kicked out of his place of security, his home because of his disobedience." I finished. Fatimah considered my words for a moment. She then sat up, I looked at her without comment. Our eyes met. And held.

"Alhamdu lillah, isn't our Creator kind and merciful?" Fatimah asked me. I nodded. "Do you ever wonder where you would be right now if it weren't for Islam?" I shivered inwardly at the thought.

"Probably still in prison, in ad-seg about to lose the best part of my mind."

"You have been through so much but yet still Allah was able to transform you into the man I am blessed to call my husband." Our eyes remained locked. "You should write about your life, I believe that telling your story would be motivational and beneficial for others who have been through some of the things you have and they could learn a lot from it."

"You think so?"

"Yes! And you should tell your story in the *raw*, don't water it down or censor it. Other Muslims probably wouldn't agree, I could only imagine the content in some areas, but I would support you every step of the way. All of the bad dreams, your experiences in the streets, everything. You should share that."

I considered that for a moment.

"Khalid has a secret admirer." Fatimah said, changing the subject with a smile on her face as if she possessed the juiciest secret in the world.

"A secret admirer?" Fatimah nodded.

"Actually, more than one. Many of the sisters in the Masjid have inquired about his marital status.   A single, young, attractive, and most importantly, *good* Muslim man is not the easiest kind of man to find in the society that we live in. Not one with morals and manners such as yours and his."

"Who is the one in particular that you are referrin' to?" I asked.   Fatimah continued looking at me without a word. Her expression told me that I could figure it out on my own. I squinted my eyes at her, thinking. It didn't take long for a certain smiling face to appear in my mind. I inhaled sharply, holding my mouth open with shock. "*Aminah*?" Fatimah nodded, smiling.

"She is... oh Atif, you just don't know! She really wants to marry Khalid but she is so *shy*. She swears up and down that he would not be interested in having her for his wife."

"What is she trippin' on? Aminah has taqwa, she is a beautiful woman and she is very sweet."

"I know! But she is afraid of rejection. I think that she should reveal how she feels to him. Will you talk to him for her?"

"Is that what she wants for me to do?" Fatimah nodded. "I will talk to him, insha Allah."

"Thank you Atif. This really means a lot to her."

Truly I had no idea how Khalid would react. He was not the easiest person to read at all. He was so focused on Ke'von and establishing a foundation for them that I feared there *was* a chance that he would not be interested in not just Aminah per se, but in marriage at all, not right then. He had never even inquired about Aminah's marital status or expressed an interest in her to me. He would greet her cheerfully and talk to her whenever they crossed paths, but that was all.

"Prophet Muhammad said that for the pious men of Paradise there will be very fair females created by Allah as such, not from the offspring of Adam and that the marrow of their bones will be seen through the skin out of extensive beauty." Fatimah looked at me. "I love you with all of my heart Fatimah, but I might have to trade you in for a couple of them!"

Fatimah sat up abruptly.

"What did you just say?" she asked me.

Uh-oh.

"I was just playin' Fatimah." I said, smiling a nervous smile. I studied her features. Her gaze was direct, penetrating, but showed no sign of anger. Somehow that made it even worse.

"No, I know you were kidding about the Hur (fair women of Paradise). I am talking about right before you finished saying what you said."

"I don't know what you are talkin' about."

"Yes you do! You said that you love me with all of your heart."

Silence.

"Okay," I said with a shrug, "You *know* that already Fatimah."

"Yes, I *do* know, but you have never *told* me. Didn't you tell me once before that you have never told any woman that you have ever been with that you loved her?" I nodded. "Not even Patience?" I shook my head. Fatimah lifted an eyebrow. "I want to hear you tell me again." She said after giving her surprise a chance to wane.

"I l-l-l-l," I tried. I then sighed. "I can't! My tongue won't let me!" Fatimah's smile disappeared from her face and she rolled over onto her side with her back towards me, pulling the sheet up over her torso.

"Fatimah?" I said, gently rocking her by the bare cold shoulder she was showing me. She ignored me, feigning instantaneous sleep. Feeling her backside against my body underneath the sheet rekindled a fire within me that had never fully gone out after "consummating" our union.

"Fati-i-i-mah? You are not sleep are you? Because if you are you won't be able to hear me tell you how much I love you. How much I care for you. You won't be able to hear me tellin' you about how it feels like I went through the fire in my life just so that I could evolve into the type of man that could fully appreciate you, this *beautiful* woman that Allah has blessed me with. This woman that I plan to spend the rest of my life displayin' a true love for that knows no bounds, a zeal and enthusiasm that can not be questioned. In my life, you are second only to my worship of Allah. I love you, I love you, I love you so much my Muslimah."

Unable to feign sleep any longer, Fatimah rolled over onto her back with a giggle, pulling me down on top of her. She then kissed me long and deep. Her features were limited in the moonlight. I watched shadows move across her face, and she seemed more beautiful than any woman I had ever known.

"Round 2?" I asked.

"Round 2, 3, 4, *and* 5." She answered in between kisses.

"Until the police come knockin'?"

"Mmm-hmm."

"Well they can ke-e-e-p on knockin' but they can't come in!" I sang, quoting lyrics from an old Cheech and Chong movie. Fatimah laughed softly and then looked into my eyes seriously, taking my face into her soft hands.

"My dear Muslim, stop being silly and get back to showing me how much you love me."

"Yes ma'am."

*****

EPILOGUE

It was a beautiful Sunday afternoon. Khalid and I were at a small park located just off of Leeds Traffic Way, not too far from the old Kansas City Tow Lot, breathing heavily after a long game of handball we had just played. I lost, which evened the tally of games 3-3. We sat in silence enjoying a brief cool breeze as it blew by.

Things were going well for the both of us. Fatimah and I had been blissfully married for a little over a year and she was in the hospital pregnant with a little brother for Destiny that was past due. Fatimah persuaded me to leave her and get some fresh air because I had been cooped up in the hospital room with her for the past 2 days, worried sick. I just knew that something was wrong. Were we going to lose our first son together? Was I going to lose her in the process of bringing him into the world?

Khalid and Aminah were engaged to be married in the spring. I thought she was the perfect mate for Khalid. Allah knows he needed someone with a soft touch such as Aminah in his life. Ke'von liked her and accepted her easily. Like me, Khalid was apprehensive about marriage at first because of how much of his life had gone by without a source of femininity within it. And like Fatimah, Aminah was more than willing to work with him. The time was right, he had established himself nicely in society and had had enough time to bond with his son.

Come to find out, Malik had been indicted for the murder of La'Ron and was actually planning to come back to the U.S.A. to stand trail. Because of the way everyone who was apprehended on the first round of indictments had refused to cooperate, the indictments against him, Antoinette and K-Red were abandoned. For some reason Malik refused to disclose, he had a lot of confidence in his ability to beat the case by acquittal.

Antoinette was indicted again once the first one was abandoned for the death of Small Balls whose body had been dug up by the Feds and re-examined, traces of the complex poison were detected that were at first overlooked. K-Red, refusing to leave her behind, vowed to stay in Libya with her. Me, Khalid, Destiny, Ke'von, Aminah, and Fatimah were planning to go on the Pilgrimage to Makkah and on the way back we were going to spend a week in Africa visiting the 3.

I was still in touch with Smack Man and all of the brothers I had left behind back in prison. Amiri (DeAnthony X) had made parole and could be seen holding security for the Minister Louis Farrakhan. We kept in touch and spoke weekly on the phone.

Siddiq, Bashir, Muhsin, they were all still in Moberly.

Skooter-B was in Crossroads Correctional Center and Cook-El was in Jefferson City, on his way out. The 2 of us had big plans together.

I saw old Knockout here and there, even hooked up with St. Joseph every once in a while whenever I visited a certain Masjid up north.

Pastor Cool Breeze was out and preaching at the First Missionary Baptist Church. I dropped by every now and then to listen to his sermons and Fatimah and I joined forces with his church with community drives and other such community building oriented programs.

I visited the grave sites of Big Mama, Darion, and my mother a lot. Sometimes Destiny would accompany me whereas other times I would sneak off and do so on my own. Allah knows I missed them all. Sometimes I cried; sometimes I smiled. Most times I just leaned against the gravestones and read the Qur'an. I didn't believe they could hear me, but I did so anyway enjoying the company of my memories with them. It is forbidden for Muslims to pray in a graveyard so I always left when it was time to offer the Salah.

Patience was working hard. I didn't see her often, only heard about her through Destiny.

Persistence was doing good for herself also. Her and Patience were upset with each other for some reason, not talking to one another. I surmised it had something to do with Smack Man.

"You know brother, I used to ride past this park all of the time when I was younger and I never even tripped

581

off of these walls or what they were for." I said to Khalid in reference to the walls of the handball courts. Fatimah and Aminah had been riding us pretty hard about speaking in broken English so we were trying to appease the women of our lives by talking with proper English, a feat I had been struggling with since around '98.

"Yeah, me neither." Khalid responded, leaning up against his blue Ford F-150 while taking a sip of spring water. I was seated on my bike, wiping sweat from my body with a T-shirt. "You were playing kind of lazily that last game brother, are you alright?"

"Yeah man, I'm good. It is just this baby thing is getting to me. She should have *been* done had him by now."

"Patience Atif, Allah is with As-Sabirun (the patient)."

At that moment we heard a car horn. Turning around we saw a red jeep Cherokee full of young women riding slowly by trying to get our attention. Two of them were hanging out of the passenger side window and another ½ way out of the sunroof. "He-e-e-y! Wha'sup! Wha'sup sexy? Can I play with you?" The young woman in the front passenger seat called out to Khalid, who was bouncing a handball off the pavement. "With your fine ass!"

"Yeah! Get off of that motorcycle and let me see that body you chocolate mutha' fucka' you!" The young woman in the back seat called out to me. Khalid and I looked at each other and shook our heads. I sought refuge with Allah silently to myself.

"Eh!" Khalid and I looked up as the young woman hanging out of the sunroof raised her blouse, flashing her breasts at us.

"Subhan Allah!" The both of us said in unison, turning away from the car and shielding our eyes with our forearms as if it was a blinding light. The ladies laughed at us and drove off.

"Brother if they would have pulled into this parking lot up on us, with the fear of Allah I would have started this bike and rolled out you hear me?" I commented.

"I would have been right behind you." Khalid responded. We chuckled softly to ourselves. "Some of the females out here in society are out of control man, ain't they?"

I nodded. "By the time. Verily man is in loss." I said, reciting the first and second verses from the 103rd chapter in the Qur'an.

"Except those who believe and do righteous good deeds, and recommend one another to the truth, and-"

"Recommend one another to patience." We finished in unison.

"I better put my shirt back on for the last game before I mess around and cause a 10 car pile up out here."

"Brother please! Now you know that it was in fact my arms them females were tripping on!" Khalid said, rising from his leaning position and playfully putting his dukes up at me.

"A-ight," I started, jumping off of my bike and putting my dukes up in response. "We are going to turn this park into *The Battle Ground* if you keep on tripping."

"*Atif!* You do not want to see me brother, I'm *telling* you!"

"The tie on the handball court ain't the only tie that still stands unresolved." I said, referring to our bout back in middle school.

"*Tie?*" Khalid asked with a convincing look of bewilderment on his face, putting his dukes down. "What are you talking about *tie?*"

"Come on man," I started, rolling my eyes and dropping my hands down at my sides. "Here we go again. You did not win that fight brother."

"You are getting old man, your memory is beginning to fail you." Khalid said. We then made our way back over to the handball court with the intent to finish our usual 7 game series. "I was reading in the Qur'an this morning after Salah and I came across the verses where Allah told the companions, may Allah be pleased with them all, to hold fast to the rope that binds them." I nodded in confirmation. "This Recitation also says that if Prophet Muhammad had all of the money in the world, he could not have united the believers; that it was in fact Allah who united their hearts in such a way with Islam even though before of which they had all been enemies one to another."

I smiled, knowing where he was going with this. He continued on.

"I couldn't help but think of us, how before Islam we too were enemies one to another. Siddiq couldn't have united our hearts without Allah's help. We were trying to kill each other out here in these streets. Then Allah blessed us with this way of life, uniting our hearts solely for His sake despite all that we have been through." Khalid then placed his hand on my shoulder.

"There is not a Salah that I offer without thanking Allah for guiding us to where we now are in life. For putting it in your heart to forgive me for what I did to you and your family. To this day I am still amazed by that. All praise is due to Allah. I love you brother and there is nothing in this world I wouldn't do for you. I would die in the cause of Allah by your side man, you hear me?" I nodded, looking into his eyes and seeing the sincerity of his words. He meant every syllable.

"Sometimes I wonder to myself if Allah will ever put it in Patience's heart to forgive me for what I tried to do to her."

"Allah is the Best Knower. It is your duty to seek her forgiveness with the purest and most sincere intentions. If she never does then there is nothing else you can do. You have already turned your life over to your Lord seeking His forgiveness and it is His forgiveness alone that will, insha Allah, grant you Paradise because He is the One who accepts repentance. Whether she forgives you or not will be irrelevant. Allah knows what your intentions are and Prophet Muhammad said that our actions are judged by our intentions. He also said that if a believer intends to do a good deed and for some reason is unable to accomplish it, then it will be recorded as a good deed in that believer's favor as if it was carried out."

Khalid nodded. "That is enough brother, don't be trying to soften me up before the game so that my mind won't be on thrashing you. Let's ride!" Khalid said, stepping into the server's box.

"Man, you are the one who started it! What are you talking about?"

"D-D-D-on't take this b-b-b...butt whooping p-p-p....personal." Khalid stuttered, mimicking a line from our all-time favorite movie Harlem Nights. I laughed out loud as he served the ball fast and hard to the right corner of the court. I returned it with a powerful shot of my own. He then hit the ball high up on the wall and it came off over my head. I ran to catch it but was distracted by my phone going off on the side of the court, losing track of the ball in the air.

"1-0!" Khalid exclaimed. "I am going to *skunk* you out here this time, insha Allah!"

"Naw, man, that didn't count. My phone went off and distracted me." I said, picking it up from the ground.

"I will give you that one. Who is it?" I read the text message and got excited instantly.

"It's Fatimah! She's having the baby!"

*****

SULTAN LANE a.k.a SOODY MAK, former rapper and song writer for 2HP Records, is from Kansas City, Missouri. He is now 31, single with no children.

For any questions, comments, or dialogue contact him by e-mail:

CagedPotential@hotmail.com

or write him at: Caged Potential
PO Box 12746
Kansas City, KS 66112

Made in the USA
Middletown, DE
05 October 2020